The Experiment

By Tony Bove

THE EXPERIMENT

This edition first published in the United States of America in 2017 by Rockument, P.O. Box 700, Waimea, HI 96796, www.rockument.com.

Excerpt from *Worlds of Music*, Jeff Todd Titon general editor, 6th edition, Cengage Learning, © 2017, p. xiv, used by permission.

Printed edition ISBN: 978-0-9989334-0-5

THE EXPERIMENT

To Pete Sears and G.E. Smith, consummate musicians
who taught me how to be one.

Note to the reader:

This edition includes musical footnotes. Whenever I read stories that include references to songs, I always want to listen to the songs. The footnotes are provided for you to find the music.

To play the songs in this novel, go to www.rockument.com/experiment, and choose a playlist.

While this is a work of fiction, you may be surprised at how many historical facts are sprinkled throughout. In this era of internet search, I encourage you to look up references to people, places, and events, and read their backstories.

— *Tony Bove, May 2017*

THE EXPERIMENT

As modern people try to locate themselves in a world that is changing with bewildering speed, they find music especially rewarding, for music is among the most tenacious cultural elements. Music symbolizes a people's way of life; it represents a distillation of cultural style. For many, music is a way of life.

— Jeff Todd Titon, *Worlds of Music*

THE EXPERIMENT

Prologue

Author's note:

The flowering of the blues and rock in American music, which inspired a cultural revolution in the Sixties, began as a seed planted by High John the Conqueror, the dark prince of West Africa, the rolling stone who carried the traditions and spirits of his ancestors to the New World. Against all odds, High John tricked his enslavers and the Corporation's ministers to raise the spirit of Legba, the Keeper of the Crossroads, in his American and Haitian descendants. Legba gave High John's descendants, including Cornell Woodrow, the courage to trick his way through the New World, and to grow a new, powerful music.

This prologue is the story of how High John came to the New World, written by Herbert Mesh, an obscure folklorist and cryptologist. Mesh could only register the edges of some elaborate ancient secret about music. His short story was never published, but was found inserted into the pages of an issue of MAD Magazine from 1956, and shared by the four protagonists in this novel: Reggie, Gilbert, Lucy, and Johnny B. Footnotes with music were added by the author.

* * *

Screams of the captives pierced the thunder and tore a hole in the sky. Out of the hole, through dark swirling clouds, fell a thunder-stone, an *otane*.

Heijande, a *jeli* poet, singer, and a *kora* and *djembe* virtuoso, born into a Gonja clan, crouched in the bush in the merciless downpour to look at the stone hissing in the damp earth. A snake appeared in his path, bearing witness. Heijande knew what it meant. The *otane* had fallen to earth to stop him from making perhaps the biggest mistake of his life.

Down in the canyon, captured members of his clan continued screaming in agony as they stumbled, the right leg of one secured to the left leg of another by the same pair of fetters, and also fastened by chain neck to neck. Dagomba slave traders were dragging them down toward the river. They were victims of tribal warfare that had started ten years earlier, in 1714, that pitted the clans aligned with Asante on the Gold Coast against the Mossi Kingdom.

Heijande had been shadowing the traders with the hope of taking out the last armed trader at the rear of the miserable procession. He thought he could free at least one, and possibly two, of his clan. Shu Lia was closer to the front of the line, but it would be suicidal to attack there first. He could disrupt the procession from the rear and try to make his way to her.

Heijande felt the blood rush to his head and fingers. He knew it was a sign that he was too angry to do this properly. Anger against the traders was nothing new, and neither was bloodshed. But the thunder-stone had fallen. There must be a reason. He imagined the first step of the attack, and then imagined each step after that. He saw clearly that he would not succeed. Members of his clan would be put to death in retaliation. Shu Lia, the most beautiful, would be raped first, and they would make him watch.

The snake bearing witness was a sign from his most powerful ancestor. The stone would draw the ancestor's power. It was still hot, but he clutched it to his chest, and rubbed his stomach with it to spread its warmth through his body. It was also a gesture of possession; he now possessed the *otane*. He began to sing and play on his *kora* the oldest song on Earth, from his Mesopotamian roots.[1]

Heijande was *nyonyose*, a descendant of the earlier inhabitants of the upper Volta River region, the Dogon *gina*, which traced its ancestry back to Dyon and the Bela Mont clan. He learned the songs of his ancestors and would still sing them today, especially the song about keeping away from runaround Su, Erzulie's wicked side who cavorted with other men, and the sad song of the Wanderer, who had brought the Dogon across the vast Sahara and Maghreb deserts to this region seven centuries earlier. Most of the Dogon had long since fled from the Mossi calvary or had quietly assimilated into Gonja clans, resisting all prevailing Muslim influences, wearing the sign of the fish head. Heijande wore the Dogon fish head painted on his right buttock, symmetrically opposed to the snake-like symbol of Aido-Hwedo on his left buttock.

As *jeli* for his people, Heijande sang the songs of his ancestors, a history of exploits and spiritual awakenings. As a descendant of griots, he was also a genealogist, and respected as a sorcerer. Heijande knew the songs that could empower and consecrate a thunder-stone and unlock its secrets.

Clutching the cow-skin covered calabash of his *kora*, he sang and played while crouching in the rain, the song of the three monkeys, loosely translated,

A stone in my path, now dark as the night
Unleashes my spirit to seek the light
With my eyes shut to evil, ears that hear only right,
And lips that are dumb to scandal, I sit in my silent might.

With stone in hand, he felt the power. He could sing a song that could change a scornful woman to feel desire for the object of her scorn. He could sing another that could stop a man's mind long enough to see the beauty of any woman, no matter how ugly, and to fall in love with her. When a cousin had been ordained to marry a woman he did not like, not even one little bit, Heijande had filled his cousin with love for this woman, so that they would be happy together.

With stone in hand, his songs would grow even more powerful.

Crouched in hiding, Heijande now worried about the fate of the boy that had inadvertently betrayed the clan. Heijande had taught the boy the song about the three monkeys, how to see no evil, hear no evil, and sing no evil, in order to evade his captors. A Mossi warlord had beaten the song out of the boy and knew its secret. The evasion song had become more than useless; it had become a trap. Heijande had not had time to warn the clan, and they were singing it when the battle of the Upper Volta erupted, Asanti against Mossi. Singing did not protect them from being captured. Before long, Dagomba traders surrounded them.

The Dagomba, known as the parasites of battlefields, sold captives from both sides of the battle directly to the English on the coast, bypassing the Dutch at the eastern edge of the Bight of Benin. They traded for beads, cowrie shells, textiles, brandy, horses, and more recently, guns, which only increased the corruption and militancy of both sides.

Heijande had sung songs about the brown-skinned clans from the north, who had established gold mines centuries ago and enslaved many clans to work in the mines. He had sung songs to their Allah spirit. Now the white clans had come, spreading corruption, turning clans like the Dagomba into traders. Heijande had no song for these white clans that traded for his people, and then took his people away, across the vast ocean from which no one ever returned.

When the white clans come, the first thing they do is take away our songs. Then they bury our shrines, and force us to worship their spirits and ancestors. If we kill them, more of them arrive. It is as if by killing them, we multiply them.

Heijande set off along a trail to the ridge that paralleled the river. From the ridge his view encompassed an endless expanse of ravines, grassland, scrub, and dust, repeating itself like waves of an earthen ocean northeast to the wastes of the Maghreb. Heijande's ancestors had come from the other side of the Maghreb, bringing musical instruments, dances, songs, masks representing the first human beings... and the story of creation. As a boy he wanted so very much to travel out there, through the Maghreb to the other side. He still imagined that distant relatives lived out there, beyond the wasteland, and that one day he would meet them. Perhaps they had survived the corruption.

The region was once fertile and rich with sheep and goats. Three centuries ago it had been cursed by Bida, the black snake spirit of the Soninke people, because he had been cheated out of his annual virgin sacrifice by the virgin's angry fiancé. Love had triumphed, but drought brought an end to agriculture and gold mining. Brown-skinned traders from the north, in Tahert, still travelled down the same trail as his ancestors, through Sjilmasa in southern Morocco, then south and inland, running parallel with the coast, and southeast through Awdaghust and Kumbi Saleh. As a boy, Heijande, like most of his people, had adopted many Islamic customs and cuisines in order to be polite to these traders, and it was a kind trader who had shown Heijande how to make a *l'ud*, stretching thin strands of the gut of a tiger over rib bones. His practice with a *l'ud* gave him the confidence to master the *kora*.

That seemed so long ago. The screams of the captives now whispered in the wind from farther away. The powerful Asante king, Osei Tutu, had ties with the legendary John Konny on the coast, and the Dagomba would likely bring them to Konny. Heijande looked due east to a distant yellow-green uprising of misty savannah woodlands, undulating to a bumpy horizon of dark brown mountains. He turned to view the southwest terrain, the Volta River snaking through tropical rain forest, about a two-day run to the tiny huts and curls of smoke that outlined the village of Salaga, the slave-trade center, a node of Konny's empire. Heijande's world was encircled by mountains and rain forest, with the only escape possible to the Maghreb in the northeast, or to the west and the slave-trade centers.

* * *

History is written in the daytime by the victors, but actions occur at night, when the English, the Dutch, the Portuguese, and the Muslims sleep.

At night, the optimists of Heijande's clan argue with the pessimists who want to prevent childbirth to extinguish the clan rather than face widespread, inevitable corruption.

At night, Heijande consults his ancestors. They are embodied in sacred stones placed at the feet of the shrine of the three monkeys, and are made immortal through song. They are fed, celebrated, danced to, and strummed into perfection by the *kora*. The white clans have what they call history, but it is a history of the dead. They allow only one ancestor to accompany them through life, the one they call Christ the Lord. They celebrate eating the flesh of this Christ, and many of Heijande's clan fear that these white clans traded for slaves and took them off to sea in order to eat them.

At night, Heijande sings a living history, the story of how his people live for all time in the bosom of all that is natural. All of Heijande's ancestors live with them and help them. Heijande songs bring their ancestors to life. His music has the power not only to heal, but to enliven everyone around him, to bring life into the world. He draws this power from within, with the help of his ancestors and with his fervent passion for the beautiful sweet-lipped Shu Lia, the muse of his songs.

Yes, history is written in the daytime but made at night. It was during the night that he had lost interest in Angula, his first wife, who no longer wanted him to travel and sing his songs for others. *Sing them for us alone, and our children, to keep us safe.* But the songs have no power unless you share them with others. We can't keep our love with this music, we must spread it to others to help them love, to enrich not only our clan but all our clans. She did not understand.

And it was during the night that he'd left her bed for Shu Lia, who now interested him more than anything in the world. Shu Lia was kin to another *jeli* and had the potential to be one herself. It would be good for Heijande to mate with her.

Angula had screamed and shouted at him the next day, in front of the others, but it only made her appear vain. The others thought, does she not understand the power of Heijande's music? Does she not appreciate that Heijande has taken on a second wife, kin to a *jeli* herself, to help with the chores?

All these thoughts lay hostage to his tired body and kept him worried all night, singing worried songs. Heijande finally fell asleep at dawn by the river, and woke up in the hottest part of the day in chains, tricked by his own exhaustion. Like his brethren, he was now a victim of this incomprehensible universe.

* * *

Black bony shapes crouched or lay flat between trees or leaned against their trunks, clinging to a scorched earth as chain gangs clinked and swirled around them, oblivious to their slow dying gasps escaping like steam from their mouths, a brownish steam of disease and starvation evaporating in the greenish gloom. In Salaga, knee-deep in the mud of the *wonkan bawa*, the bathing place of slaves, chained to a young Baobab tree with other captives, Heijande sang his songs, picked his *kora* strings with one hand and beat his *djembe* with the other, quietly, knowing he would attract more attention than if he did so loudly.

He sang in the Dagomba tongue the song[2] of John Konny, how he had used the spirits of Legba to trick the Dutch commander of Fort Hollandia. Through many contacts Heijande had learned of John Konny, the powerful black merchant and monopolist of the slave trade at the coast. The Dagomba traders stopped to listen to Heijande; many of them knew versions of this story, and spoke of Konny as heroic. Heijande used the song as a trick to associate himself with Konny, to usurp some of Konny's power and charisma, so that his captors would be pleased and his people in chains would be inspired. Heijande's performance caught the attention of the burly Noi, commander of the traders, who had strict instructions to bring any original singers, musicians, or *jeli* to the English missionaries.

The story Heijande sung was how John Konny had ruthlessly cornered the slave trade with the Asante and the Aowin. Konny staged a coup in early 1714. The Dutch sent three shiploads of armed men. Konny himself had led the charge, in the disguise of a baboon, that killed thirty-six Dutchmen and captured the fort. Heijande's song was all about Konny's bravery, cunning, and the kind of trickery that comes only from high wisdom.

Heijande's song was close to the truth. Ten years after the coup, Konny was still king of the slave trade in that region. Konny had once garroted a prisoner who had stolen silverware from a missionary family, then presented the man's blood-drenched lifeless heart to the family as an offering, but kept the silverware for himself.

* * *

The English considered Konny to be excessively violent, but easy to manipulate for driving out the Dutch. Accustomed to abominable behavior in the far reaches of the Empire, Admiral William Faithfull, stationed in 1724 on the more-or-less permanently anchored British frigate *Insoluble*, didn't think twice about Konny's torching of villages and killing women and children. This is what the tribes did to each other in their own tribal wars, and what the Dutch and Portuguese had been doing for nearly a century.

And Faithfull had no patience for the Dutch. His father-in-law and mentor, Sir Christopher Myngs, had been honorably engaging his ship *Victory* in the Four Days Battle of 1666 between the English and the Dutch when his flotilla had been surrounded and he received lethal wounds, first through the cheek and then in the left shoulder, by musket balls fired by a Dutch coward, a sharpshooter, on the deck of the *Ridderschap van Holland*. No, the Dutch could not be trusted, even though the Glorious Revolution of 1688 brought an end to their conflict.

Faithfull was there to enforce the Treaty of Utrecht of 1713, which had given Britain a thirty-year *asiento*, or contract, to supply an unlimited number of slaves to the Spanish colonies in the Americas. The triangular Atlantic trade was the most important and profitable trading route in the world. One out of every four ships that left Liverpool harbor carried manufactured trade goods to Africa, including guns from Faithfull's son-in-law's concern in Birmingham, to exchange for slaves to transport to the Americas, where they would sell the slaves and pick up a cargo of agricultural products, often produced with slave labor, for Britain. Indeed, nearly all the sugar produced in the plantations were exported to London by this route, to supply the highly lucrative coffee houses. The slave trade boosted employment especially in the copper and brass industries around Bristol and Liverpool, one of which was owned by Faithfull's uncle. A merchant ship could make a substantial profit on each leg of the voyage, which was designed to take full advantage of prevailing winds and currents. Faithfull's assignment was to ensure that these ships could conduct their trade by any means necessary.

Mumblingore and Cravingston, Anglican missionaries on station at the Gold Coast port, may have been aghast at the Konny situation but showed no interest in pursuing any other method of staying the course of the British Empire, except to hold court with Konny several times a week and keep him occupied with trivial matters. The two missionaries could be seen often, arm-in-arm like children in the dark, roaming about the port all day long with their periwigged heads so close together they seemed stuck in everlasting conference. Such imbeciles, thought Faithfull. What madness had settled in Canterbury to have sent these fine specimens of boorish incompetence! Two perfectly insignificant and incapable men of the cloth, rendered into existence by the high use of superstition and nonsense to promote the idea of civilization, the political organization of crowds. They had persisted with their beliefs and English customs in this port for several months, like gnats at the gnawing edge of a vast and dark wilderness, dull to the subtle influences of their surroundings like blind men in a large room.... All of that great land throbbing with life was like a great emptiness to them. The two understood nothing and cared for nothing except to pass the time with their moonlit ecstasies with captured native women and their shaded afternoon soliloquies made blithely insouciant by Dutch-imported opium. Faithfull had no use for them.

Ernest Mumblingore, as portly and contented as a butcher in the East End with an ostentatiously fat paunch under his black *cappa clausa,* moved about on very short legs as if rooting in a pig sty. The view through his darting, insidious brown eyes was of an inherited devastation, a clearing encroached upon on one side by a rampaging sea and by all other sides by thick forests hiding fateful complications of fantastic life, all erupting in an eloquent silence. There was no escape except by sea, either on the Admiral's ship anchored in the half-moon-shaped bay, or on one one of the merchant ships that arrived every fortnight bringing English goods and hauling away slaves. And to his mind there was no salvation for these natives except by sea; to be taken away from this fetid wash of violence and terror into the bosom of the Christian plantation in the New World.

Indeed, thought Mumblingore, the Konny situation was inevitable. Had not the rulers of these thatch-hut kingdoms supplied slaves to Muslim traders in the north and Europeans on the coast for centuries? Whatever methods they were to employ to exterminate the native beliefs in evil spirits were methods they had inherited from the previous missionaries. According to accounts, one had reported back to the Archbishop castigating Admiral Faithfull as downright immoral and beastly, and then promptly committed suicide; the other had abandoned his post at the mouth of the Volta River and set off, babbling, to find some fantastical source of wisdom in the wastes of the Maghreb. Mumblingore's reaction upon hearing this was to question the wisdom of pairing him up with someone as potentially subversive as Cravingston, but in time he came to know and like the man, if only for the entertainment of watching his judgmental convictions shatter in the face of depravity.

Richard Cravingston, all bony and angular, yellow-faced and pointy-eared, with eyes that sparkled like specs of mica, so awash within his black *cappa clausa* as to be drowning in it without his *caul* to hold his neck high, fidgeted constantly with a worried aspect. He acknowledged, ruefully, that whatever method had been employed by their pre-decessors, nothing had worked. All it did was give Konny a monopoly.

Cravingston saw the travesty right away, when he had accompanied the explorer John Atkins to Fort Hollandia on the *Swallow* in 1721, and had found the smartly dressed Konny in charge of the fort, cursing the Dutch and serving up meals of canky bread, cheese and palm wine with plates and silverware. Set around the walls of the circular chamber specially for dinner were more than thirty bashed-in heads of decapitated native warriors and Dutch soldiers, alternating black and white heads, still bleeding from all openings, many with their eyes still open, staring out in empty, hopeless vengeance. Yes, yes, it helps our side, Cravingston said, but at what cost? Dutch West India Company traders are slaughtered if they do not leave the area. These newcomers, these interlopers from Spain, from Tunis, we strong-arm them into trading with Konny. We give those blood-thirsty Dagomba chieftains a reason to collect more captives. What are we really doing here? We think we control this John Konny, but it is Konny that is controlling the port, not the British!

Squat on the western side of the Bight of Benin, the port was an opaque ring of earth encircled by jagged hills, bordering on a half-moon sheet of transparent blue water harboring three anchored ships with naked masts. The bottomless bay reflected a luminous sky. Cravingston had his counter-revelation one hot afternoon on the beach with one of the female captives Konny sent over periodically, ostensibly for a Christian conversion from their wicked ways. Konny was someone they could learn from. If the white race were to truly dig in, revel in this decadence, get to the very source of the African's primitive, dark nature, he thought as he probed with his nose the sweat-creased passages of her brown fleshy buttocks and breathed her warm smell deeply, why, we would eventually bring out jewels, priceless artifacts of human heritage, astonishing secrets of powers latent within us all. Opium from the Malay, favored among the Dutch gentlemen when smoked with tobacco in a pipe, produced a vertiginous swoon but did not connect Cravingston with these Powers Within. Nevertheless it helped him immensely to drop all his pretenses, remove from his mind all thoughts of the plump wife back home sighing over needlework and her Bible, and lay about with slave women as dreamy, pliant pillows of flesh, sweet and committed to no other purpose than to serve his need.

Mumblingore had long ago steeled himself to passionate displays and all that prancing about naked on the beach in daylight; it was not his style. His passion was for economic power, the power to make people more reasonable and more comfortable to deal with, more pliant. As a missionary Mumblingore knew only one position, on top. Inside the thatched hut that served as a chapel for the port, an enslaved Asante princess lay prone beneath his sweaty girth, spouting gibberish English at each and every one of his clumsy thrusts, English words he had commanded her to use, "penis" and "vagina" and so on, until "lord" "god" and "almighty" brought him to a flustering, dripping climax. His idea: Tame the wild beast with civilized words.

"How is that working out for you, precisely?" It was that idiot Cravingston, popping in at precisely the wrong moment.

Embarrassed as he rolled his bulk off her and pulled up his breaches, Mumblingore could not find words that could justly describe this situation. "Just fine, I must say," was all he could reply. He knew he was now in debt to his associate, as each was supposed to avoid witnessing this type of behavior by the other. He should not have engaged in this activity in this primitive chapel, of all places, and most likely at some point an unsavory favor would be asked of him in return.

But Cravingston showed no sign of caring. He had brought with him a thin little black fellow wrapped in the usual ragged, mud-smeared, hand-woven *kente* cloth. "This little devil the traders brought in could be useful, if we can get him to sing his song about Konny to Konny himself."

Ah. The Konny situation. It had such... an *immoral* side to it that fascinated him. Mumblingore scratched his gurgling stomach. "I say, Cravingston, how could the Negroes idolize this slave trader, this John Konny? And he *is* one of them, is he not?"

"Savages. They have no concept of evil, no Devil," smirked Cravingston. He was trying to coax Heijande to sing the Konny song.

* * *

Heijande knew enough of the English tongue to recognize "Devil" and "Konny" and tried to explain, *No, not Devil, not evil*. Making use of what he knew of English, he tried to explain that there is only the Trickster, and those who are tricked. He could tell that the missionaries did not comprehend, so he told them in his native tongue the fable of the Trickster, loosely translated,

Signifying monkey, stay up in your tree
You had better not monkey with me
Signifying monkey made Lion a fool
Challenged him that Elephants rule.
Lion took off looking for a fight
Elephant hiding in plain sight.
Elephant said to Lion in surprise,
You should pick on someone your own size.
Elephant stomped Lion in the grass
And monkey stuck his finger in that old lion's ass.

While they didn't understand the language, the missionaries roared with laughter as Heijande then disrobed, stood naked before them, and showed them the sign of Aido-Hwedo painted on his left buttock. To Heijande, it was all part of the performance.

As their laughter subsided in the wake of Heijande's earnestness, the missionaries pondered what to do with him. Cravingston knew a bit of the Wolof language of Gambia. He tried to get Heijande to sing something spiritual, about his religion, but there was no word for religion. Heijande assumed he meant the power of his ancestor, so he showed them the stone he had carried in his palm throughout the ordeal of his capture, the stone he had blessed with a song. Heijande spoke rapidly in Wolof about having received his first stone from his ancestor, an old man who had outwitted death, and now lived among his clan as Binu, immortal, revealing himself whenever he pleases, usually as a snake wound around a covenant-stone. Music unlocks the stone's power, the power of the ancestor within.

To demonstrate, Heijande picked up his *kora*, locked it in the crook of his arm, and announced in English that he would now sing his "Vibration Song" about the beginning of all life, the song[3] of Aido-Hwedo, Nana-Buluku's masculine partner, a snake in appearance. Writhing about like a snake and holding the stone tightly, he strummed a rhythm and sang in a wide tonal range, loosely translated,

Nummo taught the people to dance
The rhythm of resurrection
The Binu guide us back
through natural selection
Of Nana-Buluku's companion we sung
Aido-Hwedo slithers through dung
Mountains, valleys, and rivers wide
On Aido-Hwedo we take a ride

At this point Heijande stopped and held out the stone. "Hmm," mused Mumblingore, handling it. It was just a stone, but he could feel its warmth. "Good, good, good. Good vibrations, eh?"

Heijande went on singing, loosely translated,

Overburdened with animals and plants
Nana-Buluku feared the world's collapse
Aido-Hwedo ate his own tail
Forming a loop so that nothing would fail
Nana-Buluku granted his wish
To live in the ocean just like the fish
But the ocean seethes and rumbles in fury
His food runs out, that's the end of the story.

Mumblingore turned to face Cravingston, annoyed. Spirituals, religion, what nonsense! He was interested in taming shrews; he wanted to hear the songs that drove women into lustful frenzies, and wanted to work these experiments on the nubile females newly captured and detained in Salaga, the ones who've not yet tasted the white man's cock or felt his stinging lash, the ones pure enough to exhibit their true natures and fear their original demons — the only way, really. One must know the Devil's power, know His effect on people, in order to counteract His influence.

The instructions from his minister were specific on this point: root out the Devil in His natural environment, get Him to shake His rattlers and wag His tail. Listen for dissonance in their music, and for anything that hinted of the *diabolus in musica*, the Devil's Tritone. And keep a critical eye on Cravingston, whose ancestors included notable Anabaptists from the Low Countries with a tendency toward radicalism.

Of course it never occurred to Mumblingore until that moment that he'd been paired with this music historian not for any true reason, such as to dissect the native musical influences, but precisely because the man had Dutch ancestors, specifically Dutch ancestors associated with radicals. The minister wanted Mumblingore to help keep Cravingston's meddlesome arguments from stifling the progress of music censorship by the Church and to keep all debate under the stiff thumb of the Archbishop.

"I say, Cravingston, you do insist that this... this strumming and screeching is somehow in the category of... music?"

"Yes indeed," looking up from his notes. Cravingston was an expert on musical notation and the neuma system of dots and strokes placed above the text, first popularized by ninth century Roman Catholic monks. He also had studied the notation of Guido d'Arezzo, the eleventh century Italian Benedictine monk who added a four-line stave to neuma to begin to provide pitch instructions. All this had distilled down to the modern five-line stave, introduced in the fourteenth century, which coincided with the suppression of dissonance and disagreeable intervals such as the Devil's Tritone. "If we are to consider the versified Psalms, the Christmas carols, and the Gregorian chants as music, and indeed they belong in that category, then why not these chants, be it as they are, indeed, spiritual incantations? Music is not bound to any certain pitch, and *any* sort of interval is possible, though not all lead to what we would consider *harmonic*. Still, there is no reason to require spiritual yearnings of this sort to have any recognizable melody," and so on, and so forth.

Mumblingore was patient but eventually intervened. "Yes, yes, that's all well and good, Cravingston, but how do you even know the beginnings and endings of these, these performances they consider songs? More importantly, *how do you write them down?*"

It was Cravingston's turn to be patient. "Really, it is quite easy with our modern musical notation system. We can count the semitones between each of these utterances you call 'screeches' and transpose the intervals into familiar keys," and so forth and so on.

"Well of course, Cravingston," he scowled on each syllable, annoying the man, "but these songs of theirs are used to cast *spells*, and so forth. How are we to *perform* them? You see..." And so they argued on, rather politely.

Heijande recognized the call-and-response pattern of their conversation as the white clan's version of storytelling, but there were no other members of their clan to join in, and they twittered back and forth like *tingetange*, the long-legged water birds. So when they asked Heijande about the songs that turn women to desire men, and how to perform them, Heijande demonstrated again with his *kora* the song of satisfaction[4], a true call-and-response with his voice calling and the strings of his *kora* responding, loosely translated,

On the seventh hour, of the seventh day,
Of the seventh year, the seventh son say:
"I was born for good luck, and I know you can see;
I have seven women taking care of me.
But nothing in the world can satisfy
One who keeps living while others die."
Well, I wish I was a catfish
swimming in the deep blue sea
I would have all the good-looking women
fishing after me

"What the Devil?" whispered Mumblingore.

"It must be polyrhythmic," noted Cravingston, "requiring at least two rhythms to be played concurrently, at least one of which is typically an irrational rhythm on the, whatever it is, the stringed instrument, and a downbeat that does not coincide. Where one of the parts involves an irrational rhythm, the resulting rhythm could be said to be an 'irrational polyrhythm' I would think."

"What the Devil!" cursed Mumblingore.

Heijande stopped singing and playing his *kora*. "No, *not Devil*," he said in English, and then in Wolof, "*Hepi? Hip?*" Meaning, "Do you see? Can you open your eyes?"

Mumblingore stared blankly back at him, and then spoke the question of the ages. "What is... *hip?*"

* * *

Ernest Mumblingore slept the relaxed sleep of a hypocrite without conviction. The mindless babbling of these natives was not unlike the sleep-inducing babble of some of his mystical Grand Lodge colleagues back home. So he could accommodate Cravingston's notions of destiny and the literal Word of the Bible without chuckling in front of him; he could even tolerate Cravingston's passionate screeching almost every night, as it did not keep him from dropping off into dreamland.

His dream was of, naturally, himself, trudging through the snowy streets of London, entranced by the echoing sound of the Christmas carol "Gaudete"[5] spilling out of a cathedral.

The time of grace has come

What we have wished for
Songs of joy
Let us give back faithfully

At its steps he stood, listening and marveling at the great secrets of Alchemy encoded in the architecture, proving that science could be crafted to support organized religion. He would not go in, as he was on his way to the Goose and Gridiron Ale House to deliver the most sensational of his speeches, the best his peers had yet to hear.

He carried the torch of the revivalist Masons, who declared that the secrets of architecture were the only true relics of the faith of the patriarchs, before the Great Flood wiped out their early civilization. All other secrets and mysteries, including those of primitive Egypt, were but corrupt interpretations of the first primitive and true tradition.

At the makeshift pulpit in the ale house he thundered that God, Jesus Christ, and all the rest were theatrical productions, excuses to build grand cathedrals and monuments. *(Here, here! Another round for everyone!)* The sun is but a fiery furnace *(Yes!)*, the moon a cold orb that rules the night's tides *(Indeed!)*, and the stars have no influence at all *(None that we can see, m'lord!)*. We were *not* put on this Earth for some reason! *(NO!)* We simply grew here... like mushrooms.

John Locke, the hero of his youth, is now in the audience, now smiling at him, now beckoning to him to join the Social Contract. Essential Christian doctrine is belief in God and in Jesus as Messiah, yes, yes, but for Mumblingore this doctrine was also a practical political tool. Locke's reasonableness was legendary. Locke could just stretch out his arms and encompass everyone in the audience, and you would know exactly what he meant, that we must tolerate all of their nonsense, no matter if they are Presbyterians, Independents, Arminians, Quakers, and even Anabaptists, as they were all reasonable men.

But not the atheists, the so-called free spirits, and certainly *not* the primitives. We are charged with the duty of introducing the primitives to the reasonable world of Christianity, and for entry to this world, many generations must first be put to work. The men before him are the pliant, workable assets, the tools for architecture, which holds power over us all. And he, Mumblingore, solid to the core, loyal to the elite group that was now calling itself the "Corporation"... He's the man for the job.

He paused, and the Goose and Gridiron went back to work, ignoring him. The audience gulped their ale, and a peasant musician in the corner struck up a tune. Drinking was everyone's favorite topic, so everyone joined in.[6] Mumblingore felt defeated. Look at them, singing the peasant songs that make them happy. Peasant songs that were passed down orally, generation to generation, from the ancient times.

Mumblingore speculated. The primitives, what if *they* know of secrets that we the elite only *pretend* to know, and rely only on rituals to pass along? Signs and gestures considered Masonic have been found among the initiatory rites of some tribes and natives of Syria and India, interwoven with their religious philosophies, and in other forms in almost all parts of the world. Mumblingore had tried a few gestures of the Craft with these primitives, but not even Heijande, a griot, had recognized them.

Mumblingore wanted to tap the hidden side of human nature for powers that supposedly exist in all men. These powers were thought to be awakened only by those trained for many years in meditation and the occult sciences, but Mumblingore thought it could be approached, like anything and everything in life, with enough arrogance to quicken the pace. It's right there in our heads, after all, is it not? Why can we not just *dig into it*, and use it?

His modern crusade is to retrieve these powers from the dusty cobwebbed depths of antiquity, as channeled through these primitives that have kept alive the rituals and knew how to tap into these secrets. He awoke mumbling "for we are brethren of the Rosie Cross..." until shaken awake by the sounds of village life.

* * *

Not so Richard Cravingston, no relaxed sleep for the closeted free spirit, nothing but the stink and torpor of an opium fever. Every night he wrestled with the covers under the mosquito net, unable to sleep, turning finally to his coveted *Philosophiae Naturalis Principia Mathematica* by the hero of his youth, Sir Isaac Newton. Newton's description of the universe in mechanistic terms was widely accepted by Deists such as Cravingston, partly because Newton believed the Bible to be the word of God, but supported the view that the Roman pontiff was the Antichrist from the Book of Revelations.

Cravingston would read his favorite passages, humming portions of Tartini's scandalous "Devil's Trill Sonata"[7] that used the banned *diabolus in musica*, the Devil's Tritone. According to Giuseppe Tartini himself, he had met the Devil in a dream, stranded at the crossroads, not knowing which direction to go. The Devil appeared, took his Stradivarius violin, tuned it, and played the sonata. Cravingston had learned it from Tartini himself, because the Church forbade the sonata and would have burned the scholarly composer at the stake if he had tried to publish it. If ever challenged for humming it, Cravingston would claim that he needed to know the enemy to better fight them. He fancied that one day he would finally meet the Devil and *not* sell his soul, *not* make that Faustian bargain. The music was merely a temptation to steel himself against.

Cravingston hummed and reread passages until a dream took him over. A chorus of "oohs" and "aahs" accompanied this same dream he had ever since arriving in the hothouse humid, blood-rich tropics, in which night was simply a dark version of the same putrid climate. He became Rotten John of Münster, 1534, the Dutch heretic John of Leyden, who had taken over the German city, proclaiming it the New Jerusalem with other Anabaptist radicals and members of the Brethren of the Free Spirit. They were out to abolish money and private property as well as religious persecution. They wanted all heresies legitimized, which would have seriously disrupted the political framework of the time.

Cravingston's great-grandfather had participated with the local bishop in the siege of Münster, permitting no supplies to enter for over a year. The people were reduced to eating rats, grass, shoe leather, and even cobblestones before eventually resorting to cannibalism. Cravingston, in his dream as Rotten John of Leyden, unapologetically feasted on remaining supplies while his citizens suffered. He pranced about the city draped in robes and gold bracelets, executing any doubters and nailing pieces of their corpses up on posts, shouting "I yam the anti-CHRIST!" Those who agreed with him followed his every directive, even taking on additional wives. They all learned his newly reformed set of versified Psalms, which Leyden had based on John Calvin's ideas that unison singing intensified a congregation's sense of community.

Then Cravingston, in his dream as Leydon, presided over a black mass with devilish choruses of "oohs" and "aahs" simulating the pleasures of indiscriminate sex, of eating succulent flesh, of drinking blood. The cannibals' singing so unnerved and enraged the bishop's forces that, in the battle that ensued, those from the city who surrendered, including women and children, were considered possessed by the Devil and slaughtered immediately or left to die in the parched earth outside the city's walls.

Cravingston as Leydon stared across the battlements into his great-grandfather's eyes, and could feel the conviction in his throat. He wanted to speak. He wanted to say, in Leydon's words, that for those truly free of spirit, no crime was a crime and no sin was a sin; that God's grace enveloped all sinful practices, indeed *especially* those that allow the free spirit to *remain* free. He wanted to shout that he was already dead to the world and the flesh. But his great-grandfather was already climbing the battlements, the city was overrun by the bishop's forces, and just as he realized he would be tortured and put to death, he saw his great-grandfather hammering nails into the cage that, he knew, would hold his burnt corpse on display in the city's church tower.

Only upon awakening in a pool of sweat did he realize he had finally indeed fallen asleep and only dreamed all this, but still, he felt compel-led to assume the position and pray. "My God, You and I, as You know, we have an agreement. You will forget about my transgressions on the Dark Continent if I cease to question Your Judgment, Your Will. I must survive, and yes, carry out the insatiable demands of those closer to You who know better than I. But survive I must. That is all I ask of You."

The day thusly consecrated, he set out with his native songster to gather up Mumblingore and take them all to John Konny. What does it matter, thought Cravingston, that Konny's tactics are so bloody? Konny is useful.

* * *

Drums pounded a powerful rhythm,[8] the signature rhythm of John Konny, and his Yoruban slave choir sung more tales of his greatness, as the two missionaries and Heijande headed up to Fort Hollandia. Black corpses, many of them dismembered and beheaded, lined the walk up to the gates. Heijande recognized some of them as Mossi, some Gonja, and some Asante, but none from his community. Mumblingore studiously avoided looking at them and held his breath as they passed, while Cravingston whispered "Münster" to himself, over and over. Gorged flies buzzed lazily about and around their feast of blood.

Just outside the wide door, Cravingston turned to face Heijande, hand on his arm. "This is evil. Yes?"

Heijande pretended to look glum, knowing the white missionary wouldn't understand. There is only the Trickster, and those who are tricked. Konny is a Trickster in touch with bad magic, and he uses it, but even bad Tricksters can be turned to do good. The white clans, on the other hand, are purely evil, because they either know nothing about how they have orchestrated this empire of trade, or don't care. The white clans have no magic, and Heijande couldn't see how they could be turned to do any good.

Inside the innermost chamber of the fort, all was as cool and quiet as a chapel. John Konny, decked out in a starched uniform lent to him by Admiral Faithfull, lounged in a gigantic wooden chair made for a giant. He wore the standard military coat fitted to his figure at the upper body, tight at the waist — a *justaucorps*, a flattering piece of clothing for a heavily muscled black man. His vest was made from a colorful brocaded silk, which contrasted nicely with the large turned back cuffs of the *justaucorps* facings of the vest fabric, while the coat was made from a plain fabric. The vest was nearly as long as the coat, maybe only an inch shorter, tight fitting in the waist as well, and with long, tubular shaped narrow sleeves without any cuffs. The effect was as if an entire trunk-load of civilized finery had fallen onto a gorilla. John Konny was calm, cool, towering even in a sitting position in that giant chair, with all the power in the fort within his grasp. His broad face smiled mis-chievously, revealing an uneven row of yellow molars and a single gold front tooth. He wore an officer's smallsword, a light one-handed sword designed for thrusting but mostly decorative, lacking a distinct cutting edge. Or so it seemed at first; Mumblingore noticed blood dripping from its point. Against the wall leaned a Birmingham-made musket.

Heijande involuntarily gasped; the beautiful Shu Lia was entwined about his legs, stripped of the colorful *kaba* across her bosom and the expressive *asee ntoma* around her hips. Naked, incredibly desirable yet piously vulnerable, her limbs gleaming ebony with ivory undersides, her breasts heaving, her forehead perspiring. Contradictory impulses flooded Heijande's body, anger and love, lust and pity, the impulse to attack, the instinct to defend and retreat, and all this rooted him on the spot and made him unable to move.

The rolling tones of John Konny's deep charcoal voice filled the chamber effortlessly. "Ah yes, my friends from England, and how are you today? You have brought me someone, I see." Konny enunciated distinctly, with soft precision, with calculated confidence in the presence of white men, even a bit scornful in mirth, and unaffectedly condescending, as if from his throne he could survey a landscape of human folly and these two missionaries were just a small part of it.

"A singer. We've brought you a singer," said Cravingston, "who has a song about *you*, which I think you will enjoy."

"A singer! Let me see, come closer."

Heijande moved closer, and Shu Lia finally saw him. Her heart poured out on the floor through her eyes and she could not look up at him.

Heijande's contradictory impulses flattened into pure sympathy for the woman he now loved. He grew resolute, steady, sure of himself, and with concentration and deep breathing, he drew on the power within himself. He could see what would happen, and he could draw on his will to influence it.

"Please allow me to introduce myself," Konny said from his chair, without getting up or extending his hand. In his resolute eyes and through his restrained manner, one could see a man accustomed to battle, travel, escape. "John Konny, chief of this port and all lands around it," he indicated by a theatrical sweep of his arm, as if the floor of his chamber was but a miniature version of his domain. "As you can see, I am a man of wealth and taste."

Heijande felt the power within him as a lion in full crouch, ready to spring. He wanted to appear to be from outside the area, so he spoke evenly, almost noncommittally, in Yoruban. "I am honored to be in your presence, John Konny. You are well respected in every kingdom and village I have traveled through. Your exploits are well known, and your courage impresses everyone. I am Heijande, a Dogon, of the Wanderer clan of Dyon and the Bela Mont, and I have travelled a great distance, from the Cliffs of Bandiagara, to find my sister." He then gestured at Shu Lia. "It appears that you have placed her in bondage."

"But she is fine! Ha ha ha ha!" Konny's booming laughter bounced off the walls, escaped the fort and rose up to the sky to make the stars twinkle. Konny then also spoke in Yoruban. "My young beauty, you are fine, are you not? Do you not want to stay with me? I will not eat you! Ha ha ha ha!" His teeth flashed and his eyes glittered with animal lust, his dark face creased in a truculent smile, the frank audacious smile of a man who has walked barefoot in these jungles well-armed and noiseless.

Shu Lia hissed softly in Yoruban, a curse. "*Fa me nwa.*" *You have taken me as cheap and easy as the snail.*

"Oh no no no!" laughed Konny. He spread his arms wide, as if to encircle everyone in the chamber, from the quietly seething Heijande to the dejected Shu Lia to the bewildered Mumblingore and Cravingston, and spoke in English. "Come and drink with me. We're in a world full of trouble, heh heh, and I'm on a drinking spree." Sure enough, he produced a jug of the finest

English brandy from behind the chair, and passed it to Heijande, who refused to drink it and passed it to Mumblingore, who drank heartily.

"You are a *jeli*, a *guewel,* a griot," Konny spoke suddenly, sharply, to Heijande, using every word he knew for it. There was a long silence. "I know about griots," Konny said to the others, in English, and looked back at Heijande. "The griot knows many traditional songs, knows them perfectly. You carry a *kora,* so you are a worldly griot. Yes! A griot can tease out the power of these songs like grease from a lion's teeth." Then he snarled at Heijande. "Is that not right, *griot?*"

Heijande spoke not a word and gazed only into Shu Lia's intent eyes.

"You don't want our friends to know, eh? Tell me," Konny addressed the missionaries, "does our friend have a sacred stone?"

"Why, yes," said Mumblingore, nearly trembling with fear.

"He sings to it," said Cravingston, a bit too enthusiastically.

"So, my brave friend," Konny turned back to Heijande, and spoke in Yoruban, "I am *jatigi*, from a family of warrior-kings. By tradition our families are inseparable. I have the power to summon Legba, the One who guards the threshold to the spirit world, and interpret any of the songs you sing, and use that power to my advantage."

"Ahonnee pa nkasa," barked Heijande quickly in Yoruban. Its literal translation is *precious beads make no noise,* but what it means is, empty barrels make the most noise. Konny knew exactly what he meant.

"Why should I not kill you? I want your stone," Konny thundered in English. "I *will* kill you, just for that stone. And feed you to my Mossi warriors."

"You would not know how to use it," sang Heijande in rapid English, sotto voce, surprising everyone. He sang with his power, directed at Konny, in a way that he knew would penetrate the warrior's reserve and make him sick.

"Hmm." Konny appeared lost in thought or lost at sea. Some crazy energy seemed to flow through him. Stifling a rising nausea, he hissed through his teeth. "Since you know how to speak English, I could let *them*," pointing at the missionaries, as if that would be even more disagreeable than death itself, "have their way with you. You would be more fortunate to allow me to torture you, and then be eaten alive by my Mossi warriors." He gathered his strength to fight off the nausea and snarled, "You *will* hand over the stone and tell me its secrets!"

Heijande sang again with power, another Yoruban proverb. "Nipa tire nye bofere na yeapaa mu ahwe dea ewo mu." *The human mind is not like the papaya fruit to be split open to see what is on the inside.*

Konny laughed and settled in his chair, but the nausea grew in intensity and gathered around a point in his stomach, as if he'd been penetrated by a spear. "He sings proverbs in English," Konny grunted. "What kind of griot is this?"

Heijande again was firm. "If I show you the stone, and sing its power, would you let her go?"

Konny sensed a way out without confrontation, a way to banish everyone from his presence so that he could deal with his unreasonable stomach. "But how would you demonstrate this power? And why should I give up my beautiful flower?" Konny's fingers laced Shu Lia's neck as if he were about to strangle her; and as he stroked her hair he grabbed a fistful, and began to pull it like an anchor out of the storm of his nausea.

Heijande sought Shu Lia's eyes again in a silent plea, and when he connected, he sent these thoughts to her: in this world there are only Tricksters, and those who are Tricked. Then he turned back to Konny and said, in Yoruban, "I can make her fall in love with anyone, even with the fat English missionary."

Konny laughed again, and answered in Yoruban. "This woman? Your own sister? I want to see that!"

From the fold of his *kente*, Heijande produced the stone. The spirit of his ancestor. He knew a song he could sing that would give her the proper instructions, in code. His *kora* strumming complemented his voice as he sung it,[9] and a hush fell over everyone in the chamber, an overwhelming anticipation, a shared hallucination that is a part of any performance.

Shu Lia, taking her cue, swooned into a puddle on the floor, and when she rose again, as the drumming quickened, her face grew soft and pliable, gentle and smiling, and then wickedly smiling as she swept over to Mumblingore and, sighing and moaning, she parted his black cappa clausa and reached into the folds of his yellow breeches. Mumblingore quickly hardened, swooned, and lost his balance, only to be propped up by the sparkling-eyed Cravingston who could not believe what he was seeing. She pretended to fondle Mumblingore's rigid member, now in full salute, and darted her eyes to see if Konny was looking. Heijande gave a great shout and kora flourish to end his song, and turning to the missionary, started another song. Shu Lia froze in position, her eyes imploringly searching the missionary's and her mouth wide open.

As Mumblingore looked down, he began to hallucinate. Her eyes had turned blazing red in an uncontrolled rage, her face had contorted in anger, and her mouth had grown sharp incisors. Mumblingore's stiff member quickly wilted, and he backed away from her.

"Enough! Take her away!" Konny shouted in English, loudly enough for his guards outside to hear. As they came in, he shouted again, "Put her in chains!"

The Asantes who'd become Konny's guards were gentle but firm, and devoted to Konny. The Dagomba, who would eventually receive her, would not be gentle, and would ignore any message from Konny to treat her nicely. Heijande knew he had very little time, but he had to finish his trick over Konny.

Konny glared at Heijande in stony silence, nausea creeping up his chest. Cravingston wrung his hands looking like he was about to intercede in Shu Lia's behalf, then shrunk back into himself, away from confrontation.

Konny broke the silence and spoke in Yoruban. "I want to learn your songs. I will spare your life if you will teach me."

Heijande realized his trick was at hand. He bowed, gracefully, and smiled sheepishly at Konny. "I need some time to prepare, master," he said in Yoruban, and motioned with his *djembe*. "The *djembe* skin is too dry and I must prepare the *kora* for the more powerful songs. It is the practice of my clan to make a sacrifice of blood and millet porridge at a Binu shrine and to dance with Awa masks, and this may take until tomorrow to complete."

"There is plenty of blood here!" shouted Konny in Yoruban, "plenty of sacrifices have already been made. My fort is the only shrine anywhere. This is where it is done!"

"But the masks, master, I still need the Awa masks."

"And what is their purpose?"

"The dance of the masks appeases the spiritual forces disturbed by the death of Nommo. The purpose is to lead souls of the deceased to their final resting place in the family altars and to consecrate their passage to the ranks of the ancestors."

Konny had heard of this Nommo worship among the Dogon. Something queer about their spirits disturbed him, as if they knew about larger and more dangerous creatures than any of the ones Konny had known in the jungles and beaches of his land. He could taste the nausea, now seeping up into his throat, stinging with bile. He'd had enough of this meeting and wanted these people gone so that he could sip his papaya juice and relax. He cleared his throat and spoke to Heijande in Yoruban. "Very well, you will teach me tomorrow. Go then, prepare your instruments and sacrifice, make your masks. If you need human flesh, there is plenty to find, even some that is fresh!"

He then motioned to Mumblingore and Cravingston and spoke in English. "Let this one be for now. You can have him back when I'm through with him." Then, in a flourish, Konny laughed and laughed at some joke in his mind. "Musicians! They are all so alike, always preparing their instruments! What can you do with them?" His smile suggested mirth, but his piercing eyes revealed his catlike hunger and exposed his most evil intentions, while his stomach let out a low grumble.

At that, Heijande was led out of the chamber by Konny's guards and deposited in an antechamber. So far, Heijande's trick had succeeded and he still had his thunder-stone. Now all he needed were pieces of stiff tree bark to work into the shapes for his masks, the pressed juice of indigo plants for the blue coloring, and cowrie shells, beads, and bones for decoration.

Konny had put one guard at the entrance. The Asante guard was fierce but not smart. He grew weary of trying to understand Heijande's instructions, and so he agreed to take Heijande into the bush to get the materials. Heijande's rituals before cutting tree bark and pressing the indigo plants, and the various instructions for preparing the bath for the pressed indigo, so stupefied the guard that Heijande was able to disarm him and flee into the dense forest, which embraced him as a mother would her son.

* * *

"Perhaps the little wog could have told us something about his people and where they came from. We could have gone out there to find his village."

"Oh yes, Cravingston, let us go running off to find the source of the Nile and the Mountains of the Moon," snorted Mumblingore. "Ethiopia is where they came from, clear on the other side of this dark continent. Padre Páez and the Spanish have been there for fifty years now, and they have all been converted, even the Jesuits have a representative there."

"I am sorry if I..."

"No, no, what angers me is that we let that stone slip through our fingers."

"But what if it is true, that the stone has no power by itself, that you need the little wog to do his song-and-dance routine."

"But of course it is true, Cravingston. The power is right here, in your head, but you need the stone, you see. This is the rock! To unlock it."

"I do not see."

"The rock focuses the mind, it concentrates the mind's power, like our prayer bead. I believe we can use it to bring about that epiphany we all speak of, the one moment, however fleeting, that we can achieve union with God and glimpse the reality of salvation... In any case we must have it."

And so, on direct orders from the missionaries, all captured blacks bound for the soon-to-depart *Perseverance* were searched for stones, pebbles, or small rocks. Of course the missionaries were mightily relieved to find out from the *Perseverance* captain, Randolph Newman, a solid-built Jew in good standing whose family had been invited back to England during the Cromwell years, that the ship's officers routinely confiscated all objects be they religious, commercial, or of any possible utility for aggression of any kind. Even wooden combs, masks, and tiny sticks. The ship, out of Liverpool, was about to embark for America with five hundred captives.

"Some of the captives have been known to swallow stones that are precious to them," the Captain had told the missionaries, "like the ones you seek. They usually die during the voyage. Their stomachs swell and burst, and they succumb in great agony, I must say. But I cannot say why. Stupid savages. They must know that even if they survive the voyage, they will not survive having their stomachs cut open to retrieve the stones."

"Well, this one is a prince," lied Cravingston, hoping to increase the Captain's interest. "He is connected to John Konny, and well, you know, we do not want to infuriate Konny."

Captain Newman was less than impressed. He had no time for petty tyrants; his kin in America were establishing a Jewish colony in the marshy frontier of New Jersey, and he was eager to get on with the next leg of his journey, which would bring him to a point on the new continent, Charleston Bay, that was only a few days sail from the mouth of the Delaware, and then only a day's ride to the colony. Newman's great-uncle had settled there fifty years earlier, when the two proprietors of New Jersey at that time, Sir George Carteret and Lord Berkeley of Stratton, were enticing new settlers by granting small parcels of land and religious freedom. He had received word from his cousin that all was not well; that Lord Cornbury, the governor of the royal colony, had been recalled for taking bribes and speculating on land, and that the governors of New York were imposing their authority, infuriating the farming community. Captain Newman had it in mind to resign his commission upon arrival in Philadelphia, retrieve his back pay of two hundred pounds sterling, and take a few slaves with him to join his cousin. In any case, Captain Newman promised to spread the word among the crew.

* * *

Heijande had been beside himself, quivering with rage, when he saw Shu Lia and the others of his clan dragged in chains down the gangplank to a longboat that would take them out to the anchored ship. As night fell, he realized that he must calm himself, or he would never be receptive to a sign from his ancestor. Without a sign he would have no plan. Heijande stood at the cross paths near the foot of the wharf, completely naked so that he would be hidden by the darkness itself; only the luminescent strings of his *kora* reflected any hint of light. He was on Legba's hallowed ground, and it was Legba he sought, in the darkest hour of the night.

Trickster god, messenger of and spokesman for the other *orishas*, Legba was known as the guardian at the gates between the worlds, a messenger between the human and the divine. His nature can be generous or cruel, as they are aspects of the same emotion, susceptible to the aspects of the humans that seek him out. When John Konny spoke of Legba, he meant the dark aspect, Kafou Legba, the malevolent Trickster who diverts humans from their true paths. Heijande sought his bright aspect, Eshu Legba, the Trickster who interprets all languages and teaches valuable lessons, who is intelligent and, always, not what he seems.

A old black man in filthy rags approached, sprinkling the path with water from a gourd, and came right up to Heijande in the darkness. He appeared weak, but his voice was deep and strong. He spoke to Heijande by name, in Yoruban. "You have the gift of the griot. You have been chosen."

"Eshu! I have my ancestor." Heijande showed the old man the sacred stone in the palm of his hand. "I will sneak onto the white clan's ship, and sing a song to confuse them, so that I can rescue Shu Lia."

"You will not succeed," said the old man patiently. "You are just a griot; your stone, just an ancestor's power. But if you do what I tell you, if you follow what may be your true destiny, you will become much more. A legend! Your stone will have legendary power. There are sacrifices you must make. Do not be distracted by love for one woman. You must learn to love everyone and to not love anyone. You are alone in your power, and you must use it, or lose it. Now: play your *kora*."

Heijande obliged the spirit messenger and plucked the strings of the *kora*. Forthrightly, the old man took it from him. Before Heijande could even protest, the old man adjusted the swatches of animal skin that bound its bridge to the two hardwood handles underneath the neck, tuning the *kora* in a way Heijande had not heard before. Then the old man handed it back to Heijande, who started nervously plucking its strings.

A stone in my path, now dark as the night…[10]

"You must prepare yourself for a long journey, across Oshun, the deep waters that feed and harbor Aido-Hwedo." The old man pointed west, beyond the ship, into a gloomier darkness worried by winds from the north. "But be careful, the white clan searches everyone. You must carry the stone in your stomach to bring your ancestor's power to the far shores."

"*Àdóìsí loògùn*" replied Heijande; loosely translated, one who rolls with the stone, or rolling stone.

The old man smiled. "You will be a rolling stone, but your stomach will not swell, and you will not die in agony as others have. And when you reach the far shores of the land of the white clan, you will pass through the whites unnoticed, your stone undisturbed. You will trick the white clan into setting you free, and you will then be able to regurgitate the stone without being disemboweled.

"You will become a legend, and your stone will carry great power among the people there. But you must have courage. Aido-Hwedo is often angry from hunger, and Oshun pitches and tosses any ship that crosses over her. My sweet Mamarou has prepared this for you, to keep your stomach from swelling." The old man held out pieces of jalap root, which gave off a pleasant, earthy odor.

There was no question. Heijande would have sacrificed his life to free Shu Lia and his clan. Eshu Legba promised he would survive; he could trick the white captors with the power of his stone and keep them all alive. Still, he could not bring himself to swallow the stone. "Chew a bit of the jalap root first." Heijande obliged and chewed the earthy root, and his mouth and tongue were suddenly bathed in senselessness, numb to everything. The old man helped him, and the stone slipped down his gullet. He nearly gagged as he bent over, but the old man held him firmly. It stayed down, and he felt a warm glow in his stomach.

"Now you can play the *kora* and the white clan will like its sound," said the old man, his frail body already beginning to dissipate into darkness. "Play the *hootchie-kootchie...*" he said with only his gleaming teeth and lips in a smile, all that was left, and then even the smile disappeared.

* * *

Crouched in the bush, Heijande watched with interest as seamen scampered about the wharf, dancing to airs, jigs and reels scratched with great diligence and pain on a protesting violin by the ship's Captain. Before long the chief mate, belching after a slug from a hearty jug of Jamaica's finest rum, launched into a lengthy ballad at the Captain's approval; a tribute to the very instrument, the violin, that adorned his mournful voice. "The Twa Sisters" also known as "The Wind and Rain"[11] is the story of a miller who finds a drowned woman in a stream, and turns her body into a violin; roughly translated,

Made finger pegs of her long finger bones,
Oh the dreadful wind and rain
Made a fiddle bow with her long curly hair,
Oh the dreadful wind and rain
And the only tune that fiddle would play
Was a-cryin' dreadful wind and rain

The Captain bellowed the coda, sang from the point of view of the violin's purchaser,

Now pay the miller for his pain,
And let him be gone in the Devil's name.

Laughter all around the wharf, the Captain laughing loudest and longest. *There is that Devil again.* Heijande thought it must be a talisman of the power of music in white clans; they sing of their instruments as coming from their ancestor, the Devil. Another thought was forming, a stronger thought, a revelation from his ancestor in the stone, as translated through Eshu Legba: that Heijande could trick the white people and impersonate one of their griots, their storytellers. He could learn their songs and be accepted into their clans. The old man had said they would like the sound of the *kora*.

Swept into the moment, drawing power from the stone in his stomach, Heijande strolled up to the wharf naked, carrying his *kora* and *djembe*. The crew were in a good drunken mood or they probably would have tossed Heijande into the water. They all had a good laugh over the naked wog with his homespun instruments.

"Come to jam wiv us, 'ave ye?"

"Ya got strings and drums, wot's the pecker for, beatin' or pluckin'?"

"Yo, wha's the difference betwixt a dead wog drummer and a dead snake?"

"I dunno, wot?"

"The snake had a show to go to."

Much laughter, and so forth and so on, until Heijande began strumming his *kora* and singing, roughly translated,[12]

I rub my root, my luck is true,
Heijande Konner gonna mess with you
Make you lead me by the hand
So the world will know the hootchie-kootchie man

Sure enough, Captain Randolph Newman thought the performance exquisite. "Let's install this boy in the galley," he said to his chief mate, "to work as a steward and sing for our suppers. What's your name, eh? Hi-jon-de something?"

"'High John de Conker' is what I heard 'em sing," piped up a member of the crew.

"Okay then, High John de Conquer! You will sing for us anytime we want, yes? Otherwise we will put you in chains, yes?"

"Yes!" shouted Heijande in English, proud and courageous now that his trick had worked.

Some of the captured natives, chained together near the wharf in readiness for passage on longboats to the ship, had heard the naked griot charm the white captors with his music, and had seen him gather all his strength and courage to speak so proudly to them. Now the griot was draped in the white man's clothes and walked about freely with the crew. They began to whisper the griot's name, *High John de Conquer*, and spread it with reverence.

* * *

Heijande spent the rest of the night sitting pensively in the deserted pantry next to the galley as the crew slept, wearing a starched white steward's uniform. As the false dawn appeared in the heart of the jungle to the east, Heijande set out below deck to find his clan and Shu Lia. Hundreds of naked black bodies lay flat on their backs chained together, the women and children shrieking and the wounded moaning, and all heaving and drawing breath with excruciating pain, like dying animals. They stared in wonder at the griot who now wore the white clan's uniform.

Heijande spoke quietly to Ashin, a member of his clan lying on his side, chained by neck and ankle, spoon-wise, to men front and back in a row of twenty across the deck. Ashin feared the worst, that they were all bound for a place called America, where the white clans would eat their flesh, make the flags for their ship from their skins, and crush their bones to make powder for their muskets. He told Heijande about a foiled plot to burn the ship before it could hoist anchor and leave the port. Many of the younger women had been taken to the seamen's quarters to be tied up and raped, which in many ways was preferable to being chained to others in a pile below deck. The plan was for one of the women to free the others and start the fire in the seamen's quarters. But one woman, singled out by an officer, had betrayed them, and the man would not speak her name, though he knew her.

Heijande shuddered to think it must have been a woman from his clan. When he looked up to the foredeck, he saw an officer escorting a black women in a handsome English dress up to the officer's quarters. The woman was Angula, his wife, and Heijande burned with shame.

Ashin also told Heijande that he'd seen Shu Lia taken in the night by a seaman. Ashin could barely lift his arm but he grabbed Heijande's arm with a renewed vigor. He seemed not to know Heijande, or to see Heijande in a new way, though they were from the same clan. "High John de Conquer! We do not want to go to the far shore, the America lands, to be food for the white clans! Help us!"

"You must endure, my friend," spoke Heijande quietly, his shame subsiding. "We must live through this. Eshu Legba promised me we will live with others just like us, on the far shore, if we can survive the journey. We will not be eaten if we keep our spirits with us. They will protect us."

"High John de Conquer! You carry the stone of your ancestor in your belly!"

"Yes."

"You are a hero! Even Aido-Hwedo, the sea serpent, respects you. We will live through this journey, but you... you will sacrifice your life for our safety!"

"Yes," assured Heijande, but with a look of concern. He took a moment to chew a bit more of the jalapa root he carried with him, as his stomach churned and thumped like the foamy waves pounding the shore in the gathering dawn.

* * *

Captain Newton had seen much waste in his experience in the slave trade. He'd seen slaves literally packed on top of each other below deck; and consequently, from ill air, confinement, and scanty or unwholesome provision, disease occurred to such an extent that only half survived to the end of the voyage, and in a very unmarketable condition. Rather than pack them all into the holds of the *Perseverance*, the captain sent his crew through the ranks and removed any men that were already flawed and unmarketable; any men that suffered too many bruises or bad limbs. He kept all women and children, of course, unless the women were pregnant. By casting off the weaker ones, he allowed the stronger ones sufficient room and reasonable provisions, along with kind treatment.

Nevertheless, as Cravingston noted, the slaves were chained together by hands and feet and laid flat, without any room to turn over. The two missionaries stumbled over hot bodies heaving with exhaustion, looking for their singer with the magic stone. However, as Mumblingore had pointed out earlier in a protest that Cravingston had no doubt mistaken for sheer laziness, they all looked the same, unless one looked closely. Mumblingore flashed Masonic gestures at the natives without a flicker of recognition. He knew it was hopeless, and ohh! The horrid smell! Such a horrendous greeting to the nostrils, such a loathsome stench. And Cravingston, that idiot, seemed to like it.

Aft, an officer was flogging a slave that was held fast by two seamen and laid across the windlass with his feet tied. The Captain pointed at the spectacle from the poop and explained to the missionaries that the slave had tried to organize the women to start a revolt. Mumblingore thought this was an excellent moment to propose abandoning this search and moving on. "It is no use."

"What a bloody shame," Cravingston whined, looking rather longingly at one of the captured women whose chains pressed across her naked breasts. "We have this impulse to help these people…"

"Nonsense," piped up Mumblingore in a fit of misplaced enthusiasm, overcompensating for his partner's weakness in front of the Captain. "They live in Original Sin, and we are here to root it out. To root out the Devil. They need our authority, and they need to learn humility. They cannot continue to live like this!" He gestured back toward land. "Indeed, this is a fine continent, yes, full of some of the same mysteries that, in Europe, we have long-ago tamed!"

He was referring to Cravingston's ancestors, and Cravingston didn't like it one bit. His connection to the Münster revolt through his great-grandfather must be recorded somewhere, in the rectory's storage area in Canterbury, where Mumblingore would certainly have had access to it. Cravingston looked back at the shore to hide his fit of pique. "Yes, we are all so civilized now. A thousand years of progress. We are rational, reasonable, enlightened! And we are here to, wot, let us pretend it does not exist, right? Like an elephant *right in your drawing room?* Selling human beings for profit! If we were not here, would any of this even be happening? Each slave costs, wot, a guinee to five crown?" He turned to the Captain, ignoring Mumblingore's pleading look, "A-and you sell each one in America for, wot," he sneered at him, "Ninety pounds sterling?"

The Captain didn't answer, just looked away, toward the business of getting underway. He had no time for theological discussions.

Mumblingore whispered to Cravingston, in an effort to calm him down, "You *do* realize that a guinee is now *twenty-one* shill-"

"Oh stop it," snapped Cravingston, "that happened over twenty years ago." And the capriciousness of it all struck him silent, how the seemingly random forces of politics on the world stage had conspired in such irrational ways to arbitrarily control minute distinctions of value such as that of a guinee, which now determined the actual value of a black person's actual life. Was it all, simply, to reduce the price of sugar in the London coffeehouses?

A black steward showed up at that moment to bring the Captain's order of Scotch whiskey for the cast-off salute. The steward was well dressed but anyone could tell he was inexperienced, and the officers gave him a wide berth as he fumbled moves to pour the liquor. The steward cast his eye about the poop and expected a reprisal at any moment for his fumbling, but the missionaries did not recognize Heijande in the steward's garb.

And just as Mumblingore leaned forward to poke Cravingston to get him to stop talking, chief mate Anderson appeared on the quarter deck and hailed the Captain, grappling with a seaman by the scruff of his neck, who in turn held on dearly to the wrangled arm of a badly bruised and battered Shu Lia. The steward dropped the tray of whiskey, and the Captain swore at him.

"Seaman Ó Leannáin, sir!" the chief mate shouted up at the Captain, pronouncing it "Lennon," and then shouted directly at the seaman's yellow hatchet face and shifty eyes. "Freddie Lennon, they call you, is that right?"

Seaman Lennon stopped rough-housing and nodded. "Beggin' yer pardon sir, the officers 'ave already picked all the plump ones, sir, 'ow 'bout some mercy for the crew, sir?" He stood with one arm akimbo and one still gripping the girl. He was a man well acquainted with the brig, a man who'd been kicked, cuffed, slashed, and had his nose broken more than once. And yet he smiled. He knew his value as a seaman, experienced with the powerful dark forces of nature. A man who knows no other way of life; a lifelong prisoner of the sea.

The chief mate shouted up to his captain in irritation. "He had this nigger woman tied up to his bunk all night, sir. I think half the crew had a go at her, sir."

The Captain, doubly annoyed that such a display would occur in front of these missionaries of the Crown, barked his order to the chief mate. "Confine seaman Lennon to quarters, Mr. Anderson." Then his voice turned surly. "And put that woman back in the hold, in chains. We shove off in twenty minutes."

Cravingston glared at the Captain and then at Mumblingore, who simply shrugged. They argued amongst themselves as they left the ship and the pier, and the Captain was relieved. Missionaries and politicians, kings and princes, they could all go to the devil. He'd long ago abandoned the idea that any god, Jewish, Christian, or Muslim, watched over and cared for humans and their petty plots and grievances.

* * *

Heijande crept away from the cabin door and circled around and down to the quarterdeck as if returning to the galley, but stopped to look out on the quarterdeck. Chief mate Anderson and Freddie Lennon were quarreling and Shu Lia hung limp in the chief mate's grip. She looked ready to give up her life, and Heijande's heart travelled out to her. Just then the Captain's bell sounded; the quarrel abruptly ended, and seaman Lennon sullenly retreated as Anderson handed off the crumpled heap of Shu Lia to the second mate.

The chief mate grabbed Heijande by the arm and dragged him back up to the poop deck. The Captain wanted him to get his *kora* and play with the violinists for the ceremonial castoff. He joined the musicians around the Captain on the poop, and as the heave-hos and haul-aways were sounded bow to stern, the captives were brought up to the main deck in chains, murmuring, wailing, and blinking nervously in the morning sun. Any that could not walk in chains were cut loose and cast into the sea, to swim back if they could; the Captain tolerated a loss of up to twenty percent if it would mean a safer, healthier passage for the rest of them.

As the ship floated free of its moorings in glassy waters, Captain Randolph Newman looked out at the amassed captives and into their bewildered eyes without flinching, and in a booming voice addressed them: "Listen up!" He motioned to the musicians to start up a slow, stately rhythm in a 12/4/4 waltz, and began to sing in a black man's drawl he'd picked up on his last voyage across, a song that he hoped, with the grace of his singing, would conquer any last resistance, would ease their fears and make them compliant.

It was a song that visualized his hopeful future with his kin in the newly developed woods of New Jersey, a place where he could kick back on his rocking chair and count his money. He sang to the uncomprehending captives about how, in America, they'd get food to eat, sing about Jesus, and drink wine all day. In America, everybody's as happy as a monkey in a monkey tree, Captain Newman sang. Climb aboard with me, little wog, and sail away, across the ocean to the Charleston Bay.[13]

* * *

The *Perseverance* creaked and shuddered in the strong steady breeze off the land, and its sails held as much of the propelling power as they could, slicing through the Bight of Benin on a westerly passage that hugged the coast. Heijande, alone on the foredeck in his steward's uniform, felt as if he were standing on a floating rock as the coast moved from left to right. As long as he could see the coast, he was not afraid of this new land called America. Perhaps it would even be closer in distance to the Maghreb, the land of his ancestors, and this voyage would get him closer to his goal.

But then the ship dropped south out of the reeking armpit of West Africa at Cape Three Points to traverse the swells of the Gulf of Guinea. As the African coastline shrank to the horizon, Heijande shivered. He would not be closer to the land of his ancestors; the captain and his white clan were taunting Oshun by venturing out into its vast reaches, out of sight of land, and Heijande could only think that Oshun would respond with fury.

The stone glowed hot in his belly. His ancestor was angry. Heijande furiously chewed the jalapa root. Shu Lia's violation, and his wife's betrayal of the revolt, had occurred while Heijande had been tricking the white crew with his music. Did Eshu Legba really mean for him to make this journey? The white clan despised them and their beliefs. They did not fear Oshun and her prince Aido-Hwedo, squirming in his dark depths, seeking the red monkeys that carry the bars of iron for his sustenance. The white clan carried an iron strength in their unbelief; to them, day is simply day, night is night, and Oshun is water, nothing more. They understood only the things they could see, and despised everything else.

Heijande furiously chewed the jalapa root as his ancestor's anger pounded through his chest. He would go to this land of the white clan, this land of unbelief, where the dead do not speak, where every man thinks himself wise without any help from ancestors. He would use his charms and his songs to protect his people, with Shu Lia by his side.

Days passed, and Heijande went about his duties gracefully by day and stole food, fresh water, and spices from the pantry at night to deliver to his clan in chains in the cramped hold, to force into mouths that had chewed only soaked and boiled corn. Under white wings the *Perseverance* skimmed low over a sea of blue mantle shot with gold. Cries and groans of the captives in the hold swirled aloft into a marbled sky of indifferent clouds.[14]

The ship picked up the Equatorial current from the south, passing east of St. Peter and St. Paul's Rocks to avoid the currents that would have driven the ship into the archipelago's stony embrace. The rocks, pinnacles of one of the Earth's longest underwater mountain range, appeared as a jagged white outline rising sharply out of the sea. Heijande thought them to be the speckled humps of the serpent Aido-Hwedo, angry at man's defiance of nature, churning the waters and blocking any further progress west.

Equatorial countercurrents laid the ship slowly over, with reduced sail, yielding in angle but obstinate against the cold white curls of black waves. While still in sight of the rocks a heavy squall rode in, and the ship drove to and fro, reeling and rocking in pain, rolling hesitatingly over burdened waves and slicing through the invisible violence of the winds, then suddenly pitching headlong into dark smooth hollows only to struggle upwards again over snowy ridges of running seas. The captives below deck were thrown to the side and lay heaped on the top of each other, their fetters rendering many of them helpless.

As seamen scattered to their posts on the pitching deck to attend to the sails, and the officers hung on to the aft poop railing with the Captain, Heijande scampered past them into the officer's quarters, bouncing off the ladder and smashing against the bulkhead. He found Shu Lia chained to the bunk stays in the second mate's cabin. She would not look him in the eye as he wrenched and pulled at the chains to no avail.

They were discovered before anything could be done. As the ship tossed back and forth from one belligerent wave to the next, chief mate Anderson brought Shu Lia and Heijande down to a corner of the quarterdeck out of sight of the aft poop and the Captain, to confront the second mate.

Seaman Lennon spied the scene below and scampered down from the boom of the top sail.

The ensuing argument of the two officers and seaman Lennon was abruptly dampened by a heavy spray, and the ship leapt obliquely through an enormous wave. And yet another: a big foaming sea rose up and made for the ship in a madman's rush, roaring wildly. Some of the crew shouted and scrambled up the rigging, while others, convulsively catching their breath, held on where they stood.

Lennon grabbed Shu Lia's left arm, and one of the officers grabbed her right arm. Hanging suspended between them, nearly split apart by the forces of nature and greed, she stopped screaming and wriggling and opened her eyes to the storm. The listing ship gave her a clear view of the white tips of the serpent of the sea, and the rocks due west, bathed in a cold sunshine streaking from the heavens. Heijande saw her stop her struggling and hold her head erect, spreadeagled in the wind like a goddess figurehead, held back by the chains of mortal men.

The coming wave towered over the ship like a wall of green glass topped with snow and rolled over its bow in a smashing confusion, filling the ships decks. Deadeyes of the rigging churned through the great sheet of bursting froth. The ship trembled and lurched violently to windward, tearing itself from the deadly grasp of that wave, and the whole immense volume of water, lifted by the deck, was thrown across to starboard, sweeping all of them off their feet. Heijande held on tight to the quarterdeck rail as the officers and seaman Lennon scrambled for footing. The storm looted the ship's deck in a senseless, destructive fury, tearing trysails out of their gaskets, smothering the foredeck and sweeping away anything not locked down. The seas seemed to rush from all sides like an unruly mob to keep the ship from progressing, as if the ocean itself was a spirit that commanded it to yield or perish.

"Square the main yard!" The screeching yell from the Captain on the aft poop was nearly drowned out by the ocean's roar. "Haul, men! Lay on your backs and haul!"

Hanging on to the railing, Heijande, gagged by the wind and nearly dragged off by the rushing streams, could barely make out through sweeping sprays the two officers with their elbows crocked in the ladder to the aft poop deck, and the seaman flat on his stomach at their feet with one arm on the base of the ladder and the other gripping Shu Lia. A vicious thrust of wind in an outburst of unchained fury suffocated Heijande, and with eyes shut he tightened his hold. An insidious fatigue settled on and benumbed him, and he felt cold and stiff in every limb. In a momentary hallucination of swift visions he beheld his life, all his memories, all of the people he knew, and everything that he would ever know in his lifetime. He could not move to save his life or any other life.

Another wave toppled over the ship, and seaman Lennon lost his grip on Shu Lia. Her eyes met Heijande's, and in that instant, before Heijande could reach out and grab her, he knew her destiny. She was his muse, his shining light, the very reason he had developed his powers; he could not conceive of life without her. But here was that very instant in which he knew the precarious illusion of life, of human strength and weakness. We are tossed and then carried away by the very nature that embraces us, that gives us life. The white clan's notions of good and evil, of individual humans separate from this very nature, were obstinate shouts of anger in the face of the inevitable. Oshun would have her vengeance; Aido-Hwedo would have his sustenance. The white clan's arrogance would ensure that they would lose the most beautiful treasure in their possession, the most precious gift of nature, as a sacrifice for their greed.

And in that instant, as he gathered all his strength to resist the wind, as he lunged forward with the stone glowing hot in his belly, across the quarterdeck, he saw it in her eyes, that wan look of her clan when all hope is lost. As her eyes flashed in submission, Shu Lia let her body be carried off the deck in that immense, thick stream of water, to disappear into the flashing gray-green turmoil and uproar of the sea. In one moment's space, one moment's final fall from grace, Heijande could not reach her. He grasped thick air, a pounding blast of a wave, and the shock constricted his throat. He went limp; he wanted to be swept away to join her in the turbulent seas, but the stone in his belly burned hot, and his will to live prevailed. He grabbed the railing and looked for her on the leeward side.

Shu Lia was gone.

"Steady the foreyards!" The Captain could be heard crying from the aft poop, and the officers lurched aft to join him while Lennon crept slowly up the quarterdeck. Heijande saw that the seaman never looked back. None of them cared to see what had happened to her, or to him. "Steady them as best you can!" yelled the Captain. "We will hoist a hand, or drown amidst this stormy sea!"[15]

Another great wave crashed across the bow and spread out in foamy whirlpools on both sides of the deck, and yet another wave loomed. The ship ran along with it for a moment, riding its snowy crest like a thief with a woman's purse, a purse stuffed with suffering human beings. Loud cracks were heard as the ship rolled over its crest, and then swung upright. "She clears herself! She is steering," cried the helmsman. Through a sudden clear sunshine the *Perseverance* ran blindly, creaking and slovenly, spewing out foaming water gorged with debris, fleeing for its survival.

* * *

All had returned to normal. The chief mate went swiftly about carrying out the Captain's orders and the second mate organized the foredeck crew. Seaman Lennon scampered up the rigging, occasionally stealing a glance back to the quarterdeck.

No mention was made of Shu Lia. Captain Newman was in no mood for more surprises. As the captives were relieved from their pressure on each other and arranged again in the spooning position in the hold, it was found that fifteen of them had been smothered or crushed to death in the storm. The Captain was considerably vexed over the sudden loss of such marketable captives. Shu Lia had been counted as among the dead, and no one argued the count as the remaining corpses were thrown overboard.

Heijande trembled at the quarterdeck railing, burnt by her eyes as if by fire, blind in grief and senseless ire. Her beauty had been ravaged and his people were now cursed; he was cursed. He could not save her. Across the choppy black sea, perhaps only ten miles, churned the white peaks of the the sea serpent.

He cursed Aido-Hwedo's hunger and then caught himself, realizing at once that this anger was the white clan's defiance of Oshun, the white clan's burden, not his. His grief would never leave him and his descendants would not escape the curse, but his purpose only grew solid as the stone in his belly glowed hot. The ancestors had spoken of a time lost to their history, seven generations of capture and slavery, of wickedness and corruption, of revolt and escape, as the Dogon tribes crossed the great Maghreb. They had hidden, in their thoughts, the songs and dances they had learned from the amphibious ones, the Nommo. And now, Heijande knew, he finally knew, what Legba wanted of him.

The stone, the rolling stone, would inspire songs and dances that would help his people survive over the next seven generations of the curse of servitude and ignorance. Heijande would sing new songs, casting spells that would enable his people to sleep-walk, so that while they lived through horror, they could still dream.

Even now, as he walked erect in his steward's uniform steadfast through the hold among his captured clan in chains, boldly carrying extra food for them, they were starting to call him Heijande Konner. Repeated over several days and nights, it became "High John de Conquer".

As High John the Conqueror, the dark prince of West Africa, he would be enslaved as one of them, and help them find shelter when the mighty serpent quakes the Earth. For it would happen, he told them, if they were not vigilant:

Aido-Hwedo will grow hungry, much hungrier than ever before, now that we can no longer feed its loa, celebrate it, dance to it, sing along with it, and strum it to perfection. The great serpent will begin to eat its own tail, and its writhing will be so terrible that the Earth will tilt, and then slip into the sea. But we will awaken from our sleep-walk before this happens. In seven generations our people will awaken and begin again to feed and celebrate its loa and prevent this catastrophe. This is what my ancestor tells me.

Angula his wife, back in chains in the hold with her clan, pleaded with her eyes, and Heijande reached out to her. They embraced despite her disgrace, and in the days of calm sailing that followed, as the ship caught warm southerly breezes, Heijande forgave her misguided, self-serving attempt at freedom. He could no longer afford to be judgmental. His people needed him, and she had learned the secrets of Mamarou's herbs and spices. Together they would nourish their clan. The stone had infused him with the power of his ancestor and had made his spirit immortal. He was at peace with himself and his role. Legba had given him the courage to trick his way through this New World, and plant the roots of a new, powerful music.

And yet, Heijande could not put away his anger toward the white clan. He could feel the power of the stone in his gut. He knew that with a curse, he could hurt this seaman Lennon and all his descendants. His old friend Ashin watched as Heijande tightened his stomach, crouched low, and, plucking the strings of the *kora*, the strings of truth, sang quietly a song that cast a spell on Freddie Lennon and all his descendants, that they would travel the seas all their lives, lose their loved ones without mercy, and never feel at home in the world.

In the quiet gloom of the aftermath of this song, in the creaking hold as the ship swayed under warm evening breezes and steered toward the New World, Ashin quietly sung his own song of respect for Heijande, High John de Conquer. "Your power!" Ashin whispered in Heijande's ears. "You will keep Shu Lia alive, with your songs! She will be honored by our children and our children's children."

* * *

In the early light of an uncertain dawn, the ship dropped anchor in Charleston Bay. Longboats were already in the water to greet it. The *Perseverance* would be there only a fortnight to trade the captives wholesale for provisions, cotton, sugar, and coffee. Captain Newman was anxious to sail up the coast to Delaware Bay and exchange his command for a well-deserved retirement in New Jersey. So anxious, in fact, that he'd forgotten his pledge to free the musical steward; despite Heijande's prancing about like a trained monkey, spilling drinks to the amusement of the officers and grinning like a mascot, the Captain had Heijande's uniform stripped and turned him naked out for sale, to compensate for at least one of the lost captives.

Heijande cursed the Captain in a silent song that he knew would be heard one day, perhaps in two hundred years. Until it was heard the Captain would suffer a bad-tempered spirit that would roam his woods. Decades later the family would be terrorized by this spirit, which they would call the Jersey Devil.

On the return journey to England, Freddie Lennon leaned against the rail on the weather side of the ship, looking eastward towards the invisible coast of Europe. On the line of the horizon there would sometimes appear the brief stain of another ship, a breath on a distant mirror, to remind him that they were not as alone out in this vast void of ocean as it would seem. The ship was just a corpuscle in a nourishing bloodstream, a member of a vast fleet sent forth by men of enterprise and vision, engaged in the greatest commercial venture the world had ever seen, changing the course of history, bringing death and degradation and profits on a scale hitherto undreamed of. Sight of land, of England, would take away all his self-confidence, would reduce him in stature and set him once again back on the margin of existence. On the land he was just another loiterer, piss-poor and irrelevant. Only on this ship, set amidst a vast ocean, with only infinity at the horizons... only then did he feel himself at the center of the world. And yet, it was always toward land that they sailed, land they so much longed for, signifying the end of exile. Land that would land him right back on the dung heap.

* * *

To his people, High John de Conqueror had dropped all pretenses now that the journey was over. With reverence and respect, his chained clansmen had left him some slack in the chain as they were shoved into the longboats, and had then surrounded him in the boat and on shore before the massive auction block in the town square.

In the blinding morning sun and in a roar of unfinished business, each captive was shaken loose of chains and taken off to be branded. By the time High John was chosen, the most powerful landowners had taken their pick and only the weakest and least intelligent white men were doing the bidding.

Chosen by a small landowner north of Charleston, High John toiled in the bleak, troubled landscape, a slave just like the others, as wretched as any of them. But he grinned as he worked the fields, singing to the work, using the rhythm of the song[16] to power the body gracefully through the hard, physical labor. By his example the others applied themselves and worked in rhythm, making it possible to forget where they were and what they were doing. They heard the power in High John's singing, but some of them were afraid. High John posed an inexplicable threat to the order of things, and the white master needed no provocation to beat them.

Back from the fields, High John talked about the white people, how they all looked fat. "Always eating, eating. We are but skin and bone, always hungry, but according to them we were once cannibals! They are bloated from the fat of the land, with flabby chins down to their sternums and eyes clamped shut with congealed grease. But we know how to trick them for the crumbs that fall from their tables. You see, we got one mind for the boss to see, and we got another mind for what I know is me!"

Some of the other slaves couldn't handle this talk. Known to be a rolling stone, High John was set upon by the others to have his stomach cut open and the stone removed. But High John convulsed and heaved, he wriggled and danced on one leg, he slipped away from them and began to vibrate and shine like a gilded splinter, until he stopped all movement, and vomited the stone into the palm of his hand.

The women were attracted to his wriggling and dancing. They defended High John and protected him and his stone. Legends grew about the rolling stone, the dark prince from West Africa known as High John the Conqueror, who had brought life across the ocean in the belly of the white man's ship. His gift of laughter always signaled chaos or disorder.

One legend had it that he won his freedom through trickery, by pretending to love the daughter of the white Mister Charlie. To dissuade his daughter and have some fun at High John's expense, Mister Charlie pretended that John could take his daughter, but only if he completed a number of impossible tasks. John had to clear sixty acres of land in half a day, and then sow and reap the sixty acres with corn in the other half a day. The daughter furnished John with a magical axe and plow to get these impossible tasks done, but warned John that her father meant to kill him after he performed them. In a whirlwind, John completed the tasks, and a shocked Mister Charlie allowed him to spend one night with his daughter, hoping she would be afraid of his prowess. But she adored him, and was soon fast asleep in utter complacency. The original backdoor man, John snuck away from the daughter's bed, and stole Mister Charlie's own horses to escape, and although a raging Mister Charlie came looking for him, High John could not be found. They say he disappeared by shape-shifting.

The stories spread. His descendants were strong with the spirit of Legba. Harvard "Doctor" John became a well regarded Mississippi Delta root doctor and was the great- great-grandfather of the legendary voodoo queen Mama Roux. Yale "Mojo" George led a group of slaves to escape into the northern swamps of Florida, where he founded a utopia of blacks and redskins living together harmoniously until they were massacred by white settlers. His brother Princeton "Pitchfork" John-Quincy fought alongside Nat Turner in the slave rebellion. Other descendants of the High John blood line organized the Maroons for the revolution in Haiti. Penn "Hoodoo" Ulysses awakened the Deep South musicians to what would eventually be called *jez grew*. The singing pastor Dartmouth "Ragtime" Rutherford was defiled in lectures by the newly formed Negro Baptist church as the very epitome of the Devil.

Songs were written about High John the Conqueror, who always had words of wisdom for every soul he met.[17] His name became synonymous with the root of Ipomoea jalapa, which he had used to nurse his stomach from carrying the stone. Typically used in sexual spells of various sorts and considered lucky for gambling, the root acquired its sexual magical reputation because, when dried, it resembles the testicles of a dark skinned man.

And through it all, the spirit of Heijande, as High John, crept out over the land. Way back when he first arrived on American soil, he knew that the greatest song he could ever sing would be to live his way of life.

* * *

By 1890, the slave religions had been persecuted to near extinction in the hills of Mississippi along the great Delta. The spirits had burrowed deep within the Negro Christian dogma to keep themselves alive. Legba had taken on the disguise of Saint Peter, and Erzulie masqueraded as the Virgin Mary.

Cornell "Stackalee" Woodrow, strong with the Esau Legba spirit, strolled over to the Jesus side of town and into a card game to end all card games, wearing a princely New Orleans outfit of fine tweed, starched collars, a diamond stickpin, black oxfords, and a nine-gallon white Stetson hat with a silver trident pinned to its brim.[18] Claiming to be a direct descendent of High John the Conqueror, he announced to no one in particular that he was in search of the magic called *jes grew*, a type of music that was the key to the treasures of their shared primeval past.

Billy Dee Lyon was not amused. He was a principled man, a religious man, a carpenter by trade with a sickly wife and two beautiful daughters, and the host of the white man's card game every Saturday night. Billy Dee served the men whiskey from his own still, stacked the chips and card decks, procured a fresh batch of backwoods girls for them, kept watch at the door for the sheriff's deputies, and cleaned up after they left. The white men called him Billy the Lion, or just "boy" despite his age.

News had spread about Cornell before he even arrived. The black man was so bold as to present himself, all starched and perfumed, at the white man's gambling table as nobody's fool, no white man's boy, tougher than the devil. Billy Dee had tried to stop him but Cornell swept him aside. But as Cornell took a seat, the white men frowned and stopped the game. One of the white men laughed at Cornell and took a liking to his white Stetson hat.

Billy saw an opportunity, and challenged Cornell to a one-on-one. Lose, and Cornell would have to go, and leave behind his hat. Win, and Cornell could stay and play with the white men.

The game commenced. When Billy pulled the Queen of Spades to Cornell's Jack of Hearts, Cornell thought it was a trick and pulled out a knife.

"You betrayed us," Cornell spat at Billy. "You've become one of them," he gestured at the white men. "You are nothing but a sacrificial animal. You strap yourself to their wheel, and wait for a freedom that never comes. You don't feel the power of your blood, your ancestral heritage. All you feel is the darkness that surrounds your soul."

And then Stackalee cut Billy Dee Lyon down.

* * *

"This is the new thing that's happening, the work we spoke about before." Cornell Woodrow placed the refurbished cornet horn-down on the lamp table. "It jes grew from our little seed, planted right here in New Orleans, the new music, the new dances.[19] It's gonna sweep the world and lift all of us, sister, right up and out of our misery. It's the work I speak of, and don't speak of. You know it when you hear it, you know it when you dance to it."

The sweet mulatto whore nursed her Baby Louis as she listened, her eyes a mile wide and inviting for an army of Cornells, black men of stature, with outfits as good as any white man, with the intelligence to choose professions way above farming and laboring, with the cunning to win big in a world stacked against them. Cornell smiled at her son; already Louis exhibited the signs of greatness, grasping hands that knew no boundaries, a powerful shrieking scream he could summon when she couldn't satisfy his huge appetite for tit. "Got another one just like it, out in West Texas," he says, his single gold tooth glistening in the parlor gaslight like a miniature gas lamp. "And my cousin is doing the work up north, in the Delta. They's gonna be High Johns a'conquering ever which way."

Talk of other children didn't bother her. She glanced at the cornet, a powerful totem shining on the table, a key to a different future for her Baby Louis.[20]

Cornell smiled and tipped his hat, but his eyes were a warning: keep the cornet for your child, don't let me find it some day in a hock shop. She knew he would be gone within the hour, dancing his way out of the parlor and off the porch and into a waiting carriage, and off into the night just a few steps ahead of the sheriff's deputies coming to close the place down. Too much of that kickin' piano music, she was told, too much barrelhousin', too loud for the neighborhood. Whatever. Cornell had supplied the musicians, and the bulls wanted to know where Cornell had gone, but they also guessed that she would not know, so they left her and her suckling baby alone. They would close the house down, but it would reopen again in a few months, here or in some other place nearby.

And that was the world her baby, Louis Armstrong, would grow up into. Because the only way a Negro man could live in good standing, without incurring the wrath of the white man, was to be a religious preacher or a blues musician. The two occupations were as contrary by ideology as any could be; the one sings of God and the other of the sinful, devilish ways of the world. Armstrong would transcend these contradictions to become the most respected musician in America. His vocal phrasing would be copied by every jazz singer, and his solo breaks would become the foundation for all sax and guitar riffs though the next two centuries.

Music Carries Messages

"Music carries messages past the censors," he wrote in old-fashioned handwriting on the white board, his marker squeaking through the hush of sighs, grunts, coughs, and chair creaks in the full classroom.

"As long as humans have been on this Earth," he boomed, accentuating certain syllables, *phrasing* his speech, "music has carried the message of the order of the universe, of the proportions of the planets and stars, and of the proportions of the human body."

The Professor pointed to his diagram of the human form on the projection screen, superimposed with planets and stars. He hit the pad of a laptop on the desk, and atomic particles danced on the screen.

Now he spoke in a singsong, trusting voice. "You know that music is simply organized vibrations. But did you know this? Beneath the subatomic particle level? There are fibers that vibrate at different intensities. Different *frequencies!* Like guitar strings."

He paused. More sighs, grunts, coughs, and chair creaks.

"Well… the physicists say that the particles we can see are actually the *notes* of the strings vibrating beneath them. That means, if string theory is correct… It means that music is not only the way our brains *work*, as the neuroscientists can show, but also, music is what we are *made of*, in fact what *everything* is made of."

He glared out at them. This should be a "hot damn!" moment for them, or at least some of them. At least one? He stared out at the college students. Nothing. More sighs and grunts.

He continued in a serious, thoughtful, lecturer voice, standing in front of his laptop, looking down at its screen.

"Researchers agree that about 50,000 years ago, a great leap forward took place in our species, *Homo sapiens*. It was a sudden change, possibly the result of a genetic mutation or a rewiring of our brains. There were other species of humans at that time, now extinct, like the Neanderthals, the hobbit-like Flores Man, and other species of *Homo erectus.*"

That word raised a twitter and some chair creaks.

He raised his left eyebrow as he spoke, to give his voice more gravitas. "A small group, very small, started to demonstrate a range of new and complex behaviors. They started playing music! Yes, and also making jewelry, painting on the cave walls, and exchanging and bartering with other groups. There are theories that our ancestors were a very small group, about a hundred, that migrated from Africa. That they were somehow exposed to music, to an ordering of vibrations that they could identify, and generate themselves. They could play music!"

The students were quiet. They didn't quite share the Professor's enthusiasm.

Still he plodded on, eyebrow raised even higher. "Secrets! There were secrets, carried down from this very ancient civilization to our modern generations. They were carried through *music*." He looked up. Were they even listening? "Knowledge of the *musica universalis* has run like a golden thread through the teachings of prophets, seers, sages and saviors. Into the music they put the secret codes for attacking, defending, escaping, and attaining illumination through spiritual experiments."

Again he looked up, and blinked. He tried his booming voice again. "Music is the very foundation of religion! Today's concert hall was once a *cathedral*, and its stage was once an *altar*. Before that, music was community and culture. There were no performers and no audience. Everyone participated."

No one stirred, no hands for questions. He paced in front of the classroom in his trademark black suit, Hawaiian shirt, and black Stetson hat, his golden-gray ponytail dangling out in back. "Do you realize how important a role the musician plays in this world, in our lives? Do you realize what an awesome responsibility it is to produce the art we call music? It is a *holy* pursuit! Do you get that?"

The bell rang. The students scrambled from their seats and rumbled out. One, hesitant and embarrassed, stopped at his desk. He wanted to know if the Professor had ever known Phil Spector, recently on trial for his life for shooting a young and beautiful actress.

The Professor frowned. He didn't want to talk about the past that had haunted him for decades. Certainly not the musical heroes of the Sixties who had died, or succumbed to the lifestyles of the overdosed.

He vaguely remembered the mysteries. What made Johnny be good. Why all of the great psychedelic rock bands started out in the blues. Why musicians were so preoccupied with the meaning of life, so gullible as to believe in a lost chord and secrets of the ancients, so eager to blast their minds and starve their bodies, so willing to line the pockets of drug dealers. Why the country fought a senseless war in a faraway land and a holy war against its own young. Why so many freedom movements of the time, civil rights, women, gays... why they eventually turned into commercials for alternate lifestyle products.

He hadn't been to a concert or festival in over a decade. They made him feel old and useless. What was it about shows? He remembered the backstage gossip, the sharing of techniques. And of course, chasing women. What else? Playing music. He no longer did any of it, though music was once so important to him that he sacrificed relationships for it. Two ex-wives and numerous girlfriends that no longer wanted to see him, talk to him, or deal with him on any level. Two sons, locked into successful high-tech lives, who no longer remembered to call him.

The great turn in his life came when he no longer mattered to the music industry. He had joined the tribes of the defeated, migrating in gentle waves to the wilderness of the Northwest, looking to build lives outside the grid, taking spouses, shovels, pruning scissors, acoustic guitars, and a notion of the infinite goof. The churn of life had passed them by, leaving them unemployable, and they had been left to attend to nature, subvert themselves to it, examine it closely, real close — at the molecular level, permanently stoned.

Then came the crashes and the practicalities. Teaching was his only hope. His generation's kids grew up in the strip malls that bordered and eventually penetrated the wilderness, without a revolution to join or a cause to celebrate, and without much curiosity about the forces that had woken their parents from the American dream. That Sixties decade of exhilaration and experimentation, which had started with Spector's "Be My Baby",[21] was now remembered as a cliché of hedonistic, dim-witted Doonesbury characters, its wisdom degenerating into slogans and confused memories.

That night, the Professor tuned in. What was left of Phil Spector's scraggy hair, once lewdly curled but now whipped in disarray like a perplexed Einstein confronted with household chores, was tucked into a camphor-preserved wig. So spectral as to be transparent, the ghost of Sixties rock had been muttering and raving about an atonal drug that could turn musicians into zombies, no longer able to recognize melodies. He had grown even more inconsiderate and unable to empathize or even recognize the emotions of others. So, according to testimony, Spector had gone off to the House of Blues in Hollywood to find Cornell Woodrow, the only man in the world who could administer the antidote.

Back in the late fifties, Cornell had played for Spector a special recording — a vinyl record that had circulated among the rock music pioneers. An extremely powerful record that had, according to Spector, irrevocably changed popular music. This particular record, when played at a crucial time in each of the artist's lives, had completely transformed them, turning ordinary artists into geniuses. Spector wanted to see if listening to this record again, with Cornell, would reverse the effects of the atonal drug.

The video showed the ageless black dandy in court in a dark three-piece suit and somber homburg, carrying a black cane topped with a gold fish head. Cornell reminded the Professor of the "Un-Cola Nut" man in all those 7-Up commercials. There were rumors. Cornell had helped the legendary bluesman Robert Johnson develop his style, and had shown Brian Jones how to play slide guitar. He'd been there, at the Sun Studio in Memphis, when Elvis had recorded his first hit. Interviewed by reporters, Cornell allowed that yes, he'd met many of the pioneers of rock, and yes, he'd played them some records. About turning artists into geniuses, he shrugged, "I don't do nothin' like that. I don't make 'em what they already are." When pressed for more, he allowed, "I just recognize genius when I sees it and hears it. All's I do is *goose* it some." His smile grew wide and revealed a crowd of gold molars on either side, and at its center a gold tooth embossed with a fish head. "Now, you want to hear 'bout real genius?" he said, and broke hoarsely into sing-song, in a fake Irish accent,

There's a brother I know in Bel Air
Who was doin' his wife on the stair.
When the banister broke
He doubled his stroke
And finished her off in midair!

Members of the surviving rock music royalty were interviewed. Everyone seemed to know Cornell Woodrow, and yet not know him. No one cared for his limericks. He carried a House of Blues VIP card, used it like a ticket, and it got him into every green room and granted him access to everybody. Backstage dignitaries would greet him as a friend without even knowing his backstory.

Eric Clapton said he never heard of him.

"Never heard of him," growled Bob Dylan on the telephone to a reporter. "Whoever he is, he didn't have no record album to give me. I wouldn't take a record album from some stranger."

"It's not possible," Mick Jagger popped his "p" inappropriately, and in his lilting, halting voice did little to hide his contempt for the reporter. "None of it is remotely 'p'ossible. And that bit about Brian Jones, nonsense. Brian was an original. He needed no help to be what he was."

Sir Paul McCartney was unavailable for comment, but his press secretary informed The London Times that Sir Paul could not remember ever having met this Cornell person, and that his memory was quite full for now, thank you. Ringo Starr was also contacted, but said only that he couldn't remember much from that foggy period of his life, except learning to play chess.

* * *

The Professor, moved by the mention of his one-time mentor Cornell Woodrow, decided to get in touch with the musical sorcerers of his past. Dylan in Malibu was on his short list.

"Full of mystery. The songs have always been full of mystery." He could feel Dylan's sardonic sneer and piercing eyes through the phone, carried by that trademarked nasal, phlegmatic voice of the Hobo Sailor. "Most of 'em, the *Rolling Stone* writers, they didn't understand it, they couldn't penetrate it. No one's been able to. Man, these mysteries have been in music for centuries, for eons.

"And so what?" Dylan continued ranting, in deadpan. "Ain't no use bringing up the old mysteries. You can find 'em everywhere, all over the place, all jumbled up with theories, poisoned by cults. I remember listening to the Staples Singers,[22] and it was the most mysterious thing I'd ever heard. It was like the fog rolling in. The rock'n'rollers, they played music that was black *and* white.

Extremely incendiary. Your clothes could catch fire. And there must have been some elitist power that had to get rid of all those guys, Chuck Berry, Little Richard, Buddy Holly, Jerry Lee Lewis. They had to thrown 'em down, and strike down rock'n'roll for what it was and what it represented, which was a black *and* white thing. When they finally recognized what it was, they had to dismantle it, which they did, starting with the payola scandals. The black element was turned into soul music, and the white element was turned into English pop. They separated it. It's all diffused now, meaningless. It's about making a living, really. Just feeding off this nonsense, keeping the feedbag on."

The Professor steered the conversation back to the power of records — the ones that impart secrets to those who can really listen. In particular, the record Cornell had played for Bob long before his career had taken off. But Dylan didn't want to talk about it, as if talking about that record would make him some kind of accomplice. He changed the subject; he asked the Professor if he still knew how to do that trick Cornell had taught him, that trick with the feedback.

The Professor thought, did he say "feedbag" again?

It occurred to the Professor after hanging up that he should have told Bob about the level of concentration required for the feedback trick. It was the same as what was required to gain inspiration from that record.

* * *

The next day the Professor strode purposefully into the college's spring festival to test his ability to do that trick with feedback. Staring directly at the stage across the quad, he gave it the full eye treatment, concentrating for almost a minute. Just enough, just a little trouble. Fortunately it was the afternoon warm-up band for the faculty and the older folks; the hip-hop entertainment for the evening used mostly digital equipment that was somehow impenetrable.

Instantly recognizable conga samples on the back beat gave the song away, the Rolling Stones' "Sympathy for the Devil".[23] And this band of young thieves was butchering it. He concentrated on the lead singer, a Mick Jagger stand-in who looked like a human wolf, hawk-eyed, thick-lipped, cross-eyed and scraggily-haired, tightly wound in snakeskin and bristling with cheap jewelry. Just then the singer's bracelet fell off. The singer refastened it, and started in on the trademark yowls of the song, not acid-tinged but milk-fed, not from the streets but from some suburban soccer field.

So, thought the Professor, I can still do it.

But the band's rendition set the Professor's teeth on edge. They'd chosen to ape the latter-day Stones, not their early years. No Brian Jones clone. No idea, really, of where the name Rolling Stones came from. They so missed the point. The greatest rock 'n' roll band in the world was named and initially styled by Brian. Before his death in 1969, a dejected Brian had bitterly predicted that the

Stones would have to sing "Sympathy" at every show for the rest of their lives. It was some sort of payback, Brian had explained to him, like Robert Johnson's pact with the devil at the crossroads.

As the Professor concentrated, his right shoulder kinked up with the muscle memory of carrying guitars across stages during the years of touring, years that had unraveled like a lost crusade. His mind focused, this time with a purpose, on the bass player's amplifier until its hum cascaded into feedback. Grinning, he kept at it, kept gunning the otherworldly physics of his mental energy. Zork!

An electronic disturbance on stage grew into a monstrous feedback loop. The bass player was frantically twisting knobs while the other band members cringed. The loop reached the apotheosis of noise and then suddenly shut off, leaving a light and airy flute sound emanating softly from the high-powered stage speakers like butterflies fluttering out of buzzing warehouses. It sounded a bit like Brian's favorite music, the pan pipes of Joujouka.[24] The band was as befuddled as the sound engineer. The moment of awesome, bewildering unreality lingered for about a minute and then faded.

See no evil, hear no evil, speak no evil.

With this mantra, the Professor let his concentration diffuse and dissipate. It took intense concentration to draw the power from his gut to influence the vibrations colliding in the space around musicians, if just for an instant. Causing feedback was just a joke, a rakish demonstration, a piddling portion of what was possible. In a pout over something or other, he used to be able to, with one squint, reduce his band's performance to a miserable wreck of disjointed rhythms and random noise. He liked to think the power was the result, after all these years of search and anguish, of achieving a kind of transcendent knowledge, if not of the world than at least of himself. But the power came from somewhere else. It was all he could do, to play music and concentrate, in order to tap into it.

All the energy of his performance, all that sweat and spent enthusiasm, would put him in a craze, ready to trash hotel rooms. The Professor remembered earlier, simpler times, when he and his mates would climb up to perches in the rafters of a concert hall and dangle their feet, drink cherry wine, and pass joints while watching the crew flutter about fixing spotlights and placing microphone stands. When the time came, they'd take their usual places on the stage, plug in with their backs to the audience, and turn around to smile at spotlights. He'd single out a woman he could actually see in the front row, and play only to that woman, imagining that her eyes would always be focused on him, on his lithe body. After the last stance of the encore, that monstrous crescendo of pure sound, horns blaring, guitars sliding up the scale to pure screech, drums blathering in a counterpoint to the rhythm and then bopping into the final downbeats — it would take everyone's breath away.

Over time, concert halls gave way to arenas, stadiums, and outdoor festivals. The lights were all they could see as they were engulfed by the awesome, fierce roar of audience arousal. Frustrated, disconnected from his audience, he'd play to some idea of a woman, an abstract muse. The endless tours left no time for the contemplation or the discipline required for songwriting. He would be stranded at four in the morning in a hotel room somewhere, with too much nervous energy and nothing else but the readily available panaceas of debauchery and self-destruction. Where are musicians supposed to go after such a perfor-mance, before an unseen mass of humanity? Elvis practiced karate. Dylan passed out from downers to counteract the meth-amphetamines. Brian Jones and Bill Wyman took turns on the local women.

Johnny B had unstrapped his bass guitar, leaned it against his amp, and disappeared into the backstage maze while the audience continued to shout for encores. No one saw him leave. Overdose. The word usually stopped all further conversation. But no body was ever found, and an overdose was out of character for a man who knew his drugs; indeed, knew how to use a mass spectrometer for qualitative tests that would set prices in the green rooms of ballrooms and concert halls across the land. The press fomented rumors, on a par with theories about Jimi Hendrix's supposed killer, the murder of Brian Jones, and the poison dose that put Janis Joplin out, dead on the floor of a Hollywood motel. Not a word from Johnny B's real mother, if she was still alive. He had simply disappeared from the Altamont concert at the end of 1969.

Decades later, fake minks and furs replaced the ponchos and serapes in the green rooms, and no-smoking signs were propped up with bottles of apple juice. At the edge of the college festival audience, the Professor could see that the band was still in disarray. He thought he spotted Ashley, stage right. Sure enough, his former Archetypes band mate sat behind a pedal steel guitar, waiting to sit in. Rounding tables of stale tortilla chips, day-old bread, wilted salad with industrial-grade tubs of dressing, and platters of mystery meats and green-speckled cheeses, he dodged the backstage bouncer to corner Ashley Trimble.

At first Ashley didn't recognize him. Ashley himself looked simply older, chunkier, broader in the face, but still wore the headband, now holding back only wispy memories of his long blond hair, now only encircling and drawing attention to his balding pate. Still the same John Lennon granny glasses, only now he looked more like Benjamin Franklin.

"Got any antacid?"

"Gilbert!" Ashley's eyebrow shot up in a wary welcome. "Turn it down!" It was a reminder of the joke in the early Seventies when all the other members, except Ashley, had wanted the Professor to turn down the volume of his harmonica amp. Only Ashley had been supportive, and Ashley never let him forget it. "Did you have anything to do with that?"

He meant the feedback. The Professor shook his head, smiled. "You know I could never control myself."

Ashley clucked. "Just like old times. Y'know I heard you were in these parts. A professor, even! Ah, Northern California. Just the sound of it, man, and I relax, the deep forests, the tall trees, the smashing coast, all the negative ions. Man, it's like a refrigerator, calms me down. How'd you end up here?"

"Pioneer of the soul then, but now I'm in full retreat." The Professor smiled ruefully. It was like they'd picked up this conversation from decades ago. "Why are you playing with these kids?"

"Getting in practice, man. Tour coming up. The Archetypes are back!"

"How could they be *back*? They're archetypes!" the Professor corrected him. "That's not logical."

"Whatever. It's all lost on them. They call it The New Archetypes, with no irony whatsoever. One of those billionaires, Gordon MacAdam, is running it with his wife Brigit. They do your vocals, and your brother's vocals. Kinda puts a new twist on 'em with the boy-girl harmony bit."

The Professor winced. "How could they just do that..."

"Hang on, mate. He's got us in a slot. It's business. Millions of bands now, can't even get noticed. Gordon gives us a salary, a-and health benefits."

The Professor quietly shook his head.

"What the fuck are we supposed to do?" Ashley whined. "Where do we go after so many years? I'll tell you where: the rock 'n' bowl circuit."

"You find audiences out there?"

"It ain't the kids, Gilbert, it's the parents. Hell, it's the grandparents. They're everywhere. People are living longer, I guess."

"And they still come out for it, this music? Your music?"

"Why not?"

"This, this... progressive rock? Fuck, Ashley, that was *your* trip. We were a blues band."

Ashley looked guilty. "Look, this is Gordon's idea, he happens to like that period, and all the older stuff."

"And this is what it comes down to? These humorless bastards that just want to repeat everything we did?"

Ashley smiled. "We're in the Fillmore next weekend," stretching out the syllables to suggest the long line of fans that would be lingering at the door, raising his eyebrows like a circus clown. "C'mon down, I'll get you on the guest list."

Really. How ignominious to show up as a guest at your own mock funeral. You spend your entire life fighting to create this thing, and when it comes to pass, when the thing is finally realized, despite all previous defeats, it turns out to be... not at *all* what you wanted, or what you thought it would be. The resulting work carries the commercial taint of phoniness. And all your colleagues and comrades are exhausted. All they want is the payday. And another generation rises up, punks set on fighting against this very thing you wanted, calling you a phony, calling themselves the new wave. And then, irony to end all ironies, this younger generation grows up to parody your band as they go through their middle-age crises.

And he hadn't been asked to play.

Such is the impoliteness of this fast-paced age that none of these younger Archetypes worshippers had bothered to contact the founder of the band they'd expropriated. The Professor knew this feeling well, how it was to be invisible. After the fall, after his solo albums had gathered dust, and then, after the label dropped him, he once had waited in line with the rest of the crowd to get into a show featuring Ashley's new band at the time, and no one had recognized him.

* * *

A black woman in a suit approached him. She held a briefcase close to her chest, and long black hair, curled like Mary Tyler Moore, framing an innocent, contradictory black face. She was young enough to've read about the civil rights movement from the comfort of a suburban home. But her fierce features suggested confidence and competency in politics, in back-room dealings.

"Are you Gilbert Mention?"

The Professor smiled. Could it be, after all these years, someone had recognized...

Without a word, she handed him a summons and her business card.

The band, wary now of the feedback that had sprung so diabolically out of their equipment, had unplugged everything and started playing acoustic. They coincidentally struck the first guitar notes of the Robert Johnson song the Stones had pilfered, "Love in Vain",25 as the Professor studied the summons. Any and all materials related to the life of Robert Johnson, a.k.a. R.L. Johnson, a.k.a Robert Spencer, born 1911 in Hazlehurst, Mississippi.

He studied the business card. Abigail Hucke was a lawyer for the prestigious Philadelphia firm of Dewey, Cheatem & Howe.

Hucke. "I know a Hucke, and Howe," he grunted. "Any relation to Lucy Hucke?"

"My aunt, a senior partner," she said politely. "Call me Gail."

"As in hurricane?"

"Just call me Gail," she clarified, and directed his attention back to the summons.

All his love had been in vain. Robert Johnson had been murdered in 1938, at the tender age of twenty-seven, and had left behind only a handful of blues records. Virtually unknown outside the Delta region, the myth of the man had stalked the early rock scene in England like Marlowe's ghost. More than fifty years after his death, his ghost had appeared at the Rock and Roll Hall of Fame and had won a Grammy.

There were only three known photographs of Johnson, one disputed and the other two gracing the album cover and liner notes for CBS Records' box set, released in 1990, which had been on ice for fifteen years in someone's art collection. The box set outsold any other blues record in history in a whitewash of latent enthusiasm for mythic bluesmen. The whitewash continued through 1994 as the U.S. govern-ment issued a postage stamp using one of the photos, but prevailed upon the artist to remove the cigarette from Robert's sneering lips.

In the aftermath of the box set's release, alleged descendants of Robert Johnson popped up everywhere, along with various half-sisters, half-brothers, and mistresses with illegitimate or half-adopted children. A gravel-truck driver named Claude Johnson produced a birth certificate listing R.L. Johnson as the father. According to a deposition from Claude's mother, Robert Johnson himself took her by the hand and led her into a swamp near Hazlehurst, Mississippi, on a stormy night sometime in March 1931. They never met or spoke again. While at the time the affair seemed only to produce yet another black kid destined to live a life of misery, this particular swamp fuck had turned out to be worth millions.

The Professor clucked at the summons. One bluesman earns millions he never saw in his lifetime that would be spent by dubious descendants, while hundreds of other great bluesmen, stiffed of their royalties for most of their lives, still scrounged for gigs or died in obscurity.

The court sought any materials that may have been gathered by the Professor's late father, Herbert Mention, a secretive historian who once tried to publish an alternate account of Robert Johnson's mysterious death. The Professor, the lawyer assumed, had access to his father's possessions. In particular, his father's unpublished manuscript, and an acetate recording of a Carnegie Hall "performance" of a Robert Johnson record.

The Professor's first thought was how to recreate an acetate that would be a suitable replacement. He would never give up the original.

Gail was watching him for a reaction. Putting on his best deadpan, the Professor extended his hand, smiled warmly, and hummed along with "Love in Vain" while pocketing the summons. "How ironic, that they should be playing this song," he said, cocking his ear.[26]

She gave him that quizzical look black women often give older white men who are acting inexplicably. "You do understand, you have to appear. And you have to bring with you any and all materials? Including the recording, the one from Carnegie Hall in 1938?"

"If you think it will do you any good," he replied hastily, giggling nervously.

She moved closer, giving Ashley a sidelong glance that suggested he was not important. "Do you know how to find John Balzano?"

"Johnny B? Last I heard was a rumor, that he was hiding out in the Rif mountains of northern Morocco."

"You don't think he's dead?"

"No... I don't think so."

After a formal, hesitant goodbye, she was gone.

"You still got that record?" Ashley wanted to know.

The Professor shook his head, no. "Not since way back, when They started looking for it." He imagined the soft chucking rhythm of a helicopter in the distance. No, it was real, an actual helicopter, in the distance, fading away. But it was off-season for the campaign against marijuana, so what the fuck?

"Who's 'They'? C'mon, man, you still paranoid about that Corporation thing, after all these years?"

"Phil Spector mentioned Cornell and the record. He raved about an atonal drug."

"So you think those experiments are still going on. After all these years. How could that be?"

"Ashley, think about it. Have you heard a decent melody recently?"

* * *

It hadn't always been this way, performers on giant stages, playing to giant audiences. Only in the last two thousand years or so. Before that, everyone played music of some kind, instruments and voices. Everybody in the tribe. What we now think of as religion and history were passed down as secret instructions from generation to generation.

Cornell Woodrow, keeper of the secrets of the blues, had taught the Professor in his teens, way back in the early Sixties, that our most primitive impulses were guided by music. We still dream toward something unreachable, out at the limits of matter and energy. We play music in order to tap into the vibrations of the planet, the force responsible for our very nature, the vibrancy of our lives. We work together, Cornell had said, in a grand experiment. To reincarnate the voodoo spirit of Legba, an African deity, using the blues as a channel. We use the transformative power of the rolling stones, which were transported to America in the stomachs of slaves. One slave was known to have survived the extraction of the stone from his stomach. Cornell's ancestor, High John the Conqueror, prince of the slaves.

A Thunderstorm Rocked

A thunderstorm rocked and rolled eastward across the dead-hot Mississippi night in 1911 when Little Robert was born. His sound was already in him. His sister Carrie swore later on that she heard it that night, that eerie plaintive high-pitched whine he would one day develop for his voice and perfect on guitar, coming through his first whimpers and cries. The crashing thunder enveloped Little Robert's sound like orchestral accompaniment, and the pouring rain beat out a rhythm on the tin roof of the tiny painted shack.

He'd just popped right out of his mother while she screamed for help. Eight-year-old Carrie didn't know what to do. The shack wobbled uncertainly on its cedar-post supports as the wind howled around all its sides, over the top, and under the floor. The midwife from nearby Hazlehurst had dashed outside as soon as she heard the thunder. A descendant of a Yoruban clan, the midwife believed that Shango created thunder and lightning by casting thunder-stones down to earth; wherever lightning had struck, she might find the thrown stone. The Yoruba believe these stones have special powers, and they enshrine the stones in temples to Shango. The midwife was out there digging around the smoking stump of a fallen oak tree while Robert's mother gave birth.

Carrie hurried outside, leaving her mother swooning in pain and the baby, still attached to her umbilical, squirming between her legs on the straw mat. The midwife ran back from the woods holding a round smooth pebble in the palm of her hand.

"*Otane,* this is for the baby," the midwife gasped, out of breath, grabbing Carrie's hand and clasping with the other hand to give her the warm pebble. "Shango favors him!"

Carrie wanted to scream at her, but suddenly all was silent; the storm swirled up and away as if drawn to a vacuum in the sky. They both looked up to see the thunderclouds dissipate, leaving nothing, just flickering stars in the deep black sky, chirping cicadas, a croaking bullfrog. And that eerie whining sound again, a sound full of mystery emanating from inside the shack, now doubled by a harmonizing whine from outside, from a breeze rustling through the crude diddley bow. Robert's father Noah Johnson had fashioned it by driving three nails into the side of the shack high up, tying three strings to them, threading the strings through an empty whiskey bottle, and sticking a brick underneath the strings to draw them tight. Then he'd play it by beating the strings with a stick and sliding that whiskey bottle to change the pitch.

Carrie didn't think the wind could make that sound from the diddley bow, the strings had to be beaten or plucked for any sound to come out of it.

Now they both looked at the diddley bow, and then back at the sky, two heads in unison like in some kind of stage play. "Shango!" The midwife shouted, eyes glazed over. "He sings a song to consecrate the *otane*." And she clasped both her hands around Carrie's hand holding the pebble.

"Coulda been a ghost playin' it," was all Carrie could whisper, clinging to the moment, until they could hear her mother, Julia Dodds, moaning on the straw mat, and Little Robert's plaintive whine had become a louder cry. They hurried back into the shack and Carrie fingered the pebble, round and round, thinking dear Lord, God himself has come down to plant this pebble. As Little Robert grew and developed a small cataract in one eye, Carrie came to believe that the pebble might have been something bad, from someplace else, and was sorry she had ever given it to him. And when Little Robert took up playing that diddley bow and, as a teenager, harmonica, all instruments of the Devil, she knew she'd be sorry.

* * *

What did Little Robert know of his mother's travails? He was too young. All that bouncing around in her arms, rolling one place to the next, playing in the soft dank mud, laughing and giggling when she tickled him, feeling warm as she sang to him, oh Little Robert, you could be a bee to a blossom, a pear tree blossom in the spring.

Too young, he was, to know anything about his mother, the dreamily preoccupied little plantation girl now all grown up, the wife of a prominent Negro farmer and wicker-furniture maker in Hazlehurst named Charles Dodds.

Too young to appreciate the irony of a self-made black man's downfall. Dodds had been caught cheating with a mistress in town who turned out to be the unofficial property of some mean white folks, the Marchetti brothers, and Dodds had to flee in the dead of night disguised in frilly lace and a woman's dress, his head wrapped tight in a blue bonnet, as a lynch mob formed in the Marchetti's front yard.

Too young to understand why Dodds, after changing his name to Spencer and setting himself up in Memphis, didn't send for his wife Julia; instead he sent for the mistress Selena. Not comprehending, until he was much older, that he, Little Robert, was the reason.

Too young to know his father. Noah Johnson had arrived on the wisp of the wind, a tall, gaunt, ghost of a Negro with high cheekbones and a hairless face that indicated some Cherokee blood. Noah claimed to be a descendent of High John the Conqueror. Julia knew it was bullshit, but she had already lost her husband. She couldn't help it, she had no idea how to go on, and here came Noah, chopping wood and fixing the stove, trying in his clumsy way to be polite, treating her like a widow.

Picking guitar on the weekends for extra money, Noah would bring Julia to the Saturday Night dances right up to the time Little Robert was born. The music would warm her from her toes up to her bottom, and the rhythm would make her shake it, and just a sip of whiskey would take her head off, and she'd be jitterbugging and boogying, while one of the Marchetti brothers watched from a window.

For Noah, being with another man's wife had wiped out his self-respect. He didn't feel up to the challenge of defending Julia from these white men. One night, soon after Little Robert was born, Noah disappeared. Gossip had it that Noah had gone off with somebody else's wife. The Marchetti brothers had some unfinished business with Julia the night after, and tied her up and went at her, while Carrie screamed and clawed at them. The next day Julia, still bleeding, wrapped the infant Robert in blankets, took Carrie by the hand, and signed on with a Delta labor supplier.

I'm goin' away, to a world unknown
I'm worried now, but I won't be worried long[27]

Julia's trek through the lawless frontier of the Delta stripped her of any dignity. She was put to backbreaking work each day, and was passed around each night from bosses to foremen like a whiskey bottle. She dragged Carrie and Little Robert through the mud from camp to camp, forever heading north, like in the old days of the Underground Railroad, following the drinking gourd, the Big Dipper and its brightest star. She couldn't even see the miserable river from the ground. The view of the Mississippi was blocked by immense, gradually rising green levees snaking through woods, swamps, and farms, lining it on both sides from Cairo, Illinois, all the way down past New Orleans, higher and longer than the Great Wall of China, sometimes forty feet high and about four hundred feet wide, with towns and cities spreading right up its slope. She saw it as the biggest damn thing ever built to staunch the tide of nature, and it reminded her of the power of white men, far away, somewhere in government, that could force her people to build this thing.

This was a river that brought both life and death, fertile soil and floods. Tributaries would widen and then silt up unexpectedly, and oxbow lakes would appear magically one day, like God's teardrops, and disappear the next. Point bars, crevasse splays, and chute cutoffs confounded all but the most agile riverboat captains, and abandoned channels led them off-course and aground in nightmarish swamps. The Delta was one of the last holdout frontiers, a land that couldn't be farmed until the levees were built by Irish immigrants and African slaves right before the Civil War. The Irish descendants, the "Mister Charlies," ruled the labor camps with whips and chains, and hired newly freed Negros as muleskinners because they knew how to sing to the animals to stimulate them.

Julia thought she had found one to take care of them, a muleskinner respected by the bosses, until he tried to protect her from the bosses. It had been a futile effort: she got raped, he got thrown in jail. Turned out the mules were more valuable to the boss than the muleskinner.

All she could think about was how to find a way to Memphis, where Dodds must be, carrying on in the name of Spencer. To get on her feet again.

Nobody knows you when you down and out...[28]

After two seasons Julia found a way to cross that river, following rumors of higher wages in the gambling halls and gin mills of East Arkansas. On the outskirts of Helena she hid with her kids out in back behind a church, and the white preacher took them in for the night and fed them ribs. The next day the preacher took her in his arms and promised her that she would be saved, that she would walk with Jesus, if she would tell him where the voodoo orgies and rituals were held, and on which nights. Because he had heard of these things. He had heard about a Mama Roux who cooked up some brew that drove women crazy.

Julia had no idea what he was talking about. She recalled stories she'd heard from her grandmother back in the hills of Eastern Mississippi, about women going out at night to dance with the Devil out in the forest, to cook up kettles of beans, frogs legs and things. But they were just stories grownups told children, like how you got to watch out and be good or De Cunjah Man, he'll come and get ya. Stories to scare the children, to keep them in line. She told the preacher she'd heard of these voodoo things but had never seen them. And she looked up at that white preacher and saw only ragged superstition and nonsense sparkling in his eyes. So she agreed fervently to walk with Jesus, and told him nonsense about some witch-haired woman she'd met down in a nearby levee camp.

The preacher brought them to a plantation so that she could get some decent work, but not before warning her, with all severity, that if she danced, the good white folks around here would assume she danced with the Devil, and she'd be run out of the county. "Belief is a fortress. No crack in a fortress should be counted as small. We no longer live in the dusky afternoon where evil can mix with good and confound us all."

That next dusky afternoon the plantation owner's son tried to take her in the horse stall and she fought back, scratching his face. Before long deputies were on the farm and she grabbed her kids and sneaked off. Determined to set things right, she scraped together what she could in a week alongside the younger girls at a Helena brothel, a warm and friendly place where Little Robert and Carrie could get a decent breakfast, and spent all of it on train tickets to Memphis.

A day later Julia stood before the handsome residence on Handwerker Hill in Memphis, where Charles Dodds now lived with Selena, calling himself Spencer. Damn this man, he's gonna take us in, 'cause we're not leaving. Charles came out, and they argued in front of the children. Charles called Little Robert the son of a no-good field hand. Carrie cried while the mistress Selena hid behind curtains in the living room, peeking out the window.

Charles eventually relented as a good Christian should. He would take in Little Robert and Carrie, but he would never forgive Julia for having the child, and he would have nothing to do with her anymore. Julia sat on the curb crying for hours as Charles got Little Robert and Carrie settled, and they were all too busy reuniting with their brothers and sisters to go outside to console her.

Julia would not see Little Robert again until he was a teenager.

* * *

Not until he was five or six, when his sister Carrie told him all these things, did he think of himself as different than the other Negro kids. He bragged about his mother once he knew the history, talked it up about how she had worked her way up river, one levee camp to the next, to bring him to Memphis and put him in a good home and a good school. Carrie sobbed when she heard him telling these stories. The hurt in her eyes scared him, and he promised her he wouldn't tell those stories anymore.

Carrie hated and feared her father, the man who now called himself Charles Spencer, the man Carrie referred to, when talking to Robert, as "your stepdaddy." Over the years that Robert grew up in the Memphis household, Carrie refused to take on the name Spencer just to spite her father. But Little Robert took to the Spencer name easily. Being a Spencer meant living in a good house with a large middle-class family and a stepfather who made a decent living in the furniture business, and by seven he'd been taught what it meant to be a respectable Negro.

Charles Spencer had a piano in the front parlor with W.C. Handy's sheet music on the rack, and always tried his best to play "The Memphis Blues (Mr. Crump)" whenever he had visitors. And he had even more visitors when he bought a phonograph from the Victor Talking Machine Company, the only one in the neighborhood, along with red-label 78s imported from Europe, including the operatic music of Enrico Caruso, a dance-hall record by Sophie Tucker, and the first Negro composer Spencer had ever heard of, James Reese Europe.[29] He had since augmented this collection with recordings of other Negro artists, including comic George W. Johnson, The Dinwiddie Colored Quartette, and the Fisk University Jubilee Singers.

Music and comedy filled the house every night when he came home from the furniture store, and on very rare nights he'd pull out the sheet music for "Oh Didn't He Ramble"[30] by the Negro comedy team of Cole and Johnson, quickly becoming popular among the black brass bands in New Orleans and soon to become standard repertoire for their jazz funerals. It told the story of the black-sheep son of a New York Irish immigrant family, Buster, with his "rough and rowdy ways," who "rambled all around, in and out the town... 'till the butcher cut him down." Spencer would arch his eyebrows and smile wickedly at his sons and especially at his illegitimate Robert, who refused to be scared.

Usually a terse, contemplative, and detached man, Charles Spencer surprised the household one evening by coming home a bit inebriated, supported by two high-yellow gals in the gaudiest fashion clothes from New Orleans. He was accompanied by a tall, light-skinned Creole man with a massive Roman nose and a wide smile, larger than life and twice as flamboyant, in a gray pin-stripe suit, a Stetson hat and Edwin Clapp shoes, with rubies lacing his garters and a diamond in his front tooth. The Creole man announced to everybody that he was Lord Jelly Roll Morton of the Feminine Lubricants, the Original Winding Boy, Procurer of Talent and the World's Greatest Georgia Skin Player, Craps Connoisseur, Pontificate of the Poolrooms and Hot Tune Writer.

Little Robert snickered at this introduction, and the man roared and pounced on him. "Boy, you ain't old enough to be cut down by the World's Greatest! I done take money from the baddest man alive, that be Aaron Harris down in New Orleans. That man would chew pig iron and spit it out into razor blades!"

But with a twinkle of his eye and a swift change in demeanor, Jelly Roll had the boy giggling and rolling on the floor. Selena helped Charles to his favorite easy chair while another man, dressed nearly the same as Jelly Roll right down to the diamond tooth, introducing himself as Cornell Woodrow, and handed Robert's older brother a brand new record to play on the phonograph.

"We come up here," said Cornell, "'cause your daddy said he wanted to hear this. We were playing pool 'board *The Natchez*, headin' for St. Louis, just a friendly game, pocket money y'understand, and your good-natured daddy here," pointing to Charles, nodding out, "well, he didn't make the shot, and we won a place to eat and sleep for the night, so here we are!"

The recording of the Original Dixieland 'Jass' Band's "Livery Stable Blues"[31] spun around as Carrie cranked the machine. "The most important recording every made!" shouted the World's Greatest Jelly Roll. "At least until I make my own! Now that there's a Spanish tinge, a bit of Spanish seasoning, that's what you need, but you also need a powerful background, and the syncopation, know what I'm talking 'bout? That's how you get to jazz. I invented jazz, way back in 1902. I knows what I'm talking 'bout."

Little Robert had no doubt, and the rest of the household crowded around to hear it as Charles slumped, his head lolly-gagging off the fancy cushioned chair. A bottle of whiskey appeared from somewhere and was passed around, the adults careful not to accidentally hand it to one of the children. Jelly Roll kept shouting about how this was a traditional New Orleans song.

When it finished three minutes later, he whipped out some sheet music from his inside pocket and jumped on the piano, "Hey now, this is the Jelly Roll Blues! Just now published!"[32] As he launched into his stop-time rag, everybody got loose, the two gals kicked up a storm, and Selena draped her arm around Jelly Roll. Robert's older brother had his guitar out, trying to play along. The house jumped with music, the kids shouting for joy, and Selena moved in closer to Jelly Roll, tickling his neck as he played.

Carrie watched the action from over by the phonograph, frowning, and as usual no one noticed Little Robert, who'd picked up his brother's guitar, and Cornell, who began showing him a few chords. At midnight poor Robert deflated like a balloon and passed out by the couch in the midst of the party.

* * *

Robert awoke, or was rather kicked awake, as Cornell and one of the high-yellow gals made their way to the couch. Dawn was breaking, giggling female voices spilled down from upstairs, and Charles moaned on the easy chair. Cornell shook the boy and asked him to get them some food to pack for them, and a bottle or two of that whiskey if they still had some left.

These people had arrived like a hurricane and had taken over the house, or so it seemed to Robert, so he made his way through the debris to get them what they wanted.

"And I got something for ya," Cornell said when he got back, "a lot easier to play than the guitar. You can get started on this." And with a flourish, he pulled a Jew's harp from his vest. Little Robert didn't know what to do with it, so Cornell took it from him and showed him how to play it, improvising a ditty based on one of his favorite limericks,

Now this right old man was a sick 'un
He had a dozen hen ripe for the pickin'
He'd chase 'em around
With his trousers pulled down
And he'd say "Whatsa matter, you chicken?"

Little Robert giggled.

"Now don't be singing those kinda songs," boomed Jelly Roll from the stairs, with one of the high-yellow gals and Selena both leaning on him, their clothes and hair disheveled, smiling contentedly, Carrie would say wickedly in the days to come. Selena came around slowly, started to rearrange some of the debris, and hesitatingly tended to Charles, who'd passed out without a clue.

Robert pulled out his thunder-stone, the tiny pebble his sister had given him years before, the stone that fell to earth when he was born, and showed it to Cornell. Cornell took the wide-eyed boy aside and told him, in quiet tones so that no one else could hear, the story about the first black heroes that came to these shores bound in chains from West Africa. The rolling stones, who had hid these stones in their bellies to keep them from their white captors.

Soon they were off to the riverboat, Little Robert bringing up the rear carrying Jelly Roll's valise. Jelly Roll cut an amazing figure down the street, moseying with one arm swinging back and forth, his index finger out like he's pointing at something and then pointing back at himself, just shootin' the agate, as it used to be called, a kind of walk that inspires people to indulge in vices. It seemed to Robert there was nothing this man couldn't do.

Robert was out here with him, heading for the riverboat on a great adventure, and the world was turning all by itself, without any help from his stepdaddy, nobody in this new world but himself. The river marked the edge of the world for Robert, but not for Jelly Roll and his companions as they boarded *The Natchez* in all its splendor. Robert played his Jew's harp on the dock as he watched them enter the riverboat casino, Jelly Roll doffing his hat to every lady he passed. That's what a man does, thought Robert. He goes off into the larger world to make his fortune, he doesn't sit at home and fall asleep in the easy chair. Robert would have been there all day if not for the white boss who'd chased him off, but he remained in the bushes watching the tidy scene inside the riverboat's windows until the powerful honk of its horn knocked him backwards off his crouch. A mournful echo of the horn bounced off the levee to haunt him, and the riverboat drifted slowly away from the dock into the intimidating river, where it pitched and rolled like a giant log until settling into the currents and chugging upstream.

Punishment was swift and fierce. Charles was more than annoyed that his best whiskey was gone, but some twitch in his face revealed a far deeper discomfort, and Robert endured the whipping in silence, shifting his gaze to Selena and matching her silence. Eventually Charles recognized the futility of punishing Robert and also his usefulness as a scapegoat; besides, Robert's presence in the household was a constant reminder of adultery, both Julia's and his own. Selena wouldn't care for him, not in the way she cared for the other children. So Charles decided to send Robert back to Julia. He was, after all, the son of a no-good farm hand, and probably not redeemable.

So Little Robert was packed up and sent off, not that he minded at first. He wanted desperately to go somewhere, anywhere, wanted to hear that mournful echo of the riverboat horn again. The story Cornell had told him about the rolling stones convinced him that there was more to this world than what he could learn up on Handwerker Hill.

* * *

Soon Robert was back with Julia and her new husband, Dusty Willis, working at a Mister Charlie cotton plantation off Highway 61 near Robinsonville, Mississippi, some twenty miles south of Memphis and as far from the soft life of Memphis as anyone could get. Dusty kept scolding him. Get behind that mule in the morning, plow behind me all day long, all week long, all year long. You won't amount to nothing if you don't work.

Julia hid in the shadows of Dusty's wrath, stoic in the face of his stinging diatribes, solemn when confronted with her past, complacent with her role as midwife to Dusty's every need. And grateful that Dusty had taken her and Robert in, the only one she had left out of ten children. But Dusty had nothing but contempt for Robert, who was growing into a small-boned man, with long delicate fingers and beautiful hands not suitable for farm work, and a bad eye that kept him out of school. Robert's body wiggled like a woman's, and his head was too big.

A Sunday morning sun rose in biblical proportions as Robert walked the dirt road in a sweat, a road packed with decades of decadent Mississippi mud, past the ramshackle red barn and out of the plantation toward Robinsonville. A hell-hound[33] bayed in the distance, sniffing out his trail. In Robert's dreams his father was a tall man in a Stetson hat and preacher's suit with a long, angular nose and severe eyes, striding confidently out into the untamed frontier, ready for a card game, a gun fight, anything. The frontier stretched to eternity with no salvation, a hell with no beginning and no end. Just a week before, Carrie had told him that his real father, Noah Johnson, whom he'd never met, had been murdered in Helena. Some gambler had done him in after accusing him of cheating. No body had been found.

Robert walked with his head forward and tilted to one side, his body following behind, with damp dust caked in his short nappy hair, and tears welling up in his all-night reddened, deep-set eyes. He would never let anyone see him like this, never let it be known that he could be so down and out and crying. He had nothing in his greasy overalls, nothing tucked into his sweat-stained rough cotton shirt, no socks in his stepfather's worn out Oxford shoes, nothing but his harmonica, which he held tightly in his hand, his extraordinarily long and delicate, spidery fingers wrapped all around it so that you couldn't even see it. He would use his father's name, Johnson. Got these ol' walkin' blues...[34]

Well, I got up this morning
Woah – all I had was gone

Approaching a train depot, Robert saw two men sitting out in front playing checkers, with posters tacked up on the depot wall behind them for Dr. Pepper, Chesterfields, Bull Durham, Dixie beer, King Biscuit flour, Maud's Chitterling Soup. Some were defaced with hoodoo hex signs, others with mustaches scribbled on the women's faces. I'm getting away from this goddamn town, Robert thought, not gonna become just another hayseed catching junebugs and chirping like a cricket on Mister Charley's farm.

One of the men looked up. It was Cornell Woodrow, his childhood idol, wearing the same gray pin-stripe suit, Stetson hat, and Edwin Clapp shoes, with rubies lacing his garters and a diamond in his front tooth.

Cornell motioned him over. "Little Robert! Knew I'd find you around here. And you should meet my friend here, Willie Brown," Cornell introduced his checkers partner. "Well known guitar player in these parts, played with Luke

Thomson and Thomas Clubfoot Coles, did 'Rowdy Blues' with Kid Bailey — ain't that right, Willie? Even recorded with Charley Patton too, the Masked Marvel himself."

Willie chuckled. "Yeah, well, the Marvel himself coming to town, you know. So's my friend Son House. It's gonna be a whirlwind out on that old farm tonight."

Robert was checking out Willie's guitar lying on the bench beside him.

Cornell looked at him. "Boy, you learn that jew's harp I gave you, back in Memphis?"

Robert pulled out his harmonica. "Yessir, but now I play this." And he looked over at Willie's guitar. "A-and I wanna learn that."

Cornell reached over and started cranking up a record on a portable Victrola on the bench next to him. "It's a big hit now, just came out," he said to Robert as Leroy Carr's "How Long — How Long Blues"[35] spilled out of the speaker horn. "Boy, you got to listen first. Then you can learn how to play the music right."

Robert sidled over to the contraption and fingered its horn. He knew, right then and there, that his destiny was to be *on* that phonograph record player.

"The record player's yours, and these records, too." Cornell pulled out discs by Louis Armstrong, Bessie Smith, Lonnie Johnson, Tommy Johnson, Skip James, Scrapper Blackwell, Charley Patton, and Peetie Wheatstraw.

Robert handled the discs, amazed. They were like ancient objects calling to him out of eternity. He'd heard about Peetie Wheatstraw, the Devil's Son-in-law, the High Sheriff from Hell.

"You know, *you* didn't find that record player," Cornell told him. "It found *you*. It was meant for *you*. And these records can turn it into an instrument of power and pleasure. There is a power in this music, Little Robert, power in the way it was *recorded*, that can skewer a woman's heart, make her break right down, and she's yours." And then Cornell laughed and started singing in a fake Irish lilt,

Under a red Studebaker
She wanted to know if I'd make her
She put on the brakes
But I had what it takes
And flooded her carburetor!

Robert blushed, his black face burning yellow, but he laughed back. When he returned to the farm, Robert hid the phonograph in the red barn. He would steal out from his bedroom at night, when Dusty was asleep, to play his records. With all the mean things happening all around him to black people, he couldn't understand his own exuberance, that pure joy he felt when he played the records and tried to imitate harmonica licks. And he didn't understand the passion. He couldn't see the reason why he couldn't leave all those no-good women alone.[36]

Robert learned quickly how to be cute and relaxed around the girls, and his easy confidence earned him a little respect from the boys. Of all the teenage girls Robert brought out to the red barn to hear his music, only Virginia took his heart. When he first saw Virginia he felt possessed. All he could think about was her soft, ebony breasts, her wondrous delta, that earthly connection of her thigh as it met the curve of her marvelous, luscious rump, her cheeks a sweet valentine for his kisses... he just couldn't believe how much it occupied his mind. How's a man supposed to walk this earth?

All he wanted to do was crawl into the womb of her love, and play his phonograph records for her. The music made him throb with lust for Virginia, lust for any woman really. It just took him over, and everything he saw seemed altered in some way. Something magical had happened to him, certainly mysterious... possibly demonic. This throbbing power could get him into trouble. But he was dead certain this thing, whatever it was in the music, was the stuff of life. Without it he was nobody, nowhere.

For a year he listened to his music, practiced his harmonica, and worked the fields with Dusty breaking his back about every little thing, and now that he was sixteen, charging him rent. Virginia was also sixteen, and pregnant, and Robert was expected to take care of her. He spent as many weekends as he could playing harmonica for an extra dollar. On a Sunday in April of 1930 he was off playing harmonica at a white folks' social in Clarksdale, held in honor of Mister Charlie, the Will Dockery Plantation's head manager, with the Masked Marvel himself likely to be in attendance.

Virginia died that day in childbirth. They told him the child, a girl, had died with her.

Robert was distraught with guilt. Julia tried to console him, saying it was God's will. But Robert turned his back on God, whatever that was. He cradled his harmonica, shaking with fear. What evil have I done? What evil has that poor girl heard?[37]

"You *know* what that Devil music's good for," Dusty bellowed at him out by the chicken shack where none of the other children could hear, after clapping his ear and smacking his head. Robert put up with this treatment with downcast eyes and a half-smile that wouldn't leave his face. "You *know* it's sinful."

"Well I'm a sinner," Robert replied, his eyes still downcast. "And I got ramblin' on my mind."

Dusty moved to smack him, but he jumped out of range and started running down the dusty road, never to return.

* * *

Robert sat near the feet of his new mentors, Willie Brown and his friend Son House, as they played guitar in the middle of the room at the Saturday night fish fry in a shack outside of Robinsonville. Earlier they had let young Robert play harmonica with them. Willie guffawed as Robert struggled through an instrumental break, trying to keep up with Son House's impossibly arrhythmic guitar-playing[38] that could never mesh with another rhythm player.

Robert wanted to play guitar but hadn't mustered the courage to ask.

They looked a bit like the new popular comedy team of the movie houses, Laurel and Hardy, with Willie Brown's fat head and blowhard smile, and Son House's thin mustache and even thinner, pointed head and worried brow; they even had a bit of that act going, where one's an idiot and the other's a complete idiot.

As soon as they took a break, Robert was up on his feet and borrowing Willie's guitar. "Please! Let me try it some."

The racket made some of the fish fryers mad. One of them went outside to find Son House. "Why don't y'all go in and get that guitar away from that boy. He's running people crazy with it."

Son House came storming in and right up to Robert's face. "Don't do that! You drivin' them nuts. You can't play nothing 'cept harmonica, and not even *that*."

Robert set aside the guitar in shame. Son and Willie were snickering, intimidating Robert to the point where he just had to walk outside. He left town broken-hearted, his family gone, his pride shattered.

* * *

Robert wandered the Delta and saw it all with his own eyes. He saw the Devil's work in the shacks out beyond the fields, in the juke joints of Helena, in the whore houses of Jackson and New Orleans. And he saw the Devil working overtime over on the Jesus side of town, in the Negro Baptists churches, planting the seeds of institutional hypocrisy, shunting aside the righteous to make way for the ambitious, gathering alms in the name of the poor to pay for their starched white cloths, gold candlesticks, and leather-upholstered Cadillacs.

Robert eventually returned to Hazlehurst, near his birthplace, where he could dream about his father. Willie had told him to look up a guitar player named Ike Zinnerman, who claimed to have learned how to play the guitar in a graveyard at midnight, sitting atop tombstones.

Busking on the streets with his harmonica, he played a tune for a white businessman. "No, I don't want to hear the blues, boy. Play something I know. I'm from down South, the Big Easy, y'know, N'awlins." Robert remembered a song he had heard once on the radio. Heard it only once, but he knew its melody note for note. He played it for the man, "hot tamales and they're red hot!" Tap-dancing two-step and singing between harmonica breaks, "Yaas we got 'em for sale!"[39]

The man was so tickled by this that he walked down to the pawn shop and bought for Robert a Kalamazoo, a big round-hole guitar, made by Gibson. This would be Robert's guitar for as long as he lived.

* * *

For Robert, it was never a question of selling his soul to the Devil. The black man in the South had nothing to sell. He had to trick his way into some decent style of living, and there were only two ways to do that. He could either preach the white man's gospel from a well-cushioned pulpit, or travel the world singing the blues.

Phonograph records pointed the way, just like the old slavery songs with their codes and navigation aids that showed black people how to follow the drinking gourd to freedom. The phonograph is a new kind of voodoo that carries the spirit, Cornell had told him. You have only to find the subtle ways to bring it out, through recording techniques. Robert could hear them. There are records that can turn a phonograph into an instrument of power and pleasure. There is a power in the music, the way it was recorded, that can skewer a woman's heart, make her break right down, and she's yours.

Robert set out to prove it, if only to himself, over and over again. He would look for a good woman who could provide for him. "Honey, you got a boyfriend?"

"No I ain't got no boyfriend."

"Well babe," he licked his lips, "You better come on in my kitchen..."[40]

Callie had been married twice before, was ten years older, and was already taking care of three children; Robert could be like the fourth. She could fuss over all of them while he took his little book of songs out into the woods with his guitar.

He could listen to a record, or a song on the radio, just once; and then go and play the tune over and over until he got it just like he wanted it and thought it should be. And when he started getting weekend jobs at the juke joints near town, Callie wanted to be there, sit on his knee, and fend off the women that would encircle him. He would often let her fall off as he flailed his legs up and down and back and forth to keep time.

Musicians didn't take wives out on jobs. No one knew she was his wife; he gave everyone the impression that she was his mistress, taking care of him so that he could go about sporting nice clothes and well-shined shoes. But he resented this intrusion on his act.

After they moved from Hazlehurst to Clarksdale in the Delta, Callie broke down. She could no longer stand the crazed eyes of other women gathering around him as he played, and how their lips curled into a leer as if Robert's fingers were reaching underneath their dresses.

"Godammit, woman! Stop breaking down!"[41] Yes of course there were other women. "The stuff I got will bust your brains out! I'm out here doing it, doing what I know best. While you in here crying, wishing the world would just go away."

But all she could see and hear was this raving lunatic of a husband shouting at her, and the world outside just waiting to claim her life. And she broke down so far that he left her. She died just a few weeks after Robert took off. He shed her from him like snakeskin. Never again, he vowed to himself, never again make promises, never count on one woman in your life.

* * *

Cornell seemed to always show up when things were bad. Robert came across him at Ike's. "If you want to learn to play anything," Cornell was telling Ike, "or you want to make songs yourself, you take your guitar and you go out to the crossroads. A big black man will walk up there at the stroke of midnight and take your guitar, and he'll tune it for you, and show you how to play something."

Ike was having none of it. "They call it selling your soul to the Devil. Tommy Johnson talked that shit. 'Be sure to get there just a'fore midnight, so you know you be on time. Have your guitar and be playing a piece there by yourself.' Heard all that shit."

Robert joined in. "If Tommy talked that shit to me, I would have called him a liar to his face. You don't have no control over your soul. You don't even know what you gonna do ten minutes from now. You might be stone cold dead."

"Don't joke about that shit with Son House," said Ike to Robert. "He believes that shit. Come back and haunt you someday."

Cornell belly-laughed. "The idea came from West Africa. My ancestors, and yours too. The big black man is Legba, the Trickster, keeper of the crossroads, the messenger between humans and spirits. Takes care of relations, so to speak, between the spirit powers on the one road and the humans on the other, wherever they intersect. Our first African politician! But ever since we were sold into slavery, the white masters, the Christians, have been telling us that our pagan gods are devils.

"Well, just like a politician, the guardian of the crossroads can be both generous and cruel at the same time. Legba came from Dahomney, they talk about him as an evil god, who must be kept at peace, or harm will come to you. The Yorubans now, they call him Eshu. They see him differently. He's the Trickster who teaches us valuable lessons. The Haitians know him as Papa Legba. He's a kindly old man, but a mischief-maker and a seducer of women."

Cornell belly-laughed again. "Animal sacrifices! Fornication! If you believe the white folks, we're about to fuck *all* their women, if given half a chance. But we don't want their women!" And then, as was his wont, Cornell broke into fake Irish sing-song,

On the hood of an old Model T
That's where she showed it to me
From throttle to clutch
She showed me too much!
It looked like a crankcase to me.

They were doubling over in laughter when Cornell handed Robert a slip of paper, some directions on how to find it. The crossroads. "Why not?" Cornell said before he disappeared into the woods behind Ike's place.

* * *

That night, armed with the thunder-stone from his childhood and his new Kalamazoo, Robert followed the directions. They led him away from the main road outside Clarksdale and down a dirt trail to an old woman's shack in the woods. She called herself Mama Roux. A black woman of some indeterminate age and weight, with a wild mantle of tightly curled black hair framing an oval face and falling to a deep, wide body wrapped in Haitian scarves. She already knew who Robert was, and welcomed him as if expecting him.

A baby cried in the back room. "She's your child. Virginia's child. She didn't die with her."

Robert was thunderstruck. There she was, his very own child, an extension of his life. He reached into the crib to pick her up.

Mama Roux stopped him, and gave him a stern look. "You must give the child up, in order to live the life you want. I will raise her, and one day she will make you proud. I will name her Marie, after the infamous Marie Laveau, my grandmother."

Mama Roux stirred a cauldron, mumbling the name of each herb she put into the sauce, names Robert forgot as soon as he heard them, as if the herbs were protecting themselves against future mischief. Trusting this older woman, Robert drank the potion and closed his eyes. The room deepened in darkness and mystery.

"You must be careful to do exactly what I say. See no evil, hear no evil, and speak no evil," the old woman cackled in a sing-song. "And whatever you do, you must find a false reason for doing it. You must use every trick you know. Everything you like, you must pretend *not* to like, and any secret you find, you must pretend that it's *not* there."

Robert stirred, his eyes closed.

"You are a rolling stone. You carry the stone everywhere you go, and you let it out, you let it seep out, in music, the code of your ancestors."

In the pitch black of midnight, his eyes still closed, Robert heard a wolf whistle. He opened his eyes to find an old man sitting on a stump at a crossroads, playing a stick as if it were a guitar.

Robert found his voice. "What are you doing?"

The old man spoke in a croaking, bitter voice. "Trying... trying to play music, you fool."

"But you don't have a real guitar." Robert's own pathetic guitar felt warm against his back, strapped to his body with a ragged rope.

"We never use real instruments to play music," the old man rasped.

"Then how do you make a sound, other than your voice and your whistling?"

"We *don't* make a sound, *out here*."

"Well then, how do you make music without sound?"

"There is no music, *out here*."

"But you said you were making music!"

"Trying to *play* music, is what I said. We're always trying to *play*, but we never *make* anything, *out here*. Everything is already *made*, you just got to *play* it."

Robert felt conned. "How long you been trying?"

"There is no time, *out here*."

"No time? How can you play music without time?"

"What *you* don't know how to do is *listen*. You need to stop all that, stop thinking about it, stop trying to *make* it. Just listen, and *play*, for a while."

The old man disappeared. Robert was alone at the crossroads. He took off the rope holding his guitar, and as he began to strum it, he heard another wolf whistle.

"Who's that?"

But there was nothing, no sound. And then, a tap on his shoulder. A man in a black three-piece suit and a white Stetson hat. He resembled Cornell, but his face was different. "Welcome. My name is Stagger Lee."

The wolf whistle sounded again. Robert thought, it must be this man's trademark sound. But wait, the man's too portly, too short, to be the Stagger Lee of his dreams, to be his father.

"Here, let me tune that guitar for you." The man calling himself Stagger Lee reached for the guitar. But Robert instantly realized that the man wanted to rob him. It's a test of wills.

The moment of truth brought a kind of serenity. Robert heard a soundtrack, the soundtrack of his life, as he unleashed his guitar and started to play staggering, piercing notes directed at Stagger Lee's gut. Blues walking like a man![42]

With each note the man buckled over. Robert threw his entire body into it, playing a driving rhythm, and driving the stiff pointed neck of the guitar not into Stagger Lee but *through* him.

A nightmarish, muted scream escaped from the man's lips as he toppled backward. And Robert felt calm. It's not like he knew how to kill a man. He still didn't know how to kill a man, didn't really believe he *had* killed a man... not a real man anyway. There was no death, *out here.*

But he *had* killed someone. Was it Stagger Lee, or was it Billy the Lion? Which one tried to stand in his way? And is it the same evil thing, to have left your child, your only child, out in the wilderness with some witch doctor?

It's the music, thought Robert. It's the blues that took my child and tore me all up inside. And what are these blues but a heart attack, like consumption, killing me by degrees? But I just can't turn around now.

Robert walked away with his guitar. Death, he realized, is not something to fear. Death is a transformation, a resurrection to a whole new order of being, in which your previous form is nothing more than a stage play or a peep show of your own making. Everyone is part of the cast, with no longer any distinctions of black or white, rich or poor, guilty or innocent... just human energy. And you can transcend the peep show you created, and laugh at its humorous moments, and cry during the love and death scenes. Robert realized all this and more, in an instant, a flash of insight while riding the clouds of his mind.

* * *

When Robert returned to his senses at daylight, Mama Roux and her shack were gone, and his Kalamazoo was right beside him as he lay on the side of the deserted road. He remembered something Cornell had said. A good musician can play the guitar as if it were an extension of his body.

Robert took up his Kalamazoo. With just a bit of concentration, he could dispense altogether with that physical feeling that a guitar was in his hands. Instead, he played his *hands*, he played his *fingers*. He latched on to a vibration that linked his voice with his fingers and throbbed with the heat of this emotions. He could play anything. Life is but a trick to be played on your master. To keep your spirit high and unbroken among the enslaved, you must learn new tricks.

Before heading to his trial by fire in front of Son House and Willie Brown in Robinsonville, Robert learned how to dress right. Gray pin stripes on black wool, complete suit with vest, shiny black oxfords. White handkerchief sprouting from the left breast pocket. Black fedora with a wide gray band. He wore this singular outfit from street corners to juke joints, and would roll up his suit pants in a tight roll, stow it, and carry it around for weeks as he hopped freight trains or rode in the back of corn wagons. And when he took it out, unrolled it, those pants would still be pressed sharp. He would instruct his helpful women to beat his suit with a stick to dry-clean it, to shine his oxfords with pig grease, and to wash, dry, and iron his shirt.

When he arrived at the juke joint to play, the crowd parted to let him in. Son House and Willie Brown were shocked to see how good he looked, and hear how well he could play. It seemed that he had an ear for all kinds of music. Chord for chord, note for note, lick for lick, word for word, just like he had heard it on the radio. He used his bass strings to create a steady, rolling rhythm. He was making chords they didn't know. And he never looked for a chord, just naturally made them. Ninths, diminishes, augmenteds, sevenths, tenths, thirteenths, and he made them right, in all the right places. His voice changed from a moan to a whisper, or to a yell, or to trombone solo. He could sing about the wind howling, and they all could hear that wind. He could sing about going to the crossroads, falling down on his knees, and asking the lord, have mercy on me please.[43]

Robert would stop the driving guitar rhythm for a moment, and use his slide to rip the seams of the song up to a single note that raised the hair on the back of their necks. His was the Nat Turner style of blowing their minds. Where Turner saw blood in the sky, Robert saw blues falling like hail.

And then, Robert disappeared. He just thought himself *not there.* He thought: *See no evil.*

No one saw him leave. Willie suspected that he lit off in secret, out the back door, with someone's wife. Son House left the joint muttering something about his having sold his soul to the Devil.

Robert had found the power to get around. He learned that he could use this power of concentration to influence the course of events. To a point. Walking along a road, he couldn't exactly stop a car from running him down, or snap a tree limb to fall on the road like some shaman. But he could put out some kind of positive energy that would tame the beast of the road, draw a car to slow down, and even stop to give him a ride. He could charm a deputy into letting him walk through his neighborhood to get to the black section of town. Even make the weather for the day suit his clothes, rather than the other way around. And he drew women to him like flies on honey.

This was his pact. He knew that this power would last only a short time, and that his luck would run out. Not exactly a pact with a devil, just a pact with life itself. I'll trade you a few years of glory for an early grave.

* * *

The music Robert played in small, out-of-the-way places, over a period of about six years — playing bass lines, hot guitar leads, and rhythm, and singing on top of it, on a steamy stage in a roadside tavern filled with sweaty gamblers and loose women — would decades later shape the sound of rock music. It was a sound you couldn't help but stop and listen to. He could hypnotize an audience with his voice, which could quiver in a moan, seduce with a whisper, embolden with a yell, or flat-out tickle your funny bone like a trombone solo.

The music was not wholly original, but a synthesis. He *played* the music rather than trying to *make* it. He could hear no evil. Robert listened to an extraordinarily wide variety of styles on records, including all the jazz greats, before attempting his own style. The wider perspective gave Robert a sense of the theatrical and dynamic. His guitar-playing was subtly sophisticated. He could change meters, riffing styles, and tempos smoothly or abruptly, as required by the moment, making his guitar almost like an orchestral commentary on the vocals. Robert could sound like *two* guitarists playing at once. He used the bottom strings of his guitar to create a boogie bass line that echoed the upbeat sound of boogie-woogie piano, and accompanied this rhythm with lead lines on the other strings.

Other musicians heard about Robert and came to see him. Through all of them he moved as a solitary figure, cryptic and guarded, though well mannered and soft-spoken. He would speak no evil. He was protective of his style and tunings and would turn his back on them. When it was time to play, he could suddenly turn on the charm as a song-and-dance man, tap-dancing and jitterbugging, and playing the popular music of the day. He'd sing about love and passion, about squeezing his lemon so the juice would run down his leg, you know what I'm talking about...[44]

And the women would just eat it up, that gangly dressed-up boyish man with the shit-eating little Black Sambo grin, just grinning at the world no matter what might happen. "Just the cutest little brown thing you ever did see," one would say to another. Motherhood and breast-feeding urges would well up in them as they watched him carry on that way, oblivious to the men that wanted to wring his scrawny neck. Robert just carried on with a gleam in his one eye, a cataract forming in his other eye betraying the stress.

Johnson played everywhere, from the Kitty Cat Club in Helena, Arkansas, to the streets of Friars Point in front of Hirsberg's Drugstore. His wanderlust took him to coal yards, speakeasies, levee camps, and taverns all over the Delta. Seventeen-year-old Johnny Shines rode with him some of the time and described leaving a juke joint at two in the morning and hopping a freight train an hour later, not even caring where they were going.

One particular four-month trip started when Calvin Frazier, who'd killed a man in Arkansas, had to leave town quickly and Robert and Shines took off with him. They'd traveled up Highway 51 north to Chicago through St. Louis, where Robert hooked up with Peetie Wheatstraw and Henry Townsend, and played a square dance in Decatur to a mystified audience of white folks that had never seen black musicians, and were uncharacteristically respectful. In Detroit they played live on the radio with a broadcasting preacher, and made it as far as Windsor, Ontario, before doubling back to Detroit. Then New York City, where

Robert met the sax player Henry Minton, who dreamt of starting a jazz club called Minton's Playhouse that would be an oasis for visiting musicians. At Tony Mart's near Atlantic City, Robert and Shines played with a pianist, drummer, and horn player, a combination of jazz and blues with diminished sixths and sevenths that would later be called "jump blues" and evolve into full-blown Chicago-style rhythm and blues. In the middle of this performance, just as it was going good, Robert disappeared. Shines heard from a horn player that he might have gone off into the pine barrens to commune with the Jersey Devil.

Just like Robert to make up stories like that. Shines packed up and moved on. He heard some of his records that came out soon after, but he never saw Robert again.

* * *

Following the footsteps of Charley Patton, Robert eventually walked into H. C. Spier's music store in Jackson, Mississippi, seeking a recording contract. Spier sent him off with Ernie Oertle to a hotel in San Antonio, Texas, to record with Don Law, who had recorded acts all over the South. With the drapes closed against the afternoon traffic noise, Robert played his songs facing the wall. He was moody and suspicious around white folks, especially the cowboy singers Law was recording. He put down sixteen recordings in less than three days.

Don Law put Robert up in a boarding house and told him to get some sleep between sessions, but Robert had gone out and gotten roughed up and arrested for vagrancy. Law got Robert out of jail, and gave him forty-five cents for breakfast, but Robert wasn't done yet; he called Law back, whining, "I'm lonesome and there's a lady here. She wants fifty cents and I lacks a nickel." Breakfast had been the farthest thing from his mind.

The next day Robert recorded "Terraplane Blues", which appeared on jukeboxes throughout the Delta. He returned to show it to his musician friends, walking down dusty roads in his neat pin-stripe suit, shoulders high and a bit hunched forward, his Kalamazoo in one hand and, in his other hand, his first record on Vocalion with the deep blue label and gold lettering.

Robert had mastered the four-note chord, a single timeless event heard all at once, rather than in a serial fashion as pitch changes over time like a melody. He understood that to play a melody was to introduce the element of time, that yardstick of mortality, and that he could fool with the melody and thereby fool with time. But the four-note chord is timeless, and Robert understood this also; he could envision a combo of drums, bass, piano, and his guitar leading a rhythm that he could still fool with, integrating melodic lines into this four-note chord. The future. He could just see it out there, shimmering in the distance; his influence in the future. But he could not see himself in that future.

* * *

A dangerous occupation it was, being a black musician. Other musicians hated you if you played better than them. Women you loved were angry with you if you cast your eye on anyone else. And the men hated you if the women loved you. A great musician had to be careful, especially in the company of strangers.

Robert had made it with a Greenwood woman he didn't know, who happened to be the wife of the jook house manager in Three Forks, outside of town. The manager performed specific acts of vengeance for the nearby Quito plantation owner, who was well connected in the Mississippi political machine. The owner had told him to look out for this uppity Johnson boy, give him some of the white man's medicine.

On a hot midsummer Saturday night in 1938, natty Robert showed up at the joint to play with Rice Miller, going by the name Sonny Boy Williamson, who wore a belt of harmonicas around his waist. Together they played the Delta blues with more than a little musical rivalry, trading licks far into the night.

Robert caught the woman's eye at some point, and her husband saw it. Sonny Boy had been keeping an eye on the action and grew suspicious. During the break, when someone brought Robert an open half-pint of whiskey, Sonny Boy knocked it out of his hand and it broke against the ground.

"Man, don't never take a drink from a open bottle," Sonny admonished him in his gravelly voice. "You don't know what could be in it."

Robert, in turn, retorted, "Man, don't never knock a bottle of whiskey outta my hand."

The husband must have seen this, because he sent over a second bottle. This time Robert took a hearty drink. It wasn't too long after that Robert took sick and couldn't sing. "I'm playing for you all but I can't sing," he told the audience. Sonny took up the slack for him, but after a bit, Robert stopped short in the middle of a number and stumbled outside to throw up.

Eventually they got him back to town, where he was sick for several days, showing signs of poisoning, before dying. Some say he was out of his mind, raving, crawling around on all fours and baying at the moon. He was twenty-seven when he left this world, but he promised to return with a great long story to tell.[45]

* * *

News of Robert's death left many others bereft of vision. Robert Jr. Lockwood gave up playing the guitar for a long time because "I didn't know nothing else but his songs to play." The news did not travel far — not only was John Hammond still looking for Robert months later for his Spirituals to

Swing concert, but also Alan Lomax was still looking for him when he stumbled upon Muddy Waters, who had heard Robert's records and was greatly influenced by him.

Muddy said that the only time he actually saw Robert was on the front porch of a Hirsberg's drugstore in Friars Point. A crowd of people had gathered around Robert, who was playing ferociously, and Muddy was intimidated by the man's musicianship and quickly left.

The next day, still thinking of Robert, Muddy revived the traditional song about the rolling stone and the walking blues. He sang about being mistreated, and that he wouldn't mind dying, just like the rolling stone martyrs of the slave ships.[46]

A formal portrait photograph graces the cover of the Robert Johnson box set. Years before his death, on a fine day in Memphis, Robert mounted a stool at the Hooks Brothers Photography studio, cradling his battered Kalamazoo in his lap. He tipped his fedora, straightened his tie and high-riding tie clasp, and gazed into a camera lens.

He is slight, his legs are crossed, his head seems too big, and his grin too wide with too many teeth. His pinstripe double-breasted jacket and pants are tightly creased, his black dress shoes are polished, and a white handkerchief protrudes from his breast pocket. His fingers are extra-ordinarily long and delicate stretched across the guitar's neck, and he is poised to start a song. He is looking at doom in the face. The brightness in his eyes, despite the cataract, are for imagined better days ahead.

The Record Skipped

The record skipped without warning. The needle bounced, popped, stuttered and scraped across the vinyl grooves, sputtering like a machine gun, and then stopped. For five long minutes the radio station transmitted crackles of lightning from faraway storms against a background of cosmic noise.

Then, just as suddenly, a commercial broke the silence.

Brylcreem, a little dab'll do ya,
Brylcream, you'll look so debonaire,
Brylcreem, the gals will all pursue ya,
They love to get their fingers in your hair!

No apologies from the management, no word from the Philly Fryer, one of the more famous disc jockeys of 1959. Just one commercial after another for about twenty minutes.

Finally a familiar voice took over. Hy Lit, a DJ from the rival station WIBG in Philadelphia, stepped in. "Calling all my beats, beards, Buddhist cats, big time spenders, money lenders, teetotalers, elbow benders, hog callers, home run hitters, finger poppin' daddy's, and cool baby sitters! For all my carrot tops, lollipops, and extremely delicate gum drops! It's Hyski 'O Roonie McVouti 'O Zoot calling, up town, down town, cross town. Here there, everywhere! Your man with the plan, on the scene with the record machine."

Only late-night listeners heard it. Johnny B, for Balzano, was one. It was unusual for a teenager to be awake at three in the morning listening to the radio in his bedroom, but Johnny was no ordinary teen-ager. His motorcycle was still warm in the garage after returning from running an errand for his father, in fact to that very station, WYBY in Wildwood, twenty minutes down the South Jersey coast from Margate. Late night errands were gifts from his father. It's how he'd acquired the Harley, the Schwinn five-speed, a genuine black leather jacket, and black cowboy boots with pearl sequins. The errand was to deliver a sealed package to the Fryer, one of his father's steady customers.

Johnny hadn't peeked inside. He didn't need to. He already knew what it was, a package shaped to look like a stack of records. A little Turkish Lady, his father would say, and a lot of Mexican Mary.

* * *

Two hours earlier, Johnny had shared a puff of Mary, right there in the studio, the stodgy microphones leering in disapproval as Freddie held down the cough switch.

He'd tried it once before, and hadn't felt anything more than a sudden craving for Tastykake cupcakes. This time, as his senses focused and sharpened, he looked at Freddie, cool, hep, hip Freddie Falloni, the Philly Fryer. And burst out giggling.

Freddie's fat frame bustled with energy, his office chair squeaking as he riffed on songs and flung discs across the room. He was so fat that his gut overflowed his trousers, and his haunches enveloped the seat of his chair. His disembodied voice seem to come from somewhere else, not out of this ruddy pockmarked face with its shock of black grease-smeared hair and Buddy Holly spectacles riding, or rather floating, on a sea of flesh. With his lopsided beret and bunched up cravat, he looked like the eccentric curator of a dark museum who'd just been roughed up in an alley. And yet here he was, humming along and chuckling with Dion and the Belmonts, who were begging to know the answer to the eternal question, why must I be a teenager in love?[47]

Why indeed, thought Johnny, calming down for a moment. Why does anyone have to be in love? It's so unhip.

Freddie was still chuckling, and muttering "Dyon and the Bela Mont" over and over.

Johnny yelled at him, "D-yonder and the Bela Monsters!"

Freddie grinned back at the kid, who had obviously smoked too much.

"Okay, enough of that teenage bullshit," Freddie announced to nobody with the cough switch back on. "Let's cross over to the other side." And with that, he switched to "Personality" by Lloyd Price.[48]

"Jazz, bebop, rhythm and blues, electrified blues, all just code names for black music, industry labels to keep them in their places, their *markets*. So we know what's what before we play it on the air." Freddie smirked, tapped his temple with his forefinger, and propped up his one eyebrow for irony. "It's all in there."

Johnny got up and duck-walked to the song, grooving on the syncopation. He loved being at the radio station late at night, rooting out authentic records, two-minute, two-and-a-half minute, three-minute tracks with Freddie's bursts of rapid-fire nonsense, pushing this music out to the world.

Between songs he tolerated Freddie's solemn talk about the music business and how it was all going to hell. Freddie was disappointed with his former mentor, Alan Freed, who'd abandoned his "Moondog" personality in Cleveland for a string of successful shows in New York. Executives from record labels would meet Freed in the cloak room of the Brill Building and hand him paper bags filled with cash, not to demand that Freed play specific records, but just to keep him happy so that he *might* play them.

Johnny couldn't make out whether Freddie was honestly upset about the corruption, or just jealous of Freed's power, but he had no opinion, or at least none that he could give Freddie. Johnny's father, a label executive in the music business, had warned him about talking the industry talk. He'd said there were two kinds of people in the business: tricksters in on the pass, and fools on the outside. And now he could add this: only the tricksters have *personality*.

Freddie may have looked like a trickster, but he acted more like a fool, especially when he veered into the occult, or into the science of radio and his hero, Tesla, the inventor. Freddie was convinced that Tesla had rediscovered technology that had existed in ages past, including airships, particle beams, chemical warfare, even atomic weapons. Johnny didn't know what he was talking about and had never heard of Tesla, but Freddie's reverence made him curious.

Freddie always wore a gold pendant around his neck, with a pinkish stone set at the center, and he would finger that pendant as if it held some kind of power. He spoke reverently about it, that it was a gift from his ancestors, that he could use it to pick hits like a water-dowser picks wells.

After Freddie said something like that, the silence was awkward. Johnny would just look at him and blink like that bongo-beating beatnik Maynard G. Krebs on *The Many Loves of Dobie Gillis*.

Then the record would end, and Freddie would grab the mike, kick the switch, and belt out a melodramatic rapid-fire introduction about the next artist. This time he dropped the needle on "What'd I Say"[49] and started a scat-singing duet with Ray Charles. The call-and-response swung Johnny's head back and forth. Ray's gravelly voice tunneled into his soul. Freddie kicked back in his rolling chair and the station lapsed into a rhythm oblivion. Song after song seemed to walk up to the turntables by themselves, and start playing.

After midnight, Freddie grew solemn and slipped in some blues records from his own collection that the station's advertisers would normally object to, if they had been listening. He put on a disc by Muddy Waters. "Listen to this," he said to Johnny. "You know the story of the rolling stone?"

The stark guitar notes punctured the night sounds of surf and crickets. Muddy's gravelly voice stated nothing but the facts of the case: my mother told my father, a boy is coming, and he's going to be a rolling stone.[50]

"There's power in this music," Freddie told Johnny. "Decode the blues, and you find that it is really about how to find freedom. This story of the rolling stone is deeper than you think."

"Gathers no moss?" was all that Johnny could offer back.

"Much deeper," Freddie intoned solemnly. "It's voodoo. I learned about it in New Orleans, when I worked with Fats Domino. From a man you should meet. Cornell Woodrow. Finest dowser of the blues spirit. He can find it anywhere. You ever heard of High John the Conqueror?"

"High who?" Johnny started up giggling again.

Winking back at him, Freddie followed up the record with another song by Muddy, written by Willie Dixon. He's got a black cat bone, and mojo too. He's the hootchie-coochie man, all the girls lead him by the hand. Got a High John the Conquer root and he's going to mess with you.[51]

As the song cranked up, Freddie pointed to one of the new Fender electric bass guitars he kept in one corner of the studio. It was connected to an amplifier. Johnny picked it up and started picking notes. Halfway through the song, Johnny had the bass part down.

Freddie watched Johnny B in admiration even as he cued up a commercial. "How's your band coming along?"

"Still trying to get Reggie to do some rock 'n' roll."

"Reggie Mention?" Freddie blinked. "I know his father," he added softly, mysteriously, then quickly changed the subject. "They're coming after rock 'n' roll. They used to burn witches, then they burned books. Now they're coming after rock 'n' roll. That's because it's all changed! The codes are transmitted through music now."

Johnny fidgeted on his stool in the broadcast booth, wondering if Freddie was coming unhinged.

"It's true," Freddie barked at him. "They're coming after rock 'n' roll. You need to get ahead of the game."

The song ended, and Freddie wheeled around and switched to the voice of the Fryer, booming and shouting and serenading all the night people within reach of a signal that, at night, could be picked up as far away as Akron, or Norfolk, or even Buffalo.

As he cued up a set of commercials, he asked Johnny, "How long will it take you to get back home?"

Johnny cocked his head and put down the bass. "About twenty minutes."

"Okay. Tune in when you get home. I'll play something special. And while you're listening, check this out."

Freddie reached for a magazine under the control table and tossed it to Johnny. It was MAD Magazine Issue #30, from December 1956. Blasting from its cover was a color cartoon of a freckled, vaguely Irish boy with a missing front tooth, floppy jug ears, and one eye disquietingly lower than the other. Next to the gap-toothed kid, and under a cartoon of the Democratic Party donkey tangling with the Republican Party elephant, was a caption: Write-in Candidate for President Alfred E. Neuman says "What — me worry?" On the back cover was the logo in reverse and the back of the kid's head as he faces a raucous audience that includes Phil Silvers, Ed Sullivan, Dick Tracy, Little Orphan Annie, Popeye the Sailor Man, Nikita Khrushchev, Elvis, Mickey Mouse, and the Mona Lisa.

Inserted into the Elvis parody was the mimeograph of an untitled short story by Herbert Mesh that began with "Screams of the captives..."

"What's this about?"

"Reggie's father. He wrote it. Before he changed his name, from Mesh to Mention. Read it when you get home. It's a story about where the music came from, about the voodoo power of the rolling stone. The story of High John the

Conqueror. It's all in there! I'll play something in about an hour, you should read it so's you'll understand."

"Understand what? And why did he change his name?"

"Long story," barked Freddie, hand over mike, ready to plunge back into his own brand of madness. "Look for a clue. Look in the margins of the magazine."

"A clue? To what?"

"To a location. A network, all very secret," Freddie whispered with a look of conspiracy. "It's where you can find out what happened to Reggie's father. To whatever happens to *me*," he laughed. "That is, is something *were* to happen to me." He paused and smiled. "Look in the margins. Just remember to keep the stone and the key separate. Don't bring them together until you're ready. Not until you're ready, you see."

"Ready for what? I don't see."

Too late. Freddie had to spin up his next madcap monologue, a prelude to Ricky Nelson's latest hit, "It's Late".[52]

* * *

An hour later, Johnny was back in his room in Margate with the issue of MAD, trying to imitate the facial expressions and body movements in the "Elvis Pelvis" parody, wondering if any of these things were clues. Perhaps the advertisement for Genuine Height-Increasing Elevator Shoes? The references to Moxie? The Alfred E. Neuman character was always part of the cover gag, masquerading as George Washington, Abraham Lincoln, Elvis, Santa Claus, Lawrence of Arabia, and so on. The current issue, July 1959, was yet another parody of the national election, with cartoon versions of Nixon, Kennedy, Johnson and others holding signs proclaiming Alfred E. Neuman for president and "I Like Alf". Maybe the movie satire "Morbid Dick"?

Johnny always got a kick out of the marginal art. A sleeping Swiss Guard. A snake charmer tootling on a *pungi* as a snake rises higher and higher, bearing a Spanish courtier playing a guitar for a maiden on the top floor. The Hand of God reaching down to take a "God is Dead" sign from a beatnik.

The short story, "Screams of the Captives", had been inserted into the "Elvis Pelvis" parody. Johnny looked it over, thinking it to be some kind of commentary about screaming in rock and roll, screaming to a captive audience of teenagers. He glanced back at the magazine page. Three wise monkeys, one covering his ears, the next covering his eyes, and the third covering his mouth, appeared in the margin of "Elvis Pelvis" with thought balloons. The first monkey could "see no evil" in the Elvis performance, with stars in the thought balloon. The second could "hear no evil" in the melody, with musical notation in the thought balloon. The third could "speak no evil" and showed what looked like a black man in a suit, holding something in his hand. A clue? Or just more commentary about Elvis?

Freddie started raving on the radio about a new talent called the Jackal. "And now we're gonna hear his first record. We're gonna hear no evil, lemme tell you, see no evil, hear no evil, and speak no evil. This is the Jackal, listen up!" Johnny felt like he'd been here before, what was it called, *déja-vu*. He had read this story sitting on this bed listening to the radio, *before*. He began to read the short story. Was it the second time?

When the record skipped, and static poured out of the speaker, he put down the story. Had he just heard a song? He couldn't remember. He sat there, listening to five long minutes of static. Had Freddie passed out at the controls?

The commercials came on. Everything must be okay. Johnny giggled. Mesmerizing Mary, done it again.

* * *

A late night rain had left the New Jersey pine barrens misty. Down the rain-slicked street from WYBY an early riser thought she heard the call of something wild, a combination howl and whistle. A purplish blob against dark clouds in the night sky, a ghostly apparition, maybe a trick of the dawn's early light. It moved irregularly and began to take shape, two short legs with paws, swimming out of the cloud, and then a horse's head followed by its long neck, a tapered body with flapping wings twice its size, and back legs like a crane's, with horse hooves.

Detective Daniel Delatore of the Atlantic City police force wearily wrote all this down while sipping the precinct coffee, which he knew would churn his stomach. Short, stocky, overweight and sloppy, Delatore's amateurish bearing belied an almost perfect record of homicide arrests over twenty years. But now this. Ridiculous. Two more sightings of the legendary Jersey Devil, both in one night. Five already this year. This one outside the radio station just an hour or so after the homicide. Couldn't be a coincidence.

There were the usual signs, trash cans overturned, garbage strewn about, suggesting it had been the work of this crazy homeless Negro, a jungle man living in the pine barrens, who'd been spotted several times at dawn rooting through the trash bins of Atlantic City hotels. Black drug dealers on Baltic Avenue called him the Jackal, said he had grown up in the woods, raised by wolves, a black Tarzan. Delatore would believe *that* before he'd believe in the Jersey Devil.

Back at the precinct, Dominic "Big Dom" Solfeggio, an impresario on the Boardwalk, dropped by with his usual donation. When the two stood side by side, they looked a bit like Laurel and Hardy.

Delatore, as Laurel, filled him in about the latest sighting.

Big Dom replied as Hardy, with a harrumph. "Didn't some peach farmer in Egg Harbor once find the corpse?"

"Near the Blue Hole, yes," Delatore deadpanned. "It was just a dead white horse. The guy had stuck fake wings on it."

The apparently bottomless, perfectly round Blue Hole near the Egg Harbor River, filled with crystal blue water, was thought to be either the crater of a meteorite or the work of the Jersey Devil.

"Jeez, you can't trust anybody." Big Dom was sincere in a comical, slapstick manner fit for Hardy.

But now Delatore stood apart, acting serious. "You know what happened? The radio guy?"

"How would I know that?" Big Dom arched his eyebrow suspiciously.

"Just asking."

That's right, thought Delatore. Can't trust anybody. The world's full of mystery.

* * *

Detective Delatore stood erect, in all the official capacity that he could muster, at the Balzano house front door. But he couldn't hide his disgust for this grubby teenager slouching in a t-shirt and jeans against the door frame. Frank's kid. He knew it but he had to ask anyway. Looks like he slept in those clothes. "You John Balzano?"

Johnny B nodded, yawned. The pounding on the door had woke him up. It was 11 in the morning. Where was Mama Roux? He glanced back into the living room, and out the back window to see if she was hanging up the laundry.

"Mind if I come in?"

It was not really a question. Johnny just widened the door and sloughed off to the kitchen for some orange juice, scanning the backyard again from the kitchen window. No sign of Mama Roux. By the time he'd drank half of the orange juice, he was ready to throw up at the detective's news. Freddie had been shot through the head.

"You were with him at the studio, weren't you? You may have been the last one to see him alive." The detective looked Johnny in the eye, man to man. Johnny's guts churned. The unthinkable became thought. Dad must be involved. His father made a living turning screws in the music business. Dad was involved, right up past his wide lapels to his Frank Sinatra hairstyle. It took Johnny a moment to swallow. "I just delivered a package."

"At one in the morning." The detective's eyes flickered like he knew something.

"Yeah, that's right."

79

"What was it?"

"Something from my father."

"What was it?"

"I dunno, I just delivered it for my dad. Probably some records."

The detective sighed, glancing away. "Did you stay long?"

"No. Just dropped it off, and left."

"And where's your father now?"

"I dunno."

Delatore looked away. He wanted to slap the punk. That's what these teenagers need, an iron hand. But this one, what did he expect? His dad had been a punk too, and now he's a made man.

A siren whipped by on Atlantic Avenue. Delatore scanned the dining room and living room, walked over to the jukebox, fingered its buttons, looked around again, sighed, and finally headed for the door. Johnny held it open for him in the harsh sunlight. On his way out he handed Johnny his card.

Across the darkened living room a floor lamp came alive, as Johnny's eyes adjusted from the outside sun. It was Mama Roux, quietly dusting the mantel, making only calculated movements with her bony body wrapped in African cloth, slightly nodding her jet-black head spider-webbed with thin strands of white hair, and spreading her toothless grin across the wisps of white stubble freckling over her ebony face. She seemed ancient, a relic of the ragtime age.

"Hey! Where were you?" Johnny shouted. How had she disappeared into the woodwork, and then reappear, just like that?

Mama Roux eyed him suspiciously, dust cloth held askew. "Right *here*. I'm always right here. I s'pose you want me to fix your breakfast." She looked him over, as she always did in her scolding mood, when she would lapse into a Southern accent. "Waal, it's way too late for that. Almost time for lunch. You just gwine out dere and fix what you want your self. There's 'taters in the fridge."

* * *

Johnny B was alert now, his black bushy eyebrows twitching. He grabbed his jacket, mounted his Harley, and followed the path of the detective's olive Buick, which led only about a mile down Atlantic Avenue. He stopped within a block of the roped-off crime scene, squirming in his seat, resting his boots solidly upon pavement. The South Jersey summer humidity dulled his mind, flattened his duckbill, and soaked up his black t-shirt and Levi's. But he wouldn't remove his black leather jacket or his black cowboy boots with the pearl sequins. When he squinted, his aquiline nose wrinkled up its spine. Though tired from lack of sleep, his dark-rimmed eyes were observant.

Wise guys didn't grieve, he thought. Or at least they didn't show it.

Freddie's fat body had been dumped, completely naked, on a pile of freshly minted vinyl records underneath the hindquarters of Lucy the Elephant.

Lucy was Johnny's unofficial office. A tourist attraction in disrepair, and a constant in Freddie's on-air jokes, Lucy was Margate City's Eighth Wonder of the World, six stories high and shaped like a Himalayan circus elephant in carnival attire with an elaborate howdah. Lucy hung on at the edge of the tilted beach, her "eyes" round windows facing the ocean, her "trunk" a network of hand-shaped wooden slats appropriately curved down as if feeding off the sand. At different times a navigational aid for lost sailors, a saloon, and a hotel, she was visible from eight miles out at sea as a purplish wart on the line-straight coast. Its builder wanted guests to feel the wonder of the animal kingdom and get in touch with their primitive selves, so he built three of them. Lucy in Margate City, the Elephantine Colossus in the center of Coney Island, and the Light of Asia in South Cape May. And with his patent on animal-shaped buildings he successfully fought off imitators.

A cornball cash register in its day, it now stood as a monument to American trash, the "elephant in the living room" of South Jersey. The mostly upscale Italian and Jewish neighborhood of modestly plush bright-red brick and freshly-painted white homes, surrounding and protecting white-steepled churches and brick synagogues, treated it as an embarrassment, like having Louis Prima's "Just a Gigolo"[53] in your record collection.

Freddie looked like a dead baby elephant that had dropped out of Lucy's womb. He'd been shot through the mouth and the bullet had blown out the back of his brain, the brain that had a gift for picking the hits. Freddie had called rock 'n' roll the eighth wonder of the world; now someone with a sense of humor had laid him to rest here, under Lucy's bosom with his treasured records stuck up his ass.

Johnny looked away. The Earth's rotation seemed to accelerate beyond control, whipping his guts into nausea, spinning toward something awful. The level plane of the cross-hatched streets and sidewalks started to tilt. All the cars, pulsating police lights, and people gawking at the crime scene were also tilting at the same angle, something like 30 degrees. In fact the entire concrete island of Atlantic City, Ventnor, and Margate was tilted, and him with it. But nothing slid. To his right, the ocean was also tilted, its waves churning onto the beach at this odd angle. The entire friggin' world like a pinball machine gone tilt.

His father had done this. It had wise guy written all over it.

Johnny was frightened. Not of his father, not of any of that music business intrigue he knew nothing about, but of something else. Being irrelevant. Behind all his coolness and hipness was some notion, some sense of what was real, which had been planted by Freddie, the only person in the world he could really talk to. Freddie had been the source of his hipness, a mentor who'd taught him all those hip phrases, all the cool music that his peers didn't know about. Now, with Freddie gone...

Fighting his nausea, Johnny got off his cycle and crab-walked across the tilted landscape closer to the crime tape across Lucy's parking lot. Cops were shoveling records into a dump truck. The records sported red Darby Records labels, but no words. Darby Records, his father's label.

Johnny had recently overheard an argument between his father and Freddie in the back room at Tony Mart's. He thought he'd heard, "Cancel the fuckin' show, Freddie." And then, "No way, Frank. This guy's the real deal." Johnny had seen his father come out of the room with stern eyes, a frozen smile. Freddie had hung back in the room, the argument over as quick as it had begun.

No matter now. Freddie's dead. He'd been an interesting character, Johnny said to himself, steeling his gaze, making himself believe that Freddie had been nothing more than just "interesting". In fact his death was an inconvenience. Johnny kept his stash in Lucy's maintenance closet. He'd have to wait for everyone to clear out from the crime scene. He scampered like a squirrel across the tilted pavement to his cycle, and lit a Lucky Strike. Comfortably isolated on his seat, boots planted solidly on the tilted street, he gave it all some thought.

* * *

Later that afternoon Reggie Mention, dark-haired, lean and lanky in his usual prep school attire, showed up with the afternoon paper. His light brown eyes were always questioning the world before him. "I can't live with myself for taking payola," he read from the front page in his sarcastic "I'm smarter than this" attitude that always irritated Johnny. "This is from the suicide note. A-and they go on about a payola indictment."

"Not surprised," Johnny shot back, more to quiet him than anything else. "All the best jockeys are caught up in it, Alan Freed, even Dick Clark."

Johnny turned away, conversation over. He didn't want to talk about Freddie. He had no idea what to say to Reggie, how to bring up the topic of the short story Freddie had given him. Maybe Reggie didn't know about it.

"Your dad involved?" Reggie touched his shoulder and peered at him. "Well, not to worry. There's no mention of the Mafia or anything."

Johnny turned back to him, regretting what may come next. "It's not 'Mafia' you dumb shit."

"Okay then, Cosa Nostra." Reggie was persistent, always pushing buttons.

"That means 'our thing,' that's all that means."

"So what's your father call it?"

Johnny just glared at him. He'd had enough. Just last week Reggie had got on him about his nighttime activities.

Reggie glanced back at the paper. "It talks about a violation of the Mann Act. Apparently Freddie was caught in Wildwood with underage girls."

"Not surprised," Johnny shrugged again, more softly, looking for an out.

"A-and they go on about his Boardwalk rhythm and blues shows and how they instigated 'Negro violence'."

"That's *such* bullshit." Damn, thought Johnny, he got me going again.

"Ever been to one of his shows?" Reggie asked.

"Bo Diddley,[54] last summer." Johnny decided to drop his attitude, keep the talk about music. "Man, that was terrific. All these African rhythms."

"He was planning another one," said Reggie. "You hear about this new guy, the Jackal?"

"I heard he was good. Freddie played something, but I don't remember it exactly." Johnny frowned. It was one of his talents, that he could remember a song immediately after hearing it. But not this one.

"You know he's been called the Jersey Devil. He supposedly came out of the pine barrens."

"I don't believe that shit," said Johnny evasively. He thought about Skinny, a musician he knew in the black Baltic Avenue neighborhood. He'd ask Skinny about it.

Reggie fidgeted.

Johnny could tell he had more to add. "Well, go ahead, out with it."

Reggie squeezed out, "Freddie knew my father."

Johnny acted surprised. Reggie had never talked about his father before. Johnny didn't want to say anything; he wanted to hear what Reggie had to say first. "So the Fryer knew your father. So where *is* your father?"

Reggie shrugged, and paused. "He left the country before McCarthy could get him."

"Really..." So this was the big secret? He'd never seen Reggie squirm like this.

"Yeah," Reggie said, eyeing him seriously. "Freddie knew my father, and maybe he even knew where my father is now. But I think he was killed for the same reason my father escaped. For being a Communist."

"You can't be serious." Johnny couldn't picture Freddie, the fat man behind the turntables, as some kind of spy. More like an enchanter that no one would take seriously. But this connection to Reggie's father was something else, something mysterious. He'd have to go back and read that story. Reggie deserved to know about it, but Johnny needed to understand it first.

* * *

The crime scene was still occupied. On his way back home Johnny imagined all his father's cronies gathered in the kitchen talking around a pot of bubbling marinara. But no one was there. Instinctively he sat down in his father's den office, awaiting instructions, staring at the map on the office wall. It pinpointed every legitimate shop, club, and distribution point in Frank "Ballzo" Balzano's empire. Through a series of bust-out scams over the last two years, his father had legally acquired three failing record labels and their pressing plants, using the latter to make counterfeits for the European market. Suitcases of cash that couldn't be deposited in a bank were distributed to disc jockeys across the country to turn their records into hits. After skimming the action in show venues, jukeboxes, and records, exerting control through intimidation, and priming the pump with payola, pep pills, and prostitutes, the man had reached his pinnacle by running record distribution for all of South Jersey.

Johnny squinted at the map until New Jersey looked more like a fattened Italy, its southern boot tip dangling not out to sea but up the Delaware, kicking Philadelphia in its south end. And the crack from this impact would be the Schuylkill River, studded with row homes for the Italian-Americans on one side, and blackened with ghetto dwellings fronting the smoking gasworks on the other side. Yo, come on down the shore, the boot said every Spring as it kicked Philly. Come on down to nightclubs, the glitter pageants on the Boardwalk, the big bands, Liberace, Sinatra and Tony Bennett, come on down, bring the kids, spend your money. Spend your money with Ballzo.

Johnny always laughed at that name, a name his father hated. Johnny never used it to his face.

Ballzo had grown up in South Philly just a hoagie's throw from the gasworks, but he was now *Mr.* Frank Balzano. He had made his move to the vacation resort south of Atlantic City, vibrant for three months every summer but a ghost town for the other seasons, where a family could live in relative obscurity. His Margate was frozen in the suspended animation of a middle-class Jewish and Italian neighborhood, family-friendly and resistant to change.

Johnny's Margate was like the miniature town on a Lionel train set with its tiny bridges, crossroad signs, and lighted cardboard houses surrounded by those embarrassing water tanks that that popped up like giant golf balls on tees. It was a land of giant doctors and lawyers forever teeing up during the summer madness, leaving behind vacant houses and closed-up shops to bear the brunt of winter storms.

Next to the map were black-and-white pictures of Lucy awash in waves during the hurricane of September 14, 1944, the day Johnny was born. It looked like it was trying to swim back to Asia, to a land where elephants mattered, but its feet were stuck in the sand. On the same day, with a photo to commemorate it, Johnny was born in the University of Pennsylvania hospital, sixty miles away. Born in a hurricane, howling at the driving rain, with fire in his eyes and a grin on his face. That's how his father had boasted of his only son's birth.

The myths generated by that hurricane grew all out of proportion — star-crossed babies born with fiery eyes, Boardwalk pieces floating for days, even Lucy supposedly had floated out to sea, bobbing about on the surface of the ocean, a sign that all was lost... until a tugboat towed her back in. All nonsense, like all the trumped up stories Johnny had heard from his father of the golden age of the mob, of Lucky Luciano shooting up the Boardwalk in a rampage, of vendettas and retributions, of killings as Greek tragedies and political fixes as crusades. Some stories were true, like Johnny Ace, his namesake, who blew his mind out at a show playing Russian roulette backstage with a mobster sent down from the record label, Ballzo's label. Real stories embellished to the point of fake, like Lucy, Lucky Luciano's namesake, all dressed up for a carnival long gone.

Johnny B's friends were all farther south, in Wildwood, a more affordable summer resort for the black, Italian, and Irish families from Philly. Ever since the summer of 1950, when the Treniers performed their smoothly blended rhythm and blues at the Riptide, the mixed crowds in Wildwood were more receptive to black music than the clubs farther north. This was Johnny's music, Freddie's music; the music his father hated. Rockabilly had been exploding in these towns every summer since 1954, when Bill Haley and his new group, the Comets, hesitatingly stuttered into "(We're Gonna) Rock Around the Clock"[55] at the HofBrau Hotel in Wildwood. Freddie had introduced them from a backstage microphone like he was the Voice of God.

And Freddie's now gone, and rock and roll with him: bought out, raped, pillaged, and finally blown away at the feet of Lucy, the true Heartbreak Hotel, a place where lovers go to cry their troubles away, a place to deposit corpses.

* * *

His father never showed up. Early in the evening, Johnny went over to check the crime scene. The yellow ribbons were down. Johnny stole across the deserted parking lot illuminated by the August moon to Lucy's hindquarters, and with a special key opened the door of the maintenance closet in Lucy's left rear leg. The door, when opened at a certain angle and viewed from a certain distance, made it look like Lucy was peeing.

He was in and out before anyone could have seen him, pocketing two bags. Mexican Mary, Turkish Lady. He glanced this way and that, like he'd seen in the movies, momentarily distracted by the graffiti on Lucy's rear, "Free Elvis", "Bird Lives!", "Buddy Lives!", "Jersey Devil", "The Jackal", the ubiquitous Kilroy, phone numbers for blow jobs, and his own faded broken-heart valentine to an exotic blond beauty in her twenties, "Johnny and Babbs". He had tried to scrub it out after seeing her at Tony Mart's working the bar with men twice his age.

He could see in his mind her sharp, angular face, the impish smile with an upturned nose and pursed lips, the darting blue eyes, and the black-and-blue cheek, the blunt trauma caused by men who could not strike back at the world and so struck her, over and over, in the face, cursing her as a surrogate for the world. Something about her face had turned him on, much more than the simple, open-mouthed, cow-like stares of his teenage girlfriends in their unspecified, immature heat. Despite all the trauma of sex with many men, despite the age difference, Babbs wanted him, wanted his manhood at the most primal level. His cock had held its head up in sterling, severe triumph in her fingers, in her mouth; but when he came, he gushed bashfully, still a boy on his first try.

And when he saw her at work at Tony Mart's, his father saw the pain on his face and tried to be a father to him, tried to find the right words. "Son, stick with the cheerleaders. Women like that'll just break your heart." And, it goes without saying, broken hearts were for assholes.

Puttering on his Harley in low gear, slowly departing Lucy's parking lot, he counted the seconds, about thirty, to reach the street where he lived. He parked in the garage, traded his leather jacket for a Saint Cecilia High School letter sweater and his cowboy boots for Keds sneakers, and took out his bicycle. Chuck Berry was singing in his head, "You Can't Catch Me".[56] With the moonlight dancing on the waves a half a block away, he bicycled back up Atlantic Avenue past Lucy, heading north toward the mist-wrapped, floodlit city, switching to the Boardwalk at its start in Ventnor.

Faded glories shimmered down at the other end, where Jitneys stalked the Monopoly game of Atlantic, Pacific, Baltic, Ventnor, Pennsylvania and Virginia Avenues ferrying tourists clutching postcards of the Miss America Pageant. He'd played the game many times, and Reggie always went on about how you can't find Marvin Gardens in Atlantic City, because the game misspelled the real Marven Gardens, which is in Margate. Riding a bike on the Boardwalk at this hour was illegal, but it was still wholesome, something teenage heroes like the Hardy Boys might get caught doing, just out having some fun and getting some exercise, and not as risky as getting caught driving a Harley without a license.

Dominic "Big Dom" Solfeggio, his father's closest associate, met Johnny at the service entrance to Steel Pier. Just then a bikini-clad dancer on a white horse dived from a platform about sixty feet high and splash-landed in the giant barrel. Neither of them even looked up. As the crowd roared Johnny handed Big Dom the bag of Turkish Lady.

Big Dom was a very large, swarthy man bulging out of a seersucker suit. He peeled tiny hundred-dollar-bills from a wad completely dwarfed by his large hand, and handed them over. "How's your father?"

"Fine," Johnny replied with a smirk. "Haven't seen him tonight."

"Well you give him my best. And look what I got for you." He handed Johnny some clear acetates. "This one's been played a few times, but you can still get a few more plays out of it. They're for your father, tell him I did what I could. And here's something for you, for your trouble." He peeled out another hundred for Johnny.

A pause, then Big Dom hummed in the scale of C, do-re-mi-fa-so-la-ti, a thing he did when he was agitated. Johnny grinned; with his capacity for discerning absolute pitch, he could tell the gangster was flat. Big Dom cleared his throat. "You knew Freddie, right? Had business with him?"

"The Fryer," chuckled Johnny, distancing himself, "he owed my father, not me. Don't know shit about it, but suicide? That's a good one."

"You know this singer he was talking about?"

"The Jackal? My dad said something. The Fryer had a free show scheduled for Central Pier."

Big Dom smiled. "Not any more. They're gonna run that jigaboo out of town. Ask your father if you don't believe me."

"Well, I don't give a shit," Johnny cursed, pretending to be carefree as a silent accomplice, just along for the ride, y'see. Big Dom was still his favorite gangster confidante. A record plugger, Big Dom enforced part of the Ballzo empire of gambling, prostitution, drugs, and the construction workers union. Ballzo and Big Dom were both made men, connected to the DiAngelo family in South Philly. Johnny once had a thing for a DiAngelo debutante but thought better of it.

"Good," Big Dom poked him. "Tell your friends there's gonna be all niggers all over that pier, and they're gonna get their heads broken, so stay away." He paused for a second, and grunted. "Hey, Ricky Nelson's coming to town, I can get you maybe six passes. Bring your little girlfriends, they'll love it."

"Ricky Nelson? He wears a cucumber in his pants."

"Don't get smart with me, kid." Big Dom seemed to grow bigger suddenly, eyeing Johnny, rooting him to his spot on the edge of Steel Pier. "Jungle music's out. People want entertainers. You wanna do something big? Find yourself a singer, one that looks good, bring him to me and we'll put it together."

Johnny threw his head back and laughed, and kept laughing, as if he'd smoked Mary again. Big Dom smacked him in the back of his neck. "Fuck's a matter with you? What's so funny? You think I'm funny? You been doing any of this shit?"

"No," Johnny cut the laughter and frowned back at him. "Nothin's funny." He rubbed his neck and looked up at Steel Pier as the scantily clad lady on the white horse prepared to make another plunge. No, not funny, just ridiculous.

"Don't get wise, kid." Big Dom put his arm around Johnny's shoulder, but Johnny flinched it off. "Y'know, you look just like your father." Big Dom paused as if his message took time to sink into this kid's brain. "Alright kid, stick it to those cheerleaders for me an' give 'em something to really cheer about. Just remember what I said. Talk to your band mates, look around the school, find a singer. You can use your band to back the singer. Bring me the package and we'll get you a deal. You do that. Talk to your father about it. He's gonna tell you to come to me anyway."

Meaning, of course, train the singer in a style, record a song that has the copyrights already set up for the skim, and create a package for the disc jockeys that they can't resist.

Johnny had heard about payola one time when his dad was in a good mood and they'd gone out for ice cream. It's the grease that makes the engine roar, his dad had explained, the prime for the money pump. "You like to listen to those late night jocks, well they're shuckin' and jivin' with the rest of 'em. They think *they* break out the hits. *Fuck* them. They give themselves too much credit." Johnny had just shrugged, not giving anyone credit.

Johnny's patented shrug got him away from Big Dom and back on his bike, and he headed uptown through the stark, rough ghetto that encircled Atlantic City, singing "you can't catch me, no you can't catch me" again. Couldn't get it out of his head. Maybe the band should try it, he thought.

His unnamed band consisted of Johnny on bass, Reggie on acoustic guitar, and a pimply kid from Wildwood named Alger, who they'd nicknamed Scotty because he could do a fair imitation of a Scotty Moore lead on a Fender Telecaster. No drummer yet; for their first and only gig, at Saint Cecilia High, Johnny's father had brought in a professional drummer from the Cool Cats who were playing that night at Tony Mart's. None of them could sing worth shit. Scotty wouldn't even show up for practice half the time, he was only fourteen and couldn't get a ride. And Johnny's standup bass, inherited from a jazz player pal of his father's, was too heavy to carry and always seemed to fall out of tune at the wrong moment; the bullet hole through the neck could have had something to do with it, supposedly put there by Lucky himself attempting a hit on a junkie bass player who displeased him. Another one of his father's stories.

Johnny had one more stop to make, to see Skinny at the corner of Virginia and Baltic.

"Yo. Joe College." Skinny in a white sleeveless wife-beater shirt and porkpie hat stepped from the shadows, his black skin carrying some of the shadow into the streetlight.

Johnny, still straddling his bike, handed him a rolled up plastic bag. "Right on time."

"No shit. Where's the rest?"

"Next week."

"Your *dad*," Skinny spat the word, like it was a white word, "is playing some tricks. You tell 'em he's *late*."

"You got a problem, take it up with him."

"No problem," Skinny backed off, smiling. "You the man with the Mary."

Johnny grinned, baring his teeth, and got off his bike, sensing that Skinny wasn't properly respectful. He took out his pack of Lucky Strikes and lit one up. Why do Italians, his father and all his friends, hate blacks? Hating the Irish he understood, as they competed for work here in America. But the blacks were here *before* their dads got off the boat. Why do they talk about them like they're animals? But you mention Sammy Davis, and they turn respectful, because Sammy hangs with Sinatra. They call all the rest of them *niggers*, except the ones who are sports heroes or singers. In Catholic school the nuns told a story that black people had all descended from Noah's son Ham, after the Flood, but were banished to the wilderness.

He stared at Skinny for a long moment. Then he asked him. "Hey, what do you know about the Jersey Devil?"

"He's the Jackal, one and the same."

"What, some wild crazy black man in the woods?"

Something snapped in Skinny and his smile turned mean. "The Jackal, he got the *voodoo*. Possessed, man, by the spirit, the Jersey Devil. He's the next Johnny Ace. You watch. Jackal's gonna bust out, ain't gonna be no more of that greasy Frankie Avalon shit. You watch." Skinny was poking his finger at him.

"What, he some kind of punk?"

"Man, you hear that 'Stagger Lee' on the radio? Man, *he's* Stagger Lee, motherfucker. Take *that* back to your dad. Jackal's the next motherfuckin' Stagger Lee. Tell your gumbah friends, they come by the show, they gonna get stomped. A-an' you tell your *dad*, we don't care 'bout no whitey disc jockey motherfucker, tell him he can kill 'em all, we don't care. But he fuck with us, he gonna get it back in *spades*, know what I mean?"

Johnny, taken aback, recovered quickly. He focused his penetrating smile. "Yeah well, y'know he ain't gonna like hearing this shit."

"Then don't *tell* him, motherfucker. I don't care." And with that, Skinny merged back into the shadows.

Johnny felt his grin, his entire face, was floating in thin air, detached from his head. How much did it look like his father's? That look of certainty, eyes amused, mouth wry and tight? That infamous kick-your-balls grin, framed by a scar down his left cheek. He took a knife to the cheek. Would I be able to do that?

Johnny shivered, alone now out on Baltic Avenue. His only protection in this neighborhood was his father's reputation. His father was grooming him for the business. And really, what else could he do? School was a joke. He couldn't see himself as a doctor, a lawyer, an accountant, an insurance salesman. Reggie, hell yes, Reggie would go to college. But my father is setting a place for me at his table. A place of honor in his community, a made man, civilized, with an army of henchman at his beck and call.

The wash of the distant ocean seemed to disagree. *This is the world*, it whispered. *You are not responsible for it, it is not of your doing.*

* * *

When he reached her house, he hid his bike in the bushes at the end of the front lawn and silently entered through the unlocked basement door. She was waiting for him in a nightshirt that hung on her spark-plug body like a tent, revealing through the dim light the dark spots of her nipples, the shadow of her pubic hair. She looked and spoke older than her age, a hulking woman-child of sixteen, hungry for love, but like a character out of a fairy tale, with wide, sparkling eyes and an elfin face with a low nasal bridge and turned-up nose, cute as a button. Another Lucy.

The mulatto daughter of a black musician and a white ex-dancer now married to a white middle-class insurance salesman, Lucy Hucke Whittleman settled into herself, resigned herself to be a half-breed, a mutant, without a true home. She ignored her stepfather and dreamed of her real father out there in the jazz world. She read books voraciously, about jazz, about the new beat generation, about the new pop art in Britain, and spoke softly in measured tones, in a practiced way, about French poets she adored, American beats she considered to be *poseurs*, beboppers that couldn't find work. Cultivating an air of the unconventional, she could be reclusive in the middle of a crowd. Her basement was cluttered with books everywhere. She had been to a state institution for the criminally insane. That fact encircled her head like a halo of smoke, turned her eyes into mirrors.

In the dark of her basement Johnny could surrender to her like a baby suckling at her breast. Her large dark hindquarters were velvet to his touch, to his cheek; it was a warm place to dissolve into, a different sort of closet to hide secrets. He didn't want to use condoms with her. She let him come inside her anyway, treasuring his moment of surrender. They were nymph and bushman of the forest, under a brilliantly starry night sky.

By day Johnny kept his distance from Lucy. He pretended not to know her, which was easy, since the other high school kids mostly ignored her except the occasional pranks and wiseass remarks, whispering comparisons to Lucy the Elephant. And, well, she didn't help her case, he thought, with that elaborately curled high head of black hair that looked every bit like the elephant's howdah. She brings it on herself because she's got no sense of style.

At night they would meet in her basement, in secret. She would talk, and Johnny, uncharacteristically, would just listen. Though she was the same age, she knew more about the world than he did. She would remark about the kids sniggering at her, the adults frowning and staring, the silent treatment in the hoagie shop, the practiced air of pretension around the school... but all in a sing-song voice that was oddly soothing. She idolized her real father Archie Hucke, a black jazz musician lost to time. She couldn't stand her stepfather, but it was he who had paid for her therapy sessions, the damage to the waiting room when they had led Lucy away the first time, the six-month "vacation" in upper New York State, the shock treatments. She said all this with a mock girlishness and twisted her black spit-curl with her finger.

She said she admired the simple folk of the Himalayas because a person could spend a lifetime getting one thing right. She said American men were easy to understand. She said this as if she were not from America, though she had lived in New Jersey all her life. American men start out as American boys. Johnny knew she meant white boys. When you're a kid, she said, you pretend to be a cowboy or Indian, and when you're a teen you pretend to be black. It's when you grow up that you start acting like an American man.

She said a lot of things.

This time, she asked him about Freddie. "Don't you feel anything? Why aren't you upset?"

"I'm upset," he deadpanned. "I'm angry. I think my father had something to do with it."

She brought his head to her bosom and stroked his hair. She knew about the errands for his father. She spoke soothingly. "You can't work for him anymore. You just can't. You know that."

"If he's involved, that means I'm some sort of an… accomplice."

"Some people think it was the Jersey Devil," she said to change the subject.

"Oh c'mon, we all know that story. Mama Roux used to scare me with that, tell me she was going to leave me in the woods. Told me the Jersey Devil took my real mom."

"It's the devil child of a witch," Lucy intoned solemnly. "I read about it. The witch lived near Hanover, before the Revolutionary War. She was a friend of the local Indians, and she would dance with them for the spring planting. She learned all sorts of things from the Indians, like how to be a midwife. But the British were building a colony for Jewish refugees, and its leader, Captain Newman, banished her, and she went to live in the pine barrens. Which is not as bad as what they were doing up in Salem at the time, which was burning the midwives, calling them witches."

Johnny couldn't quite follow this. His hand slithered up her nightshirt but she ignored it.

"Anyway, she got her revenge. She gave birth to the Jersey Devil, and it massacred Newman's colony. Newman had been the captain of a slave ship, so he probably deserved his fate."

Johnny remembered something in that short story, something about a Captain Newman.

"The Jersey Devil is supposed to have helped the revolutionaries," Lucy continued, in all seriousness. "The Devil protected people hiding in the barrens. Religious dissenters, fugitives, slaves, deserters from the war. The revolutionaries were just smugglers back then. They were looting British ships and moving the stuff through the barrens to Camden and Philly."

"I don't believe it," said Johnny flatly. He was hoping she'd feel his hand, now resting firmly on her naked buttock under the nightshirt.

"Lots of people believed in the Jersey Devil, still believe it," she continued, oblivious to his hand. "It was spotted in the last century. President Monroe even sent up a party to kill it. They shot at something they saw, a pale white horse with wings. Lots of people witnessed it."

"How about since then?"

"Last year a telephone lineman in Absecon said he shot it in one of its legs, and it limped into the woods."

"I don't believe it."

She gave him a sorrowful look, the look a nun would give to an errant child.

* * *

After midnight, back at home and in bed in the empty house, his father still out, his hormones still raging, he caught on the radio the song Skinny had been talking about. Dialing past the schlock crowding out the rhythm and blues on Philly's WHAT and South Jersey's WYBY, Johnny tuned between stations to pick up signals skipping across the ozone, broadcasting out of Memphis, Cleveland, and especially Jack the Cat and Poppa Stoppa in New Orleans, all this music infiltrating the night sky across America, inspiring the "late people" as the jockeys called their late-night listeners, the anxious teenagers staying awake to hear dirty lyrics, weird rhythms, heartbreak songs.

That night Johnny heard the song on WNNR's Poppa Stoppa show. Lloyd Price's "Stagger Lee"[57] came tumbling out of his radio, bobbing and swinging with a wicked syncopation. Stagger Lee is ready to shoot Billy, and Billy cries to him about his three little children and a poor old sickly wife.

The bold, swaggering story about a rakish gambler shooting his way out of a bad judgment call touched a nerve in night listeners like Johnny, hinting at a freedom beyond the strictures of the day. Here was a man who could take the law into his own hands, dispatch a soul to hell just as quickly as look at him, follow that soul to hell just to continue bedeviling him.

Skinny had meant to scare Johnny by invoking this evil character.

What should Johnny say to his father? Should he ask who pulled the trigger on Freddie? Would it matter anyway?

His father trusted him. It had been Johnny's idea to move the merchandise. It solved a problem his father had with the New York and Philly families, who'd decided to leave the drug trade to the black neighborhoods. Problem was, the mobsters didn't trust the black dealers. Too many were like Skinny, sloppy in their lives, putting routine distribution in jeopardy. Too apt to get themselves all tied up in vendettas and unnecessary gunplay. His father needed someone inconspicuous, someone he could disavow with sincerity. The organization would believe a made man, a father, who's frustrated with his teenage son's indiscretions. And if Johnny got caught by the bulls, his father could fix things downtown.

Johnny thought about all the drug users, dealers, pimps, hookers, and other undesirables among the nighttime radio listeners, the "late people" jumping in the night to fast rhythms. That vast disorganized mess of people out there who plod along with their lives by day but thrive with the music at night, tuning into secret mysteries over the airwaves, mysteries more exciting than sex, more satisfying than dope. The late people. What secrets do they know?

A Phonograph on a Pedestal

A phonograph on a pedestal was set like a pivot in the center of the vacant stage of Carnegie Hall. They tested it with the record "The Heavens are Telling" from Haydn's *Creation*.[58]

Commanding the southeast corner of Seventh Avenue and 57th Street, two blocks south of Central Park, Carnegie Hall is one of the last large buildings in New York City built entirely of masonry, without a steel frame, rising to the equivalent height of a 30-story building. Its exterior is rendered in narrow Roman iron-spotted bricks of a mellow ocher hue, with details in terracotta and brownstone. Inside, the foyer offers a high-minded exercise in the Florentine Renaissance manner of Filippo Brunelleschi's Pazzi Chapel, the white plaster and gray stone forming a harmonious system of round-headed arched openings and Corinthian pilasters supporting an unbroken cornice, with round-headed lunettes above it, under a vaulted ceiling haunted by the ghosts of Mahler, Nikisch, Stokowski, and Bruno. Designed so that it would not require steel support beams that would ruin the acoustics, the edifice was built using the Guastavino process, with concrete and masonry walls several feet thick, no doubt inspired by chapels and temples built by Freemasons to capture Mozart's *Gesellenreise (A Fellowcraft's Journey)* or *The Magic Flute,* or other sounds and reverberations considered to be sacred. The overall message of this architecture was that it housed secrets of antiquity.

At first regarded as a heathen instrument of rent parties and juke joints, the phonograph in 1938 had begun to replace the piano in the parlors and living rooms of the upper middle class, accompanied by a respectable collection of classical music. Freddie Falloni worshipped the phonograph, understood its technology, and made his living off it. He would tell anyone who'd listen that it was really a time machine that transported you into the vibrations of the recorded past.

Freddie was John Hammond's sweaty nineteen-year old engineer, one of a rare breed of prodigy field recording experts who'd grown up with and took for granted the technologies of audio transformation that older people considered to be magic. And he was repelled and even insulted by Hammond's request to put a phonograph on a pedestal in front of this particular audience. The wealthy Park Avenue crowd boasted of having the best models in their parlors, so what was the point?

John Hammond, the show's champion and producer, didn't care to waste time making the point, and certainly not with Freddie, who after all was just an employee. He not only wanted this phonograph to be rigged to the loudspeaker to fill the hall with sound, but he also wanted it wired for recording. He wanted a *recording* of the record playing on the phonograph in the hall. This was what he wanted, and John Hammond, spawned in the Vanderbilt family pond, always got what he wanted.

Backstage, all manner of chaos amplified anxieties beyond reason, from power brownouts and a missing trumpet to fainting spells and a drunk master of ceremonies. Hammond made a beeline for the front of the hall, past musicians blinking inwardly from lack of sleep, avoiding Count Basie's exasperation about the late piano tuner, and sidestepping a haltingly sincere Sonny Terry, stiff and awkward in his new store-bought pointed shoes, hat in hand, blind behind his sunglasses, "I done come all the way from North Carolina to do this thing, a-and thank you, suh, thank you." But Hammond was already out the door, seeking fresh air, pulling out his pack of Lucky Strikes, letting go a late-afternoon coffee-scented sigh and fart, leaving just for a moment this baptism in progress.

Out front, a squat immigrant in a rumpled suit and bowler hat, wearing a sandwich sign bearing the Commodore Music Shops logo from East 42nd Street, bellowed to the ticketed crowd, "This Blues music will never die, for it is life itself! We know this to be a fact! For we at Commodore are the first to promote authentic Negro Blues in the North. Yes! We pushed it when others couldn't give it away, back in the year B.S., Before Swing! Ours is the only shop where you can easily procure records by the great Bessie Smith, and Pine Top Smith, and Meade Lux Lewis! All the performers here tonight as well!" And so on.

John Hammond's Hudson Terraplane was parked at the curb, surrounded by admirers sneaking a peek at one of the first-ever car radios. Hammond, grinning through his Lucky smoke, opened the car door and set the radio's tuner to a swing station in Queens that ventured occasionally into the blues and had programmed a set to promote Hammond's concert, "From Spirituals to Swing."

The handsome, tall and gangly blond photographer and writer Carl Van Vechten, flush with controversy over his recent best-seller *Nigger Heaven* that portrayed Harlem's "dark inhabitants" in satire as debased, lecherous creatures, cabaret hounds and thirsty neurotics, leaned against the brownstone watching Hammond's performance with the Terraplane and then with an interviewer from *The New Masses*.

"Serious audiences have neglected this music, and it has to find its followers among uncritical groups," Hammond shouted over the sidewalk din at the interviewer. Dressed casually in double-breasted tweed, blue oxford shirt and matching tie, with newspapers tucked under one arm, Hammond looked more history professor than concert producer. His Brahmin accent identified him as a native New Yorker, inheritor from the wealthy class, conservatively dressed yet liberally outspoken; with an upstate, almost countrified accent that had surrendered to skyscrapers and garbage and was now as flat as Flatbush Avenue.

Hammond was determined to showcase talented black musicians for the downtown audience that still thought of them as vaudeville darkies with slapstick gags. "This music we will present here tonight has thrived, even in an atmosphere of detraction, of oppression, even distortion," he lisped, glancing a critical eye toward Van Vechten. "It is uniquely American, the most important cultural exhibit we can give to the world. What you will hear is the most sincere and valid representations of this music our research could find, the real thing, from some of its best Negro practitioners.

"You have to understand, the greatest of these artists die of privation and neglect, they are world music idols and, ironically, paupers at the same time. Meade Lux Lewis, for example, works in a garage. Big Bill Broonzy is a laborer, a ditch digger. Between the Jim Crow unions and the unscrupulous night club proprietors, this industry has denied Negro musicians a living wage and a rightful place in music.

"Now, this concert is dedicated to Bessie Smith, who died recently after being injured in a car accident, and who would probably still be alive if the first hospital they took her to hadn't rejected her for being a Negro."

Of course that last part wasn't strictly true, but the interviewer was just eating it up, perfect fodder for *The New Masses*.

Carl Van Vechten knew all about Hammond's argumentative nature, his penchant for justice, his crusade to integrate jazz bands, but... *really*, another bleached liberal, a Vanderbilt heir no less, who secretly wants to be a Negro. Not endure the hardships and the racism, just be black and tan and cool, just be spiritually one with them. Carl disliked the "uplift-the-race" sanctimoniousness of his lily-white patrons of the East Side, though he never let on. But he sensed a kinship of amateur voyeurism in Hammond. He imagined all sorts of situations where Hammond might push his voyeurism too far, might even trade his boy-scout enthusiasm for a go at Negro cock. But no, if confronted at a rent party, such as Bessie Smith's wild rehearsal night in the Harlem railroad flat before her last studio session, Carl knew Hammond would do the same thing he always does, crinkle his nose at the marijuana-laden air, show a bit of disdain for the arrangements, turn a blind eye to the public copulation, and leave early.

Carl was here to take stock of the proceedings, make a report, and if possible, find a way to sabotage Hammond's success, or at least make him look like an idiot. With Hammond's boyish, toothy grin, regarding him as an idiot was not a stretch and the cartoonists would have a field day. All Carl needed was a catalyst.

It turned out that some of Carl's patrons were upset about Hammond's column in *Down Beat* three years earlier, which had excoriated Duke Ellington for deliberately ignoring the plight of his downtrodden race, and for turning a blind eye to his own exploitation in the hands of white promoters. "He has the completely defeatist outlook which chokes so many artists of his own race.... He has very real fears about his own future." As a result, Hammond had written, "Ellington's music has become vapid and without the slightest semblance of guts... The Duke is afraid even to think about himself, his struggles, and his disappointments and that is why his 'Reminiscing' is so formless and shallow a piece of music."

The Duke had stewed these last three years without replying but growing richer and more famous as the leader of the house band at the segregated Cotton Club in Harlem, performing for an all-white audience on an elaborate set built to resemble an old Southern plantation, just us ole darkies cavorting in the moonlight.

Carl could agree with Hammond that politics has no place in the music industry, though Carl was not deterred about music having a place in politics. There was a subtle difference. Hammond worked the "left" side of the money river. Record label executives, some of them his best friends, thought he was a loose cannon. Apparently the pursuit of money was unimportant to him. He had his causes, and Carl could empathize. Hammond had driven all the way to North Carolina just to sign Blind Boy Fuller, but when he found out Fuller was in jail, he would not give up, and just for spite he auditioned the Negro fella next door, Sonny Terry.[59] As Hammond's luck would have it, the fella could really play the harmonica. Hammond signed him on the spot. "Geniuses everywhere out here in the back country," he had enthused. "Alan Lomax had been right about that."

When the interview finished, Carl Van Vechten slithered over and eyed Hammond up and down, nearly licking his lips. "You going uptown after the show?"

"I doubt it," Hammond grinned, revealing molars all the way back near his ears, like he couldn't wait to shatter this guy's illusions. "We're all going downtown, to Café Society, in the Village. It's opening night. Some of your writer friends will be there." His grin dripped with sarcasm, but in truth Hammond felt ill at ease with the fiery rhetoric of the black Harlem Renaissance writers, and he had no idea what to make of Carl Van Vechten. His sphincter tightened and he was ready to wage verbal warfare whenever Carl was around, and around he was a lot these days, always chauffeuring white society matrons up to Harlem for jazz outings. Hammond could sense his faggotry with a keen eye the same way he could sense musical genius with an attentive ear. Hammond hadn't seen much of Van Vechten's photography except his portraits of Bessie Smith; he also hadn't found the time to read *Nigger Heaven* but thought he knew what it was about. Hammond knew most black intellectuals were furious with Van Vechten. The man had been going behind their backs and collecting material in order to write this sensational thing and boost his own reputation. Bessie Smith, not one to be patronized, had thrown Van Vechten's wife Fania to the floor at a posh gathering. Still, Hammond trusted Langston Hughes, who'd defended the work.

"Of course, I'd love to attend," replied Carl Van Vechten, deftly turning John Hammond's offhand comment into an invitation yet remaining cool and elusive about following up on it. One should not telegraph one's anxieties if one wished to be part of the new cool. The new integrated club was the latest brainchild of the leftists. They'd painted murals mocking the bona-fide members of the real café society, as if to give the finger to the all-rich, all-white Stork Club uptown. Carl, a habitué of the Stork, didn't feel welcome in Greenwich Village, which was fast becoming a haven for anarchists and bohemians that were practically Negro in all but color. Carl loved the Negro artists but knew better than to act like one; he thrived instead on the tension, the fear that patrons had about direct contact with the Negroes. As long as the social friction and guilt kept them wrapped tight in their furs and locked securely in their limos, Carl could escort them, be their tour director, make an extravagant living. Hammond, on the other hand, had no such anxieties, and his exuberance was infecting. "We're not so different, you and I," Carl leaned in to whisper. "I just think it most important for Negro artists to understand that they must take advantage of the situation at hand, and exploit the white interest for their own benefit."

Hammond backed off disagreeably from Carl Van Vechten, saying "I read your piece in *The Crisis*. 'How Shall the Negro be Portrayed in Art?' Right? That was the title?"

The cultural organ of the NAACP was a bit too wishy-washy for Hammond's taste. He wasn't too happy with the NAACP, either, since the organization he'd helped so much had refused to provide the funding for this show. Some of these middle-class blacks leading the organization were influenced by whites like Van Vechten. They were too embarrassed by the primitive forms of their own native music. And they weren't militant enough about segregation.

"I don't even agree with its premise," Hammond continued. "Who are we to say how *anyone* should portray themselves, for the sake of art?" Hammond pronounced it flat, an "aart" far removed from the Met.

"You disapprove of commercialism, I know," Carl offered. But Hammond just frowned at him. "Look, I'm no Charlotte Mason," Carl suggested peevishly, "I'm not from old wealth and I don't have my 'charges' call me Godmother... or Godfather I guess it would be... I don't have them kneel before me on my throne in my lavish New York apartment and kiss my ring. You don't either."

Not a ring, but they're certainly kissing something. Hammond had just that afternoon driven his Terraplane through a Harlem seething with secrets, disorganized crime, hoodoo, rent parties, music spilling out of dingy clubs, to pick up Ruby Smith, Bessie's niece by marriage, who would make her debut tonight at no less than the finest venue in the land, to take Bessie's place on the stage. Hammond had even arranged to have his childhood hero, James P. Johnson, elder statesman of the jazz piano, writer of "Charleston"[60] and regular accompanist for Bessie, guide Ruby through her first performance.

Her eyes had been moist with gratitude, her magnificent bosom heaving with nervous energy when she swung her hips into the Terraplane seat, exposing thighs of gold, and Hammond knew about this kind of sex the way a man knows about a monster behind the door without ever having seen it. It would have been a gross injustice to take advantage of Ruby. She had learned everything she knew from her aunt. The insatiable Bessie Smith had once beckoned to Hammond with hips grinding and thighs open and eyes revealing that she had only one thing on her mind. And Ruby, so vulnerable, opened her arms to the powerful white man who could make her career. Hammond had sternly extricated himself from her grasp, and then smiled.

It was all right. Perhaps they should be grateful. Big Bill Broonzy had ridden the bus all night long, singing to himself, about how grateful he was to be invited to play. Count Basie, proud of his heritage and of his middle-class upbringing, worked his magic for nickels and dimes, was grateful now to be getting dollars.

Robert Johnson's body lay out there somewhere in some unmarked grave.

His Negro friend Cornell Woodrow had taught him how to listen for the singular voice, and to not be thrown by cliché or to use his intellect. Just listen for that distinctive voice that comes from someplace in particular and speaks with a certain kind of emotional force. Follow it anywhere, trace it to its source.

"You were saying?" Carl Van Vechten prodded him.

Hammond didn't like the scheming, conniving look in Carl's eyes. "Doesn't your sponsorship, your patronage of black authors take something away from the integrity of their art?" Again, "aart" suggesting it could only be found in the streets or up in the hills. "Or is it, in fact, you know, just some sort of necessary evil?"

"Well of course it is."

Just as quickly Hammond blurted back, "Well I don't think so. And I'm not happy that Louis Armstrong, the great Louis Armstrong for godsakes! Has to play stunt music for these breakfast-food people. Who the hell do they think they are?" He gestured toward the East Side. "What I want," he said, pointing at the majestic apartment buildings, "is for these wealthy friends of ours to see these performances. I want them to hear this music just as it is, without any pretenses or, or," pausing, "ar-arti-tificial nn-enhancements," he stuttered thickly. "Without any meddling from whites, not from musicians, not from conductors." He paused, gathering strength. "And I'll tell you why. Because this music will redeem the Negro. It will redeem all of us, you watch. This music, it... it *transcends* racism."

That statement would have elicited one hell of an argument on any other day, but Carl needed the subterfuge of friendship to ensure his task would succeed, so he tacked, politely. "Oh, so you don't meddle? I don't think that new young singer you discovered, Billie Holiday, I don't think she would agree, now would she?"

"We get along fine," grinned Hammond. "She's maahvelous, just a maaaahvelous singer," one of his common expressions that would be picked up by Jewish comedians in later years. "It's just that... well you ask her. I don't like all that... I don't like some of her friends."

"And your, ah... dismantling? Of the Count Basie band?"

"Well now, you talk to Bill Basie yourself if you want. He'd agree that the band is much better off now." Basie in fact had agreed with Hammond with the retooling of the band when they arrived in New York. However ruthless they think I am, thought Hammond, my instincts are correct. "The Count trusts me. I drove all the way to Missouri to meet him, you know."

It had been another tip from Cornell Woodrow. After leaving the Crescent City to give blessing to zydeco developments in the swamps and sugarcane fields, Cornell had learned of Hammond's interest in blues performers and had headed north through the Delta, with stops in Clarksdale, across the river in Helena, back across to Memphis, and on up to Kansas City, to scout talent. Cornell spent some time with William Basey, started calling him "The Count" as he pulled up a chair next to Basey's piano bench at the Reno Club. After Basey's show Cornell told Hammond to drive on down, and a week later they were prowling the brawling clubs and seething streets of Big Tom Pendergast's riotous Kay Cee with the Count. They stopped in to listen to Big Joe Turner shout the blues, and this jamming, in a relaxed, drunken atmosphere, transported Hammond to a new level of sophistication and appreciation for improvisation. In Basie's "One O'Clock Jump"[61] the jamming would soar above the short, rhythmic bursts of repeated melody known as *riffs*, adding a counterpoint of flight to the foundation. This completely free and riffing thing blew away Benny Goodman when he first heard it, and they'd argued about how it would be the next new thing. Hammond recognized the power in that music and how it moved people.

"And you don't see the conflict of interest," Carl wouldn't give up, "when you're promoting this show, and promoting its performers, in articles and columns you write under another name? Henry... Johnson, is it? Without mentioning that you are the show's producer?"

"I do that sparingly," Hammond replied, annoyed. "You mean the Robert Johnson piece. I had to do that. The man deserves to be known for his music."

"Ah yes, the mysterious bluesman who died before he could show up." Oh yes, Carl had heard of Robert Johnson. The fellow was quite direct in his music, antagonistic even. "And you hear that it was murder?"

"That's what we heard, yes. And let me tell you, the records I have of this man, they are just maaahvelous. They're on Vocalion, you know. Hard to find the race records, except maybe at the Commodore. But I think it's amazing luck that this man even recorded in the first place. I have a few copies in my Terraplane, given to me by my good friend Cornell. It's the most basic blues I've ever heard, and the best I've ever heard, and yet it's modern, one song is about a car! I'm going to play some of his records tonight, for the audience, right from a phonograph on the stage, in the slot I had reserved for him."

"Play a phonograph record? To the audience?" Carl was taken aback. He sensed disaster; his wealthy patrons would walk out during the performance. "You're not serious. I thought you already lined up a replacement, that Broonzy fellow." Indeed, Big Bill Broonzy was far more mannerly, about as threatening as a butler with that Negro "done got wise" sense of humor.

"Well of course we got Broonzy." Hammond was annoyed by Carl's pretense that he really knew anything about blues musicians. "But I want to demonstrate the power of Robert Johnson's performances. I want them to hear a proud black man sing his blues the way he meant to sing them, without any white audience to intimidate him. And I think I can only find that on the few records he made."

"Well, it hardly matters now, does it?" Carl backpedaled. "I mean, unless you're selling the records."

"I don't know what you're insinuating, but I receive nothing from this, nor from any of these artists' recordings."

"I meant your career, it's based on —"

"I know what *swing* is based on," Hammond shouted, "and I want to get back to the roots of the thing, I want to reveal its power. That's the point of all this. If you drive a stake into the heart of popular music, kill off everything commercial about it, strip it of all the pretense, dismiss all that technical virtuosity, and get right down to what *moves* people... what you have is something maaahvelous!"

"But your career, man," Carl took his arm, a bit seductively. "Swing is popular, you ought not go backwards, not this far. Don't play that Robert Johnson record, it's not suitable."

Hammond shook his arm free and eyed him suspiciously. "I work in this industry, but I don't have to take the money. I can play by my own rules because I *don't* take the money." Hammond was fierce on this point, a stand-alone man.

It's impossible to describe that feeling, when you're young, that you can shake up the world. Hammond's ancestor Cornelius Vanderbilt shook it up quite thoroughly, and he did it without using his own money. He couldn't help but think of Cornelius whenever he mentioned the Commodore Music Shop. The real "Commodore" had been a notorious skinflint and cheapskate, which are traits Hammond secretly relished. But he'd also been a stubborn bully, which is something Hammond never recognized in himself. Cornelius believed that anyone could change the world through sheer will power.

Hammond took it upon himself to demonstrate that will power. He'd balked at a Yale education and had combed the streets of Harlem for records, sneaking out of the East Side mansion. He sensed, even then, the reason why this music was so deeply passionate, and to Hammond, it couldn't be explained simply as the outburst of a downtrodden people forced to live in a harsh world where the color of their skin kept them perpetually at the bottom rung of society. The vast class difference between him and his genius artists made him blind and indifferent to these harsh realities and at the same time opened his eyes to the potential of the music itself, particularly in recorded form. He recognized the power of these records he'd been collecting since he was ten, to his father's initial amusement and eventual consternation.

The power of the blues from Broonzy could move an audience, but Robert Johnson and his "Terraplane Blues" was something from another world, alchemy of a different sort, and he knew it would go right over the audience's heads. No one could comprehend the simple magic of its lines, comparing a woman to a car, "I'm goin' get deep down in this connection, keep tanglin' with your wires…" Hammond perceived it as a rite, an "old" wise man of twenty-seven initiating the audience into mysteries, opening fissures in their intellectual foundation, conjuring spirits that would follow them home to their nightmare beds.

* * *

Back inside and backstage, his anger only slightly cooled by the empty gloom of the hall, he shouted for Freddie. "Why is this phonograph not set up for recording?"

"Huh?" Freddie blinked. "You can't record the playing of a record."

"Why not?" Hammond was indignant. Technical people always sought out limits to his desires rather than appeasing them.

"Well it won't sound right. I mean, it will sound like a record on a phonograph, played in a hall. With these acoustics, everything will be in there, needle noise, people coughing, clapping, everything."

"But think of it," Hammond's protuberant eyes brightened, his anger gave way to a toothy grin. "A recording of a performance consisting of a record being played to the Carnegie Hall audience, from a phonograph on the stage. This is something that has never been done before." Hammond was excited at things that had never been done before.

"I'm not even sure it's legal, according to union rules," thought Freddie out loud.

"Damn them! Record it anyway. We may not use it, but nevertheless," Hammond's eyes twinkled, merry with insanity, "it will be a work of aaart!"

But will it capture the power? Hammond thought not. It would merely capture history. There would be no alchemy, its power would not be doubled, tripled, or otherwise amplified by the process of reproducing it. If anything it would be diluted. Sigh. But still…

When he'd called Don Law, the talent scout that had recorded Robert Johnson, and asked him if he could round up Johnson and get him to New York, Law couldn't believe it and told Hammond he was making a big mistake, that Johnson was so shy he'd freeze up in front of a white audience. Hammond wondered whether Law had been talking about the same bluesman; so many of his friends couldn't tell them apart.

Law had passed on second-hand information about Johnson's death, but maybe Law was wrong and he was still alive, Hammond hoped, cutting other guitar players and stealing women from their men at Saturday night fish fries all around the Deep South. His singing and his guitar were so eerie and unearthly, they spun such an intricate web that at times it sounded as if there were two guitars playing at the same time. The record demonstrated that he could play guitar like that, and sing like that, and make love with his eyes to all the women in the room like that, all at the same time; it was superhuman. The constant bass line, the echoing treble strings and unconventional timing would frustrate any but the most dedicated apprentice, who'd be too busy looking at the fretboard to notice the audience.

No, there was simply no way Hammond could communicate to his people the ribald passion of Robert Johnson's blues. They'd have to be satisfied with the record.

* * *

The vast interior of Carnegie Hall brimmed with the furs and jewelry of the upper crust of East Side society mixed with some of the wider-lapel Europeans from the West Side and a sprinkling of Negro intellectuals from Harlem, some wearing formal kaftans. The hall was so packed that temporary seating had been set up on each side of the stage, bringing almost a down-home feeling inside this church of Western music.

Hammond paced the backstage area and watched through the curtains for his parents. With the master of ceremonies absent, Hammond had been tapped to make the introductions, and he was terrified, having never spoken from a stage before. But he knew all this, Carnegie Hall, was an astonishing achievement for a man in his twenties, and that his father could not but be proud of his son finally, after all these years fretting over his bohemian taste and the scuttling of his Yale education. Perhaps he could give his father a taste of that rage he'd seen during his stay at The Millionaire's Club in Georgia, recuperating from Yale, walking through angry Negro streets as the son of the president of a private club. And his mother, well, she'd feel the exquisite discomfort that only a Vanderbilt would feel as a guest in the rival house of Carnegie.

The audience cackle fell to a murmur as the curtain rose, presenting the inexplicable sight of a phonograph on a pedestal, its horn pointed outward. Hammond was about to introduce recordings from H. E. Tracey's West African expedition a few years earlier. Once again his information was faulty. Hugh Tracey had taken fourteen young Karanga men to Johannesburg, five hundred miles to the south of their homeland, to create the first ever recordings of indigenous Rhodesian music. Hammond's objective was to demonstrate the roots of jazz and blues in West African music, but when he learned of his error, he cracked that wide smile of his and said what the hell, Rhodesian music would suffice, the audience would hardly know the difference.

But now that compromise seemed to haunt him. Hammond's first words through the microphone, in an effort to quiet the audience, left him panic-stricken as no one could hear him. The fix was in. The phonograph's rig had been connected to the loudspeaker channel. Carl Van Vechten's associate, a burly cab driver from Queens who doubled as a stage gaffer, had seen to it. And now, on a cue from the cabbie up in the rafters, Carl shouted "Louder!" from the front row of the audience. Hammond gestured to the sound technician to increase the loudspeaker volume, and of course, he was drowned out by rough African singing.

Carl had hoped for a massively disgruntled audience, but the mishap had the opposite effect, or perhaps it was Hammond's toothy grin from the stage: the audience roared in laughter and came a bit undone as everyone loosened up. Maybe they wouldn't have tolerated such incompetence with the Philharmonic, but these were Africans, by God, and that's what they came to hear, the Negroes, and who would expect them to behave properly? Hammond sensed the playful mood, allowed the African recordings to finish without further ado. He'd wisely set up the Count Basie Orchestra[62] to start playing at the end of the African singing, and the place started jumping. He caught the eye of his father in the audience, smiling.

As audience members recalled afterwards, Hammond took a moment before bringing on Broonzy to announce that Robert Johnson, a featured performer, was unfortunately unable to appear because he had recently passed away, under the most unfortunate of circumstances. All that was left of Robert Johnson's influential legacy were a handful of records. Hammond then played "Walkin' Blues" for the respectfully silent audience, followed by "Terraplane Blues" and "Phonograph Blues".[63] "What evil have I done?" Robert cried from the grave.

The heavens did not part. Hell did not rise up to claim anyone. But Robert Johnson's spirit was fed by all the attention of high-class white society. Johnson's spirit reared up and took notice, scanned the horizon and looked for young blood. Dead, but still kicking, he could see no evil, hear no evil, or speak no evil. He could do no wrong.

Cornell felt the chill and welcomed the unleashing of the spirit. Unbeknownst to Hammond, Cornell had listened from the back of the hall with his new friend, Herbert Mesh, a code expert for military intelligence, who had decoded ancient Sumerian tunings and had discovered that their pitch frequencies could affect our bodies, and how our bodies vibrated with them. Hammond wasn't the only one interested in the recording of the phonograph performance. Herbert, at Cornell's insistence, had helped Freddie fine-tune the recording mikes. It turned out that Robert Johnson had also somehow stumbled onto these Sumerian frequencies, and the recording would capture the resonance of the audience vibrating with the music.

* * *

No one quite remembered hearing the Robert Johnson records from the stage. No one spoke of having realized any impact from them. Some could remember the music emerging from the phonograph only as an acoustical storm that had somehow been contained in a bottle.

Hammond had nodded ecstatically during the performance, and the other musicians had bowed their heads to listen in respect. To Hammond, by playing these records on a phonograph on the stage of this revered hall, in all its religious awe, he was playing the audience itself as an instrument the way Picasso would play with his nude models. To the audience, Hammond was merely demonstrating that peculiar kind of eccentricity common to American blue-bloods that devote an hour every Tuesday afternoon to feed the poor. They tolerated this embarrassment until the records were over.

Count Basie would later remark that the "boy" Robert was sure enough unique in many respects, and not so embarrassing as some of the other primitive blues musicians who'd managed to get recorded. "Must've been listening to Leroy Carr, he's got a bit o' that crooning goin' on." Like many blacks who'd grown up with phonographs, Basie liked more sophisticated music than country blues.

The records themselves disappeared after the show, though copies of "Walkin' Blues" (backed by "Sweet Home Chicago") and "Terraplane Blues" (backed by "Last Fair Deal Gone Down"[64]) on the Vocalion label could be found in Harlem and at Commodore's on 42nd Street.

The transcription disc of the stage recording Freddie made also disappeared, under Freddie's arm, right under Van Vechten's nose, who searched in vain long after everyone backstage had split for Café Society with a deeply satisfied Hammond, who knew that he'd pulled off the most amazing concert in American music history, a revelation for all of the white world to see.

A revelation that would prompt the Corporation to respond with the force of a window slamming shut.

* * *

Meetings with high ranking members of the Corporation were rare, which made them far more exciting to anticipate. Transatlantic air travel rarer still, with war in Europe about to break. Even in flight across the Atlantic, ensconced in the womb of technology that defies Newton's physics, he could feel a Dark Age settling over 1939, and could sense that the Forties would be a decade of senseless atrocities and ignorant political ravings, starting with this maniac Adolph Hitler in Germany, rumored to have tapped an ancient reservoir of power shrouded in the mysteries of the Tibetan highlands and was prepared to use them to conquer Europe.

Would Archbishop Spellman be there? Do I kneel when I kiss his ring? These thoughts propelled young Will Cravingston in his tweed jacket and rumpled wool slacks up the steps two at a time and through the front entrance of the Masonic temple, rising like the Sphinx above the brownstones and mid-19th Century Italianate and Eastlake architectures on Clermont Avenue in Brooklyn's Fort Greene neighborhood.

Behind Cravingston, huffing and still puffing a cigar, Justin "Tony Just" Tonatio in his usual three-piece pin-stripe approached each step with trepidation. He didn't like meetings in the daytime, too bright for cloak-and-dagger. He felt relieved as he entered the dark interior of the temple, intoxicated by the cool rush of air, his kind of place, museum-like, tomb-like, dank with ancient secrets.

Deep in the center, a solitary light shone directly on a roll-top desk that was old enough to have been Benjamin Franklin's. Behind the desk stood a distinguished-looking elderly man, tall, lean and cadaverous with a scholarly stoop, who could easily have been a professor of archaeology at Yale about to deliver a dissertation. He cleared his throat as they approached, and spoke in a surprisingly flat and nasal Manhattan style, slurring his 'r's to come out 'ahs' like a cab driver on a dirty street outside a fancy restaurant. The voice seemed a bit inappropriate for a professor.

"Yes, yes, thank you Tony for bringing him in. Will Cravingston, I presume? Please sit."

Will nodded, and waited for the man to introduce himself. He didn't, and after an awkward pause, he confirmed "Yes."

"Good." The man floated elegantly down to his seat behind the desk, and Will and Tony Just took their seats out in the gloom. "We know all about you, Tony's filled us in. What we want to know first is... what you know about your friend, Herbert Mesh."

"And who is this 'we'?"

The Manhattan man smirked, and Tony Just shuffled his feet and uttered a low growl. "You know who we mean."

Puzzled, Will kept to the facts. "We travelled the upper Nile together, more than two years ago, April of '36. I was stationed in Cairo in the Foreign Office."

Manhattan Man frowned. "You were not accepted into the F.O. You were, in fact, collecting ancient manuscripts for the Knights, using Mesh to get them. Look, we don't have time for lies."

It was Will's turn to shuffle his feet.

"Mesh has disappeared," Manhattan Man snapped at him. "He took some things of value with him. We want to know if you know where he is."

"Last I heard he was off to India, in search of more manuscripts. Symbols, he's obsessed with them. We traced the swastika, among others, to ancient texts."

After an uncomfortable pause, Manhattan Man cleared his throat. "Yes, we know all about your translations, your *interpretations*. In fact it's the reason you're here now, for this project."

At the word 'project' Will took notice of the binder on the desk. Symbols embossed on its front told a story. A simple circle, then a circle with a dot in its center and rays extending all around it, undoubtedly Lower-Nile Egyptian. Then wavy lines and a solid circle without rays, a simple cross followed by a looped cross, and a winged circle followed by a winged eye, all from the infamous Mexican Tablets, surrounded by controversy since their discovery in the Valley of Mexico by William Niven in 1921, deemed as possibly Scandinavian petroglyphs or even the sacred writings of a lost civilization.

Underneath all of these, the cosmogonic diagram of the Lost Continent of Mu, as drawn by James Churchward in a book published six years earlier, illustrating the twelve gates to heaven, the twelve virtues man must acquire before entering, the twelve temptations man needed to overcome, and the eight roads that man must travel to get there. Churchward claimed to have found it in a temple in Uxmal which Le Plongeon had called "The Temple of Sacred Mysteries" and had interpreted it to be the diagram of man's first religion, estimated to be 35,000 years old. Herbert Mesh had been obsessed with Churchward's theories, Will not so much.

"Do you know about the legend of the Nine Unknown Men?" The man had followed Will's gaze to the binder on the desktop.

"Another of Herbert's obsessions," murmured Will, still fixated on the binder. "The keepers of ancient technologies and secrets of nature and the universe, a society of nine formed by an emperor of India, about two hundred years before —"

"In 273 B.C., yes. The Emperor Asoka. He unified India, and he saw to it that the techniques of liberating energy, sterilizing by radiation, and psychological warfare — fascinating techniques that are truly advanced, even by today's standards — he saw to it that these things would be cloaked in mystery and mysticism. The Nine Unknown were the high priests of Asoka."

Indeed, Herbert Mesh had gone off to India in search of evidence. But Herbert thought the initials, NUM, meant something else, something co-opted by these Nine Unknown Men. Something about numerology. Turning to Churchward's book, Herbert had connected this legend of the high priests with descendants of the original Naacals, who had supposedly saved the Sacred Inspired Writings from the destruction of the lost civilization of Mu.

"We know about Mesh, his research, and what he's looking for in India."

"Yes," volunteered Will, thinking it would continue the flow of information. "He's gone off a number of times about music, the power of music, and where it comes from."

"In fact he has a translation of some of the earliest sacred writings of these Nine Unknown," continued Manhattan Man. "Look here." He opened the binder to a page decorated with mandalas, and turned it to show Will. "Read this."

O'er the door of the sacred Temple
They sit in their wisdom the three —
The little deaf Monkey,
The little dumb Monkey,
The Monkey who will not see;
With their eyes shut to evil,
Ears that hear only the right,
Lips that are dumb to scandal,
They sit in their silent might

"The origin of the three monkeys," said Will. "Mizaru, covering his eyes, sees no evil. Kikazaru, covering his ears, hears no evil. Iwazaru, covering his mouth, speaks no evil."

Manhattan Man smiled.

"And we know about his transcriptions, the Sumerian scales," piped up Tony Just in a voice coated in sawdust.

"The point is," Manhattan Man cut in, "We want you to find him. We want you to bring him back into the fold. These symbols," he pointed at the binder, "are just the beginning. You know what the Nazis are up to, we have intelligence working on their codes, but this business with the symbols..." He looked at Tony Just. "We have reason to believe the Nazis are working with ancient techniques, including a primitive form of atomic energy, that are coded in ancient manuscripts."

"Find Mesh, bring him back," growled Tony Just. "We've got projects lined up for him, and for you, in the Army, the OSS. Our man Donovan, you know of him, he's another Knight."

"Listen, I'm no hero, and Herbert is certainly no —"

"No, no. You misunderstand," replied Manhattan Man. "We work with engineers, not soldiers. The engineer, you see, is like a magician to some, but to us the engineer is the hero of the future. Drawn by some magic attraction, to see behind or beyond the walls of science, to go to the moon or Mars, to capture thunder, to transmute the elements and make gold. The engineer seeks to expose the mysteries of the universe. Heroically."

Tony Just looked uncomfortable with this talk. Manhattan Man just smiled as he continued. "And yet, like the hero of a Greek Tragedy or one of those ancients sagas, a fatality hangs over the engineer, and a painful end awaits him. It is *we* who eventually control science, guard its secrets, and manage its... applications."

Tony Just snorted. "Manage *them*, you mean."

"It's true, they need our guiding hand, *your* guiding hand, Mr. Cravingston. Some would go mad otherwise, like Tesla. And we couldn't keep Edison from trying to construct a machine for communicating with the dead, or Marconi from claiming that he'd intercepted messages from Mars. The price of our authority is constant vigilance."

"Indeed." Will tried to look thoughtful, but his thoughts were elsewhere, the deciduous forests of the Himalayan foothills... Herbert talked often about evidence of an ancient civilization in these Tibetan monasteries, of powerful techniques for controlling vibrations that could liberate energy and transmute metals. Alchemist manuscripts had been found dating back to the earliest of times, before writing. Both architecture and music preceded writing, and both may have even been used for coded messages. Herbert had said that adepts have been transmitting over centuries, through architecture and music, the message of alchemy dating back to remote antiquity.

Comforting thoughts, but Will had his doubts. Over a thousand books and manuscripts on alchemy were ignored by real scientists. Perhaps they contained the secrets to energy and matter, but the intellectual climate of the times, Catholic in the past, rationalist in this day, forbid any attitude other than scorn. Only mystics and would-be prophets had explored them, seeking confirmation of their spiritual beliefs, or the odd eccentric like Mesh, seeking answers to questions no one even thought to ask. Much of the literature of alchemy bore the stamp of madness, filled with unbalanced writings taken to be supernatural revelations or inspired prophecy. Were the alchemists mad to begin with, or were their minds transmuted by their experiments into a genius we can only decipher as madness? Perhaps this madness was caused by the mercury vapors?

"It is the power of music that we must turn our attention to," continued Manhattan Man. "The ancient secrets of how to use music for psychological warfare."

Psycho... wha?

"Learning everything about our target enemy, their beliefs, likes, dislikes, strengths, weaknesses, and vulnerabilities," explained Manhattan Man. "Once we know what motivates our target, we are ready to begin our, ah... *psychological* operations. A war to capture their minds, so to speak. Our primary weapons are sight and sound. We must also look into the techniques of manipulating vibrations, audio vibrations to be specific. Recorded music, and other sounds."

"Radio?"

"Radio broadcasts are especially effective as a means of influencing the public," replied Manhattan Man, "but we can also use them to pass on coded messages. We want to devise new methods of communication, to evade our enemies' listening posts. In fact we've put on your team an engineer who designed, all by himself, with no help from anyone, a sophisticated ship-to-shore communications system. He was a cab driver at the time, he hid it in the trunk of his cab! In Seattle, he drove his cab and spotted for the rum-runners, ferrying their cargoes past the Coast Guard."

"Al Hubbard. The kid from Kentucky," rasped Tony Just. "And Freddie Falloni, that kid who recorded Hammond's concert. He's also missing. We want him found."

Will stood, bewildered. "You will have me work with engineers on radio communications, while looking for Herbert and, and —"

"Freddie Falloni. That's right. We have plans for all of you," said Manhattan Man. "Soon we'll have more control over radio in this country."

"What do we do with Hammond?" Tony Just suddenly asked Manhattan Man, who now seemed to obviously be the boss here.

"He'll be in the Army soon. We'll have him down in Louisiana, working the camps, raising the morale of the Negroes. And when he comes back, he'll be right back with his friends at Columbia, where we can keep an eye on him. And you, my friend, will lead Hammond to the concert hall of his dreams, a place to record natural sound through a single microphone. This place!" Manhattan Man gestured around the empty temple that echoed back his voice in stark undertones. "Built in the true Masonic tradition, in perfect proportions, with a thirty-five foot-high ceiling and a sturdy wooden floor. Perfect acoustics. So don't worry about Hammond. Swing is over. We have other worries."

"Swing maybe, but not jazz, not these jump blues outfits," growled Tony Just. "Once that shit got started…"

"It's our own fault," Manhattan Man interrupted, "we allowed this recording industry to flourish. The publishing houses don't know what to make of it. They've lost power, you see. And we've lost a vital monopoly on history, on thought itself. Together we exerted control over what was published in the world, and persecuted the heretics who stirred up trouble. Now, with all this recorded music springing up everywhere, you've got these, these…"

"Poets?" Will ventured in jest, thinking "Hey bop a-rebop"[65] could be considered…

"Yes. Poets. Coming out of the woodwork," spoke Manhattan Man serenely, without a hint of malice. "And alchemists who work with sound, who can bend the mind with startling revelations."

Herbert had talked like this. Will secretly hoped that something like this power existed. Like Herbert, he also hoped that one day he would wake up to an utterly new world, his spirit rejuvenated. Unlike Herbert, he didn't think he'd be so lucky.

"What most engineers don't realize," continued the Man, "is that the real weapon is not *how* the power is transmitted. We can work with real shamans, if we need to. No, the real weapon is the *message* it carries, and how that message affects the *people*. Upward mobility!" The Man's sudden shout startled Will. "That's the message we want to hear. Carl Van Vechten, Charlotte Mason, *they* are the ones doing the good work! They are elevating the Negro's art, bringing it up to our level of sophistication. They're helping in many ways to eliminate this, this uprising of *primitivism*. This primitive mentality, spiritual and superstitious, incubated by this, this *coloration* of our culture, not so much in literature or fine art, but certainly in music. These elements they call... jazz," he spat out, mindful of its nasty sexual connotation, "blues... country *hill*billy, for god's sake! Even gospel, they are all so infused, now, with this primitive mindset, this effusive sexuality, if you will... We must find a way to eliminate it, or make *use* of it."

What kind of perversion is this? thought Will. "*Eliminate* it?"

"Well my friend," Manhattan Man smiled knowingly, his eyes sparkling, "culture would survive just fine without music. Sounds stimulate our brains, they can be quite pleasurable. But we can learn to anticipate these feelings and tap directly into these reward centers in our brains, without music."

"Bullshit." Tony Just's gangster growl bounced heavily off the walls of the chamber. "Music is everywhere. We sing these goddamn songs in our heads now! 'Hey bop a-rebop!' And I bet some day we'll be walking around with music piped directly into our ears from some gizmo we got attached to us like some goddamn space helmet like that *Buck Rogers*."

Manhattan Man just smiled.

* * *

Will Cravingston took a seat at a table far in the back at Café Society. There was John Hammond, greeted by the manager as if he were visiting royalty even though he owned a piece of the club, strolling through the in-crowd and stopping at practically every table to schmooze with many of New York's leading writers, artists, and show-biz people, giving a warm welcome to writer S. J. Perelman, stopping to shake hands with screenwriter Budd Schulberg, and pecking the well-rouged cheek of puckish playwright Lillian Hellman. The place was crawling with communists and left-wingers of every stripe.

At the opening cheers for the boogie-woogie musicians, Meade "Lux" Lewis, Albert Ammons, and Pete Johnson,[66] who'd bowled over the audience at Carnegie Hall, Cravingston knew the Manhattan Man and his cohorts had missed something. Here was a sophisticated crowd going crazy over jungle rhythms more appropriate for a Kansas City cathouse. The music infected everyone; wealthy white folks were bouncing in their seats like the Negroes during the *jez grew* menace a decade earlier.

Cravingston thought about his handler, Dr. Eugene Mumblingore, a portly and pompous Corporation fixer who had tried to explain what had gone wrong with the Van Vechten plan. Will had stopped him before he could gather wind. "Such a frontal assault would never have worked," he had told this Mumblingore, with the authority of a field agent. "Your man simply turned Hammond into a tragicomic figure, and the audience sympathized with his plight. It doesn't work, to make a leader look ridiculous in front of his own people. You must try to *engineer* things," he had used Manhattan Man's words, "so that the leader acts ridiculous, or suggestive, or even decadent."

Although Cravingston had a feeling that his destiny already included Dr. Mumblingore, he'd done some quick research on the man who had experimented with mind-altering substances on human subjects, under federal contract. The good doctor had tracked down and detained famed occultist Aleister Crowley under the false pretense of wanting to publish a new edition of *The Book of Lies*. His Tammany connections had given him the coroner's job when he needed access to corpses. For a man of science, Dr. Mumblingore was unaccountably mystical about certain beliefs, such as the notion that the secret of immortality was somehow conveyed in music; in particular, *recordings* of music. "If you know how to listen to them," he said in a heavy whisper. "And if you listen over and over and over again, which is something you can't do at a live performance or over the radio." And yet he despised overt tricks and strategies, priding himself on knowing the limits of fraud. The good doctor might catch a medium in the act of cheating a dozen times in a séance, and yet refer to some of the phenomena of that séance as evidential. He liked to say that although a medium might have his hands free to cheat, that fact did not explain "the earthquake in Messina" he'd somehow caused.

Cravingston didn't think Mumblingore was up to the task. A pompous man is, without exception, a fool; especially if he insists on stopping every moment to admire himself. The man had no imagination or real magical perception, no glint in his eye when the discussion turns to strategy. He seemed comically ignorant of the alchemy and pharmacology in which he boasted scholarship. Will, on the other hand, saw himself with the capacity for measuring the limits of error in any investigation with great accuracy. Just as the skilled climber can make his way on rotten chalk by trusting each crumbling fragment with *just that fraction* of his weight which will not quite dislodge it, so he could prepare a sound case from worthless testimony.

So the Manhattan Man was hedging his bets, thought Cravingston, pairing such a harmless egghead, an agnostic academic, with a steeled operative like himself. The good doctor could spend his time concocting his potions and arranging fixes. Cravingston could mollify him by keeping him informed while he worked on his own.

"What may work is a coordinated subterfuge," he explained to Mumblingore's chagrin. "It worked before. You know your history? The Anti-Masonic Party? The first time in American politics that a third party appeared? Andrew Jackson had been branded a Mason, and the Freemasons knew that the best way to guarantee his election was to split the opposition. The Anti-Masonic Party was the perfect vehicle for this, and of course the Freemasons were secretly running it. Pandering to fear has always worked in politics, and so has the planting of the seeds of false opposition."

Cravingston was about to prove this point at Café Society. Its owner, Barney Josephson, a former shoe salesman from Trenton, had a brother mixed up with some prominent left-wingers, and the café had been written up by society dame Helen Lawrenson, a self-proclaimed Communist and spy. Lesbian as well. She'd called it "the right place for the wrong people," and Josephson used the phrase in his advertisements in elite magazines and on matchboxes. Communists, socialists, and leaders of far-left labor organizations socialized at the Café Society to listen to jazz, the melting pot of all things progressive.

Cravingston had convinced Barney Josephson to approach Billie Holiday with a subversive, political song. "Strange Fruit"[67] was a song about the lynching of two black men in Indiana in 1930. It had been written by a Jewish schoolteacher in the Bronx under the pen name Lewis Allan, which just happened to be the names of the stillborn children of the executed Rosenbergs. The "strange fruit" hanging from trees, with "the bulging eyes and the twisted mouth," were black men hung by racist white men.

Will thought the song to be suitably controversial; it made the listener aware of a form of racism not restricted to the Deep South. And with this song, Holiday would self-destruct. The question was whether she would be too scared of retaliation to sing it.

Barney Josephson knew better. During a pause in the stage performance, Barney ordered the waiters to stop serving, and turned the lights in the club off, with just a single pin spotlight illuminating Billie Holiday on the stage. During the musical introduction, Holiday stood with her eyes closed, as if she were evoking a prayer, and then she gave it everything, softly and gently, singing like the wind. She sang about the strange fruit hanging from the poplar trees, with blood on the leaves and blood at the root, and black bodies swinging in the southern breeze.

Her audience was so stunned that for several long moments no one applauded until one patron began cautiously clapping, after which the applause was deafening. It became a staple of her repertoire.

Cravingston realized that a turning point had been reached. The Corporation's attempt at sabotage had, once again, failed.

* * *

The transcription disc of the stage recording, Robert Johnson's music in Carnegie Hall, piqued Freddie's curiosity. In a normal recording, vocal and instrumental signals are put through a transducer, a microphone... the energy form itself is changed, from audio to electromagnetic. The signal drives a phonograph cutter head, which carves the record grooves. The phonograph needle and cartridge is another transducer, changing minute physical displacements in the grooves back into electromagnetic signals. The continuous vibrations are preserved, but what if we now record the electromagnetic signals... a sort of double-reverse transducer?

Despite the complexity of his physics and his inability to articulate them, Freddie recognized the power his electrical alchemy had wrought. It was his friend Herbert Mesh who suggested that musicians would be drawn to it in an unblinking rapture. Music of this sort, Herbert had pointed out, this combination of fast rhythm and blues, could in fact be harnessed by special recording techniques that could wield a power over people: a compulsion to dance, a vibration to resonate with, a force to fornicate with.

Herbert felt innately the need to keep this power a secret; having worked for the government and the military, he had a feeling that shadow men would try to steal the transcription disc from them, perhaps even hurt them in the process. When Cornell Woodrow met up with them, he verified Herbert's paranoia with news that the FBI, under its new director J. Edgar Hoover, had taken a special interest in John Hammond after hearing about the record played on a phonograph on the stage at Carnegie Hall. The bureau's New York office had received instructions directly from Hoover to conduct an investigation "to determine whether this person should be considered for custodial detention... in the event of a national emergency."

"They want to shut us down," Cornell added, subtly drawing Herbert and Freddie into his circle, at the center of which was his experiment to reincarnate the voodoo spirit in music. "That's where this record can make a difference." Cornell pointed out that its effect may only help musicians who weren't black. "Records of all kinds affect *my* people, the blacks of my generation," he said, "the ones who remember the hoodoo spirits. They already know how to listen, hell, they listen all the time, and some of them, like Robert Johnson, it comes natural to them, they got the music in their bones. It's *your* kind, the white musicians, who need this particular live wire shoved up your butts."

So the record, when played at a crucial time in a white musician's life, could turn that musician's life around. Make him into a genius of the black rhythms and blues. Herbert asked Freddie to make a safety copy, but Cornell had warned that copies of the original would not hold as much power. The subject would require concentration.

Freddie and Herbert strolled up through Harlem looking every bit the odd couple, chubby and whimsical Freddie like Abbott to Herbert's lanky, practical Costello, arguing over this and that, frightening the black folks around them. For the first subject, Cornell had pointed Herbert to his own cousin, uncle Bernie's son Milton, who had become a clarinetist and saxophonist going by the name Mezz Mezzrow, developing his own style in the Chicago jazz clubs. He'd led a few swing-oriented dates with his integrated band The Disciples of Swing. He was happy to hear that Cornell had sent them over. "Man, he taught me the real blues, the roots of it, how to play like Louis. And he introduced me to my new wife Mae!" Sure 'nuff, Mezz and his black old lady turn out to be the first interracial couple Herbert's ever seen.

They settled down near the phonograph, and Freddie pulled out the copy of the acetate. Cornell had warned that copies of the original would not hold as much power. The subject would require a more concentrated effort at listening, perhaps drop into a meditative state first.

"A little extra concentration? That all you need? Lemme lay somethin' on you. Cornell got me some 'tea' from the lady herself, Mama Roux." Mezz brought out the mixture, Herbert produced the copied acetate for the turntable, and Freddie sat himself down for the ride. Herbert gave the crumpled envelope a sniff. "No, no," Mezz out with some cigarette papers. He could roll with one hand. "You smoke it! Once you do, man, you feel happy and sure of yourself."

After the first listen, Mezz said to put it on again, and he puffed some more. The combination had a peculiar effect on him. "I hear my saxophone like it's inside my head! The vibrations of the reed against my lips! I can slur much better, put just the right feeling into my phrases. I'm really coming on! All the notes come easing out of my horn like they'd already been made up, greased and stuffed into the bell, so all's I gotta do is blow a little and send them on their way! One right after the other, never missing, never behind time, all without an ounce of effort. And with my loaded horn I can take all the fist-swinging, evil things in the world and bring 'em together in perfect harmony, spreading peace and joy and relaxation to all the keyed-up and punchy people everywhere. I can preach my millenniums on my horn, leading all the sinners to glory!"

Herbert coughed on his first puff. "Hey, I think this is marijuana!" Muse of Morocco, fumes from the Delphic Oracle. An otherworldly presence in this world.

"Yeah, well, not just for the Mexicanos, y'know. Louis loves this stuff, Fats, ain't he misbehavin'? We're the vipers, y'know, the Vipers Club. We be on a whole other plane, my man, on another sphere altogether, not like those bottle babies, always hitting the jug and then coming up brawling after they get loaded. We like things relaxed! And easy! Mellow and mild, not loud or loutish! Not that scowling chin-out tension of the lush-hounds with their false courage! Those lushies don't even play good music. Their tones come hard and evil, man, not natural, soft and soulful. We members of the viper school are for playin' music that's real foxy, all lit up with inspiration and her mammy!" And over at the Lafayette Theatre they were smoking acres of it, the audience and the performers lighting up as they please.

Soon it became a ritual, smoking and listening to the acetate, something to use to get all fired up. Except Mezz now also considered *himself* to be Negro, and even cut his nappy hair to look more Negro. His performances now echoed the wildness of the juke joints, and in the subsequent jazz madness that allowed his career to flourish, he recorded his signature tune, "Really The Blues,"[68] with the Tommy Ladnier Orchestra.

Only problem was, the Mezz got too popular. "You've got Dutch Schultz's boys tailing you," Herbert pointed out. Sure enough, word had spread that the nappy headed jazz clown had the best golden leaf "muta" from Mexico, two dollars for a full Prince Albert can. Dutch Schultz, Vincent "Babyface" Coll, just wanted the Mighty Mezz to expand and cut them in. Dutch knew quality. Cab Calloway had vouched for the product, calling the mezz supreme and genuine. But each day the wise guys got less good-natured, their voices got harder, and their demands more insistent.

"Hey there, Poppa Mezz, is you anywhere?"

"Man I'm down with it, stickin' like a honky."

"Lay a trey on me, old man."

"Got to do it, slot," and it was off to the next Harlem joint with a juke.

The authorities eventually caught up to him before the Dutchman did. Mezz was busted trying to enter a jazz club at the New York World's Fair in Flushing Meadows, Long Island, with sixty rolled "muta" reefers. They found him "with intent to distribute" which meant two years in Rikers. Herbert found him in the segregated prison's Negro section, because he had insisted to the guards that he was colored while pointing to his nappy head.

It didn't occur to Herbert or Freddie to be suspicious that Will Cravingston would suddenly show up at Rikers one day, at the same time as their visit with Mezz. How coincidental. Herbert's old botany-expert friend from military intelligence was running a program at King's County Hospital to study the effects of marijuana. "All the reefer you can smoke," he promised Mezz. "All the newest tape recording equipment at your disposal," he promised Freddie. And to Herbert: "All the research you will ever want to do, funded for eternity."

* * *

Secrets softly bubbled to the surface of the amber liquid in the hermetically sealed flask in the darkened laboratory financed by the Corporation at Mumblingore's insistence. For Armand Barbault, the highly analytic and detailed aspects of science were now fused with a unity and spontaneity of vision, which to him was the mark of real knowledge.

What had fused science with vision was the atomic blast, first as a test in New Mexico, and then in the mightiest blast of death and destruction ever seen on Earth in recorded history, which leveled Hiroshima. Barbault thought back to that moment, watching the way Oppenheimer had strutted across the parking lot after the test blast like Douglas Fairbanks in *The Thief of Bagdad*. He had done it. He could see no evil. But Barbault had been filled with trepidation.

"The liberation of atomic energy is easier than you think," warned Fulcanelli before the war. The last of a line of alchemists with secret knowledge of the past, Fulcanelli had hoped Barbault would carry the message to the great atomic physicist André Hellbronner, tasked to bring this power to the German forces. Time was short, war in Europe was imminent, and Fulcanelli could see what would happen. "The radioactivity artificially produced can poison the atmosphere of our planet in a very short time, a few years. The alchemists have known this for a very long time."

Barbault had been curious at first, but grew skeptical the more he heard about alchemy.

"No, you must listen," admonished Fulcanelli. "The secret of alchemy is important to this new discovery. You see, there is a way of manipulating matter and energy to produce a *field of force*. You can use this field of force, to see, to gain access to, *other* realities, which are ordinarily hidden from us by time and space, matter and energy."

"Field of force."

"Yes. We who work this field, we call it the Great Work. We don't need electricity, or even a vacuum. We can do this with certain, ah, *geometrical* arrangements of the highly purified materials we gather, and these are enough to release atomic forces. Forces you would not believe were possible."

Barbault could not believe what he was hearing, this from a man considered a genius.

"Many thousands, perhaps millions of years ago," Fulcanelli added, pointing his finger at the ground, "nuclear weapons were used against humanity. The result was total destruction."

As far as Barbault could tell, Fulcanelli's message had gone unheeded. Never in the history of humankind had so much knowledge and power been withheld from the many by a precious few. Dr. Hellbronner was eventually assassinated by the Gestapo. Fulcanelli disappeared after his conversation with Barbault, leaving no traces. Barbault had heard that he survived the war and celebrated the Liberation of Paris. But every attempt to find him failed.

After Hiroshima and the second blast at Nagasaki, the threat of nuclear annihilation hung over every aspect of human life.

Before these blasts ended the war with Japan, Herbert Mesh, an operative in London for the American Army's OSS, the Office for Strategic Services, asked Barbault how to find Fulcanelli. Barbault could not say at the time, and still did not know. All Fulcanelli had left behind were two books: one about the mysteries of cathedrals, and the other about the dwellings of philosophers. The books were written in a cryptic and erudite manner, replete with Latin and Greek puns, alchemical symbolism, double entendres, and lectures in Argot and Cant, all of which serve to keep the curious in the dark. An even more mysterious third book, about the end of the "glory of the world," was withdrawn from publication by the author.

By then it was well known among scientific circles that radioactive elements gradually decay, giving off radiation and producing "daughter" elements which then decay even further. One such chain starts with uranium and ends with lead. The question was, could the process be reversed? Or, if you start with another element, what might you end up with?

By 1947 Barbault had finished writing his astrological handbook, which he knew would be published and could make him fashionable among the society ladies and politicians. Having adjusted to the idea that Evil had been defeated by the "atom" bomb, people were not only ready for astrology as a meaningful force in their lives, but were also ready to accept the idea of a vitality serum. They had adopted the lingo and dance moves from the lively forms of music performed by the colored descendants of slaves. They snapped their fingers to

"Daddy-O (I'm Gonna Teach You Some Blues)", a hit for Dinah Shore. They em-braced the sweet orchestration of Guy Lombardo's version of "Frankie and Johnny". They could sing along with "How are Things in Glocca Morra?" and they were learning how to play "Good Rockin' Tonight"[69] and "We're Gonna Rock, We're Gonna Roll" on the parlor piano.

It was Barbault's second wife, who'd also worked for the OSS, who had convinced him, with practically no argument or pout but just the serene nature of her attitude, to abandon his comfortable urban life for the anonymous countryside. For Barbault, the turn towards the study of ancient alchemy was not a free, deliberate choice. It was an act of obedience to a call, maybe even a command, that had been transmitted through the woman. The role of the woman in alchemy is traditional and fundamental; this he already knew. She is the guide, and the channel for superior forces. And for Barbault, no training had prepared him for this command better than astrology, which showed him the reason why. His destiny was to perform a Great Experiment to prepare a form of liquid, potable gold.

With his wife's guidance, he made the decision nearly a month after the broadcast of a UFO crash-landing in Roswell, New Mexico, and one week after the National Security Act established the CIA, to start the experiment to make the elixir. He identified the site for his first sample of soil at the very moment when the grand conjunction in Leo (the opposite sign to Aquarius), together with the crowning of the sun, signaled a very important planetary influx, one that would be earthed and so would prepare the First Matter for the moment six months later when it would be acquired. Several male children would be born in six months and would be instilled with the power of this transformation. He knew it would take at least 13 years for this elixir to reach maturity and the boys to reach puberty.

He began with the acquisition of the First Matter, the *Prima Materia*, by digging several centimeters underground. However, much of this matter had to be of celestial as well as terrestrial origin. The process needed a long-lasting cycle such as that of Saturn or Pluto, beginning the very day of the conjunction of the two planets. The Work would not reach perfection until the moment Saturn had completed one-half of its revolution; that is, had reached Aquarius. Allowances also had to be made for the combinations of subsequent cycles, particularly the grand conjunction of Uranus and Pluto in opposition to Saturn, which would occur in the summer months of 1967, and which would also mark an important stage in the Work.

That is, if the Corporation doesn't shut him down. Mumblingore had been wary of his loyalties, and Cravingston thought the vegetable gold experiment was dangerous, that it would unleash a power and radioactivity on such levels as to mutate humanity itself.

Barbault's fear was not paranoia. Fulcanelli had left no trace, on purpose. Some of the most important thinkers that worked for the OSS and eventually the Corporation were dropping out of government work, and some, like

Herbert Mesh, had simply disappeared. Al Hubbard, who had supplied the uranium, had become a rogue element, taking samples of mind control substances on a kind of Johnny Appleseed mission to enlighten the cognoscenti. Even Herbert Marcuse had left, taking refuge with other professors at universities sponsoring "Russian Studies" and economic discussions in coffee houses brimming with folk music.

Restless Spirits Know

Restless spirits know no boundaries of time or space. It could have been Robert Johnson's body that was put to rest in an unmarked grave just north of Greenwood, on the "Money Road" that links the town with the hamlet of Money, Mississippi. It just as easily could have been some other young black man in that grave. No one knows for sure where Johnson's body was laid to rest. It could be the small cemetery on the Money Road in the backyard of the Little Zion Missionary Baptist Church, or the Payne Chapel Memorial Baptist Church cemetery in Quito, or the one in back of the Mt. Zion Baptist Church in Morgan City.

Robert himself had sung his will. Bury my body down by the highway side, he sang, so his old evil spirit can get on a bus and ride.[70]

Perhaps it didn't matter, or as Cornell Woodrow told Sonny Boy a month after the tragedy, perhaps Robert Johnson needed more than one grave. Cornell had said that if you die with success in your hand, you multiply. Your spirit invades and transforms babies and youngsters across the land.

Sonny Boy, sophisticated as he was in the ways of business and enter-tainment, a former radio DJ, nodded slowly and listened solemnly, for he knew he had success in his hand. And Robert Johnson's spirit was especially strong, Cornell told him. His spirit probably multiplied, and one spirit went off with the wind and swirled around the Earth until joining up with the massive hurricane of 1944 that pummeled the East Coast of the U.S. Another spirit, an "evil" version of Johnson, festered in one of his graves, feeding off the crime of his death, until 1955, when this spirit erupted to foster racial violence in the area of Money.

Emmett Till, a poor 14-year old black boy from Chicago, just visiting his uncle, fingering candy in the Bryant Grocery and Meat Market in Money, was distracted for a moment by an attractive white woman, Carolyn the shopkeeper, sashaying to the music on the radio. Big Mama Thornton belting out "Hound Dog." All Emmett could think to do was emulate his older friend Willie whenever Willie saw a girl he liked; he wolf-whistled, just like Robert Johnson would have done.

Emmett Till was kidnapped from his uncle's house that night and dragged screaming through the streets of Money by Carolyn's husband and half-brother, down to the Tallahatchie River mud bank, where they proceeded to beat the shit out of him, leaving him with one eye gone and the other dangling by its entrails and rolling around his bruised cheek. The pride of Southern white manhood then fired several rounds to make sure he was dead. His body was found three days later; no one was ever convicted. Coming as it did on the heels of the Montgomery Alabama bus boycott, the murder of Emmett Till more than anything else galvanized the nascent civil rights movement of the late 1950s.

It was as if the power of Robert Johnson's restless spirit and music had stirred a subtle revolt that would seed the best minds of the next generation, not just in America but also back to America's white motherland, Europe. It didn't matter where this spirit travelled; Cornell Woodrow would follow it, and help it along on its quest, nefarious or redeeming, whatever it may be.

* * *

Cornell was surprised to see the white kid from Tupelo, the talent scout winner, at Sam Phillips' Memphis Recording Service at 706 Union Ave. It struck him odd that this young cracker had adopted Negro body movements and dress. The hillbilly guitarist and bass player wore jeans or work pants, boots, and short-sleeved shirts, but this kid with the science-fiction name, Elvis Presley, wore a pink and black drape jacket, dress pants with a pink stripe down the side, loafers, and a black shirt, all from Lansky's on Beale Street. To top it off he seemed to've dumped an entire bottle of Rose Oil hair tonic on his head to slick up his hair and sideburns.

From his swagger and sneer Cornell could tell the boy held that Stagger Lee fantasy in his mind. It didn't matter where he got it, thought Cornell; he probably grew up around black folks, but it must keep him at arm's length from his peers. In pink and black he stands out in the crowd, girls wondering what he's like, boys sniggering that he looks like a carhop. He was a good boy, an earnest boy who worked to help his parents, a young girl's sweetheart who never acted out the impulses he heard on records. There was no doubt he'd listened to a lot of blues, but he was a ballad singer, a white gospel singer, with a bit of hillbilly still in him.

As Cornell talked with Sam in the control booth, the boy led his two instrumentalists through all the popular ballads he knew. Sam was disappointed, tapping his fingers absentmindedly on the console. A fierce-looking man with luxuriant, carefully sculpted chestnut-brown hair and a severely knotted tie, Sam Phillips sat at eye level with the musicians in his control room, not high above them as in other studios. Set under fairly prominent brows, his eyes always seemed to be squinting, but his steely gaze would bore right through to your very soul. This hard, unceremonious man could nevertheless talk sweetly, even cajole and croon to his musicians, to get them to feel comfortable and at home in the studio, but also to keep them alert. He knew that long hours in the studio could have a mind-numbing effect, that it would smooth rough edges and banish the very spontaneity he was trying to capture.

Finally they decided to take a break, and Elvis thought maybe they should just give it up for the night. Cornell strolled out to say hello, to tell the boy to loosen up a bit. "Y'all know the woman named Alice?" Cornell chuckled as he shook hands,

Who used a dynamite stick for a phallus?
They found her vagina in South Carolina
And bits of her tits in Dallas!

Laughter all around as Cornell sidled up to Elvis. He'd seen the boy shaking his leg in a heady anticipation before each take, but then bottle up all that loose energy before approaching the microphone. "Go ahead, son, shake your leg, shake your whole body if you have to," he spoke soothingly to Elvis. "Put some of that shakin' into your performance. Go ahead and shake it, that's all right."

Perhaps it was because the black man carried himself far more confidently and stately than any other Negro Elvis had met, that Elvis answered "Yes, sir," in a tone that surrendered to a higher authority. And as he shook Cornell's hand, an old bluesman's tune popped in his mind, a song he'd hummed since childhood whenever he felt put upon or blamed for something. *That's all right.* A child's song, really, nothing important. He even thought that *maybe he'd written it,* and he told Bill the bass player's brother that he *had*... but really, he'd just heard it somewhere as a child and never forgot it.

So the song came into his head, and he started shaking his leg again. As Cornell took his bow and returned to the control room where Sam was rewinding tape, leaving the control room door open, Elvis jumped up and started scat-singing the melody, acting the fool, shaking all over. "That's all right, mama! That's all right for you!"[71] Bill picked up his bass fiddle and started acting the fool too, slapping away at the root notes, and Scotty joined in on guitar tentatively.

In the control room Sam could hear the ruckus. "What's that you're doing?" he yelled out to them.

"We don't know," Scotty called back, a bit tersely, as if reprimanded at school.

"Well..." Sam thought for a second. "Back up. Try to find a place to start, and *do it again.*" Absentmindedly he began to roll tape.

When they started up Sam recognized the tune and was amazed that Elvis even knew it. "That's All Right, Mama"[72] had been a minor rhythm and blues hit a few years back for Arthur "Big Boy" Crudup, who'd sounded tired when he sang it. But the way Elvis handled it, with his good-natured tomfoolery bubbling through it, the song came across with a freshness and an exuberance that Sam was looking for. And Scotty and Bill fell in behind Elvis with an easy, swinging gait; the combination defied categorization. Something different, indeed. They worked hard on it, several takes, and afterwards, as they heard it the first time, they couldn't believe they'd done it.

"Well that's fine," Scotty said, putting down his guitar. "But they'll run us out of town!"

* * *

Later that night, with everyone packed and gone, Sam and Cornell kicked back and listened to the recording several times.

"You got something here," Cornell kept saying.

"But what am I to do with it?" Sam kept repeating. "I need something to follow it up."

After another listening, Cornell smiled sheepishly. "You got a problem. Now I know black singers can go white, they can do their own stuff and sing white music too, but... you can't.... white singers don't usually *go* in the black direction."

Sam grinned. "You mean I got to pull him back."

"I mean you got to balance it out. You got some cracker song he can do? Somethin' hillbilly for the white folks?"

Sam thought about it, squinting as he usually did, indicating some kind of distaste for any kind of tampering. But Elvis had run the scales on Bill Monroe's "Blue Moon of Kentucky"[73] while practicing, and you couldn't get any more cracker than that. The boy really wanted to sing ballads, gospel, spiritual stuff. When he first showed up, he'd sung every damn pop song he knew. Sam had kept telling him to relax, you're doing fine, but the boy had locked up. Sam searched for signs of what he thought was there, looking right into the boy's eyes through the plate glass window of the control room. But the session had been a dismal failure, he hadn't even recorded it. He didn't know what he had on his hands, it was so damned hard to tell when you're dealing with a bunch of damned amateurs.

Cornell could just about read Sam's mind. "That boy can't walk into a club full of rednecks dressed that way, like he just stepped off Beale Street. He'll only make it with records."

Sam nodded in his taciturn way. He sensed in Elvis the same insecurity, he could see it in his stance and demeanor, the same insecurity he sensed in the great Negro bluesmen he'd recorded. It was that social and psychological inferiority, bred from institutionalized racism, and instilled in seemingly all Negroes born in the South. Even that great bull of a man, Howlin' Wolf, had been humbled by this white man's simple, unpretentious studio. This boy Elvis had grown up poor, and somehow he'd retained this Negro humbleness in a generation cocky with racial prejudice. And so he really didn't fit in with his peers. He was a quiet and introspective boy, devoted to his mother and nurtured on gospel quartets and the spirited sermons of black and white country preachers. And with an almost feminine preoccupation with his hair and his outlandish outfit, and the strange name Elvis Presley, he seemed to come from outer space, from some pink and black planet.

So *this* was the future, of white *and* black music. By now it was possible to sell almost half a million copies of a rhythm and blues record. Sam had licensed his recordings to Chess and other labels and had seen them take off, based on the appeal to white youngsters. And yet, the southern youngsters still showed resistance to buying Negro music. They liked the music, sure enough; they just weren't sure that they were *supposed* to like it.

Sam believed in records as a great equalizing force. In the future, people won't care what color the singer is, they'll just buy the records if they like the music. Sam truly believed that records could liberate black people and integrate the local culture, but he couldn't explain it, not to sweet Marion at the front desk, nor even to his best friend Dewey Phillips on WHBQ, who recklessly spun sides from race labels and boasted about having the largest Negro radio audience in Memphis.

But Sam could talk to Cornell Woodrow. The man seemed to know outer space, he could even be the godfather of all Negroes in America. The man was above it all, especially above all the prejudice. As a child, Sam first met Cornell while attending the Negro Methodist church in Muscle Shoals to listen to the *a cappella* singing, in the company of Uncle Silas Payne, a worker on his father's farm who told him fantasy tales of the Molasses River in Africa with battercake bushes and sausage trees, and sang him the old Negro spirituals and work songs. Cornell was a proud visitor to the church who'd brought with him a gospel quartet made up of prisoners from Parchman Farm. Uncle Silas had introduced young Sam, and Cornell had given the boy a 78-rpm record of "Cool Drink of Water Blues"[74] by a country singer named Tommy Johnson. It had been Sam's prized possession for many years and one of the reasons he'd gravitated into the music business: to record the Negro talent.

Cornell seemed to be the same age now as he was then. His ageless wisdom came with no pretensions, and he brought Sam artists and songs and news from the outer frontiers of the music industry. Sam could talk to him unintimidated, about the Negro artists, about white radio DJs who drew Negro audiences, about anything. He could tell Cornell that he sensed in Elvis a kindred spirit who shared the same secret, an almost subversive attraction to black music and black culture, and a belief in the equality of man. "But I have to keep my nose clean," he whispered to Cornell as he rewound the session of "That's All Right" in preparation for cutting an acetate. He meant that he tread a high wire, trying to get this music played on the radio.

Cornell agreed. "They'll call you a 'goddamn rebel who's turned his back on good Christian white folks.' They'll say, 'why give this nigger-loving sonofabitch a break?'"

"They'll run us out a town," Sam replied, using Scotty's words with as much good humor as he could muster.

* * *

Dewey Phillips, popping open a Falstaff in Sam's control room and sprinkling salt in it, kept quiet as he listened to the acetate of "That's All Right", which was so uncharacteristic of him that Sam knew his interest was real. If Dewey had just blurted out that the record's a hit, it would have made Sam suspicious that Dewey was just patronizing him. Sam wanted some kind of advice from Dewey, because he just didn't know where to go with this record. It's not black, it's not white, it's not pop, and it's not country. What the hell is it?

Without regard to Sam's reserved manner and the formal atmosphere of his control room, Dewey had propped his feet up on the desk and farted. Tall, loose-limbed, sloppy-looking with his shirttail out and unapologetic about it, Dewey always seemed too large to inhabit the space he was in. He knew how popular his radio show had become, not only with the Negroes of Memphis but also with the white population too timid to buy Negro records.

Daddy-O-Dewey played "the hits" as he called them; mostly boogies, blues, and spirituals, the Soul Stirrers followed by Muddy Waters and Wynonie Harris, and he'd have fun with it, playing 78s at the wrong speed, mangling the names of advertisers and telling everyone to say "Phillips sent ya!" Before anyone had even thought of stereo he'd put two copies of the same record on two turntables and try to start them at the same time, but of course they were always off a bit, creating a phased sound that added dimension and intrigue. He was getting up to fifty telegrams a night and three thousand letters a week.

One night he asked his listeners to blow their car horns at 10 p.m. and it seemed like the entire city complied, to create one supersonic blare. The police chief (who of course had been listening to the show) called Dewey to remind him of the anti-noise ordinance and pleaded with him not to ever do that again. Well of course Dewey went right on the air, told his listeners that the chief had called and would not let him do it again at 11 p.m. And of course Memphis once again complied with an even louder-than-supersonic blare, if that was even possible.

"He's a man who just happens to be white," said rhythm and blues singer Rufus Thomas, a DJ on rival WDIA. Everybody on Beale Street knew Dewey, and they'd just as soon crack up over his Dizzy Dean impersonation as over his constant pitch for everyone to buy "a fur-lined mousetrap." Dewey had no sense of time and would just as likely call you at three or four in the morning as any other time. Even his best friends wondered if there was a real Dewey deep inside.

More than anything, Dewey loved his show and could hardly talk about anything else. Marion didn't like him, even perceived him as a threat for Sam's attention. Dewey and Sam would argue for the fun of it. But not this time; Dewey could sense Sam's nervousness and how serious Sam was. Sam kept on, asking Dewey to just *listen* to the damn record and tell him it's not something that never before existed on this planet Earth.

Dewey knew the song. He'd played Arthur "Big Boy" Crudup's version a number of times over the years. He was proud of his gut feeling, and he generally discounted local talent, preferring performers from exotic locales. And dammit, when he picked a damn record, he didn't want to be wrong.

But this was something else. The boy's falsetto didn't crack, it just flowed right over the high notes with a confidence he hadn't ever heard in a young white singer. And when his voice descended into masculine territory, it did so with a fullness of purpose. Goddamn, this record was serious, not to be trifled with. Dewey didn't say anything as they listened to it several times, pausing only to take a gulp of Jack Daniels followed by a chug of Falstaff. What stifled his usual boisterous behavior was the recognition that this record might be more important than his radio show, more influential than anything he or any other DJ might play or say on the air. And whatever it was, it was going to pass him right by if he didn't get serious about it. At 2 a.m., a bit earlier than usual, Dewey put down his Falstaff, noticed the time, gave Sam a pat on the back and went home.

First thing the next morning, Dewey called Sam. "I couldn't sleep a wink, man." He wanted that record for his show tonight. In fact he wanted an extra copy of the acetate so that he could play them on two turntables at once, and he didn't want Sam to tell anybody else about that record.

* * *

Sam Phillips had alerted the boy that the record might be played that night, and Elvis fixed the family radio on Dewey's station for his mother and father. Fidgeting, pacing about the living room, he was too nervous to listen and finally fled to the local movie house to watch the flickering screen and pretend it all wasn't happening.

Dewey fondled the acetate of "That's All Right"[75] as he announced it on the show, not a new record exactly, just a dub of a record coming out next week, and it's gonna be a hit, gee-gaw, ain't that right Myrtle? (A moo from Myrtle the cow.) On it went, and the response clapped back like thunder following a lightning strike. Over 50 calls and 14 telegrams rolled in as Dewey played the record seven times in a row. Daddy-O was beside himself, encouraging his radio audience to join in the discovery of one of Memphis' own sons. We *up*town, Dewey cried, we *way* uptown, 'bout as *far* uptown as you can *get*.

Gladys was so shocked to hear her precious boy's name, Elvis Presley, on the radio that she hardly even heard the song. By the time it was over the phone was ringing, Dewey on the line asking for Elvis. She told him Elvis was at the movies. "Well Mrs. Presley, you just get that cotton-pickin' son of yours down to the station!"

Elvis was scared to death, shaking all over when he arrived. Dewey got hold of him and told him to cool it. "Sit down, I'm gonna interview you." Dewey quickly put on some records while they talked to loosen him up, and Elvis didn't know the microphones were on. Dewey managed to get Elvis to mention his high school, Humes, so that the listeners would know the boy's white, not colored like he sounded. But Dewey could tell that most of these dad-blamit birdbrained callers didn't know the difference, they'd called without knowing one way or the other. Maybe they just didn't give a hoot anymore. Hell, it's 1954 already, and here in Memphis, they just like what they hear.

News travelled fast.

* * *

Dixie received the mysterious telegram at her cousin's house in Florida where her family had gone on vacation. "Hurry home, my record is doing great," it said. What record? The one he'd made a year ago as a surprise for his mother? Elvis had never played it for her, but explained that he'd heard "Just Walkin' in the Rain"[76] by the Prisonaires on the Daddy-O-Dewey show and then, coincidentally, had seen an item in the paper about the Memphis Recording Studio on Union Avenue, where it had been recorded. He drove by the place a few times, and then one day he decided he'd go on in there and make a surprise record for his mother. They had asked him what kind of singer he was. They thought he was just a hillbilly singer, but he told them that he could sing all kinds of music. And they asked him who he sounds like, and he'd told them that he don't sound like nobody.

She so adored Elvis when he talked like this. He'd get so excited and his leg would bounce so fast, he would just melt her heart. But his disappointment was also just as fierce. He'd done this, he'd made a record, two songs, but nothing happened after that. The studio had not called him back. He wanted to tell somebody, and Dixie wanted to listen and sympathize. He'd talk to her about things he'd never say to anyone, not even his mother, even though there seemed to be no secrets between him and his mother.

Dixie would join in his family life and it was like playing house, in a doll's house of three. Vernon, his father, would have been handsome had he not been so dour, inconsolable and suspicious about everything. What an odd couple; Vernon's wife, Gladys, was just the opposite, vivacious, sociable, ready to exchange recipes and small confidences. Dixie got along with her just fine and simply avoided Vernon. Elvis told her that his father had been through a lot, and that he had every right to mistrust the world. The world had put his daddy in jail, Parchman Farm no less, for eight months for the crime of forgery. But it had been a mistake, a misunderstanding, just one lousy lapse of good judgment. And it was no wonder they lived in their own insulated world.

Elvis could so easily be hurt by teases and gibes, like the time he had to get a haircut for work and he was so embarrassed about it he didn't want anyone to see him, and Dixie's uncle kidded him about it, just kidding really, but he got so red-faced and nearly burst into tears. He just was more sensitive than any boy she'd ever met, and maybe that's what made him so appealing. And yet, he was not outwardly courageous, as you would expect a boy to be. Afraid of the dark, full of fear on the darkest of nights, he'd cuddle with her as a child would suckle at a mother's breast. He so feared the world and how it might take his mother or father away. Dixie remembered the time they were all swimming and how Elvis got so upset and afraid when his father took a deep dive. He was nearly inconsolable, then so angry that he scolded his father the way his mother would have scolded him.

They went to the First Assembly Church together, though not as often as Dixie would have liked, and they'd sit in back so that they could sneak out during the sermon and head down a mile away to the Negro church at East Trigg to bask in the singing of the Golden Gate Quartet,[77] or Rev. Brewster with Queen C. Anderson and the Brewsteraires. They sang songs that were out of this world. Often James Blackwood himself would come with the Songfellows. At home Elvis would pick out a popular tune or hymn on the piano and Vernon and Gladys would join in singing, and even Dixie would sing, though she was shy about it. She'd seen Elvis' face grow luminous as he sang like the gospel singers, as if possessed by a spirit.

Elvis was the center of attention in that family and he basked in the warmth of that attention, which came mostly from his mother. It was only when he stepped out to meet the world that his fear of rejection would take hold. He stammered out once that he'd auditioned for the Songfellows and they'd turned him down. He was so deeply disappointed that it clouded his view of the world, almost as if he were being treated as badly as his father had been.

So Dixie was surprised to hear about the record. Was it "Tomorrow Night"?[78] This was the song he'd sing to her all the time, the one he sung better than the original version by a colored man, Lonnie Johnson. But she wasn't surprised that Elvis would have gone another step with music. Cautious or not, he was determined to be a singer, not just sing in church gatherings, or play music as a hobby. While they knew James Blackwood and loved the Blackwood Brothers, Elvis preferred the more rousing Statesmen. "Listen to Jake," Elvis would whisper to Dixie, as Jake Hess would soar to a high note with his controlled vibrato. And Big Chief was a commanding presence, everyone watched him from the moment he first walked out on stage, and when he started to dance around and shake his leg, the crowd would go wild, about as far wild as a white audience could go.

Dixie was nervous about all this. She'd sensed a change in Elvis when he had startled her with news that Eddie Bond and his band were looking for a singer, and that they had to go to the Hi-Hat on South Third. This was a real, scary, nightclub! She hadn't expected this, what if someone saw them? When Eddie Bond had dropped by the table and asked Elvis what he did for a living, Elvis had blurted out that he was a truck driver, and Dixie had been embarrassed for him; it made him sound more masculine, like a tractor-truck driver, rather than the driver of a small truck for Crown Electric. Elvis didn't look like any truck driver; he had been wearing his bullfighter's outfit with a pink shirt, about as queer an outfit as you'd find anywhere in the South, except on a Negro. His two songs, accompanying himself on guitar, had gone unnoticed in the hurly burly atmosphere of the club. Eddie Bond had come by afterward and told Elvis that he'd better stick to driving a truck.

Dejected, Elvis had listlessly gone through the motions of having a good time picnicking with her in Overton Park. He'd been driving by the studio on Union in the electric truck, stopping by once in a while to chat with Marion at the front desk while still in his work clothes. To Dixie it all seemed hopeless that he would ever make another record, and even if he did, what of it? She didn't understand what would happen next, if anything would. Then, about week before Dixie would be leaving with her family for a vacation in Florida, he had gotten the call from the studio. Marion had asked if he could be there by 3 p.m., and Elvis had replied that he'd be there before she could hang up the phone.

Later, when Dixie saw the exasperation in his face, she knew it hadn't gone well. He had told her that the man in charge, Sam, had him sing everything he knew, and apparently he hadn't liked any of it. Elvis had taken out his bitterness on her, getting picky and aggravated about the smallest things. And jealous when Dixie talked with other boys, even though their relationship hadn't progressed beyond heavy petting. Then there was the day, just before she was to leave, when Elvis switched from morose and bitter to sweetness and piety, and they had talked about marriage. They could just drive to Hernando, Mississippi, where anyone could get married in a simple ceremony. But Dixie was still in school, and about to start a summer job in the cosmetics department of Goldsmith's, and Elvis' job was uncertain, and what would we do? Where would we live?

The evening after his first tryout at the studio, news of a disaster overwhelmed Elvis, Dixie, their families, and all of Memphis. Two of the Blackwood Brothers, the most progressive of the gospel quartets, had died in a plane crash. The funeral was one of the biggest in Memphis history, and Elvis and Dixie held hands, crying through the entire ceremony. They were still crying and hugging even as Dixie's parents awkwardly packed for the trip, and they promised to remain true to each other, and to write. She told him that when she returned, everything would be the same, they'd have the rest of the summer together, but she had doubts she couldn't even express to her mother. Something had changed in him.

The telegram made her anxious all the way up to and after her return to Memphis. She didn't see him that first night she got back; eerily enough, she only heard him. The song "Blue Moon of Kentucky"[79] by one Elvis Presley was the first song her family heard on the car radio as they approached Memphis. Dixie could hardly listen. Elvis now seemed to be someone else entirely, as if he'd joined the circus and she'd arrived too late to stop him.

* * *

It was a hillbilly song, right up their alley, a beautiful waltz familiar to anyone who'd listened to the Grand Ole Opry, and revered by every string picker in the South. But Bill Black couldn't treat it so reverently; after so many hours of working it, with nothing to show, he just turned on that goony charm, jumped up and down and clowned around, beating on that bass and singing in a high falsetto to break up the tension. Elvis picked up Bill's buoyant mood and strummed a rhythm that the song had never met before. Bill's clowning had a way of energizing Elvis, and in a heartbeat the two were off on this crazy tangent, banging out "Blue Moon of Kentucky" not like a waltz but like a sacrilegious romp, a roaring freight train heading for derailment. Elvis drove it with his ringing rhythm guitar, and Scotty propelled it further with chording riffs and single-string filigree. As they finished one recorded take the studio equipment seemed to melt as in a blast furnace, and visible heat waves bounced off the walls. The band shuffled out wasted, limbs akimbo, as if from a steam bath.

"That's fine now," Sam crooned smoothly to console them with his voice of reason to their backs as they hung their heads. "Hell, that's *different*," his voice registered a higher notch of approval. "That's a pop song now, nearly about."

After everyone left, Sam Phillips went about the task of adding an echoing feeling, what he called "slapback" — an echo created by running the recording signal through a second Ampex machine to get an almost sibilant phased effect. Sam thought it to be a special trick that was his alone, a way of injecting excitement into a blues recording. Hell, this recording didn't need an injection, but he did it anyway, delayed the signal a tiny bit longer to get even more of the effect.

* * *

Gladys put on a brave face, but deep down she was terrified. Her mama had told her a long time ago that if she paid close attention to things, she'd develop a sixth sense. And her sixth sense was telling her that something was wrong, and it was connected somehow to that Cornell Woodrow. Somehow she knew he had been in that studio with Elvis. She didn't know where she got this idea, and she'd never tell anyone, but that proud colored man had something to do with it.

She'd met him once only, and that was enough; he came to pick up her friend Mabel at the Tupelo Garment Factory one day. They were from the black quarter of Tupelo known as Shake Rag. Gladys had been burning to ask Mabel about a colored midwife she'd heard about, Mama Roux from down in the Delta. You don't want that, Mabel told her with eyes downcast, she's not right for white folks. Cornell had shown up at that moment, and he must have heard everything because he was laughing. His was a booming guffaw that filled up the entire plant to the rafters.

"White midwives are fools," he said in a deep voice, followed by a chuckle at her embarrassment. Smiling, he touched her belly. "You have twins." Grinning broadly, he spread the fingers of his hand across her belly. "They are both male, but one is weaker than the other." He paused, and frowned. "One may not survive."

"My mother-in-law's a midwife. She's not a fool."

Cornell smiled and nodded like a sympathetic politician. "It is good luck, regardless. May you have healthy twins, but if one is stillborn, the other will absorb his talents and be much stronger."

Gladys was so shocked by this remark that she couldn't even sputter a reply. But she didn't have to. Cornell tipped his Stetson hat, and Mabel quickly ushered him out of the plant.

The encounter left her strangely aware of her twins, in ways her doctor could not explain. A twinge of pain here, a subtle kick there, and suddenly an agony of convulsions. She could not get out of her mind the simplistic Biblical view of good and evil. She had been touched by this man, and what if his prophesy was true? It wasn't that Cornell was colored, or that she thought anything more or less about colored people. She worked side by side with them in the plant, this was the New South. It's just that colored folks were more in tune to those primitive, base desires. Colored folks needed to go to church more often than white people, just to keep those desires from rising up and taking them over. They needed to sing in church louder than white people so that God would hear them.

Cornell was a proud colored man, too proud of his primitive nature. Why had he touched her? What good or evil came from that touch?

When Elvis was born, his twin brother was stillborn. Gladys remained silent in her anguish. She would love this child, this one child, just as God intended. The child would fill her life with joy. He would take the place of two sons, one good and one bad, and she would help him fuse these energies together. And so he would have a special, God-given talent, thanks to his stillborn brother. And Gladys would remain cheerful about it to the end of her days. She would tell others that "when one twin died, the one that lived got all the strength of both."

* * *

Sam was late getting to the Overton Park show, Elvis' first real public exposure. The hillbilly audience, save a raucous group of Memphis teens, really had no idea who "Ellis Presley" was; they were there to hear Slim Whitman and Billy Walker, the Tall Texan. He spotted Dixie rooted to her spot, scared to death. Elvis looked pitifully unsure as he came up stuttering, "I-I-I-I just don't know what I'm goin' do!"

"Look, we'll find out, that's all," Sam patted him paternally. "We'll find out if they like you or not. And y'know what, I think they're gonna love you." He'd said it, but couldn't shake the scent of failure that permeated the air behind the band shell.

Cornell Woodrow arrived out of nowhere to stand at Sam's side. The two of them standing there, arms folded in confidence, calmed the boy down. But even Scotty's knees were knocking as they took the stage, and after Bob Neal's hasty introduction, they were out there on their own.

Elvis twisted the mike so hard his knuckles turned white. About to hesitate, a look crossed his face, a look of defiance, not against the audience or anyone in particular, but against his own fear. As he struck the opening chords of "That's All Right" and Scotty and Bill fell in behind him, barely in the rhythm, the defiance turned upward into a sneer, almost a leer. Elvis moved forward into the mike and his legs began to quiver.

Scotty saw it first as they did "Good Rockin' Tonight",[80] how Elvis jiggled and shook his legs, and how the pleated front of his loose-fitting pants made it look like all hell was breaking loose underneath. Girls in the front rows were screaming, and guys were laughing and yelling, and Elvis seemed to think they were all making fun of him, which only made him shake more as he backed off the mike on an instrumental break. Through "Blue Moon of Kentucky" he was so nervous he slammed the rhythm like a jungle drum and Bill had to slap his bass double to keep time. As soon as it was finished, with a quick sweep of his forelock and a look of panic in his eyes, he scrambled offstage and ran right into Cornell. "They-they-they're laughing at me!"

"No they're not, son," Cornell spoke incisively to Elvis through the crowd roar, with Sam at his side nodding, smiling to himself. "They want you back for an encore. They're hollerin' for you to wiggle some more. Go back out there and keep doin' it."

Out they went again, and this time Elvis kept his sneer in place, a calculated sneer, and he wiggled some more, and the more he did, the wilder they hollered. Cornell caught the dull brown eyes of a teenager in the front row, a white farm girl, as they turned pink and blazed hot. Cornell recognized the loa, mounting the girl, taking her over. Erzulie! Seeking a love forever unrequited, scenting her mount with the sweet-ness of sin. And the next girl down the row, the same transformation of her eyes to hot pink. Erzulie worked her way up and down the rows, turning them inside out, throwing them into such a ribald state of exhilaration that their boyfriends and families trembled. Erzulie, drawing the spirit and power of Yemayá, the majestic maternal energy of the ocean, the one known in Brazil as Yemanjá, who can arrive without warning and flirt mercilessly as the girl with the red dress on.

This boy had the power. Like Robert Johnson, the boy could raise Erzulie, and just like Robert every woman wanted to mother him. That sweet vulnerable face that every once in a while betrayed the sneer of sin. Elvis seemed to be on a tightrope, all at once killer predator and loyal puppy dog, and every once in a while a hound dog. The boy would soon be a man with success in his hand.

Cornell had found one aspect of the Robert Johnson spirit, had figured out what to feed it, and had gone ahead and fed it.

It was up to the boy now, how he turned into a man and what he did with his power. Cornell's work here was done.

Sam Phillips loved the record business and the radio business, even when he had to deal with mobbed up label owners who stole his acts, like Robey. But he knew firsthand and abhorred the crass phoniness of the touring and booking side of show business, the carny atmosphere of the Hayrides and the Grand Ole Opry itself, and the blustering fools who ran them. The worst of the lot were the most successful, mountebanks with titles like "Baron of the Box Office" Oscar Davis, "Lord" Jim Ferguson, and "Colonel" Tom Parker, who thought nothing of exploiting their stars and radio DJs and leading the entire industry down the road to perdition.

They came down from their adult positions to see this nineteen year old boy wriggle his legs and excite the teenagers. They came down with dollar signs in their eyes. They didn't understand the music, Sam knew that. They didn't understand what he was reaching for. Hell, they didn't even listen to the records he'd made. They just wanted Elvis.

Sam didn't know where this "Colonel" Tom Parker had come from. Must have just crawled out of the woodwork. He said he had witnessed the Johnny Ace shooting, and he understood the Negro spirits from old fairy tales learned from his nanny in South Africa. The Colonel saw the music industry as a carny would see it. Everyone's a mark, and Elvis is his boy. Sam had to work with him. Parker was fond of saying that he never signed a contract he didn't like. "Yeah I always get a 'kiss my ass' clause in the contract."

"What's that mean?"

"It means you can kiss my ass."

* * *

Herbert Mention heard Daddy-O-Dewey's broadcast that night as he motored down Highway 51 toward New Orleans to meet up with Freddie. He knew exactly what had happened. Here was another chosen one, chosen by that Stetson-topped black dandy, Cornell Woodrow, the muffled mystery. The savage with an innate sense of delicacy, the primitive who exhibits the utmost politeness. He treats the civilized in a most courteous and considerate manner. How had he survived in a white-dominated world for so long? What kind of half-hinted influence did he have on Robert Johnson, on countless other bluesmen? On this new kid Elvis?

Cornell was like a creature that artists and musicians see only in their dreams, and then only dimly, as a traveler from primitive countries that still, even in this modern era, preserve much of the ghostly aboriginal essence of Earth's primal generations, when the memory of the first man was a distinct recollection and all men his descendants. Those who can see Cornell Woodrow for what he truly is can also perceive the primitive human consciousness that is on the borderline of the natural and supernatural.

Herbert would find out. He thought he knew how it worked. The talented kid would become a traveling musician because he was driven from within, most likely due to the lack of a father, or mother, or both, like Robert Johnson. But here was a boy with a solid family background, religious almost to a fault.

* * *

Tony Just squirmed in the swivel chair in Randy Wood's chintzy wood-paneled office at Dot Records in Gallatin, Tennessee, a sleepy cancerous town with Bull Durham advertisements everywhere. His wool slacks stuck to the seat of the swivel chair, his hemorrhoids throbbed, his forehead burned hot and his mouth seemed filled with mud. The stinking muggy South. A swampland harboring miscreants, black and white. First, this Elvis hillbilly. And now this nigger, a raging queer, a frequenter of the homosexual bars outside Atlanta, and a song about... he couldn't even say it. Sure, the lyrics had been cleaned up at the last minute, Wood had told him, but still, "Tutti Frutti"[81] was about taking it up the ass, no doubt about it. "Tutti Frutti, good booty, if it don't fit, don't force it, You can grease it, make it easy." Chrissakes.

They talked about the move to Hollywood. Certain parties back in New York would make sure that the money flows, as long as Dot Records takes on these nigger songs and wipes them off the charts with clean versions. Randy told him this kid Pat Boone looked like their best shot. "A descendant of Daniel Boone, can't get more American than that. Been on *Ted Mack*, hell, even *Arthur Godfrey*. He's a natural. We got him to redo that Otis Williams song and he turned it out, y'know, lily white. He even wanted to change the title of 'Ain't That a Shame' to 'Isn't That a Shame'," laughed Wood, "'cause he didn't want to offend his parents. Now that record is beating the shit out of the Fats Domino original."

"Thanks to our friends in New York, let's not forget," Tony Just reminded him sternly. "Everything has a price."

Right. Randy Wood was to make a deal to fund his move to Hollywood. Tony Just had lined up manufacturing and distribution with Ballzo in New Jersey. All Randy Wood had to do was confront this radical music head-on, lyrically and stylistically.

* * *

In the front row, Charles Hardin "Buddy" Holley could almost taste the sweat pouring off this kid Elvis on the stage. Buddy's stint that afternoon, at

KDAV with his Western and Bop Band, had ended on a sour note when a tall, square-shouldered black man all dressed up in a gray pin-stripe suit and black Stetson hat entered the studio with demos of this new kid. The hat was Texas, but everything else about him looked out of place in Lubbock. Some kind of black carpetbagger, promoting records out West that should be kept in the East. We don't want it out here, we're rebels of a sort, we like cowboy music, not this big city stuff.

Cornell Woodrow smiled. "This boy Elvis is from Memphis, he's got country grit under his fingernails. You got to check him out."

But Buddy was too jangled by this weird juxtaposition of a successful black man promoting records in a country music radio station in Texas. He didn't see what the man was aiming at, but he agreed to go check out Elvis that night at the Cotton Club.

Cornell was pleased with himself. It was like taking a graft from a healthy apple tree and planting it into a young sapling of a different color. Now that sapling could taste success. It was that hiccup that Elvis used to break up certain words, that hint of vulnerability peeking out through all that bluster and vigor. And that high voice he used to glide over rough spots, like walking a tightrope over a swamp.

There was something to it. Buddy didn't know what it was. But damn if he wasn't going to use that hiccup. His last recording for Decca in Nashville, after changing his name to Holly, was a country swagger called "That'll Be the Day"[82] based on a phrase that John Wayne kept repeating in *The Searchers*.

It had been rejected. It sounded too much like everybody else, and not as good. He could try it again, maybe rock it up like Elvis, but he needed a new band. All this was going through his mind as he soaked up Elvis performing "Heartbreak Hotel".[83]

Cornell dodged the jumping screaming girls, grinning like a guilty pimp, to join Buddy in the front row. Elvis doesn't come out on stage, he *arrives*. Turning this way and that, shaking his body as if forces were carrying him one way and then another, like some herky-jerky whirlpool and he's smiling all the way down into it. He's smiling at everyone, right and left, smiling directly at Buddy as the song begins, but regarding everyone and including everyone in the song and dance.

* * *

"You make a record, it becomes a hit, and the next thing you know you're working every night, driving all day, getting no sleep at all." Elvis, at the wheel of his pink Cadillac, was talking to the night; the boys were asleep in back. "It's getting to the point where I have to hide from all the girls. This urge to please, to pour it on, to do the put-on and watch 'em squeal... I mean, what, eventually, is the point?"

Scotty stuttered a sleepy response. "And what happens when you get too old to put it across?"

Elvis was scared. The moment would soon arrive, he knew it. The moment when everything would spin out of control. He drove that Cadillac hot all through the Mississippi night toward Texarkana. About halfway there, at the very moment that his mother Gladys was awakened out of a sound sleep in Memphis with the feeling that something was wrong, the Cadillac caught fire and nearly exploded.

Elvis, Scotty, and Bill got out just in time and watched from a hillside. Elvis saw it as an omen. This is what happens on the other side of success, after you've pushed things to the limit. If you stay on one side, the poor side, you just keep going, keep your mind on what you're doing, like an electrician, you can't be the least bit absentminded or you're liable to blow somebody's house up. But if you cross over, become famous, you need to stop and look around. All the forces of nature are coming at you, coming to strip you of your humanity. The cruel winds fan the flames that burn you up.

The dream of being everyone's likable boy had burned up with his first Cadillac. Elvis was a man now, expected to take sides in adult dramas like racism and politics, expected to do all that was necessary to make the business run. The Colonel had arrived in his life at just the right time to take over the steering wheel.

* * *

Hibbing inhabits a wide open space, flat as an iron plate, dusty from one end to the other, a scabrous landscape shaped by intensive strip-mining, with the largest man-made pit and the largest slag heap in the world. Everyone has to shout until they're hoarse to be heard above the wind. Bobby Zimmerman would walk past a huge abandoned iron ore dump to reach the Willows, where he'd hide with Bill and his other friends in a makeshift fort in the high weeds. The old days were gone, the iron ore nearly tapped out, and every minor business dispute would grind the town's economy down to a halt. Bobby was growing up in a dustbin loaded with discarded dreams and the stationery of failed enterprises. Many years later he would tell a reporter, "I was born very far from where I was supposed to be."

There's no reason to go anywhere. That's what his father would say. But his father was weak, spent. Polio got him, and now all he could do was mind the appliance store. And the only good thing that ever came out of that appliance store was the mahogany radio with the turntable on the top. He'd listen to whatever came on, Hank Williams singing about a cold, cold heart[84]; John Jacob Niles, singing like a songbird.[85] The sound of a record made Bobby feel like he was somebody else, not even born to the right parents.

He dreamed of faraway places, of railroad stations where bluesmen said their goodbyes to their wives and kids, of honky-tonks out West where singers sang for whiskey, of back-room poker games where the winner takes the dancer, of long lonesome highways where he stuck out his thumb to hitch rides with eagles. One night he dreamed of St. Augustine, and that he was part of the crowd that killed him.

On his first trip on his own, to Duluth, Bobby was drawn to strippers, dancing girls. The image of her bare midriff, white and subtly rippled, all-too-human, would seize him. The act of opening up, showing just a slit of white nakedness in this cave, while outside the wind kept blowing... it was just too tantalizing. He knew some girls, but these strippers were real women, experienced, sad. And if he could take them... And so he does. With all his heart in it, he makes love to the stripper in Duluth, hoping his love would be something she'd never had before.

But of course, afterwards, just a cigarette or two, it all becomes plain. She's just another working girl, lumpier than most, with stale dreams and no real future. No different really than the other girls, only older, with less and less to accomplish as the years roll on. He'd gone out looking for pleasure, all he could get, but he found that the more pleasure he got, there was just as much pain. He began to see it as a balance.

And so he went back to Hibbing to date girls his own age; with this experience, he'd be bolder. He was attracted to the poor, the non-Jewish. The daughters of miners, farmers, and workers were more interesting. For one thing, they had more interesting names. Glori Story was the first, that was her real name. Then Echo, what kind of name was that? Like she's only an echo of a person, an echo is all that can exist out here on the Iron Range. That's all I can find, anyway. Just an echo of a girl, an echo of a life, a life I don't want to live.

* * *

By the winter of '57 Cornell Woodrow and Jim Dandy had made it as far north as Virginia, Minnesota, just east of Hibbing. Cornell had felt the shift, the winds of rock 'n' roll blowing across the prairie, scattering new rock 'n' rollers across mainstream America, bypassing the visceral electric blues of Chicago. Way out there in white folks' places like Fargo and Duluth, cracker singers worked the songs that had done so well for Elvis and Carl Perkins. They kept following that Highway 61, parallel to the great Mississippi, all the way up to its very source, Lake Itasca, and proceeded East, past the much larger Leech Lake and through Cohasset, Bovey, Nashwauk, Hibbing, and Chisholm, to arrive at the hotel in Virginia, the road's end. The only directions were North, toward Canada, or South, toward Duluth and the tip of Lake Superior.

"What you gonna find up there?" Jim Dandy's half-brother and partner, Jim Crow, had snarled at Cornell. Jim Crow was determined to stay in Helena and try to make it the way Sonny Boy had.

"Talent," answered Cornell, in a faraway voice. "Talent is not skill. The bluesmen today, they've got the skills, the techniques. And they've got mojo. But it's not getting over on the white folks. White rock 'n' rollers are imitating Elvis, or they're trashing the blues. I got to find some white talent. Out there, the sound of the wind blowing across the range."

"Sounds like you lookin' for that honky stuff. Hank Williams."

"I knew Hank. I helped him record his preacher songs as Luke the Drifter, 'Be Careful Of Stones That You Throw' and 'Ramblin' Man'[86]. No, I think a bit of Hank is just what I need right now."

Jim Crow harbored a fierce resentment. They were working together, Dandy and Crow, with a repertoire of Robert Johnson songs, when up came Cornell Woodrow, their new Teacher. After learning many things from Cornell, the two split up. Dandy headed north with Cornell, while Crow stayed behind, and took on the moniker of the Jackal. Crow wanted to kick back at his tormentors. Dandy, on the other hand, wanted peace and tranquility, the source of all wisdom, and was happy to be a singing, dancing, grinning fool on the radio.

* * *

Bobby wanted to sing and play rock and roll, but just as he got a band going, the Golden Chords, he lost its members to other bands that were making money, getting gigs. Just about to give up, he heard Jim Dandy on the radio. Dandy had a show east of Hibbing, not far, in Virginia, Minnesota, and he just didn't fit out here, probably the only black guy within fifty miles out here on the Iron Range. Bobby couldn't understand what it was about these songs, this music, that was so powerful, that bowled him over. It made him angry that he couldn't understand it, couldn't get to the bottom of why he liked it so much. "The bluesman can move you from the rear, grab you from your fear, bring you through the mirror," he heard Dandy say. "He did it all through the South, and he can do it here." With a single phrase, a nod of the head, a blues progression, and then another phrase, Jim Dandy had just about summed up everything there was to know about the bluesman's life. It suddenly was all plain to see. America is wide open, and anything is possible. He talked one of his friends into going out there to see the bluesman, staying at some big hotel.

Jim Dandy met them in his room filled with all kinds of records. Some were blues recordings, some "rhythm and blues" as they were called on the radio. Some were decades old but still composed on American soil. Some were derived from ancient Scottish, Welsh, British, and French songs, but were transformed in a century of reinterpretation to be uniquely American. "Barbara Allen" and "Wild Mountain Thyme" mixed with "Stagger Lee" and "Wreck of the Old 97" and dozens of other songs recorded in the Mississippi Delta, in the Piedmont and Appalachian mountains, and in West Texas. Jim Dandy even had records by Robert Johnson. He called Johnson's music "the only true, valid death you can feel today."

One record after another caught Bobby's attention. Here was Uncle Dave Macon's "Way Down the Old Plank Road,"[87] heading out of town in celebration, unburdened by fear or responsibility. He sang about building a scaffold on the mountain just to watch the girls pass by. He sang about how his wife died on Friday and he got married again on Monday. He yelled "Kill yourself!" in the middle of all this, a huge apparition now hovering above the story and commenting on it, judging it. Indeed, go ahead, it can't get no better than it is, might as well kill yourself! It sounded like a good idea, maybe even fun.

"My Teacher, Cornell Woodrow, told me to play you some of his new recordings by this cracker from Oklahoma, Woody Guthrie.[88] You got to read his book, too." And there it was, *Bound for Glory*. And the songs Jim Dandy played were like keys to other doors that led to other countries or other selves. It was strange music that carried with it the call of another life. You could listen to his songs and learn how to live. Bobby knew these songs contained some truth, the truth of being, that lasts from birth to death, even past death. Jim Dandy said the truth would be plain to everyone, if only the songs were sung the way they were meant to be sung, and heard the way they were meant to be heard. Then he handed Bobby a small polished stone. "Cornell meant for you to have this. It's a thunder-stone, came down in the last storm. It carries power within it."

"What kind of power?"

"Keep it, you'll see. It will help you hear, as well."

As Bobby pocketed the stone like a lucky coin, Dandy played a Robert Johnson record. A passion lifted the song with a yearning so fierce that it was hard to listen to.

But then, he could conjure visions of heaven, a bountiful earth, women. A pretty dancing girl, conjured into being. She began to shout, move her hips, smile at him through lascivious eyes. The room going warm, red, and pulsing with a jungle beat.

Outside on the Iron Range, nothing but wind.

Next day, they went back to see the bluesman, but his door was wide open and he was gone. And the pretty dancing girl could not be found. So they watched the sun rise over that little Minnesota town.

* * *

Bobby saw *Rebel Without a Cause* at the Hibbing theatre during a blizzard. The rightly cold weather equalized everything, he had to wear layers of clothes, even sleep in his clothes that night. Couldn't see through the storm, couldn't feel anything, couldn't even be a rebel in that cold.

Not long after, Bobby saw Buddy Holly at the Duluth National Guard Armory. With the royalties still withheld and the rent due, Buddy had been forced to go back on the road with a pickup band to replace the estranged Crickets back in Lubbock.

In the front row, Bobby was catching every move Buddy made, watching him sweat. He caught that hiccup Buddy picked up from Elvis to break up certain words.[89] Bobby sang along, imitating Holly's sweet, naive, almost childlike voice, awed by the finger-style flamenco guitar picking that Holly had picked up in New York, and how Buddy used it to charm folks out here in the heartland. At a certain moment Buddy moved on stage to a position where the stage lighting made a halo appear around his head, and at that moment Bobby saw Buddy looking right at him, right into his eyes, and playing for him. Bobby had the unmistakeable feeling that a torch was being passed from Buddy to himself.

And so it was. Cornell Woodrow had gathered the Crickets and were on their way to meet them, but they kept Buddy in the dark about it, to make it a surprise for them to join him onstage. But it wasn't to be. Two days after Duluth, Buddy Holly died in a plane crash. In Fargo, the concert manager desperately searched for a fill-in act for Holly. He found the Velline brothers, calling themselves the Shadows, in nearby Moosehead, Minnesota. Led by Bobby Velline, who had shortened his name to Bobby Vee, the Shadows needed a piano player, and someone suggested Bobby Zimmerman, the part-time busboy at the Red Apple Café in Fargo, whose band had just left him. Bobby Vee thought he played fine, even a bit like Jerry Lee Lewis, as long as the band stayed in the key of C. They played two gigs in Fargo and cut four sides for the Soma label in Minneapolis, including "Suzy Baby",[90] a minor hit in the midwest. But the band couldn't afford the extra member. Bobby came home one night in the rain on a bus from Fargo, and told no one that his first professional chance had failed.

Afterwards, Bobby Zimmerman traded in his electric guitar for an acoustic, and decided to go on a musical expedition, to immerse himself in these records, especially Guthrie's, which were as rare as hen's teeth out there in the midwest. The photograph on one record showed a gleam in Guthrie's eyes, something that said "I know something you don't know." And so he pocketed his dog-eared copy of *Bound for Glory*[91] and escaped from Hibbing, and from the stultifying business of rock and roll. But he was not truly committed to this Woody Guthrie ramblin' persona. An artist has got to be careful, he thought, not to arrive at a place where he thinks he's at somewhere. Got to realize that you are constantly in the state of becoming. As long as you stay in that realm, you'll be alright. As long as you don't have a past. Nothing matters except what you are doing now.

Talent Grew Wild

Talent grew wild in the American backcountry. Herbert used to say this to her as he packed his Studebaker in the clandestine years after the war, heading off from Margate on the southern coast of New Jersey to parts unknown, with Freddie. And if they didn't find it right away, someone named Alan Lomax would beat them to it. Sure. There's always a reason. She knew all about husbands who could not stay home and be a parent to children, who could never resist the call of the wild.

The last trip wasn't announced as such. It was just another trip, as far as she knew at the time. She had been standing in her perpetual position at the stove, with apron on and her wispy brown hair tied back into a bun, all prim and proper. Freddie, before heading out to jump into Herbert's Studebaker, had whispered to her about pursuers, gray-haired men in black overcoats, and had even told her not to answer the door for a week, an entire week of nervous anticipation. Freddie had returned quietly, without telling her, to a job at the local radio station. She found out when she heard his voice on the radio. Herbert did not return. And nothing else happened.

Until now. Beatrice quietly moaned at the news. Suicide had been ruled out. Freddie Falloni had been executed gangland-style, according to the police. The newscast flashed photos of Freddie working the dials at the radio station and announcing acts on the stage at Steel Pier. Here were photos from his past, including one with labor leader James Caesar "Prexy" Petrillo, president of the American Federation of Musicians, taken in New Orleans about a month before the infamous recording ban of 1942. In a bit of news editing that would make a textbook case of "guilt by pronunciation," the network followed mention of Petrillo with the report that Falloni had ties to organized crime, keeping the photo of Falloni and Petrillo front and center.

This bit of editing made Beatrice gasp.

As she recalled it, Freddie had fought Petrillo's union strike and recording ban, to no avail. He had complained that the ban would put radio in a bind and keep extraordinary musicians out of the studios. After the ban went into effect, he laughed about the unintended results. Singers were exempt, so the small record labels began recording *a cappella* singing groups that scat-sung an all-new repertoire of nonsense syllables like "dit dit doo wop" and "sh-boom".[92] Herbert had to laugh at the Corporation's embarrassed engineers who failed to decipher them.

Ballrooms, supper clubs, and the larger dance halls all darkened, but tiny nightclubs sprung up in their wake, in New York, Chicago, Los Angeles, and even outside of Atlantic City. Scab musicians avoiding the union-controlled venues started to play a vexing new jumping style of blues that she liked very much. All that was needed was a small combo; typically piano, bass, drums and perhaps a saxophone. She'd get together with other abandoned wives and dance up a storm at Tony Mart's, where Dizzy Gillespie and Charlie Parker were hiding from the union watchdogs.

After the war, it may have been their first trip, Herbert and Freddie came upon a fledgling mulatto singer and guitarist in one of those tiny clubs, soft-spoken in manner but absolutely crazy on stage. Called himself the Jackal. Freddie told her how he had played this singer a special recording, and the effect was as if he'd unleashed a genie. Now the Jackal was in town, and Freddie…

"What is it mom?" Her chubby, golden-haired 12-year old son interrupted her reverie with eyes wide and astounded.

"Your father knew him," she sobbed, breaking the silence she had maintained over the years about Herbert. "They were friends at one time."

"You mean the radio guy, a-and my dad?" Gilbert jumped for joy at any mention of the father he assumed would come home someday, from his work.

"Yes, they worked together." She paused. "He must be devastated by this."

"When's he coming home? It's been years! I'm not even sure I'd recognize him."

"You'll recognize him." But it was only a soft scolding. She knew better than to deflate her son's optimism. In any case, Herbert, if she ever encountered him again, would look the same. He'd always worn a three-piece suit and tie, creased trousers he could never really relax in, fedora right off the head of Humphrey Bogart in *The Maltese Falcon*.

So Herbert and Freddie would go off into the bush and hill country of southern Mississippi or someplace, searching for a maker of authentic pan pipes, or a blind kid who could play two harmonicas at once. Searching for whatever they called it, that juvenile term, *mojo,* using Robert Johnson's life and lyrics as their guide.

Once they brought back a maniac they'd found in a medicine show in the deep South, a white drifter and hillbilly who called himself Harmonica Frank.[93] The man could chew on his harmonica in one side of his mouth to play it while singing and playing guitar. The kids loved him, especially Gilbert. He could also flirt like the devil when Herbert wasn't looking, cupping her rear as she brought a second helping of pancakes. After helping Frank get a short-term gig on the Boardwalk, they took him back down south, to Sam Phillips at the fledgling Memphis Recording Service, who had recorded black musicians. Sam was known in distributor circles to be restless, always looking for something different in music. She remembered that trip because Herbert returned all excited about a piano player they found in New Orleans, a black man with the silly name of Professor Longhair.

Herbert's obsession about the power of music, the ancient tuning scales and how their pitch frequencies affected our bodies and minds, were beyond her understanding. He had walked out of her life, out of a house littered with children's toys, away from whatever had held them together: love, tradition, property, loyalty... to search for clues. She could picture him joining the ranks of alcoholics, inveterate gamblers and con artists, casualties of the poverty class, even the truly psychotic. Dangerous people in desperate circumstances.

He had walked out, with her betrayal of him to Cravingston unresolved.

Freddie had kept her informed. He was still occasionally in contact with Herbert, and he promised her that Herbert would surface one day and forgive her this one mistake. The clues he found would redeem him as well. But now Freddie's dead, likely killed by the same people who were after Herbert. Last word from Freddie, several months previously, placed Herbert in a summer cottage in a seaside resort town, the original Margate, in the Thanet district of East Kent, England. Margate, of course. It demonstrated Herbert's sense of humor about coincidences, and how he assumed his pursuers would never make the connection. There would always be pursuers for people like him, he would say with a twinkle in his eye.

How she had loved his masculine confidence in the face of the unknown! But his appetite for conspiracies would never be satiated by a simple conspiracy of two people in love, or even three or four, as Reggie and then Gilbert joined them. Was it all too much for him, was it because he no longer occupied the center of attention?

No, it was never that simple. He wanted children as badly as she did, wanted them badly enough to go AWOL, an Army officer deeply in love with a Liverpool gal skipping past the exploding bombs of the London raids in early 1944, and escape to neutral Ireland just one day before the British suspended all travel to the Irish Republic. Reggie had been conceived in a warehouse on the Liverpool docks hours before the journey. Over the nine months of peace in the Irish countryside Herbert read, to the unborn child in her growing womb, passages from Plato, Aristotle, Hegel, Locke, Hobbes, Marx, and Engels. He explained that he was training the fetus to accept a completely Western way of life, to survive. He would rail on about how the War in Europe was just a civil war among factions of the Corporation, as he called it, a battle over the Corporation's tactics of ethnic cleansing, a correction to squelch a particularly dangerous faction known as Fascism, and so forth.

Nothing she really understood, except that toward the end of their stay in Dalkey, she sensed a secret collaboration behind the scenes, an unmentioned agreement among neighbors to keep an eye on them, rifle through their garbage, make notes about their grocery purchases.

By the time the infant Reginald was ready for travel, the erstwhile family had packed up and gone to America under assumed names: Herbert Mesh transformed in a forged passport to Herbert Mention, discreet Englishman. They kicked around New York for a spell, visited Atlantic City, and found this peaceful beach community where Herbert could quietly resume the research the war had interrupted.

Postwar America held many opportunities for postwar Army officers, but not for Herbert, whose AWOL identity changed to MIA status as his former employers wrote off the dead or missing. As Herbert Mention, he had no past; the war had cleansed him of it. But he never relaxed. While she welcomed the anticlimactic adjustment to peacetime and a family life enhanced by washing machines, supermarkets, and television, he suited up for an ambiguous challenge, packed a suitcase of records and field recording equipment, and drove off on research that would keep him away for weeks.

Will Cravingston showed up while Herbert was away. They were colleagues, or had been. She had met Will before, in London during the war. He was looking for Herbert, and all he needed was a look at Herbert's notes. He said he would be generous, and she needed the connection, any connection, to whatever Herbert was doing. Later, Herbert called from somewhere, and she told him about Cravingston. At first he was angry, then distant and incommunicative, and finally, gone.

Life progressed and children grew up. Her bank account accumulated deposits from sources she never questioned, assuming it was either Cravingston's generosity or her gone husband's guilt. But now, there'd be no more word from Freddie. Would the deposits also stop?

She watched her son now, escaping into the embalming light of the television tube. The newscast ended with a medley of rock 'n' roll songs, a bit heavy on the Bill Haley and His Comets stuff that Freddie had promoted back in the day, and it brought a scowl to her face; she involuntarily crossed her arms and held herself tight. Gilbert rocked to the music. She gave him a thin-lipped smile and retired to her bedroom to light her candles.

The ritual every night, when Reggie and Gilbert were asleep, and repeated twice in church every Sunday, included a prayer as she lit ten candles: two each for Herbert, Freddie, Reggie, and Gilbert, and one for herself, and one for Christ. At night she sat by the window in her closed bedroom kneading her apron, crying into an imaginary rain the feelings she kept suppressed all other times.

* * *

Dreaming, with one hand on his penis and the other gripping the headboard, Gilbert Mention wallows in a passion left over from an afternoon of peeking up at bikini bottoms on the beach — globes of jiggling flesh, mysterious darker spots, wrinkles of cellulite and wisps of pubic hair — all memorized so that he could play it all back in his head. Except that his Catholic guilt comes crashing down, and he feels the heart-pounding anxiety of being late. If he doesn't make it on time, he won't be allowed to turn thirteen.

Sister Mary Deirdre, a Sister of Mercy, guards the locker room exit. His future is out there. They can't decide, his mother, the nuns, perhaps even his father somewhere out there, they can't decide where to send him, whether to Reggie's prep school, or somewhere else... or make him stay right here. In this hall of mysteries, in this locker room of shame.

Sister Deirdre looks up at him, stops her prayers, drops her rosary to the floor, and looks away, toward Charlie Flaherty, who is horsing around with the other half-naked boys behind him, shooting towels at each other. Charlie's penis dangles out through the slot of his jockey briefs. Gilbert moves forward to join them, but immediately recoils. Charlie smells like a disease, his body odor precedes him like a wave of bad kelp. Charlie already dated girls. How could any girl tolerate that smell? Sister Deirdre kneels before Charlie, eyes darting back at Gilbert, whose penis begins again to harden...

With a squeaking cry the nun takes off. Gilbert hesitantly follows, up the mysterious winding staircase behind the cafeteria that students are not allowed to use. It ascends to the convent's cloistered living quarters. He creeps further up to peek across shoulder-high cubicles. He sees the nuns denuded from their habits, revealing their pearly white, grey, blonde, and brown close-cropped haircuts, some nearly bald. One hears him, or somehow senses him, and with a wry smile walks sideways, crab-like, as if hiding something behind her back, toward the far end of the room.

Gilbert tumbles backwards down the stairway, bouncing off its railings. He lands outside, in the street in front of Mad Records on Keystone Avenue, a block from the Boardwalk. He quickly scrambles inside the record shop. He can hide there until dark, relieved by the smell of shellac from the old 78-rpm record bins in the back mixed with the odor of vinyl from the 45s arranged in the front, a mixture that reminds him of when he was five or six, watching a man he thinks is his father, standing quietly in a dark room staring out a window.

Dream scenes jump quickly. Gilbert emerges from the store into a twilight street, static fills the air like snow flurries. He has records under his arm. Did he pay for them? Aunt Mary will scold him, she thinks the records are obscene. Aunt Mary and his mother loom together, arm-in-arm, in the shadows across the street, at the entrance to a granite Church with gargoyles across its arches and twisting spires that spike the sky. Where to run? The record shop has turned into a salt-water taffy store, all done up in red and white stripes. The street glistens with a light rain, and no direction seems to make any sense.

Rocks begin to fall out of the sky. A huge rock lands just a few feet in front of him. Out come the derelicts and drunkards to surround the rock and cry their prayers to it. Gilbert remembers this from the Gilgamesh story he'd read in class. My namesake, Gil. In Gil's dream, rocks fall from the sky, and Gil befriends a wild man of the forest who teaches him the meaning of life.

So where is the wild man? Gilbert whirls around and thinks, where is Johnny B? He looks at the rock, and the beggars trying to lift it. A secret is supposed to be underneath it, and if he can learn this secret, he might become powerful, and his father might come back to him. But even as he shoves beggars away from a corner of the rock and tries to lift it, he knows he can't. Is this some stupid Arthur and the sword thing?

Out of nowhere, his mother glides across the street to him, carrying a glowing Jesus statue with a bright red and pulsing sacred heart in the statue's chest. "A man of great force and strength will come," she says softly with a voice that pours honey through his body. She takes him back across the street to a door, and leaning against the door is an electric bass guitar. Does she want me to pick this up? I can't play this. No, she motions away from it. "He will help you, and you will help him." How could his mother know about an electric bass guitar? She hands Gilbert a harmonica. Is this a joke? A joke instrument. He puts it to his lips…

Gilbert slowly became aware that he was awake, and heard the sound of life, normal life, coming from the kitchen. His older brother Reggie had already made it down to breakfast first. He heard Reggie talking to his mother. Damn! He had wanted to get down their first, but not in his pajamas. Now it was too late, his heart was still pounding. Boy's dreams are supposed to be like the Beave's in *Leave it to Beaver*, and Reggie is supposed to be like Wally, willing to listen, sympathetic even. It's supposed to be alright to be scared after a dream that big, that deep…

Right Wally?

Golly, Beave, I don't know, why don't you ask dad?

Well, where is dad?

Gee, Beave, I don't know. Now quit botherin' me.

* * *

Oatmeal, pancakes, country scrapple and smoked bacon from the Pennsylvania Dutch country, Taylor pork roll from Trenton, and chipped creamed beef. These were the primary reasons why Johnny B dropped by the Mention household many a weekend morning, leaving his bike in the garage and walking over.

"Yo, Bert," Johnny B nodded as he came in, sheepishly dragging his feet across the kitchen, all his swagger deposited outside the front door. Johnny liked having a fan, even one so annoying as Gilbert.

Johnny's arrival was always an event for Gilbert, though Johnny was Reggie's friend. When Johnny called him "Bert," Gilbert felt older, and capable of ignoring Reggie's pejorative "Gilby" and other put-downs.

"Siddown, buddy." Reggie, in white bucks, chinos, and a button-down shirt open at the collar collegiate-style, turned cool in Johnny's presence, more worldly and experienced than usual. Gilbert noted the change and prepared for his older brother's onslaught of sarcasm. "Get a load a Gilby over here, wants to go see Ricky Nelson[94] at Steel Pier this weekend. Hey, *Gilby*, gonna go in your *PJs?* Poor little fool! Uh-huh!"

"Don't start up again," mother Beatrice Mention warned in a guttural groan as she ladled the chipped beef onto toast, then switched to sweetness and light. "Johnny, how's your father?"

"Just fine, m'am." Johnny never ventured any more than that. He didn't think Mrs. Mention had ever met his father. And of course, no one talked about Johnny's mother. There was no proper ground for the two dismembered families to meet as one, to fill the void of the missing *mama* Balzano and *pater* Mention. While Johnny was out at night running his father's errands, the Mentions were slouched in front of the television, like most people, with the gray shades of *Ozzie and Harriet, Leave it to Beaver,* and *Father Knows Best* on one side of the tube, and the color of reality on the other.

It was easy, then, to tell the difference. The Mentions, in color, matched the Nelsons — Ozzie, Harriet, David, and Ricky — in black and white. Except that Herbert Mention, the Ozzie character, was long gone, a voice of reason now silent and hypothetical. He left behind the stone statue of Beatrice at the stove in her perfect bubble coif and apron wrapped around a flower print dress that fell below her knees. Beatrice could invoke paternal wisdom as vividly as if the mythical father had just left the room and it was now up to her to enforce the rules. To Johnny, who could not remember his own mother, Beatrice was a more powerful dose of TV-style motherly love than even the Harriet model, baking pies and making breakfasts and calling everyone to the table but with a louder, much shriller voice.

"Ricky Nelson's better'n Elvis!" Gilbert raged at his brother. "Ricky's so cool he could even dress up like Elvis for Halloween."

"Gilbert, stop shouting," commanded Beatrice from the frying pan.

"A-and when Ricky's date heard an Elvis song on the radio, and she liked it so much, Ricky decided right then and there to record his own song!"

"Shut up Gilby," Reggie kicked his leg under the table.

"They all laughed," Gilbert sputtered, "all his buddies and even David laughed, even Ozzie laughed, his own dad didn't believe him. But Ricky went right into the studio and came out with a hit. 'I'm Walkin','[95] yes indeed and I'm talkin'!'"

"Ricky Nelson's a fake," snickered Reggie. "That whole show is a fake, he doesn't sing for real, they got his record on and he's just moving his lips."

"No he's not! Ricky sings great, he's bigger'n Elvis. He's not a fake."

"They call it *lip-syncing,* you fool, he's singing to his own record. And what does Ozzie do for a living? How come he's always home? Poor little fool."

That stumped Gilbert. Ozzie always wore a sweater, never a business suit, and he was always home. Dads are supposed to go to work, and moms are supposed to stay home and take care of the kids. But my Dad's always at work. And I'm hoping, as Ricky sings in the song, that he'll come back to me.

* * *

They adjourned to the Mention family garage where Johnny had left his stand-up bass leaning against the wall of gardening implements. Reggie cradled his Gibson acoustic guitar, bought with savings from selling hula-hoops on the beach the previous summer. Gilbert had picked up several harmonicas in different keys at the Mad Records shop. He had seen Delbert McClinton playing harmonica on Bruce Channel's "Hey! Baby"[96] on American Bandstand, and was determined to prove himself to Johnny, going as far as to imitate Harmonica Frank, the Boardwalk Hobo, playing the harmonica sideways in his mouth and singing at the same time. The harmonica got all saliva-yucky, but eventually Gilbert learned to play something. Reggie, ever the commanding older brother, let him practice with them as long as he played softly in the far corner facing the wall.

Wildwood Scotty couldn't make it, which suited Reggie fine. Scotty favored rockabilly, which was just too hard for them to get right. Johnny had brought Scotty in, and now Johnny was out on some other planet with his rhythm and blues. Reggie preferred the sea shanties and bad whiskey folk songs of the college circuit. Reggie strummed the Kingston Trio arrangement of "Worried Man"[97] and started singing the chorus as Johnny took up the bass. It takes a worried man to sing a worried song.

With a smirk, Johnny put the bass notes exactly where they belonged. He was a master of rhythm that could make folk music swing. After a while, with Gilbert tootling harmonica notes in the far corner, Johnny warmed up and began to improvise verses over Reggie's strumming.

Reggie's huggin' porcelain, barfing up last night's brew,
Bertie's on the kitchen floor tangled up in glue,
Well I'm here in the bedroom, goin' down on flat-foot Sue,

Frowning, Reggie joined in harmony for the last line:

We're worried now, but we won't be worried long!

Another chorus and more strumming as they let Gilbert falter through a harmonica riff. Reggie frowned at Gilbert and smirked at Johnny. At least the kid's in the right key. Johnny smirked back as if to say, fuck you and watch this. He thumped a quick blues walk-down to bring it home to the chorus. After the chorus, with a mean look in his eye, he took Reggie to task with another set of lyrics, the third line in stop time.

Yo, Gilbert wants to learn about the dad he never knew
Brother Reggie, sure is edgy, wonder what he'll do
And Johnny's got no mama, oh... lord... I'm... feelin'... blue!

Gilbert and Reggie joined in, first in stop time, then in exuberant time:

We're... worried... now...
But we won't be worried long!

This time Reggie added syncopation to the repeating chorus:

It takes a worried, worried man to sing a worried, worried song...

And Johnny surprised him with a double-time walk-down, suggesting a backbeat. Sure enough, it was rock and roll as they wound up the song.

Reggie was not happy. "You can't do shit like that. Not at a gig anyway."

Johnny glared at him. "Like we even have a gig."

"That's not the point," Reggie was serious. "People don't want to hear that, they want to be entertained." And he launched into the current folk hit "Tom Dooley"[98] about a man who stabbed his girl up on the mountain and was about to hang for it.

"Oh boy, you're bound to die. Nice, let's all go to a hanging."

"Johnny," Reggie replied sternly. "It's a good song. Easy to play."

"So are Chuck Berry songs. 'You Can't Catch Me'."

"I'm tired of Chuck Berry. Everybody does Chuck Berry."

"Let's do Ricky Nelson!" Gilbert shouted from the corner. The mock argument between Reggie and Johnny had given Gilbert legs. "Let's do 'Walkin'."

"We need a piano for that," was Reggie's smart-aleck response.

"No, we can do it, Reggie, stop being so literal," Johnny snapped, then caught himself, puzzled at his own outburst. "Let's try for a groove somewhere between Fats Domino and Ricky. Bert, you sing it."

Once again Johnny had called him Bert, and once again Reggie had called him a poor little fool, but Gilbert put his gut into singing "I'm Walkin'", half-expecting his father to walk in the door to catch his finest moment.

* * *

151

Low waves from a peaceful Atlantic lapped the sands in front of Lucy the Elephant. Overweight families, pale-white and squeezed like albino sausages into their bathing suits, crowded around Lucy's legs and up and down the beach. The few local residents stood out as tan, rested, and ready for vigorous action, some volleyball or body surfing. The lifeguards were bronzed, buffed and bored.

Reggie and Gilbert trundled down to the beach in the newest fashion, Hawaiian shorts, with their oversized beginner surfboards. Johnny watched from the steps, slapping his thighs in time to the music in his head, Duane Eddy's "Cannonball"[99], and keeping an eye on the locked door of the maintenance closet in Lucy's hindquarters. Eyes wide open in mid-stare and frozen for decades, Lucy dominated the misty beach with her hulk, displacing a massive amount of space and air, but in a way that was completely unnoticed.

Johnny's watchful gaze did not go unnoticed by a group of local cheerleaders from his high school, blushing and posing in the latest fashion, the two-piece *bikini*, popularized first by Brigitte Bardot in *And God Created Woman,* and named after the atomic test site in the Pacific, Bikini Atoll, vaporized into no Bikini at all in 1946. They gossiped in anxious, conspiratorial tones. Johnny remained aloof in his street clothes, too cool to look directly at them, too hip to join them. He worked it, the long tall strong dark-haired brown-eyed biker, not yet 16 but going on 25, worked it up and down his body by tensing and releasing various muscles. He would never join the athletes, never pit his coolness against their sweaty enthusiasm. His right hand shielded his eyes as he looked out at suburban surfers in mock salute.

Maxine, the one with a doomed Jayne Mansfield look, blonde, blue-eyed, sweet sixteen, waved to Johnny. He'd spent a few hours working his charms on her in history class, after basketball, and right before a school band session (and though he stood in the back of the stage, on stand-up bass, she kept waving at him, embarrassing him). To be cool, one had to acknowledge her only casually, as one might notice a chrome-plated Harley. Hip, on the other hand, was about getting laid. Balancing the attitude with the ambition, he beckoned her over for a conference. The girls twittered, and he glanced once more at the maintenance door in Lucy's hindquarters before pausing, leaning his head back, taking a wild sniff of the mid-afternoon's hot breezy decadence that was sure to set off more girlish twittering, and descending the wooden stairs toward the street. Maxine followed several steps behind.

With Mama Roux off to visit kin for the afternoon, the house was his. The Wurlitzer jukebox in the Balzano living room shook the house with the thumping bass notes of "Gee"[100] by the Crows, the original version. This was the very same jukebox that had once graced the bar of the CR Club in Philly. Johnny's father had taken him and Reggie, still in elementary school shorts and white sox, to an early afternoon dinner at the CR Club before a show. They were served slabs of filet mignon that, despite their protests, were cut up by the waiter into cubes. Elvis Presley, that night's entertainment, stopped by to say hello and talk about his deep gratitude for his fans. One day his father brought the jukebox home, and it was like Elvis again, right in his living room.

A striking ray of sunshine peeked through the bay window and settled on the delta of Maxine's bikini bottom. The grunting lyrics, "duh duh de duh" moving up the scale, mapped to a part of her brain that remembered caves in the deep earth, moisture and fungus, sweat and genital funk, a heady atmosphere of abandon. How she wanted to just dissolve into a puddle in his lap. She lay against Johnny, her nearly perfect ass in his lap, arms outstretched and head thrown back, lips parted, eyes closed, in the pose of an Empress.

This was what she really wanted: to tame him, bring him out of the wild of his youth and domesticate him, to be Delilah to his Samson. She wanted jewelry, furs, new shoes, a decade of glamor before settling down with kids. To live the rest of her life in a fur-lined cocoon, never in need or want. To make the boy into a man who would do her bidding. Her mother had explained these things one night in her bedroom when her father wasn't home. How to get a boy to devote his life to you. How to use sex to instill that insatiable desire. Maxine considered Johnny to be an inexperienced philanderer, a lover only in his mind. Always grinning, even when it makes no sense. This is how he flirts. "Give in to the grin." He interprets her every gesture, every sigh as a sign of romance. Like any boy, he misinterprets the most perfunctory blow job as a vow of devotion, a swallowing of his fealty with a pledge of allegiance and undying love. And then, she would have him.

Johnny had no idea it would be this easy, the music seemed to be doing all the work. His finger, illuminated by the light, gently separated the flesh at the top of her thigh from the seam of her bikini and probed a bit further, appearing as a dark shadow against the white polka-dots illuminated by the sun ray, stroking the fine hairs above her julie. The jukebox switched to "I Only Have Eyes For You"[101] by the Flamingos as he pulled down her bikini bottom and entered her from behind.

My love must be some kind of blind lust, I only have cock for you... He pushed slowly with the music and then deeper with the dramatic key change in the chorus, timing his thrusts to each note of the confident bass walk-down. The timing was mathematically precise and yet flowing easily, so easily that he could finesse the timing of his thrusts to coincide with the single piano note, constant through the song, over and over, the same note through all those changes, as constant as a fiercely beating heart. He was *working* it, working the music almost as much as the musicians playing it, and he could feel a power surging from his groin.

Maxine came to her senses, found herself bent over with her fabulous naked butt pressed against his stomach, her hands on his knees stabilizing her body for each thrust, and she could see underneath to his testicles squashed against the leather couch. "P-pull out, pull out, before you c-come," she murmured unconvincingly, nearly disturbing his momentum, but the roll and bounce of his balls with each thrust, perfectly timed with the rhythm of the music, cast her back into the swoon, and all she could sense were the song's nonsense syllables, *shlub-blub*, whatever it was, it sounded like sex, like the plumbing noises you make, in and out, *shlub-blub*, with a bass line descending into a heady oblivion, right back into that puddle. She fought the impulse to come, but came anyway, surrendering to another *shlub-blub*, surrendering again to the next with a tiny growl from her throat. In response to her call he responded, came all over in a hero's welcome, all gushes, crowds, ticker-tape...

As if on cue, the song ended. The intensity of the moment demanded a silent pause of contemplation of their awkwardly connected bodies.

Then, in a fit of pique the jukebox fought its own mechanism, clicking and clacking and stuttering. It seemed to have a mind of its own. In fact, the jukebox knew its own history, and the history of the records it held. It knew the lengthy path of corruption that this particular song had traveled to get into its stack. It "saw" the scars on the record label, the names of imaginary songwriters. It was a black man's country song written for white people, titled "Ida Red" but then retitled, to avoid copyright issues, after a brand of cosmetics.[102] The record company added extra songwriters to the royalty stream, including Alan Freed, the popular DJ who had promoted it, and a distributor who'd never heard it. So the jukebox hesitated. Perhaps it knew its owner's role, Johnny's father's role, in this process of stoking the hit-making machinery behind the popular song. Perhaps it resented its destiny as a monument to payola in the mobster's living room.

With a shrug or perhaps a kick from the spirit of Ballzo himself, the mechanism finally worked, but with one last angry gesture, the jukebox skipped the record at the raw guitar intro. "Ida Red", changed to "Maybellene", came roaring out stuttering at first and then solid, Chuck Berry never sounding better than on his first hit. *Why can't you be true?*

Johnny's right in there, in Chuck's V8 Ford, nothing can beat him, he's been chasing this girl in the Coupe de Ville all day. Just why, he can't say. It looks like Maybellene's standing still, I can still catch her at the top of the hill...

Maxine's scornful look brought Johnny back. She disconnected and got off him with a grunt, spilling juice across his bare legs.

"I'm sorry," was all he could say.

"You pig!" She wiped herself with her bikini bottom, exposing a bit of animal brown within the crack of her perfect white butt. "What do I do if I get pregnant?"

"I can arrange something," Johnny spoke soothingly, aroused again by the glimpse inside her butt crack. "The Bahamas, or Barbados. It's legal down there. You know what I mean."

"I know what you mean. That's just *so* romantic."

"That song was romantic, wasn't it?" Trying to calm her fears, he leaned forward to kiss her, but he caught a whiff of his own semen mixed with her body chemicals, hairspray and perfume, way too much perfume, and backed off.

"Romantic is Frankie Avalon. 'Venus say you will.' *That* was something else." Perplexed, she scratched her stomach, and her absent-mindedness made her appear almost ape-like.

Johnny could have caressed her tenderly at that moment, but something stopped him.

She noticed. "You're wrinkling your nose. Do I have on too much perfume?"

Johnny grimaced.

"You bastard." She swung her arm at his face, smacking against the side of his head as he ducked. A knock at the front door saved him, sending her scurrying naked to the den with her bikini top and bottom in her hands.

* * *

At the door was a black man, age indeterminate, all duded up in a three-piece suit, somber homburg, black shiny oxfords, and a black cane with a gold fish head at the top, right above the man's grip. Johnny could see a shiny-black hearse, a Cadillac Eldorado stretched to fit a coffin lengthwise, resting like the cloak of death at the curb, reflecting all of the remaining light of the suburban street. He looked east down the street to the darkening ocean, and then west up the street to a sunset that was wrapping up its weak medley of golden oldies and settling into bleak retirement in the bay. How long had this character been out here on the porch? Everyone on the block can see this hearse.

"Nice music you got on here." The black man smiled widely, flashing several gold molars and a gold front tooth embossed with the same fish-head icon.

"Nothing but the originals, none of that Pat Boone stuff, no covers," replied Johnny, pointing in the direction of the jukebox. To contradict him, the jukebox started spewing Elvis Presley's "Hound Dog".[103]

"What you talkin' 'bout? That's a cover right there. You got the original, the *race* record, as you folks call 'em? Big Mama, Willie Mae Thornton? She was a bull dyke, you know what that is? Like a man, she preferred women. And she wrote *that* song about a man."

Johnny shot back, "Peacock label, 1953. Of course we have it."[104]

The man deftly bounced his black cane and caught it with his elbow so that it rested on his arm. "Elvis heard it at the Sands hotel in Vegas. Only it was these white kids doin' it, and they messed up the lyrics."

"I know them. Freddie Bell and the Bellboys. Freddie Belo, *paisan* from Philly."

"That's right," said the man. "He's on Cameo, Bernie Lowe's label. But it was two white kids, Jewish kids, who wrote the original version. Leiber and Stoller. Those kids had it right. But this Philly boy took out the best line. 'You can wag your tail, but I ain't gonna feed you no more.' He changed it to something about chasing a *rabbit*."

"OK, well..." Another blues purist. Johnny looked at the hearse. "You here to see my dad?"

"No, I'm here to see *you*." The man smiled widely again and held out his hand. "Cornell Woodrow, at your service. You are Johnny Balzano, right? And you're looking for an electric bass guitar, am I right?"

The man said he'd been informed of Johnny's desire for an electric bass from the band teacher at the school. Johnny was immediately suspicious. Couldn't have been that teacher; she had threatened to kick him out of band class for playing boogie-woogie piano, that day when he lost the piano chair to an Irish kid from Absecon. Stand-up double bass was the only chair open, so his father pitched in with the jazz player's double-bass with the bullet hole. Ballzo would have bought him a hot-rod Chevy before getting him a detestable *electric* bass. Besides, Ballzo considered the stand-up with the bullet hole to be sacred. So Johnny took it on, and took it over. He learned Bill Black's slapping double-bass line on Elvis' "That's All Right" after only one listen. And that's what did it. It was not alright with the teacher, who made good on her promise to kick him out.

"I've got one in the car," Cornell Woodrow prodded him. "A Fender Precision. Used, but in excellent condition." Johnny flashed on this, the very bass played by Bill Black for the first time on "Jailhouse Rock". "Well, not actually used much. Just once," Cornell smiled, flashing his gold tooth, "on a record by the Jackal." He paused for effect. "You've heard of the Jackal?"

"I've heard of him."

"But you never *heard* him. Have you?"

Something new stirred on the jukebox. An Elmore James riff on a National Steel guitar, sliding up, all the way up, past what was reasonable. An electric bass started up the walk slowly and then brought it home to a hypnotizing fast rhythm, a Bo Diddley beat multiplied onto itself in syncopation. The song surged through the speakers, nonsense Little Richard-style syllables repeating "nummo, nummo, nummo..."

"The fuck is this?" Johnny postured, hand on hip.

Cornell just held up one finger to his lips, quiet, just listen. He went off to his hearse to get the Fender bass. As the man left, Johnny smelled fish, a whiff of tide from the ocean a block away. No, it seemed to be coming from inside. Could it be Maxine? As he entered the living room the song infected him and the scent knocked him out. He came around at the song's abrupt ending, an interval of three notes that suggested dire consequences. What the fuck just happened? He couldn't remember having heard the song.

So Johnny went over to the jukebox and pulled the plug. He wrestled it sideways and opened up the back to see the record that had caught him by surprise. The needle had just come off the Peacock label of "Hound Dog" by Big Mama Thornton. He searched through the jukebox's records.

"You won't find it there." Cornell Woodrow was back at the front door carrying a black travel case sized for an electric bass, the Jackal stenciled on one side, the fish head symbol on the other.

"How'd you *do* that?"

"Did you like it? The Jackal *has* somethin' don't he?"

"I don't know. How'd you *do* that?" But Johnny had a feeling the man wouldn't say. Something about this song goes too far. Johnny would remember this moment, years later when anarchy ruled his life; a moment of otherworldliness. This Jackal *had* something, didn't he? That bass part, or what he remembered of it: just incredible. Johnny looked down at the bass case.

Cornell Woodrow smiled at his rapture, and spoke lowly, in a chocolatey velvet voice. "This bass is important. It has power. You need to give it respect, play it well." The man's gold front tooth glowed suddenly a bit too brilliantly, given the angle of the sun behind him.

"What do you mean, power?"

Cornell belly-laughed and gestured toward the back of the house where Maxine had fled. His voice came back up to a normal level. "Looks like you got all the power you need!" And then he put on a fake Irish accent, strange for a black voice, and sang,

The lass I brought home was a prize,
With alluringly bright blue eyes.
Her bottom and breasts had passed the tests,
But her penis *was quite a surprise!*

Cornell belly-laughed again. Johnny was at a loss for words.

"Take this bass with you, learn how to play it," Cornell instructed. "But you got to go elsewhere to make something happen with it. It can't happen here. You're a musician, I can tell. Musicians have the *gift*.

"Now remember this. If a musician plays something, there's always another musician that knows what to play next. You plug right into it."

Johnny didn't know what the man was talking about, but he sure did want that bass. "What's the price?"

"It's yours. For a favor."

* * *

Frank "Ballzo" Balzano, living up to his ballsy moniker, moved swiftly to cut off a Dodge Valiant in the left lane while dodging an oncoming Ford Falcon blaring its annoyance, just to get ahead of them both and make his left turn. *His* left turn, into *his* street. Off Ventnor Avenue, the street of his dreams, with the ocean at one end and the bay at the other. Ventnor to the north was predominantly Italian, Margate predomi-nantly Jewish, and the two met along a straight border that included a stretch of stores that catered to both tastes. Jewish and Italian mothers were basically the same except for their accents, their places of worship, and their grocery lists. Jewish and Italian fathers were shrewd, practical men who knew the price of everything and liked the same vices; that's why Jewish mobsters and the Cosa Nostra got along so well. Ballzo's boss worked with Morris Levy. That's one reason why the South Jersey business had been all but handed to him. Another reason was this little side mission, a favor for Tony Just in New York, to keep an eye on a certain Margate household right on his street of dreams.

Ballzo's blue Cadillac Coupe de Ville, a roaring lion when it cruised up and down the commercial strip, hesitated and nearly choked a cycle when it passed the Eldorado hearse parked in front of his house. By the time he'd finessed the Coupe into the driveway and slammed its door, Cornell Woodrow had come out of the stately brick house with a look of finished business. A black man looked distinctly out of place in this community; this black man in particular looked out of this world.

Ballzo strolled up with his elbows out, all mean and lean like Sinatra, his hawk eyes scanning every which way before settling on the black man. "You Screamin' Jay Hawkins[105] or something? His uncle?"

"Mr. Balzano." He extended a deeply wrinkled black hand, which Ballzo did not accept. "Cornell Woodrow, at your service."

"Cornell. Woodrow. Heard the name. The Jackal's lawyer, right? Or undertaker?"

"Agent for his lawyer, Mr. Balzano," he spoke in an elegant but very deep voice.

"Listen, he can't break his contract," Ballzo declared as he slid his right hand inside his jacket to his wallet pocket and fingered the handle of his snub-nosed .38 armpit holster.

"I don't think that will be necessary," the black man replied smoothly, moving his hand behind and inside his jacket to the waistband at the small of his back. "I've brought your son a gift, a peace offering, if you will."

Ballzo noted that the black man held his ground, did not quaver, did not back down. Just smiled. Probably armed. "You tell your client if he breaks the contract we'll pave the street with his records, right out in front of Darby, we'll pave Race Street. We'll take all of 'em down there and put 'em under the steamroller. He's *nobody*. He's nothing if he don't play ball. You got that?"

"Yes boss," the black man growled with a smile, flashing his gold tooth.

"And you can forget about American Bandstand. We already got a replacement."

The black man did not smile at this. "Come to Tony Mart's tonight," he said in a dark, cryptic voice. "I *know* you know where it is." Hanging this challenge in the air like a target, he turned and strolled over to his hearse. Looking back at Ballzo, he smiled again. "Some people will be there tonight, you oughta meet."

"Let me tell you something," Ballzo barked, working up a steam, marching toward the hearse. "If the Jackal's got balls enough to come to this town and play, I can assure you he won't have balls when he leaves." On that last remark Ballzo pounded the hood.

The black man did not reply, just got into his hearse. Ballzo straightened up and lightened up; his point made, he could afford to be jocular. "You really are Screaming Jay's uncle, ain't ya? I seen that hearse before." Ballzo talked black the way Sinatra might have, joshing with Sammy Davis. "I heard your boy got himself locked in that coffin one time on stage, so scared he shit in his pants."

The black man smiled, looked away, put the hearse in gear, and drove off, saying and signifying nothing.

Johnny watched this standoff of pure evil from the living room through the picture window, two Stagger Lees from their respective cultures. Fats Domino[106] hit the jukebox as Maxine tromped in, back in bikini and ready to kill. Baby, Johnny thought, what are you going to do? I'm sick and tired…

"I thought you said your father wouldn't be here! Hey!"

Johnny paid no attention until she threw the James Dean pin at him, the one he'd given her back in history class, the covenant sealer, the current fetish. Girls went ape-shit over this stuff, she was even a member of the James Dean Society, worshipping the dead star nationwide with a magazine, a newsletter, and pages of certified authorized merchandise. What would James Dean say if he could, having lived and died for this? The pin sailed across the room, missing him by a mile.

* * *

"So what happened here?"

"Nothing." Johnny sheepishly looked over to the couch. He knew his father wouldn't be mad about Maxine, but he *would* be mad about that bass guitar hidden behind the couch.

"Didn't expect me home this early, right? Did I interrupt something?" His father was leering at him.

"No, nothing, forget it."

"So what did that guy bring you? He said he brought you something."

Johnny thought fast. "C-note. That's all." He pulled out the hundred dollar bill Big Dom had given him the night before. "Wanted me to bring my friends down to this show he's putting on, the Jackal, or whatever his name is."

Ballzo looked his son over very slowly, from head to toe and back again. "Don't go near that show. You hear me?"

"Yeah."

"You heard me, right?"

"Yeah I heard ya."

"OK, let's go. We got work to do. Bring an empty box, I got some more records you can have for the jukebox." Johnny would help his father move record boxes in a dimly lit warehouse in Camden, a city of devastating unemployment just across the Benjamin Franklin Bridge from downtown Philly. Johnny loved to spend time in the cool dark warehouse. It reeked of shellac, freshly stamped vinyl, and musty card-board, as if ten record stores had been compacted into this dank space.

That evening Johnny had to load a truck with boxes of records. Ballzo was on the phone to Darby Records, cursing someone out. "We'll see if he's got the balls," he said to the telephone. "There's this new kid from the same neighborhood, it turns out, he's over at Cameo, we call him Chubby Checker. Fats Domino, Chubby Checker, get it?" Johnny loaded the truck and waited for his father to finish by stretching out on a cot near the loading dock, immersed in the aroma emanating from a new shipment of records from the cutting plant.

In Johnny's dream a grease-slicked black man from the bush, hair sticking straight up as if electrified, appears naked in front of several large refrigerators, holding a turkey baster as if it were a microphone. He knows it's the Jackal, but the man's thick flaccid penis and prune-sized balls are chunked up with clay; his body is slowly turning into a statue. He can feel Lucy in the audience, Babbs somewhere backstage. Johnny's father appears next to him, toothpick bouncing on his lips, ever the Ballzo, counting worn dollar bills no longer green but some shade of tarnished copper. "Better move fast kid," he murmurs, tooth-pick bobbing, and Johnny realizes he's holding a revolver, a snub-nosed .38 Special. Black surfaces reflect the Jackal as a statue with flood lights trained on his naked, muscle-rippled body. "Too late," says his father.

And then he awoke, his father shaking him. "Too late for this shit, wake up!"

* * *

Dawn brought out his curiosity, and Johnny couldn't stay in bed. Some kind of gospel music[107] floated upstairs, out of the jukebox in the living room.

"You's up early," was Mama Roux's only comment when he stumbled into the kitchen. She was fixing her tea and humming along.

"What's this? John and a radiator." He didn't remember there being any gospel music in the jukebox.

"John the Revelator."

"Why they call him that? Which one is it, John the Baptist, or John of the Apocalypse?"

Mama Roux laughed. "Don't matter which one. Could be High John de Conquer."

"Who?"

But just then the music faded away. Mama Roux kept humming, and then singing softly, a verse without music, but Johnny could hear drumming in his head. Oh children run, she sang, here comes the Cunjah man, he'll work his trick and make you sick.

Just as she finished, the jukebox kicked on again. "Conjur Man"[108] by Memphis Minnie, one of Mama Roux's favorites.

Johnny sighed. "You're always trying to scare me with that boogie-man shit."

Mama Roux looked up sharply. "Watch your tongue."

"So how do you do that?" Johnny smirked. "How do you disappear so suddenly when someone's at the door? A-and then reappear when he's gone? What's the trick?"

Mama Roux softened, looked down, and couldn't stop that shit-eating grin from creeping across her face. Johnny warmed up to that feeling of being part of her family, maybe just like one of her grandkids. But then she straightened up and looked him in the eye. "You got to *concentrate*, that's all, concentrate." She said it like it was a new word, like in "concentrated orange juice" on the television commercial. Like it was a *white* word. "Just stop everything, and think. Think yourself *not there*. Can you do that? I don't believe so, you kids today. Don't have the time, you kids today, gotta go hop on your bike, go rushing off."

"What do you mean, 'stop everything'?"

"*You* knows it. You *do* it every time you sit down and listen to that jukebox, every time you play that guitar."

Johnny sat there quietly at the kitchen table, and tried to think himself *not* there. He felt like an idiot. Mama Roux finished her tea. "You *knows* it," she repeated, "but you should try listening and playing some *other* kinda music." And with an uncharacteristic belly laugh she got up to start her chores.

* * *

Reggie pressed his white chinos for his date with Lucy: miniature golf around the corner from Maggio's Seafood, where Reggie had made a reservation thinking, how ironic, a socialist in the guise of an entitled prep-school prince, making a reservation in a fancy restaurant.

Gilbert comes in, "Ohhh, I'm a getting all misty," a phrase borrowed from the bongo-beating beatnik Maynard G. Krebs on the hit TV show *The Many Loves of Dobie Gillis.*

"Get the fuck outta here."

"Johnny called, wants you and Lucy to meet him at Tony Mart's later tonight. Hey, how come you guys get to go there?"

"We go in back, Johnny's father lets us in. We can't go out in the club, we gotta stay in back. Johnny's got a buddy, gets us rum and Coke."

"So why can't I come?"

"'Cause you're a poor little fool. At least we look *almost* old enough."

Gilbert had no argument to that, so he fingered the condom on Reggie's bureau. "Think you'll get lucky tonight?"

"Shut the fuck up. That's just for emergencies."

"Oh yeah, like an emergency *fuck.*"

"Like you even know what you're talking about. Leave it alone."

Wrinkled and frayed at the edges, the condom had spent a lonely year in Reggie's wallet pressed flat in the seat of his pants. Reggie had no expectations of getting past first base with Lucy, but just in case he didn't want her to see this worn-out condom. She seemed way too intelligent to have sex on just a normal date. They had met in the library on a rainy summer day, in the music section where Reggie would read about music history and prehistoric musical instruments. Lucy had been wandering around, pondering the massive shelves of books but not taking one. Reggie imagined her to be one of the new beatniks he'd read about, obsessed with art and bebop, Kerouac and Ginsberg, like the sole Jewish kid at his school, Hammond Prep on the mainland, who wore a beret and was growing a faint goatee. He was not disappointed to find out that she was a classmate of Johnny's at the local Catholic high school. The popular kids at the Catholic schools were mostly jocks weaned on football, greasers destined to become car mechanics, and cheerleaders preparing to become the matrons of large families, but there were always exceptions, one or two weirdos neither Italian nor Irish, who would never fit in. Reggie's dialectic analysis put her in the same class as the downtrodden artists, the fringe element.

Awkward in his pressed chinos and shiny Oxfords, he took notice of her casual look of light blue capri pants and a pink wool sweater that did nothing to hide her bulky midsection and bulging rear end. They shook hands outside her door like hospital attendants in the midst of a crisis. Over miniature golf he talked musical theory, linking it to Emma Goldman's remark about not wanting a revolution unless you could dance to it. He talked about what was hip and what wasn't hip. She said being hip is a male obsession, like record-collecting, like keeping score at miniature golf.

He noted that she was winning. "It's man's quest for truth. We yearn for deliverance from chaos. You understand this."

"Ha. I do," she said impishly, maybe even bashfully, in almost a curtsy.

"Yes, and at the risk of sounding like a jerk, you're not like other... women," he stammered politely, though she was only a girl of sixteen. Maybe she would recognize how sophisticated he is. "They only see what's happening to *them*, day-by-day, they can't see what's going on outside their irrelevant lives."

"I know," she sighed. "The President comes on TV to warn us about the military-industrial complex. But they pay more attention to the hairspray commercial."

"Yes, the Bomb could suddenly turn us all to dust." Reggie looked conspiratorial. "And they'd be yakking and gabbing, about boys and prom dances."

"And we'd be..."

"We'd know about it. We'd be talking about it right before it hits."

"And that's a good thing?" She hit a hole-in-one through an obstacle that resembled a Venetian palace, shooting through the center canal.

"You'd rather not know. You think, 'what can we do about it.' Am I right?"

"Oh Reggie, you have no idea how 'irrelevant' this conversation is." She laughed her way to the next hole, a windmill affair with a middle-hole through the structure that led straight to a hole-in-one. Naturally, she got it in one.

"What you mean is — "

"What I mean, Reggie dear, is that people believe they can change things. They'd be willing to die, or kill, for their beliefs. The rest of us just die when the time comes. So what does it matter anyway? I just don't believe in anything."

She'd called him "dear". Reggie's confidence grew along with his penis. "I thought you were supposed to die for your beliefs. Like, you didn't need them confirmed, you just believed."

"Really." She faked a pout but couldn't help giggling.

His penis wilted. He started whining. "Being willing to die for your beliefs should make your life richer than it would ordinarily be, should give it a point that it wouldn't ordinarily have."

"Well put." She then grew thoughtful, as if rain clouds had formed above her. "Are musicians willing to die for music? Let me ask it a different way: does a musician fear death, not because it is death, but because there is still more interesting music to make?"

"We believe in... something." Reggie didn't want to represent all musicians everywhere, but he had to stand up for his art. "Why write songs you don't believe in? Why stand alone without beliefs?"

"It ain't about whether you believe in something, like God," she answered sensibly. "It's about whether you believe in yourself enough to put those songs *out* there, to stand up on a stage and *deliver* those songs to people."

Reggie thought, she's toying with me. She's placing miniature golf obstacles in my course, windmills, moats, drawbridges, castles with secret passages to her inner sanctum. "Do you believe in love?"

"I believe in fucking," she said, as a matter of fact.

Reggie smirked as if it were a joke.

"Let's do it right here," she cajoled, smiling warmly, freckles dancing on her brown skin. "You can have *my* hole-in-one. A miniature fuck for a miniature life." She shrugged, and gave her money-maker a shake.

But it all took Reggie by surprise, and he was speechless.

* * *

Johnny could tell right away from Lucy's manner that she had not been laid. Her eyes burned, her legs were splayed out on the seat. Her mouth managed to find the shape of a pout, an O, no matter what she said. Johnny's cock stirred from the memory of their times together, on weeknights when no one would see them; that mouth of hers on him, that burning look in her eyes.

Reggie is a complete idiot. How could he have failed?

All three shared the back seat of the blue Coupe de Ville as Johnny's father drove across the Ocean City causeway. The intense traffic streamed around the Somers Point Circle in a rousing cacophony of horns and shouts. Locals mixed with the Philly crowd in the parking lots of bars and nightclubs, dulled to a stupor from a day at the beach, many still in sandy bathing suits and tank tops. The sun had long ago taken a powder somewhere in the pine barrens to the west, leaving only streaks of pink party streamers in the sky.

In the 1920s the nickelodeon in the Bay Shores Cafe jumped with South Philly Italians and Germantown Jews doing the boogie-woogie and the jitterbug. World War II brought girls in gowns and soldiers in browns, swaying to the big band sounds of Tommy Dorsey, Benny Goodman and Glenn Miller, breaking out into the Lindy Hop, hands and feet flying. The rafters would shake and the dance floor seemed to tilt toward the bay. The floor had once extended out into the bay until the storm of 1944 swept it away, leaving only the pilings slurping in the muck, silently condemning nature in still waters. After the storm, local entrepreneur Tony Marotta opened Tony Mart's across the street, increasing the competition for music and energizing Bay Avenue into a popular entertainment strip that by this time included Steel's Ship Bar, the Under 21 Club and the Anchorage. When Bill Haley and the Comets and Conway Twitty played Tony Mart's, the Bay Shores countered with Rocco & the Saints, Frankie Avalon and Bobby Rydel. When the music stopped at 2 a.m. you could still make the scene at Dunes on Longport Boulevard, Ballzo's after-hours office, owned by a former bootlegger turned beer baron.

A boxy three-story white wooden structure with an added reddish-brown shingled roof entrance, Tony Mart's looked more like a lodge for Italian miners in northwestern Pennsylvania. You expected a pizza aroma and dark rooms with clear glasses of Frangelico. The marquee, a giant red sign stretched lengthwise along the roof, visible for miles, screamed TONY MART, with the words "FOLLOW THE ARROW TO" along the top and an arrow pointing down to the "T" like an apostrophe. You couldn't stop yourself from going in. The place held three stages, eight bars, two dance floors and a low ceiling, with wall to wall people, most of them dancing where they stood, drinks in hand.

Ronnie Hawkins, billing himself the King of Rockabilly, took the main stage with his ragtag group the Hawks, dark hillbillies in black suits with starched white shirts and thin black ties, pinched waists, skinny lapels, and pegged pants over pointy black boots. The band launched into the menacing hoodoo anthem "Who Do You Love"[109] accelerated by a chopped Bo Diddley beat on overdrive. Ronnie's screeches and howls erupted like a night train to disaster, and then he suddenly pulled a front flip, landing in a perfect split, then slipped into a vaudeville step known as the camel walk, moving while appearing to stand still.

Reggie poked Johnny. "Is that 'hoodoo y'love?'"

"I think it's '*who* do y'love' but I'm not sure. Look at that guy play!" Johnny pointed to the lead guitarist who was tearing stark chaotic rockabilly licks out of his Fender Telecaster and grimacing in agony with each note. If the drainpipe-thin drummer hadn't kept up his quirky, slipping-between-the-lines beat the song would have fallen apart, but that slipping beat just propelled it all further into madness. Hell, this is *more* than perfect, thought Johnny. This rock 'n' roll thing is way bigger than I thought.

Johnny, Reggie, and Lucy hid on the side of the stage behind a curtain. Johnny's father, at the front and center table with his crew, had made the arrangements and had even sent back Gretz beers. They set them on an empty drum case decorated with a sticker that said "The Jungle Bush Beaters, from Marvel, Arkansas."

Johnny fingered the bag of pills in his pocket. His father had given him a name and description of the contact, with instructions to hand over the pills and collect $200. He scanned the crowd from side-stage and caught sight of a shapely blonde woman at the corner of the bar. When she turned, he was surprised to see it was Babbs, her arm casually draped around a chubby fortyish man in a Hawaiian shirt and goofball shorts.

Johnny recalled what she'd told him that night, about her work. A whore sizes up a person in an instant, she had said. It's an advantage, in that swift business, to be quick about perceiving anything wrong, up front, as soon as possible. So it seemed to Johnny at the time that a whore like her could teach him this trick better than anyone else, even tell him things about himself that he simply wouldn't know any other way. He admired her, even in his anger. Whores have a clear picture of the stark facts. This guy in the Hawaiian shirt is either a fat Ozzie from the Philly suburbs with cash from the family cookie jar that he will soon spend entirely on her. Or he's a cop, local, state trooper off-duty, or even an FBI tail on one of the bosses meeting with his father. In which case, by the usual arrangements, the blow job would be on the house.

As Johnny silently seethed, Reggie fidgeted on the drum case and Lucy fixed her gaze on the musicians. The Hawks were a live jukebox of rockabilly, country, and electric rhythm and blues, looking for their own sound somewhere in the mix, the drummer pulling and pushing, expressing their weary and fatalistic sensibilities, blurring the edges. Lucy was engrossed, her right shoulder twitching to the beat, not dancing in a heavenly pose like other girls, but seriously analyzing the music.

Reggie stewed over the argument they'd had on the ride over. He had tried to explain the struggle between art and commerce, the good of artistic creation as compared to the evil of money and capitalism, the free artist as compared to the exploited. Artists that refused to work under the terms of the rip-off businessmen were never heard from again. There is no impact you can make on this world without dealing head-on with greed.

Lucy had wanted to shush him, but she also wanted dearly to help him with his music. "Reggie, dear, what you need is *mojo*."

"What's that? You sound like Maynard."

"My dear, *mojo*, got my mojo working, mojo in your hand, like that Muddy Waters song.[110] Makes me want to tear off my panties."

Reggie had been embarrassed, of course, while Johnny had snickered and Mr. Balzano drove them in silence.

Now side-stage, Reggie elbowed Lucy. "Does *he* have mojo?" Referring to Ronnie Hawkins, the Hawk himself, a windjammer of the worst sort, blow-harding his way from one song to the next. "Been ever'where, known ever'body, done ever'thing, rolled more jelly than Jelly Roll Morton, and folks, our next number's the one that took us from the hills and the stills and put us on the pills!" Hardly anyone paid the Hawk any mind at first, but the place started rockin' when his band kicked in.

"No, it's the drummer," she hissed over the roar.

"What, such a sloppy beat. And look how young he is. Looks like a dork."

"He's perfect," she hissed back, and blew the drummer a kiss.

Johnny came up behind Lucy close enough to let her feel his heat. She didn't even need to turn around to see who it was; she reached back with one hand, the back of her palm against her butt, her fingers lacing out to tease his package. Reggie shot Johnny his trademark look of wounded righteousness, eyes that pleaded, I know she's not mine, but why does she have to be yours? You have so many, it's like you can just snap your fingers...

* * *

A gloom had gathered around Ballzo's table, the gloom of a golden age dissolving, of a team lagging in the playoffs. They passed the ceremonial cognac around the table from one to the other, Big Dom to another equally large capo known as Vic the Dick; to an anxious *cugine* working for Vic; to a big earner named Giuseppe "Joey Tart" Tartini backed by his two young Turk bodyguards; to Randall Cheatem, the hard-on with a suitcase from Dewey, Cheatem & Howe, angling to be Ballzo's *consigliere*; then over to the invited guests, Manny Yunk, chief of Darby Records, and a tall white-haired man in his sixties, strong-boned, hearty for his age but thin, dressed dapper in a pin-stripe three-piece suit and "die if you touch them" two-tone shoes. They called him Tony Just. The man from New York.

The shop talk was about disc jockey Alan Freed's testimony in the star chamber, which according to Randall was a doomed effort. Another DJ, Dick Clark, had held up to hours of grilling and eventually charmed the committee with his aw-shucks manner. Clark was just following the rules of the game; he was a product of the industry's practices but certainly, *your honor*, certainly not the cause. Manny pointed out that Clark had cashed in his chips, and had divested his interests to include music publishing companies, record labels, and pressing plants, to show his good faith. Across the nation DJs were scrambling to sign affidavits disavowing payola.

"Respectability," laughed Big Dom. "This is the thing."

"That fucking Irish bastard, up in Boston," Ballzo puffed hard on his cigar.

"Tip O'Neill."

"Yeah, someone oughta tip *him*."

Well that sounded almost like an order to do a piece of work, but not quite. Big Dom looked to Vic for some guidance, but Vic wasn't too sure either. On the record, sanctioned by the *borgata*, or off the record, like Johnny Ace? Ballzo would have to be more specific, such as a time and a place, and that wasn't likely. O'Neill was a politician with legs. It was just a political move to make speeches against pop music, to sound the depths of this new issue to see if it held votes. O'Neill's targets were mostly the new vocal groups. What was that quote? "Not so much the devil's music but music for simpletons, foisted on the public by sleazy disc jockeys greased by payola." O'Neill was talking about them, the Philly and South Jersey crowd.

Tony Just removed his cigar in a pose copied from George Burns, leaned forward and took his time to lick his lips, and then spoke in a gravely voice with the hint of a Brooklyn accent. "My advice is to leave him be. We might find a use for him." And with the slightest hint of a smirk, he leaned back again out of the light, into the smoky air surrounding the table. Ballzo glared back at him but said nothing.

After a pause for this little mystery to soak in, Joey Tart got back to business. Ballzo needed to sign off on a merchandise deal for the Boardwalk stores. Colonel Tom Parker and H. G. Saperstein and Associates had worked up thirty different Elvis products for the Jersey shore: hats, T-shirts, black denim jeans, handkerchiefs, bobby sox, canvas sneakers, skirts, blouses, belts, purses, billfolds, wallets, charm bracelets, necklaces, magazines, gloves, mittens, stuffed dancing dolls, stationery, greeting cards, sweaters, statues, bookends, guitars, cologne, and even stuffed hound dogs.

"Elvis cologne?" Big Dom gave a hearty laugh. "That *cafone* don't even take baths."

"Hound dogs. Can you believe it? That sick fuck. You hear about that show in L.A. a few months ago?"

"Not now," Ballzo looked up from signing the papers, looking warily at Tony Just for any reaction.

But Joey Tart was unstoppable, he had a story by the tail and wouldn't let go. "Pulls out this stuffed dog, calls him Nipper. Got him from the record company, some kind of gift. Well he starts humping it! Right on stage!"

"Wha?"

"I mean *humping*, like he was ready to pull out the bacon. Singing 'Hound Dog' and humpin' a dog, the sick fuck. The place went wild. All this screaming and it wouldn't stop, they couldn't get the kids to leave at the end. Announcer comes out, sez 'Elvis has left the building.' Kept repeating it, 'Elvis has left the building.'"

"So that's where that 'left the building' thing started."

"I hear the Colonel wants to trademark it."

"So the cops show up the next night, see. They're ready to bust him. But Elvis is hip to it. When he pulls out Nipper, the place goes wild, but all he does is play around with it. Doesn't get it anywhere near his groin. Draws a halo around its head instead."

"What the fuck for?"

"Who the fuck cares? Shut the fuck up," Ballzo had had enough. "I'm trying to concentrate." Looking again at Tony Just to see the man's reaction, but can't make it out. Ballzo's pissed at something in the contract, pissed at his crew, pissed about Tony Just. Sent down here with cash from Morris Levy, rubbing his nose in it. And now he's pissed at the band. The lead singer, all he does is scream and snarl, and jump around like a nigger with a hotfoot. Who the fuck booked this act?

As if on cue, the owner of the club, Tony Marotta, showed up with a young girl on each arm. "My daughters!" He announced to everyone's amusement. "You guys doin' okay?"

"The fuck you got on here?" Balls pointed at the stage. "Stinkin' up the joint with this hillbilly shit."

"I got stuck tonight," yelled Marotta as the music swelled. "Billy Duke didn't show. Ronnie Hawkins is a good man, man of his word, he showed up on time.

Band's a little loose, that's all. Morris sent them down, they just packed 'em in last night down in Wildwood, drew almost as much as Sammy Davis."

Ballzo leaned into Tony Marrotta to whisper something.

"Naw, it was the bass player. Strung out, they had to sober him up. But hey, this is a good band, Morris signed them on Roulette, he thinks this guy could be the next Elvis. Down at the Rainbow they packed in twice as much as Frankie Laine."

Ballzo leaned in again to Marotta, again whispered something. The owner of Tony Mart's laughed nervously, taken aback by whatever it was, and gathered up his girls. Whatever Ballzo had said, Marotta didn't take it seriously, or took it seriously enough to want to drop it.

As Marotta moved on, a tall black man in a dark three-piece suit materialized out of nowhere. Black homburg in hand, and a black cane with a gold fish head at the top hooked to his arm, grinning up a storm, flashing gold molars and a gold front tooth embossed with a fish head. That golden grin was about all anyone could see from far away. Cornell Woodrow had stayed out of the light as he made his way through the vast club filled mostly with white folks, moving unnoticed, dressed too well to be a black family man on vacation, but well enough to pass as a maitre-d, a head waiter, or even a foreign diplomat.

That is until he grinned, and his menace glowed in gold.

He startled Ballzo. The others at the table switched to red alert. Cornell looked each member in the eye, going around the table, grinning madly, stopping his gaze at the empty chair. Tony Just had disappeared.

"Your friend seems to have vacated." Cornell spoke in a thick low grumble, and gestured with his homburg at the empty chair. "May I take a seat?"

"Suit yourself," said Ballzo. "But you must know, your kind is not wanted here."

Cornell spoke up, loudly for everyone to hear. "I have 'suited' myself, thank you. Heh heh." Grinning at everyone. "My kind, in fact my kin, which is the root of the word kind, you know? They've asked me to be here. Representing them. My kind. Heh heh heh. My name is Cornell Woodrow. They calls me 'Stackalee'."

Ballzo rolled his eyes, looked around the table as if to say, get a load of this. They all went off red alert, sighing, shuffling feet, moving about in their chairs, grabbing drinks or burning cigars. Cornell took the empty seat. For a moment there was no conversation, no more passing of the ritual cognac, only a settling in, as a quizzical waitress took Cornell's order. Kentucky bourbon, straight up.

Ballzo straightened up in his chair and turned his full attention on Cornell, pointing his cigar at him like a schoolteacher pointing with chalk. "You got some nerve, coming to this town. I hear you're still planning to go through with this thing, on the Boardwalk." He waved his cigar around the table. "We all think it's a bad idea. Everybody in this town is against it. Ricky Nelson's coming to Steel Pier, it's all set. You won't have an audience. They'll all be over at Steel

Pier." He pointed his cigar at Manny Yunk. "Even your record company's against it. That is, if you still have a record to put out." Ballzo smirked, glanced at the others and received appropriate reinforcement. "Your boy, the Jackal, right? Stupid name for a *schwartz*. Maybe he wants to reconsider, for the sake of his career."

"Heh heh. Mr. Balzano," Cornell stopped to sip his bourbon, "you know this is not Monopoly, and you don't own Boardwalk."

"You'd be surprised, sir," piped up Randall Cheatem, the mob lawyer. "Boardwalk, Park Place, Ventnor, Atlantic, Pacific, all the railroads, —"

"Even the jail," intoned Vic in monotone, looking daggers at Cornell.

"But it's always free parking, my friend, right?" quipped Ballzo. "So let's stop the bullshit. We tolerate your kind if you stay where you are."

"Heh heh, I love this country," Cornell snickered, gazing at each member of this round table. "People can say anything, do anything, risk everything, and still come back for more. You all heard that story about Charlie Parker?"

Ballzo shifted in his seat. Parker was an original hero. Ballzo cut his eye teeth in this business with bebop records. Charlie "Bird" Parker was the first to cut loose from the mainstream and make the break to the very edge of jazz, way out where Benny Goodman never dared to go, and that had appealed to the young Ballzo's rebellious instincts.

Cornell had their attention. "Parker, back in '48 at the Argyle in Chicago, had broken one of his own rules." He lowered his pitch to intone, voodoo style. "Never take Seconals and play chromatics."

Laughter all around, uneasiness abated.

"And on this winter night Bird was noddin' out on stage," Cornell continued, "playing out of key but not on purpose, playing the wrong tune, pissin' off Miles Davis and the rest of his band. Man, Parker was so far gone, he stumbled off the stage and took a piss in a phone booth, thinking it was a urinal."

"What the fuck," Ballzo remarked. More laughter.

"Heh heh, yes sir, the white man, owner of the bar, came out and fired his ass. Fired the whole band. Kicked 'em right out." Cornell paused.

"But then months later, Parker's on a roll, see, a dominant force in music, thanks in no small part to white folks, like you, running the music business. He comes back to the Argyle, back to that white man's bar, who's now grateful to have him back. Charlie Parker, man, you know what I mean? Blowin' the sweetest, the finest and most complex music that place had ever heard. Only this time he shuffled offstage and went straight to that phone booth on purpose and left his mark, zipping up on the way back to the stage with a smile on his face. Then he blew some more. Charlie Parker, *he's* my kind."

Silence. They didn't know what to make of it. Cornell just smiled back, eyes wide and the color of moonshine.

Ballzo cleared his throat. "Good story. Though I don't get the point."

"You know what I'm talking 'bout. You dump all that heroin in our black communities, get all those jazz musicians hooked, but you can't, you know. You can't stop the music."

The sudden quiet around the table coincided with the band going on break. Ballzo shot each of the round table members a glance that captured their attention. "So, you paid a little visit to my house yesterday. You talked to my son. What was that about?"

"Why don't you ask him?"

Instinctively Ballzo looked over at the side of the stage, to see if Johnny was there. Cornell followed his gaze. Ballzo caught him following it, and got up. "Let's take a walk."

* * *

The band came off the stage weary, bone tired. The drummer with the unlikely name of Levon Helm, still wearing sunglasses, stopped to impart some of that good 'ole southern charm on the teenagers. Levon's grin, a triangle of mischief taking up most of his face, seemed wider than that shock of dirty blonde hair plastered to his head with sweat. "Y'all come here for the music or the girls?"

"Both," giggled Lucy, moving in close. "I like his hairdo," referring to the spit-curl pompadour hanging down Ronnie Hawkins' forehead.

"Yeah, Ronnie calls it the Big Dick Look. C'mon back to the green room and meet the rest of the boys."

They all crowded into the tiny backstage room, chairs stashed against the walls and a table with a rancid deli platter in the center, gobs of food and beer bottles everywhere. No one could hardly move, all pressed against each other. Why is it called the green room? Reggie wanted to know. There's nothing green in here. No one volunteered an answer. Someone shouted more beer. The conversations ratcheted up a notch in sound and took up more space as people used their arms and hands to gesticulate, nudging and bouncing off each other. Ronnie Hawkins held court in one corner, sitting back-saddle on a folding chair, talking earnestly with a tall white-haired man in his seventies, dressed dapper in a pin-stripe three-piece suit and two-tone shoes.

Levon was face-to-face with Lucy, smacking his lips. "We've been up and down this Jersey shore, just barely makin' it. Yessiree, but we're happy to be here, leastways we don't get beat for the pay. Ronnie always told us, this is just hamburger money. Soon we'll be fartin' through silk."

Lucy couldn't get enough. "You really like it down here? What's it like on the road?"

"Waal, it sure is hard on the road, 'specially when your broke," Levon laid on that Southern accent thick. "Y'know we carry the Arkansas credit card, know what that is? Siphon, rubber hose, and a five-gallon gas can! Yessiree, sometimes during breaks when the crowd is gettin' their beer, we're outside stealing their gas."

"These are tough crowds you play too?" Reggie had squeezed in to get a word.

"Hell, son," Levon talked down to him, though he was only a few years older, and Reggie was taller, "Some of these roadhouses, you got to puke twice and show 'em your razor just to get in."

Someone nearby asked about records. "They didn't like us up in New York City. We played a tad too fast for them." Levon played that awe-shucks grin for all it was worth.

Johnny asked him about the guitar player.

"That's Jimmy Ray 'Luke' Paulman."

"How many first names this guy have?"

"Well I guess his momma couldn't decide," Levon chuckled. "Used to be with Conway Twitty, but Ronnie stole him."

"How 'bout the bass player?"

"Oh that's his brother George. He's having a bad night. Something wrong with his bass."

"How come he only got one first name?"

But Levon had been drawn away to another conversation about the upcoming weekend's concerts, Ricky Nelson's and this guy they call the Jackal. "Ricky's got Joe Osborn with 'em, and Jimmy Burton, man he's one hot guitar player." Yeah, but someone wanted to know about the Jackal. "I knows 'em," Levon said smartly. "We know his agent too, my man Cornell." This perked Johnny's ears. "He plays our kinda music. Don't know what that is, they don't have a name for it yet."

Cornell. Johnny looked over at George Paulman, the bass player, wiping off his Fender. Same model as the one Cornell Woodrow had given him yesterday.

Johnny sauntered over, tapped Paulman on the shoulder, and commenced to talking about bass guitars, eventually cajoling Paulman to hand it over and let him try it. Paulman shrugged, said something about not being able to hear it without the amp, but Johnny stood with bass in position. And something powerful came over him. His stature grew with each silent plucked note. The dull roar in the green room quieted down, and everyone turned to watch. The faint sound of thunder from outside punctuated the scene, all transfixed to watch the kid with the bass guitar.

Then, as Paulman winced, Johnny reached up and began to tune the Fender without a sound, as the electric bass was not plugged into anything. Paulman frowned, how could he even hear what he's doing? Now I'm gonna have to get back up on that fuckin' stage early, to tune it again.

All at once Lucy was beside Johnny. "It's just a tiny bit flat but I think I know what you're trying to get."

Johnny looked at her shining eyes. Lucy has absolute pitch, she can feel it like I can, and she's not even touching the strings. But I've heard her try to sing, she can't sing worth a damn, can't hold a note. How could she know?

Levon broke through the gathering. "You have a feel for it, don't ya?"

Johnny broke into a run on the bass in a quick tempo. Only Lucy, and now Levon, seemed to hear it.

"Y'all have a feel for it, that's for sure," Levon congratulated Johnny, patting him on the back. "and you got the Gift. The Gift of Time. Know what I'm talkin' about? Somebody plays somethin', and there's somebody else that knows what to play next, and you plug right into it."

Johnny'd heard this line before. Sure enough, the man himself, Cornell Woodrow, appeared in the doorway of the green room, holding his cane high, casting some kind of spell. The thunder outside seemed closer. Cornell moved closer, and the people parted for him to make his way inside the circle around Johnny, Lucy, and Levon.

"Ever seen talent like this before?"

"Why yes, Levon," Cornell replied, but stared at Johnny. "Boy I knew once could play a diddley bow. Know what that is?" He seemed to be asking Johnny. "That's one string nailed to the side of a barn. Only this boy, he stretched three strings across the side of a barn and played it as a guitar. Went on to be the greatest blues guitarist of his generation."

"You must be talkin' bout Robert Johnson," said Levon. "I never got to see him, he was before my time. Heard he drank some poisoned liquor in a juke joint and dropped dead."

"That's true, Levon. Gotta watch what you drink in 'em juke joints." And then Cornell reared his head and belly-laughed, and adopted a fake Irish accent as he sang...

On the tits of a barmaid named Gayle,
Were tattooed prices of beer, stout, and ale.
And on her behind,
For the sake of the blind,
Were precisely the same, but in Braille.

Laughter all around. Cornell put his arm around Levon. "Now's the time for *your* music. And you got to play all night, don't you?"

"Waal, we're gettin' pretty ragged —"

"My boy here, he can help. Ain't that right Johnny?" Cornell wielded his cane, tapped Johnny on the arm.

Johnny gave up the bass to a muttering Paulman, reached into his pocket, and pulled out the bag of speed pills. Without thinking, he handed the pills to Levon, whose eyes widened beyond what seemed possible.

"Woah! We're in *high cotton* now!" Levon quickly rolled up the bag like a thief rolling up a stolen Persian carpet. "What do we owe you for this?"

Johnny replied, looking at Cornell as he spoke. "Nothing. Knock yourself out. You guys sound great, now you can go all night." Cornell seemed to approve. Already Johnny was thinking of this father, of the need for some excuse for not having $200 to show for the bag.

Lucy and Reggie both caught this action and were surprised, not that they didn't already know about Johnny's father and the many errands Johnny ran for him, but because they'd never seen the actual product in question, the suspiciously wrinkled and unkempt plastic bag, the powdery pills; they'd never even witnessed a payoff. But before either could say anything, a commotion that had started in the hall outside the green room triggered a mass exodus to the corridor and back door to see what was up.

A beating, that's what. Three tough guys stood over a black man sprawled in the dirt on the rough end of the parking lot. Ballzo stood a distance apart, barking orders. When the black man raised his head, one of the goons kicked it with his patent leather shoe, caught the man's ear by the tip of the shoe, and blood spurted up into the night. The black man collapsed with a groan and didn't move again.

Ballzo saw the audience they'd just gained, heads bobbing for a look out the back door, mostly the musicians but one of them looked like his son. Goddamn it, that fuckin' Cornell should be watching this, where the fuck is that asshole? Just wanted to do a favor for Tony Mart, teach this nigger bass player a lesson, and give that Cornell asshole a message.

Inside the back door, the people surged forward to stick their necks out and look, then one by one they would peel out, having seen enough. Johnny stuck his head out between Ronnie and Levon. When his father yelled "Hey, Johnny!" and started across the parking lot toward the back door, Ronnie grabbed Johnny's arm. "Son, you in trouble? 'Cause if y'are, see that white '59 Sedan de Ville over there? I got the *difference*, right there in that glove box."

The thought of being involved in a shootout with his dad crossed his mind. It had happened before in mob circles, son killing father, nephew killing uncle, brother killing brother. Maybe he deserved it, and maybe Johnny needed to make the first move. The fucker'd made his mother disappear, just like that, snap of his fingers. Then Freddie, just like that.

But no. "No, no. He's my father."

Ronnie and Levon backed off, and so did everybody else, leaving Johnny standing in the doorway waiting for his father with a perplexed look.

Somewhere inside Ballzo's rough exterior was a heart pierced with disappointment and regret. I did this to my boy, like my father did it to me. He put me in early, taught me how to earn before I knew anything else. My mother didn't know, it was like she wasn't even there. Pop never had more than two words for me. I saw him kill a man before I was even, what, 15? Johnny's age.

So now Johnny's got no mother. So what. How much more does this kid have to see, before he'll grow up?

Ballzo steeled his gaze, calm but forceful. "So, you wanna be a musician?" Johnny knew his father's question was rhetorical, so he didn't answer. "Here's a lesson for ya. Show up on time. It's a job like everything else. This nigger fucked up his band's reputation by not showing up on time. Junk. You know what I told you about it. You mess with that shit and this is what happens. He fucked his own band, that's what he did. Now his band *don't deserve* to be headlining Tony Mart's!"

Johnny narrowed his eyes and set his jaw. "Is he dead?"

Jeez, thought Ballzo, the kid looks confident. Maybe he's coming around. "He's lucky I'm in a good mood. He'll sleep it off, probably forget all about it tomorrow when he jabs another needle in his arm."

Christ, thought Johnny, he probably got it from Skinny, who got it from... A prickly fear crept up Johnny's spine as he recalled the bag of pills he'd given Levon.

His father seemed to read his mind. "You collect it yet? I saw him in the audience."

"Red jacket, white pants, name is, uh, Gigliotti." Johnny pretended to rustle a nonexistent bag of pills in his pocket. "Haven't run into him yet."

Ballzo sensed that something was wrong. "Don't ever let me catch you using that shit." God forbid this kid would throw away his life, his career, he'd seen too much of it, especially in the music business.

"No dad, never. I don't like it." But Johnny knew he'd said too much. How would he even know he didn't like it, unless he'd tried it? So maybe he had, but he didn't need it; he was up all night anyway, couldn't sleep worth shit.

His father gave him that look, that dissatisfied look before getting furious. Then he made a move to slap Johnny, but held back for a moment. Then he pointed at his son like Uncle Sam on those posters, I want YOU for the U.S. Army. "We're a team, son. Let's keep it that way." And with that he was off to the show floor, passing the very door, Johnny noticed, to the back room, the scene of that argument with Freddie the Fryer. No longer part of the team, see, *that's* what happens. The Fryer, dead at 40.

* * *

By the time Johnny got back inside the band had started up again; he could hear already that Paulman hadn't changed the tuning. He joined Reggie and Lucy at the side of the stage to watch. Ronnie was doing backflips and the camel walk, putting everything into it, but didn't seem to matter. All attention focused on the band, which had turned solid gold. The violence they'd seen outside had not scared them so much as emboldened them to make it or break it, kick this audience in the ass or they'll get *their* asses kicked. So they made a sound that was so much more primitive and emotional than before, a driving force, that it dwarfed Ronnie's antics, nearly made Ronnie irrelevant.

"It's all in how you tuned that bass," Lucy said to Johnny, loud enough for Reggie to hear, her eyes flashing brilliance. "That bit of flatness makes it sound behind the tune, like it's a hobo always trying to catch up to a moving train."

Wow, exactly, thought Johnny. She's got it. Maybe she's not so batshit like everyone thinks. She's got this whole other level, deeper, not appreciated.

Just then, coincidence engines working overtime, Babbs appeared in the far corner of the bar, her face turning away from Johnny's direction back to the family guy in the Hawaiian shirt she was working. She must have seen Johnny, she must have been looking at him and Lucy. How would she size him up now? Dreamy adolescent on the scent of love? Incurable romantic, still too young to understand the crap he's about to live through?

Crap comes to haunt him. Now this guy Gigliotti is backstage, looking for him, sent no doubt by his father who was probably pissed about getting involved. Johnny was supposed to handle this shit, keep his father's name and presence out of it.

Johnny looked for a diversion. He leaned into Reggie, who was regarding Lucy, who was enrapt in the music. "Look, she's always been yours, you gotta just do it. Get into her pants tonight, man, the coast is clear. And I'm outta here, got to go. Get a ride back with my old man if you want, but tell him I got sick or something. Tell 'em I left, okay?"

And before Reggie had time to answer Johnny hightailed it right past a confused Gigliotti, through the corridor and out the back door. At the edge of the parking lot Johnny started running for his life. Thunderclouds billowed over the city across the bay, holding it down like a mantis with its prey, stinging it with lightning to paralyze it. Rain streamed with tears down his face as he settled down into a steady jog across the causeway, ducking out of view of passing cars, running for hours until he reached Margate, and Lucy the Elephant, where he collapsed in the maintenance closet, the first overnight tenant this hotel had seen in decades.

* * *

Ballzo stayed tight-lipped on the drive back, watching the kids in the back seat for signs of speed behavior. The chocolate nut case, Lucy, he'd already heard about, and the Mention kid was quiet. The Mention father had also been a quiet type, kept his secrets to himself. Some kind of drug researcher, had worked for the government, had learned too much, had gone AWOL. Ballzo's side mission, on orders from Tony Just, was to keep watch on the household, to see if Herbert Mention ever came back to visit his precious wife and sons.

Scanning the back seat in the mirror, Ballzo wondered what Johnny saw in these two. Where's that leadership quality that was supposed to be passed down, father to son? Must be the black in him. Conceived in haste, a tryst with one of the hired help, Marie, and raised by her mother, Mama Roux. By then, his wife Sheree had wounded him. She was a snitch, she became a problem. Even Ballzo didn't know what happened to her. She just disappeared. Word may have gotten out; the job was probably handed over to another *borgata* in New York out of respect, so Ballzo wouldn't have to know. She had been a mistake anyway.

Angelina was the one. His first true love, the brown-eyed brunette angel he adored, the one he would have gone to the mattresses to fight for, the woman with the strong Roman nose, purebred Sicilian, the one he wanted to have children with. Gone, dead at 24, from a mysterious stomach ailment after eating, of all things, soul food in New Orleans, on one of her outings as a singer for a jazz combo. How he hated the world then, especially that New Orleans style of jazz and the second-line rhythms, how he tore apart that roadhouse out on Lake Charles, kicked Professor Longhair off his piano stool midway through the instrumental break in "Tipitina"[111] and shot holes in the piano with his snub-nosed 38 as everybody scattered, wild white man on the loose, no tellin' how many black folks'd have to die before they come for him. How he'd come back home to his father's business, taken over South Jersey, and taken his father's *comare*. Sheree at that time was an exotic dancer and waitress at Palumbo's, easy for a young man to fall for. His father had told Ballzo the same thing Ballzo had told his son about Babbs: she'll break your fuckin' heart.

By the time they'd reached Lucy's house, Ballzo had decided that Reggie, the Mention kid, was some kind of closet fag. What kinda name was Reginald, anyway? Must be a fag, his father too. And Lucy, well, she's gonna bust her panties in public one of these days, get her ass sent back to the nut house. It was only a matter of time. And Johnny needed to get his head out of his ass. But maybe, he thought, just maybe sonny boy was running a scam on his old man. It seemed out of character for Johnny to be on speed, he didn't seem to go for the random hooliganism of the other kids his age. Now he's out there somewhere, probably scared. What do I have to do to bring him in? This is nothing, what he did. But he don't know that.

Looking for his son, Ballzo circled the island that held captive the swank Atlantic City metropolis and the Ventnor, Margate, and Longport resorts, then cruised down its wide avenues, one end to the other, through an uneasy night of stormy weather into a crimson-streaked dawn.

* * *

Gilbert was laughing hysterically, nearly convulsing with each smack of Bugs Bunny's lips in the animated short called "The Big Snooze" that satirized Raymond Chandler, though Gilbert didn't know it. Bugs doses Elmer Fudd with sleeping pills, as if to get rid of him, but really Bugs has to push this to the limit, so he takes a dose himself in order to continue tormenting Fudd in his dreams. Duh, what's up, doc?

By the end of the short Gilbert's on the floor, rolling in laughter toward the TV, and reaching up at just the right moment, a Brylcreem commercial, to switch to a rerun of *Ozzie and Harriet* that was just ending, and there's Ricky Nelson singing "Travelin' Man"[112] and fronting a backdrop of picture postcards and scenes from exotic locales, in what was essentially the first-ever music video. *Pretty Polynesian baby, o-over the sea.* Gilbert by this time was plucking a tennis racket as a guitar, up against his groin like Ricky Nelson. Even if he had stopped his antics and turned around to see his mother watching him, with her head in her hands and tears streaming down her face, whispering "not again, not again," he wouldn't have known what to make of it.

In any case, Gilbert had no time to register his mother's hasty retreat to her bedroom as car doors slammed and hoarse whispers from the outside walk testified to Reggie's return from Tony Mart's. Gilbert quickly put down the tennis racket, but not quick enough for Reggie, alone, to see it as he opened the front door. Aha, thought Reggie, let the teasing begin.

* * *

A woman in her thirties, all in white, with white flowers in her brown hair, dances by herself in a darkened ballroom, vast and unnaturally empty of people. Somewhere music is playing a song Johnny'd heard many times in his mother's womb, "You Always Hurt the One You Love"[113] by the Mills Brothers. The street chimes of an ice-cream vendor mimicked the notes to blend with the song, and for a moment the woman seemed in ecstasy, her back arched, her face turned to the ceiling, but still not familiar; he couldn't register the face in his mind. In a very short time the ice-cream vendor's chimes grew louder, over-powering and then finally dissolving the song, the scene, and the dream.

"Okay you creep!"

The shriek startled him. A dark mass haloed by a mess of blonde hair came into focus as Maxine, her head shielding the sun from Johnny's eyes, just as the ice-cream vendor rolled by with his cart. Johnny lay on the sand in shorts and t-shirt near Lucy the Elephant drying from his morning bath in the Atlantic, and drying out from the adrenaline-soaked nightclub activities of the previous night.

"Now it's for real!" She screamed at him.

Johnny rolled up in a sitting position and squinted at her.

"You know what I'm talking about," she said more calmly, but with a frightened catch in her throat, which told him all he needed to know.

He staggered to his feet. "How could you possibly know in just two days?"

"I know. I can just feel it."

Christ. His father had warned him, of course. Now he would have to ask his father for help.

Maxine's hair was mussed, her eye shadow streaked. He'd never seen her looking so forlorn. What would it take to turn her back into a cheerleader again?

"Remember what I said. We fly to the Bahamas, get it taken care of in just a few days. No one would know, not your parents, not your friends, nobody. Our little secret."

Her downcast eyes and fluttering lashes told him something new. She was serious about having the baby. Panic crept up his spine and ionized his mind, but he did the only thing he could think of: he wrapped his arms around her and held her tight, straining against her sobs to force back a tear of his own, a choke in his own throat. Marriage to Maxine would enslave him to his father's career, because only a chump would try to work a clean life without a college education. His father would probably insist on marriage as a way to lock him in. But maybe, just maybe, I could persuade her to get the abortion, and get Big Dom to help me. He owes me, at least he said he did, way back when his mother disappeared. He had said, "If there's anything you need, anything you can't get from your father, you come to me."

At the Italian deli, at the supermarket, in church on Sundays with his father, at all these places where mothers gather and talk, Johnny would look for a mother of his own. But if I saw her on the street someplace, he reminded himself, I wouldn't even know her. One more middle-aged woman buying groceries. But he was curious about what these older women wore, how they carried themselves, how they moved and spoke, what music they liked, whether it be Sinatra or Benny Goodman or Louis Prima or even the Pennsylvanians. Whatever detail he could register he was desperate to remember, constructing false memories of what his mother would be like today. Wherever she was. His father had said she went upstate to be with her family, that she couldn't take the life down here. Johnny gathered that she went crazy and is still in the care of someone, "upstate" being code for either prison or asylum. He wouldn't allow the thought to cross his mind, that she was killed to be silenced. Practiced at putting this thought out of his mind, Johnny could now banish any highly-charged emotion, at least temporarily. Enough to get Maxine back to her senses and in a calm enough mood to leave her with her friends on the beach.

Mrs. Mention had a plate of warm bacon and eggs in the oven for him. Today's rehearsal, again without Scotty, fell apart before it started as Reggie and Gilbert gathered around Johnny and his new Fender electric bass, which he had stashed in the Mention family garage. Indeed, it was the same make and model George Paulman of the Hawks used, the one Johnny'd tuned in the green room at Tony Mart's. Johnny told Gilbert and Reggie about how he'd met Cornell Woodrow, the man who'd told that Diddley Bow story, at his house earlier in the afternoon, and how he'd given him this bass, without mentioning that it was in trade for a favor. "The man says this Jackal is the next Johnny Ace."

Reggie was skeptical. "So who is this guy, Cornell Woodrow?"

"He says he once managed this guy who wrote a song that Elvis tried to sing when he went to record for the first time, called 'Without You.' This black singer from Nashville who disappeared before the record company could find him. Cornell says he knows what really happened. Says he knew Elvis and he knows Muddy Waters and all them bluesmen."

Johnny started playing his new Fender Precision to "Jailhouse Rock" and then Junior Parker's "Mystery Train",[114] the record slowly gathering steam to turn into a locomotive force no one could stop, roaring down the tracks of fate with Parker's mocking vocal already gone to echo, half-dead and cursed, rising in misery with the mournful sax mimicking a train whistle up from the echoing gorge.

But if it's the train I ride, Johnny's thinking, the train *I* ride, how could it take my baby and be gone? Only if it leaves me dead on the tracks.

This is the way of the incomprehensible world, these songs tell the truth, that there's no escaping fate. The Carter Family knew this truth, warped as it was by the Southern white gospel culture, when they revived the old folk tune of the "Worried Man" and sang these very lines that found their way onto the Mystery Train, the train to nowhere. It took my baby, Parker moaned, it's gonna do it again.

Not Elvis, he wouldn't let that happen. Johnny put on the Elvis cover of "Mystery Train".[115] Elvis quickened the pace of the song, oblivious to its mystery, remembering only this: that train's got his baby. Damn! Johnny thumped his bass as Elvis turned that train around and took it over, riding new rails of fate off into the night. Once it had taken his baby, *but it never will again* he shouts, *no not again.* Elvis screamed at the end, *whoo-ee!* And he was gone, taking the Mystery Train with him, taking that celebration of life known as the blues in a new direction, through a tunnel and out into the promised land.

Elvis the sensation had never meant that much to Johnny. Though he wouldn't admit it, he leaned more toward the emotional hothead Buddy Holly, who sounded like he was chained down for his own protection. He liked Buddy Holly because, as the story goes, Buddy wouldn't compromise, wouldn't allow producers to put studio musicians behind his ragtag trio. He got right up in the face of an industry executive, all dorky with his homely black-framed glasses, to say *No!* to the man's explanation of the way things work. The man was so angry his spittle got away from him as he blurted out, you get your songs from the songwriter, the arrangements from an arranger, and the producer puts it all together, y'know studio time is expensive we can't let you go in there without supervision. Buddy just got up in his face and told him that *I* write the songs, *I* do the arrangements, and by god *I'm* gonna to produce these here *records.*

That kind of arrogance set Johnny's spine a-tingling. And he liked the slow-fuse Roy Orbison, who built his sound up from a smoldering manly growl to a girlish falsetto that set hearts a-flutter, and he did this without embarrassment.

Roy could walk the land and feel the pain, and tell it to you straight up, without pretensions. Not insincere, like Elvis in those movies.

When Johnny was younger Elvis was too much at once, a shock like a cold milkshake headache, and by '59 Johnny'd had enough of the modern crooner and movie star. But now with this bass in his hands, it all took on new meaning. Johnny could feel how Elvis went up against the old meaning of the song because they had to make it their own. Elvis saw an opening and took it. And I need to do the same, he thought, or I'll end up on this train to oblivion, riding the rails my father laid before me.

All at once it occurred to him that he needed to honor the deal with Cornell Woodrow for the bass. It was an audacious con for a fifteen-year-old, and Johnny was amazed that Cornell thought he could pull it off. Johnny would go to Darby Records, convince the manager that his father had sent him, and pull the Jackal's master tapes and contract from the files. Cornell had even told him what to say: "The contract needs some alterations, a change in the songwriter's name and music publisher, and the master tapes needed editing."

Then he'd turn them over to Cornell. Maybe it was a good deed, maybe Cornell was going to do something right. Somehow it didn't matter. His father had a grip on this Jackal material and a grip on Darby for a reason, and even if Johnny didn't know the reason, he knew that a betrayal on this level would set the record straight. That the father's son is a man on his own.

A betrayal on this level could also get a man killed. The ghost of Freddie the Fryer shimmered before him as he practiced scales on his bass.

* * *

Back in the Mention garage, Reggie had shifted to a new level of Gilbert-teasing. "I saw you, yes I did, workin' that tennis racket, weren't ya!" Reggie impersonated a faggot version of Ricky Nelson, leering, holding his real guitar tight against his package, "bom bom bom bom, hey, I'm a travelin' man."

"Fuck you," Gilbert whimpered.

"Whoooo! Poor little fool!"

"Hey, c'mon." Johnny was impatient with this nonsense. He needed to get to Philly, and he needed some kind of diversion, some way of making everything seem normal when he got to the Darby Records office. He could see how it would go: he'd bring Lucy and Reggie with him to the office and he'd say his father's out in the car with Gilbert, they'd just returned from something. Then Gilbert would come running up and say 'hurry up, your dad's waiting' and that would convince the office manager that everything was okay.

It all clicked into place. The truck would still be parked at the warehouse in Camden. It couldn't be filled with blank discs; they had to be the Jackal's first run of records, destined for the dump. He could pick up the contract and the master from Darby, then cruise right over to the warehouse and get that truck. Deliver it to Cornell, truck and all. At fifteen his driving experience amounted to a few weeks with his Harley, and once, backing up the truck to the loading dock while his father smirked with pride. But it would be night. He would have to take the backroads through the Pine Barrens to not get caught.

How much of this plan could he tell Reggie? Not that Reggie wouldn't understand rebelling against a father that didn't act like one. But there was a level of detail past which Reggie's attention would wander into a pastiche of soul-searching, of debating the pros and cons of crossing their elders.

So Johnny kept it simple: we're going to Philly tomorrow, check out American Bandstand, run an errand for my father, be back home before midnight. Gilbert too! And Lucy, let's bring her along. Reggie frowned, but Johnny just slipped another record on the turntable and took up his bass, and sung along to Buddy Holly's "Down the Line",[116] "Gotta go (go) go (go) go (go) go..."

   * * *

Lucy bounced on her seat, giggled and shrieked, and generally let just about everyone else on the Greyhound bus know how excited she was to be going to American Bandstand. Reggie kept silent, all the way to the station at Market in Filbert in Philly, even through the idiotic mustard antics outside the station with the hot soft pretzels, flinging gobs of the spicy yellow paste just missing each other, speckling the sidewalk.

"This is fuckin' great!" Gilbert kept repeating, as if he'd never been out in public before. Reggie scowled. Johnny led them through the passages to the Market-Frankford line, a surface trolley to Market and 69th Street, and then to the headquarters of American Bandstand at WFIL-TV.

There they joined a crowd of teenagers that poured into a huge studio all lit up like a basketball court and reeking of body odor. Rock 'n' roll blared from tinny speakers, providing the giddy atmosphere of a high school record hop. A main section in front of the stage, shimmering in the intense lighting, was cordoned off with ribbons and video equipment, behind which dour-faced technicians with clipboards eyed the crowd with disdain, sometimes barking orders to what looked like crew-cut college students or members of the same football team, but were actually bouncers, in white letterhead sweaters stenciled AB. The crew-cuts meandered through the crowd outside the barriers, selecting couples and girls to bring inside the circle and into the dazzle of television lighting, in what seemed to be a ratio of three girls to every two guys.

Reggie, concerned, eyed Lucy, who had edged forward toward the bouncers. "They're not selecting any Negro kids."

Johnny hadn't noticed at first, but now that Reggie mentioned it... There were a few blacks around the perimeter; there had been a lot more outside from the neighborhood. They seemed to know enough not to try to come inside, content to hear the music through the open upstairs window, playing craps on the sidewalk, hustling sheepish college kids out of their monthly allowances. As Johnny scanned the crowd and then the stage, he spied Big Dom exiting stage left. Following him was the maestro himself, Dick Clark, a mask of teen frenzy plastered over his perennially frozen smile.

"There goes Frankie Avalon!" As Gilbert pointed, girls around them shouted and screamed, and it was indeed Frankie in the flesh, oily and sickly pale with black hair greased up like a candle wick, making his way through the grasping and clinging arms of teenage girls held back by two letterhead bouncers. Avalon passed right by Reggie and Lucy, his scent of Coppertone and Jean Naté heralding his arrival and clearing a path.

All of a sudden one of the bouncers grabbed Reggie, who grabbed Lucy, and together they were pulled into the circle as the lights behind them went dark. The crowd and music hushed, center stage blazed in bright white lights, and Dick Clark materialized in front of the microphone like a science teacher in the School of Oz.

To Johnny it seemed as if the selected kids had been chosen for some kind of white-light illumination, a ritual of ascension to an elite level, the chosen people, set before Dick Clark as a microcosm of the teenage world beyond. Out in the dim perimeter, Johnny could see the reality of show business, its paint-caked surfaces and false props, a frenzy controlled by cue cards and timed to fit within commercial breaks. Dick Clark started off by cueing up the latest hits. The crowd swayed in unison to the Wah Watusi[117], then swung in earnest, arms akimbo, to a local favorite called the Bristol Stomp.[118]

Almost immediately the clipboards and crew-cuts spotted Lucy, her brown body popping out of the pale white crowd like a raisin in a bowl of cream of wheat. Stern faces and nods sent a technician running backstage, and as Dick Clark watched from the stage half-amused and half-disgusted, a producer with headphones appeared side-stage, draw-ing his finger across his neck in the customer fashion to signal "cut."

More bouncers approached to surround Reggie and Lucy. At that point Johnny lost it, shouting "No!" He jumped the cordon, slammed against a television camera, and dove into the selected teenage audience frozen in their dance steps.

The scuffle was over before it ever really got started. Reggie, scared out of his wits, was no help at all as the bouncers dragged them away. Lucy's blood-curdling scream was caught by the recording equipment, so thrillingly piercing and clear that it was eventually included in a Darby Records LP compilation of the finest horror-movie screams.

They regrouped outside. Reggie was nearly inconsolable, babbling on about racism. Johnny steered them to a cheesesteak shop. The lunacy subsided, and Lucy shrugged and scarfed down her cheesesteak smothered in onions and sweet peppers. Eventually Johnny got them back on the Market-Frankfort line heading to Center City, and told them about the favor he'd promised Cornell Woodrow. "I'm going to grab that record master and take off. All I need you to do is go with me. Once I get it, we split up and meet back in Atlantic City."

Reggie, cooled out by talk of conspiracy, asked the all-important question. "This is why Freddie the Fryer was killed, isn't it?"

Johnny's empty stare spoke volumes. Lucy gasped.

"Like, wow!" Gilbert was totally on board. "It's like, we're the Hardy Boys! Reggie, you're the dark-haired older brother Frank, and I'm the blond kid, Joe."

"Thought it was the other way 'round," Johnny B snickered.

"And our dad's Fenton?" Reggie snapped. "What, is he supposed to've been kidnapped or something?"

"Well," Gilbert won't give it up, "maybe the record describes a treasure map, like *The Secret Warning*."

"Or maybe it describes a rare book, like *The Twisted Claw*," Reggie clucked at Gilbert, slapping him on his head. "A-and it sends code words over the radio, like *The Short Wave Mystery*. Give me a break."

* * *

Darby Records was on Race Street just north of the Greyhound terminal on Market. At the steps to the record label, Johnny stationed Lucy outside with Gilbert. But at each step up his nausea grew, his sweat beaded on the back of his neck, his skin prickled.

Johnny and Reggie approached the secretary in the front office who was munching on pizza. After a brief introduction, explaining how he was Frank Balzano's son, his dad's outside in the car, she said fine and put the half-eaten slice back in the pizza box. "I need the, the Jackal, the Jackal's contract," Johnny stammered, "a-and the master tape of his last session, please."

It finally registered on Reggie that Johnny had just mentioned something about his dad being out in the car, and he was about to say something when Johnny cut him off by stepping on his foot.

The secretary smiled sweetly, put aside the pizza box, and went off without even a glance back. By now Reggie was just about to burst.

"Stay cool."

"What the fuck?"

"Just stay cool..." Johnny had Reggie by the lapel of his jacket. "I know what I'm doing. Look, go outside and make sure they're okay." He gave Reggie a shove, who needed no further encouragement.

Johnny leaned against the front desk and waited. Minutes seemed like hours. He wiped the sweat from his brow with a napkin next to the pizza box. And then he could hear, coming down the stairs in back, the heavy footsteps of a big man; no, two men. The unmistakeable humming in the scale of C, do-re-mi-fa-so-la-ti, told Johnny all he needed to know: Big Dom, and as usual, the gangster's singing was flat.

Run? No time. Somehow, someway, he had to disappear. He remembered what Mama Roux had told him. Think yourself not there. That's not going to work. What the fuck do I do? He grabbed the pizza box, shut it closed. Underneath it was the receipt, and he tore it off the bottom of the box and just stood there, pizza box in one hand, receipt in the other.

Think yourself not there.

Big Dom rounded the corner with a college-age kid. "Fabian's a great name," Big Dom was telling the kid. "All you's gotta do is watch these films, and take some lessons, y'know, about how to move on stage and all that." But the kid, Fabian, looked like he'd rather have been out on a football field.

Johnny inhaled and stood stock-still, glancing at them furtively, looking back at the desk, looking bored. *I'm not here*, I'm the pizza delivery boy.

Big Dom came within two feet of the front desk, still talking to Fabian, then he looked up to see the pizza delivery boy.

Johnny, holding his breath, stared at his shoes.

With a grunt Big Dom shuffled out the door with Fabian in tow. He hadn't recognized Johnny. His only thought was of stopping at Fazzio's on the way back to Atlantic City, to get the pepperoni special, only be sure to first take some Tums.

* * *

Johnny exhaled. He put down the pizza box just as the secretary came back with a package containing a manila folder and the master tape in a sealed tin, lightly whispering the melody of "Mack the Knife"[119] and frowning at him, thinking he was after her pizza. She handed the goods to Johnny. "Here ya go, sport," she said sardonically.

"Sure enough, thanks m'am!" Johnny fled down the steps and out the door.

Reggie stood poised like Marshal Dillon on the sidewalk, hands at his hips. "I'm going with you."

"No no, my man." Johnny was all business. "You get your brother and Lucy on that bus. We meet at the Egg Harbor at midnight."

Gilbert was ecstatic and started singing, "It takes a worried man…"

"Alright, alright," snapped Reggie, "enough already, rilly, ya sound like shit."

Leaving the merry trio at the Greyhound station, Johnny tucked the package inside his leather jacket and set out on foot, east on Market and then Race, lighting a cigarette to calm his nerves, shivering as he passed Independence Hall, a glowing sepulcher illuminated from within by electric candles, and stopping for a breath at Benjamin Franklin's grave. Now there was a great man who knew about secrets and codes. Hip for his day, a runaway at a time when running away was illegal, a prankster who wrote letters under pseudonyms to provoke newspaper publishers, a tireless campaigner against hypocrisy. And when he could find no work in New York, Franklin is supposed to have walked all the way across New Jersey. How he got across the Delaware River is not mentioned in the history books.

He certainly didn't have this bridge. Johnny stood under gathering storm clouds at the brink of the Benjamin Franklin Bridge walkway, the package burning a hole in his gut under his jacket. He'd done it once; could he make himself invisible again? The truck too? This bridge carried U.S. Route 30, part of the old Lincoln Highway, which at one time divided America into north and south more accurately than the Mason-Dixon line. From this point on the bridge, it was a straight shot out the White Horse Pike to Virginia Avenue and the Boardwalk. Johnny knew a bit of South Jersey history. He could avoid the Pike and its cops by following the same route through the Pine Barrens used by American privateers before the Revolutionary War.

That's what I'm doing, he thought. Pulling a Franklin, acting out the revolt with this stolen contract, this half-baked plan to steal his father's truck filled with the Jackal's records from a Camden warehouse.

Johnny scampered off the bridge and down the darkened Camden streets, feeling feline in his limbs. The truck sat stoically in the parking lot, unmoved since Johnny had loaded it days earlier. Johnny knew it would be unlocked and that its keys would be, natch, under the floor mat. How cliché, he thought, and quickly got in behind the wheel, wondering what other clichés might pop up in this dubious under-taking, like if his father's warehouse manager kept a dog for security.

And yes, just then, a dog howled at the raging wind, and Johnny jumped. Did I think that? Did I make it happen by thinking that? Jeez, calm down. He lit a cigarette and calmly smoked, sitting in the driver's seat, waiting for his blood to stop rushing and his heart to stop pounding. *Think yourself not there.* He covered his eyes, then his ears, and then his mouth with his hands. *See no evil, hear no evil, speak no evil.*

Then, in low but unmistakeable tones, he heard a howl, the call of something wild, and then a shrill whistle. Through the windshield, Johnny could make out a purplish blob against dark clouds in the night sky, a ghostly apparition. A trick of the city's lights? But it moved irregularly and began to take shape, a nightmare vision of two short legs with paws, swimming out of the cloud, and then a horse's head followed by its long neck, a tapered body with flapping wings twice its size, and back legs like a crane's, with horse hooves.

Ridiculous, and yet sublime. All at once he understood. In his feverish scare he'd conjured up the Jersey Devil, the infamous creature of the Pine Barrens, legendary protector of religious dissenters, fugitives and military deserters; often described as a flying biped with hooves. Johnny's imagination had made the

Devil real. Horribly real. The stink of fish now, rotting up his nose. A roaring sound, the beating of wings. The creature swooped down, its shadow enveloping the truck and obliterating Johnny's view through the windshield for a tense, charged moment. He couldn't flee, he couldn't move. Most of all he couldn't see, or speak. He could only *hear*.

He resolved to go with it, trust in what he heard, not what he could see. The beating of wings. A roaring sound. He thought it not a real creature but an apparition, a transmogrification of his own dream, the dream of the dark spirit that inhabited his tumultuous birth. Freddie had talked about occult practices, witches and demons, and how a demon could possess the soul of an embryo in its third month. The result was usually a miscarriage or stillborn, or the birth of an idiot; but in some cases, a monster...

Born in a cross-fire hurricane, howled at my mother in the driving rain. And then my father banished my mother. Was it for bringing *me* into the world? Johnny, seized in shame, began to pray. The Jersey Devil is my protector, I shall not want, I shall not...

The momentary phenomenon subsided, and the dark sky appeared again, stars shining through a hole in the clouds. Johnny saw a star fall toward the region of the Blue Hole. Something in that area that draws meteorites out of the sky. Franklin would have checked it out.

Then he heard thunder. Lightning scorched and illuminated the barrens like a scene out of a Bela Lugosi movie. It was a response! Nature is responding to my thoughts! If I think of rain, or rather... if I *hear* rain? Sure enough, it began to pour, thunder followed, and Johnny felt the entire world shake as the truck shuddered in the wind. He cowered, wrapped his coat tightly, bowed his head, and waited it out.

After what seemed like hours but was only minutes, the pounding rain tapered off. Glancing up at the night sky, seeing no devil or angel, he started the engine and gingerly swung the truck around and out of the parking lot. The wind picked up again as he double-clutched out the back streets of Camden, and every leaf that blew against the windshield startled him with a brief glimpse of that hoofed, flying devil.

* * *

A half-hour after calling the number Cornell had given him, Johnny sat in a row with Lucy, Reggie and Gilbert in the Egg Harbor Diner on the outskirts of Atlantic City, with Cornell on the other side of the table. A storm raged outside.

Johnny spoke for the group. "The truck's in the parking lot, and here's the rest of it," handing Cornell the manila folder containing the contract and the master recording acetate.

"More than I expected," Cornell chuckled, "so now your karmonics are in balance."

"My wha?"

Cornell smiled at him. "Johnny my boy, Johnny be good, Johnny guitar. You have paid a karmic debt for your heritage, for something that is an accident of birth but still a burden you must overcome. And you are ready, as they say on game shows, ready for the big challenge."

Johnny gave him a hesitant smirk, not quite understanding what the man meant.

Cornell gathered the others in his gaze. "You are all ready." And then, to Johnny, "You can be the next white boy who stole the blues. I can see it in your eyes. Your sparkling eyes! Heh heh. You have omnipotence at your command, and eternity at your disposal."

Reggie was unconvinced. "Hmph. What are you going to do with the truck?"

"Don't you worry," Cornell assured him. "The truck will be left somewhere obvious, just another stolen truck. And you, my friend," he reached into his jacket pocket, causing Reggie to jump in reflex. "You can all have these, passes to the show tomorrow night. The Jackal will start at the moment the Steel Pier show ends. Bring your friends. This show will astonish everyone."

"Not if my father..." but Johnny stopped himself.

Cornell lowered his head. "You've betrayed your father for a nobler cause. For every karmic turn of justice there is always a counter-turn. For every advance, a small retreat. You will learn how to deal with these difficulties."

Johnny looked at him blankly. Cornell reached again, this time into a side pocket, and brought out three misshapen pebbles. "They fell from the sky," Cornell told them. "Did any of you see it?"

"That?" Johnny frowned. Yes, he had seen something while driving the truck through the Pine Barrens. A falling star, a meteorite. They burn up in the atmosphere.

"That. Touch this one. Go ahead, pick it up."

Johnny hefted one of the pebbles. It was warm, but not too hot. Reggie picked up another one, and Gilbert picked up the third.

Lucy smirked and looked away. Just another boy's game.

"They're called thunder-stones," said Cornell, "and you can use them to direct, or rather, *re*direct your power."

"What power?" Johnny had turned suspicious.

"Didn't Freddie tell you? Didn't he tell you about *their* father?" Cornell gestured at Reggie and Gilbert. "Our experiment? He must have mentioned the MAD Magazine. 'See no evil, hear no evil, speak no evil'?"

Johnny was startled. Reggie, Gilbert, and Lucy were all wide-eyed.

"Our ancestors tell us that the spirit of all goodness is asleep, and hungry," explained Cornell patiently. "The hunger brings harm to the world. The experiment is to awaken the spirit and celebrate its goodness. But there are those who want to block the experiment. And the only way around them is to see no evil, hear no evil, and speak no evil, but to pass along the information."

All four of them had the same uncomprehending stare.

"You don't know what I'm talking about? You probably think it means to look the other way, to refuse to acknowledge evil by feigning ignorance. But it's true meaning is like the golden rule, only it's even older than the golden rule. It's the most important rule, from the very first religion, what they now call Zoroastrianism."

Reggie perked up. "Huh?"

"That's right," Cornell continued in a soothing baritone. "1200 years before Christ, they used the terms 'Humata, Hukhta, Hvarshta,' which means 'good thoughts, good words, good deeds.' When we see evil, we digest it, and when we digest it the evil becomes a part of us, which means eventually the evil needs to find its way *out*. If it doesn't, the evil wreaks havoc on our bodies and minds. Same as when we hear evil, it becomes part of us. Our bodies absorb it like a sponge. It must *come out!* So you must convert that evil to information, and pass it along."

Johnny B nodded. "That copy of MAD Freddie gave me. The three monkeys cartoon, in the margin of the Elvis parody."

"Exactly. And where have you seen that before? Maybe on a sign somewhere?"

Johnny looked around, puzzled. Reggie looked hostile. "What copy of MAD?"

"The record shop!" Gilbert shouted. "It's the sign above the Mad Records shop."

"Mad Records..." Johnny mused. "On Keystone, isn't it? Freddie had said to keep the stone and the key separate."

Cornell smiled. "An old way of referring to a safe house. A stop on the Underground Railroad. Ever hear of that?"

"Yes," piped up Reggie, ever the scholar. "From before the Civil War. Slaves were using it to escape to the North. But... New Jersey is already the North, right?"

"Many of them were on their way to New England," said Cornell. "It's one of the oldest escape routes still in use, but today it's used for other reasons. There are tunnels underneath Keystone Avenue, and one leads to the bay."

"What other reasons?" Reggie wanted to know. "What's this got to do with these stones?"

Cornell looked at Johnny questioningly, and then realized what was up. Johnny hadn't told Reggie and his brother about their father's story. He sighed, and turned back to Reggie. "I suggest you take a close look at that magazine that Johnny has. Can you read music? Do you know what the devil's tritone is?"

"Of course," said Reggie, though not too sure of himself. "It's a harmonic interval of, of, what is it? C and F sharp, right?"

"You got it," said Cornell darkly. "Look closely at those thought balloons. And when you see those musical notes, think of them as *numbers*."

Reggie looked at Johnny, who shrugged.

"Now, keep these stones," Cornell gestured to them on the table. "You will eventually figure out how to use them. You'll find information at that location. About the power to see no evil," looking at Reggie, "hear no evil," looking at Johnny, "and speak no evil," looking at Gilbert.

Cornell gathered up his cane, and stood to leave. Only when he was ready, clothes adjusted, hat on head, cane in hand, did he speak, and only to Johnny. "Your stone brings luck. Hear the thunder?" Sure enough, thunder seemed to peel off the roof and put it back on again. "It's calling you. It's telling you to leave! Decipher this code in the magazine, and take it with you to the record shop. You'll figure it out. Do it before the show tomorrow. Central Pier. You're all coming to the show, right?" And then he winked at the group, and cane in hand, soft-shoeing a jig, he sang in a contrived Irish accent,

There was a young fellow named Perkin
Who was always jerkin' his gherkin
His father said "Perkin,
Stop jerkin' your gherkin.
Your gherkin's fer ferkin' not jerkin'!"

And Cornell laughed that booming laughter of a man unafraid of anything in this diner, this town, or this life. Then he paused, smiled, and spoke once again, soberly, to Johnny. "Seriously, work on this. Find the clues their father left behind," Cornell pointed to Reggie and Gilbert. "And leave as soon as you can. I myself will be off soon, heading across the Atlantic. To England, where the slave trade started."

"Whoa! Take me with you, when you go," Johnny pleaded in a singsong voice.

Cornell tapped his cane on the floor three times, and repeated three times, to Johnny, Reggie, and Gilbert, "Keep your stone! It brings good luck." And he was off.

"What's this about my father?" Reggie was madder than Johnny had ever seen him.

"I got to show you something Freddie gave me. It was tucked inside this MAD magazine Cornell's talking about. A short story. Your dad wrote it."

* * *

Morning brought relief to Reggie's troubled mind. He'd spent the night in a waking dream, walking among the scenes of his father's story, looking for Cornell Woodrow and his ancestor, the black Methuselah, High John the Conqueror. The rolling stone who had brought the African spirits to the New World in the form of music.

The Mention household was quiet, awash in an incomparable strangeness, their scheduled band practice merely an idea floating above Reggie and Gilbert as they talked in hushed tones, instruments in hand but nobody playing. Johnny showed up with Lucy, and the hours rolled by like imperfect waves as they waited for Mother Mention to go out to the store. They talked about the issue of MAD magazine, what the balloons above the monkeys meant, and what might be waiting for them down at Mad Records... everything but the elephant in the room, Father Mention, still on the run.

When Beatrice departed, they headed out to Mad Records. Gilbert bubbled with enthusiasm, repeating, "Just like the Hardy Boys" and looking at Reggie with the usual "I told you so" glare. Reggie had taken the lead in deciphering the code. In the magazine, above the monkey that could see no evil was a thought balloon showing stars arranged in a constellation which looked like the Big Dipper. The thought balloon above the speak-no-evil monkey showed a bluesman holding something in his hand. A thunder-stone? From the stars?

But it was the thought balloon above the hear-no-evil monkey that provided a code, in the form of musical notation that Reggie could translate. It started with a treble clef symbol, with three measures: a melodic interval A C with D.S. al coda, another melodic interval E F G A B C D E with S/sign, and a final harmonic interval C and F# and C and G, with 0+ sign.

"The treble staff begins with the first line as E," Reggie explained as they entered the store. "The first measure, the interval A C with D.S. al coda. That must be Atlantic City, and Del Signo al coda means 'go to the sign, and from there go to the coda.' The second measure is the S/sign, the melodic interval E F G A B C D E, that's E followed by rest of octave, or 'E8'. Maybe that's where we're supposed to start looking. The third measure has the the 0+ sign as a coda. That means use integer notation for the chromatic scale. Remember? Cornell said that when you see those musical notes, think of them as *numbers*."

A black woman dressed in multicolored scarves and wearing a Zulu headdress sat by the cash register, looking for all the world like she belonged right there. And maybe she did; this was Mad Records, an odd little store that closed or opened whenever it wanted to, stuck between the large brick monstrosity of a bus station and a cement box department store perennially going "out of business" on depressed Keystone Avenue. The record racks were lined with blues, rhythm and blues, jazz, and some rock 'n' roll. Johnny was amazed to see copies of the Jackal's blank-label record featured right by the register.

"You-all looking for something special?" She looked them up and down with disdain, the way a black mother would look at her wayward sons.

"Three monkeys!" Gilbert blurted out.

Reggie shushed him, and turned to the storekeeper. "Would 'E8' mean anything to you?"

"Sounds like a locker. The self-storage, right behind the store," she said, looking at them funny. "You can use the back door."

Sure enough, the self-storage business was right in back, across a narrow alley. Johnny headed inside, past a vacant front desk, with Reggie and Gilbert following.

As they left, the woman fumed, but then a puzzled look came over her. She rummaged through the drawers of the desk behind the register and pulled out a framed photograph of a young boy of about ten, in a cowboy suit. "Robert's grandson!" she exclaimed, and looked thoughtfully at the back door.

* * *

They found locker E8. Reggie decoded the devil's interval C-F# and the C-G interval in the integer notation for the chromatic scale and came up, after some trial and error, with the combination for the lock: 0 + 6 + 0 + 7.

Lo and behold! Inside was a steamer trunk, dusty with cobwebs along the bottom but recently wiped on top, especially around its lock.

The four of them carried it, walking crablike, out to the street. The storekeeper leaned against the storefront and watched as Reggie hailed a cab. "You better bring that back," she warned them, "if you know what's good for you."

They took it straight back to the Mention house. As they arrived, Beatrice stood at the door with a stoic expression and her arms crossed. "Well," she concluded, "perhaps it's time." And with a sniff she withdrew to her bedroom, and returned with a key for the trunk.

Beatrice started rummaging through the trunk with Gilbert at attention, Reggie anxious, and Johnny looking on. Her eyes brimmed with tears as she pulled out the pieces of Herbert Mention's life, research notes, clippings, pill bottles, canisters of mysterious liquids, bone fragments, dried roots, unknown ointments, feathers and hand-carved statuettes from West Africa, the beak of an eagle, three polished stones, a diatonic "blues harp" harmonica in the key of A, and two 78-rpm records by Robert Johnson: "Sweet Home Chicago" backed by "Walkin' Blues" and "Last Fair Deal Gone Down" backed by "Terraplane Blues" on the Vocalion label, and another record, a 78-rpm acetate with "Special from Spirituals to Swing" handwritten on a blank label.

And, of course, bound in dusty leather, The Book.

* * *

Over every secret hovers a betrayal, wrote Herbert Mention on the first page of The Book, titled "Introduction", *and in my case, I do it to unburden my soul. And to pass along what I know, so that others can continue from where I was forced to stop.*

This is what I know, but not allowed to say or demonstrate (beyond my own private experience of it): That a network of adepts of higher intelligence exists and functions throughout our planet and, I suspect, extends even farther than our Earth, and they communicate with each other in code. Music has always served as a medium for these codes, in ancient times and even today.

Herbert Mention's "Introduction" spanned many sloppily typed and smudged pages strewn with incomplete sentences and childishly misspelled words, mixed in haphazardly with mimeographed song lyrics, all sorts of maps, illustrations, handwritten notes and typed letters. It never really resolved to an ending, making the entire book an introduction, and a true picture of the man's mind at work.

Herbert started off with mention of *his* father's manuscript, left to him when his father was marched off into the sugarcane swamp of southern Louisiana, never to be seen again. Gilbert Reginald Mesirow's manuscript, according to Herbert, had detailed some of the coded instructions found in Negro songs dating back before the Civil War. The Ku Klux Klan was active in those parts, and Gilbert Mesirow had been called out as a nigger-loving jew for associating in a congenial fashion on his porch, indeed even in his living room, with some of the most troublesome and disreputable blacks in the county, especially the whiskey-drinking banjo pickers. Young Herbert had eavesdropped from the stairs and picked up a few codes, Negro slang, and snippets of songs. As he grew older he took on his father's protective attitude about black music players. There was something about this music that begged attention from white people, that revealed the soulfulness of all humanity. Why was it so difficult for white people to understand?

His father, cursing the deputies as he was dragged from the family home, had warned Herbert to keep silent. His mother insisted on traveling light, and off they went, shortening their last name to Mesh, and joining the rambling, hoboing ranks of America's white trash discarded at the start of the Great Depression. As Herbert described it, mother and son fought off drooling, battle-scarred men, rode the rails of the locomotive age, sought shelter from sympathetic guards in train yards, slipped into slowly-moving boxcars and disappeared into their empty interiors. Young Herbert met apostles of nonconformist paths, anarchists and bomb-makers exiled from the Colorado mines, countless jobless refugees from the industrial North, gypsy followers of the Russian *stranniki,* even raggedy ambassadors from Shambhala in the Tibetan wilderness who thought highly of their spiritual selves, and thought holy their crusade to illuminate the world through poetry, song, and exotic plants and herbs.

"I've read about them," Lucy snickered in delight as they read through it, "the *stranniki*, the wanderers in Russia. Nonconformists. Just like today's beatniks."

* * *

With Reggie excitedly turning the pages, they reached a section that Lucy helped to translate: haphazardly inserted recipes for brewing teas from exotic plants, a brief on the myths of ergot use in ancient Greece by Plato and Aristotle, and reports of a shaman in the Yucatan who could levitate thatched huts. References to someone named Fulcanelli were sprinkled in, along with a close friend from his wandering days, Al Hubbard, who had invented some kind of energy transformer. Reggie paged quickly over this material, including a lengthy section containing the charter for something called the Uranium Corporation of Vancouver, which seemed too dense to penetrate.

He stopped on a page torn from the People's Songs Bulletin, an arrangement of "Follow the Drinking Gourd"[120] published in 1947 by Lee Hays, a member of the Almanac Singers and the Weavers. Long understood to be a blueprint for the Underground Railroad, sung to teach antebellum slaves how to escape to the North, Hays claimed the song conveyed much more information than the version passed down. It "told the slaves... when to go, what rivers to follow, what mountains to pass over, what turnings to make, who to ask for..." The lyrics outlined an escape route from Mobile, Alabama, up the Tombigee to the Ohio River and freedom in the North, as long as one followed the "drinking gourd," the Big Dipper, the constellation whose North Star was a beacon for this journey. Herbert's father had met the son of a famous Underground Railroad operative known as Peg Leg Joe, who moved around as a journeyman laborer from one plantation to another just north of Mobile, but whose real mission was to teach slaves the "Drinking Gourd" song and mark the escape route. In the margin Herbert had scrawled, "See no evil, hear no evil, speak no evil."

"The constellation, the one above the monkey that sees no evil!" shouted Gilbert referring to the clues in the issue of MAD. "That's the Big Dipper."

Next, a page of scrawled musical scores. Herbert Mesh, before changing his name to Mention, had learned some kind of secret about the origin of music. He wrote that he could play ancient songs with mysterious tunings on a banjo left behind by one of his father's associates, and that he learned how to do it without any help from anyone. *No one should expect me to get the dates right*, wrote Herbert, *I'm not a scholar. No one should expect strict musical composition, notes in their perfect places, I'm not a professional musician, and I'm not an expert at tritones or diminished sevenths. The math may not work out. There are discrepancies leading back to Pythagoras and even before.* But he couldn't find the words. Sentences would simply deteriorate before his eyes. The nature of this secret, as all secrets, was to be elusive.

Herbert had submitted some of his research on sorcery in the blues to anthropology journals, but they had rejected the pieces, so he'd given up on publishing any of it. The Book would be his only grip on the history of this thing. Let others continue where he left off. Let them continue from these scores, these notes. Some kind of spiritual experiment had started in America in the last century, perhaps much earlier but all we have to go on are the recordings, and the stories, and the predilection to use secret codes.

One story in particular stood out in Herbert's fevered imagination: Stack-a-Lee or Stackolee[121] or Stagger Lee gunned Billy down, all for a nine-gallon Stetson hat. What was the true meaning of this? Herbert had interviewed people from the Biloxi area, taking extensive notes. The man they called Stagger Lee had swaggered off the levee and had blown away the sheriff.

Juxtaposed to these interview notes, and scribbled in the margins, were Robert Johnson's lyrics, with more scribbled questions: How could musicians like Johnson wield power? Incompetent in social situations, in raising families, in staying true to their spouses… how could they keep clear of drink, drugs, and self-destructive patterns? What made them so adept? What secret did they know and share with only a select few?

Herbert did not scribble any answers to these questions. The sections that followed, that made up the bulk of The Book, appeared to be travelogues accompanied by graying photographs of a grizzled Herbert Mesh with unknown persons standing in front of pyramids, in the jungle at the purported source of the Nile, at the Taj Mahal, in a Himalayan ashram.

After these travel notes, it seemed that pages were missing; Herbert wrote a letter to Freddie Falloni in 1938, but there is nothing again until 1948, when Freddie, at that time at Columbia Records, joined him on a haphazard crusade through the Deep South to find what the old bluesmen called *mojo*, the lucky hand, the spell that puts women in that state of rapture that men can't resist. The performer's mojo could be harnessed, thought Herbert, to drive forward a blues uprising, a salvation for the black man in America.

They worked together, but split up to cover more territory. Freddie thought the thing had surfaced in New Orleans, with Professor Longhair,[122] and he followed that thread to J&M Studios to watch Dave Bartholomew conduct Fats Domino sessions. The war had been over for a few years, and various black studies that had been interrupted were cautiously resumed, the most impressive of which was the Fisk University study of the folklore of the Deep South, in which Lewis Jones and Alan Lomax recorded rural blues in Mississippi. But Freddie thought that the study had failed to locate the cultural wellsprings of this black underground society. *There's a mystery here in New Orleans,* Freddie wrote to Herbert in one of his many letters included in The Book. *People come here looking for it, listening for it. They know it's in the music but they don't know what it is, and they'll keep searching for it. But I'm sure it's right here.*

Indeed, the signs were obvious that Freddie was on to something and frightening the local power structure. Cards with "The Eyes of the Klan are

Upon You" were inserted in the windshield wiper of his parked car. And one night in a Negroes-only club in Baton Rouge, where he'd come to field-record a handsome black curly-haired singer, a legend in those parts, someone had planted a time bomb and the whole stage blew up just as he walked in.

Herbert wrote warning letters back to Freddie, alarmed at his mishaps. A conspiracy theory had taken shape in Herbert's notes. He alluded more often to something called the Corporation, a group that had engineered the commercialism of jazz in an effort to stamp out primitive music. Blue notes were incorporated into big-band arrangements as musical jokes and rendered politically harmless like comic strips on the back pages of serious newspapers. But the primitive blues grew as it gained more listeners in the juke joints. Its transcendent effect couldn't be ignored.

Herbert sought its roots in the Mississippi Delta. He wrote about the rumors of Robert Johnson's meeting the devil at the crossroads, and how that rumor had hovered over other blues performers as well, including a distant cousin Tommy Johnson, and that the name "Johnson" seemed to have something to do with it.

Freddie's reply to Herbert concerned the recording of Johnson's records on the stage of Hammond's "From Spirituals to Swing" concert. Reminding Herbert of the fact that the man himself, Robert Johnson, had been murdered before he could appear in the concert, Freddie wrote about dark forces hovering around Hammond. Leftists were starting to feel the heat, and Hammond's connection to the *New Masses* put his other work under a magnifying glass.

And it puts you under that glass, Herbert wrote back to Freddie. *There are people who don't want this type of music to gain any more popularity. Be careful.*

So Freddie and Herbert shared this special recording of a Johnson record played on a phonograph on a stage, background crowd noise and all, and everyone seemed to want to get it from them. They kept it floating in the U.S. Postal Service, mailed back and forth for more than a decade, and to friends and colleagues with strict instructions to mail it to someplace else. Eventually Herbert hid it under lock and key, "lost in the funhouse along with my other papers" according to Herbert's last letter in The Book, dated January 5, 1950.

Freddie's reply, stuffed into The Book's jacket at the end, indicated how nervous he was about making sure this recording stayed lost in the funhouse, and how a certain contact of theirs, Cornell "Stackalee" Woodrow, had given him a key, and a pendant with a special stone, a "thunder-stone" as he called it. A lucky charm from this spiritual experiment. "We know where it's going now," Freddie had wrote at the end of his reply. "We can now see the vision, hear the future, and speak truth to power."

* * *

Beatrice was uncharacteristically snapping her fingers and humming "That Old Black Magic"[123] softly, at a much slower tempo than usual, as if she were skimming the handsome bachelors at a Park Place cocktail party. Johnny couldn't comprehend how, or why, he knew this song, even this particular arrangement. Another trick of the womb? Did Mrs. Mention and Johnny's own mother grow up at the same time and have babies, at the same time, listening to the same tunes? At some point in the song she stopped humming and said, echoing the black storekeeper at Mad Records, "You better put it back where you found it, if you know what's good for you."

But by now Reggie had grabbed one of the old records from the trunk, the one with the red label marked "Special from Spirituals to Swing," and had set about getting it started on the record player in the garage, so they could jam to it.

The sound, curling out of the speaker like smoke, was Robert Johnson's "Terraplane Blues",[124] one of the songs played on a phono-graph on the stage of Carnegie Hall, with chamber acoustics blending the audience's murmur and scuffling with the music. Reggie could only guess at the level of political intrigue behind this event, recorded in so haphazard a fashion. It was the audition of primitive black music before the ruling white audience. Robert Johnson's plaintive voice and the sound of his guitar pierced the buffeted clouds of opinion, distaste, and loathing, and cried its soulfulness into a wilderness of skyscrapers and subways. Blues, yet modern, the song compares the car to a woman. He's going to check her oil! Get down in her connection and tangle with her wires! Mash down her little starter, set her spark plug on fire!

To Johnny, the recording was pure musical enlightenment. Robert Johnson's guitar strokes jabbed at him with precision. Right in the middle it seemed to slow down for a verse as the guitar strokes softened, but the timing was perfect, and the effect was like gliding through a dip or wash on a desert road, and then it came right back up out of the wash, guitar strokes jabbing again, back on the road.

Reggie said he's hearing two guitars, a completely independent bass line and two-part chords along with high-string riffs. It took a while for them all to realize it was just one guitar, one player, and he was singing at the same time. Robert Johnson didn't obey the rules of rhythm and harmony. You couldn't find a way into his music, if you wanted to play along with him. He was playing for himself.

As Reggie gathered everything up to return to the record shop, Johnny reached a decision. The music had helped him make up his mind. He was going to escape from his father's grip. Something in the music was calling him.

* * *

Searchlights poked the dusk sky, prematurely blackened by the waning storm, seeking out the moon through the clouds. The spectacle at the Boardwalk had grown way beyond the usual proportions. An unheard and uncounted nation of teenagers had emerged from an underground of shadows. 43,000 was the last estimate, straining the wooden piers with their weight and threatening to topple entire sections of the creaky Boardwalk into the dirty sand. They bobbed and angled for a peek at Ricky Nelson, proclaimed now by the local media as the champ of Atlantic City, having broken Sinatra's previous attendance record at Steel Pier. Enforcement agencies double-shifted the entire weekend, clocking in overtime. The police presence increased tension in the city, spooking drivers and snarling traffic downtown in a cacophony of car horns and backfires that set teeth grinding for every cop in earshot.

Ballzo, Tony Just, and the Chief of Police stood at a railing at Virginia Avenue and the Boardwalk, the terminus of Rt. 30, watching a police copter fly over the crowd carrying Ricky and his entourage to the backstage area.

"We got a barricade up between our kids and the jigs," said the Chief, addressing Ballzo's concern about the storefronts stocked with mob-distributed merchandise. Thousands of white kids had gathered south of this barricade at the entrance to Steel Pier, and thousands more black kids and adults gathered north of the barricade above Virginia Avenue to await the coming of the Jackal to Central Pier. The Chief had called for reinforcements from as far away as Cape May and Camden. The New Jersey State Police, out in force working overtime with traffic problems, carried riot gear. The National Guard had been put on alert. The aircraft carrier USS *Tarawa*, a world traveler displacing over 27,000 tons that had narrowly missed action in the Pacific in two wars and had been placed in reserve at the Philadelphia Navy Yard, steamed out of Delaware Bay to a point in the Atlantic about 40 miles east of Longport, ostensibly for routine maneuvers and coastal attack practice, sighting Lucy the Elephant as ground zero.

"A bit overboard, maybe?" Ballzo was irritated by Tony Just's presence, the fact that Tony Just put him out of the loop. "We don't need the military, we can handle this."

Tony Just anticipated this, and kept his response smooth. "We rely on you to handle it. Your job is the Jackal. But as you know, our client has more at stake here."

"You mean that nigger Cornell Woodrow."

Tony Just winced at the low-class slur, but his lack of response confirmed it.

The Chief eyed them both with suspicion. Some kind of dissension in the ranks?

"How could that nigger be that important?" Ballzo enunciated on purpose, hoping to push a button in this friend of ours from New York.

Tony Just turned to fully face him, his eyes piercing the dark. "He has 'the touch' they call it. We don't know the extent of it, what may come out of it. Your boy, for example. He and his friends found Mention's papers. We think your son might have learned 'the touch' and is starting to use it."

What of it, Ballzo thought, proud of his kid. "Well maybe he *should* use it, a-and maybe *we* could use it. What difference does it make, as long as we get our cut?"

"It makes a big difference to our friends in New York. We want those papers."

Not for the first time Ballzo suspected another agenda, one he was not privy to.

"We need to... neutralize their effect." Tony Just talked in pauses. "And your boy... if he has them... you need to take care of that. Our friends in New York... They are depending on us to fulfill this... contract."

The Chief had averted his eyes midway through this exchange, not wanting to be seen as having heard anything. The roar from the Boardwalk grew louder, and minor scuffles were breaking out everywhere, so the Chief had reason to excuse himself. Jeez! What kind of clients do these wise guys have?

* * *

Johnny B crouched under the Boardwalk in the rendezvous spot, scowling, while Lucy caged a cigarette from members of the Irish gang from school. Johnny knew some of them, knew also that they scorned all the Italians, which outnumbered them at the school. They slouched like Puerto Ricans, had ripped their clothes straight off the soundtrack album to *West Side Story*.[125] They'd twisted their tobacco cigs into what looked like reefers.

Earlier that day, before they had returned the stuff to the locker, Johnny had snatched a bit of the herb which had the same texture as Mexican Mary, and rolled his own reefer, a real one. Johnny had the passes Big Dom had given him for Ricky Nelson, but he wasn't going to show his face; his father would have told Big Dom to keep an eye out for him. He also held the passes to the Jackal show. So he'd talked Lucy into going down the Boardwalk to the Jackal gig early, see what's happening. He shared the strange reefer with Lucy. It was bitter, and they were coughing uncontrollably, drawing attention from the Irish kids. One of them grab-assed Lucy and started smooching with her, and Lucy was giggling, enjoying it a bit too much. It looked like Johnny would have to intervene.

Instead, Reggie's unnerving cries of anguish intervened. He showed up wailing for Gilbert, where's Gilbert? Johnny had time to grab Lucy's arm and pull her back from her fun.

Reggie was out of his mind. He'd lost Gilbert in the massive crowd at the gates to the show on the Boardwalk above them. "Twelve, he's only twelve! What if they know we found that trunk? What if they're after him?"

"Man, don't worry," Johnny said soothingly. "Gilbert can fend for himself. He's probably waiting at the ticket gate." Johnny brought out his fifth of Johnny Walker Red, offered some to Reggie, who didn't even see it, so wrapped up in his trauma. Lucy grabbed the bottle and took a long swig.

"So let's *go!*" Reggie started tugging at Johnny's sleeve.

"Yo man, just *cool it,* watch the jacket." Johnny's head suddenly reeled; the booze seemed to be fighting whatever that stuff was that he'd smoked. In another moment he might just puke.

Reggie wrung his hands, twirled in tight circles, babbling. His kid brother. All he's got, really, in this world.

Johnny could see everything was falling apart. They might not even make it to the show. He straightened up, swallowed hard, and grabbed the bottle from Lucy. He was jealous, and he had no right to be jealous. "Hey, leave some for the rest of us." He pretended to take a swig but didn't let the evil liquid pass his lips. Instead, he frowned over his shoulder at the Irish kids circling like hyenas.

Lucy let out a tremendous whiskey belch, then giggled. His obvious jealousy made her tingle. Was she filled with delight because she felt a different love coming from Johnny? Had she graduated from being his mistress of the night? Was he accepting her as a friend, perhaps even a real lover? She smiled sweetly at him.

Johnny, caught in her smile, felt a wave of shame come over him, and on cue, a rogue wave dashed up the simple sand, its roar galloping behind. The wave nearly reached their feet. What had he been doing all these months to this poor girl? It was rape, pure and simple, even if she didn't know it, even though he was underage himself.

A distant roar, much louder than the ocean, rumbled overhead on the Boardwalk, and they could hear Ricky Nelson's band starting up, the opening bars to "Hello Mary Lou"[126] and the roar of the crowd doubled, if that was even possible. Reggie shrieked about having to go find Gilbert and took off.

Johnny took Lucy in hand and they made their way down the beach to steps north of Steel Pier, toward the Jackal's gig, with the Irish *West Side Story* fakers skulking behind them.

* * *

Gilbert knew his brother would be looking for him. Reggie was frightened, the first time Gilbert had ever seen him that way. Scared of what may happen, now that they knew about the steamer trunk. "Don't tell anyone, not *anyone,*" Reggie had shouted, "and especially don't say where it is." But Gilbert was not scared. His father! He'd left them a treasure.

And now he'd just seen his idol, the pop star Ricky Nelson, in a blur of motion all glowing white and shimmering around the edges, leaving a trail of white mist as he scooted on by with his entourage at the back entrance. Gilbert had been drawn to the back to watch the helicopter; now he stood nailed to his spot, gazing in dumbfound infatuation at the long-legged blonde that emerged from the mist of Ricky's entourage. The twin globes of her perfectly round bottom, squeezed tightly by her diaphanous dress, seemed ready to burst at a touch. The dress outlined the contours of her body, showing no hint of underwear. Gilbert relished every twitch, and fell into a swoon as her swinging gate revealed her exquisitely bulging bosom. She looked at him, at *him!* And he felt his feet leaving the boards, floating in the power of her glance.

What dragged him back to earth were the hands of Johnny's father. Frank Balzano had come up from behind and grabbed his shoulders in a firm but fatherly way. "Ain't you a bit young for that? Where's your family?"

Gilbert blinked and trembled a bit. This was his first encounter with the infamous Ballzo. He knew mobsters carried guns but he didn't see one. He could sense, however, the connection to the treasure his father had left behind.

"What're you doing here? Where're your little friends?"

"I wanted to see Ricky Nelson," Gilbert blurted out. "Reggie and I, we're meeting Johnny and Lucy, they got passes to get in."

Ballzo quickly looked around for his son. "So where are they?"

"I dunno, I lost Reggie. He said he'd meet me at the ticket gate."

"That's around front. We'll never get through this crowd. C'mon," he grabbed Gilbert, "I got a pass for ya. We'll meet them inside."

Ballzo took the kid in through the back entrance and into the green room, filled to capacity with an odd assortment of local dignitaries in full evening dress, wise guys in bulging double-breasted suits, letter-sweater jocks from the high-school football team, assistant producers in cardigan sweaters wearing headphones, brightly-dressed paraplegics in wheelchairs, work-shirt stiffs with long hair and mustaches carrying guitar cases ...and the band, all dressed in black suits with cowboy ties, surrounding a bemused Ricky Nelson sheathed in a blazing white tight-fitting suit spangled with ruby sequins and topped with a turquoise-studded cowboy tie.

Gilbert's heartthrob, the perfect blonde in the diaphanous dress, had draped herself around Ricky like an exotic scarf. Gilbert had entered the inner sanctum, the back room of power, the tiny control center for the universe, and they're roaring outside, stomping their feet in time to some tinny amplified music, waiting for their star to appear. And here he was! What would Reggie think?

"Hey," Gilbert shouted without even thinking, "My older brother think's I'm a poor little fool!"

Laughter all around, and Ricky himself took notice. "Hey, little man. You're not a fool. Atlantic City, sure can be a lonesome town." Ricky paused, his blue eyes radiating sincerity as he regarded Gilbert as the little brother he never had. "You play an instrument?"

"Sure do, harmonica! A-and I'm in a band! With my older brother."

Ricky brought Gilbert into the fold, introduced him all around. Gilbert told everyone that his father was a giant in the music industry, over in England, and that he was saving up to run away and find him, and start a band of his own with his father's help.

Ricky was amused, and the blonde bent down to look directly at Gilbert. He bathed in her musky aroma, greeted with a smile her blue stare, and adored every nook and cranny of her smiling face… even the faint hint of a bruise on her cheek. She whispered her name, Babbs, to his ear, and brought her hand to his face to brush away an errant lock of hair on his forehead and look deeply into his eyes. Gilbert nearly passed out.

* * *

The Ricky Nelson concert was well under way as Reggie worked concentric arcs through the tumultuous crowd around the front entrance, oblivious inside his shroud of doom to the pushing and shoving, focused on finding and cursing out his little brother. *What the fuck is it about him? No common sense, and he doesn't listen. Don't lose sight of me, and if you do, meet me here. Don't wander, don't let anyone take you anywhere else. Goddamn it.*

A sob worked its way up his throat; *what if Gilbert had been kidnapped or something? Holding him to get his dad out of hiding?* In this city you could get snatched just a block away from the Boardwalk. The city was scary enough to keep Reggie and all his friends, all the kids he knew, isolated in this dazzling stretch of Boardwalk with throngs of other kids just like them. Venturing west into the actual city, past Pacific Avenue's row of seedy motels, was unthinkable. Only Johnny. He said he'd done it many times, even has some black friends out there. He could use Johnny's help now, but Johnny was hiding from his father.

Reggie kept scanning, feeling guilty that he'd not been more responsible. Now the kid's missing his favorite pop star. Reggie could hear echoes of Ricky's band starting up another song, a sad one, and Ricky's voice floating in the ether above the echo, singing about being a teenage idol and how people envy him. *But they have no way of knowing how lonesome it can be, to be alone, just a rolling stone.*[127]

God, how many times had he criticized Gilbert, mercilessly, for no other reason than to try to get laughs? Calling him a fool when we're all fools, all of us. All I've got is a basket case for a mother, and for a father? A phantom of the night on some kind of historical quest. What if I never see Gilbert again?

Reggie was tearful, nearly choking on this thought, when his last concentric arc intersected the police barricade separating the pre-dominantly white teenage crowd from a menacing confusion of blacks, all ages and sizes, scrambling to stay one step ahead of police batons. A swirl of rowdy white kids pushed through the barricade, carrying Reggie with them, to attack the cops from the rear. Reggie threw up his hands in surrender, yelling help, and stumbled toward the police line hoping for rescue. Amid shouts of "get back" and "nigger lovers" Reggie got whacked by a baton to the forehead, knocking him senseless.

* * *

Drums along the Boardwalk. Sounding at first like a Mohawk uprising, the rhythm morphed into a steady, extended "walkin' the boogie" beat,[128] with the Jackal's entire audience rippling in rhythmic syncopation. Johnny was higher than he'd ever been, just out there, on whatever that stuff was from the trunk. And Lucy? How to protect her? Johnny cleared his thoughts enough to round up his entourage, a few young toughs from the high school who'd follow him anywhere, just for the adventure.

Now they gathered in a tight group around Johnny and Lucy, the only white kids in an ocean of dark-skinned people that kept arriving in waves, as if out of the dark Atlantic, to watch the Jackal fire up the makeshift stage at Central Pier. Many of them held records with no label and no credits; Johnny recognized them as the booty from the warehouse he'd unloaded on Cornell Woodrow. Must have been 10,000 discs in that truck.

All at once, the smell of fish got up his nose like nobody's business, and he couldn't avoid it. People all around were asking the same question, what's that smell of fish, oh baby! The scent was a prelude to the Jackal's new song.

With sweat pouring down his face and streaking his blue serge suit, the Jackal launched the song like a rocket from his National Steel guitar, sliding up the frets like Elmore James into the opening of what at first sounded like an accelerated "Hawaiian Boogie"[129] but exploded into a rhythm four times faster, driving home a set of nonsense syllables, all anyone could remember from the song, "nummo, nummo, nummo..."

The sheer raw energy pulverized Johnny. He gasped for air during the entire performance, which may have lasted four minutes but seemed more like 400 years. The audience came alive, a mass of writhing bodies bouncing like balloons in a wind tunnel, as the Jackal preened, danced, and thrashed his guitar about the stage, coming on wilder than Screamin' Jay Hawkins; combining everything, Presley, Berry, Little Richard, Jerry Lee Lewis, and Bo Diddley rhythms all into this one song. Midway through, on some kind of bridge, the Jackal turned the song around, changed the tempo, and drove it home, pointing the neck of his guitar at the crowd in front like a submachine gun perpendicular to his right hip.

Just then a teenage white girl climbed the lip of the stage and, on her knees, reached out to grab the Jackal's crotch. The Jackal leered at her and thrust out his pelvis; her hand splayed across the crotch of his tight blue serge pants. A photographer's flash momentarily blinded everyone; a young Phil Spector, stage right, had captured the moment on his Nikon F, the first single lens reflex camera that introduced Nikon to the world.

The cop standing next to Spector, thinking him a reporter and enraged that this spectacle of a white girl grabbing a black man's crotch would probably make the morning news, ran out to intercept, grabbed her about the waist and hoisted her up in the air, kicking and screaming.

The Jackal drove it further than home, straight into the gullet, once again chanting what would be the final chorus. The audience roared back "nummo nummo nummo..."

"The fuck are they saying?" Johnny screamed to Lucy, "is it 'no more'?" But Lucy's attention had already been drawn to a fight out on the perimeter. Black police batons flickered in the Boardwalk lights, then slammed down on heads with a sickening bop sound. In a flash she disappeared into the thick crowd. Johnny dove in looking for her, elbowed his way through it and staggered to its perimeter, falling out into a space bathed white in klieg lights and rimmed with sparkling helmets. He nearly ran right into Big Dom, who dwarfed the police captain with the bullhorn next to him. Big Dom, midway through swinging a baseball bat at what looked to be Skinny's head, did a double-take and glared at Johnny. "Yo! Get that 'fucker!"

Get that 'fucker? Johnny barely had time to stand before the bluecoats had him by the arms, and dragged him before Big Dom, who dispatched an officer to go find Frank Balzano, quick. Then he leaned into Johnny's face. "Johnny, you got to come in. You don't come in, you gonna be a problem."

Johnny choked back tears. "That what you call a favor?"

Big Dom softened a bit. "Listen kid, I promised I'd help you out, 'cause of your mom. But this thing..." He looked up to see if Ballzo had arrived yet. "It's out of my hands. You take this beef to your father."

Johnny strained to look around, and that's when he saw Reggie, crumpled up on the boards and bleeding. "Reggie!" he yelled, struggling with the cops, who had him firmly by both arms. Then back at Big Dom, with all the anger he could muster, "is this what you fuckin' wanted?"

"It's not what *I* wanted," barked his father, who'd just arrived like the eye of a hurricane, bringing calm with him, a vortex of silence at the heart of the riot. Ballzo continued in a lower tone. "This party's on account of your friend Cornell. Y'know, that black fella, gave you that new bass? Wha, you think I don't know these things?"

Ballzo then turned to the police captain and nodded, as if the captain were a waiter at a garden party. The cops let Johnny go, and Ballzo put his arm around his son. "Don't worry, we'll get Reggie taken care of." He motioned to another officer, and several cleared a path to Reggie, now moaning in a fetal position. "Call Beatrice Mention," he told another officer, "she's in Margate, tell her to meet her son at the hospital."

Johnny worked up the courage to ask, "You in control here?"

Ballzo smiled at his son. "I wish. This thing's outta control. Listen, what you did, I can forgive. But you need to come in, tell us what you know. About that stuff you found, from your friend's dad."

Ballzo looked back at the cops. Then he leaned forward to whisper to his son. "You're under suspicion, you know. The last person to see Freddie alive. They think you had something to do with it." Then he straightened up and spoke louder, in case anyone was listening. "Forget about the money, the truck. You can make restitution. But you gotta get back on my team."

"I hear ya," Johnny smiled ruefully, and quickly added, "Dad." The truth was, he was startled by the news about the cops. Would he be safe on his dad's team?

Ballzo relaxed. "Okay, look, you go with your friend, to the hospital." He pointed to where the cops were half-dragging Reggie to the side of the Boardwalk.

"What about Lucy? She's..."

"Don't worry son, we'll find her and get her out."

Johnny sighed, and just as quickly felt deeply ashamed. What kind of hipster was he? He'd betrayed his father before, and he was about to do it again. He'd deceived Lucy all these months, and now he'd abandoned her to the ravages of a full-blown riot.

* * *

Through the rumble of loud music, the screams of the badly beaten, and the roar of a crowd sensing and reacting to the very idea of wild-ness, Lucy gazed up through the glow of the Boardwalk lights to a flat-black night sky. She saw a point of light, so close to the moon that it couldn't be a star or a planet. It must be one of those new satellites she'd read about in the newspaper. We humans are so intelligent now, we can hang our own stars in the sky. We are so good we can do anything.

At first Lucy didn't feel it when hands grabbed her every limb and she was borne into the air, closer to this fabulously beautiful night sky. The jiggling and abrupt changes in body posture didn't bother her so much as she was carried high above the crowd to the ocean side of the Boardwalk and down the steps. The sand felt cool and damp as they lay her underneath the Boardwalk, a part of the beach that never sees the sun. There were six of them, maybe eight, that had carried her, and more showed up, she couldn't count. Her clothes came off easy because she didn't want to resist.

One by one, they penetrated her, and after a while it didn't hurt so much; but deep down inside her, in a place she could never explain to anyone, not even her shrink, she could feel the bright fire of her determination to survive, the molten core of her being that was unassailable from the physical world. No one could penetrate this core, not multiple penises, not even the electrodes at the hospital. They couldn't touch her there.

And when she was finally left alone, hardened to the breeze off the ocean, she examined as much of her body as she could see, for bruises or cuts, and she fingered the sticky moisture between her legs. They were teenagers, black, hispanic, and white. With her racial mix, what did it matter?

When the nausea abated and her brain stopped whirling about like a dervish, she picked herself up, wrapped around her as much of the clothes as she could find, and followed the shoreline south to her beach, about five miles away.

* * *

Gilbert left Steel Pier charged with energy but nowhere to go with it. Figuring his brother had left him behind for more promising adventures, probably with Johnny at the Jackal show, Gilbert felt liberated. Alone in the promised land. But... with only a few dollars in his pocket, and Million Dollar Pier's pinball machines closed at this hour, there wasn't much to do for a kid his age, except to go home, close the door to his room, and succumb to the fantasy blonde. He loved the Jitney buses, so he took one to the edge of town, and walked all the way through Ventnor to Margate and a darkened house. No one home!

Gilbert found the spare key near the back door. With the house all to himself, he was so thrilled he didn't know what to do first. Sneak through Reggie's drawers, snatch some of his condoms? But all he could think about was Ricky Nelson's blonde, her bosom, the curves of her gorgeous bottom... his memory of her body was quite clear, and he could pretend she was right there with him, in the house all by them-selves, and as he pulled off all his clothes and stood naked in the sunroom, bathed in the yellow light of the desk lamp in the corner, he felt her eyes on him, and his penis grew erect. He caught his reflection in the bay window, his glowing white rippling torso, his cock poised for climax, and for an instant wondered if anybody outside could see him... but this indescribably delicious feeling that came over his body, of being watched, only made him grow larger, only brought him closer to this primal exhilaration. Each ticking second sliced away another layer of guilt, guile, and shame, leaving uncovered the primal urge. Here it was, the dominating force, the goal of all ambitions, the dark corner of all drama, the warm center of all comedy, the true agenda lurking behind every encounter, the entire point of fashion and dressing up, the very reason for existence... this penis that has guided him to the cliff-edge of climax.

Well of course someone had seen him, and it happened to be Mrs. Quotidia, the grumpy deli-slicer at Barcana's Grocery, who'd once met Beatrice Mention and didn't like anything about her except her Italian handbag. Mrs. Quotidia would always clutch her rosary, the one she bought at the Vatican decades ago, in her right hand whenever she walked the six blocks from the store to her home at night, and on this night she held up the rosary, all balled up in her angry fist, the way an exorcist would banish the Beast, to block out the image of naked Gilbert. Quickening her steps, fearful of some kind of penis uprising, of naked boys running amok in her community, she reached her home, secured her multiple locks, and breathing deeply to calm herself, dialed the police, choking as she described the house and what the boy had been doing, that perversely reoccurring image that so frightened her, an image she could not ignore.

The Margate City Police dispatcher knew how restive the troops had been all night, sitting on their hands, waiting for any sign of the riot to reach south as far as the city line. She radioed the incident as not just indecent exposure but also a possible statutory rape-in-progress.

It sure looked suspicious to the first officers who showed up. Training their police-car spotlights on the front lawn of the Mention house, they caught a half-naked pudgy teenage girl, leering in an obscene manner at a completely naked younger boy in the open bay window. One officer shouted "Hey!" and the boy crumpled in painful shame and slammed down the window. The girl turned to face them wearing only a shirt ripped open down the front, with her breast popping in and out, and ripped panties. The officers froze, and took deep breaths, and finally one came running from a police car with a blanket to put over her.

She said her name was Lucy. The unmistakeable stench of sex floated off her like butterflies tossed in the winds of intrigue.

* * *

"OK, son, you can tell me. Were you playin' with your peter?" The fat, pizza-faced Sergeant who, sans uniform, could have passed for an insurance agent, spoke quietly to the boy with a put-on lily-tongued Irish accent.

"I'm not your son," mumbled Gilbert, hugging himself against an imaginary chill. They were seated in the Sergeant's office. The Sergeant loomed from behind his massive blond wood desk as Gilbert trembled on a folding chair, vainly seeking comfort in the beige walls, brown carpeting, blond wood trim, and bronze balustrade that separated the office from the rest of the activity. The precinct was built in the same modern style as the new Catholic church, all cinder-block, bronze, and blond wood trim.

"Son, y'know what I'm talking about. Were you pullin' your peter, or what?"

"I dunno," was all Gilbert could mumble. He couldn't bring himself to admit it, couldn't even look the Sergeant in the eye.

"Alright, son, just tell me what you were doing."

"I was just getting undressed for bed," Gilbert blurted out.

"You didn't see the girl outside, looking in at you?"

"No!" he lied, a little too quickly he suddenly realized. "Uh, what girl?"

The Sergeant grunted impatiently. "You were home all night? Where're your parents?"

"I dunno, my mother's out. My brother Reggie and I went to see Ricky Nelson at Steel Pier. I lost Reggie and came back home by myself."

"You weren't down at that other show, the Jackal?"

"No!" Now Gilbert felt a bit relieved. His excuse about undressing, that was logical, wasn't it? Lucy outside, what could he do about that? He fought back the thought, how she had touched him through the open window, how it had been so delicious, so exhilarating, so...

"And you don't know this girl?"

"Uh..." But there was no escape. Shame slammed him down. "Yeah, she lives down the block I think. My brother Reggie knows her."

These kids today. Jesus Christ. Probably fornicating in the bushes. Listening to that jungle music.

The Sergeant left the boy in his office to get the latest report on the goings-on downtown. The riot outside the Jackal show was contained. Kids were brought in and questioned, but no one could remember the song that triggered the chaos. They did remember the fish scent in the air while it played, a strong decaying smell of dead fish. Of course they were near enough to the ocean to explain that. But there was no explanation for the kids, the way they all of a sudden just acted wild. The music seemed to affect even the kids outside the show who could barely hear it. Roving gangs had committed vandalism and started rumbles, and two rapes were reported but never investigated. The men had joined Balzano and his henchman, with clubs to attack the Jackal audience. So a few white kids got beaten as well, so what. Teach 'em a lesson they'll never forget.

Christ. He didn't want to do this, but Detective Delatore had ordered him to start a file on this kid Gilbert Mention with an official warning for indecent exposure. Delatore had some theory about the Freddie Falloni homicide, that it was connected to the kid's father, the missing Herbert Mention, and his brother Reggie knew something, and so did that mobster's kid, Johnny. They were all up to something.

* * *

The creep of cold dawn gave Johnny the shivers out on the sidewalk, about halfway between his father's home and Lucy's, blackness giving way to a metallic pink at the far edge of the Atlantic. His weariness felt like a graduation from the late-people life; he'd stayed up later than everyone else.

An hour earlier he'd helped Mrs. Mention serve snacks to tamp down on the high-nerve energy and get Gilbert and a bandaged Reggie to bed. Reggie had been all wisecracking about civil rights and police brutality. Pestered by the cops surrounding his hospital bed about his association with the Negro population, eventually one particular leering officer attempted to provoke him by asking when he was gonna stop loving niggers. Reggie had wanted to respond, but he had lost all power of speech, too weak to fight. As he told the story in the brightly lit kitchen his mother was horrified, muttering to herself as she served more food.

Gilbert sat morosely contemplating his hands, offering no comments, cowering before some imagined onslaught of teasing contempt from Reggie. But it never came. Maybe Reggie didn't know what had happened last night.

Something happened last night, Johnny thought, something that goes beyond all reason, an inexplicable change, after which nothing would be the same. He could no longer even think about love with Lucy. It was no longer a young world.

The police car that had been in front of Lucy's house for hours was quietly joined by an ambulance with its lights out and siren off, as if a war had ended. White coats had scurried in the predawn darkness to carry a drugged Lucy out on her back, tied tightly to a stretcher, as her step-father watched from the front door, arms folded in resignation. They inserted her, stretcher and all, into the softly padded interior of the back of the ambulance. Shock treatments, Johnny thought. They'll experiment with her brain, disconnect the important parts. She won't be able to recognize melodies in one experiment, won't recognize rhythm in another.

"You'll get over it." Ballzo, his father, caught Johnny by surprise. Somehow he had stepped out of the shadows behind him without being heard. Stiffening, Johnny turned, ready for battle. "Take it easy, son." He carried a paper bag with something large inside, a mason jar. "Justice is already served." He motioned Johnny to take a look.

The mason jar held a viscous liquid, formaldehyde, and inside, bouncing in the murk, were a pair of testicles.

"The Jackal left something behind." Ballzo smirked. "I'll have it gift-wrapped, sent to your friend Cornell."

"He's not my friend," Johnny blurted out, reeling in nausea.

Ballzo put his arm around his son's shoulders. "Take it easy, take it easy. Your little stunt didn't do any damage. Took balls though." He looked again at the mason jar in his paper bag, and smirked at his own joke. He'd kept the jar for years, a souvenir, the testicles of the late great Johnny Ace,[130] taken from his corpse after the "accident" backstage. He was surprised that his son hadn't understood the joke, that it really wasn't the Jackal's, but he left it alone. Maybe it will keep his son on his toes and watching his back. "I'm kinda proud of you, takin' the initiative like that." Then he squared off Johnny's shoulders. "Just don't do it again. They're watching you, watching both of us."

Johnny looked up at his father. "Who do you work for?"

"Don't ask questions," Ballzo snapped at him. Then he softened, and looked around to see if anyone was watching. "Look, as you get older, you'll have friends, you'll be an associate. Get to be a big earner, you'll get your button, be a man of honor." He paused. "And you can keep the bass guitar. Just forget that nigger."

"Why all this?"

"Why?" snapped Ballzo indignantly. "The man was dangerous."

"Dangerous? A rock 'n' roll singer?"

"It's more than that. It's family business."

"Like Freddie?" The instant Johnny said it, he regretted saying it.

Ballzo frowned and looked hard at his son. "That wasn't me, and it wasn't family. But the cops... they may need to arrest somebody." He looked away then, leaving his son hanging.

Johnny heard something in his head, a singer in a high-pitched weary voice, not an old bluesman's but a young, imploring voice. "You'd better come on in my kitchen, babe it going to be raining outdoors."[131] And then a muscular guitar riff. It replayed in his head, he couldn't shake it. Where did that come from? Freddie had once told him that our earliest exposure to music is our most profound, that it forms the basis of our understanding of music and influences our musical tastes.

What Johnny didn't know was that he'd heard this song, over and over, while still in his real mother's womb.

* * *

Reggie bolted upright in his bed. "Johnny!"

Johnny and Gilbert stopped their impromptu practice and came upstairs.

"Johnny, it suddenly hit me. We've got to get that stuff out of that trunk."

"Why would we wanna do that?" Johnny didn't want to risk going out and running into the cops.

"I don't know, it was in a dream. I saw a note, pinned to the trunk. A note from my father."

Johnny and Gilbert set out for Mad Records. Johnny didn't like it, he didn't have a plan. Risking everything on a dream! As if Reggie could see the future in his dreams.

The black storekeeper in scarves was at the store cash register, just like before, only with a smile on her face. Her lively eyes met Johnny's, and she beckoned them to the rear of the store. She picked up a brown knapsack in the corner, drew Johnny to her, and whispered in his ear. "My son, use this. You must hurry. I'll show you a way out."

My son? Who was this woman? Johnny nervously glanced back toward the store windows. A black Cadillac was parked across the street.

Gilbert, wide-eyed, tugged at Johnny's arm. They went out the back door to the storage lockers, and quickly got out the trunk. A note was pinned to the wooden frame, on stationery that showed the three monkeys.

Take everything. Reggie, my son, keep the book safe. Gilbert, my son, keep the acetate safe. Divide the rest among you. Come back for more later. HM.

Gilbert was thunderstruck. *"Gilbert, my son…"* He held the note dearly in his hand, while Johnny started filling the knapsack. By the time Gilbert snapped out of it, Johnny was ready to split.

"This way," the storekeeper beckoned to a closet. Inside was a trap door propped open. "It's a secret entrance to an underground river to the bay. Make a right on the walkway and follow it about twenty minutes. Don't go left, that leads to the old train station. Go right, about twenty minutes, and you'll see a ladder that goes up inside Lucy the Elephant's maintenance closet. There's a trapdoor you can push open, near the circuit breakers." She handed Johnny a flashlight.

Johnny knew exactly where she was talking about. He had opened the trapdoor in Lucy's closet to hide his stashes, never suspecting that a tunnel lay beneath it. They scampered down the ancient wooden ladder into the depths below, Johnny lugging the overfilled knapsack. They crouched and stepped gingerly through the dank tunnel, following the sound of running water, as hundreds of escaping slaves had done before them over a hundred years earlier. They eventually found the ladder leading up to Lucy.

After they left, the woman closed up the record shop and locked the closet. Smirking, she glanced out at the black Cadillac. It still waited to see what the boys would bring out. She laughed out loud. "My son, my son! Oh Robert, Daddy, you sure would be pleased." Then she went back into the storage area to tidy up.

* * *

Detective Delatore slurped the precinct coffee, now cold, and thought about his perfect record of homicide arrests over twenty years. He knew all about Balzano and his associates. They didn't need to murder radio personalities. They could just buy them off, like they've been doing. Big Dom coming around the precinct when he did, the morning after, seemed like they were fishing for information, not covering up their tracks. And Balzano himself, taking orders from someone else, last night on the Boardwalk. Another family? The name Tony Just. He'd done some research, it's a mob name. His real name is Justin Tonatio. But that name didn't ring any bells.

And this Jackal fella, now disappeared. Looks like Freddie had an appointment to make a recording with him, right before the killing. The Jackal would have been eager to get his recording done. Did he do it? That didn't make sense. Johnny, the Balzano kid, might have been there at the same time. Did he do it? Under orders from his father? That also didn't make sense, no motive, no reason to put his son at risk like that. Did someone else show up? Did they both scamper out of there when they saw someone else do it? That would explain the overturned trash cans. Their shadows could have resembled the Jersey Devil.

And there's the coroner's report. Red, blistered skin on the tips of his fingers. Rigor mortis had set in quickly on his fingers and hands. All of the... what did the coroner call it? "Adenosine triphosphate in his muscles"? Whatever that is... All of it had been burned off, causing his muscles to stiffen. If it wasn't for the obvious gunshot wound, the coroner would have decided that the man had been electrocuted.

Now who could have done a thing like that? Could the electric current have been reversed, suddenly, so that when Freddie touched the microphone...? Static for five minutes, then, somehow, the commercials reel started up. It played until the substitute disc jockey, Hi Lit, showed up. Who called Hy Lit? Who started up the commercials reel? The only fingerprints he could find were Freddie's, Hy's, Johnny's, and... another pair of prints on the radio control panel that he couldn't identify.

Delatore frowned. He couldn't let this dead-end case ruin his perfect record of homicide arrests over twenty years. He'd leave it open for awhile, to see what else might develop.

* * *

It seems that what Mrs. Mention had in mind, ultimately, now that Reggie was set to start at Harvard, was to return to England. To the real Margate, where her aunt Mary now lived. She'd had enough of New Jersey. She'd already made arrangements to sell her house and move her things back to her aunt's. Gilbert and Reggie absorbed the news in an air of serious fatality; it was the wake of Freddie's funeral, it was the revelation that their father was still out there, and they didn't argue. Reggie, for one, was looking forward to going up to Boston. Gilbert was still in a daze.

Reggie had hidden the Book among his belongings to take to Harvard. At that moment he didn't think about how easy it had been for him to be accepted at this institution. He only hoped that he would find someone at Harvard that would understand what his father had written about.

Gilbert stashed the "Special from Spirituals to Swing" acetate for safekeeping. Reggie and Johnny B split the two Johnson records, and Gilbert kept most of the dried roots, pill boxes, and liquid canisters, and what he wanted most of all, the harmonica. He imagined that it had been played by a blues man with an awesome past. All three kept their polished thunder-stones, still faintly warm at the touch.

During the nearly three weeks of dodging his father and the cops, it had become clear to Johnny that he needed to split. South Jersey would not be his future. He had been treated by the Mentions as a real member of their family, eating almost every meal with them. So he had only one thing to ask Mrs. Mention. "Can I come with you?"

* * *

Mrs. Mention paid a visit to Mr. Balzano.

"I know you've been watching us, so you know how it is, with Johnny coming over so often," she said immediately, without a moment's hesitation, as she crossed the threshold into the Balzano living room.

He glared at her, which confirmed her suspicions. She hesitated, then went on. "These children! They talk strangely. They go into the garage to play their music, where they think I can't hear them."

"What do they talk about?"

"Who knows, who really understands what these children talk about. But you know you can't hold Johnny here. You know that. You can't hold him with the motorcycles, the leather jackets."

Ballzo was taken aback. "What do you want?"

"I want you to release Johnny to my custody."

"And why would I allow that?" Ballzo leveled his gaze at her.

She sighed. "You know this life is not for him. You knew it about your wife, too."

Ballzo flinched. He could have killed her on the spot, were it not for standing orders, from Tony Just himself, to leave her alone. "And if I don't?"

"Very well," she said in that English way of saying, all right then, I'll show you. She steeled her eyes directly at him. "The boy is already at the top of the detective's list. They think he had something to do with Freddie, under your orders. I know that Cravingston will know what to do."

Ballzo thought for a moment. He'd heard of this man Cravingston. Tony Just had business with him. He smiled at Beatrice. "You realize," he told her in a smooth voice that covered his menace like a velvet sheath covering a dagger. "They'll find you. No matter where you go, there'll be someone else watching you. They'll find Johnny, and they'll find your husband's papers."

"Of course," she said. "But leave my sons alone."

Ballzo paced around all four corners of his living room like a tiger in a cage. He finished standing in front of the window, his back to her. "Go," was all he said.

A World of Permanent Novelty

A world of permanent novelty shimmered and vibrated in the Paris twilight. Seventeen-year-old Brian Jones uncurled from the fetal position, awakened by the sprightly jazz music[132] spilling out of a café up the street. He breathed it all in, the novelty of the moment, the rich coffee-scented air, the gay laughter, the preposterous music. He breathed slowly and haltingly to avoid the asthma attack that always accompanied stress.

Sleeping by day and carousing about at night. This was the way to take advantage of Paris in 1960. He sought out American jazz and bored housewives in the clubs. The novelty exhilarated him. A demonstration, a crime, a clown scene, a riot, or anything at all could be happening on the next corner.

A scuffling noise to his back caught his attention. A dark unshaven man in a gray trench coat was scratching out an inscription in the wall of the rue de Seine, next to graffiti calling for a demonstration seven years earlier, NE TRAVAILLEZ JAMAIS.

"What does it mean?" Brian asked him peevishly, in English.

The man swirled around, revealing that he wore nothing at all underneath the trench coat. He tightened the coat around his needle-thin hairy body, leering at Brian. "Never work!" He spat it out in a French-accented English like a chewed lump of tobacco. "Never get a job, never start a career." His teeth gleamed white in the twilight. His name was Franco and his friends were nearby. Brian could sense immediate adventure.

Brian had run from a scandal in his quiet home town of Cheltenham in the Cotswolds. He had begged, borrowed, and stolen his way around England. An old gentleman had tried to pick him up on the train, and he watched in fascination as the man mimicked cocksucking by sucking his thumb. Here is a fine example, he would have told his dad, another one of these hypocrites of your generation.

But why not take advantage of this? He hadn't wanted it to go very far, had never in fact gone that far before. Nothing at school had gone beyond the usual slap and tickle of English boys. The gentleman led him to a private compartment, and Brian let him have at it. Soon Brian was thrusting into the gentleman's mouth, mechanically, hearing Charlie Parker's "Scrapple to the Apple"[133] in the clickety-clack rhythm of the train in motion.

Afterwards he vomited. As the gentleman held him around the waist, guiding his slumping figure so that the vomit would fall away from them, Brian turned around and punched the man in the face. He'd never done anything like it before. He reached behind to grab the man's wallet, and then sprinted off to the next car, and then the next, tearing money from the wallet, laughing hysterically to the Charlie Parker sound track in his head. He finally hid in a WC to await the next stop, and jumped off.

With this pocket money and a few coins from busking with his cheap guitar on street corners, he'd traveled around Sweden. Teenage girls would gather around him as he played. He basked in the attention, so unlike the isolation he felt in Cheltenham. He could use his power without anyone disapproving. He could just look at the girls, and inevitably one of them would take him home to a hot meal, a place to sleep, and a frenzied midnight grope.

He'd made it through Germany thanks to a widow he looked at in a cafe one hot afternoon, nearly as old as his mum, who subsequently took him back to her empty house for "piano lessons". This experience seem to balance out his involvement with the queer gentleman, make him whole again. The next week found him walking the streets in Paris with his battered guitar slung over his shoulder and a change of underwear in his alto sax case. He couldn't stand being unclean and wearing tired clothes.

Back in Cheltenham his mates had teased him about his cleanliness, his smart suits, his pruning. Are you a poof then? So Brian overcompensated. He needed to prove he was better than the others at shagging birds. And he *was* better, the first of his friends to score. He could give a girl a look, just a powerful look with that impishly innocent smile, that precocious, cheeky charm.

Valerie, one who could not resist, eventually got pregnant. Only 14, she spurned Brian's attempt at a marriage proposal, reasoning maturely and correctly that she'd be better off alone. The scandal erupted and found its way into every corner and conversation in Cheltenham. Brian had done the worse thing a boy could do in a tight community. Nothing would be the same.

Lewis Jones had screamed at his son, "You think this makes you a man!?"

"You just don't like me," Brian yelled back. "Because I'm a constant reminder of what a real man should be."

His father retreated to his pint by the telly, as if his son no longer existed.

Brian thought about how his outburst stung. Mum suffocates his father, she *surrounds* him at every step at home, no wonder he goes to the pub every night. And then he yells at me. Stop sniveling, s-s-stop all that l-l-lisping, stop being so p-pathetically girlie. If I don't, he says, I'll turn into a full-fledged poof. But why, then... why didn't he stop mum from treating me like a girl? Pamela, my sister, died an infant. So mum goes after me, dresses me up in women's clothes, brushes my hair in a woman's curl. Says if I don't behave I'll disappear, like Pamela. But I got her turned around now! I pretend, look shy, make with the limp posture and cocked head, and plead with my eyes, and she melts into my arms... And then she came after me, to touch me, and I had to push her off.

Valerie's family had sent her to France to have the baby. Brian would never be allowed to see the child. Isolated from his former chums, and with disapproval looming around every corner, he fled Cheltenham. At the time, he had no expectations of passing through there again.[134]

During his travels Brian called home three times, and each time his father had answered and had hung up. Across the Continent, busking on street corners, Brian adapted to the lifestyles of the homeless. He shared his pocket money with Franco for apples, cheese, and bread. Eventually Franco brought him around to an alley where he knew some friends would be squatting against the brisk night.

Never once did Brian ask *why* Franco was naked underneath his coat, but Franco could sense that Brian was curious.

"Don't question why you need to be so free," Franco told him. "He'll tell you it's the only way to be."

The "he" in this case turned out to be an older man who called himself Yves Dormant, Grand Subverter of Dreams, his title a pun on the Grand Master titles of so many manufactured occultists. Dressed smart in an overcoat and waistcoat reminiscent of the turn of the century that barely contained his rotund, wine-swilled belly, Dormant exploded with passion when he first set eyes on Brian.

"You! You are Saint-Just!" he exclaimed, wiping spittle from his handle-bar mustache. "You look just like him! You *must* be his reincarnated soul."

Brian just blinked and cocked his head.

"Saint-Just! You know, the Angel of Death, the Archangel of the Revolution. He was a beautiful man, Saint-Just. Such an indescribably soft, pensive face. So much energy locked up in that face! You look just like him. Look!"

At that he pulled out, from somewhere in the folds of his overcoat, a scrapbook of pictures, and opened to a page with an illustration of Louis de Saint-Just, Robespierre's associate and leader of the revolutionary Jacobins, whose fiery speeches in 1792 called for the head of the French king. Brian did seem to resemble Saint-Just, in the illustration a very young and exceedingly handsome man, with a pale, oval face, brilliant blue eyes, and brown hair well tended. His white skin and stiff clothing suggested an aristocrat, as did also a certain disdainful haughtiness in his manner. Like Brian's, his mouth was sensitive and somewhat feminine.

Dormant idolized Saint-Just and devoutly quoted him, mixed with passages from Albert Camus's philosophical essay on the Jacobin leader, *The Rebel.* "Those who would make revolutions in the world," Dormant spoke with his index finger pointing up, then gestured around the dingy alley, "those who want to do good in this world, must sleep only in the tomb."

They passed around wine and bread, sharing everything. Franco borrowed his guitar and strummed some unrecognizable chords with an enthusiasm that didn't quite make up for lack of talent.

Brian was ecstatic at this total acceptance of him by these people who were so representative, it seemed, of the lunatic fringe. Dormant spoke, with the voice of authority, about banishing authority. Saint-Just had arrived at exactly the right place at the right time in history, and had nearly single-handedly pulled Europe out of the dark ages. He had demolished the political notion of a king as divine.

"He spoke for the people," Dormant added solemnly. "With his fair long hair dancing on his shoulders! He demanded the trial and execution of the king, as an enemy of the people. He was the first to step forward, towards enlightenment and freedom." It was a fairy tale that Brian could adopt as his own, if only for a day.

Referring to each other as Brothers, Dormant's group traced their intellectual roots to the Brethren of the Free Spirit, a dissident move-ment that sprang up in the 13th Century all across Europe, preaching an alternative view of Christianity. Antinomian and individualist in outlook, the Brethren came into conflict with the Church and were ruthlessly persecuted, their leaders burned at the stake in Paris and London; a pattern that would be repeated with other heretical secret societies throughout the ages. Dormant wanted to know if Brother Brian had ever heard of the Ranters, a radical English sect in the mid-1600s with pantheistic beliefs, who were often associated with nudity as a manner of social protest and religious expression, and as a symbol of abandoning earthly goods.

Franco grinned; his trench coat was still buttoned but his chest hairs protruded at the top, and his bare lanky legs stuck out of the bottom.

For a few days these outcasts were Brian's family, rampaging through the cafés and nightclubs at night, sleeping in doorways and alleys during the day, begging for change, pick-pocketing the tourists on the rue de Seine, even conducting a second-story operation, with Brian on lookout, and splitting the take communally. They all ran with a crazy crowd in Paris, including a larger, mysterious group called the SI, Situationist International, whose members scrawled crazy graffiti all over famous cathedral walls and gates, *God is dead, The words that we have spoken shall never perish from the earth, Happiness is a new idea in Europe,* always just a few steps ahead of the police. Brian liked to paint *Bird Lives!* just underneath the other slogans. Dormant had actually caught a Charlie "Bird" Parker performance and told Brian that some of the professionals, including Mingus, believed that Bird still lives, somewhere in hiding, and that he'll come back with some new shit that will scare everyone to death.

"Little by little, the City robs you of certainty," Dormant breathed heavily through his syllables, leaving traces of a sour wine smell. "There can never be any fixed point, and you can survive only if nothing is necessary to you. Nothing!" He spit with a flourish. "Without warning, you must be able to change, to drop what you are doing, to reverse. You must learn to read the signs."

Indeed, jazz is Dada on instruments, Dormant liked to say and repeat, thinking Brian was so hooked on jazz as to miss the point. Working to cure themselves and their civilization of their discontents, the Dadaists, he lectured

Brian, had built the first laboratory for the revitalization of everyday life. It was in a Zurich café in 1916.

"The group was a funnel, sucking up all the trivia and rubbish cluttering up the world. And this was right on the eve of Worldwide War!" The word Dada itself came from an advertisement for soap. According to Dormant, Dada is the theory and practice of being in the right place at the right time, and jazz does the same thing: It is a performance of random notes that happen to fall in the right place at the right time.

"Unless it's the wrong song," observed Brian.

At that point a slinky pockmarked woman of indeterminate age in an all-black caftan, with a shock of white hair falling everywhere about her shoulders, sashayed up to Brian and wrapped around his neck a white silk scarf dotted and sprayed with yellow paint, and tucked it seductively into his coat.

"High priestess Dahlia!" Dormant exclaimed by way of explanation. "A true pioneer of graffiti! She works with new technology: spray paint!"

She whispered in Brian's ear. "Saint-Just had a delicate face, like yours, the face of an archangel. A pensive face," she continued, her "p" full of promise, "full of energy, with an air of indescribable softness." She stroked Brian's neck. "And his cravat, it would blind you, it was so white! Saint-Just's cravat would choke him!"

And just when Brian thought she really *would* choke him, or do something equally wild, she backed off, leaving him with the scarf. She grabbed Brian's alto sax out of the case, spilling his only change of underwear into a puddle. She began tootling random notes.

"You can never be too sure," said Dormant, continuing from wherever he left off. "Hugo Ball wrote that the libraries should be *burned*. Even his own writings! He was *that* sure of Dada. Even after the Cabaret closed and their grand experiment... expired!" He wiped spittle from his mouth. "He wrote that if the libraries burned, only the things that everyone knows by heart would survive. A great era of The Legend would begin! This is what is happening now, except the libraries didn't burn, they were bombed during the War. Legendary architecture, beacons of illumination and mystery, destroyed! And then they were... ignored! They turned to dust, just as everybody started turning on their televisions. And so the great libraries are gone, and music is the only thing left for us to know by heart. And so it is from music that our legends will emerge."

Indeed, it is the best and the brightest that die early, Dormant lectured the drunken lot. He told the story of Luciano Pozo y Gonzales, better known as Chano Pozo, a devotee of Santería, who introduced West African chants from his Cuban *lucumi* religion into bebop with Dizzy Gillespie twelve years earlier.[135] "The audience was embarrassed! A jazz audience! Negroes! And they were not ready for it. They were not ready for their African past. They had in fact been taught to be *ashamed* of it." According to Dormant, Pozo had tapped into the true rhythms of the Earth, that synergy of Afro-Cuban rhythms, that syncopation. And for that, he was killed over a bag of marijuana, in the Rio Bar on Lennox Avenue in Harlem.

Brian could hardly follow any of this, but the mention of marijuana brought everyone around in a huddle. Dormant produced a hashish joint half-filled with tobacco. A dull headache seemed to creep up the back of Brian's brain stem as he smoked.

"But are these pioneers really dead?" Dormant asked rhetorically. "Or have they become immortal, somehow, through their music?" Giggles all around as the hashish dealt its hand, the Fool card. "Does reverence for the dead make them alive, still, in some cosmos beyond our perception?"

They had wandered a bit into a seedy district, spellbound, and eventually gathered outside a nightclub with a marquis showing three monkeys in the classic "see no evil, hear no evil, speak no evil" pose, from which emerged a raucous blues guitar and harmonica punctuated by perfunctory grunts and howling moans of a perfectly mysterious African origin.[136] Dahlia mimicked the howls on Brian's sax, and Franco strummed incoherently and at odd moments. The cacophony impressed Brian, and he began to understand what it meant to be in the right place at the right time. Was it jazz, to accompany this performance in the club from outside on the street?

"It is a *situation!*" Dormant roared. "They can't stop us! Not the neo-Dadaists, not the Fascists, or even worse, the Surrealists! None of them can stop us. They're all inside, but they can't stop us out here."

Out of a dark alley there suddenly materialized a tall, thin man with jet-black skin in a dark gray pin-stripe suit and fedora. Brian saw him first. It just occurred to him to ask, "Do you mean to stop us?"

The tall black man spoke in a deep baritone as he held out his hand. "Cornell Woodrow, from America, from Memphis." As he smiled, a single gold tooth glinted, reflecting the streetlight. Inside, the music shifted. A gruff Negro voice belted out something about a little red rooster, to lazy to crow for day. Cornell Woodrow caught Brian's eye and could see he was interested. "You here for the Howlin' Wolf?"

"Well, I'm Brian Saint-Just, mate," he put on with a Cockney accent, "and I dunno, what's a Howlin' Wolf?"

"Let me show you. Back door," he pointed. A teen no older than Brian was holding the door open. He looked Italian-American, with black bushy eyebrows and an aquiline nose, but with a rocker's leather motorcycle jacket.

Cornell introduced them. "This is Johnny B, from America." But the boy just nodded back at Cornell and left them at the door, heading straight for Dormant, pulling something out his pocket. Dormant seemed to know this Johnny B and was quite pleased to see him.

Cornell beckoned, so Brian followed him into the dark alley and inside, backstage at the club. This was the "blues" that Brian had heard about, only he had heard it refined and polished, and played smoothly on a piano, as on the one blues record he'd heard, *Blues from the Gutter* by another black man with a strange name, Champion Jack Dupree. Brian hadn't yet realized that there were musicians who played *only* the blues; he thought that those who played the blues were really jazz players pandering to some baser instinct while apologizing for it at the same time.

There was no pandering or apologizing here. At six foot three and close to 300 pounds, the Howlin' Wolf stomped in a controlled fury across the stage like a gorilla in farm coveralls, grimacing with the perturbed look of a natural being in an unnatural world, a King Kong trapped in a Paris club surrounded by impeccably dressed women. He growled with the impatience of a conqueror, his bazooka shouts could overpower a tank, but then... he put it all aside, whispered like it was all just a stage act, embarrassed, like everyone else, at his ungainly bulk; a cartoon bull in a china shop. This subtle self-deprecating move pierced the moist deltas of those impeccably dressed women and sent them a-vibrating. Cornell shouted into Brian's ear. "The mighty Wolf!"

During "Little Red Rooster"[137] Brian caught the Wolf's quizzical glance backstage, as if something evil was about to overtake the band. Brian watched closely as the Wolf's massive hips began to shake. He was a monster with grace. The Wolf's voice could drown the song, but he was also gentle, acutely sensitive, even concerned that the audience could hear the lyrics. He stubbornly repeated a verse over and over, whispering and then growling, and finally chewing on the line until he'd extracted all its flavor before spitting it out. And when he howled, it was a real howl, long, drawn out to the rafters, and full of frustration, bitterness, and rage. That voice hung in the air and made the room rumble with echo.

Brian understood it. The Wolf had the audience in his hands. That power can really work, especially over women. When Wolf pointed to the middle of the audience, Brian could almost see bolts of lightning pulsating out and blasting the crowd. Dormant had said that the basic Dada act is a performer's attack on an audience. But this Howlin' Wolf was much more. He could cast a spell over the audience, channelling the hoodoo chants and modal harmonies of his African ancestors through his electric amplifiers.

"The Wolf, he completes the triangle of Atlantic trade," Cornell spoke in a low tone to Brian's ear, somehow cutting through the bass of the roaring music. "Bringing it all back to Europe now, all that power taken from Africa so long ago, captured into slavery and brought to the New World, all to support the economy of Europe. And now he's come back, the son of a slave's son, come back to the halls of Europe for his due."

Brian registered the pain behind Cornell's assessment, and the historical fact of the slave trade. But mostly he watched the younger black guitar player with Wolf, who maintained a perennially lopsided grin plastered on his face, curling down a bit on one edge of his mouth; a grin Brian started immediately emulating.

Cornell leaned toward his ear again, and spoke in a way that cut through all the sound, reading Brian's mind. "That's Hubert Sumlin. The Wolf practically raised him. He always plays for the Wolf. If you listen carefully, and yield your mind to the sound, you can hear with the musician's ear."

Sumlin pranced about with that idiotic lopsided grin, his fingers dancing on the fretboard with a smooth bottleneck on his pinky, playing wrenched, shattering bursts of notes, then suddenly delving into cliff-hanger silences brought up abruptly by daring rhythmic suspensions. This was a form of jazz *inside* the notes, *within* the structure of a 12-bar blues. Brian was transfixed. Jazz as he'd known it live, in England, had been fake, a false promise, a type of music Europeans could not do because they had not sacrificed for it.

"Where did this music come from? This is better than any blues I've ever heard."

"I don't think even the Wolf knows where it really comes from," Cornell answered, with his chuckle cutting through to Brian's ear. "He'd say it comes from the heart and the gut, and from the traditions of his people. Others might say it comes straight from the Devil."

"But *you* know where it comes from, don't you?"

"One of the oldest secrets. It goes way back, farther even than the primitive tribes of Africa. There is a power in this music that defies the erosion of time, and it offers immortality to those who can wield it."

"What are you saying...?"

"I'm saying you can tune into it. You got your guitar, right?" Cornell smiled and his gold tooth gleamed.

Brian was suddenly embarrassed that he'd let Franco play with it, a crazy naked guy, he might ruin it.

"That's all right," Cornell spoke soothingly. "I know you want to play music. Play like the masters. Right?" He reached into his jacket and pulled out a 45-rpm record. He was about to give it to Brian, but then pulled back. "You're not just playing music to get girls, are you?"

"I... I want *every*one to like me," Brian smiled back at him, his blue eyes sparkling.

Cornell chuckled. "Well here, let me lay this one on you. Elmore James, a true genius of the slide guitar. He learned directly from the master." Cornell handed Brian a record called "Standing At The Crossroads" on the Fire label, credited to Elmo James due to a printing error.

"That's very generous of you. Why me?" Brian was naturally suspicious.

"Well, just *look* at you!" Cornell chuckled again, and his gold tooth seemed to mock him. "Blond hair, green eyes, lily-white skin. Man, you could have walked out of an ice age. You're as Aryan as they come! The perfect white boy to learn the blues. Now you learn this record, learn it well. Concentrate on listening."

And Cornell winked at him as he bent down to whisper in his ear, like a dirty secret,

There once was a man from Madrass
Whose balls were made out of brass
When he'd bang 'em together
They'd play "Stormy Weather"
And lightning shot out of his ass!

Brian didn't know what to say.

"Study that record," Cornell grew a bit more serious. "And when you think you're ready, I want you to look up a friend of mine in London. His name's Alexis Korner."

Brian had never heard of them. Alexis Korner. Elmo James. When he looked up to thank Cornell, he was gone, like the apparition of a long-dead friend.

As the set ended Brian tripped over gear backstage in his rush to get out. He joined Dormant and the others out front, jamming to melodies in their heads, passing around more wine bottles that seem to come out of nowhere. The tourists ignored them as harmless drunks. Franco flashed a smile. "He got more hashish," pointing to Dormant. Johnny B was gone.

* * *

Dahlia told Brian that she had a record player, so Brian followed her back to her apartment. Once inside, with a sweep of her white hair, she wrapped her long silk scarf around Brian's neck and dragged him into her bedroom. With another sweep she turned to face him and shed her caftan to reveal her creamy naked body, with tattooed thorny vines rising up from her stomach and underneath her breasts to gather at each nipple. Brian had a hard-on before he could get his shoes off. Stumbling over to the bed, he fell face first into her fragrant buttocks, which were splayed with a swirling tattoo of dragons and snakes that encircled her portal of orgasmic bliss. She arched her back to give him more access, and Brian was initiated into the vast pleasures of purely decadent sex.

He emerged from her bedroom wearing only a sheepish grin to find Dormant and the others in the living room, puffing on a hookah. Turns out Dahlia's place was their safe house. Franco frowned at Brian, and Brian reached for his clothes. He thought, was Dahlia Franco's girl? Or perhaps Dormant's? She had told Brian about Dormant, in a flat, disgusted monotone, "il est bisexuelle." What kind of situation have I got myself into?

As if reading his mind, Dormant beckoned Brian over to take a puff and check out his collage-book, titled *Situations*, published in 1957. It was comprised of scores of paragraphs, sentences, phrases, single words, all cut out of magazines, books, and newspapers, and adorned with splattered blotches and colored lines, spots, and drips, in collage with photographs, advertisements, comic-strip panels, blueprints for buildings and cities, reproductions of woodcuts and engravings, repetitions of the three monkeys... a mad, precocious conceit. But Brian could see himself doing this, exploding the syntax of everyday life and then rushing out to the street to pick of the pieces and make pictures out of them, songs... catalysts for new passions, new performances, new acts of courage, new *situations*.

A world of permanent novelty. In such a world, the seemingly meaningless words and pictures of *Situations* made sense. Dormant accompanied this message with his own credo. "In times when each day creates its own nihilism, meaning has to be created, made up, out of anything, out of everyday life situations involving love, betrayal, broken hearts, and mortality."

Brian thought, is he talking about my dalliance with Dahlia?

Again, reading Brian's mind, Dormant repeated his last phrase. "Love, betrayal, broken hearts, and mortality. Did you know," suddenly upbeat, "that Dahlia is a Gypsy Woman? A very special one, indeed! From a long ago race of magicians and entertainers, descendants of the Argonauts. Yes, the quest for the Golden Fleece! They came from east of Persia and settled in North Africa. They were the Christian nobility of Egypt. Around the year 990 they abandoned their possessions in order to escape the Muslims. They came to Europe and infiltrated the noble families of Europe with their music. The gypsies are a magical people, they use spells and rituals to harness the power of nature, and communicate with the elemental spirits that are all around us."

Brian shivered. He may have known everything about her private parts, but nothing about her life. He could still taste her. She had enveloped his manhood, had brought him almost literally into her womb, while chanting some evil chant. Her essence now lay all over him; his every breath carried her scent.

"She can still speak the language, the Gypsy language, Romani," lectured Dormant. "This language carries traces of an ancient tongue, a language that Jesus revealed to his Apostles, a language that teaches the mystery of all things and unveils the most hidden truths. The language of the quest for the Golden Fleece is the foundation of all initiations. It is the common language of illumination for the Christians, the Incas, the Medieval troubadours, and the ancient Greeks. It was the language spoken before the fall of the Tower of Babel!"

Dahlia slinked in and leaned against the doorway in her satin pink slip, smiling at Dormant, and licking her luscious lips.

"Do you know Fulcanelli? The mystery of the cathedrals?" Dormant seemed determined to make Brian understand. "He discovered that the great cathedrals of Europe are really *books*, expressed in stone. It is the same language. The great secrets of alchemy, the pinnacle of western occult science, is plainly displayed by the walls and structures of the Notre-Dame Cathedral. It is the Philosopher's

Book. The medium it-self, the architecture, is the message. And traces of this ancient language can be found in the language of the Gypsies, and in the Tarot."

"Andre Breton said that the alchemical process could be expressed artistically," add Dahlia in her husky, sexy voice. "He said that Surrealism was nothing but alchemical art. The *adepts*, those who know how to express the alchemical process, can use the power behind music to stir the masses into a patriotic fervor, or a revolt."

"The Surrealists are traitors to Dada!" screamed Dormant.

"No, they just learned properly how to use the masks," replied Dahlia, intent on correcting Dormant. "The masks were a clue to an ancient power, a power humans," she winked at Brian, "could not resist."

"Hugo Ball wrote about the masks, about putting them on. He wrote, 'Something strange happened. Not only did the mask immediately call for a costume, it also demanded a quite definite, passionate gesture, bordering on madness.' So Ball and Huelsenbeck, they'd put these masks on, and then walk about silly, with the most bizarre movements and ponderous asides, elbows akimbo, you see. They had masks, they were festooned and draped with chisels, iron plates, bells, impossible objects, each trying to outdo the other. And they studied the occult virtues of sound. The potency of sacred names. Huelsenbeck broke them down to the most important of all sounds, the phoneme, the smallest articulable sound. They all knew this, that noise is a direct call to action. But the Surrealists pandered this idea, sold it for their own enjoyment, for the money. They are pimps!"

Dahlia smirked. Brian wondered, what would the Gypsy Queen say about the Voodoo King? "Let's play this record," he said as he pulled out the Elmore James record Cornell Woodrow had given him.[138]

The opening slide guitar crackled like lightning. A sax kept up with the rockin' rolling rhythm. "People, I was standing at the crossroads," called Elmore James with such a high pitch and tight throat that it sounded like he was up a tree with a noose around his neck, "with my head hung down and crying." The response was a slide guitar frenzy that sliced through his brain like an icepick. Brian could see his entire future all wrapped up in this kind of music.

* * *

The basic Dada act is a performer's attack on an audience. Dormant wanted to reenact Michel Mourre's assault on Notre-Dame Cathedral on April 9, 1950. Ten thousand people from all over the world had come to the greatest cathedral in all of France to hear Easter High Mass. Mourre had mounted the altar in the disguise of a Dominican monk, and taking advantage of a pause after the credo, he began reading a sermon in which he proclaimed, "Verily I say unto you: *God is dead*." The event had made headlines in newspapers all around the world. This had been a modern Dada moment, according to Dormant. One burning moment that had defined the 20th Century.

And now, a hush falls over the many thousands in attendance at the cathedral. Playing the character off the false Dominican Mourre, Dormant mounts the altar in the disguise of a monk, his silver-tipped sword swashing in its leather sheath underneath his robe. He begins to read a sermon, business as usual, Ephesians 6:12, "For we do not wrestle against flesh and blood, but against the rulers, against the authorities, against the cosmic powers over this present darkness, against the spiritual forces of evil in the heavenly places."

He suddenly turns to face Dahlia on the side of the sanctuary. She raises her baton and starts the heavenly choir of ladies singing "The Hallelujah Chorus"[139] and everyone joins in.

At the shimmering finale, Dormant as Mourre shouts, "Verily I say unto you: God is *still* dead!"

The audience draws its breath in shocked silence.

Brian, cast by Dormant as Saint-Just, takes the opportunity to jump up to the altar to protect Dormant.

The cathedral's Swiss Guards draw their swords. This is clearly not allowed. This is subversion of the worst kind.

Brian as Saint-Just is supposed to say "The words he has spoken shall never perish from the earth." But something else pops into his head. "Living well," he yells above the shouting. "Living as art! Living is the very thing!"

Dormant grabs Brian from behind. "But living like this?" Something is wrong. Dormant is too rough, is he changing the script? Some kind of spontaneous theater? Now he's ripping off Brian's shirt, tugging at the back of Brian's pants. Out of nowhere Franco dives in to grab Brian's legs and paw off his shoes. Outstretched, held struggling by Dormant around the shoulders and Franco around the legs, naked with his trousers in a bunch around his ankles, Brian becomes the sacrificial lamb. Was this what Dahlia had meant about Dormant's latent tendencies? His bisexualité?

Dormant holds the cold steel silver-tipped blade an inch from Brian's crotch. "Don't anybody move, or I castrate him!"

The audience hushes in silent sympathy. Brian is frightened but also elated, ecstatic... even aroused! From all around, even from the back of the cathedral, they could see Brian's writhing body white as fleece, drawing all attention to the light brown spot of genitals.

The Swiss Guards are trained in all forms of stealth warfare. Within seconds a Glock appears at Dormant's temple, held by a Guardsman at Dormant's back while another Guardsman, crouching, upends Dormant's arm from the wrist, sending the sword clattering over the altar.

Dormant, crazed and babbling, is led away to jail. Brian is helped to his feet and helped with his trousers, and then he too is led off, not to jail but to the train station, with a ticket to Calais and a ferry pass for Dover. Franco disappears.

In a world of permanent novelty, performances are like daydreams in that they produce nothing, show no consequence, but rule our hearts. "Daydreaming subverts the world," Brian remembered saying to himself back when he was just skipping along the *rue de Seine* with a guitar in one hand and a sax case in the other. Now he knew that what he meant was to *live a life* of permanent novelty. He would make a spectacle of himself.

* * *

Look at me. Who am I supposed to be?

Alone at the mirror in a sort of trance, a Liverpool teddy boy shapes his hair in front like an elephant's trunk, combing it down over the forehead, and in back like a duck's arse, greased to come together, and runs the comb once through the side whiskers extending well down his face. Despite his aunt's scornful look he wears very tight drainpipe trousers, bright socks, brothel creepers, and a long drape jacket.

He wears the clothing and adopts the swagger because he really needs to be someone else, someone special. Someone with a purpose. The swagger, the way he walks and carries himself, is like Elvis the King crossed with John Wayne the Duke. He looks like he's ready to draw a gun. He wears these clothes to school to stand out, to show off his independence with clothes that other kids aren't allowed to wear. He is portraying something that he wants to be.

He thinks he can write a song that would explain everything. Dad was never good enough for mum, he pissed off and went to sea. Mum took off with an Army officer and left me.

He dimly remembers his sailor father in a high moment, impersonating Louis Armstrong and Al Jolson and playing a banjo. The memories fill his head as he hears Lonnie Donegan on the radio singing the "Rock Island Line" song.[140]

Donegan starts out slow, talking about this train. The railroads in Britain hold no charm, but American railroads are full of adventure, travelled by wild men who opened up the wild West. What'cha got on board? Donegan sings I got sheep! I got cows! I got horses! Pigs! All livestock! Alright, the toll man says, you don't have to pay me nothing. As the train runs through the toll both, it builds steam, goes faster and faster. I fooled you! Donegan laughs. I got pig iron! We-ell, the Rock Island Line is a mighty good road, it's the road to ride!

It is called *skiffle* in Britain. Probably because Ma Rainey, out there in the American wilderness, had called her music skiffle. It was black American country music back then, and Donegan now performed it on guitar with two others on washboard and tea-chest bass, playing a variety of folk and blues songs, particularly Lead Belly's, in a lively jug band style that preceded rockabilly.

That bouncy rhythm fills the teddy boy with a pure joy. There is nothing like this song, nothing that came before holds a candle to it. It's more than playing cowboy or train conductor, he knows it as a way of life, a life his father knew. Even Auntie tolerates it, the song is on the BBC and all.

One day he gets up the courage to ask his Aunt. "All the boys my age are getting guitars, could you lend me the money to get one?" He knows the answer, but still he asks.

And then his real mum arrives like a hurricane, back from some-where, and carrying on with a hotel waiter called Dykins. The boy calls him Twitchy behind his back, always nervous, always twitching. Mum wants me, her son, to be *friends*, and she wants me to call her Julia. She gives me ciggies when Auntie isn't looking, and she buys me a banjo on a whim. But where is she now?

Like Elvis was supposed to have done, the boy carries his guitar to school every day and plays in the cafeteria. He listens religiously to *The Goon Show* and any American records he can get his hands on. They are like portals to another reality, where nothing of practical value, not job, religion, or conformity, makes any sense. He finds these songs on Radio Luxembourg, and he finds six shillings to spend on the 78-rpm record of "Rock Island Line". After playing it nearly to death he turns around and sells the record, for two shillings sixpence, to his schoolmate who has a banjo; together they form a skiffle band named, ironically, after the school he hates to go to, Quarry Bank. They are the Quarry Men, but mostly they are *men*.

Music thrills the boy and holds him in its hypnotic sway. Music transports him to a special place, a soft dreamy place of cushiony release that can suddenly turn hard and as concrete as desire. A different world snaps into place when he hears music. It takes his body into a new geometry of interlaced emotions, new laws of a different nature. The chords imprint in his memory; he only has to hear something once or twice to know it and play it in his head. It's just that his fingers stubbornly resist putting them down on the guitar.

He plays in the cafeteria for the girls, but mostly he plays for attention. People react to music in a somewhat predictable fashion, they totter through the immaterial trivia of the misfortunes that make up their lives, glancing up only briefly in wonder, eyes unaccustomed to the light, when they hear music.

I thought I had my mum back again, but she got run over by a police car.

So that's who I am. Now, *what* am I supposed to be?

* * *

Stu Sutcliffe and Johnny Lennon peeing against a wall. Stu says to Johnny, "Ever look at it? The mark you make on the wall? Mine's like a mushroom cloud."

"How gloombily," mumbles Johnny. Both are quite drunk. "What're ya gonna say, mate, that's art?" They look so incongruous together, Johnny the unruly rocker with vestiges of the teddy boy look, Stu the stubbled beatnik wearing dark glasses at night.

"Why not," Stu replies, shaking out the last of the drops. "Duchamp called a urinal 'art' and named it *Fountain.*"

"Fucking Duchampion nonsense. All that bloody crap Ballard and Burton go on about, all their hot air and shite, only good it does is warm the bloody classroom. You can't just pee on the wall Stu. You've got talent and you've got to show it, mate. Fuck all that, trying to fit into a *style.* Do what you want! You already won an art show and made millions."

"75 pounds."

"More than you'll make in a month with that Höfner bass. You're shite, you know!" Johnny's grin belies the truth, which is, in fact, that Stu's bass playing is not his best work, and Stu knows it. His style is elementary, mostly sticking to root notes, serviceable for rock 'n' roll but not good enough for Johnny or the other band mates.

Still, unruffled, Stu shoots back. "I get more applause than you *or* Paulie when I sing 'Love Me Tender' you sod."

"The audience are fucking idiots, they applaud for cripples, they scream at Cliff Richard and they don't even see the fat scab growth on his head."

They both laugh at the idea of a crusty scab on the sweet-faced Richard that only they could see. In moments like these they feel close to each other as the only two fully realized human beings in the world. They can tell each other anything.

"Well," says Stu, "it's fine that you still believe in me."

"That's a curse," growls John. "'Cause everyone I've ever believed in are dead. My Uncle George, me mum and dad, Buddy Holly, Eddie Cochran. Or they're dying, like Elvis in the Army singing 'Love Me Fender' or Chuck Berry in jail singing 'You Can't Scratch Me'."

"You miss your mum." Stu knows how to find John's kind and gentle heart.

"Yes I miss her, I miss Julia. She wasn't a mum at all, really, my Aunt Mimi is really *that.* Julia was my friend." John pauses, then snarls in a disgusted tone to disguise his distress, "She taught me banjo chords, she meant well, but now I've got to unlearn 'em to learn real guitar chords."

Stu lets it go. "You know your dad's not dead, or you would have heard. I feel differently about my dad, John, I don't blame him. It's what he does, it's what he has to do."

"That's all well and good for you, Stu, your father's a war hero and he sails home once in a while. Alf's a drunken merchant seaman out shagging natives off the coast of Africa or somewhere." John softens his tone. "My only memory of him really, is when he wanted me to go with him. I was four or five, and I remember we walked along the docks. And he goes and tells me about the fuckin' slave trade! He tells me that all these big houses and docks, all of Liverpool really, was here because of slavery. The ships left here for Africa, took the slaves to America, and brought the money back here. What kind of fucking thing is that for a dad to tell his son?"

* * *

They shuffle along. In the embarrassing silence John has a vision of the ship Perseverance, brand new in 1723, and its owner the Liverpool merchant McNamity, watching it glide gracefully down the greased slipway stern-first, then wallow massively, unseemly, ducking her rear into the dark cold 'Pool, then be pulled abruptly, herky-jerky, by a merciless tug. Her figurehead is the Duchess of Devonshire, re-imagined in long yellow hair flowing regally down the back of a royal blue gown, voluminous at the skirts but leaving her white shoulders and her great smooth breasts bare, her arms drawn back in a poignant pose, her brilliant crimson nipples pointing the way, not toward a prosperous journey but back again toward shore. A decrepit crew member in the bow, Alf "Freddie" Lennon, reaches down with raggedly sleeved arms to fondle the figurehead's breasts, catching her crimson nipples in his filthy fingers. The sailor, his ship, and her figurehead, dissolve as captive giants in the gloom, awaiting masts to be fitted midstream. McNamity watches the duchess and her tormentor intently as the ship is tugged away from shore, yearning for rescue with each jagged pull. As the ship neatly disappears in the fog of the 'Pool, the bare-breasted figurehead with Lennon's fingers wrapped around them would be the last of her the ship's owner would ever see.

* * *

"Fuck him," John broke the silence. "Just like his bloody ancestors, all of 'em called 'Freddie' and all of 'em shite. I was forced to make a choice. Bloody hell, I went crying back to Julia. And then she went off with some twitchy, and handed me off to me Auntie. I always wanted Alf to come back home. But he wouldn't, would he? Doesn't even fucking remember me except in his bloody drunken nightmares."

"How bloody awful," Stu remarks in a comic tone, changing the subject, "about the Negroes, I mean. We took their bodies, now we steal their souls, singing Negro music. It's like another outbreak of primitivism." Their shared lectures in art history comes to the fore, with Stu as usual leading the discussion, drawing meaning from history. "The Europeans artists did it many times, revert to a primitive nature. In the Cabaret Voltaire in 1916, the Dadaists took to a stage and sang Negro poems, just grunts and whoops to an improvised beat, 'umbah-umbah'..."

"A-wop-bop-a-loo-bop, a-wop-bam-boo! Nothing's changed," says John. "We're all primal beasties. But that's Paul, he's the one that wants to sound like Little Richard. Not me, I want *me own* sound. I want to be Elvis, and more. Bigger than Elvis. Bigger than Jerry Lee Lewis and Elvis *combined*."

"Ahh, Elvis. From the moment you hear him, every pop song that was ever done before him is suddenly, nothing! He blows them away like chaff. He just walks out on that stage, on the telly, and all he has to do is just stand there, just be Elvis! He's got it, he's Dada, assaulting the audience."

"But he doesn't play an instrument, not like Jerry Lee Lewis who can bang the shite out of a piano. There's nothing out there that has improved on 'Whole Lotta Shakin' Going On'.[141] He sings like there's nothing out there in the world that can challenge him. And that's how I sing, mate." John glares at Stu. "I must be a genius but nobody's noticed. Or mad, which is it? If there is such a thing as genius, which is just... what? What the fuck is it? Well I am one, and so are you, unless there isn't any such thing, and then I don't care."

And that seems to be that. "Yeah, well... 'I love ya, Johnny, the Beetles love ya, we *all* love ya,'" Stuart mimics Lee Marvin, the leader of the rival Beetles motorcycle gang that gave Marlon Brando a tough time in *The Wild One*. "'I've been looking for ya in every ditch from here ta Fresno, hopin' you was dead.'"

John cracks up. Stuart goes on to imitate the small-town daughter in the movie, asking the moody Brando character, "Hey, Johnny, what are you rebelling against?'"

"'Whaddaya got?'" John spits back, trying but failing to imitate Brando with his gum-chewing, eye-popping grin.

* * *

Staring at them from the end of the alley were three young dockworkers in leather jackets and winkle-picker shoes. One of them was angry about these punks pissing on the back wall of his uncle's garage. The other two were looking for the guitarists who'd got their girls all worked up with their playing inside the Jacaranda. In a sudden, menacing moment all three confronted the giggly pair. John could not as much as sneer before a punch gutted him. Stu, trying to come to his aid, was toppled by another punch, and one attacker kicked Stu in the head, nearly slicing his temple open with this winkle-picker shoe. As Stu lay unconscious and John slumped forward with a groan, the dockworkers took off.

A Leap of Faith

A leap of faith is what Reggie saw in the eyes of the singer and guitarist, a bright-eyed leap of faith. At first, Ohio State dropout Phil Ochs couldn't even face his audience. He'd begun hesitatingly, like any folk singer, strumming the mournful chords of a desolate intro in the key of A, then down to E, the blues train, and then up to a foreboding G that prefigured the song's first verse.[142]

But then, like someone flicked a switch, Ochs leaped right into it, throwing caution to the winds, and a wildness burned bright in his eyes as he strummed powerfully, almost idiotically, in the key of C, the "People's" key. He wants everyone to take a walk with him through this land of power and glory, a power that rests on the strength of freedom. We're only as strong as our love for this land. Only as tall as we stand…

It was so thrilling to hear this that Reggie unconsciously brought his hands together as in Catholic prayer. Here was the very gem of the idea that had been crystalizing in his mind for some time. You approach the idea of democracy with the religious fervor of a soldier of Christ. You take all that goodness associated with God, and all that pride and patriotism for Country, and you apply it to a new order, a patriotism of the *land*.

And, like prayer, it didn't matter how good a song was, only how good a song *does*.

Those were Pete Seeger's words. Seeger had been recently convicted for contempt of Congress because he'd refused to answer questions and name the names of Communists among his friends. On stage, the gangly man himself, a thin giant always stretching his neck and turning his face to the sky like a giraffe, shook Phil Ochs' hand and clapped him on the back, beaming at the audience. Then they started singing together, some old work song, Ochs keeping regular to the melody while Seeger soared above and beyond, humanity's ambassador to the galaxy, and bellowed like a prisoner at some invisible guard tower.

Two centuries earlier Reggie would have joined the colonial revolutionaries massing on the rough cobblestones outside Johnston Gate in Harvard Square, clamoring for justice. He flashed on Jesus Christ, Gandhi, Abraham Lincoln. The folksingers looked just as fiercely optimistic as these role models must have been. But behind these features, they shared the same pale sense of doom that the gladiators felt at the gates of the Coliseum.

* * *

A year earlier, clutching a knapsack with his father's Book, his stone, and the Robert Johnson records close to his chest, Reggie had entered Harvard Yard, a place of fantasy rendered real, encircled by real ivy-infested red brick buildings trimmed in white, and teeming with real intellectuals in cap and gown. Decisions made here affected the entire nation, the entire world. He stumbled over decorative cobblestones in the twilight of an autumn evening, retracing the ghostly footsteps of presidents, senators, barons, philanthropists, scientists, theologians, the stalwarts of American culture; hearing through the traffic cacophony outside the Yard the ghostly clip-clop of horses and the rattle of Brattle Street carriages en route to conspiratorial meetings, shadowed by Tory spies.

Decisions made here would affect his entire life. One in particular would come to haunt him.

"Ethno-musi-cology?" Counselor Garfink had drawled out the syllables as if he'd never heard of this study, arching his thick eyebrows that seemed plastered to the face of a death mask. "Music Theory, Archaeology, Creative Writing…" The counselor paused, twitched those massive eyebrows, and squinted through them at Reggie. "What do you think you're doing?"

Reggie was puzzled.

"Do you know why you're here?"

Reggie fidgeted. "To study folklore, and music, and possibly go to graduate school for a degree. Like Francis Child, collector of the Child ballads, who taught here at Harvard."

"That was a different time. Child was one of the best writers and speakers of his day, a mathematician actually. Class Orator when he graduated. But why do you think it was so easy for you to get into Harvard?" The counselor pronounced it "Haa-vaad" with blood on his breath, under the passive oil-painted eyes of John Quincy Adams, Theodore Roosevelt, Louis Brandeis. "Someone pulled strings to get you here, and it's because of your faaa-ther."

"What about my father?"

The counselor's eyebrows rose to form an arch worthy of a Gothic cathedral. So, the boy hadn't been told. "Your faaa-ther worked for the government."

"My father researched folklore," Reggie replied with defiance.

The arch of the counselor's eyebrows formed a question mark as he regarded the student. "Indeed, the Smithsonian Institution is part of the government." Quickly, he changed tack, and his eyebrows dropped like sails in a fierce wind. "You are here to pursue a degree in political science. Now, you can keep attending 'Ethno-musi-cology' if you must, but I insist you take history, political science, and at least one foreign language, preferably Russian."

"How do you know what my father wants? Have you heard from him?"

"Your mother was quite clear about it. A degree in political science, followed by law school."

What would my mother know about political science? Why hadn't she talked to me about it?

Now he could add the ghost of his father, who may or may not be dead, to this ghastly roundtable of presidents, senators, governors and judges. He never shows his face but he somehow pulls the strings. Reggie had dim memories of being roughly handled by a man, his father, on a beach while his mother laughed. He'd seen photographs, of course. One of a young man in a rumpled suit and hat with spectacles reminded Reggie of a book cover photo of James Joyce. That similar pensive, insatiable look of a man who's been through a world war and a drug habit. *Over every secret hovers a betrayal,* his father had written. And he had betrayed... whom? And why? *To pass along what I know, so that others can continue from where I was forced to stop.*

So his father had worked for the government. The thought flashed in his mind like lightning, and when his eyes refocused the world appeared in higher brightness and contrast, as if someone had adjusted the knobs of a TV set. The same man who had befriended musicians, who had collected blues recordings in the South and had written about music as *a medium for codes, in ancient times and even today...* who had written like a lunatic about a network of secret, powerful people. Who had been *working for the government?* Who had subsequently disappeared.

Play along, said the voice in his head. Find out what you can. And so he found a way to accommodate Counselor Garfink. Still, he chose French over Russian, and he combined political science with history in a course about the French Revolution of 1789. He agreed to report weekly to a Foreign Affairs department head who doubled as a career counselor. His name was Cravingston, and he wanted Reggie to supplement his regular courses with a Social Studies course that would combine philosophy, sociology, psychology, and music, with an eye toward acceptance into the most important fraternity on campus, Phi Beta Kappa.

* * *

Will Cravingston had the suave, unruffled air and wore the same wash-and-wear bluish gray suit that Cary Grant wore in Hitchcock's recent thriller, *North by Northwest,* with the same world-weary eyes, as if accidentally caught up in some intrigue but willing to see it through, and with style. His drab office in the basement of the Center for Personality Research, disconnected to the frenzied comings and goings of students upstairs, did not seem to be his real office, just a temporary post as the Center's "chaperone" and budget link to the department head. No matter how powerful the insights on human behavior the Center's students and professors gained from their lab experiments, they still needed to knock first at Cravingston's black door, gain permission to enter, and assume subservient positions before his desk to hand over the required paperwork.

Reggie had been startled to see the framed photo, the only photo, on the wall behind Cravingston's desk. He would wonder later if the man had set it up that way on purpose, or perhaps the man's assignment was so temporary that he'd had no time to put up other photos, or worse, he carried it around with him. It was the same photo he'd seen in the Book, the tall man in a rumpled safari outfit in a jungle at the purported source of the Nile, only now he recognized the man next to him in a military uniform, caught in the full bloom of a laughing spasm, as a younger Cravingston.

"Yes, I knew your father," Cravingston spoke evenly in a slightly British manner. "We haven't spoken in a long time. We travelled the Nile, you know. Spent some time together in India. You have his journals, right? You've read them?"

"No," Reggie shot back, too quickly though; Cravingston knew he was lying. "I-I mean, I've seen them. Not read them. My mother keeps them locked up." But why should I hide my father's writings? Why not seek help in understanding them? "I could ask her for them..."

"I knew your father well. Your mother, also. In '37 your father and I worked together for the Army, the Signals Intelligence Service. I was on loan from the Special Operations Executive. I remember when he met your mother in London, and I even took care of her for a few months while she was pregnant with you, while Herbert was on assignment."

And so it was, so smoothly, with talk of friends and family, that Cravingston wore down the young man's defenses. He would turn Reggie and have the Book in due time, and even more, he would orchestrate the son's career in becoming his eyes and ears among the tumultuous youth.

* * *

Winter storms raged outside Reggie's red-brick cocoon of study. Revolutions were breaking out in Cameroon, Somalia, Togo, and the Belgian Congo. Black students in Greensboro, North Carolina, were refusing to leave a segregated Woolworth's lunch counter after being refused service. France was about to test its first atomic bomb in the Sahara. Elvis was returning from Germany, and Harvard's own wayward son, Senator "John F. Kennedy '40" as he was called in the *Harvard Crimson*, had just announced his presidential candidacy with the promise of "a more vital life, for all of our people."

It was rare for Reggie to scan the television in the dormitory lounge, but the news was getting more interesting every day. The other students would glance at the TV and just decide they were too busy. This was Harvard, after all, a highly competitive path to the lofty pinnacles of knowledge, business, and science. There was work to be done. Reggie could see in these students a die already cast. Harvard had lost its charm and had begun to reveal the toxic layer of aristocracy underneath. It was less an institution of discovery and learning, becoming more and more a factory for turning out Harvard Men, gentlemen but not scholars, except perhaps inadvertently. The "education" would eventually cripple them with the sort of soft, reflexive, and humorless caution that was required for leading a company or a nation.

Not Reggie. He was not cut for that kind of cloth. He would never look like these fellows in their casual sweaters over buttoned-down Brooks Brothers shirts and dress slacks. He would never be asked to join the exalted ranks of the privileged who would grow incalculably rich at the expense of the legions of the working class. How he knew this, he couldn't say. It was almost as if he could sense the future.

Cravingston had suggested that they meet each Wednesday afternoon at Winthrop House. A number of very senior faculty at Harvard, with the enthusiastic encouragement of McGeorge Bundy, Dean of the Faculty of Arts and Sciences, had been meeting for some time to plan a new interdisciplinary undergraduate major in Social Studies. It had a strong theoretical emphasis, grounded in the great tradition of European social thought. The reading for the first week was *An Inquiry into the Nature and Causes of the Wealth of Nations*, by Adam Smith.

"All of it?"

"It's not for a test, son," said Professor G. B. Martini. "You are reading it because it is a brilliant and very influential book, and we think you will find it interesting."

Reggie plodded on through the semester, making nominal progress in French and Political Science, Music Theory and Archaeology, while also moving through Martini's reading list, from Smith to Mill's *Political Economy*, a selection of Marx's writings, de Tocqueville's *L'Ancien Régime et la Révolution*, Tyler's *Primitive Culture*, Nietzsche's *Genealogy of Morals*, Freud's *Civilization and its Discontents*; and after reading these and three hundred pages of Max Weber, Collingwood's *Idea of History*, and Whitehead's *Modes of Thought*, he was ready for Durkheim's *Suicide*.

Professor Martini was insane, of course.

When Reggie finally reached the critiques of Marx and Freud by Herbert Marcuse, it was like a vacation in a foreign resort. He bathed in *Eros and Civilization*, its sensual language of sexual freedom, the end of repression, and the instinctual drive toward happiness, articulated in such pursuits as philosophy and art, and in such habits as daydreaming.

Daydreaming in Cravingston's office of a nude Lucy emerging from the ocean waves, Eros naively greeting Civilization, Reggie snapped back to attention at Cravingston's remark. "You know, your father knew Marcuse," pointing to the book under Reggie's arm. "They worked together for the government, the OSS. The two Herberts, one demystifying the Nazis and the other demystifying secret codes. Both with the initials 'HM'. Did you know that they used to pull practical jokes on their superiors? You know, switching assignments and initialing them 'HM' in the same style."

And like so many left-wing OSS associates, Marcuse ended up teaching at Harvard and had recently held a chair at the Harvard Russian Research Center around the back of the Yard on Cambridge Street, an institution for which the Carnegie Corporation, not Harvard, determined overall research priorities, and even named the personnel who would operate it. "At the Center, he was known as our 'Marxist-in-residence,'" smirked Cravingston.

"My father and Marcuse were friends? Marxists? Is that why he left the country, Joe McCarthy?"

Cravingston waved his hand, dismissing this notion.

"McCarthy was more interested in deposing stars in Hollywood and the bureaucrats at the State Department rather than engage in any kind of meaningful debate with Harvard intellectuals. Besides, he never had that kind of information. They were OSS. Everything McCarthy got was from J. Edgar Hoover at the FBI, and Hoover knew better than to turn over his files about a rival agency."

Cravingston continued, smiling at some inside joke. "No, your father had other reasons for disappearing. Did you know that he changed his name, before you were born? His name, and your real name, is Mesh. It's on your original birth certificate in England. Why your father changed it to Mention, I don't really know. But I know that your father wasn't born Mesh, either. *His* father, your grandfather, was Gilbert Mesirow, the socialist. An unknown hero, really. He was hauled off and killed for organizing a Negro revolt in the Deep South."

Reggie furrowed his brow, pretending to have not read about his father's father in the Book.

"So it's not surprising, really, that your father would fall in with Marcuse, another true believer. They were both disillusioned with governments, the treacheries, the assassinations. Even as they worked at the OSS, tracking former Nazis that your government and my superiors at Whitehall wanted to recruit, they would argue. Argue all the time, about the similarities of the Western and Soviet systems, how they were simply two sides of the same bad coin. What did Marcuse say? 'The present communist spirit resembles the capitalist spirit' or something like that. At least, that is what I thought he said; he had such a thick German accent."

Cravingston paused to clear his throat. "And I would argue with both of them. What kind of plans do the left-wingers have, the communists and socialists? Would they make our lives better? How can you argue *against* using our scientific knowledge, our most up-to-date technical expertise, to make our lives more comfortable and secure? The answer is, they didn't know! They had no real plans. They couldn't argue back. They couldn't say where to turn, for solutions to real problems. Should we not trust science? In this modern age? In the technical intelligence that built this system in the first place?"

Cravingston sighed as if he really didn't want to believe his own theorem. "The truth is, the workers they so desperately wanted to help are now becoming obsolete. We are replacing their function with machines. We are all becoming managers. We share in the commonwealth of the machine age. You know, when the first nuclear weapon was detonated, and I remember exactly the date and time, July 16, 1945, at 5:30 in the morning... *at that moment*, the *technocrats* took control of our culture. And now we are all becoming technocrats."

Now it was Reggie's turn to sigh. "Marcuse saw technocrats behind everything, behind *all* evil. But if his views were so radical..."

"Then how did he end up here, in this factory for making technocrats? Is that your question? Or is it, why did he end up in academia, like so many others from the OSS? These wartime friendships go very deep. They're faculty members, bitterly opposed in their political views during the day. But at night, they're back in the pub, all warm and friendly over pints. You see, they *are* technocrats, all the same."

After a pause, Cravingston continued. "Or is your question, why are Marcuse and others here, and not your father? I don't know the answer to that. The Herbert Mesh I knew was obsessed with secret societies, and the secret wisdom of the ancients. Another friend in the OSS, Norman O. Brown, or 'Nobby' as his friends called him, is also now a professor. Nobby was an important influence, he grew up with occultists. Madame Blavatsky was a friend of his family, and so was Aleister Crowley. You know those names?"

Reggie, puzzled at the name Crowley which had appeared in the Book, tried hard not to show recognition.

"It was Nobby that introduced us all to a deeper understanding of Freud," Cravingston went on. "You see, he was trying to find in Freud what was missing in Marx. He insisted that Freud had not gone far enough with psychoanalysis. He said the hardest thing was to follow Freud into that dark underworld he explored, and *stay there*. What he was looking for, and what I've spent a good part of my life researching, is a synthesis of psychoanalysis, anthropology, and history. Here, look at this."

Cravingston lobbed a thin, leather-bound book into Reggie's lap. It was a published speech by Brown, delivered the previous year to graduating members of Phi Beta Kappa at Columbia University, titled "Apocalypse: The Place of Mystery in the Life of the Mind." Reggie assumed it was yet another purely scientific exploration of psychology and the physiology of the human brain, perhaps an explanation of the biochemical reaction that occurs when people encounter mysteries. He also understood that he had to please this man Cravingston, who meant to indoctrinate him into a new clarification of reality, and most importantly, into the Phi Beta Kappa chapter at Harvard. And so he read.

And read again, the first sentence of the second paragraph, twice, for he was not sure he'd read it right.

Our real choice is between holy and unholy madness: open your eyes and look around you — madness is in the saddle anyhow.

The opening lines of Allen Ginsberg's "Howl" floated into his mind. The best minds of his generation, destroyed by madness.

"Amazing for a history professor, isn't it?" Cravingston was enjoying this. "Nobby considered Freud the analyzer of unholy madness, and Nietzsche the prophet of holy madness, of Dionysus, the mad truth. He was arguing, in effect, that students should fight against the tyranny of science. Here, read on, this passage."

And Reggie read on.

The great equalizers dispensed by the scientific method are the tools, those analytical tools. But fools with tools *are still fools, and don't let your Phi Beta Kappa key fool you. Tibetan prayer wheels are another way of arriving at the same result: the degeneration of mysticism into mechanism — so that any fool can do it.*

"You see his point?" Cravingston had watched Reggie's eyes and felt the interest growing in his young student, growing as an almost sexual kind of awakening. "He is saying that true wisdom will not be attained by scientific analysis or by dwelling in libraries, but only through the pursuit of the Dionysian spirit. And this is what stodgy Marx didn't understand, and what Freud would never admit. Neither of them knew how to sing and dance in the face of his own mortality."

Cravingston laughed, then turned serious. "Nobby saw our culture as pathological, and wanted to restore that psychic wholeness that, he felt, must have existed in ancient times. And your father, well... He went off into some kind of death-defying history project, what he called 'psychic archaeology' that would delve into the mysteries of the ancients, and reconcile them with the visionary imagination, which to him is the *real* world. He could not accept this world, this tangible world we feel, a world of the elites repressing others to keep their privileged positions. And this is, perhaps, where your father made his mistake."

Reggie could feel the seduction in Cravingston's fatherly tone. Oh, so it was only a *mistake*, was it? My father changes his name and disappears from a normal family life and a professional career. Meanwhile, his buddies in wartime espionage go on to successful academic careers. They continue to debate about untying the knot of repression, but they never get loose of the knot within, the scientific world view that keeps them employed. And one of them, now in a position of power, is trying to recruit me.

And why not? Here was something Reggie felt he could sink his teeth into. He could fake servitude to his country, or rather, to his country's elite, in order to learn something, gain some leverage. Use his power of thought. "So what does it take to become a technocrat?"

"Prepare yourself," replied Cravingston without missing a beat. "You have three years to develop a distinguished record of performance in the arts, humanities, languages, mathematics, natural sciences, and social sciences. Election to membership in Phi Beta Kappa is an honor typically conferred upon fewer than ten percent of each graduating class, and you don't apply. They select you. If you are worthy, you are called in your senior year, although there have been exceptional juniors admitted."

A knock on the door brought the meeting to a close. A tall, gaunt man in blue jeans with pig-shit stains, carrying a banjo, looking for all the world like a slice of the American countryside lost in the corridors of power, peered into the office. He had a puzzled look as if peering into an empty barn after the horses had already scattered. "I'm looking for Professor Timothy Leary."

"And you are?" Cravingston rose upright behind his desk.

"Mel Lyman. I have an appointment."

"Upstairs, down the corridor to the end. When you see the plaque with the three monkeys, make a left."

* * *

When Reggie got back to his dorm room, it seemed to have been swept by an unseen wind. Books were out of place, drawers were left half-open. The satchel that had held his father's Book had been tossed aside. Now he thanked his luck that the Book had not been in the room. He had lent it to his new friend down the hall, Clay Jackson, who wanted to transcribe the Negro folk songs in it.

Some cursory research into the secret Phi Beta Kappa society revealed that most of America's forefathers had been members, including Harvard's own John Quincy Adams and Theodore Roosevelt. Its oath of secrecy, Greek mottoes, ritual of initiation and handclasp of recognition gave it a mystical aura, and more than a few historians had traced the origins of these rituals to the Bavarian Illuminati Order of Freemasons, a secret society within a secret society, linked to both the American and French revolutions. This group, in turn, traced its lineage back to King Charles Martel of France, Hiram of Tyre, Solomon, Euclid, and Pythagoras.

Reggie recalled in his mind the words from his father's Book, which had not only footnoted Freemasonry but had hastily explained some of its more profound symbols. "A network of adepts of higher intelligence exists and functions throughout our planet and, I suspect, extends even farther than our Earth, *and they communicate with each other in code. Music has always served as a medium for these codes, in ancient times and even today.*"

The depth of these connections displaced his mind and left him unable to concentrate. In literature classes he diagrammed the sentences; in logic, he wrote poetry. His father's exploits, if not the man himself, had followed him to Harvard to haunt him, to hover over his shoulder and confound his thoughts. There was that rude snobbery underneath the sophisticated air of the campus, and with all these former government agents and bureaucrats in position as deans, a sense of a Gestapo hiding in the rose bushes.

He'd met Clay in Martini's class but really hadn't said two words to him until they bumped into each other at a Radcliffe mixer of highballs and caviar. Reggie had gone to forget his cares, hoping to meet a young girl; all he met were assembly-line goddesses, austere and inhuman in their sparkling evening dresses, posturing and talking sarcastically about fashion while furtively seeking out material to mold into future husbands. As a freshman he had no accomplishments to speak of, nobody's shoulder to cry on, no one like a Lucy who would hold his hand and talk him out of his feverish self-pity. What he needed, he knew, was a real friend.

Clay Jackson was a tall, handsome, hard-faced shit-kicker from Texas who'd outgrown his father's Grand Ole Opry and his gospel-singing sisters, learned to play the ukelele like Roy Smeck, and lovingly carried his Nat "King" Cole records with him to Harvard. At the mixer he was as out of place as a kazoo in an orchestra. He had snuck in a fifth of Jack Daniels and staked out a corner to watch the action. Reggie and Clay blended into the gold-leaf wallpaper and ignored everyone, focusing on that fifth. Somehow the conversation drifted from the insane reading requirements for Martini's class to sea shanties and Negro folk songs, and Reggie had told him about his father's Book. Clay wanted to learn the songs.

Leaving his dorm room unlocked — why not, they'd already been through everything — Reggie took off for Martini's class and spotted Clay in the back of the lecture hall, innocently copying lyrics from the Book right out in the open, ignoring the other students pulling out notepads to prepare for the lecture. Professor Martini held a stack of the final papers at the podium, and was preparing to read from some of them. The Professor could bear to read only the first paragraph of the first paper before declaring it to be an unmitigated disaster, and placing it aside. But it was the second paper, Reggie's own essay on conspiracies at work behind the scenes of the French Revolution, that aroused his ire to a fever pitch as he read the first sentence, dramatically crumpled up the first page, and launched the paper ball across the room toward the waste basket. And missed.

Readying his stare directly at a shame-faced Reggie all the way in the back row, Martini launched into his diatribe. "You seek heroes and villains!

"You blame conspiracies," continued the wiry professor in a lower tone, calmly adjusting his cheap wireframe glasses over his stupendous nose, supported by a waxed Zapata mustache. He never took his glance off Reggie. "But when we have falling wages and rising prices, we have a *calculus for revolution*. The ratio of these two variables, falling wages and rising prices, could be considered the index of revolutionary potential..." He went on, a bit too fast for the class to write it down in their bluebooks. Clearly beside himself with glee, Martini had recently returned from the nascent Cuban Revolution and had reported its success to his peers, including Marcuse.

"And even as there are conspiracies and secret societies that believe in their own power to bring about revolution, they are not in any more control of the conflagration as a match is in control of a spark, or a spark in control of the fire." Amused by his own erudition, he forged ahead with his point about the French Revolution. "And this is why Robespierre, considered mad, was justly executed by those he sought to serve. In the midst of a speech! He was warning them that the bourgeoisie had already killed the revolution. And this is why he is a tragic figure: Robespierre did not understand why the revolution could not deliver what it had promised."

But what of these secret societies spreading ideas about freedom? "Granted, they were perhaps the channels that spread the ideas of Enlightenment, but would these societies have that much power? You can't grow wheat on stony soil." This time Martini, certain of his wit, paused to allow note-taking. "The fact is that over 90 percent of the French population were peasants. Very few were ever recruited into Freemasonry, before the 1770s. These ideas would not have taken root if it weren't for the rising population and its inevitable wage-price differential. While it may be true that secret societies were plotting to overthrow governments, it's also true that the rebellions in Switzerland and Holland were falsely blamed on 'radicalism' or 'subversion' and not to economic desperation, which was their true cause. The Gordon Riots in London were attributed to anti-Catholic hysteria, which was only its façade, since virtually all of the rebellious were unemployed or marginally employed. They were men seeking an outlet for rage and despair."

And they lose, thought Reggie. They reach a point where they can't break through. Spend their entire lives fighting for the noble thing, but when they come closest to realizing what they think is their collective dream, it disintegrates into hypocrisy, turns out to be not at all what they wanted, or what they thought it would be. The dream becomes a commercial for a new Elvis movie. It carries the commercial taint of phoniness. "So what becomes of the true heroes and villains?"

"We mythologize them," Clay answered, on the way out of the hall, handing Reggie back the Book. "We paint them, write about them. We sing songs of their exploits. That's *folk* music, buddy."

Reggie recognized a kindred spirit in Clay. Despite his stated intention to live as a wealthy intellectual, and after two long years of trying to be an intellectual and trying to get laid at the same time, Clay finally resorted to skipping classes to hang out with a folk group.

"We work to make others rich," Clay summarized the lecture, the class, the university, the city, state, and country. The world itself. "The reason why life seems so tough is because it's so *pointless*. We serve the Beast of Commerce. It doesn't make any difference who's in the White House, whether he came from Harvard or Duke. The orders still come from Wall Street."

In any case, Reggie wanted, more than anything, a friend to listen to his records and delve into these fascinating mysteries. There was a little bit of Kerouac's Dean Moriarity underneath Clay's placid, studious nature. It would emerge only when he was outside the gates of the campus, in staccato outbursts of philosophy and rascal remarks to the girls in the record stores. With his roommate John Cooke, the three of them would go out to the stores to find ancient records that sounded *real*. Real people playing wooden instruments and *not* wearing gold-lamé outfits.

Rare records were a badge of honor, and Cooke's large collection gave him authenticity, while Clay's eclectic choices revealed a higher appreciation for hip. Reggie qualified for membership as the Jersey kid with the Robert Johnson record whose father had known Woody Guthrie. Exploring the roots of American music took on the quality of a quest for a holy grail. Reggie thought they were a small group, a secret society of three, just three white college boys seeking anti-intellectual truth in dirt-poor country music, clutching Folkways records hidden like pornography in plain sleeve wrappers. Then Clay introduced him to the fourth member, a clever graduate who'd formed an old-timey folk group called the Charles River Valley Boys that every once in a while took over the campus radio station for a few hours.

Eric Sackheim had come from a well-to-do family in New York and had already spent four years at Harvard, single-handedly turning the others, one by one, into lifetime lovers of rural music. He'd created an entire department of "language studies" consisting of himself, and had been awarded *summa-cum-laude* for his thesis on Folk Music, which no one understood or even read. His class was a rich cul-de-sac of intellectualism, sanctioned by Harvard, and accountable to no one.

"What kind of career can you have with a Folk Music or Ethnomusicology degree?" Reggie wanted to know.

"You won't need to worry about that," winked Eric. "You'll be graduating from Harvard. No one looks at what you actually studied."

Seven of them would meet in the Woodbury Music and Poetry Listening Room in the Lamont Library and compare Library of Congress recordings by Woody Guthrie, Lead Belly, and Sonny Terry. Bob Siggins, member number five, was the proud owner of an Obray Ramsay record.[143] Sackheim had everything from Uncle Dave Macon and Charlie Poole to the rare collections recorded by John and Alan Lomax, and the very rare Mention-Falloni recordings.

Mention? Would that be Herbert...? Sure enough, Eric Sackheim knew something about his father's quest and had a reel of field recordings he'd done with Freddie Falloni in the wilds of Arkansas, of a jazzy bluesman who called himself the Jackal.

Eric had also bought nearly every country blues record ever made, including a few authentic Robert Johnson records from 1938. Back in Eric's filthy apartment, amidst piles of records and tapes and surrounded by overstuffed bookshelves and dangling exotic instruments, they gathered to listen to the holy grail, the *Anthology of American Folk Music* collected by Harry Smith for Folkways Records, a collection of 84 performances on six LPs. The cover looked like it had been torn from a page of Leonardo DaVinci's notebook: an etching of a single-stringed instrument superimposed on a globe, in the process of being tuned by the hand of God.

"The etching is by Theodore de Bry," Eric told them, pulling out a book of alchemy and mysticism by Robert Fludd in which the original drawing appeared. "'The Celestial Monochord' goes all the way back to 400 B.C. Supposed to be invented by Pythagoras. The word for 'monochord' is the root of the English word 'accord' and this drawing shows all of creation," Eric drew his finger around the outer globe, "balanced, by the monochord, into separate spheres of energy for reason and sensuality. A-and get this, the record labels are blue, red, and green to symbolize air, fire, and water."

Reggie stared at the record cover with the titles and names of blues singers, hillbilly bands, and gospel chanters printed irreverently over the exquisite filaments and ornate Latin captions in the etching. Inside was a booklet with songs marked by oversized black numbers that suggested an obscure, ancient mathematics lurking beneath the surface. On its cover appeared a drawing of a long-haired, bearded minister holding a great book, with the words "All please sound" printed alongside, as if the book contained hymns. The commentary on each song — and many were ballads handed down from medieval times — reduced volumes of scholarship to wry one-liner newspaper headlines: "The Butcher's Boy"[144] described as "Father finds daughter's body with note attached when railroad boy mistreats her," and "House Carpenter" as "Wife and mother follows carpenter to sea; mourns babe as ship goes down."

"Or my favorite," pointed out Eric, for "Ommie Wise"[145]: "Greedy girl goes to Adams Spring with liar, lives just long enough to regret it."

This mysterious, occult textbook on folk music brought forth previously forgotten recordings on commercial labels from the 1920s and 1930s. These were decidedly *not* the Lomax-style field recordings of farm hands and prisoners, but commercial recordings. Many of the songs had had an original pressing of only 500 copies and were, at best, regional collector's items, never to be reissued again. They were already old when they were recorded. They issued out of the fissions and cracks of American culture like curdled steam, only to vanish in the air.

"The anthology is really a bootleg," said Eric, "legal only if you take the position that this music needed to be captured and reissued by eminent domain."

For one thing, Harry Smith hadn't commented on whether the performers were black or white, and there were no photographs. Race records of the period were assumed to be black, and popular records white, but this was something else entirely. The project mysteriously slipped by the licensing attorneys at the record labels that owned the masters. The anthology was released without fanfare and without any legal battles because no one really knew what it was. The songs were hidden in plain sight, just like the mysterious America of the farmlands and levees it documented.

A single listen through all the recordings took over four hours and several jugs of wine. The music rose right out of the ground, like clods of rich, dark, timeless earth. The guitars were out of tune and you couldn't understand the words in their rural vernacular, but you could sense that they were sung by outcasts, antiheroes, bad men and underdogs, hanged murderers, scorned lovers. Singing about the hopelessness of our times, such as that silly cry, "peg 'n peg 'n peg... and awl"[146] — the last whimper of the artisan class, with Harry Smith's wry comment, "Technological unemployment hits shoe industry in the year of 18 and 4." Through some kind of alchemy Smith had combined just the right set of songs that could turn your mind around. Reggie heard the call of another life.

In the very back, Harry Smith had listed a bibliography accompanied by advertisements of record albums from commercial labels. At the very end, printed along the side of the advertisements, was presumably Smith's opinion of them, flipping off the very adversaries that could have stopped the project cold: "The advertising on these envelopes gives a good idea of the companies' attitudes toward their artists." Indeed, one showed a fiddler on a stool outside his farmhouse, and another, from Vocalion Race Records, showed a happy-faced Negro guitarist picking away on an acoustic guitar as a white lady socialite dances erotically with her dress hiked up above her knees.

Accompanying this, a few quotations: "Civilized man thinks out his difficulties, at least he thinks he does, primitive man dances out his difficulties." (R. R. Marrett)

And this, which took Reggie by surprise because it was accompanied by that symbol, the one used as code in the MAD Magazine, the three monkeys in the "see no evil" pose:

"Do as thy wilt shall be the whole of the law." (Aleister Crowley)

Eric explained. "I think it may be a mistranslation of Crowley's famous words, 'Do *what thou wilt* shall be the whole of the Law,' or else Harry Smith wrote it that way on purpose."

Reggie thought, more coded messages? Hiding in plain sight?

This "whole of the Law" theme snaked its way through all these stories masquerading as songs. Here was "Stackalee"[147] in an earlier form, sung in a country voice neither black nor white, but not so far removed from Lloyd Price's current version on the R&B stations. The traditional song told the story of a gambler shooting another over losing his Stetson hat. Billy DeLion or Billy the Lion pleads for his life, for his three kids and poor little sickly wife, but Stagger Lee, or Stacker Lee or Stackalee, shoots him anyway, shoots him so bad the bullet went right through him and broke the bartender's glass. Harry Smith's one-liner headline put it cynically: "Theft of Stetson hat causes deadly dispute, victim identifies self as family man." Leaving one to doubt the victim's veracity, to wonder how a gambling loss could be considered theft, and to dismiss the entire story as an aberration, a misinterpretation from some other culture where black is white and wrong is right.

But Reggie didn't want to dismiss it; he wanted to wallow in its contradictions, and that's what Harry Smith's message seemed to be: to treat these songs as codes, just like the coded Negro slave songs in his father's Book, for learning a different way of life hidden beneath the American dream, to learn about underworld heroes that carried on their own personal revolutions by living as criminals right out in the open, under the noses of the authorities. Heroes masquerading as villains, like John Johanna, Bandit Cole the Younger, Charles Giteau, and the desperate little man John Hardy. And here was John Henry,[148] dying heroically as he tried to beat the speed of a steam drill using only his own hand drill. "And Joe Hill," added Clay, "he's the left-wing Stagger Lee, taking the fight right into company territory. They couldn't stop him honestly, they had to frame him for a murder he didn't commit."

It hit Reggie that real folk music did more than champion the underdogs. Folk challenged conformity in a way that the Kingston Trio, in their collegiate striped shirts, could never get across; it challenged everything that's intellectual and phony. "How did this guy get away with this?" Reggie gestured at the archaic drawings, the crude booklet and packaging that looked ancient, the weird sayings, the previously released songs by racist record companies.

"No one was looking," laughed Eric. "Those songs were released in a different time, before the Depression. The pop music labels today are embarrassed by them, so they didn't even bother with it."

What could it have been like, Reggie wondered, when the ordinary people of 1929 encountered these records? Did they ask, what is a record? At early listenings to Edison's phonograph, young women fainted. Scientific experts were convinced it was a trick of ventriloquism. A Yale professor pronounced this machine that could "steal" a human voice to be a flat-out hoax. What was this thing, this *record*, that could make absent people present, could bring the dead back to life, even now?

"These musicians," Reggie pondered out loud, "they're all long dead by now."

"Don't be too sure of that," whispered Eric. "Wait and see what I bring back from my recording expedition this summer."

It was only then that Reggie noticed the dusty plaque on Eric's wall, practically hidden behind a bookshelf: the three monkeys. Once again, haunting him. See no evil, hear no evil, speak no evil.

* * *

Pursuing records had led Reggie outside the gate that is not a gate, just the impression of one bracketed by decorative fenceposts. He greeted the modern traffic outside the ancient walls with an air of pretense. He was, after all, a Harvard student, a wealthy and prized customer for the brick commercial establishments that blurred cobblestoned history into the steel and glass of Mt. Auburn Street.

A coffeehouse had been crammed in between the steel and glass, from which music spewed forth like the steam from the espresso machine. Tulla's Coffee Grinder was an Italian-flavored room crammed with small tables and many chairs, set on a level several feet below the sidewalk, so that Reggie had to bend over to peer inside. He found, to his amazement and amusement, a bearlike man with wild hair sprouting in all directions from behind wire-rimmed glasses, in an untucked work shirt and baggy pinstripe trousers hitched up to show his ankles, singing about muleskinners.

Passing a hat for spare change, the bear introduced himself as Eric Von Schmidt, Ric for short, and started reciting a song he'd scrawled and illustrated on torn notebook paper, titled appropriately enough, "Grizzly Bear",[149] and managed to get through the first verse before Reggie stopped him with a quarter in his hat. A statuesque Norwegian blonde of indeterminate age serenely poured an espresso behind the counter; presumably Tulla herself. On the wall, a news clipping from the *Harvard Crimson*, published Nov. 28, 1956. Reggie scanned the opening paragraph. "Two interesting people have opened a new coffee shop on Mount Auburn Street that smacks not one twit of the desperate degeneracy one sometimes associates with such places on this street."

What places would these be? Reggie didn't exactly want to participate, but wouldn't have minded watching a bit of degeneracy. He watched Ric shuffle out unselfconsciously, his zipper partway down, his guitar slung over his shoulder with a rope for a strap, carrying a large bag of something, which turned out to be artichokes.

Out on Brattle, a souped up roadster with its lights off zoomed up and screeched its brakes, nearly hitting Ric, who paused his rollicking mellow gate to smile back. The driver, about the same age as Reggie and wearing a Harvard warm-up jacket, sneered back, "Fuckin' townie," and gunned his engine, and, just as Ric was extending a friendly artichoke through the driver's window, zoomed off, spiraling Ric through a rain of artichokes and leaving him prone on the street with a cracked rib.

The driver was part of the new generation now swarming Harvard. They were the sons of Gatsby's careless friends Tom and Daisy Buchanan, embarrassing the intellectuals, and tripling the ranks of its sports teams. They felt entitled to cause a ruckus and then retreat into their money while others sorted it out. Reggie knew the student vaguely as one of many arrogant jocks in the locker room that left puddles of shaving cream and shaved hair around the sinks and dirty bandages in the showers, disgusting representatives of our nation's elite, leaving it all to the Negro janitor, they call him Narcissus, to clean up.

Reggie valiantly gathered up the artichokes and helped Ric back to the apartment Ric shared with his wife Helen, just off Harvard Square. Helen's folksinger brother Robert L. Jones showed up, and then more friends from Boston as well as a few Harvard students Reggie had seen around campus, gathering around the von Schmidt record collection, including Eric, Clay, and Bob Siggins. "Y'know," Ric, in mid-conversation with someone else, kicked

Reggie in the shin, and pointed to a fifth of rum on the bookshelf, "coffee's not my idea of a real drink." Helen frowned as Reggie poured, but before long the kitchen was as loud, bright and jovial as a bowling alley.

Wincing from his cracked rib, Ric still couldn't help grabbing a guitar and launching into an old blues tune, "He Was a Friend of Mine"[150] — a kind of weird rebuke to the arrogant kid that had almost run him over. Reggie was startled by the authentic sound of this white man's bluesy voice. The subtle poignancy was beyond anything he'd ever heard before. Before long he was in an argument with Eric Sackheim about the meaning of folk music. "It's not the Kingston Trio, it's not even Pete Seeger," Eric yelled over the din. "The real folk music is the country blues, the Appalachian hillbilly songs."

And what about Woody Guthrie, Joe Hill, the songs of struggle and resistance? Topical songs?

"Lots of these older tunes were topical, if not political," Ric growled at them. "Woody himself said he was the biggest song stealer of them all. Now, you wanna hear a topical song?" He launched into "When That Great Ship Went Down".[151] The rich would not ride with the poor, so they put the poor below, and they were the first to go. Yes, it was sad when that great ship went down...

But not too sad. The party jumped a notch higher as a boisterous contingent arrived from Greenwich Village, which turned out to be two people: a tall, dark, fidgety artist with a mischievous grin popping out of his black turtleneck sweater, Bobby Neuwirth, and the most handsome woman Reggie had ever seen, Debbie Green, in peasant blouse and jeans, carrying her acoustic guitar, only about a year or two older than him, maybe twenty. Reggie couldn't take his eyes off her. She carried herself earnestly, with long curling brown hair framing inquisitive eyes peeking out from high cheekbones, square-shouldered and full-figured, with a bashful good-time smile revealing her upper gums and slightly crooked teeth. She melted Reggie's heart.

Joining Ric, Debbie threw her body into playing the guitar in a masculine style, fingers popping up and down the entire neck, finger-picking rather than strumming chords as Reggie had seen most women folk singers do. In contrast to her earthy playing, she sang in a misty voice, penetrating and serious, covering traditional English and Appalachian ballads.

Bobby Neuwirth, muttering about the uptight New York scene, asked Helen, has Geno arrived?

"Been here and gone, like the force of nature that he is," she said, reaching behind the counter for a baggie of some vegetable material. Neuwirth went off with it to the bathroom; within minutes, pungent smoke spilled out from the cracks in the doorway.

"You better not bring any of that down to the club," yelled Ric before starting up a verse of "Fast Acne"[152], another of his original songs, this time about teenage angst. Concerned looks all around.

Reggie turned to Eric Sackheim, what club?

"Club 47, it's a folk club, we're going to see Ric perform." This was all news to Reggie. "And no one wants to jeopardize the club's very tenuous existence," sneered Eric, "by bringing down the heat." Odd that a Harvard grad would use Negro slang for cops, Reggie thought, and why would they care about folk music?

Debbie sighed at the interruption, put aside her guitar, kicked off her sandals, and smiled at Reggie like an old friend. Too smitten to say anything clever, Reggie started out stammering about college life, but she must have sensed his nervousness and just talked and talked, and her words just washed over him. She'd just recovered from mono-nucleosis, and had got back just in time to join her best friend Joanie Baez, to play at the club tonight. They both went to Boston University, she majored in drama, but mostly she majored in staying up all night and playing at the nearby Café Yana, where the Charles River Boys had made their Boston debut. As a teen she'd learned at the feet of the best café guitarist in New York City, Dave Van Ronk.

Reggie thought, Van Ronk, Von Schmidt; who are these aristocrats in peasant clothes, they know so much about American music? Ric Von Schmidt must be at least thirty. Are they all just chasing college skirts?

Debbie kept going and going. "Joanie and I do these old traditional ballads because there's so much drama, mothers protecting their daughters from evil men, a woman condemned to death for carrying the king's child, they're all so dramatic. And I learned them from a book, it's called *The English and Scottish Popular Ballads*, by Francis Child, you know? My mother has a whole bunch of trouble in her life, she's very emotional, you know? She does a lot of crying, so I have all this heavy weight on me. So when I play guitar and sing these songs, all about unrequited love," she sighed, putting her hand on her breast, as Reggie's heart fluttered, "it's a release, you know? From all that sorrow."

Reggie thought he knew. He sure wanted to know. He wanted to cuddle up with her all night so that he could know.

"So why don't you come with us to the frat party, it's right on campus."

And so it was. By the time they arrived, the house reeked of stale beer; the "Go man, go" sax enthusiasts had crowded the basement, bopping to the bop. Ric was telling Reggie that a fat mystic named Leopold ruled this house, always cooking up wondrous meals, but he was some kind of magician who knew a lot of card tricks. Eric Sackheim whispered about Leopold's connection to Aleister Crowley, and that a respected and credible witness had testified at the Pledge Week Bash that Leopold had made lightning appear in a closed room.

Who should appear at that moment but Cravingston, bright-eyed and blinking furiously like Cary Grant in a rumpled suit in the hotel lobby in *North by Northwest*. "He's upstairs," pointing at the stairs. "Go have a look."

What kind of 'frat party' invites faculty? Nevertheless, Reggie climbed, followed by Cravingston, to the top of the stairs, and was about to knock on the heavy oak door at the landing, the only access to the entire floor, when the door swung open of its own accord. Inside, the overture to Mozart's "The Magic Flute"[153] had just begun, with its heavy reiterated chords sounding for all the world like someone knocking on a heavy oak door.

"The sorcerer's apprentice must knock three times," whispered Cravingston into his ear, uncharacteristically mischievous. "The magic flute will protect you, and sustain you in the greatest of misfortunes."

Leopold, fat and swarthy in a foul-stained terrycloth robe, held court in his sanctuary brandishing an iron skillet like a conductor's baton. The room smelled of something peculiar and it wasn't all coming from the dead frogs in formaldehyde he kept in his closet. As Mozart's music ennobled even the dull and unpoetical passages of Schikaneder's libretto, lending to the whole a touch of the mysterious and sacred, Leopold quietly addressed a mixed group of students in matching terrycloth robes, steam rising from their bodies. They'd just come out of the wet sauna in Leopold's spacious bathroom.

"Three ladies tell Tamino of the powers of the Magic Flute," intoned Leopold in a low voice. "With it he can change the passions of people. The sad will become joyful and the bachelor will accept love. Emanuel Johann Schikaneder, who wrote the libretto, was a friend of Mozart and a member of the same Masonic Lodge. Together they constructed this expression of a cosmology, in which the essence of life is the energy of opposing forces, a dialectical tension between night and day, woman and man, nature and culture, emotion and reason, odd numbers and even numbers, fire and water, and so on. It is completely unprejudiced and impartial; it is Nietzsche's *Beyond Good and Evil*, but without the philosopher's polemic tone and biting cynicism. The story itself portrays the education of mankind, progressing from chaos through superstition to rationalistic enlightenment, by means of the trials of Tamino and the errors of Papageno, ultimately to remake the Earth as a heavenly kingdom." Leopold then dropped to a whisper, and with a twirl of the robe's sash, "And to remake mortals into gods."

And with this pronouncement and another dramatic flourish he put down the iron skillet and retrieved from his robe a flask containing an amber liquid resembling whiskey. There were a few twitters and stifled giggles beneath the hoods and robes of the group, behind fake angelic smiles.

"The great alchemist of our times, Armand Barbault, curated this mixture from an experiment that he started in 1948, on the night of the new moon in Aquarius," Leopold proclaimed, lifting up his tiny arms, reminding Reggie of illustrations of giant, fat dinosaurs with scrawny, pickled limbs. "The seeker was up before dawn every day, for months on end, to gather dew from the meadows and young plants swollen with sap. Then came twelve years of curation, sublimation, and putrefaction. Twelve long years of preparation, a labor of love, to conjure this elixir of the First Degree, the liquor of vegetable gold."

And with that pronouncement, Leopold took a cautious sip of the liquid.

"The secrets of life," he intoned sonorously. "Whether you seek them with drugs or sobriety, you must attend to the eternal mysteries, and experience with your heart the meaning of death and the triumph *beyond* death. Like a Greek Tragedy, or like the music that is the special glory of our age, the music that goes beyond mere beauty to challenge us, to inflame us, to inspire us to be more glorious beings than we ever thought we could be."

The subtle seduction of Mozart's music intervened, impregnating Leopold's pause with meaning. "You see, all art constantly aspires toward the pure state of music."

Reggie turned back to see Cravingston's response to all this, but the man had somehow quietly sidestepped Reggie to enter the room unnoticed, and was now also in a robe, seated yoga fashion. Cravingston was leaning into and obscuring the face of a woman whose body shape vaguely resembled Lucy's. Reggie caught Leopold giving him the evil eye reserved for unsophisticated intruders. Just outside the nearest window, roof turrets aimed their loads of psychic energy toward Boston in the east. It was time to leave.

"It's weird up there," Reggie said to Ric Von Schmidt downstairs in the living room, who had set himself up on a straight-backed chair, guitar in hand, ready to sing the blues.

"And it's weird down there," Ric spoke like a carnival barker, pointing downstairs toward the basement of jazz. "Mozart up there, Miles[154] down there. So different, and yet so much the same. As above, so below! And what we got right here, on this floor, is the middle ground." And he started picking blues notes.

Eric Sackheim joined them with his banjo, having come from the jazz basement. He sniffed and coughed with a knowing wink at Ric. "I think Geno's down there."

"Been there and gone," intoned Ric in a bluesy voice, "been down so long, it looks like up." Then he stopped playing and looked up. "You know Geno. He buys the supplies. First rate, too."

An embarrassed pause as Reggie blinked at them both. Something going on here?

"You know, I think jazz is burning itself out," Eric changed the subject as he tuned his banjo. "It's like a war against itself, against its own limits. Bebop, now there's a catastrophe! Way out there, reveling in the outer limits at the expense of harmony. The beatniks are just as lost as everyone else. Their scene has turned into a vaudeville show."

"Like that Maynard G. Krebs and his bongos," piped up Reggie.

Ric picked a fast-paced "Stewball"[155] about a drunk racehorse, then suddenly stopped. "It's elementary. We needed some kind of primitive music to cure ourselves of the frenzy of our times. So we all caught the Boogie-Bug. It started with a little R&B here, a little C&W there; Lord Lord Lord, that old Amazing Grease! Behind many a mild-mannered middle-class façade the Boogie-Bug is still alive and thriving. The twin symptoms have already appeared: the Itch to Twitch, and the Urge to Hanker. And it all began so innocently. A ukulele given by an aunt. That chromatic harmonica that made a funny bulge in the Christmas stocking," Ric lowered his voice and arched his eyebrows. "All those seemingly harmless *kazoos*."

Debbie appeared at Reggie's side, her feathery fingers resting on his arm. "I'm so nervous. I need to practice my set."

Ric continued playing "Stewball" and Debbie chimed in on harmony. At the end, Ric handed her his guitar. "You'll do quite well, my little pretty!" Sniggering like the wicked witch. "They'll eat you alive tonight."

Reggie ached for her. Lust pierced his chest as she trilled soprano notes with the coal-mine sadness of Appalachia. Her voice told him that life is for living, that love is everywhere, and that nothing is a promise; beauty exists, yes, but it must be hunted for. She sang of the magic in our lives in the face of an indifferent world, as hungry students flailed about looking for more beer. Shouts and drunken curses filtered up the stairs, neatly drowning out her anguish, as if she were a still life, Folksinger in Performance, torn from its frame on the wall and dumped with the detritus in a living room demolished by a hurricane. She took no notice of the chaos, singing through it all until she was done with the song. But when she looked up, her eyes could not meet his. She was still far off in a distant thought, and he could think of nothing to say to bridge that gulf.

A shout from the stairs preceded her roommate Joanie's arrival, a lank beauty in long dark hair with an impish, Spanish smile. She inserted herself into the group and got right up next to Debbie. "Show me that chord again, the one after 'can't be your bride.'"

Debbie, suddenly embarrassed, patiently strummed the chord structure, demonstrating it over and over. She then handed the guitar over to Joanie, who clutched it eagerly as if it were a bone snatched from a rival dog. Joanie copied Debbie's arrangement closely, humming the song softly without really singing. Flashes of a her wild grin punctuated each successful chord, but she never looked up from the guitar; she was pleasing herself. All eyes were drawn to Joanie like compass needles to the north pole.

Reggie wanted to reach out and touch Debbie's hand, but Joanie's presence had deadened her. The still life, Folksinger in Performance, went back into its frame on the wall. And in the commotion surrounding Joanie, as Reggie shifted his gaze around to take it all in, the still life in its frame had disappeared, stolen away by an older, intense man in tortoise-shell glasses and a big nose named Rolf, who had gathered up Debbie in his arms and whisked her off early, leaving her guitar in Joanie's hands and only frayed impressions on Reggie's heart.

On the way over to Club 47, Eric raved about how Leopold had disappeared from the upstairs room in a flash of smoke. "'I am not my body,' he said. 'I am not here at all.' A-and then he said something about the teachings of the Rose Cross, and that if it wasn't for that wisdom, he would have been dead two hours earlier. I assume he was talking about that elixir or potion."

Reggie stopped him. "You mean that gold liquid?"

"Elixir of the gods. Fountain of youth. A liquid form of gold you can drink."

"The man is out there in the stratosphere," grunted Ric.

"But that's just it!" Eric raved on. "He just disappeared. He said, 'Now I must go away again and not be here,' and with that, he disappeared, only to reappear on the rooftop."

"It's a trick, of course."

"I dunno. He stayed out on that rooftop. Looked like he was blessing the moon. He didn't come back in."

"What happened to the people in the room?"

"They all scattered, quietly muttering some kind of mumbo jumbo."

It was indeed a mystery that would never leave Reggie, because Leopold disappeared after that night. Ric thought he had simply stumbled out into the dimly lit Cambridge streets, inebriated on whatever it was he had drunk from that flask, and either passed out, passed away, or was mugged. Whatever happened, no word got back to his fraternity.

* * *

In performance, Debbie's friend Joanie Baez was something else entirely. Her controlled and graceful quiescence gave her a sort of reverse-psychology sex appeal, a sad virginal princess. You knew that she would never appear in a Hollywood beach movie. Her delivery gave the words of the songs a more penetrating meaning, a more vivid portrait. Barefoot on the tiny Club 47 stage, with long straight black hair hanging down, the princess seemed to have taken on the weight of the world, of all women and all their sorrows.

All the girls miserable with their lot in life were dying to cry along with her. The songs were not about how she loved someone, but rather, how she will never marry. Don't sing love songs that will wake her mother, she sings, because in her mother's right hand is a silver dagger.[156] All the girls know that all men are false, they'll tell you wicked loving lies, and the very next evening they'll court another, leaving you alone to pine and sigh.

The performance made just about every man in the room feel guilty. Staring into Joan's eyes as she sang, Reggie could tell that she shared a form of love with everyone she sang to, but not a love anyone could possess. None were worthy, none could be with the virgin princess who lives in the sky. Reggie contrasted this feeling of hopeless anticipation with the hopeless lust he'd felt for Debbie of the earth, also beyond his reach.

Joan followed up "Silver Dagger" with nearly every song from Debbie's repertoire. Watching from the kitchen that also served as a backstage for guitar cases, alternately seething with anger and then with despair, Debbie stuck her guitar in the sink and sobbed into Rolf's work-shirt, "I didn't see this coming,

254

you know? I go away for a few weeks, I get sick, I come back, and she's taken everything!"

Reggie watched the action leaning against a pillar on the side of the club, and could see Rolf comforting Debbie. Joan's delivery had been so complete that it was difficult to imagine how Debbie could follow her. It occurred to him that he'd witnessed the two different archetypes of the folk music experience, the personal and the professional. Debbie, Ric, and the Charles River Boys were entertaining, competent, even inspirational, but held no view of themselves, and no anxiety about how they dressed or appeared in public. Joan, on the other hand, performed for the mirror, and swooned in the majesty of her ascetic grace. She had a brooding style that suggested a Hollywood starlet, yet portrayed the negative image of that starlet. She was, in fact, the antithesis of starlet: thin, dark, strong, smart, and seemingly virtuous. And yet she could clearly command the attention of every man in the room.

Waiting his turn on stage, Ric shook his shaggy head, not quite contemptuously. "She sings like a bird, but not an ancient bird. She makes these songs contemporary, but they lack something... authenticity. She's gonna be a star, I know it."

Reggie blurted out, "What about Debbie?"

"Oh, she'll be alright. Rolf'll take care of her. He wants to take her out West, to Berkeley, start another club like this one. You know, he escaped Nazi Germany and enlisted in the Army during the War, and ended up in the OSS, the Ossified Spy Service, y'know, the CIA. Man, he used to parachute behind enemy lines to blow up bridges. He knows German, Chinese. He's like our rabbi, a dispenser of Talmudic truth, and when he's not teaching guitar, classical, flamenco, whatever, he's teaching karate, the martial arts. We just finished recording an album together, we wanted Joanie to sing on it, but she had other plans."

It was hopeless. Reggie had thought that just being a Harvard student should get him some attention as it did with the Radcliffees, but here were hardened, experienced, grown men chasing the same skirts. Offering dreams of clubs and careers in entertainment. What girl could possibly be interested in just another student who hadn't figured out yet what to do with his fortunate education?

Eyeing Rolf, he wondered if the man's OSS connections were still active. Had he known his father? He made a mental note to ask, but just then Joanie got his attention by announcing a song she learned "from Pete Seeger's friend Cornell, you all may have heard of him." The reverential audience hushed, straining to hear every word. "And Cornell sat me down and taught me this African song, 'Mbube', or 'The Lion', which Pete had recorded with the Weavers.[157] They called it 'Wimoweh' from the chorus, which is really 'Uyimbube' or 'You are a lion' but we can't seem to pronounce it correctly."

She stifled a giggle, grew serious again. "The song refers to an old legend down in South Africa, the last king of the Zulus, who was known as Shaka The

Lion. The legend says, Shaka The Lion didn't die when the Europeans took over our country; he simply went to sleep, and he'll wake up some day."

Cornell? She used the man's first name only, and seemed a bit like Scarlet O'Hara as she pronounced it, a subliminal reminder that the man is black. Reggie connected the dots. This must be the same Cornell Woodrow mentioned in the Book, the man he'd met, the man Johnny had helped back in Margate. He leaned into Ric as Joanie yodeled the chorus, "Who's this Pete Seeger friend everyone's supposed to know, this Cornell?"

"The man showed up here in Cambridge once with Blind Sonny Terry. His partner Brownie McGhee was tied up in a contract with Manny Greenhill, our local impresario, so Cornell got Sonny a gig at the Golden Vanity, downtown. And he came around to Tulla's, saw me playing, and asked me if I'd play with Sonny. Well! Does God make honky-tonk angels? Was Lead Belly the King of the 12-string? If a bear shits in the woods and you don't hear it, did it really happen? It ain't rocket surgery, it ain't brain science. Of course I'll play with Sonny!

"Well we got down there, and the place was rigged up like a whaling nightmare catered by Melville. The tables were huge barrels, and nets were hung all over the place. A ship's wheel hung behind the stage. Well I went upstairs, unpacked my guitar and two bottles of gin, and introduced myself to Sonny. This is one of my heroes, you know. It just blew my mind that I was actually gonna play with him. Cornell introduced me, and then introduced Sonny to the manager. And I'll never forget it. Sonny, blind as a bat, said he needed money first. And he spelled it out, M-O-N-E-Y. Cash, baby. Before going on. And Cornell talked the manager out of that cash, and then placed each bill in Sonny's hand, telling him what kind of bill it was, until he got up to a hundred dollars. And then Sonny said, 'Let's go.'

"Well, you know, the Golden Vanity is a coffeehouse, but that night everybody was juiced and feeling no pain. And that's also where I met Bobby Neuwirth and Robert Jones, who's now my brother-in-law. They were drunk on their asses, supposed to be washing the dishes."

"Okay," Reggie sighed, "but what's his last name? This Cornell?"

Ric just shrugged. But just then a commotion grew in the back as Joanie finished, drowning out the subdued applause. A small tornado had whirled like a dervish through the front door right past the cashier, heralded by war whoops and whistles as the crowd thronged around the disturbance. The tornado resolved into a tall young man with Greco-Roman features suggesting an actor of the stage, tromping through the crowd in goat-herder boots with no socks, covered in what looked like a sealskin coat over a turtleneck sweater and giant wide-wale corduroys, and topped with an eskimo hat.

Ric bellowed, "My god, it's Quinn the eskimo!"

The goat-herder parted the seas of the audience as if it were God's will. His eyes burned straight at Joan, and he took the stage without interference, grabbing Joanie's mike, and turning to the audience with an evil grin framed by his villainous handlebar mustache. "Keep on truckin' mama!"

Next he grabbed Joanie's guitar, and Joanie cracked up giggling like a kid at the circus. He had on razor-sharp fingerpicks and shredded the guitar's sound hole as he tore into the song. His blues came out at top velocity, and Joanie hung on for dear life, harmonizing on every other measure. Together they seized the audience in rapture.

"That's Geno," said Ric loudly into Reggie's ear. It's a scene in the making. Outside, motorbikes were revving up, Super Rockets and a Vincent Black Shadow. "And that's Geno's entourage," Ric yelled. And the way Joan was looking at Geno seemed to say, eat your heart out, college kids, here's the rebel and I'm his queen.

The roar of the audience seemed to cause the lights to flicker. No, it was the management, signaling the end of the show. The bikes outside had drawn out a phalanx of cops, mostly Irish and Italian, inflamed by a sense of concern about these new beatniks, as they were called in *Life*, going about despoiling virgins and shooting up drugs. The Cambridge blue laws included one that prohibited more than three stringed instruments in a place that served food and beverages, which must have been been bought and paid for by competing Boston establishments a century earlier. This permitted the cops to close the place down for the night. The lights flickered on and off, the cops stood guard at the door, and Reggie thought he caught a glimpse of, no it couldn't be… Cravingston? Talking with the cops?

"To Bick's!" came the cry, echoed quickly across the audience. Reggie had heard about but had never ventured into the Hayes-Bickford eatery, "a center for the gathering of peculiars," according to the Cambridge Rambler in the Boston *Record American*. "They gather late at night and in the early morning hours over coffee, exhibiting their Castro beards, short-haired women sport near masculine dress…"

It seems like everyone from the club turned up at the Bick, some to crow their defiance of authority in the late-night air, others to watch the unbridled caffeinated activity that persisted after every club gig. Located on the corner of Holyoke Street, just past where Mass. Ave. makes its end run around Harvard Yard, the Bick was always in view of the cops patrolling the Square, and its late-night patrons were forever goading them with witty theatricals. The fried-egg special was the thing, half an English muffin, one piece of bacon, one egg. An entire meal for students and the older streetwise bohemians. "Worst coffee in the world," said Ric.

The place was already lively, but Geno blew in like a slow-motion explosion, hopping from table to table acting out a phony interview show, getting diners to hoot like owls and whistle like trains, scooting around the waitresses to pinch their behinds.

"Come now, what masques, what dances shall we have to wear away this long age of three hours between our after-supper and bedtime? Where is our usual manager of mirth?" Geno yells back at the kitchen where the help are frantically serving up breakfast, casting sideways glances at the madman. "What revels are in hand? Is there no play to ease the anguish of a torturing hour?"

His Haughtiness stopped before Reggie. "I am that merry wanderer of the night," he quoted Puck. "I'll follow thee and make a heaven of hell, to die upon the hand I love so well." With that, Geno picked up the lemon slice from Reggie's ice tea, and attempted to squeeze lemon juice into Reggie's eye. "Churl, upon thy eyes I throw all the power this charm doth owe!" Geno squirted the juice in the general direction of Reggie's face. "When thou wakest, let love forbid, sleep his seat on thy eyelid."

The folks at all the surrounding tables were laughing hysterically as Reggie pretended to fight back. He was mostly amused at Geno's great good nature; the intellect was evidently developed to a high pitch for someone who seemed to be his own age. Behind his youthful blue eyes, Reggie could see the huge force of his soul, and the passionate desire for experience that boiled in his brain. Reggie could conceive him capable of monstrous deeds, for Geno would let no one, no prejudice of men, stand in his way.

Despite Reggie's best efforts the lemon juice found its mark on his cheek, and Geno was instantly apologetic, though once again quoting Puck. "If we shadows have offended, think but this, and all is mended — that you have but slumbered here, while these visions did appear. Do you have a car?"

"Uh, well, no."

"We need fish. A man may fish with the worm that hath eat of a king, and eat of the fish that hath fed of that worm. You don't have a car?" And as suddenly as he arrived, Geno was off to other tables looking to borrow someone's car to drive down to the Boston docks and pick up some fish. Within minutes he dangled keys in front of Reggie's face. "Lovers and madmen have such seething brains, such shaping fantasies, that apprehend more than cool reason ever comprehends. You, my friend, are cool and reasonable. I need you in this escapade, for balance. Come!"

And off they went in a beat-up Dodge only partially owned by an assistant professor of English who realized, too late, that he'd loaned his car to a maniac, and was last seen tearing out of the Bick in hot pursuit.

But Geno was already driving furiously down Mass. Avenue and passing to Reggie a lit joint. "Dope. You know what dope is? You smoke it?"

Reggie nodded vigorously, caught in the daze of adventure, and holding it between his fingers, puffed on it like it was a Chesterfield. In the Book, his father had likened the smell to burnt lawn clippings, masking a very deep, very pungent essence of skunk. Reggie suddenly realized that the Book was also a veritable Merck manual of potions, charms, spells, secret recipes, and yes, methods of curing weed. He'd have to share some of this with his brother Gilbert, who'd taken the raw materials from the trunk with him to prep school. "Geno, where do you get this?"

"I get it from Connecticut, a jazzbo friend of mine. This guy knew Mezz Mezzrow, you know, the *Mezz*? The best shit, all the jazzbos love it. And the girls love it, man, just a few puffs and off come their skirts. Hey, don't Bogart it, man, pass it back."

Reggie passed it over between his fingers again, like a teenage girl proffering a puff. "My buddy back in South Jersey used to get it. His father's in the Mafia."

"Whaaat!?" Geno drove over a curb, but quickly got it back on the road.

"My friend. You even look a bit like him."

"Where's he now?"

"Europe. England, I think," said Reggie.

"We gotta get in contact with him. I could really use a good Mafia connection."

Geno drove crazily but kept precisely to an awkwardly straight path through Boston's radial grid of crooked streets down to the lower docks. Sure enough, Bobby Neuwirth was waiting for him, a bottle of pills in hand and halibut in a bucket. A friend of his, Buzz Marten, took off in the direction of Long Wharf to lose any cop tails they might've picked up at this notorious smuggler's hour.

Reggie, giggling as Geno and Bobby whispered in conspiracy, couldn't understand what the fuss was all about; the joint didn't seem to effect him. And then it hit him. A powerful urge to eat! Even that stinking halibut was fair game. Bobby saw it coming and directed Geno to Buzzy's Roast Beef, and eventually the three dock warriors returned triumphant to the Bick with the fish, the pills, and the car in one piece. And in the celebration, as waitresses scurried around them to keep cups from spilling and plates from cracking, Reggie understood that he was an actor in a play, in which they had all come together to watch *another* play, an amateurish comedy. And that this is all a dream, or at least, he should remember it only as such.

* * *

"So you met Geno last night." Cravingston's casual remark emerged from under his desk as the counselor was bent over, reaching underneath with a key to a hidden drawer lock. Reggie's wariness drowned out his morning headache, but only for a moment as the ache returned like a *basso profundo* punctuating the downbeats of his heart. "And also Leopold."

Reggie, puzzled, didn't get the connection.

"Two opposite poles of the same, ah, *bohemian* energy. Like sulfur and mercury."

This left Reggie even more puzzled about which was which.

"Or perhaps more like Tamino, which would be Leopold, and Papageno, which would be, of course…"

Reggie dimly recalled Leopold's lecture on *The Magic Flute*. "Progressing from superstition and chaos to…"

"Enlightenment," Cravingston completed the thought. "To make the Earth a heavenly kingdom, and turn mortals into gods." He rose from his crouch under the desk, sighing wearily. Reggie wondered if he'd also been up all night. "Do you know anything about alchemy?"

"Wha, turning metal into gold?" Reggie remembered that Freddie the Fryer used to talk about alchemy as a joke, turning records into hits, *gold* records.

"Turning *lead* into gold is the original myth." Cravingston sighed again, the weariness of a teacher with a truly dumb student. "Transmutation of the elements, causing changes in molecular structure. All radioactive elements gradually decay, giving off radiation and producing what are called 'daughter elements' which then decay even further. You start with uranium and end up with lead. So the question is, can this process be reversed? Or, if you start with another element, what might you end up with?"

Reggie shrugged, his tongue swollen, tasting a metallic dryness, the iron in his blood. "Gold?"

"Nuclear physicists can make gold," Cravingston said matter-of-factly. "They did it in 1941; they transmuted a radioactive isotope of mercury into gold. But these are only applications, particular cases. The essential thing is not the transmutation of metals, but that of the experimenter himself. It's an ancient secret that a few men rediscover, perhaps once a century. Barbault is one. When he started his experiment to make liquid gold, what he called 'vegetable gold', in 1948, he knew it would take at least 12 years for his elixir to reach maturity. Leopold was hired to be one of Barrault's assistants, but he was really reporting on the work to the OSS. I've heard that Barbault learned to walk through walls, turn invisible."

"The OSS again," Reggie drawled sardonically. "They seem to've had their hands in many things. I suppose this Barbault also knew my father?"

"Of course. But his real work is in nuclear physics. He believes, just like your father believed, that it's possible to produce an atomic fission by means of a relatively common ore. In fact, alchemy is not magic as many people believe; it hasn't disappeared, either, though it hasn't become popular, like astrology. Alchemy is very much with us today, in the form of modern physics and chemistry, especially astrophysics and nuclear physics. The alchemical techniques, boiling to hasten, sealing to retain, burning to reduce, trapping the distillate with an alembic, gilding by quicksilver — in general, imitating and hastening nature — have all become part of modern scientific practices."

"My father worked in nuclear physics?"

"Well…" Cravingston pointed to the sole photograph on the wall. "You see us together, in that picture, in Africa. We were still scientists, at least he was still a scientist at that time. Investigating the Dionysian spirit? Yes indeed we were! But we were also on assignment. Not to find the source of the Nile. Exploration was just our cover. We were investigating reports of uranium in vast quantities, in Central and West Africa. And what we found was far more interesting."

Cravingston shifted position in his chair to put his elbows on his desk in a stance that suggested getting down to business, secret business. "A natural uranium mine in the Oklo region of Gabon contains an abnormal amount of U235. It means that many self-sustained nuclear fission chain reactions took place at this mine about two billion years ago. It may be a relic from a prehistoric civilization. In other words, two billion years ago there was a fairly advanced civilization in Africa that knew how to split the atom."

The look of recognition on Reggie's face told Cravingston what he needed to know, that the son still had possession of his father's notes.

"Your father, you see, had some interesting friends in the uranium business. Tell me, did his journals mention Al Hubbard?"

"Yes," Reggie hesitatingly replied, "but only in passing."

"The Uranium Corporation of Vancouver," said Cravingston. "Your father and Hubbard were business associates. Uranium was not well known at the time, before the war. Fermi had not yet won his Nobel Prize. There was a French physicist, André Helbronner, working for the Germans, who had an assistant who claimed that he'd received a warning from a real alchemist, a man named Fulcanelli. The warning was that the entire world was in danger from their nuclear experiments. This man Fulcanelli told him that the liberation of atomic energy was easy, and that the alchemists have known how to do it for a very long time."

Cravingston shifted in his seat and continued, in a lower, conspiratorial voice. "Well, at that time, we were all fearful of Hitler's inner circle. All these rumors, about how they were tampering with ancient formulas for power. Our counterparts in Germany, the Abwehr, were scrambling for sources of uranium and looking for this Fulcanelli. So your father and I were sent on a mission to Africa to find uranium deposits before the Germans acquired them. Hubbard set up a processing facility in Vancouver."

Once again, Reggie gave away his hand with a look of recognition. There were indeed passages in the Book about the Uranium Corporation, Hubbard, and Fulcanelli.

"He disappeared, you know, this Fulcanelli. Some say he never even existed, or that it was a fake name. But we were looking for him nonetheless. Your father believed that modern alchemists knew about ancient civilizations that had made the same nuclear discoveries."

"Ancient civilizations?"

"They were quite serious about this. Serious enough for the OSS to mount a search for Fulcanelli as the war escalated. They thought Hitler might have captured him. By then your father had been transferred from Signals Intelligence to the OSS. They needed a signals expert. Know why?"

"I give up," Reggie snorted contemptuously.

"They assumed that alchemists would be communicating in code. Your father, of course, was already known for his work on Magic, the cryptanalysis project that broke the Japanese codes. In fact, your father was the one who'd coined the term 'Magic' for the intelligence."

Cravingston paused. "You know, there *was* some kind of magic involved in decrypting the codes. He never told me, but I always thought he'd learned something from the adepts."

"Higher intelligences?"

"Wisdom of the ancients," grinned the mischievous counselor as he rummaged through the now unlocked drawer. "Not so far-fetched as you think. Even Isaac Newton believed in the existence of a chain of Initiates, going back to very early times. Newton was also an early Freemason. He looked into these theories, the secrets of transmutation and the disintegration of matter. Of course, if you ask me to summarize for you many thousands of years of philosophy and the efforts of many lifetimes... well, I can't. I would have to translate these concepts using ordinary language, which is not intended to reveal these secrets."

Reggie's suspicious look told Cravingston that he was losing him.

"Look. What you need to know is that the role of the observer is more important than you think," Cravingston said with some impatience. "Relativity, the principle of indeterminacy, shows how the observer intervenes in *any* phenomenon. The secret of alchemy is simply that there is a way of manipulating matter and energy, to produce what our scientists today call *a field of force*. This field acts on the observer and puts him in a privileged position with respect to the universe. From this position he has access to... let's say, 'realities'. I mean the powers of reality that are ordinarily hidden from us by time and space, by matter and energy.

"This is what is called 'The Great Work'.

"But your father, and Leopold. They were more interested in the split that occurred in the Seventeenth Century."

Cravingston lectured more quietly, arching his eyebrow in an effort to gain back Reggie's trust. "That's when alchemy split into scientific and occult traditions, the occult alchemy of Robert Fludd and John Dee, and the Rosicrucians. From the scientists, we have what we now call nuclear energy. But from the occult tradition, we have the Freemasons, the Theosophists, and Aleister Crowley and the Golden Dawn. They look upon metals as living things, still capable of being transformed into some permanent form. They shared the beliefs of the ancient alchemists, that one's inner being is changed by participation in chemical experiments. They spoke of the Philosopher's Stone, the com-pound that can produce gold from mercury, and the liquid gold elixir of life, useful for rejuvenation and possibly for achieving... immortality."

That last word hung in the air between them, frozen in the cold vacuum at the center of a nuclear reaction, a blasphemy any God-fearing person would shudder to hear. From certain passages in the Book, Reggie had considered his father to have been duped by mystic charlatans, devil-worshippers, and all sorts of anti-religious fanatics, straying far from the acceptable courses of life.

"You see, the alchemist knows that there is a very solid link between matter, life, and consciousness," Cravingston continued. "Most of the others who claimed knowledge of alchemy kept its nature secret, and spoke of it only in the most enigmatical and allegorical language. They formed secret organizations such as the Golden Dawn, or the OTO." He drew out the letters on an imaginary blackboard. "You must have come across the name Aleister Crowley in his notes? I believe your father was initiated into one of these orders. I think it's one that mixes alchemy and oriental philosophy, with a bit of our own European magical traditions, for political gain."

"Initiation? You mean like a fraternity."

"That's what we do *here*," Cravingston smirked, gesturing around to include all of Harvard. "This is all part of an initiation."

"To learn secrets." Reggie frowned, sensing that fatherly seduction again.

"Yes. And to keep them secret, but also, to pass these secrets on to the next generation."

By that did he mean Gilbert?

"What you need in order to penetrate the secrets of alchemy is a *leap of faith*," said Cravingston in a half-whisper, for emphasis. "That's what Nobby believed. That's how we become immortal, you see, by encoding these secrets within our great works, for future generations to be illuminated by them."

"And that explains why songs have hidden meanings, maybe even coded instructions?"

"You have no idea," Cravingston enthused. "The greatest artists, the greatest writers, even the greatest composers! Haydn and Mozart were initiates of the Craft. You heard *The Magic Flute* last night. Remember the three knock-like notes at the beginning? The way it all reverses on itself in the finale? The whole opera is a magnified Masonic initiation!"

Swept up in a cold passion from his seat, Cravingston stalked the circumference of the office, talking as much to the wall as to Reggie. "Even the greatest architects! Fulcanelli wrote about the Gothic cathedrals in Europe. He interpreted their symbols as codes for the secrets of alchemy. The secrets were contained in the stone structures, carvings, and so forth. It has been hinted at for centuries, but Fulcanelli actually *wrote it down*."

Cravingston had paced around the entire office in a circle around Reggie, only to end up behind his desk in the posture of lecturer.

"Your father's book. Does it include any notes about Fulcanelli?"

Reggie shrugged. The man wanted more than just information about his father. He sensed that Cravingston was trying to recruit him. He could tell by that crafty look in the man's eyes when he pretended to be distracted, just like a priest behind the veil of a confessional. Not just to pull up his grades so that he could make it into Phi Beta Kappa; something more.

"I understand your distrust of politics and history," Cravingston spoke authoritatively. "Yours is the first generation, really, to no longer identify with the adults. The first to even think about a nuclear war, an armageddon! Not one fomented by an angry God, but by humans acting out their fantasies of power with the irrational misuse of physics."

"Thanks in part to the geniuses of *your* generation," Reggie shot back.

"Yes, well, perhaps the new geniuses, the new alchemists of *your* generation are keeping their discoveries for themselves. There is an extreme power in the concentration it takes to perform music that captures the imagination, the soul, of its listeners. There is the power to persuade, which is so useful in negotiations of any kind. The power to see all aspects of the universe at once. And so it was with your father, who may have been way ahead of his time."

Okay, well, Reggie already knew these weekly meetings were a lot more than professional chit-chat about alchemy and secret societies. This was getting personal.

"And I think that maybe *your* generation's geniuses are acting out the bohemian life," continued Cravingston, "just a few hours of work each week to provide for the necessities of life, but spending the rest of the time working on projects and ideas of which we can have no conception."

"Now *you* sound paranoid," Reggie smirked.

"Do I? You've seen some of this work. Harry Smith's anthology is an example."

It was Reggie's turn to feel paranoid. He recalled the record cover with the titles and names of blues singers, hillbilly bands, and gospel chanters; the booklet proclaiming "Do as thy wilt shall be the whole of the law." All those songs about heroes masquerading as villains.

"Yes, the trials of Tamino and the errors of Papageno," Cravingston spoke amusingly. "If you combine them, you've got to keep them in balance. Watch them like a hawk, see who they influence. Do you know who Geno's father is? Clark Foreman. Your father knew him. He's the founder of the Emergency Civil Liberties Committee. An old lefty who worked for Roosevelt. He *still* has a lot of enemies, to this day. So Gene grew up in politics. He knows things, he knows people."

Cravingston paused again, and put a fatherly hand on Reggie's shoulder, a cajoling hand. "So I'd like you to do me a favor. Keep an eye on Geno. Tell me what he does, who he talks to."

* * *

If any of this shit is even remotely true, thought Reggie, then his father, the elusive Herbert Mention, was some kind of hero. Drowning in recollections of passages from his father's Book, Reggie sank back to his dorm and dug out the Book from its hiding place. His father's words, from the "Introduction":

This is what I know, but not allowed to say or demonstrate (beyond my own private experience of it): That a network of adepts of higher intelligence exists and functions throughout our planet and, I suspect, extends even farther than our Earth, and they communicate with each other in code. Music has always served as a medium for these codes, in ancient times and even today.

And even today. Music passes these secrets on to the next generation. Reggie surmised that his father must have been at least partly a lunatic about his references to a network of adepts, and paranoid to boot. Maybe now he was on the run. Maybe that Book was written in some kind of code. To describe music as a medium for these codes, in ancient times and even today... His father was pointing at today's music as the key to the code. Perhaps it is about politics and power. Maybe the key can be found in the music of the oppressed, what they now called *protest songs*. One needed to understand music as a chain of communication from one generation to the next.

He remembered Martini's lecture about the role of secret societies in the French Revolution. The chains of communication, not the means of production, were responsible for kicking off social change. Marx had been wrong, like the engineers of Marx's time who thought of electricity in terms of *work done*, before Marconi thought of it in terms of *information transmitted*.

Harry Smith's *Anthology* was a place to start, where voodoo meets Aleister Crowley in songs coded for future generations. A severe fatalism seem to bleed through all the songs in the *Anthology*. It started with the second song, the melancholy "Fatal Flower Garden"[158] by Nelstone's Hawaiians. The boy is enticed by the "tipsy gypsy lady" to enter the forbidden garden, offering an apple, a tangerine, and finally a diamond. She takes the boy by his "lily-white hand" to a room where no one can hear him call out, and she performs unspeakable acts on him. But he does not seem to care too much. "If my dear mother should call for me, tell her that I'm asleep... If my dear father should call for me, tell him that I am dead." Here was an entirely different view of Eden, a song that carried a sacrilegious message out into the open, with nary a peep from the establishment. Recorded in 1930.

Eric Sackheim knew the details. "Loosely based on a set of ballads collected by Child dating back to 1255. Songs about a boy stolen by a gypsy have been reported all throughout England, in parts of Scotland, in Ireland, in the Canadian Maritimes, and in all parts of the U.S. east of the Mississippi. Child follows the story back to the year 419 in Syria, and a similar story set in Spain was the inspiration for Ferdinand and Isabella's creation of the Spanish Inquisition."

But what these accounts don't explain is how, and why, the boy succumbs willingly to the charms of the gypsy. Reggie finally knew why when he succumbed to his own "gypsy," a voluptuous Radcliffe redhead named Rachel Vanderbilt who initiated him into the mysteries of oral sex. He would arrive at the women's dorm every night, hat in hand, standing in the lobby dripping from rain as the matron on watch recorded his name, and skip upstairs gleefully to her room for an hour of mouth-to-mouth and mouth-to-genitals, coming at least twice, before sitting up in bed to discuss things. She was waiting to meet the aristocrat of her dreams, so she wouldn't do intercourse. She might fall in love, but she would never marry a Catholic. He tolerated everything she had to say while cozying up to her ample bosom. She hated her first name because it sounded Jewish.

"It is Jewish," Reggie responded. "Maybe some of your ancestors were Jewish." That remark ended the relationship.

And so he finally knew why the boy stayed with the gypsy, and he knew how the power worked, and he had even learned the guitar parts to that song, but it would take a lot more concentration to figure out its code. So the next stop would be Ric's, to show him the chords, get off on some of Geno's grass, and ponder the situation. He gathered up the Book and the Robert Johnson record and slipped them into a boy scout knapsack, the forerunner of the stylish accessory to be seen on campuses everywhere in the coming decade. From now on he would carry this knapsack everywhere; if They came for it, he could find out who They are.

* * *

Reggie's fuzzy-haired roommate, a taciturn guitar player named Tom Rush, had been the one to point out the poster tacked on a telephone pole in Harvard Square. It advertised a rally, sponsored by the Committee for a SANE Nuclear Policy, with Pete Seeger and Joan Baez performing. Reggie had heard Phil Ochs sing about the land of power and glory, had clasped his hands together in a leap of faith, had squirmed under his vision of the gladiator slaves of doom and the martyred heroes. He'd jumped to his feet to sing along with Pete Seeger and everyone else in the rousing finale, a tribute to Woody, "This Land Is Your Land",[159] including the forbidden lyrics about a high wall with a sign that says "Private Property" but on the backside, it says nothing. This land was made for you and me.

Reggie finally met the great man backstage, where he'd gone to see Joanie after her performance and commiserate about Debbie. She took his hands in hers, and peered earnestly into his eyes, as if he were the only person there. "Debbie is better off with Rolf. You know that. You have to move on." For a brief moment Reggie thought he should make a play for Joanie; she seemed to want men to flirt with her. But after hearing Debbie sing the same songs, Joanie's sad virginal princess act no longer worked the same magic on him. What he really wanted to find was a gypsy to lead him to that fatal garden.

Joanie introduced him to Pete Seeger, who was tuning up his banjo and discoursing about Woody Guthrie and the encore song. "He wrote it because he was irritated by Irving Berlin's 'God Bless America' sung by Kate Smith, which seemed to be endlessly playing on the radio in the late Thirties. In fact, he first called it 'God Blessed America for Me' before renaming it to 'This Land Is Your Land'."

Reggie was in the habit of introducing himself with his last name, Mention, loud and clear, to see if it would ring a bell.

"Are you related to Herbert Mention?" Pete Seeger smiled paternally.

Reggie nodded, shrugging a bit. "My father."

"Well I knew your father. Back in 1940, at a recording session for the Almanac Singers. We were doing "Follow the Drinking Gourd"[160] as I recall, which we later recorded with the Weavers. Woody was there, and so was Alan Lomax and your father. They were highly charged, on a mission so to speak, to bring the authentic country blues out to the rest of the world. I remember it well. That's when I first met Cornell Woodrow, an associate of your father's. Cornell is an alchemist of the blues."

Another mention of the elusive Cornell. "I met him once."

"I know Cornell," Joanie interjected, looking first at Pete and then at Reggie. "He taught me 'Wimoweh', the lion sleeps tonight. But that lion," she smirked, then laughed out loud, "that lion is waking up now! He's waking up in the Deep South. And we're singing for him, we're singing to wake him up."

Pete Seeger nodded. "Both of them, Herbert and Cornell, talked about waking up the spirit of Legba. They sang songs about it to the Student Non-violent Coordinating Committee."

Of all the political groups carrying signs and setting up makeshift donation tables around Harvard Square, it was the Student Non-violent Coordinating Committee (SNCC) that truly captured the imagination of the student press and the folkies. Their heroics in the Deep South were legendary. Their members always looked like they'd just come back from the front lines, in raggedy overalls and grimy denim work shirts. Cravingston had given Reggie his opinion. "The workers they so desperately want to help are becoming obsolete. We're replacing their function with machines."

Cravingston may be right about that, thought Reggie, but he had been wrong about this new "civil rights" movement, just as he had been wrong about Geno being some kind of threat. Pete Seeger was far more of a threat. Corny, yes, in so many ways. Naively nostalgic for that Thoreau way of life, simplicity, living in nature and all that. But Seeger understands the power of music, and how it can be used to fight back the evil of our times. Reggie had read about him in his father's Book. Seeger has been out there and is *still* out there, despite all of his career setbacks due to his political affiliations, *still* singing about technical solutions, like higher wages and worker's unions, and about a better way of life for the disenfranchised. And the government was probably *still* tracking his every move.

* * *

In 1941, Herbert Mesh met up with Cornell Woodrow, his source of research on the country blues musicians, outside a theater in New York City. The film version of *The Grapes of Wrath* was playing, and Cornell had brought with him the Oklahoma-born songwriter, Woody Guthrie, to see the film, along with Woody's Almanac Singers partner Pete Seeger, going at that time by the name Pete Bowers.

A Corporation operative, who had seen a performance of the Almanac Singers at a longshoreman union meeting in San Francisco, had told Herbert they were "extremely untidy, ragged, and dirty in appearance," and claimed that the union's enthusiastic participation in a sing-along had been involuntary, the effect of some sinister "mass psychology". The operative's mistrust and disgust had conversely tweaked Herbert's curiosity.

Cornell wanted Herbert to record Woody. They set up a session, and while doing so Guthrie went to see the film several times. The night before the session, Woody stayed up all night writing "Tom Joad",[161] a seventeen-verse ballad that adroitly and powerfully complemented the film. Herbert recorded the song for Alan Lomax's folklore archives of the Library of Congress.

"We got to bring American folk songs up to date," Woody was saying outside the theater. "This don't mean to complicate our music a-tall, but simply to industrialize, and mechanize the words. We need songs of the wheels, whistles, steam, boilers, shafts, cranks, operators, tuggers, pulleys, engines, and all of the well known gadgets that make up a modern factory."

Cornell beamed at Herbert. "You see? Even white people can be infected with the spirit and find their own *mojo*."

Woody was earnest, talking especially to Pete. "We got to include a *timeless element* in our songs. Something that will not, tomorrow, be gone with the wind. But something that tomorrow will be as true as it is today. The secret of a lasting song is not the recording of a current event, but this timeless element, which may be contained in the chorus or last line or elsewhere."

They were momentarily startled by the appearance of a prostitute at the street corner. Cornell belly-laughed. "The timeless element is right here with us!" Then he spoke in an uncharacteristic sing-song voice with an Irish lilt,

Girls in this way fall every day
And have been falling for ages
Who is to blame?
You know his name.

The boss that pays starvation wages.

It was the beginning of a beautiful friendship. Cornell explained the progress of his Great Work, and Herbert signed on indefinitely, even if it meant hiding all of his activities from the Corporation.

As the year careened toward a war in Europe and the Pacific, Herbert knew a crackdown on leftists was coming. And yet, at Almanac House, New York's left bohemians — poets, musicians, intellectuals, writers, lovers of folksong and scholars of folk culture — blithely gathered to eat proletarian food and discuss the next benefit concert for *New Masses* as if nothing cataclysmic was about to happen.

It wasn't lost on Herbert Mesh that several of the Almanac Singers, Pete Bowers in particular, were not of Woody's threadbare cloth, and were as far from the poor Okie consciousness as they could ever be. Pete had defected from the aristocratic life, had dropped out of Harvard and tuned in to the folksong movement, had even changed his name from Seeger to protect his father's government job. But Pete, in the face of alarming censorship and hatred of communists, had found the courage to reestablish his Seeger name, and with a tremendous leap of faith he made a strong commitment to the Communist Party. His longing for a morally consistent life, which is a venerable Yankee tradition not to mention a Calvinist doctrine, found fulfillment in a peculiar kind of authenticity that comes from aligning musicianship with ideology. Similar to John Hammond, he embodied the paradox of the gentile son from a rich Yankee family embracing the working-class black culture of the Deep South.

To Herbert Mesh, Seeger even *looked* like a banjo. A most anachronistic instrument, the banjo always seemed to be on the verge of disappearing from popular music, forsaken by the Gilded Age parlor society that had given it some cachet, repudiated by jazz musicians as their gigs moved uptown. Pete Seeger looked like and played an instrument that history had left behind. It had even been abandoned by black culture, which had originally reconstructed it from a series of African stringed instruments.

At Cornell's urging, Pete, Herbert, Woody Guthrie, and Alan Lomax were compiling a book of all of the most militant topical songs — industrial ballads, protest songs, and blues — from the the 1920s and the Depression. These were songs of the migrants, the unemployed, the auto workers and sharecroppers that were trying to unionize. From the coal miners of Kentucky to the union organizers of the Rockies and the Northeast, wherever working people united, they sang. The book was titled *Hard Hitting Songs for Hard-Hit People.* But no publisher was interested, and then Pearl Harbor happened, and Herbert had to go to war.

* * *

The Peekskill Riot of 1949 was a turning point for Herbert Mention, or rather the ending of a wide turn that had started when he went AWOL in Britain, from Army Intelligence, for reasons he could never explain to his new British wife. He'd changed his name, like so many musicians did, from Mesh to Mention. Herbert had long fantasized about disappearing into the woodwork of the industrial world, and his new identity would conceal his tracks.

These were trying times for communist sympathizers. The war had raised the task of purchasing to a patriotic level. The wartime economy had become the peacetime public culture. Thrift had become un-American. Purchasing, especially among the new suburban housewives married to the returning heroes of the war, was no longer an appeal or a seduction; it had become compulsory. His own new wife, Beatrice, presumably untainted by the American Dream, had begun to show signs of compulsive buying, of dresses, cosmetics, the new appliances.

The war had pulled the rug out of the Popular Front so favored by Pete and Woody, an alliance of liberals and leftists. The New Deal had given way to Truman's Fair Deal, and it was, in Robert Johnson's prescient words, the last fair deal gone down. A system of agreements between government and business, cultivated by the Corporation, had built up the military-industrial complex. The House Committee on Un-American Activities acquired permanent status in 1945, contributing, along with Truman's loyalty oath for federal employees and the attorney general's list of subversive organizations, to an atmosphere of social and political paranoia.

From Herbert's perspective, uncluttered by the official sanctimonies and allegiances of the older leftists, something had to be done, and folk songs were one way to do it. Folk singing was a symbolic as well as a practical instrument that was capable of stirring hearts and embodying ideals.

Folk songs did not need trained singers. Indeed, Seeger's voice betrayed a network of contradictions, a lower Hudson Valley accent delivered in the tones of a school headmaster and affecting the idiom of a ranch hand with overtones of the Broadway stage. The Almanac Singers had been fanatically democratic, virtually unregulated, youthful, and collective. They would compose songs with everyone contributing lines while one member dashed them out on a typewriter.

Herbert saw it coming. The Corporation was striking back at the folksingers and radicals. Paul Robeson, the first black man to become an international star of the stage, had been outspoken about trade unionism and was promptly called before a Senate committee and questioned about his affiliation with the Communist Party. Refusing to answer did not help, nor did Robeson's speech at a Soviet-sponsored World Peace Conference in Paris. The Corporation handily discredited him by rewriting the transcriptions before they reached the press.

As Robeson arrived in Peekskill, New York, for a concert, a mob of locals attacked concert-goers with baseball bats and rocks. Robeson was lynched in effigy. Herbert, Cornell, and Robeson were stopped by a jeering crowd throwing rocks and chanting "Dirty commie"and "Dirty kikes." Herbert had to restrain Robeson, who'd played football at Rutgers, from getting out of the car to confront them.

Fifteen thousand people sat on lawn chairs and picnic blankets. The stage was a sound truck parked under an oak tree, and surrounding it was a line of union men, black and white, shoulder to shoulder. The concert played out while a helicopter hovered overhead. Word went out backstage that a sniper's nest had been discovered. Robeson walked out on stage in a dark jacket, gray pants and a tie, surrounded by 15 bodyguards, and flashed everyone a winning smile. The audience cheered, and he began to sing.

When Israel was in Egypt's land[162]
Let my people go...

Herbert was nervous. He sensed an ambush. He was absolutely sure that his old crony Cravingston was behind this. Along the road on the way in he'd noticed that about every 20 feet were cairns of stones, ready to be thrown. The police were doing nothing about it.

As the performers tried to leave, rocks crashed through the windows of cars and buses. Splintered glass flew into eyes, rocks hit foreheads and shoulders. Blood flowed from cuts. Herbert drove a car with Robeson, and Guthrie drove a car with Hays, Seeger, and Seeger's wife and kids right behind them, past houses displaying American flags, and on the lawns were men and women yelled "Jews, commies, niggers!" and tossed stones. Policemen on motorcycles rode along and did nothing. Seeger's car was hit, showering glass all over his two-year-old son. Guthrie pinned a shirt to the inside of the window to stop it shattering — a red shirt, of course.

"You've got to understand," said a police officer to Herbert as he directed traffic. "They're just regular Americans, the kind you might meet going fishing."

Herbert looked out on the suburban landscape at pretty housewives holding outstretched hands with thumbs to their noses and pinkies pointed at them, the most obscene gesture they knew how to make. And then, across the road, Herbert spotted him. Will Cravingston in his G-man suit, holding up a photo for a sheriff's deputy. It must be a photo of me, Herbert thought. He quickly ducked down and drove on through, barely able to see above the dashboard.

* * *

It was a mutual decision to declare a stalemate. Herbert and Will Cravingston needed to meet without one having to put the other into handcuffs.

Following Herbert's instructions, Cravingston got out of a cab in New York City and headed up Essex, past the window of a kosher restaurant. Located under the kitchen, Chernoff's was a former speakeasy run by a Ukrainian Jew who emigrated shortly before the Romanovs were shot in the snow.

Cravingston walked down the alley, through the kitchen door, past two Chinese men at large steaming sinks, past boiling pots of winter cabbage, and down a set of narrow steps to a basement with a walk-in freezer. He pulled the brass latch on the heavy freezer door, stepped inside among hanging meats and ice blocks, and tapped his shoes against each other to knock off the sawdust. At the back, a false door opened to reveal a nightclub with a copper-topped bar and leather banquettes. A jazz quartet bleeped and blooped softly from one corner.

"Such an unorthodox place for a meeting," smirked Cravingston. "A former... speakeasy," spitting the last word.

"Just wanted to demonstrate the folly of your goddamn organization's meddling," snapped Herbert. "Just like Prohibition. You build a wall but the smart people find ways to navigate around it. That's what will happen every time."

"Really. So now you're a leftist? A communist, perhaps?" Cravingston was just needling him for a response. "Changed your name, did you? Did you think we couldn't find you anyway?"

Herbert stared back without a word. At Chernoff's they never ask for your order. The waiter just arrives with plates of pierogi, herring, and tongue, and shot glasses for the middle of the table. Vodka distilled in a bathtub, despite the repeal of the 21st Amendment. The food was cold, the vodka medicinal, and the service abrupt.

Cravingston grew impatient. "And you're here to tell me..."

"Why are you chasing me? Why should you care so much about me? The war's over."

"We're not chasing you," said Cravingston smoothly, smiling, gesturing around the restaurant. "We're just observing you. You're like a divining rod, turning up all sorts of interesting things. Magic potions, fascinating music, revolutionary ideas... You're what we think of as *hip*."

What Cravingston wanted to say, he couldn't. That Herbert was the Corporation's only lead in tracking down Cornell Woodrow. That for some reason they couldn't just go out and get their hands on this elusive black mentor of musicians. They would set up a stakeout and Cornell would just evaporate. One officer even put it down in his report that the man had vanished before his very eyes.

Herbert's eyes shifted around the restaurant to divine the truth. "It's Cornell you're after. Well you can try all you want, but it won't work." He knocked down a shot and looked inside his empty glass.

"So Cornell's little experiment... continues?"

"You bet," Herbert met his eyes evenly. "We're only getting started."

Cravingston looked down at his own shot glass. By the time he looked up, Herbert had silently disappeared.

* * *

And so the great work continued, still just a fly in the Corporation's ointment, but important enough to devote manpower for surveillance. Cornell convinced a music-sheet printer he knew that worked in Tin Pan Alley in New York, one George Margolin, to take his guitar down to the Washington Square Park fountain and play some of his hillbilly mountain-folk tunes, the ones he'd learned from Clarence Ashley.[163]

It seemed so incongruous, in the hubbub of Greenwich Village all bent out of shape with cool post-war jazz, to see this backwoods bumpkin in the park singing in a full nasal twang, and strumming without pretense songs from a pre-war era better left buried in the Appalachian mud. Within weeks Margolin had imitators that gathered around the fountain. And more people came to hear them play, and then went home and got their guitars and came back. Within two months the New York News had run a feature on the "Washington Square Folk Craze" and Pete Seeger and Woody Guthrie, alone and together as the Almanac Singers, started to appear regularly.

Greenwich Village quickly came into focus as a folk haven. The location of New York State's first penitentiary, the Village grew as a bohemian enclave centered around the Hotel Albert and Café Society, the first racially integrated night club financed in part by John Hammond. Allan Block's Sandal Shop, only twenty feet wide and forty feet deep, wedged among the regimented commercial establishments on West 4th Street, appeared as a time tunnel to an ancient culture of leather, hand tools, a shop table with a buffing wheel, and a few pine stools against an exposed brick wall with pencil drawings of sandal designs. Allan piddled away on fiddle amidst the odors of leather, tanning solvents, glue, and pipe tobacco. Musicians jammed the place on Sundays, comparing instruments.

And Alan Lomax and Herbert Mention were at it again, arguing in the din about the value of some of the records Cornell Woodrow had brought him. Lomax in his prickly style took the position that authentic music could not be found on popular records. Mention argued that field hands were just alright with him, go ahead and get those prisoners on wax, but the performers on stages and in the streets were the ones with testicles, and the best of them managed to get themselves on *record*.

Harry Smith, agreeing with Mention, had even put aside his film projects to round up a collection of the best of recorded pop music of the 1920s and 1930s, only he craftily called it "folk" to get it sold as the *Anthology of American Folk Music*. Harry had been trying to stop time in his films by hand-painting each frame. Codes could be transmitted through a single flashing image at 24 frames per second — the same mysteries of life that were transmitted through Native American music. He hadn't realized, until Herbert explained it to him, that these codes were embedded in black music, even white mountain music, the music of the "folk" that had never succumbed to sophistication. The records made by these musicians had survived.

"There's a power in these records," Smith quoted his mentor, Cornell Woodrow, who'd provided him more than half of his collection. "That is, if you make a leap of faith, and you learn how to listen."

A Power Defying Time

A power defying time, a power growing with each passing year, blazed lightning across the predawn Liverpool sky and bellowed peals of thunder. John Lennon had wailed at the semi-conscious Stu Sutcliffe until a mysterious man in a black cloak had appeared, gathered them up, and got them back to Stu's Gambier Terrace bedsit. That was all Lennon could remember later that morning as he limped with a bandaged Stu into the Jacaranda on Slater Street, a coffee bar famous for its bacon butties, just a few blocks from Liverpool Art College, and downstairs into its basement world of heat, sweat, and loud conversation. Immediately they ran into Allan Williams, the café's owner, a Welsh-born hustler burly with oversized ambition and a bit unconventional, a jack of all trades and master of none, who kept a jaundiced eye on everything.

Williams lightly punched Lennon in the chest. "What happened to you? And why are you still looking like a ted?" He ran his fingers through Lennon's duckbill. "A bit late with that Elvis bit, aren't you? You're fucking middle-class, a ted pretender."

"Lay off," Lennon sneered back, but not too harshly, because Allan Williams was the only connected man in town for gigs. "It makes me look tough so I don't have to get into any more fights," he grinned. "I'm a bloody coward you know. So Al, what have you got lined up for us next? Come on, Al, we need the money."

Williams grinned, always more comfortable in the company of layabouts and dreamers. A few months earlier he'd been knocked out by the reaction of the teenagers at Liverpool Empire's show with Eddie Cochran and Gene Vincent,[164] goggle-eyed in an erotic spell as he watched girls caress their inner thighs and moon over these scruffy performers, all of them only about ten years younger than him. A potpourri of young pussy! He could smell the money. He'd come away with a half-baked plan; anyone with a telephone could be an agent, but Williams had a telephone and a Jaguar, and that made him a potential manager for these sputtering groups busking in the Liverpool 8 cellars for cigarette money.

Stuart Sutcliffe was special to him because Stu had helped with the floats for the Mersey Arts Ball, so Allan had hired Stu to paint the ladies' lavatory at the Jacaranda. Stu brought his friends and they went on to paint elaborate voodoo-themed murals on the downstairs walls. Williams gave Lennon credit for having a good friend in Stu, but he also gave him credit for acting the part of the performer. Of all of them, only Lennon had it in him to make it, and Williams could see that. Lennon knew just what to do, how to get the the right effect. When Williams sent that photographer around from *The People* to Sutcliffe's flat to promote the new Liverpool groups, Lennon laid flat on the floor amidst the debris for the photo, inspiring the editor to title the article

"The Beatnik Horror." Williams had tacked the article from the paper on the wall in his tiny office.

The flat, Stu's Gambier Terrace bedsit that John frequented with his girlfriend Cyn, was a horror of filth. Dust and dirt found its way into everything, their paintings, their records, their lovemaking. Stu heard the sound of dust and grit in Elvis' early records. Country music from the States was all over Liverpool at the time, brought in by droves of American servicemen, serving the entire community, rich and poor, cutting across lines of age and class. The country songs taught Liverpool sons about the heartaches and heartbreaks of American parents, of anyone's parents — the father who couldn't feed his family, the wife who lost her husband to a Saturday night honky-tonk angel or the bottle, or the family that lost everything in harsh economic winters. Most of all, Stu heard the promises his parents could never keep.

John heard the horror of loneliness in a world vastly populated with fools. The country music of Elvis' childhood was steeped in Southern fundamentalist tradition. That honky-tonk energy of Saturday night was dragged down on Sunday morning by songs of fear and resignation.

Stu agreed, but also recognized that this atonement for Saturday night was false. Elvis demonstrated that Saturday night could be the whole show. That's the kind of show they should put on, that's what Allan Williams really meant by "make a show." Not these noontime folk sessions, but Saturday night full throttle all night long.

John, leader and founder, knew about making a show, knew it instinctively, knew it when he started the group three years ago. On guitar, and singing lead, Lennon was all brusque attitude and sheer confidence, wavering on the line of talent.

But it was Paul McCartney who actually showed Lennon how to tune his guitar properly, and Paul who had something like a photographic memory about music and lyrics. John had doubts about his guitar playing, but deflected criticism by pointing out that Stu was worse, that he couldn't keep the beat. It was such a contradictory thing to say, because it was Lennon's idea that Stu should remain in the group. When Paul began to echo the same sentiments about Stu, John's gut reaction was to defend Stu. Round and round they would go, with Stu alternating as scapegoat and Svengali, and somehow remaining necessary to John to stroke the algorithms of his ambitions.

Back in Allan Williams' cramped office at the Jac, Lennon winced at pictures of other Merseyside "beat" groups that Allan had booked in cellar clubs around Liverpool. Rory Storm and the Hurricanes, Derry and the Seniors, Gerry and the Pacemakers... so many groups trying to make it, and such a crowded island, how is he ever to rise above all this?

"You need work then?" Allan snickered. "I have just the job for you punters. Come along." Ever alert for business opportunities, Williams had wanted to open Liverpool's first strip joint in the midst of its shebeens and hidden brothels, after visiting a successful one in Manchester. He had teamed up with a colorful character from Trinidad who called himself Lord Woodbine after the brand of cigarette that always dangled from his puffy lower lip. As the founder of the Royal Caribbean Steel Band, Allan's regular act at the Jacaranda, and as a prominent resident of Liverpool's Toxteth black community, Lord Woodbine knew everybody in the Liverpool 8 district.

They set up business in a dim, cramped cellar with a tiny stage, an even tinier bar, a sticky floor littered with cigarette butts, an unused coatrack, and the grand name of New Cabaret Artistes Club. The local hookers were not buff-shop bait, so Williams contacted a stripmeister in Manchester who sent over a candidate. Shirley descended into the dank, urine-smelling basement and swiftly removed her gear for Allan's approval. "Her tits stuck out like train buffers," Allan would tell his friends, "no spaniel ears here!"

But Shirley demanded a live band, and Allan's arguments turned feeble in the face of her heaving breasts and musky aroma as she grew more adamant. A band it would be, even if they had no drummer. With her equipment the audience would never even notice the band.

"All it is, twice a night, twenty minutes a pop, and ten bob for each."

John was disgusted, Paul was upset. Stu pointedly asked Allan to raise the ante to a quid each, for the bloody indignity of it all.

The next night found them playing in matching lilac jackets in front of a mangy curtain that served as Shirley's dressing room, for the original ten bob each. Shirley nonchalantly handed them the sheet music for "Sabre Dance" and Lennon, without further ado, stuffed it in the waste basket. They played, repeatedly, "Moonglow", "Ramrod",[165] "September Song" and "The Harry Lime Theme" as she wantonly shook her booties for the geezers and lurkers in raincoats.

They all got a laugh over it, though Stu acted moody, you've seen one nude, you've seen 'em all. John and Stu had sketched and painted with a nude model at college and had acted like it was no big deal. Paul was a bit disdainful, as if his girlfriend might see him leering at Shirley. Cyn and the other girlfriends were not allowed, obviously. They'd be waiting for the boys back at the Jac, talking condescendingly about their "boys' night out" and other rubbish.

John had a theory about all this. Love is wonderful, warm and fuzzy, but this relationship business brought it all down to the level of boredom. If you think you're settled with someone, you stop trying so hard to please them, and it all goes zip. Then you're just leaning on each other, protecting each other from the storms. You close yourself off to everything and end up in a cottage somewhere, going to work every day and drinking gin every night with no hope of doing anything else. And why doesn't everyone see this? I must really be sick, he thought, because I'm the only one who sees it. Drop a few pounds here, smooth over a few wrinkles there, and Shirley could become Brigitte Bardot. Do it the other way, and she becomes the Hag of Spinster. It's whatever attitude they have at the time that changes them, that turns one into a sexy stripper and the other into one of those old women with fat growths under their armpits.

At one point John gave Shirley the raised eyebrow, but she ignored him. Truth is, she fancied the youngest member, the gangly flop-eared Georgie Harrison, all teeth and flashing eyebrows, who couldn't conceal the delight growing in his pants.

Nothing to do to save his life, call a pint in. Lennon sidled up to the bar during a break, light-years away from Cyn, from Mendips, from everything in his formal world. He was thinking hard about what he was doing. He couldn't sit around and wait for lightning to strike, playing the bleeding piss cellars the rest of his life.

Just then, lightning struck, not far away, illuminating through the tiny window above the bar everything inside and outside the club in a shattering electric-blue incandescence. Everything just as suddenly disappeared into deep blackness, and then the lights flickered back on and thunder rolled across the area. Now that was startling, thought Lennon. Did I think it up or did it just occur naturally?

Lord Woodbine, impeccably dressed in a black turtleneck and silk suit that lent a sheen to his panther-black skin, appeared behind the bar brandishing an ornate cutlass no doubt stolen from an East London antique shop. He looked menacing enough but everyone who knew him called him Woody; he had a soft touch for the beat groups, and would often cajole Lennon into joining him on one of his lordly bouts in the local brothel. "The storm brings good luck. Your friend Geoff will be here presently." Woody grinned, demonstrating some of that cheap clairvoyance he was known for.

"Yeah, well, how 'bout it, mate? It's just an ordinary day, nothing unusual about a naked lady outstanley on the stage, grumbling to the tune of the sour mash, everything's quite navel, i'n'it? How 'bout a lucky pint for a sore loser. My dad's gone, my mummy's dead, I failed lettering and they chucked me out of college."

"Ah, but your name is Lennon, you already have the luck of the Irish." Lord Woodbine's lilting, singsong West Indian accent was a narcotic, a stepping stone to something exotic. In another flash of lightning Lennon could see through the grimy window out across the street to the second-story window of a flat occupied by an extended Japanese family living quietly, in cultural isolation. It looked like they were preparing something in a bowl and passing it around. A scene from an absolute elsewhere. Could these things really be going on right under our noses? Are we sleepwalking through this life, while all around us are signs that more powerful forces are at work?

"The *chado*," said Woody quietly under the rumble of faraway thunder, with reverence, as he followed John's gaze out through the high window. "A way of preparing and drinking tea. It is a moment that must be fully experienced and appreciated. It demands complete attention, helps you focus the mind to achieve a kind of super-awareness."

As in super-wakefulness, if we could only awake from this reality. Lennon's trancelike state dissolved into puddles of stale beer and cigarette smoke.

Nothing outside of this world could be happening in a crappy striptease club, now could it? "I'm super-aware, all right. That I was born in the wrong place at the wrong time. Stu and I, were both fucking geniuses and we just don't fit in, they chuck us out of their mental institutions they call college."

"There are other ways you can be a genius, John."

Just then Geoff Mohammed, his college friend who'd always skip out and wile away the afternoons drinking and joking around at Ye Cracke, materialized at the door of the club as if conjured by some voodoo magic. Lennon shot Woody an incredulous look.

Lord Woodbine shrugged. "You see, man, even I can be a genius. I have a gift, I don't know how to use it properly, y'know, I can't predict the future, man, I just see what is happening, just tune right into it, y'know."

"I know what he's talking about," warbled Geoff with a half-Indian, half-Italian accent. "People can make coincidences happen. They can create their own realities." He brought out his right hand. "The unique patterns of lines and signs in the hand are a direct result of the way we think, that's why palmistry works. The gypsy fortune teller can read these lines to know how you think, and from that, predict your future."

"Right, pull the other one," snickered Lennon, "It's got bells on."

"I'm serious!" laughed Geoff. "Palmistry goes back thousands of years, my Hindu ancestors practiced it. They studied hands to judge people and their relationships. It's written in the earliest sacred writings. The lines never lie. They are the blueprint of your experience in this reality."

"And what do the calluses tell you?"

"That you'll never make it as a guitar player, you poof!" Geoff turned his wrist limp and swiped it at John, who in turn pulled the face of a spastic, with arms akimbo, bent over like a cripple. With shouts and giggles the other boys came off the stage to spill some beer and join in the fun, leaving Shirley fuming in the middle of unwinding a fur boa.

Suddenly the club door opened and lightning flared across the room, transforming bodies into bluish skeletons. The thunderstorm, rare for these parts, had whipped up a steady downpour, and out of this torrent came a tall silhouette in a gray raincoat and homburg. He removed both as the lightning flare dropped off, revealing an ageless black man in a three-piece suit. Like magic, a black cane with a gold fish head for a handle appeared in his hand, and he tapped it against his black shiny oxfords, one at a time, to knock off the rainwater. Only after doing this did he look up and smile at the bar patrons, flashing gold molars and a gold front tooth.

"Cornell!" Woody was beside himself with glee. "It has been such a long time!" He grabbed a bottle of rum and sprinkled drops before the man leading up to the bar, like some kind of welcoming carpet.

"Yes, my friend," Cornell spoke thickly in a deep baritone, and turned to the boys at the bar. "I am Cornell Woodrow, and this..." He gripped his cane with one hand, and held out the palm of his other hand that held a wet stone, gray like lead. "This is a thunder-stone. It dropped out of the sky, and it belongs to someone here. The Yoruba believe these stones have special powers." The man looked deeply into Paul's eyes, then Stu's, and then George's, before turning his attention to Geoff and John. He then placed the stone on the bar in front of John. He grinned again, revealing the fish head icon embossed on his gold front tooth.

They were all speechless, except John. "Is it good luck, then?"

Cornell grinned at Lord Woodbine and leaned against the bar. "From ancient times, well before history was written, stones that fell from the sky were collected and consecrated with songs, sacrifices, prayers, words of blessing and power. Each stone is blessed for a single person and carries his ancestors, who help him focus his spiritual energy to achieve great things."

"Right here in Liddypool?" John relished an argument. "Talk Hall is very hysterical with old things wot are fakes!"

"Looks like some kind of prehistoric writing," said Stu, once again trying to defuse the situation, pointing to chalky inscriptions of geometric designs that appeared on the stone as it dried.

"Watch it now," Lennon reverted to humor, made a snarky face. "Anything you can say can be used in Everton against you."

Paul stepped in, introducing himself as Paul Ramon. "But what kind of trick is this?"

"No trick," spoke the confident black man, his gold-toothed grin now plastered into everyone's minds. He turned his attention back to the scruffy ted with courageous eyes and a sarcastic mouth. "Lennon. That's your name, right? The stone is for you. It connects you with your ancestors, who sailed the Atlantic and traded in African slaves to make their fortunes in sugar. You know, of course, that around the time of the American revolution, half of Liverpool's sailors were engaged in the slave trade. The legends speak of an Irish-born seaman named Lennon, whose descendants are cursed to travel the seas all their lives, lose their loved ones without mercy, and never feel at home in the world."

John flushed, momentarily speechless, then hotly arrogant. "Did you know my dad then? Go too far with him, did you, to the infernal ends of the earth? Did you imigrateful from some little slum in Jamaicaland and then land yourself a cozy job over 'ere as coachman?"

Stu and Paul looked on, embarrassed by John's racist remarks. But Cornell was not fazed. "It holds a power that defies the erosion of time, that connects you with your ancestors to give you a measure of control over the cosmic forces. With this power you can truly see through the veil of space and time. Some can predict their destinies," he nodded at Woody, " and some can turn base metals into gold," he said, pointing at his tooth. "Some can play music that can cause women to weep and moan, and others can compose a song that can stir masses of people into a patriotic fervor, or a revolt. It is a power that acts like a rocket, propelling your spirit to the highest level of your abilities, ambitions, hopes, and fears. It offers immortality, but only to those who are worthy enough, confident enough, and focused enough to wield it."

Paul was gaining strength and having none of it. "He's just a wind-up merchant, John."

"As false as his wallies," murmured John out of the side of his mouth. But still, he picked up the stone and hefted it. "Let's all go have a wank with our ancestors."

"Wait." Stu snatched it from John. "Let me have a closer look."

John regarded Stu's keen interest. "If only it could help us get more work. Maybe improve our playing, somehow. Something that would take us to the top."

"The top?" asked Cornell. "Where's that?"

"The toppermost of the poppermost!" John shouted, and the others giggled and knocked their heads together like stooges.

"You're a pop group, then," Cornell spoke thickly, with eyes narrowed in a hint of disapproval.

"Yes, we do rock 'n' roll, Chuck Berry, man. Elvis, Eddie Cochran. But a lot of it is rubbish, really, 'cause we're not Americans. We can't go on imitating Americans and make a living out of it."

Paul leaned in with a let-me-explain-it smile. "The basis of our beat is off-beat, accompanied by a faint on-beat. It's like the four in the bar of traditional jazz."

"No, no," protested John, "we're anti-jazz. I think it's all shite. All those educated jazz followers, students in Marks and Spencer pullovers. Jazz never *gets* anywhere, never *does* anything. It's always the same and all they do is drink pints." He punctuated this remark by guzzling his own pint.

Cornell was not impressed. "You're not inspired by jazz? How about the blues?"

"It's *your* fucking music, what do you think?" John challenged him. "How do you like having English blokes like me sing 'Baby Please Don't Go'?"

"No, no, my man!" Lord Woodbine, ever the ambassador, sought to bridge the culture gap. "Music is universal, it belongs to no one! You make it with whatever is at hand, in whatever style they want," pointing at the meager audience sitting on their hands waiting for Shirley to return to the stage. "My steel band, we start at the junk pile. This is our history. The British take away our drums, so we find abandoned gas drums and oil tins, we cut them down to make our steelpans. And we play music you might think is out of character for us, Beethoven, Toselli, Schubert. But the audience loves it! And when we want to cut loose, we do the *Soja Man*."

"Ah, the *Soja Man!*" Cornell bowed with respect.

As if on cue, Bones, a member of the Lord's steel band, blew in from the storm carrying his steelpan. He set it up near the stage and came over to stand behind the bar, saying nothing but nodding at Cornell. Lennon could see some kind of invisible message passed between them, a query and an acknowledgement.

Lord Woodbine turned back to Lennon. "You have no drummer, man, how you expect to make it with no drummer?"

"We make it fine," Lennon shot back in a mocking Jamaican accent, "just pour us another pint if you please."

"We don't need one," said Paul as a matter of fact. "The rhythm's in our guitars."

"But there's not enough bottom," pointed out Woody, and Paul and John both stole a glance at Stu, who held the stone at eye level the way a painter holds his brush to point at the canvas.

"In the African tradition, drumming and dancing are inseparable components of the same activity," lectured Cornell. "Dance-drumming is like having a personal conversation with your wise ancestor. It is magical, to describe it in your terms. Dance-drumming puts our bodies on display, it boasts of our achievements. It is the drama of our people performing well in our lives. The smithy beats out the rhythm of the universe, and dancing becomes the new world order."

"Yes, yes," added Woody quickly, to get to the point. "But really, without drumming, you don't have that magic, you can't penetrate a woman's body to capture her heart."

Geoff snorted a laugh, spurting beer through his dark lips. "I thought it was about music."

Woody ignored him. "You can't go on like this, pulling drummers here and there. You need a drummer that provides a structure for your sound. Why don't you talk to the drummer in the Hurricanes? The one who wears all those rings."

"Oh, Ringo?" John perked up. "He's a professional, why would he want to put up with us? Anyway Johnny Hutch is a better drummer. The Cassanovas have that powerful drum thing."

"No, I've heard him," said Woody. "Too strong for your sound. You should try Ringo."

Stu gave out an exasperated sigh as he put down the stone. "I think he's right, John." He looked over at Lennon with a sly grin. "Maybe I should have taken up drums rather than bass." He grinned sheepishly. "Look, I'm not feeling well, this headache's come on."

"So go on, then."

"George or Paul can use my bass, give whichever one my ten bob."

"You give up too easily, Stu."

"I'm not giving up," he shrugged. Paul watched Stu leave, and turned to look at George, who muttered that he wasn't going to give up lead guitar to play bass. Paul looked at him incredulously. Wot, not even here, in this dingy strip club where no one's listening anyway?

John picked up the stone to avoid looking at either of them, and tried to see right through it. Solid rock. My group is disintegrating without Stu. What am I supposed to be?

Cornell had been watching Lennon with interest. "You need to see it for yourself, this power? Let me show you. Gather your group, and let's hear you play. But first, take the stone, rub it gently, and put it in your pocket."

"A-and play pocket billiards wi'it?"

Cornell smiled. "A cheap shot, yes. But let Bones sit in with you, and watch the girl as she dances."

"Our bass player's gone," said Paul. "I wouldn't mind playing bass but I'm left-handed..."

Cornell strolled over to Stu's bass, took it out of its battered case, and brought it over to Paul. "Flip it upside down," he said as he handed it to Paul. "And spread your fingers over the frets spatially opposite, low to high to note. It's like learning to drive in America, on the right side, rather than the left side. You just reverse your polarity."

Bemused, Paul began to practice playing the right-handed bass upside down. Once again they took the stage, with Bones pitter-pattering a rhythm on his steelpan appropriate for "Ramrod" as Shirley meandered out and started going through the motions. Dispirited, bored, even disgusted with Shirley's nonchalant business-as-usual approach, Lennon shot hard glances at Cornell, who seemed to be mustering his energy to do something, concentrating hard on the dancer. The thought occurred right then to Lennon that something more was called for, some kind of truth. What is Shirley really dancing for? What is her final purpose?

Of course! John started to bang out a rudimentary version of a recent hit called "Money (That's What I Want)".[166] He could see Paul grinning, appreciating this bit of humor that ran deeper than typical wanker jokes.

So with Paul on Stu's bass leading the way, Lennon started grinding out the opening blues riff with George hanging on behind him, right on up to the stressed, suspended plateau, and down into the canyon of the first verse, which Lennon belted out in a renewed ferocity. "The best things in life are free," and he strummed the backbeat chord savagely. "But you can give 'em to the birds and bees, I want *money*."

The others joined in, "Money, money." Lennon returned the favor: "That's what I want." He glanced at Shirley, who was starting to move seductively. "That's what I wah-ah-ah-ant oh yeah," John sang, finding his meaty voice in the lower registers and driving that masculinity straight home to her quim. "That's what I want."

Cornell's somber face cracked into a watermelon smile as he gazed at Shirley. Lennon felt suddenly that the room, the entire club, floated on a cloud in something unreal. Time didn't stand still but started to wave, like ripples in a river, and as he concentrated on his grinding blues riff, the timing of his strumming matched these ripples.

The riff began to infect and then possess Shirley. She gathered her body in a rush of euphoria and flung her arms to the ceiling, her breasts bouncing as if the stage were a trampoline. In sync with the rhythm, she twisted her body in jerks and spasms, forming a spiral as she hunkered down, thighs wide, vagina aimed at the stage floor. With a single thumb she snapped the G-string, squatted, and pressed her naked pussy's lips to the wood. The crowd roared. They'd never seen anything like it. Lennon could feel the power of his strumming move her body, trigger her to gyrate and thrust, to squirm and grind.

The ecstatic display shattered the mind of a middle-aged man in a raincoat and bowler hat standing near the stage. Groping at invisible phantoms he made his way to the stage and flung himself at her lower torso, face and mouth open, arms flailing, bowler hat rolling around at the band's feet. Shirley was amused and leaned back to give him a whiff, but Lord Woodbine across the room was not; brandishing his cutlass, he strode with quick purpose through the crowd to the stage and threatened to cut off the man's head. Lennon kept on grinding the chords behind all this, grinning idiotically, giving the hat a kick, and thinking that he was manipulating this scene and they were all his puppets.

But George stopped playing, and then Paul, both taken aback by the cutlass in Woody's hand gleaming brightly in the stage lights. Bones pitter-pattered a soft flutter on the bongos and stopped. A hush fell over the audience; the show had knocked the wind out of them. As Woody firmly escorted Shirley's assailant out of the club with his cutlass held high, Lennon stopped his manic strumming and Shirley slid back on her haunches in exhaustion. The audience cleared their throats, fingered their wallets, checked their timepieces and collected their coats, mystified by it all and quite ready to forget it had ever happened.

"Was that the demonstration, then?" John snapped at Cornell as he came off the stage, his guitar slung over his back and his aggression barely under control.

Cornell met John's stance squarely, but with a smile and a twinkle of his eye. "You'll know it when you feel it." Perhaps this English boy is a white Stagger Lee. Turning to Lord Woodbine as he put on his coat, he placed his hand over Woody's on the cutlass handle. "I must leave now, my friend, and take Bones with me. We're off to Hamburg. Something is starting up there, along the Reeperbahn. A mixed crowd, gun-runners, gangsters, black American G.I.s. There may be... opportunities." He spoke the word as a talisman in his deep, dark voice. Then he turned back to the room, still holding Woody's hand-on-cutlass, and, still in a dark voice, said, "And I leave you all with this." And with a swirl of his overcoat and a smile as large as the room, he began to sing, loudly...

A pirate, history relates
Was scuffling with some of his mates
When he slipped on a cutlass
Which rendered him nut-less
And practically useless on dates!"

And with that, belly-laughing, Cornell Woodrow swirled out the door and was absorbed into the abating rainstorm.

Well, *that* was something. Lennon had felt something new, something unpredictable. Now that he possessed this stone, whatever it was, he had a choice of whether to believe in it or not. And yet he understood that he could do both: believe in it as something to concentrate on, to better his skills; and disbelieve it, treat it as simply a lucky piece, and don't expect anything from it. Either way there was an unexpected demand that he must now obey new laws of nature, laws he'd never known before. New laws for a new universe, parallel to this one, into which this club had been transported. And as he thought this, the room, the street outside, Liverpool, all of it grew increasingly insubstantial, like sand castles dissolving in the relentless waves of an ocean from another universe.

He knew that a true miracle had just occurred, a small one, but then all great things seem small and insignificant at first. But it was not the thunder-stone, that was just a bit of fake magic to disrupt your usual thoughts and point you in the right direction. No, the power came from concentrating on the rhythm of the music, on finding the meat in his voice and singing from his stomach, on overcoming fear and just laying it out there, for all to see. His rhythm had meshed with Paul's bass in a way he'd never heard before. Their different guitars, rhythm and bass, were somehow linked on another plane of experience. This is it, he thought, something to be taken seriously, for the first time in his life. He'd heard it tonight. Everything started to click.

Everything started to click with Paul on bass.

John couldn't talk to Stu about this. Stu wanted to impress John with his bass playing and would do anything to continue with the group. John didn't know how to let Stu down easily. He could talk to Paul about it, because Paul knew how important it was to get the music and the rhythm right. Paul knew how to hide his feelings; Paul had also lost his mother and seems to understand how important it is to make it, to make a business of it, to live the life of it.

It turned out that John didn't have to talk about how the music clicked; Paul wouldn't stop talking about it as Stu quietly sulked. Paul had tasted the magic of the bass guitar, and thought it no coincidence at all that Richard Starkey, a.k.a. Ringo from the Hurricanes, had showed up at the Jac the next day during the Silver Beetles gig. Ringo showed up at just the right moment, as if conjured by voodoo, that Paul had stepped in on bass while Stu took lead vocals. Ringo sat in for a while on congas that were lying around, and the rhythm grew as perfect as John's smile.

Paul talked to Ringo afterward, but Ringo couldn't be bothered with joining this primitive group; he was keenly aware that there were over a hundred groups in this province alone and practically none of them had a chance of ever being heard in London, let alone the rest of the world. Except perhaps the Hurricanes and another group, Denny and the Seniors, which were preparing to bypass London and go to Hamburg.

* * *

Allan Williams sensed a change in the air. As the other members of the Royal Caribbean Steel Band slipped away to Hamburg, he recognized that something this unpredictable must be pointing the way to new opportunities. He'd heard some stories about Hamburg's Reeperbahn. British teenage girls swooning at the feet of someone as ugly as Gene Vincent was one thing; adult women in Europe carrying on with wild abandon to Caribbean steel music was something else entirely.

His connection with Larry Parnes guaranteed that even more groups in the area would be at his disposal to manage. The Parnes tour packages, and the ever-growing club scene in Liverpool and now Hamburg, all seemed to Williams to be plum pickings. With the steel band gone, he could afford to give more time to the Silver Beetles, and even suggested a drummer. "I'll see what I can do to arrange an audition for Parnes, but John, you really need a proper drummer. Why don't you give Tommy Moore a go?"

"The fork-lift driver? He's too thick for us."

"Aw, give 'em a go, and I'll arrange something with Parnes. He's coming to the Wyvern, mate, just a week from now."

"Ol' Parnes, Shillings, and Pence?" It was a quid pro quo, no doubt. Lennon was, as usual, suspicious of Allan's motives, always helping them, and for what? Allan will give Parnes an arse-licking for sure, but did the man also owe Moore a favor? It seems that to get anywhere, you have to put up with these cripples.

At the Wyvern Club audition for Parnes, Paul's impatience with Stu came to the surface. An American bass player, about the same age as the rest of them, popped backstage amidst the clatter and confusion to give them a hand with their gear. He called himself Johnny B, from New Jersey, played bass with the Ancestors, a rhythm and blues group out of the Cheltenham-Tewkesbury area that only recently started playing matinees at London jazz clubs. He also worked part-time for Larry Parnes as a road tech. Lennon caught a whiff of the underclass about him, a street kid, glaring and inquisitive. Not at all what he'd thought an American teenager was like. Turns out he not only knew about that Cornell Woodrow character, but he also knew Lennon's friend Geoff.

"You know Geoff, then," Lennon broke the ice wryly.

"Yeah, he told me to look you up."

"Did he tell you all about India and his father, his ancestors? All that bloody nonsense about sorcerers and holy men and the healing power of the Ganges?"

"Yeah, he's a wild one," Johnny B answered matter-of-factly.

"He's a practicing maniac," retorted Lennon.

Johnny B had heard their audition. Like his own band mates in the Ancestors, these Brits were caricatures of the rock 'n' roll heroes back home. Even so, this bunch articulated themselves with panache. They were cheeky, they didn't take themselves too seriously. How could they? Playing music from another country? But like most vulgar expressions of caricatures, these were overblown.

Paul wanted to know about his group, the Ancestors, how they thought up that name. "We're Johnny and the Moondogs right now..."

"No we're not," snapped Lennon, thinking quickly how absurd the name would sound to a hip American. "We're the Silver Beetles."

"I dunno, Ancestors, it's just a name," Johnny B's voice seemed to slither out through a rangy grin. "A friend of mine back home suggested it, before I came over here. I needed to get a group together, just to keep my sanity. But I'm sick about what's happening back there, all this Frankie Avalon shit making it while the real music, the black music, is stuck in the clubs. All we have is our records, a-and my father, he's a big distributor back there, but everything he distributes is shit. You got the same thing going on over here, this creeping commercial shit, Cliff Richard and all that, I've seen enough Elvis imitators to last a lifetime. Hell, I met Elvis, seen him perform. You got nothin' like the real Elvis over here."

"Fuck Elvis." Lennon didn't believe this Yank; he would have been just a kid when Elvis last toured.

"Yeah well, I played with the Hawk, Ronnie Hawkins, and his band, even helped him come over here to appear on that TV show back in December."

"Yes, 'Oh Boy!', I saw it," said Stu. "Gene Vincent and Eddie Cochran, too. We caught them at the Liverpool Empire in March."

A moment of pause for Eddie Cochran, who'd died the previous month on tour in England, the same car accident that put Gene Vincent in the hospital. Then Lennon spoke sarcastically, "Another dead loser. Now *he's* Something Else," joking on the title of one of Cochran's songs, "and Vincent's a cripple, can't dance to the bop no more."

"Eddie was a genius," countered Johnny B. "There wasn't anything he couldn't play after hearing it once or twice. He wrote his own songs, he could play that Chet Atkins bass-melody picking style. Lemme show you."

With a subdued chuckle, Johnny B demonstrated the bass line Eddie Cochran had employed on "Twenty Flight Rock",[167] a percussive slapping style pioneered by Bill Black on Elvis' Sun recordings. The song was more or less a pastiche of early Elvis mannerisms, and McCartney knew it well, had in fact taught the song to Lennon, but he watched Johnny B's playing closely. His timing was so perfect; Paul had never seen anything like this up close. All the Merseyside groups seem to rush through their songs, but Johnny B held on to the rhythm, reinforcing it with a laconic style. Johnny B suavely coasted through "C'mon Everybody", "Something Else", "Summertime Blues", and then "Jeanie, Jeanie, Jeanie"[168], which clicked in Paul's head, and it came to him how to play the bass part and change the arrangement for the newest Lennon-McCartney composition, "One After 909".[169]

Stu, meanwhile, had been watching and perfecting Johnny B's sneer, and hadn't even thought to grab his Höfner. Paul noticed and elbowed Stu. "You ought to take lessons from him, y'know."

Stu reddened. Lennon pounced for the kill. "Sutcliffe, just turn your back to the audience, so they can't see that you can't play."

Johnny B winced at the remark and felt some sympathy for Stu. These Northerners, as the English called people from the northern provinces that included Liverpool and Manchester, could be cruel to each other and to everybody else.

The audition call came just as Tommy Moore showed up direct from his forklift job, all rumpled and dirty, and they used up valuable audition time setting up his drums. Stu had time to think about Lennon's remark and decided that he'd take a more aggressive stand, sneering under his Ray-Ban sunglasses and facing the audience solidly with the body of his Höfner bass centered against his chest. It was a pose Lennon would imitate, if only to embarrass Stu.

Larry Parnes was not so impressed with the drummer for the Silver Beetles who had arrived late, acted surly, and looked ages older than the rest of them. This Tommy Moore character would scare the teenagers if they got a good look at him. No way would he let this outfit back Billy Fury on an island-wide tour, not until they found a proper drummer. Until then, he could use them for the Johnny Gentle tour in the North. But he wanted to hear the group without the bass player. The two guitarists were fine, but he had another bass player in mind, and besides, Stu looked a bit too beatnik for his tastes.

The humbling experience of standing down hurt Stu worse than any other rejection of his life. He never regained his enthusiasm for the music. Stu had been experiencing, off and on since the kick to his head, severe headaches and acute sensitivity to light. At other times he suffered a fathomless hurt buried deep inside his head. The deeply ingrained pain brought drama to his dreams, and he had dreamed giant bass notes turning into the scaffolds of an executioner.

Scotland in May 1960 was cold and rainy, but Lennon was bursting with energy at each performance and actively engaging the other tour groups, exercising his dry wit by criticizing everything, especially Stu's playing. John's exuberance greatly increased with his inner feelings of failure. He was about to drop out of school, while Paul and George were going back to the Institute.

Aunt Mimi wouldn't stop scolding him with "You must think about getting a job instead of messing about with the guitar." And Stu seemed more distant than ever.

To avoid the tension between John and Stu in the shared hotel rooms, Paul would grab Stu's Höfner and visit the Ancestors' room to learn a few things from Johnny B. The tutoring helped Paul to slow down his energy. Johnny B taught him to concentrate, to capture the timing by feel, and to tune his bass in a more accurate way to produce the right vibrations. Paul's fingers were raw, sliced up from the piano strings Stu had bought for the bass to save money. Paul was in a hurry to learn and hadn't developed proper calluses for bass strings.

* * *

Johnny B awoke in a supine position on a couch in the beautiful white-haired Dahlia's bedroom in Paris, a copy of Dormant's collage-book *Situations* on his lap. He vaguely remembered his fascination with the overall idea of the book as a slice of current life exploded to the point where every spot, drip, photo, comic-strip and blueprint image is pregnant with meaning. It was a meaning you had to make up yourself, make it up out of anything, out of everyday life situations.

Dahlia had flown somewhere. Dormant himself was snoring on a floor cushion in the living room. Franco was working on another French poster, translated into English as "Live without dead time, indulge untrammeled desire!"

Johnny sensed meaning in everything, but he was not so mystical about it. Cornell had taught him to be practical. Also, to not be impatient. "It took over seven generations for our people to awaken and begin to feed and celebrate its loa. Take your time, and feed it right." Feed the musical serpent, as Johnny interpreted it. And he had some ideas for this Liverpool band, the Silver Beetles, that he'd met a month before, that was now cutting its eye teeth in Hamburg. They needed to break out, and in order to do that, they needed something new, a new image. He would start with a decent photographer.

Dormant had pointed him to a group of existentialist friends in Hamburg, "Sartre and Camus are their patron saints. They're just students, going around wearing black clothes and looking moody." The city was a northern port like Liverpool, and even on the same latitude, but twice its size and ten times its wickedness. The Reeperbahn main street had more strip clubs than any other street in the world. As a free port Hamburg harbored gun runners during the Algerian crisis and attracted foreign gangsters, who mingled with British and American servicemen. As the Berlin Wall went up, East German illegal immigrants fled to Hamburg to get drunk and conduct gang warfare in the clubs.

The *exis* included several artists and photographers, including Jürgen Vollmer and, as Dormant put it, "the Mata Hari of monochrome" Astrid Kirchherr. Dormant put Johnny B in touch with Astrid's current boyfriend, an illustrator named Klaus Voormann.

As soon as Johnny B arrived in Hamburg, he brought Klaus to the Reeperbahn. The band now called themselves the Beatles, "Beatles with an 'A'" as Lennon put it. They were playing the Indira club, named after India, which had a large elephant sign as its symbol. Klaus, whose student friends were more into jazz, had never been to a club like it before, all noisy and menacing. They sat at a beer-drenched table in the back with the Beatles on a break. Klaus was amazed at their black-and-white check jackets and long pointed shoes, and one of them, Stu, really looked the part of a rocker, with his hair piled back and high, and wearing those clip-on sunglasses all night. The waitress dropped by with their Prellys, and Johnny B couldn't help but notice the label on the drug bottle — Preludin, the same pills he used to peddle for his dad back in Jersey.

Back on stage, the Beatles put on an energetic show of raucous, screaming vocals and driving rhythms. The music was so exciting for Klaus that he brought his girlfriend Astrid the following night, and promptly lost her, as she fell in love at first sight of the moody, inarticulate Stu, a James Dean replica right there in Hamburg.

Astrid felt motherly to Lennon and the others, despite their sexual overtures. John was clearly all for himself and his penis, boisterous and rowdy but inexperienced in sensual matters. Paul was a bit more sensitive and caring, but there was this rude side to him that didn't really accept women on their own terms. George was too shy and prac-tically a virgin, and Pete the drummer, well, he was earthy and kind, but not as intelligent as the others. It was Stuart she was drawn to, overtly shy but capable of loving on an entirely different level. She knew he could pierce her veil and discover her secrets and she could almost feel him going down on her as he stood there, like a stone, playing his bass.

Johnny B persuaded Astrid to experiment with the Beatles, and she started with Stu, changing his hairstyle to be more like Klaus, bringing the hair forward, over his brow. Stu was thin enough and the same height as Astrid, so she gave him her leather pants and collarless jackets, over-sized shirts, and long scarves. The overall effect was feminine, but Stu could pull it off with his jutting masculine chin and dire, mysterious eyes. And despite their witty gibes at Stu about looking girlish or wearing his mother's clothes, both John and Paul were jealous of the new look. Even Johnny B adopted it, and Astrid eventually gave them all the "moptop" look except Pete the drummer, who could sense already that he didn't fit it.

With the coming of Astrid, Stu was ready to graduate from his great "wallow" in the gritty life of rock and roll. He was now ready to pursue realism, before prying open the escape hatch of abstract and surrealism. Stu had heard the call of the wild in the early works of Max Ernst, in the "kitchen sink realism" of John Bratby, in Eduardo Paolozzi's "I was a Rich Man's Plaything", which — Johnny B had pointed out — was very popular among Dormant's group in Paris.

This move to the primitive in his art was the same, he tried to explain to Lennon, as the latter's pursuit for that raw feeling of rock and roll, the primitive music. But John, stung by his friend's newfound interest in someone far more intellectual than him, told Stu on no uncertain terms to decide. Painting, or the band.

Astrid eased the tension by taking long early morning walks with John, sped up on Prellys after the shows. After a few embarrassing attempts at hitting on her, John stopped acting like a idiot and started talking to her. All he really cared about, he told her, was to get on with his rock and roll.

The next week Johnny B arrived with Ringo Starr from the Hurricanes, who were playing up the street. Stu had felt sick and stayed for a few days at Astrid's house, so left-handed Paul had taken to playing Stu's bass upside down, as Cornell had shown him. Johnny B took over on bass for a song, and Ringo took over from a moody Pete on drums, and they launched into the best version of "Some Other Guy"[170] that they'd ever played, with Lennon beaming as he sang, using a stance borrowed from Stu with his guitar at his chest, his chin held up high, and his eyes in a squint so that he could see without glasses. His body faced the world without fear, as if overnight he had become the spokesman for all of rock and roll.

It was impressive work, and Johnny B was proud of his role as a talent scout and Cornell's protégé. He'd hooked them up with an art crowd of sophisticated tastes, and he'd arranged a recording session for them in Hamburg, with Ringo in tow, to be the backing band for Tony Sheridan singing "My Bonnie".[171] He was taken by surprise when the authorities showed up to deport the Beatles. Had he been followed? Cornell had formidable enemies who could coerce the German police to raid the club. A pretext, some ridiculous shenanigans in the cubbyhole backstage involving a flaming curtain, had put Paul and Pete in the slammer, while George was summarily flown back to England for being a minor.

Lennon limped back to Liverpool without a cent, all contrite to his Aunt Mimi, but still optimistic. Ringo was going to join the band, and Johnny B had talked Bob Woolton into setting them up for regular noontime gigs at the Cavern club. Lennon wouldn't die of starvation, but he also wouldn't die of boredom.

Stu, however, would tragically die of a brain hemorrhage in Hamburg the following year, stemming from that kick in the head back in that Liverpool alley. He had been a trend-setting artist, the first of many to wear the hairstyles of the new hipsters. John Lennon would always think of him as a martyr for his pursuit of the primitive and his willingness to experiment in rock and roll.

* * *

A week after Paris, Brian was back in Cheltenham, Gloucestershire, with his sax, guitar, and Elmore James record, eating humble pie, doing his mum's bidding, and trying to keep from lisping in front of his dad. At least they hadn't thrown out the picture of his dead cat, Rolobur, the one he'd painted blue with food coloring. But he found his old school haunts to be as drab and dreary as his old suit and his old room.

The beatnik phrase "hang out" had finally reached Gloucestershire at the foot of the Cotswolds, and Brian hung out as much as he could between odd jobs, mostly with older jazz players and bohemian revelers at trendy coffee bars like the Aztec. Soon he was playing sax with a local band and practicing his "look" on the local girls. It worked: misting up his eyes, pouting, cocking his head, thrusting his chin, folding his arms, and leaning nonchalantly to one side. He was utterly seductive, and yet he trailed bitter victims behind him like Hansel his breadcrumbs. His only way back home was through a thicket of apologies he would never make. Right and left he violated girls bareback without a thought to the consequences, trying to get some satisfaction for his insatiable appetites. He could hear former comrades whisper warnings to girls behind his back. "He's a creep." "Girls just feel sorry for him because he always looks so lonely and depressed." "Don't give him money, you'll never get it back." And it was no surprise to anyone but him that he would father a second illegitimate child, this time by a 23-year old married woman who caught his eye when he played sax at a dance.

Pat, a dark-haired handsome girl of 16, felt sorry for him, but was also intrigued. She found him clever, well dressed, and even a good listener, a rarity among the teenagers. She knew his history, and more importantly, knew that he was experienced. The thought of his experience gave her the hot flashes. Before long, she too was pregnant, with Brian's third illegitimate child, and Brian sweetly sold his meager record collection to buy a bouquet of roses and carnations for her hospital bed. But she'd met his austere mum and stuffy dad and had serious misgivings. She wondered if Brian's sweetness would ever be more than just a coverup for his personal rebellions. For his part, Brian wondered if he would be forever trapped in a hopeless domestic life.

The would-be bohemians of Cheltenham gathered late at night in the basement of Mrs. Filby's house on Priory Street, or over in the Wheatsheaf public house on the Old Bath Road. Brian often sat on the door collecting admission money and issuing membership cards. He wanted so desperately to have a close friend, and to talk about music and sex. His former friends thought the talk creepy, but he eventually met up with Dick, a fat bumbling nincompoop, ambivalent about his sexuality, who hung around him like a puppy dog, obviously smitten, hanging on his every word.

"We copy American jazz, but jazz itself is just a trick," Brian told Dick, "a false promise, a sort of tawdry compensation for the blacks who first created the sounds that gave it form and substance. The sounds of the blues." Dick could only agree. They hit it off like a house on fire, and after perusing Dick's collection of Muddy Waters records, Brian decided to take advantage and move in.

On a night of a severe thunderstorm, the Chris Barber jazz band played the Cheltenham Town Hall, with Alexis Korner's skiffle band[172] as the opening act, and Sonny Boy Williamson II[173] as the middle act. Lightning struck the hall's tower as the show started, scattering sparks across its rooftop like a shower of gold, and momentarily freezing everyone who saw it. Inside, Brian recognized the American kid, Johnny B, from that Howlin' Wolf show in Paris slouching at the backstage entrance. Blended in shadows behind him was the familiar tall, thin, jet-black Cornell Woodrow in a dark gray pin-stripe suit and fedora. Cornell beckoned to him to come backstage to watch the show from a musician's perspective.

Sonny Boy, ratty, ugly, scowling and cajoling in his three-piece suit, bowler hat, and armor belt around his waist, looked like a sales rep for the Devil's snake oil. Brian was fascinated with Sonny Boy's armor belt with harmonicas in different keys occupying the slots normally used for bullets. The Barber band rolled out a magic carpet of horns and drums, and Sonny Boy's harmonica slithered across it like a greased king cobra let loose from its cage.

Brian invited Sonny Boy, Johnny B, and some of the band members back to Dick's apartment after the show, and they whipped up a frenzy in the kitchen all night. Johnny B demonstrated the proper method of combining hashish with tobacco in a rolled cigarette, and passed it around. Brian got out his guitar to demonstrate what he knew of Elmore James' techniques, using the jagged neck of a Penderyn whisky bottle that would scrape his finger, drawing blood. Johnny B told him that Elmore had learned "Dust My Broom" from the late Robert Johnson. "You got to hear this," he raved. "Johnson sounds like an entire orchestra but he's only playing guitar by himself."[174]

Sonny Boy's eyes glittered from the smoke and his demonic stare softened to a smile as the record played. "I was with Robert when he got poisoned," he told the rapt audience overflowing the kitchen. "A woman. Y'know? It's *always* about a woman. Her husband was the bartender, and he offered Robert an open bottle of whiskey. I told Robert not to drink it, I even knocked the bottle out of his hand. I said 'Don't ever drink from an open bottle, you don't know what's in it.' And he got mad at me, told me, 'Don't ever knock a bottle out of my hand.' And he took a swig from another open bottle that was offered to him. Man he was so sick after that! And in a few days it was over for him, he died, crawlin' around on all fours, barkin' like a dog." Sonny paused, retreating into his mind for a minute.

Cornell unravelled his booming laugh and unleashed another limerick, thus:

Your mammy don't wear no drawers
Got another man doin' her chores
Wouldn't be my bitch

'Cause she's got the itch
And she crawls around on all fours!

Everyone chuckled. This was Robert Johnson's legacy, his bald-faced lying humor, his scatological asides, his obsession for lusty women, his laughter at the cruelty of life. It all made no difference anyhow. But, as Sonny Boy pointed out, "He had a sound you couldn't help but stop and listen to. He could hypnotize an audience."

Brian was already hypnotized. He could hear that slicing slide guitar riff that Elmore James had picked up from Johnson's version, and a whole lot more. The sparse details of Johnson's murder only deepened the mystery. He wanted to know more. "They say he sold his soul to the Devil, is that true?"

Sonny Boy sighed. "Son, we all sell our souls to the Devil. That's why his music is so powerful. That's why we can still hear him. No tombstone could hold him." He paused again, lost in thought. "Robert had that flair for the dramatic, you know. He told everyone he'd been down to the crossroads. The way it goes is, if you want to make this powerful music, you take your guitar and you go to the crossroads. A big black man," Sonny Boy's eyes twinkled, "will walk up there at the stroke of midnight and take your guitar, and he'll tune it."

Cornell chuckled, and held out his hand to Brian. A shining wet stone glittered in his palm. "It fell out of the storm tonight. Take it. It belongs to you."

"What is it?"

"A thunder-stone," replied Cornell in a low, Bella Lugosi voice. "The Yoruba believe in thunder-stones. They carry spirits. This one was consecrated by tonight's performance." He turned the stone over in his palm. "This here's the spirit of Robert Johnson, and it's for you." He then handed it to Brian, whose blue-green eyes widened in disbelief.

Sonny Boy slapped his belly and guffawed. "Just look at that boy, he's turned pale as a greyhound! Well, my mother told my father," he began singing in a raspy imitation of Muddy Waters, stomping his foot, "just before hmmm, I was born, I got a boy child's comin', he's gonna be, he's gonna be a rollin' stone." He blasted through notes on his harmonica, guffawed again, and shouted, "Sure 'nough, he's a rollin' stone!"

"You know the story of the rolling stone? One who rolls with the stone?" Alexis Korner peered at Brian. "The high priests of West Africa, when they were captured to be brought to America as slaves. They would take their sacred stones and swallow them, to keep them. They'd carry those stones in their stomachs across the sea. And they'd get sick, sicker than dogs, carrying those stones. And when they got to the New World, they'd be killed and have their stomachs eviscerated. They were considered holy martyrs, sacrificing their lives so that their people could keep their gods with them."

"Oh well," Sonny Boy continued singing the song and playing the harmonica.

"Rolling stone," Brian mused. "So, what? It's a metaphor, a, what, an analogy —"

"Allegory," corrected Alexis. "And yes, it's all those things, and more. It's real."

Thunder echoed in the night, and all the lights blinked. There was a moment of silence in the bright warm kitchen, finally broken by Johnny B's halting attempt to pluck bass notes from Brian's acoustic guitar. He fiddled with the tuning and handed the guitar back to Brian. "Try this," he said, pulling a metal tube out of his blue jeans, a Sears socket wrench. "Better than the bottle neck. Doesn't cut your finger, and it sounds better, you get that steel sound."

Brian's confidence on slide guitar improved immediately; before, his fingers would hesitate on the frets and he could not avoid wincing as he anticipated blood. Now he could slide up and down the frets with abandon and a wicked grin.

Johnny B had something else up his sleeve. "Try this," he held out a Preludin tube of pills from Hamburg, and shook one out. "It'll wake you up, give you some energy."

Sure enough, from that point on Brian couldn't stop playing slide guitar. They stayed up all night discussing tunings. "My friends back in America," Johnny B told him, "their father was some kind of wandering historian, and he uncovered something about music. These ancient Sumerian tunings, how their pitch frequencies could affect our bodies, and how our bodies vibrate with them."

"Yes, I've read all this stuff about the role of music in our ancient past, it's all beyond what we knew before," Brian replied. "The ancients used music in more ways than entertainment. It was the basis of *all* communication at some point, before language. It's all resonant with our bodies, our bodies inherently know all about harmony, disharmony, and dissonance."

"Yes and there is a secret my friend's father uncovered," Johnny B went on, "something that has been suppressed for thousands of years, having to do with these musical tunings. How they can affect people directly, without lyrics, without context, without meaning or politics or religion. How they can transcend religion, in fact. But we lost this power in the music when the tunings were 'corrected,' first by Pythagoras, and then by what they called Just Intonation. They added what they called a 'comma' that produced a barely audible flatness in all the perfect fifths, so that they are really not as harmonic as they must have been back in Sumer."

"And we add it back in, subtly, with harmonica, sax, slide guitar," said Brian, catching on quickly, "with blues licks that bend pitches to notes that are not on the scale."

"Exactly. *That's* mojo."

"So what are you saying?"

"That there are some people out there like me, like my friends, like Cornell. Out there planting the seeds of mojo in the music. Mojo that can turn girls crazy."

That was all Brian needed to hear; that and the baby's cries and Pat's pleadings. And the fact that Johnny B could set him up to sell tubes of Prellys to support his music-making. Franco, the trench coat nudist in Paris, was Johnny's courier, relaying the drugs from Germany. When Franco first showed up in Johnny B's company, Brian didn't recognize him because he wore regular clothes. The arrangement gave Brian enough pocket money and confidence to fast-talk his way out of his domestic situation, and in the early wintry days of 1962 he finally escaped Cheltenham.

Groups were springing up everywhere like mushrooms. Brian sensed that he had to get in front of this thing. Determined to start his own group, a *band*, Brian entertained fantasies of basking in the jazz clubs every night and sleeping it off on Alexis Korner's floor.

His first stop was Oxford to see Johnny B's new group, with Paul Pond on vocals. Johnny B had left the Ancestors just as they faded into obscurity, and was now laying down a throbbing Bo Diddley beat in counterpoint to Paul's angelic singing. They called themselves Thunder Odin's Big Secret, named after a Lightning Hopkins record "Santa Fe Blues".175 The Odin part came up in another late-night Phenmetrazine rap as they listened to the record over and over while perusing Johnny B's new crop of American comic books from his buddy Gilbert. And so the band was named after Odin, the Norse god whose big secret was the power of his son, Thor, god of thunder and Marvel comics hero. Brian understood the connection to thunderous rhythm and blues, even if he didn't quite understand the Big Secret. Most attractive was the comic Thor's shaggy blond mane, and the defiant look that could kill if someone so much as mentioned how feminine his hair looked. Brian could use his secret power to become Thor, a sort of Super Saint-Just.

Brian briefly joined the band, and even recorded a demo tape for Alexis Korner, in an Oxford club, playing the derivative "Dust My Blues" with a scathingly gritty slide on an acoustic guitar behind Paul's wobbly voice and Johnny B's relentless bass. Brian connected with Johnny B's rhythmic bass lines in an interlocking pattern, surprising them both. If only they could perfect this method of weaving guitar and bass guitar patterns in the same volume range, without all the noise from the sax and drums. Brian knew he could arrange the music so that a band could play their instruments as one sound, with every different timbre and voice adding spark and flavor, sweetness and light, to the main melody. Rhythm and blues could be done tastefully.

To the others in the Big Secret, the point of all this was to catch birds, as there were so many cute ones dancing in front. It was a hobby, not a living. Most were in college studying to be architects or accountants, or in art school practicing their craft for the advertising industry. Paul Pond was semi-serious, calling himself Paul Jones onstage because Brian had decided to call himself Elmo Lewis. But he could only devote part of his time to music. Brian sensed this, and when Paul asked him to join the Big Secret, he made up a reason on the spot. "I don't really want to be in a band unless I'm the leader." That sounded pompous enough to divert attention from the real problem: these young men weren't serious, except for Johnny B. Maybe Brian could pry him loose and start a band with him.

"I've got another gig," Johnny B told him. "Right now, I'm spread out between the Big Secret and a group called the Roosters." The Roosters had just recruited another fantastic guitarist, a youngster called Eric Clapton, who'd flipped over a Robert Johnson record Johnny had played for him.

Brian's next stop was a club west of London that Johnny B told him to check out. Brian found the Ealing Club, a tiny drinking establish-ment in the back of the ABC Bakery, down the steps between the teashop and the jewelry store. What a fantastic scene! The Blues Incorporated sound was chaotic. A large burly panel-beater from an auto body shop by the name of Cyril Davies, referred to as "Squirrel" onstage, seem to devour his harmonica, honking in the heavy backbeat of the Chicago blues, while Alexis alternated strumming and finger-picking in a style more in line with Charles Mingus.[176] The result was a cacophony that sometimes worked, held together by a taciturn, well-dressed nineteen-year-old drummer called Charlie Watts. With all the courage he could muster, Brian handed Alexis Korner the tape he had made as Elmo Lewis. Korner was so impressed with Brian that he give Brian his home number and address, and asked Brian to sit in with the band the following week.

All across the British Isles and Europe at this time, teenage kids were awakening to a rising siren song and putting on the clothes and attitudes of self-made American hipsters. Movies like *Rebel Without a Cause* and *The Blackboard Jungle* had given them a frame of reference, Elvis had given them a taste of freedom, and the atomic bomb had instilled in them an urgency to get on with their lives quickly and passionately. Eleven-year-old Ray Davies felt suffocated by normality as he obsessed over American records and, at his Eleven Plus exam, feeling tested on some level higher than normal intelligence, decided to sign his name at the top of the paper and do nothing for the rest of the test. An angry fourteen-year-old Roger Daltry, transplanted from the grimy industrial Shepherd's Bush to tree-lined Bedford Park, got expelled from grammar school for smoking and formed a working band to cover Eddie Cochran hits. Seventeen-year-old habitual truant Keith Richards, hooked on Chuck Berry, kicked around art college setting fire to dustbins and feeding pep pills to the cockatoo in the aviary for laughs. These three would eventually start the Kinks, the Who, and the Rolling Stones. And a sixteen-year-old Donovan, in Hertfordshire, paid homage to James Dean by scrapping up junk from a car graveyard, a carburetor, a mirror, a smashed speedometer stuck at 90 mph, and lots of plywood, stretching a sheet of polythene over it, and lighting the bugger up in flames.

* * *

Ding ding free ball. Gilbert snapped his wrist in a stylish flair as he pulled the plunger and released it, as if to put some english on the act of striking the ball in the entry lane. Up it zoomed into the inclined play field, missing static targets and bullseyes, bouncing off all five jet bumpers and a rebound kicker, sliding past slingshots without triggering them, and rolling down towards the bottom, without scoring any points.

Gilbert let it roll down with supreme confidence, a chill maneuver, never even nudging the machine, until it fell to the left flipper. He deftly held the ball in place, trapping it on the flipper for nearly a second before juggling the ball in a "dead flipper pass" to the right flipper. He twisted his entire body into the pounce with his right index finger on the right flipper button, and with a grunt, shot the ball straight up to the top of the play field again, where it promptly hit 10 rollover buttons to the center drop target. The target, to Gilbert's surprise and amusement, consisted of three holes in the laps of the three monkeys that see no evil, hear no evil, and speak no evil. Gilbert's strategy all along was to get the ball into the left hole, see no evil, where it would pop directly into the center hole, hear no evil, and then the right hole, speak no evil, racking up more points than any other targets. The ball then dropped into one of the eject holes on the side to raise another drop target, and popped out to smash both targets before drop-ping down the side alley into the drain. The machine finally erupted in a frenzy of bells, buzzes and rings to announce another free ball.

The other kids were amazed. Gilbert seemed to ignore all the buzzes and bells, the glittering lights and other distractions. According to the back-page article about youth culture in the *News of the World*, provoked in part by the rioting in Brighton Beach, the Yank "pinball whizz kid" showed up every afternoon at the machine still in his Dartford Grammar School gold-trimmed maroon blazer and tie. Gilbert would buy some malt-soaked chips, keep to himself, and consistently slash all records on the Williams Vagabond, with a Winston dangling from his sneering lips, a popular new brand in America named after Britain's own Winston Churchill. The sneer would give way to a wry smile after winning a free ball, but then he'd light another Winston and reach for the plunger again, grunting in rhythm to the newest Lonnie Donegan skiffle hit blaring over Radio One.[177]

The pinball machine happened to be one of the Vagabonds shipped illegally to England by one of Frank Balzano's jukebox companies, but Gilbert didn't know that. Pinball, banned in many places around the world, persisted in provincial bowling alleys, billiard halls, and art college hangouts. There was the outlaw romance in playing the machines. It worried his mother. Beatrice remonstrated about hoodlums who hung out at those places. It's the Devil's playpen, she would say. It's morally corrupting, a gateway to gambling. Of course she couldn't stop him.

In late summer they'd arrived in the faded Victorian seaside village of the original Margate in Kent, northeast of the medieval majesty of Canterbury Cathedral, just mother and teenage son, to find cramped quarters in her aunt's cottage. That weekend the entire peninsula, from Ramsgate to Westgate On

Sea, was invaded by East Londoners on Lambretta scooters dressed in flash custom-tailored suits, fur-collared anoraks, Cuban heels, and white jackets with side vents up to five inches long.

Gilbert caught up with some of them in a fish and chips shop, chasing this new culture in his new world. Mods, they called themselves, meaning modern. They were singing *a cappella* the Buddy Holly song "Rave On"[178] and acting cool for the sake of their male friends, but dismissive of the girls hanging around, their jaws set hard against the cruel world. He could see how obsessed they were with fashion, and how seriously they took their music. It was *their* music. Mad, they were, with everything and everybody, not accepting that they would have to eventually act like adults. Pure mod was about being one step ahead of everyone else. What you wore last week was no longer flash. The dance steps changed from minute to minute. Being cool was more important than anything. Cool for its own sake; even just *trying* to be cool was cool. The "faces" were the leaders of cool, and the "tickets" were followers.

Above all, Gilbert wanted to be cool. Think yourself to be cool, and you become cool; others see how cool you are, and it makes you even cooler. The entire purpose of a teenager's life is to be cool.

Cool, even in the face of violence. Some of the tough uncool local kids, rockers in black leather jackets and motorcycle boots, kicked the shop door in and pounced on the invaders. They rolled and tumbled out into the street, where a pitched battle was raging all around the cafés and pubs and on the beaches. Gilbert got punched before he could seek shelter under a table. It was more than just a disagreement over clothes, styles, and music. The rockers, only a few years older and stuck in a proletarian life of greasy work, motorcycles, alcohol, and Elvis-style rock-and-roll, hated these mod poufs from art college and office jobs, and didn't want them ever to be larking about *their* turf again.

More bemused than afraid, Gilbert saw how important American music was to these Brits who'd only heard its raw sources second-hand. They were bored with Cliff Richard and the other British acts that aped Elvis. They all wanted to hear the more authentic music from America, the black rhythm and blues music that most white Americans knew nothing about.

The Brits also knew next to nothing about pinball, the most popular teen game on the Boardwalk back in Atlantic City. As the odd American, pinball and authentic music were Gilbert's keys to being cool. Pinball is a lightweight's game, an underdog's game. You don't have to be smart or athletic to play it. It's a great equalizer among different skill sets and economic classes because anyone could get really good at it.

Before leaving New Jersey, Gilbert had prevailed on his mother to let him take his favorite records with him. Gilbert had raided Mad Records looking for harmonica players of all styles, but he was mindful of his father's record, so he also looked for Robert Johnson. The black woman in scarves behind the counter pointed him to a Muddy Waters record featuring a Robert Johnson song and a harmonica player named Little Walter. Within the week he was imitating Little

Walter's more rocking numbers, "Juke", "My Babe",[179] and "Mellow Down Easy", and had picked up on the lazy, behind the beat style of Jimmy Reed, who wore a harmonica in a rack around his neck while playing guitar.

Margate was temporary. Beatrice wanted employment, peace of mind, and a decent school for Gilbert. Her aunt had pointed west, down the Thanet Way through ranks of indistinguishable suburbs toward South London, and they had settled in Dartford amidst shopping centers, squat terraced streets, and commuter rail stations about thirty minutes from Victoria Station. Though Gilbert hadn't taken the usual Eleven-plus exams, his American status and some behind-the-scenes maneuvering by his mother placed him in Dartford Grammar School rather than the mediocre state-sponsored secondary modern. Gilbert navigated his way through a strange terrain of ritualized athletics, ceremonial speeches, masters in gowns, house captains, societies, and secret clubs. By the second year, Gilbert had finally made a few friends among the clandestine smokers who gathered during breaks in the downstairs loo, united in a common need to show cool. Pop stars, movie actors, and television personalities all smoked. Smoking gave them a look of thoughtful contemplation and a way to fill the anxious silences between conversations.

One of the older kids, Dick Taylor, smoking a Player's Weights, had started singing the Roy Orbison song "Only the Lonely"[180] that had recently topped the charts, and the other smokers joined in. Gilbert surprised them by joining in on harmonica, matching the singer note for note. At the end of the song, he added as a coda the riff from Jimmy Reed's "Ain't That Loving You Baby".[181] The juxtaposition of these songs attracted a friend of Dick's, Michael Jagger, to join in the applause.

Afterwards Gilbert pulled out a Winston and leered in utter coolness.

"So you're the Yank, the pinball wizard," said Jagger. "Where did you learn how to play that?"

Gilbert looked up at him with a sneer. Jagger was older. But his skinny frame draped in a loose cardigan bordered on effeteness, and his somnolent eyes, retroussé nose, and wide sagging lips locked in a scornful grimace, suggested weakness, even vulnerability, and certainly gullibility. Gilbert was not intimidated, but rather attracted to Jagger's cool way of flouting Dartford's dress regulations, substituting French slip-on moccasins for the prescribed black lace-up shoes. "I learned a lot of stuff, back in America, before I got here," replied Gilbert, puffing away on his Winston. "Had a rock 'n' roll band back there. We played the summer resorts in New Jersey."

"Rock 'n' roll?" Jagger sniggered in distaste.

"That's just what the kids wanted," countered Gilbert with a bit too much distance for someone just barely a teenager himself. "When we practiced, we'd play country blues, and rhythm and blues. I got some rare records I brought with me from America."

Unconvinced, Dick asked him, "You know Chuck Berry?"

"Of course. You know Bo Diddley?" And on it went.

Later that day Michael and Dick visited Gilbert's home and listened to a number of records, including the Robert Johnson disc from his father's trunk. Despite the age difference they formed a secret blues club. Jagger borrowed Gilbert's *Best of Muddy Waters* long-player to learn how to sing "I Can't Be Satisfied",[182] a song that echoed his attitude of never getting satisfaction, and "Rollin' Stone", a song that flitted in the back of his mind as the *reason* why he would never be satisfied.

* * *

It was, always, all about records. Months later, Jagger was carrying that record and *Rockin' at the Hops*, a Chuck Berry record, when he bumped into his childhood pal, Keith Richards, at the Dartford train station. Newly enrolled at the London School of Economics, Jagger had affected a broad Cockney accent and a vaguely bohemian style, arming himself with words like "capitalism" and "proletariat" and dropping "Mike" for "Mick" to identify more with the working class. Keith was feeding cockatoos pep pills, setting fires in refuse bins, and generally rampaging about at Sidcup Art College. They hadn't seen each other in years, and the talk about music led to afternoon practice sessions. It seems that music, once again, could bridge the gap and forge a friendship between polar-opposite personalities from different classes.

Gilbert took a perverse interest in Keith, a thin, slouching creature with a bullet head that accentuated protuberant ears, and a raw red nose and blistered lips that made him look pinched and cold in any weather. Keith lived in the council housing project on the wrong side of Dartford. An arrogant teddy boy with a chip on his shoulder, Keith would spit in his beer to prevent others from drinking it. At twelve he'd been chosen for the school choir, one of the three best sopranos, and the teachers would let him out of class for choir practice. But when his voice broke at thirteen, he was kicked out of the choir; they also demoted him to repeat a year at school because he hadn't learned his math.

Keith's anger grew, though he didn't show emotion, couldn't show emotion or talk much at all, because why bother? No matter what he did, they would fuck him over. He would never whine about it. But no fucking way was he going to be agreeable. No more haircuts, no more regulation flannels. He started wearing tight blue jeans, winkle picker shoes, the same denim jacket every day, and a violet shirt that never seemed to get washed. Anything to annoy them.

He landed at Sidcup Art College, where his father hoped he would eventually learn a useful trade, a last chance for a teen with failing grades to learn commercial art for the advertising industry. Instead, he incessantly practiced Scotty Moore licks from Elvis records. It was the sound, a totally different way of delivering a song, stripped down, burnt, no bullshit, no violins or ladies' choruses. The American music was far more interesting than Britain's first rocker, Tommy Steele, whose records seemed so tinny and insubstantial. By the time he reached Sidcup he had started to imitate Chuck Berry's bare sound. He was mystified by it, by how it was done, and how it could sound like that. So hip and cool. Music from the past, yet way ahead of its time. And so he searched, more and more, for authenticity.

Despite the difference in age, Gilbert knew more about the authentic American blues than any of them, and was occasionally invited to sit in on harmonica. Jagger showed no interest in guitar and would sing diffidently until he could find a singer to mimic, such as Richie Valens. Keith was a more visceral rhythm guitarist than Gilbert's brother Reggie, slicing through Berry riffs with ease and perfect timing.

"Timing is everything." Johnny B dropped by on leave from a Parnes tour, in part to partake in another Beatrice breakfast, this time crumpets, fat greasy slabs of English bacon, black pudding, and scones. "But it takes a break, to get noticed. Do you have a singer?"

At Johnny's urging, Gilbert talked to Jagger, who'd named the band Little Boy Blue and the Blue Boys, about putting together a tape and sending it to Johnny's friend Alexis Korner. With Gilbert manning the reel-to-reel, they captured a ragged version of Chuck Berry's "Little Queenie"[183]. Johnny B was impressed.

* * *

"Cornell has been here for a while now, looking for white musicians that can play rhythm and blues." Johnny led Gilbert to a dark corner at the pinball arcade, shifting his gaze about as if someone might be listening. "I've been working with him. It's, like, some kind of experiment."

"Is he in touch with my dad?"

Johnny winced. "I don't know." He looked hard at Gilbert. "Look, you can't trust anybody, not anybody over thirty. Not back in America and not here, either."

"Freddie was over thirty."

"And look what happened to him," Johnny pointed out.

"Are you saying…"

"I'm saying, watch your back, Bert. Whoever came after Freddie, they're not going to stop. Look, this experiment, Cornell says they'll always be coming after him, like they came after Freddie, and came after me, and probably came after your dad, too."

"But I thought…" Gilbert hesitated. How far could he take this? "I thought *your* dad was involved."

"He is," sighed Johnny. "But I think he had orders to be in the radio station, to make it up to look like a mob hit. I think Freddie was already dead when he got there."

"Well then, who…"

"I don't know. Maybe Reggie knows something. Have you heard from him?"

Gilbert shot him a look. He didn't want to say why. He'd just had enough of his older brother. All that teasing and condescending attitude. Yes, Reggie had written to him a few times from Harvard, he told Johnny. The last letter started out as "Dear Beave" as usual, but had quickly grown ominous and as serious as the diary of Anne Frank. *I've learned more about our father, and who, or what, is pursuing him, and why Freddie was murdered.*

Johnny B grabbed Gilbert's arm. "And he told you about his power?"

"What power?"

"*See no evil.* That's Reggie's power. He should have made the connection by now, he has the Book and everything. Mine's *hear no evil.*"

"What's it mean?" And what power do I have, thought Gilbert.

"I don't know what it means for Reggie. Maybe he can see into the future or something. But for me, it means *hearing* the future. Helping bands get started."

"Well, what's it mean for *me?*"

"Dunno, Bert. Yours must be *speak no evil.* Or maybe it's *sing no evil.* I bet it's something to do with Cornell. At least that's why I'm here. Cornell and I, we got our own thing now. 'Our thing,'" Johnny gestured with his hands, each with two fingers curling into quotes. "*Cosa Nostra.* It's the new music, man! It's getting that rhythm and blues thing *over* on them, filling the old jazz clubs, bringing out the *black* thing, man. Cornell's got bluesmen coming in from Chicago, from St. Louis. Not twenty miles from here, in London, Muddy Waters is in town."

A few weeks after Gilbert sent off the Blue Boys tape, Johnny B rang him up to tell him about a new club opening in Ealing, west of London. "It's a blues club, can you believe that? Probably the only one in all of Britain. And dig this. The bandleader's a friend, and he lets amateur singers sit in, so bring your singer." Although Gilbert was underage for a drinking club, Johnny could get him in if he carried equipment.

Gilbert rang up Jagger about it. "Think about it," Gilbert told him. "People are out there, playing the blues, to an audience, for money!" Jagger gathered Dick Taylor and Keith Richards to catch a train up to London.

* * *

In the smoky downstairs room between the ABC Bakery and the jewelry shop adorned with a marquee of a piece of cardboard with "Ealing Club" scrawled on it in crayon, Alexis Korner, looking dangerous in a white business shirt and tie, sat in a rickety chair on a tiny stage under a grubby tarpaulin canopy fingering a Spanish guitar. Flanking him were Cyril Davies, the burly car mechanic in pleated trousers sweating through a harmonica solo; Jack Bruce, a fresh-faced youngster in a Scottish sweater twirling a stand-up bass; and Charlie Watts, a taciturn, nattily dressed young man with an old face, brush-stroking the drums. They called themselves Blues Incorporated. Invited to join them for a song, Jagger, looking every inch the London School of Economics student in his white poplin shirt, half-unknotted tie, and chunky bohemian cardigan, stuttered and stammered his way through the opening of Chuck Berry's "Around and Around",[184] a bit out of key and nearly paralyzed with fright.

The other musicians were bemused at the choice of the Berry tune, its simple vamp, far below their caliber, and Cyril actually felt sorry for the kid whose love of the blues had taken him far beyond his limitations. But the audience applauded, and Jagger was offered the role of second-string vocalist for the gigs when Long John Baldry couldn't make it, for a fee of fifteen shillings, plus beer. Alexis liked the way Jagger threw his head around and how is hair shook when he did it, moving quite excessively for typical student haircut.

The next few weekends, Gilbert, Jagger, Richards, and Taylor visited the Korner residence in Bayswater before the Ealing gigs, to sip Bobbie Korner's tea and hear Alex rave about all about the blues greats that he and his friend Cornell had brought to London. They heard about how Big Bill Broonzy had slept in the Korner kitchen and woke up thinking he was in Paris, and how Muddy Waters had been confused about what to play to these English traditional jazz audiences mixed with students and teddy boys who wanted rock and roll. Should it be the Delta country acoustic blues by himself, or set up his electric band? Korner had advised Muddy that the blues purists in jazz wanted the authentic Delta sound. "The jazz people are hostile to rock n' roll. They consider it a fad, not real music."

Keith Richards weighed in. "Really, rock 'n' roll lost its edge when they put Chuck Berry in jail, man. Now it's all this tame stuff, Cliff Richard *shite*, imitating Elvis."

Jagger agreed. "It's too middle-class," he lisped. "What we want is the real blues."

Alexis roared at Jagger. "Mike, *you're* middle class! An LSE student no less."

"It's 'Mick' now. I don't like 'Mike' or 'Michael'."

"Oh, you prefer Mick now, do you?" Keith jabbed him. "Bohemian now, are you?"

And so it went, each weekend, until the night of April 7, 1962. Keith, Mick, and Dick showed up at the Ealing Club, and Johnny B had brought Gilbert in through the back. They gathered at the bar. Brian Jones, who'd sat in with Blues

Incorporated on guitar a few times, also appeared with Paul Pond, and were invited to join the stage as Elmo Lewis and Paul Jones.

Brian, in a dark suit and even darker oversized sunglasses, cautiously held his acoustic guitar with electric pickup, and peered out at the audience holding his breath. He turned his back to them and counted out the song with Charlie the drummer, who'd softened his disgusted visage to give this kid from the hills a chance. Brian knew that these London musicians thought him to be a pretentious little sod from Cheltenham, and Charlie had all but confirmed it, but he would show them.

Brian adopted a stance facing sideways on the stage, away from the audience. With no warning to the band, he slid his socket wrench up the guitar's neck to stinging, piercing heights and back down to degrading depths, improvising an opening to "Dust My Broom",[185] the Elmore James classic.

Gilbert, entranced by the cool, detached Brian, poked Jagger at the bar. Johnny pointed at the stage. Keith suddenly came alive, yelling "It's Elmo James! It's fuckin' Elmo James!" Gilbert didn't have time to correct him, that Elmore James was a black bluesman, not a white Englishman with blond hair. They were all transfixed by Brian as he shook the song inside out and sliced it up to serve it. The audience cheered, and Brian felt vindicated. He turned to face them and bowed three times, grinning like a fool.

Whooping and hollering, the group at the bar caught the attention of a shadowy character who materialized out of a dark corner of the club, an ageless black man in a gray pin-stripe suit, a black Stetson hat, and Edwin Clapp shoes, with rubies lacing his garters. The man took off his hat, bowed, tucked a black cane under his arm, and smiled widely, flashing several gold molars and a gold front tooth embossed with a fish head.

"Cornell!" Gilbert gasped.

"Cornell Woodrow, at your service." Acknowledging Johnny B, and then smiling at Gilbert, he said in a voice steeped in coffee and dark chocolate, "Your father sends his best."

* * *

"So he's alive? Where is he?"

"Last time I saw him he was very much alive," chuckled Cornell as if Gilbert's concern was unimportant. "And you know I can't tell you where he is. Not yet, anyway."

Brian Jones bounded off the stage and came over to say hello to Cornell and Johnny B. "Hey man, you were right, the spirit of Robert Johnson."

Gilbert grabbed Johnny's arm, remembering the records from his father. "What's he talking about?"

Cornell put his arm around Brian's shoulders and turned to Johnny and Gilbert, including them all in the conversation. "A strong musical influence. It can be like a spirit invasion." The others gathered around to listen to Cornell's dark, smooth voice. "The musician starts to adopt the same muscular reflexes, to replicate the instrument patterns, to play the guitar lick or the sax riff exactly the same way, or to sing the same way. The musician begins to *think* the same way, apply the same theories to life. Elmore James idolized Robert Johnson to the point of duplicating the way he played, with an unusually strong *concentrated* effort. Even *living* like him, on the road." And then Cornell patted Brian on the back. "And you can evoke Robert Johnson's spirit until that spirit inhabits *you*."

Keith, enthralled with Brian's playing, whispered to Jagger something about a band. Brian, ever aware of competition, took the initiative. He announced to everyone that he was forming a band and about to hold auditions.

"Great way to catch birds," remarked Dick Taylor, and Mick Jagger grinned from ear to ear.

Keith eyed the room suspiciously, looking to see if there really were any girls in the club. "Sure of that, mate? What would birds want with the blues?"

Cornell's belly laugh brought everyone to attention. "Rhythm and blues? My boy, it's about women. It's *always* about women." And then he launched into an Irish singsong, punctuating each line with his cane:

There once was a man from East Kent
Whose tool was so long that it bent.
To save her some trouble
He folded it double
And instead of coming… he went!

Guffaws all around. "You boys'll have no trouble catching birds," Cornell chuckled. "When you learn to put it *out* there, when you can conjure up that secret power, when you get that *mojo hand* and break out, that's when you'll become dangerous. And women *love* dangerous men! But watch out. The overlords get anxious. Be careful." And with a tap to his Stetson, he was off.

Jagger, Richards, Taylor, and Gilbert left the club mystified by this Cornell character, but certainly in awe of Brian Jones. If anyone was going to make it, it would be Brian, the consummate musician.

* * *

One day Gilbert's mother trembled and cried as she shooed him off to school. The morning and midmorning break was typical, smoking in the downstairs lavatory and talking about the latest records. On the way back to class, the hall monitor handed Gilbert a note to visit the office.

Inside, the headmaster eyed him suspiciously. On the desk was a confidential "closed" report with the emblem of a precinct in New Jersey. Gilbert squirmed in the wooden chair. Out the window, in the distance past the red brick ramparts of the school, he could see the blurred skyline of London. He was now in the serious world of adults. He felt shamed by his childish action of two years previous. The indecent exposure was a scarlet letter that had crossed the Atlantic to find him.

The headmaster gave him the frozen smile of a bureaucrat and began a lighthearted conversation. "Your mother tells me that you waste all of your spare time playing those infernal pinball machines."

Gilbert slumped in his chair and said nothing. The headmaster looked down his nose at this precocious fourteen-year-old. "I called you in here for several reasons. You know why. We don't go for long hair on boys here," referring to Gilbert's blond mane that bristled around his ears. "And we don't go for smoking in the lavatories. You know smoking is forbidden at school."

Gilbert grunted.

"Now. Let me have your cigarettes."

Gilbert nonchalantly handed over a semi-crushed pack of Winstons, and started to get up.

"No, sit down. There's another reason I called you in here. I want you to meet someone. He knows your family."

At a signal from his intercom, in walked a lanky, athletic man in a gray flannel suit, thin face, angular nose, and scrutinizing eyebrows. The headmaster introduced him as Professor Cravingston, from Harvard, visiting with colleagues from the Royal Geographical Society. "He came all the way down from London to see you. He is counseling your brother at Harvard, and he knew your father."

"Indeed," said this man Cravingston, producing a photograph of a younger version of his father wearing spectacles, a rumpled suit, and a tattered fedora, standing on the banks of the Nile with a jaunty adventurer in a seaman's cap that looked vaguely like Cravingston.

"Your father and I worked together once, for the Society," said Cravingston cheerily. "We even explored the source of the Nile River." He got closer, and then he bent forward and up into Gilbert's face, so close that Gilbert winced. "So, you have more than a passing interest in archaeology?"

"Not really," said Gilbert, awkwardly leaning back away from him. Archaeology?

"Hmmm. Well, why not?" Cravingston gave him a broad, dazzling smile, then backed off. He started pacing the office, which Gilbert found annoying. "Did you know your father was obsessed with ancient civilizations? The Atlantis legends?"

"Uh... no?"

"Have you seen this?" Cravingston stopped at the headmaster's desk and laid down his briefcase. He pulled out a *Life* magazine. Its cover showed an oceanographer named Jacques Piccard with a bathyscaphe. He opened it to a color spread of Piccard's boat and crew, and pulled out enlarged photographs of the bottom of the sea. "These were classified by the United States Navy. They're from the floor of the Mariana Trench, in the western North Pacific. You can just about make out the grid of streets. Looks like a city, doesn't it? And right there, the remnants of a pyramid. And it's right where Churchward placed his lost continent of Mu."

"Mu." Gilbert blinked.

"Yes." Cravingston blinked right back.

The murky shapes in the photographs revealed nothing. The crosshatch pattern shimmered at the bottom like the exposed skeletal framework of a zeppelin. The spongy blob could be a decayed pyramid, or it could just be a spongy blob.

"I'm here for a few weeks. We're giving a report to the Society about these findings. Your father investigated Churchward's theories. Don't you think he would want to see these?"

"I guess," Gilbert replied, cautiously.

"But you don't know where to find him."

Gilbert just shrugged. "Maybe you should ask my mother."

"Ah, yes," nodded Cravingston. "Your mother..." he paused in reverence. "She tells me that you like to play the harmonica, is that right?"

Gilbert looked down at his dusty Oxfords. The man had pronounced the word "harmonica" as if it were a toy, a prop for one of those novelty songs. Gilbert's face reddened, and even though he wasn't looking at the headmaster, he could feel the heat from the headmaster's glare.

"And you're in one of those 'beat' groups, with your school friends, am I right?"

Gilbert glared back at Cravingston defiantly. "We're rhythm and blues, and we're a band."

"That so! Well, let me be the first to congratulate you on choosing an American style of music." Cravingston started pacing again, annoying Gilbert further. "And let me also say that I think you should continue this pursuit. Yes, I know, you probably thought I was going to try to talk you out of it." Cravingston shot a glance at the headmaster, who looked quizzical and annoyed at the same time. "But really, I want you to go as far as you can with this band, group, or whatever you call it. And I'd like to know how it's going, and which of these groups you think are going to be popular. If you help me, I can help *you* by making it easier for you at school."

Another quick glance at the headmaster showed Gilbert that Cravingston was clearly in charge. "And I can explain things to your mother, so that you can go up to London more often and check on these other groups. All you have to do is report back to me every month or so. Tell me about your progress. That's all I ask."

* * *

With a few pounds pilfered from his day job at Whiteley's, Brian Jones arranged rehearsals in the back room at Bricklayer's Arms. Ian Stewart arrived on his racing cycle looking nothing at all like a blues pianist, all muscular and thickset with his long, pugnacious jaw, wearing leather shorts and munching a pork pie. But he could slam out boogie-woogie piano riffs, even while keeping an eye on his cycle outside the window. Geoff Bradford, a blues purist, played lead guitar in the style of T-Bone Walker.

Together they made a noise that was altogether insignificant until the tornado of Blue Boys appeared, mostly the whirlwind of the gangly Keith looking to plug in somewhere while Dick Taylor hefted his new electric bass and Mick lounged around with his somnolent, slightly arrogant grin. Gilbert sat in back nursing a clean set of Hohner Marine Band harps in the essential blues keys.

Gilbert, absolutely entranced by Brian, could see that Brian was increasingly annoyed at the other members' lack of competence on their instruments, save Geoff, who could play very well but wouldn't stray from the tones and inflections of his bluesman heroes to play something as mundane as Chuck Berry riffs. On the other hand, Ian Stewart, or "Stu", could play anything on the piano and get along with anybody. The first drummer couldn't find the off-beat, couldn't pick up on that Jimmy Reed lazy style. The second drummer overplayed everything as if were auditioning for jazz band. Charlie Watts, Korner's drummer, was the one Brian wanted but he couldn't afford him.

Cornell and Johnny B appeared at the auditions, and together helped Brian make his decisions. He had all but decided to cut Geoff out, and work with Keith to intertwine their guitar licks. Johnny recommended a rock solid bass player, a former member of the Cliftons who called himself Bill Wyman. Typically, Brian was more interested in Wyman's huge amplifier that could accommodate several guitars.

But Brian wasn't satisfied until he could get Charlie Watts. Cornell pulled this off by convincing Alexis to pair Wyman with Watts, just to see whether they could sync up. Under Cornell's spell, and with coaching by Johnny B, the two locked into a monster groove that foretold the band's future, an edgy mix of blues and London fog driven maniacally by the fused rhythm machine of

Charlie and Bill. Johnny didn't even need to supply the hashish to convince Alexis to counsel Charlie to join.

By the time the final lineup had its first gigs, Brian had named the band "The Rollin' Stones" in honor of the high priests of West Africa who had carried the sacred stones in their stomachs when they were taken as slaves across the sea.

Survival was the utmost concern. Brian had been kicked out of three flats in London in little over a year, and Keith was still stuck out in the suburbs with his mom. Mick, still unconvinced that music could pay the rent, was attending the London School of Economics. Subconsciously the three of them knew they needed to bond, so they pulled together to live in a rangy, rundown flat in Edith Grove. Brian's only possession was a combination radio and record player. With Mick off studying, the decrepit flat was left to Brian and Keith to play guitars, nick the neighbors' beer bottles to get the thruppence deposit, and raid the markets for potatoes. Brian chortled about how they occupied the middle floor between respectability and vice; in the top floor were two male schoolteachers who'd throw Duke Ellington parties, and on the bottom were four aged hookers from Liverpool.

For the first time in his life, Brian Jones had a purpose. He'd even given his roving eye for women a rest, and pushed for the band. Keith and the others considered him barmy, but Brian was on a crusade to get the band on the stage in a club and be paid, and most importantly, to be billed as a "rhythm and blues" band. In the months that followed, Brian cajoled club managers to accept them, many times meeting them eye-to-eye with a searching, unyielding stare and a vulnerable mouth suggesting sex. Not that he actually had to give anyone a blow job, but it came to close to that. The men who were promoters and in a position of power over the band's future were attracted to him, no doubt, because he seemed to cross the line somewhere. Months later, when the other band members found out that Brian had been skimming five pounds off the top of each gig for "expenses," it was just one more reason for them to be resentful of him.

* * *

At the Crawdaddy Club, the Stones began to be brilliant.

The lead singer of a band usually got all the attention, but Mick Jagger was slightly off from center, and forfeited some of the attention to Brian Jones. Mick was hunched in a sweater that was forever slipping off his right shoulder like a tea gown, his smear of a mouth parroting a black man's words as his opaque eyes searched for his reflection in the imaginary mirrors surrounding him.

But it was Brian, bouncing around the stage with a cool insouciance, who agitated the crowd with his stinging guitar, injecting the airless claustrophobic club atmosphere with a malevolent energy all his own. He moved with the rhythm all the time, making it part of his body, playing his body so that the guitar was merely a receptacle for his energy that translated it into musical notes. Even the boys were pulled into Brian's aura, while their girlfriends fantasized about his disturbingly seductive eyes. Brian teased the audience, dancing forward to leer at them and snap a tambourine in their faces to get them aroused. He would stick his tongue out in a nasty way to make the girls scream. Some of the boys would then try to land a punch on him, but he danced back, continually playing, never missing a note, whipping his slide guitar into a frenzy on "I'm a King Bee"[186] that upstaged Mick's singing.

Mick began to resent Brian's popularity and castigate Brian for his love of the limelight, but he also noted the effect of Brian's body moving to the rhythm. Keith, who usually stood stock still while playing and didn't really want the audience near him, was noncommittal about Brian's popularity and in any case considered Brian, the musical pioneer, to be the leader. But Keith enjoyed a good prank. So while Brian remained on stage after the encore to bask in the glory of the screaming fans, Mick and Keith got the others to split, leaving Brian surrounded by the growing mob at the backstage door. Suddenly frightened, Brian swung his guitar to clear a path, and ducked and bulldozed his way out to the back alley, losing his jacket and shirt and a few tufts of hair in the process. Chased by the very fame he craved.

"When you've got three thousand birds in front of you that are ripping off their panties and throwing them at you, you realize what an awesome power you have unleashed," Brian boasted to Gilbert later, who couldn't help remembering the glimpse he'd had of Brian's rather large penis in the shared bathroom back in Edith Grove. How many of those girls had grabbed hold of it? Gilbert was enchanted by the prospects of becoming a player, and had come to emulate Brian. Like Brian, he wore tight black jeans, black roll-neck sweaters, and Anello & Davide black Spanish boots with Cuban heels. Gilbert's blond haircut made him look like Brian's protégé.

"You know, the bluesman never wanted to compromise, but he did," Brian continued. "He played the chitlin circuit whether he liked it or not," he said unconvincingly, as he had no idea what the "chitlin circuit" was, he'd just read about it on album covers. "And so do *we*. It's not that we want to be famous. It's just that we've *got* to be famous, in order to do what we're doing. To plant that seed. And that's our deal, the one we've made, at the crossroads."

Sure, thought Gilbert. He envied the way Brian could glad-hand his way through the backstage area, a preening peacock, gregarious, artistic, winking at girls and even older women. Someday, Gilbert hoped, they'd be throwing their panties at him. In the sex-charged atmosphere that surrounded the band, anything was possible, including getting laid at 14.

* * *

Maggie May, a shapely brunette in her late twenties hooked on the youthful energy of these club shows and eager to tease, even possibly deflower, the most popular of the teenage boys, had crawled out of Brian's side of the bed at Edith Grove to pose thoughtfully in front of the mirror, wearing only panties. I'm a king bee, thought Gilbert, buzzing around your hive. He watched from the doorway as she caressed her perky breasts and ran her hand over her slightly bulging belly. Her flimsy panties barely concealed the smooth curves of her gorgeous ass. She was posing for him! The moment had come. Gilbert modestly shut the door behind him, nearly lost his hard-on completely as he fumbled with his belt. That's when she turned to face him, nipples at attention, and with a knowing smile she reached for his cock inside his pants and started to stroke him… He came before he'd even got out of his underwear, but her tender fingers brought him up again, straight and to the point. She helped him fumble through the awkwardness of losing his virginity.

At some point, having released much of his nervous energy, Gilbert grew stronger and more confident. He thought about how thrusting was the opposite of pulling the plunger in pinball, but required similar finesse. And the more he licked her nipples, the more points he scored with her, as if he were bouncing a pinball off the jet bumpers. Foreplay was a process of hitting a few targets and slingshots first, and then letting the ball drop, letting it drop nearly all the way before trapping it on the flipper. It's like *defying time*, and then you flip it to the right flipper, it's called a 'dead pass', and then you hit that right flipper! This is how you get across to her, get her to come, light up her center drop target. She comes, bells, buzzers, rings! Smash all the targets, perform like a sonofabitch, hold it back until you can't anymore, then drop the ball down the side alley into the drain, leaving her wasted.

Gilbert came away with a newfound confidence. The next few weeks at school were surreal. He knew it was hopeless, but he could see Maggie May's face in every window, smell her body with every breath.

Back again at the Crawdaddy, Brian saw the starstruck look in Gilbert's eyes as he searched for Maggie, and took him aside to give him the benefit of his experience. Brian explained to him how any woman would be his, without even asking, if only he would learn to be seductively, extraordinarily charming. How to greet people by repeating their first and last names, and then inserting their first names in your conversations, so that they would be flattered by the personal attention and recognition. Girls wanted his eyes to undress them. Boys, especially mods, wanted to be around him to be infected by his unbridled, evangelical enthusiasm. Brian said that he should turn aloof at the right moment, leaving them all feeling like they'd been in the presence of a superstar.

Gilbert learned another trick from Brian, and one day he tried it out on the train to London. The woman stood with her back to him, facing the window across from him, carefully adjusting her sweater. She was middle-aged, and seemed mild-mannered, not at all on the make in any way, just minding her own business. Gilbert stared at her back, and then slowly let his gaze fall to her bottom that was vaguely framed by her skirt. She squirmed as if she could feel his gaze. Moaning under his breath, he bore a hole into her ass with his staring eyes, and she started to twitch and react, absentmindedly scratching the left cheek. When she turned to look behind her, she held a slight smile of interest, but unsure of what, exactly. Gilbert averted his eyes at just the right moment. She didn't quite know what was happening, glancing this way and that, but she straightened up and thrust her chest a bit, putting her breasts front and center, as if ready for anything.

With newfound confidence, a power defying time, Gilbert swaggered as he carried equipment for the Stones into the Crawdaddy, checking out all the older girls, imagining fucking every one he sees. When it was over, he was back on the train to Dartford with a hard-on that wouldn't quit, and dreary weeks of school to get through before the next break.

* * *

Less than a month later, Johnny B had news from Liverpool about an explosion of bands, and the Beatles were leading the charge. "Turn on your radio!" Johnny B shouted at him over the phone as "Please Please Me"[187] hit number one. "And go check out the Alan Price Combo, they're calling themselves the Animals. And you should see the lead singer of the Yardbirds, he looks just like you and Brian."

Gilbert's mother had taken a new job in Shepherd's Bush and had moved him to Acton Grammar, where he was once again the odd Yank with the pinball moves, Winston cigarettes, and blues harmonicas in several keys. Young John Entwistle was impressed, and in turn let Gilbert show Johnny B his homemade mahogany bass guitar. In the Detours, now calling themselves the High Numbers, Entwistle played thunderous bass runs loudly, front and center, driving not only the rhythm but also defining the melody.

One night out in Shepherd's Bush with Johnny B, the guitar player for the High Numbers, Pete Townshend, a gangly, pimply-faced kid with a long nose and a pointy head, approached Gilbert before the show. "You're the pinball wizard, right? I hear you can play harmonica. Why don't you give it a go?" Proudly, as Johnny watched, Gilbert took the stage to sit in on "I'm the Face",[188] a song about the "faces" who set the styles and chose the dance steps for the "third-class tickets" who wanted to be mod.

Gilbert was aware that the birds were watching his every move. He could feel their eyes on him, and he began to twist his body as he played the harmonica, languidly rolling his rear end the way he saw Brian do it, and peering out from underneath his sheepish blond bangs. At first it seemed pretentious and cute, not something a man would do... but gradually the rhythm took hold of his body. He grew euphoric as his body settled into the rhythm. He used his body to project the rhythm and the melody, shifting with the notes, raising his eyebrows, shaking his head, crouching down as the notes tumbled, rising up as the notes reached a crescendo.

He realized how playing the harmonica was really playing his body — he sucked air in and blew it out with the rhythm, using his diaphragm and entire body. He selected the holes for pitches with his tongue and lips, and used his powerful mouth muscles to bend the notes. The harmonica was just there to translate his body energy. And he could control the feedback that emanated from the speakers when he subtly pointed the microphone at them sideways. Girls swung their hips in rapt attention, cocking their heads each time he drew out a bent blues note, swooning when he dangled a note into caustic feedback. Gilbert could feel the sap rise, he could almost taste them out there, hungry for him, expecting him to come at any moment.

Afterwards, over a pint with Pete and Nik Cohn, a young journalist from the music trade press, Gilbert explained his pinball theory of sexual prowess.

"You need some confidence to start with an opening line," said Gilbert, "which is like pulling the plunger and releasing it."

Nik joked about how so many guys would just let the ball drop. "But still, anyone can play pinball, and anyone can become a great lover."

Pete, the moody literate High Number, disagreed. "Not everyone," he announced prophetically. "Some of us are deaf to the sounds of the machine, dumbfounded by the way it works, and blind to all the flashing lights and targets."

Gilbert could feel a bit of resentment coming from these older kids. They always talked about catching birds, but 14-year-old Gilbert was already a man because he'd had an older woman. He had mastered Brian's attitude of not needing to do anything but act in a charming way, and the girls all wanted to catch *him*. The roles were reversed. He had only to say a few words, and the girls, most of them older, would swoon over him.

Gilbert didn't realize at first that it was this resentment coming from the other males of the tribe that prevented him from sitting in with the band again.

* * *

Brian Jones had heard from Pete that Gilbert had made quite a debut on harmonica. At the Stones' first recording session, Gilbert stammered out an explanation for his method of bending notes, but Brian had had enough talk.

"Mick's been trying to play one for weeks. Let me try it." He snatched the harmonica out of Gilbert's hand. Gilbert pointed out that a harmonica player routinely slobbers all over his instrument. Brian just smiled back at him and wouldn't stop playing it until he could completely mimic Gilbert's style.

That very same afternoon Gilbert watched as Brian Jones played a flawless riff that Gilbert had shown him, on "Come On"[189] to accompany the simple

Chuck Berry guitar strumming. The next day, Brian played a harmonica solo on "I Want to be Loved"[190] that took Gilbert's breath away, better than any lead guitar could have done to capture the emotion of the song.

Gilbert was amazed at how every musical instrument came so easy to him. Brian's guitar swaggered through "Everybody Needs Somebody to Love"[191] and melded in perfect rhythm with Keith's lines in the sparkling "You Can't Catch Me",[192] galloping along at twice the speed of the Chuck Berry original. Gilbert could just see Brian grinning as he effortlessly pulled these riffs off.

Under Johnny B's influence, the recording engineer placed the bass front and center in the mono mix, and Bill Wyman, who'd been coached by Johnny himself, rose to the challenge. His bass and Charlie Watts' drumming, inspired by bebop, came to define the foundation of what came to be known as "rock" music. No other band could put it across quite so effectively, like thunder and lightning, and total immersion in the sweat and blood of carnal desires.

Lennon came away from a Stones show during the first year, murmuring to the other Beatles, "They really know how to play those guitars, especially Brian." That's the damn thing about them, Lennon pointed out. They looked so surly and unruly, ready to pick a fight, but they could really play their instruments better than any of the Mersey beats, better even than the blues purists in London. The band had substance and carried a great weight, the weight of playing well.

But Alexis Korner pointed out the fact of the matter: there is only so far you can go in the London club scene. If you stay in that club circuit you eventually get constipated. You go round and round so many times, and then suddenly you're not the hip band anymore. The High Numbers would take over, or the Yardbirds. Mick agreed, and Keith went along on principle, because they wanted to get out of the clubs and into the larger ballrooms, where the kids were. They were still sleeping in the back of the van. Just an engine, one passenger seat in front, and all that equipment, guitar cases piled on top of drums and amplifiers.

In short, they had to learn some pop songs for the teenagers, and maybe write some of their own. Keith and Brian protested. They wanted to play rhythm and blues, period. But Mick saw how easily John Lennon and Paul McCartney had knocked off the number "I Wanna Be Your Man",[193] finishing it off right there in the studio as they stood around watching. In a moment of generosity befitting the new kings of pop, Lennon and McCartney gave the song to the fledgling Stones.

Still, Brian had found a way to twist the song into a stinging slide-guitar blues.[194] Listening to them side-by-side, the two versions reflected the personalities of the two bands, with the Beatles as the wholesome boys next door mooning about being a girl's lover, and the Stones as the wicked beatniks down the street ready to rape her.

Brian's point of view about the blues was eventually vindicated when their version of the old Howlin' Wolf standard, "Little Red Rooster",[195] flew up the charts on the wings of Brian's howling slide guitar. Through it all, Brian and Keith developed the early Stones signature sound, interleaving guitars to the point that neither could tell which was playing lead and which rhythm. They had listened closely to the teamwork in Jimmy Reed records, and how they could play together with two guitars and make it sound like four or five.

Careening through the countryside, the Stones would arrive at the outskirts of a village knowing full well that the populace awaited them. Girls on the street would point at them in hushed excitement as they drove by. Parking in the rear, they would unload the gear and settle into cigarettes and pints in the dressing room, enduring the excruciating boredom of nonchalant conversation with some locals and their girlfriends as they awaited their hour of destiny. And through all of that, their ascendance to god-hood was assured. They would walk out on that stage to have every pose, gesture, swish of hair, every pore, every molecule of their bodies under intense scrutiny.

And then, they would start to play, and the world dropped away. Nothing feels as powerful as rising to the role of minor gods.

* * *

The group meets four times a year in different places each time; places that require a security clearance, places that people of considerable wealth and power have no problem getting into. A sort of Western Culture Appreciation Society, its members drew from the ranks of the Knights of Malta, the Freemasons, and other secret orders, even the Jesuits in a vulgar, unholy alliance. This quarter the meeting was held in the dining room of the Yale Club in Manhattan. Presidents peered down from framed portraits as they gathered with their cigars and drinks.

Cravingston led them through an impromptu welcome speech to identify the participants to each other. As he spoke the names of important people, an older man in a gray flannel suit whispered to his companion, a younger man in a three-piece pin stripe. Both wore their college ties. "We work for one another, I suppose. No ranks or titles, or even a chain of command, really."

"Really," his companion answered. "So how do you plan operations?"

"Well, we just know what has to be done, that's all. We rely on common sense."

His companion nodded. Cravingston finished, and motioned everyone to follow him. "We will now see the extent, the *damage*, that has been caused by the rogue experiment involving that black shaman Cornell Woodrow and his most recent stooge, our own Herbert Mesh, now going by the name Mention."

Cravingston led all of them through the foyer, Mumblingore bringing up the rear and chatting with the Manhattan Man. "We thought we had them with Presley, Gene Vincent, that lot. But the intelligent ones over here, and especially in New York and Boston, have moved on, and now they're listening to acoustic instruments again, what they call the 'country blues', all this jug band, calypso, and slave music, *sea shanties* for christsakes…"

"Songs of revolution," commented the Manhattan Man. "In any case, Elvis is under control. He got too famous too quickly, and the Colonel had to sidetrack him, put him the Army, in Germany, where he can prepare to make movies."

Cravingston opened a heavy wooden door that provided access to a control room overlooking a lounge and dancing parlor. Casually dressed students were sitting at tables sipping Cokes, laughing and flirting quietly, and listening to Pat Boone. The suited gentlemen filed into the control room to watch this party.

"So, as you can see, we have an orderly scene, with the kind of music we think young people like. And you can see that they do; it's a pleasant scene, one in which a boy might meet a girl, or vice-versa."

The control room voyeurs grumped and fidgeted to get a better view out the control room window at the scene.

"But what would compel these nice kids to go crazy? What I have in my hand is a record by the new British sensation, the Beatles, and what's important is not what you *hear*, which is a group of white boys with funny accents covering a rhythm and blues record by the Isley Brothers, but what you *see*, the effect this record has on these kids."

And with that, Cravingston slipped the record on the turntable with a malevolent grin. They heard a crackle and pop, three strokes of a guitar, and then…[196]

You know you make me wanna (Shout!)
Click my fingers! (Shout!)
Throw my head back! (Shout!)
Kick my heels up (Shout!)
C'mon, now! (Shout!)

The young people were suddenly up from their chairs, jumping on the tables, ties askew, jackets tossed off… They were going crazy, the girls shaking their hair loose and kicking up their heels, exploding their pent-up frustrations, and it looked just like one of those Negro revivals, with men doing backflips and women prancing about and thrusting their hips. The control room voyeurs were shocked into silence at the awesome display.

Cravingston shouted above the mayhem, "What is this impulse? Why do these white kids respond to this in such a manner?"

At the end of the song, Cravingston switched off the turntable. The young folks gathered themselves up off the floor, off the walls, and off the ceiling, and returned to their chairs.

A British operative, a member of Parliament, cleared his throat. "Our lads are just copying your negro music, and now this negro thing is popping up everywhere, infecting our popular music. It's running trad jazz right out. We thought we had some control, with trad jazz. All those banjos! Nice, clean, wholesome music. Now it's all negro wildness and dirty lyrics."

"Yes, how ironic," pointed out Mumblingore. "It all comes back to England's shores, like the original Atlantic trade, arms and goods from Liverpool to Africa, slaves from Africa to America, sugar back to England." He gave Cravingston the Eye, as if to say, what nefarious scheme are you planning now?

"And speaking of England," Manhattan Man interjected, also looking over at Cravingston. "What's going on with all this nonsense? What's all this about beetles?"

Cravingston smiled at his partner Mumblingore to silence him, and provided an explanation. "The Beatles, sir. We're directing their career, you see, like the Colonel is doing with Elvis. We think it's more useful to ride along on this bandwagon, and steer it our way. Our friends in the business," and he gestured at Tony Just and lapsed into vernacular street slang, "they just want a chance to earn, you know? And as we learned with Elvis, the merchandise business is worth a fortune."

"But they are wild, unpredictable. How can you be sure you can move this in the right direction?"

"I have a good man working on it," Cravingston replied to Manhattan Man. "The young Jew who runs a branch of the North End Music Stores in Liverpool. Epstein's his name. It was simple, really," flashing a glance at his more scientific partner Mumblingore. "No need for drugs or any of the other mind control techniques, except gentle persuasion. All I needed to do was send one of the layabouts into the store to ask for their first record, and I knew Epstein would follow up and find it. And I knew he'd be captivated by the band, once he saw them play."

"I've heard of him," interrupted the British operative. "Isn't he a homosexual?"

"Yes," Cravingston sighed, "and that should prove useful in the future. He loves his 'boys' as he calls them. But he's meticulous. He got them to clean up, dress alike, and make their music a bit more wholesome."

"Are the kids going to buy that?"

"For a while. But we're not stopping with the Beatles. There's a raft of these 'beat' groups in the Liverpool-Manchester area. And we also have a handle on those ruffians that call themselves the Rolling Stones. They're in London. They have a critical following, and other bands are trying to follow in their footsteps."

Manhattan Man blinked at him suspiciously.

"But we have a plan for them, too," Cravingston assured him. "One of Epstein's associates, Andrew Loog Oldham, just picked them up for management."

"That's his name?"

"Wants everyone to call him Loog, but that's his full name."

"Another homosexual?" The British operative seemed obsessed with this line of questioning.

"Not really, but he can put it out there, you know what I mean? He dresses up nice. But his plan, really, is to make the Rolling Stones out to be the bad guys. The opposite of the Beatles. The band for street thugs and the like."

Manhattan Man looked at him quizzically.

"So the bands, they'll compete with each other. They'll both want to get to the top of the pop charts. And with both bands locked up, we can control the scene better. Especially the merchandise."

Manhattan Man smiled. "You're turning lead into gold."

At the Crossroads

At the crossroads of Harvard and folk music, Reggie found a synthesis in radical politics. Although Marcuse's theories had given him the mindset, it turned out to be a horny college girl, finally, that radicalized him.

Bernadette, a raven-haired Irish Catholic beauty from Radcliffe with a fierce pride radiating out from her sharp, pointed face, was distributing pictures at the Harvard gates in faded blue mechanic's coveralls with her sleeves rolled up and her hair tied back. The pictures were of a burning bus, with rioters beating up Negroes. The first Freedom Ride, organized by the Congress of Racial Equality (CORE), had broken down on the road outside Anniston, Alabama, where it had been set on fire and its black and white student occupants beaten. "We must help them this summer," she intoned solemnly. "Remember what Kennedy said at the inaugural. 'The torch has been passed to a new generation.'"

A torch indeed. Her fiery green eyes mesmerized him. Ever the rationalist, Reggie suppressed his lust. He had to impress her first. "Why haven't I heard about this?"

"The newspapers, TV, you get to see only what They want you to see." She flashed him a heroic smile, just back from the front lines of the war against injustice. And she took him up on his offer to continue the conversation over coffee at Tulla's.

Reggie thought her naive, but so cute! He was helplessly enchanted by her eyes as she spoke breathlessly about her faith in the power of democracy. He gathered that she hoped this new administration, after Ike, would be an activist one. She wholeheartedly believed that Kennedy was on her side with his statement that "man holds in his mortal hands the power to abolish all forms of human poverty *and* all forms of human life."

She was willing to accept that the administration was right about shifting from direct action to voter registration in the Deep South. She took the Bill of Rights at face value, but the writ of the First Amendment, with its freedom of speech and assembly, did not run through the Deep South. "Why, in one Mississippi county, Negroes are the majority and over 3,500 hundred of them are of voting age, but only *one* Negro has succeeded in registering."

Despite her naiveté, she was remarkably fluent in American history. "The white profiteers subverted the 14th Amendment. The very idea that a corporation can be treated as a person was founded on the backs of the Negroes. Think about it. A corporation is a legal person, a figment of the imagination, but really a special kind of person with no moral consciousness, no soul to save, and no body to incarcerate. Be-holden only to their stockholders, who are protected from prosecution. And all this was founded on the backs of African slaves."

Reggie leaned into her, silently sniffing her faint aroma as she explained.

"It happened right after the Civil War. The 14th Amendment was supposed to protect blacks, you know, from having their property and liberty taken from them. But along came a former senator, Roscoe Conkling. One of the worst carpetbaggers of all time! He was the architect of the North's strategy to buy up all the Southern property during the Reconstruction. So Roscoe goes and makes his own copy of the committee's journal, changing the original intention of the amendment to apply to corporations as well as human beings, and forging the signatures. Then he lies to the Supreme Court, claiming his copy is the real thing.

"And only a handful of people challenged this," she continued. "Two of them filed an appeal but failed to win, and then they both disappeared. One was described in the newspapers as a Negro hoodoo witch doctor by the name of Cornell Woodrow, and the other was a white lawyer from the South, Gilbert Reginald Mesirow."

Reggie, startled, dropped his cup into the saucer, spilling hot coffee on his pants. "My God, you're talking about my grandfather! In fact I'm named after him. Reginald. My parents changed their names to Mention. I read about him in my father's book."

What he didn't mention was his familiarity with the other name, Cornell Woodrow.

"Your father's book?" Her impish look suggested an opening. Eager to impress, he brought her back to his room to show her the Book and serenade her with folk songs. Halfway through "Wade in the Water"[197] she rubbed his knee and wrapped her other arm around his neck, pulling him to her.

* * *

Many white Harvard students had paused long enough in their relentless pursuit of success to feel guilty enough to donate money to the Student Non-violent Coordinating Committee (SNCC) and CORE for its upcoming Freedom Ride to Mississippi. But only a few had actually boarded the bus with Reggie and Bernadette; in fact only one, a black educator named Bob Moses.

Reggie was going for the adventure. Here was an opportunity to build his character in preparation for the upcoming struggle. He would learn all about the victims of capitalism, as portrayed in the writings of Steinbeck and Dos Passos, and in the songs of Woody Guthrie. "And don't forget Joe Hill,"[198] added Clay, "he was the left-wing Stagger Lee, taking the fight right into company territory."

And if it didn't work out, he could meet up with Eric Sackheim, who would be trekking across the Delta looking for old bluesmen.

Reggie and Bernadette held hands all night, all the way to Memphis and into the ragged daylight of the sidewalk outside the bus station. A crowd had formed of solid white citizens, Christians, with hands on their hips and lines of hatred etched into their faces. The crowd shouted at the neatly groomed black Freedom Riders in their somber jackets, serious ties, and black wingtips as they emerged from the Negro side of the segregated station.

Reggie, in Geno-style khakis, a turtleneck sweater, and hair curling over his ears, felt halfheartedly white and stupidly collegiate. He mentioned this to Bernadette, who wrinkled her cute nose and asked if he'd like to see her in blackface. "But don't you see the contradiction? We're down here in a perverse kind of Spring Break, to get our heads broken, in the name of, what, justice? For blacks? And back at Harvard, how proud we are, we talk about civil rights in the lecture hall, but we're hypocrites. We depend on Narcissus, the black janitor, to clean up after our parties."

But her blazing green eyes gave him confidence. They got in line with the Freedom Riders for the next bus, politely letting others in front as if it were a Sunday outing for a church social. Reggie was acutely aware of the aroma rising from the two joints he'd stashed in his pocket, now realizing what a mistake it had been to bring them. With Bernadette leading, they went straight to the back of the bus to see how it felt.

Just an hour of a bumpy ride out of Memphis, Reggie had a premonition. He saw an angry mob with bats and bricks smashing the windows and sides of the bus, dragging "nigger lovers" out into the street. He saw his own body dragged out and beaten, saw himself crawl under the bus to get away from his tormentors, and saw Bernadette's legs pulled apart and a burly white man stick a bat like a giant phallus into her crotch.

Turning whiter than white with this vision, he clutched Bernadette's hand on the bus seat. The song from the SANE concert returned to him. We're only as tall as we stand.

Bob Moses, the black educator from Harvard, came up the row to the back and sat next to them. The soft-spoken Moses was the leader of this expedition, but the man's disarming attitude and familiar jokes about Harvard broke the ice. Bernadette swooned in admiration until Moses, a bit uncomfortable with the fiery brunette's attention, excused himself, and went up to the front of the bus to deliver some news about the other Freedom Rides.

The first bus had burned up outside Anniston, Alabama. The second bus had reached Birmingham only to be stopped by a Klan mob carrying chains, pipes, and baseball bats. No police were in sight. Rumor had it that one of the Klan was an FBI informant who had briefed his handler about the Klan's plans, and the FBI office in Birmingham had contacted J. Edgar Hoover's office to tell him that Bull Conner would be giving the Klan free rein. But Hoover's men did nothing to stop it. The mob beat them senseless; one sixty-year-old Freedom Rider was left permanently brain-damaged.

His light brown skin, slight frame, and large somber eyes gave Moses the look of an ascetic. He spoke slowly, plainly, with a mild, even-toned voice; a soft voice that commanded attention as if in church. He made quiet assertions. Great currents of moral perplexity ran through him as he spoke. "We are going to try to make it to the Birmingham bus station. And we must act *as if* the bus terminal is free. We must act *as if* the federal government should be taken at its word, that they will protect us.

"If anyone wants to withdraw," Moses continued to the hushed bus, "you can get off before we reach the Alabama state line. You have every right not to participate, especially if you aren't ready to get hurt. No one will think any less of you if you withdraw. You all have to remember now, that down here, the cops don't need us, and *man*, they expect the same."

No one moved. Reggie quietly reached for his shiny Martin guitar, and began strumming while Bernadette shyly squeaked the opening lines to "We Shall Overcome", attempting the Joan Baez style.[199] And suddenly, like a flower opening in a fast-motion picture, the bus erupted in song. Moses smiled like the father of a lost tribe that had just found its way out of the desert.

Armed state troopers in Jeeps, and the President's representative, John Seigenthaler, in his own car, met the bus at the Alabama line and accompanied it to the Montgomery city limits while the passengers sang "We Shall Overcome" and a spirited "Wimoweh" complete with corny yodeling. But once inside the city, the state troopers disappeared, leaving only Seigenthaler's car and the sound of yodeling diminishing in a doppler effect off into the night.

Down the street Reggie could see a crowd. Hatred came of it like a fog rising from a river. The world, the entire universe shrank to a bubble, a finite earth and sky, with Reggie frozen at its violent center silently mouthing "We shall not overcome after all."

A brick smashed through the window to his right, scattering glass all over passengers and launching a roar from the crowd. A young white boy in coveralls bashed in the emergency door with a baseball bat. Suddenly the bus itself was rocking side by side, more windows were smashed, and the front door caved in. The driver was dragged out into the street, and everyone was on their feet.

As Reggie had seen in his mind only a few hours before, a small army of white men in dirty coveralls boarded the bus with chains and bats, bashing their way up the aisle and carrying off black and white Freedom Riders, shouting "nigger lovers" and "black bastards." A white man in a flannel shirt pulled Reggie out the back door and punched him in the face. He could taste the blood flowing out of his nose. Another man grabbed Bernadette and dragged her off the bus, and then several white men surrounded her. Reggie tried to get up and someone bashed him on the head, driving his face into the asphalt. Bernadette was screaming and repeatedly choking "Get off me!" As Reggie began to crawl toward the underside of the bus, he saw her getting poked in the crotch with a baseball bat.

Bob Moses, reeling off a beating, staggered into the middle of Bernadette's tormentors and fell on her, covering her with his body, which proceeded to get pounded by more baseball bats. The fleeting thought occurred to Reggie that this was America's favorite past-time, this game with bats and balls, and now with bats and human balls. Flat on his stomach and choking in the dust underneath the bus, he recalled that end-of-the-world feeling from the beating he got a few years back on that Atlantic City Boardwalk. He welcomed the sudden and complete blackout, with streams of bright colors arcing across his eyeballs.

* * *

Through the blackout came a shout, and a thought entered his head: something was coming to save him. He saw in his mind a pink Cadillac, and looked up from under the bus to see a commotion in the middle of the intersection. Someone was driving a wedge through the mob from the other side. He thought he saw a whirling black cane wielded by an arm in a charcoal suit, gripped by a black-gloved hand, spinning like a helicopter blade. The crowd parted, and Reggie could see it was a black man, duded up in a three-piece suit and Stetson hat, twirling his black cane like a Texas cheerleader, shouting hoarsely, "Whoa! Stagger Lee! Make way for Stagger Lee!" Amazingly, the white men held back, tightening their grips on their baseball bats and chains, dumbfounded by the sight of this bold and untouchable black man.

As he reached the bus, Reggie recognized him from the Boardwalk: Cornell Woodrow. The man himself. His eyes sought out Reggie's, and he beckoned. Then he swiftly gathered a bleeding Bob Moses and a nearly unconscious Bernadette into his arms and wrestled and dragged them back through the wedge in the crowd, which had now gone quiet. Reggie stumbled out from the under the bus to follow them.

At the far end of the wedge across intersection sat a dazzling pink Cadillac with a white roof, a '55 Fleetwood Series 60. On its door was an elaborately carved ivory crest of the three monkeys.

Cornell pushed the couple into the back seat and motioned Reggie to follow. Just as Reggie climbed in, the crowd came to life again with a low rumble and a few shouts. Cornell turned to the crowd and held up his cane, gripping its gold fish head at the top, and pointing skyward. "Heaven help the fools!" he shouted in his rich, coal-black voice, and then pointed his cane down the block where Seigenthaler had parked and was helping a battered black woman into his car. "Kennedy sent his man down here!" The crowd surged down the block, and its front line swarmed over Seigenthaler.

At that moment another car, a black Cadillac Coupe de Ville driven by another charcoal-suited black man in a somber homburg, pulled up between Cornell's car and the back of the mob, and some of the bus victims crammed in. Within seconds Cornell floored his pink Fleetwood and raced down the street, with the Coupe de Ville close behind.

* * *

Reggie, squeezed into the middle of the front seat, gazed in wonder at the car's white interior. Large foam dice dangled from the rear-view mirror, and diamonds studded the gold-inlaid steering wheel.

Cornell spied him looking. "Got this car from Elvis."

Reggie cocked his head and stared back. "Hey, I know you. Summer of '59, in Atlantic City. The Jackal concert."

"Of course you know me," chuckled Cornell, then changed his tone to mock serious. "What are you college kids doing down here?" He said "college kids" like "collard greens".

"We believe in civil rights, in freedom. We're down here to help the, uh," he almost said "Negro," his face coloring, his speech faltering. "You know, black people."

Cornell snorted and laughed. "Like your grandfather, eh? You white folks sure do crack me up!" And then, in a singsong voice:

A bear taking a dump asked a rabbit
"Does shit stick to your fur as a habit?"
"No," said the hare,
"It's really quite rare!"
So the bear wiped his ass with the rabbit.

Bob Moses chuckled in the back seat. "Stop it, Cornell, you'll frighten 'em." Bernadette was clinging to him.

"'Bout time you caught on," said Cornell back to Moses. "We got to put the fear into 'em."

"That why you sent them off to grab Seigenthaler? I know you have the power to do it."

"Got to give those liberals up in Washington a taste of what it *is*," said Cornell. "They're tip-toeing around this mess."

"My brothers, they say only the young black men can fight this fight." Moses sounded wistful. "The white students are ineffectual, even as white shields. My brothers say to them, 'you-all go on back up North where you came from,'" looking directly at Reggie. "'This is our struggle.' That's what my brothers say."

"But that's not what you say?" Reggie squirmed. "And by the way, you got me wrong. I'm down here because I love the music."

Moses looked daggers at Reggie. "I say we can use some help. We are down here, and we're gonna stay down here while you and the other students are back at school. All these debates about nonviolence and direct action and voter registration, and whether or not whites should be a part of SNCC, they're all really about whether love or power is the answer."

"You talk about 'Snick' and it sounds like Snickers candy," chortled Cornell. "It don't work to tell white people about this hatred against black people. Half of them don't know about it, and the other half don't care."

"Yeah, well, what are you doing here?" Moses retorted. "You're like Jim Dandy to the rescue! Ol' Zip Coon himself, got your fish head cane and your Stetson hat. Well I'm going to Mississippi to organize voter registration. We're gonna put together an alternate delegation for the next Democratic convention. A *black* delegation."

Cornell looked to Reggie. "What do *you* think of his chances?"

Reggie could suddenly feel the future. "They'll deny them access. They won't allow them to be seated."

"Hmmm," Cornell smiled at him. "You're demonstrating the power."

Reggie didn't know what he was talking about. But he had another disturbing premonition. All these courageous black men would be led down a happy path to a fake freedom. Why should they care about integrating restaurants and hotels when they don't have jobs and can't afford to enter them? Why should they risk getting killed, just to register to vote? Reggie saw the movement move toward more violence. Its founding fathers, Bob Moses among them, would never see the promised land.

"I'm going with you," cooed Bernadette to Moses, who was startled and suddenly at a loss for words.

"Bernadette…" Reggie also couldn't find the words.

"Let 'em go," said Cornell in a kind, fatherly voice, as he pulled up to the bus terminal. Wounded and frightened Freedom Fighters cowered in the black section of the segregated terminal. Bob Moses, Bernadette clinging to him, strode in with a purpose and a speech, and tried to rouse them into an organized action to integrate the white areas of the terminal. But the fighters were exhausted and were not having any more of it.

* * *

Cornell drove on with Reggie in an uncomfortable silence louder than the passing traffic. After entering the black part of town and passing a rundown church, Reggie broke the silence. "You knew my father. Where is he now? Is he alive?"

Cornell kept driving on in silence for a minute, and then spoke. "Your father is a great man. We traveled together. I do believe he is alive, but we haven't spoken in a long time." Cornell leveled his eyes at Reggie. "He's on the run. The Corporation has been trying to find him for years."

"But why? Is it the government that's after him? Is he a spy, a Communist?"

"It's not that simple," said Cornell. "He didn't want to end up dead, like Freddie, y'know, the DJ."

"I thought Freddie was killed by the Mafia."

Cornell eyed him suspiciously. "You still have your father's notes?"

"Yes. The Book."

"And the records?"

"The Robert Johnson records, yes. We split them up between us, me, Gilbert, and Johnny."

"What about the acetate from Carnegie Hall?"

"Gilbert's got it."

"And the thunder-stones?"

"We split them up."

Cornell drove on for another minute in silence. Then, "Have you been contacted?"

"There's a counselor at Harvard that used to know my father and wants me to find him."

"Cravingston, no doubt."

Reggie was astonished. "You know Doctor Cravingston?"

"Doctor," Cornell chuckled. "Doctor of what? Psychology? Heh heh… So, you didn't see him, lurking in the shadows while the Justice Department man, Seigenthaler, was getting beat up?"

Cravingston, down here? Reggie was aware that the man had many connections. But what the fuck…? "Did he follow me down here?"

Cornell shrugged. "Don't matter if he did or he didn't. But what do you think's gonna happen?"

"Why do you keep asking me that?"

"You got the power. *See no evil.* You can see into the future."

Reggie puzzled this over. "I know what you mean, I can feel it come over me, but it's fleeting, it just appears in my mind and then disappears. What the fuck is happening to me?"

"It's like you're on a bus," Cornell began to lecture, dropping that down home accent, but then picking it up again. "You just got on a-ways back, you can't remember when. People keep getting on and off the bus, and you travel with them. At some point you realize that your stop is coming up. You realize, everything you've lived through was on this bus, everything that was important to you was on this bus. And you are about to step off it. So what does it matter, all that you lived through, all that was important? *Not important.* That bus just left! You're at the stop, waiting for another one.

So you get on the next bus, and it's the same one. The same life, only you don't remember it. You go through your entire life again. Everything you did, you do again. It's not a do-over. You just don't remember, and you repeat your past over and over again."

"So…"

"So at some point, you look out the window and see that other bus, with you on it. Only you see it at some point in the future."

"Okay…" Reggie let that sink in a second. Then he had to ask. "What do I do with this?"

"Well, you have a skill," said Cornell, matter-of-factly, completely dropping the down home accent. "Not many people have it. But talent is not skill. You can develop skills, with practice, to build up predictability. You can get real technical with it. You can practice the chords and scales until you get them perfect," he smiled and reverted back to the down home form. "You the tech wiz kid, ain't ya? Ain't the future in your hands already?"

"You mean I make it happen? The future?"

"No no no," the laughter coming from deep in Cornell's stomach, like errant bass notes. "You just got to find the groove. Go with it." Glancing over at Reggie to see if that registered. It hadn't.

"Think about how you get there with music," Cornell went on, dropping the accent again. "As you listen, your brain constantly updates its estimate of when the next beat will occur. And when your brain's estimate is right, you feel a sort of satisfaction in it. Satisfaction in matching a mental beat with a real-world one. But when a talented musician *violates* that expectation in an interesting way, you know, tells a musical in-joke, or speeds up or slows down to suggest that the music is breathing… Well then, your brain is delighted! It's the cerebellum, finding pleasure in adjusting itself, to stay synchronized, y'know. And so, you *feel* the groove in the subtle violations of timing. And you find that groove *not* by aspiring to be technical, *not* by joining the ranks of the so-called experts who decide what is real and what is not real, the *technocrats*," he spat, "but by *feeling* it."

Reggie frowned, confusing this talk with a lecture Cravingston had given him back at Harvard.

"You see, your R. D. Laing, he was right," Cornell went on. "We don't need theories so much as we need the *experience*, the source of the theory." He looked over at Reggie, who looked annoyed. "What? I'm using your own language, ain't it right?"

"Right." Reggie nodded with eyes downcast, ashamed at his own prejudice against black people, against all forms of the poor and outcast. Of course they could understand, but how could they know what was in these books? How could they spend such a luxurious time learning to read them, when they were so caught up in basic survival? Then a thought occurred to him. "Why was my father so interested in Robert Johnson?"

Cornell had stopped at a crossroads, and he looked both ways. "They say Robert Johnson sold his soul to the devil, at some crossroads like this one, 'round about midnight, to get that talent he had, to play guitar like that. You're raised Catholic. What do you think?"

"I think if the devil wants my soul, it's gonna cost a lot more than some guitar lessons."

Cornell belly-laughed. "And I thought you wanted to learn something."

"Well, my guitar's gone." Reggie's guitar had been bashed over someone's head and lay in pieces back inside the bus.

Cornell took a left at the crossroads and continued onward. Eventually a dimly lit music shop materialized out of the fog of night. Cornell skipped inside and came out with a vintage 1938 Martin D28. The fog parted, and they were standing at the edge of another crossroads over a hundred miles away, outside Hazlehurst, Mississippi. The night was inky black. The time was close to midnight.

"Jeez…" Bewildered by it all, Reggie fished in his pocket for the two joints. "Maybe we should light up one of these."

Cornell's grin, his pearly mouth surrounding a shiny gold tooth, shown through the darkness. "Gimme one." He took one joint and pocketed it. "Keep the other one, you might need it later. Now let me show you how to play this."

A wolf howled. Cornell picked out a blues riff with his long, slender fingers. "Legba, the trickster, some call him Esu. Guardian of crossroads and entrances. You wanna go someplace? Got some important decision to make?" He picked a refrain for the riff. "Why you down here anyway?"

Reggie was going to say, again, it's the music. But he knew it was far more than that. More, even, than fighting the raging injustice of ignorant whites beating up blacks, burning their churches, and destroying their hopes. More than just the world's predicament with the Bomb and countries bickering on the brink of total destruction. Something deep inside him was festering, unsatisfied with just about *everything*, unsatisfied especially with his chosen path through Harvard and on to… what? "Technology or politics," he could see Cravingston's grinning face. "Even better, the technology of politics."

Cornell was looking at him funny. "Why you down here? Cravingston send you down here?"

Cornell's question startled Reggie. "I didn't tell him anything," he said defensively. "I came down here to help out, and to learn about the music. But something else, I don't know. I just don't know what I'm supposed to do, what the future holds."

"Most people, they think about the future," said Cornell in a fatherly voice. "They think about all the possible futures. But you have a glimpse of the real future. You know something about it, but not enough to change it. It's that feeling of destiny you have. You can't really envision any other possible future but what you can glimpse of the real thing. So tell me, what do you see yourself doing in a few years?"

Reggie concentrated. He could see a recording studio, lots of guitars strewn about, someone he didn't recognize on a piano, someone else playing an acoustic guitar and harmonica at the same time, the harmonica attached to a bracket hung around his neck.

"Y'know, a good musician can play the guitar as if it were an extension of his body." Cornell stretched his fingers out. "You don't play strings, you play your fingers."

Reggie's vision vanished back into nighttime darkness. Cornell started strumming the chords to "We Shall Overcome" in a stately pace. "Wonder why you cringe a little when you hear that?" Cornell spoke between notes. "Why it seems so cloying, so sweet, almost too sweet? Why it's not so 'cool'? It's because there's no *danger* in it, no *pathos*, y'know. Everybody sings together, everybody's *in* this together, and it sounds like we're all in Sunday school. But if you change some of these notes..."

Cornell bent a note so that the three notes together formed a tritone. "You can make it sound a little dangerous. It's a classic blues sound, hidden in that dominant seventh chord we use for turnarounds. And the diminished seventh, you know, C to E flat to F sharp to A. That's two tritones. In medieval times, the Church banned it, calling it the *Diabolus in Musica*, or Devil's Interval, because when monks used it for harmony, it took them to a place where they were in touch with the Divinity. Beyond the Church's control, y'see. It aroused them, *sexually*, y'understand? Now that song started out as a hymn, by Reverend Tindley of the African Methodist Episcopal Church, and somewhere along the line its lyrics were transposed to the gospel song 'I'll Be All Right Someday'."[200]

As Cornell played the song, Reggie saw a wood paneled, white-steepled church materialize in the darkness. From inside he could hear a black chorus singing freedom songs in their original forms, using that same Devil's Interval. Woke up this morning with my mind stayed on Jesus, go tell it on the mountain, keep your hand on that plow hold on, we shall not be moved. Among these intervals were ample space for improvisation, all blue thirds and sevenths, and frequent short refrains in which the congregation could join. Reggie knew he'd be welcome in this hot rural church, the motherlode of black experience, where the pressed weight of suffering and resistance had formed a bedrock of faith... far more welcome here, than in any of the cold brick churches up North.

He could still hear Cornell picking the older version that focused on individual triumph. And yet the song itself had yielded to a white culture that had left the black man with nothing but hope for a paradise *after* death; it had been simplified to "Yes in my heart, I do believe."

Cornell took the theme of the individual further back in time, now echoing the opening and closing melody of an even older, more powerful song, the brooding "No More Auction Block For Me".[201] Reggie realized he held in his hands a catechism of some other, unknown religion, with a handbill tucked into it advertising the next auction, right off the boat, 48 vigorous negro males and... 36 fertile females! He dropped the handbill to scrutinize the catechism. Arranged as hymns were familiar blues lyrics set in an ecclesiastical typeface with coded instructions for blue notes, call-and-response patterns, and contrapuntal rhythms. Etched illustrations accompanied the text, showing a can of hot foot powder, a sprig of jalap root, a gypsy woman, the Seventh Son, a mojo hand.

"The world's first religion," Cornell peering over his shoulder at the catechism. "The ancient musical notation is part of the lettering. You know, music is found in every culture, past and present. It originated with the first humans in Africa, and these humans started dispersing around the world 50,000 years ago, spreading music, the first religion, the only true religion. There's a natural foundation to what we now call the diatonic scale, and harmony, and it goes back to antiquity, to Africa. And it has always had a sacred purpose, and a power that has all but diminished today."

Cornell continued playing stinging blues riffs. "Beneath the deep flowing vibrations," he solemnly intoned at each refrain, "beyond all your fears, lies the secret. The Seventh Son of the Seventh Son carries the Secret. The decibel of your soul's vibration, the timbre of your personality, and the pitch of your triumphs and fears, are what make up your song."

Reggie could hear it now. He always thought of the blues as a very simple form of music, just three chords in 12-bar sequences in infinite variations. But singing the real blues, stomping away the real pain and suffering behind you, is something else altogether. It is the ultimate escape key, coded with lyrics and riffs, to make it possible for the slaves and the oppressed to live a life of some sort. Decode the blues, and you find that it is really about how to find freedom. And he saw the slaves chained up in the dusty compound, the merciless ship awaiting its cargo at the docks, and the griot singing to his people, providing them hope.

"These songs are like the sacred stones from your father's collection," Cornell continued as he started on a new song. "They cultivate the spirit and give it housing. They transform people's lives and infuse them with power. The Africans have been dispersing around the world throughout history. The slave traders bringing them to America, that was just another wave. But they brought their songs, and their sacred stones, to America, because this country is where the spirit will flourish."

And with a flourish he sang the rolling stone song that the bluesmen in the Delta would play while Muddy Waters was growing up, called "Catfish Blues". My mama told my papa before I was born, got a child coming, gonna be a rolling stone...[202]

Cornell twanged a flatted fifth. "A holy man would be chosen to serve as a carrier on the slave ships, you know. They called him a rolling stone, and he had to carry the sacred stones to the new world." Cornell hit the seventh. "This man would be a martyr!" he shouted angrily. "A hero! Sacrificing his life! So that his people could keep their gods with them. Many of them died choking while trying to swallow them, and others died in agony during the voyage, as their stomachs swelled and burst. But even when that happened, a dozen volunteers would come forward, eager to carry the stones, to become rolling stones, even though it meant certain death. When they got to the new world, their stomachs would be cut open and the stones removed, and then hidden from their white captors."

Reggie can see them, slaves hiding their stones in their tar-paper shacks as the white preachers gathered the little slave children for Christian church services on the back lawns. It is 1781, and "Black" Harry Hosier has taken the sermons to heart with a gift for memorization that extended to quoting entire hymns and passages of Scripture from memory. He starts a tradition of encoding African spirit talk within the sermons and hymns. Legba hides in various disguises as St. Peter, St. Anthony, and Lazarus. Erzulie, goddess of love, hides in the sky-blue cloak of the Virgin Mary. Time skips to 1867 to show one of the first all-black Christian churches, where former slave John Jasper preaches a gospel laden with references to the spirits of Africa, sliding into lyrics and song like the griots of old. "If you is what you was, you ain't," he shouts to the congregation. "Amen!" They shout back.

Outside, a white crowd is gathering for a minstrel show. "It's a coon show," Cornell whispers in Reggie's ear. Bearing songs from their mentor, Stephen Foster, and their own "Ethiopian melodies,"[203] the Christy Minstrels rub their faces black with burnt charcoal, just as Thomas Dartmouth "Daddy" Rice had done in a New York theater, and set up in a semicircle in front of the audience with the tambourine player, Mr. Tambo, at one end, and the bones player, Mr. Bones, at the other. Mr. Interlocutor sits in the middle and begins to sing:

Come listen all you gals and boys,
I'm gonna sing a little song.
My name is Jim Crow.
Wheel about and turn about and do jes so,
And e'bry time I wheel about I jump Jim Crow!

"Heh heh," Cornell whispers, "Daddy Rice invented a lot of these blackface characters, Jim Crow, Black Sambo, Zip Coon, Jim Dandy. White folks got to think of blacks as singing, dancing, grinning fools. The minstrels were white boys trying to play the blues. They put it out there for everyone to see, that blacks were lazy, stupid, or not even human."

The Christy Minstrels fade into the raucous Five Points of mid-19th century New York, and Reggie, following the sound of music, peers inside a tavern to see a corpulent black fiddler and tambourine player stomping the boards of a small raised stage. Leading the dancing is a lively young black man performing the first known version of the tap-dance. The dancer, Master Juba, rallies his brothers into a minstrel formation, all wearing blackface makeup over their black faces. Their clothing is a ludicrous parody of upper-class dress: coats with tails and padded shoulders, white gloves, monocles, fake mustaches, and gaudy watch chains. They primp, preen, and strut before the swooning white women in the front row.

Cornell again whispered in Reggie's ear. "Blacks imitating and fooling whites, whites imitating and stealing from blacks, blacks re-appropriating and transforming what has been stolen, whites making yet another foray on black styles, and on and on. This is what America's all about. Master Juba, he tricked the white boy who stole the blues. Well that's just the point, isn't it? The 'white negro' hipster doesn't want to be black. He wants to be *both*. Now maybe your father's cousin Mezz wanted to be black. But that's not hip."

Now the diorama unfolding in Reggie's mind reaches the 1940s. Stagger Lee devotees line the streets, like the Harlem hustler they call Detroit Red, always in the flashiest zoot suit, yellow knob-toe shoes, and wildly conked red hair, saying "Ya dig?" and "Daddy-o, let's go down South and organize, kill us some crackers." The tricksters have turned mean. Snapping their fingers to bop, jazz for the outsiders. Reggie could hear the music of Dizzy, Bird, Monk. Very difficult to listen to, let alone master technically and play emotionally. There seems to be a message in bop: whatever you go into, go into it *intelligently*.

"Here's that wild, frantic, not just crazy but *mad* crazy music," whispered Cornell, "not to be dug unless you had lived through the dark days, when a *bop* was a policeman's nightstick on a black man's head. But it's just another one of those nicknames white people invent, like bop, bebop. Or jazz. Or country blues.

"Y'see," Cornell continued, "As long as the secret of the power of music remained buried within the black population, the white rulers ignored it, allowed it to fester, or maybe they simply couldn't root it out. So it grew in mystique, as *mojo*, as *high john de conqueroo*, the performer's voodoo, as any number of things. But it's still, *to this day*, buried in black culture, in the lingo, rhymes, and rhythms. And that's what your father and I disagreed about. He thought, just like the owners of the race record labels, that as long as the secret stays buried in black culture, everything'll be fine. But if it breaks out, into the white world, them rulers are gonna get anxious, and bad things'll start happening."

Reggie could see a rundown church burning, a black child screaming. No one was paying attention. He could see the anxious puking of white college students just like him, on the Delta levee, about to be tortured to death. And then, blood red skies over a city ghetto.

"You can see it now, can't you. You can see something about the future." But Cornell didn't wait for a reply, he just brought the tune back around, playing the guitar opening to Sister Rosetta Tharpe's "Rock Me".[204] "It's a fascinating story," Cornell talked over the song. "the secret nonofficial musical life of this country. You can hear it now, that sly, devil-may-care attitude," Cornell bent the note to a flatted fifth. "It sounds 'cool', it sounds like a curve ball, like a baseball pitcher putting some english on the ball. As American as baseball! You can slide the note up to the regular pitch, or slide down from the regular pitch, and it's like you're adding english to it. You take any three regular tones in the song and bend one of them, or slide one of them, and it turns into something else, something 'cool' and wiser, more experienced, than the Sunday school sound." He continued playing, enjoying himself. "You may even feel a little wicked listening to it."

Cornell handed the guitar back to Reggie, who immediately tried to play the Robert Johnson song he'd heard on the record from his father. "No no no," Cornell wised him up. "You got to play what *you* feel, not what someone else felt. Otherwise, you're just being tricked."

Reggie took up another song, this time the Civil War song about the slaves escaping through the Underground Railroad that Pete Seeger had performed, "Follow the Drinking Gourd".[205] He sang it with all the full-throated emotion he could muster. In his hands, the song took on the mantle of a yearning Homeric epic by mixing major and minor chords, and the chorus promised salvation from freedom.

"That's good," Cornell said, "but it's too white. Lemme show ya." Cornell took back the guitar and started in on playing his own version of "Follow the Drinking Gourd".[206] In a low, weary voice, Cornell sang about the path of the drinking gourd as if it carried you through the last valley in the world to a freedom that seems like death. The subtle interplay of blue notes throughout the song gave it an entirely different meaning, not of hope for freedom but a final deliverance from life itself.

"What's this song really mean?" Reggie asked.

"Oh yes, there's a kind of encoding going on," said Cornell as he picked out its melody. "Your father was an expert on it. But the lyrics, coded messages in the lyrics? They're not that important, they're like a ruse, a red herring, ya dig? They're in there to throw you *off* the track. What was it, one of your white folks, T.S. Eliot? Pointed out that the camouflage function of 'meaning' in a poem was like the juicy piece of meat carried by the burglar to distract the house-dog of the mind, so that the poem could do its work."

Cornell slowed it down to a Delta pace, picking each note with interest. "The real coded message is in the sound itself. The relationship between the tones as you hear them. The frequencies go right into your ear and your brain responds directly to them." He demonstrated with a few notes. "Certain relationships between tones can make you feel happy, sad, brilliant, depressed, confident, scared, whatever. Your body resonates to these frequencies."

It was a revelation. Reggie could feel these emotions. "You see," Cornell continued, "the languages of the part of Africa my people come from, they're all *tone* languages. The relationships between the pitches provide the meaning."

"But what about the coded messages?"

"Well, they set up the context. This song just about defines what the flight from slavery was like, to find your freedom. You have to follow the drinking gourd, the Big Dipper, pointing North. Maybe you ought to do this, retrace the steps by following the lyrics, you start from Mobile Alabama, head on up the Tombigbee River. The riverbank makes a mighty good road. The dead trees show you the way. Ole' Peg Leg Joe marked those trees with mud, the outline of a left foot and a round spot in place of the right foot. The river ends between two hills, and there's another river on the other side, the Tennessee River, then downriver to where the great big river meets the little river. That's the Tennessee and Ohio rivers in Paducah, Kentucky. Just follow the drinking gourd."

Reggie smirked. "Is that where they got Dorothy's yellow-brick road?"

"Of course. Oh it all exists, all right. Not a hoax. It exists because the white folks wrote it down, published it. Otherwise the hymn would be unknown today, like all the other hymns with instructions and maps. These songs were not supposed to be passed on after the Civil War ended. White folks were not supposed to know about them, the instructions, the maps. Otherwise they'd start analyzing them, and the field hollers and work songs next. Then all us niggers'd be in trouble," he joked.

"But the gospel music, the blacks who are Christians…"

"Just fooling everybody," Cornell quipped. "This is the deep South, what did you expect? This here is apple pie and Bible country. But our black churches down here ain't like any of your white churches. Lemme tell you 'bout the white churches down here." He strummed an awkward Irish air and sang,

There's some pretty black ladies in Birmingham
And here's the story concerning 'em.
They lifted the frock
and sucked the white cock
of the bishop as he was confirming 'em.

But the Bishop was nobody's fool —
He learned about racism in school.
He took down his britches
And butt-fucked those bitches
With his twelve-inch Episcopal tool.

But that didn't bother those two.
They laughed as the Bishop withdrew:
"The Vicar is quicker,
and thicker, and slicker,
and longer and stronger than you!"

"Ha ha!" Cornell handed the guitar back to Reggie and rubbed his hands with gleeful eyes.

"This is what Robert Johnson learned, a-at that crossroads they all talk about?"

"Well now," Cornell gave Reggie a look. "Don't you sound Southern! Where's 'at accent comin' from?" He paused. "The black vicar is quicker than the white bishop, y'see. It's all a trick. You get your trick together, ya dig? That's what our young Robert learned. Get that trick together, take it on the road.

"Now *you* need to go on the road," Cornell continued. "Go back north, follow the drinking gourd. Follow that trail, see what you can see, and take your trick with you. And when you get to New York, look up my friend Dave Van Ronk. And you got to find this kid, he's in New York now, Dave will know. You'll know if you meet him. He'll say he knows Jim Dandy, the radio jockey, from back in Minnesota. He plays and sings like Woody Guthrie, but he's got this black attitude, like an old bluesman in a young kid's body. And when he sings, he sings with words that mean more than one thing. He's *signifying*."

"Okay, but you were going to tell me something more about my father. You said the Corporation was after him. Which corporation? Does it have anything to do with my grandfather, and the fight about the 14th Amendment?"

"Not any corporation. *The* Corporation."

"You mean the Company?" Cravingston had called it that. "The CIA?"

Cornell chuckled. "That's just a subcontractor."

* * *

It was Reggie's first dive into and out of America. He'd hitchhiked, crawling up from the Deep South with just a tinge of Southern Drawl in his voice, just another college-age white kid with a guitar, easy to get rides, following the drinking gourd twinkling in the impossibly beautiful southern night sky. He rode a whirlwind of trucks across the strip-mined landscape, hitting all of the truck stops… down to the rolling green hills and deep, dark forests, and past tar-paper shacks, from which emanated the thin nasal strains of the music of poor Americans, white and black, generations that had shared riffs and lyrics. Reggie felt the Long Memory of Pioneering America haunting this countryside, wallowing in the pastures of plenty, whispering through the pines of the deep forests, and echoing over the rolling hills. The Long Memory still controlled us through dreams, and through visions that are but newer versions of the same secrets.

He rode on through Matewan, Mingo County, "The site of the last great civil war in this country, the West Virginia Mine War of 1920," drawled the heavyset driver of a long-distance eighteen-wheeler. A quarter of a century earlier the farmers had been compelled to sell the mineral rights underneath their land, for pennies, to a group of cynical Northern con men. Within a few decades these residents of the fog-shrouded southern mountains became serfs. They were miners paid in scrip and marooned in debt in company housing, just like the black sharecroppers farther south, and discarded and evicted when injured.

Detectives hired by the coal companies had come to Matewan with a phony warrant to execute another round of evictions, but the local mayor and sheriff, allied with the striking miners, stood their ground. When the smoke cleared, ten people were dead. The coal company detectives retaliated by assassinating the sheriff, and thousands of armed striking miners faced off against thousands of mercenaries hired by the coal companies in a ten-mile skirmish line that snaked across the forbidding twin peaks of Blair Mountain. This was Frank Hutchison's country, hiding in his brooding "Stack A Lee" and "Train That Carried the Girl From Town",[207] who started recorded in 1926 and finished in 1929 when the Depression killed off such marginal enterprises as phonograph records for the blues and hillbilly jukeboxes.

Reggie could see why Pete Seeger and his followers romanticized this music and the innocence of the peasant folksinger. We've fallen in love with these organic communities of the poor, out here in the wasteland of the strip-mined countryside, where each song belongs to everyone. And each song embodies the mysteries of life and a yearning for peace and home, and more… a yearning for justice, in the midst of all this modern progress, noise, and upheaval. Reggie could hear this purity, an oasis of freedom unsullied by commerce or greed, an essential goodness in the ballads and blues of the country, recorded by people from small towns and tiny settlements in Appalachia, in the Deep South, and in the dustbowls west of the Mississippi. This was the new world to discover, to bring back to life, this country within.

But that's not what truck drivers in this part of the country wanted to hear. Asked to strum a few, Reggie drew on his Woody Guthrie repertoire with "Sowing On The Mountain"…[208]

God gave Noah that rainbow sign
Won't be water but the fire next time

Long after the driver had sighed and stopped singing along, when silence had crept inside the truck's cab to fill Reggie with guilt, the guilt of a civilized person with his first discovery of extreme poverty, he put down his guitar and tuned in the radio. WWVA out of West Virginia boomed 50,000 watts from sunset until dawn, playing the songs of Woody and Lead Belly. At some point Reggie realized that he was retracing his father's steps. According to the Book, Herbert had returned from the Deep South and reached Harlan County, Kentucky, in the early 1940s, where he heard Aunt Molly Jackson in a tavern singing songs about the plight of the miners and passing the hat for the union. Many of her songs were simply new lyrics applied to older Appalachian tunes derived from even older English ballads, blended with the music and vocal styles of the local black singers.

It was hard to reconcile how these poor white miners, treated like blacks by the mine owners, would be kin to the redneck racists in the Klan. The white folk singers sang about another America, of tolerance and kindness. They were beautiful, simple, relatively uncomplicated people living in the country, close to the soil. And yet, ever the sociologist, Reggie could sense the contradictions. Harry Smith had finessed these contradictions by blending white and black music in his *Anthology* in such a way that the two could not be separated. Listeners could not tell which musicians were white and which were black. Even some of the performers were ambiguous about race differences. Clarence Ashley, like many of the *Anthology* musicians, had played banjo in medicine shows and had even performed as Jim Dandy in blackface.

Reggie's path led ever north, back to a North he could no longer trust, a North that would no longer abide his new sensibility, a North whose promising career in Harvard-sponsored politics meant a betrayal of everything he'd just learned. The professors, snug in their fireplace-lit anterooms of history and mystery, would smile in relief or cluck in disbelief and never take him seriously. The college girls, smirking their way into suburban dramas of marriage and infidelity, would never understand him or even care to. His own brother might not recognize him.

Just seven years before, when he was 10, he thought he had glimpsed his father out through the kitchen window, in the shadows of their Margate driveway. Mother Beatrice had been out there sweeping, and was bent over her broom, weeping. By the time he beat a path outside, his father's shadow was gone.

Have I now turned into him? Another shadow named Mention? At some point in his journey he took pen to paper, another "Dear Beave" letter to Gilbert.

I've learned more about our father, and who, or what, is pursuing him, and why Freddie was murdered. And I've been to the crossroads, with Cornell Woodrow. Remember our vow: hold on to the stones.

The Liberated Energy

The liberated energy of the spirit of Legba could not be bottled up like a genie. Back in the North, Reggie drifted restlessly through the haze of late summer, taking up folk blues finger-picking as well as banjo to augment his strumming, his father's Book always in reach for quick reference.

He got good enough to play with the Charles River Valley Boys, and practiced with Mel Lyman, the tall, gaunt pig farmer who'd poked into Cravingston's office that day looking for Dr. Leary. A good-natured picker, a student of Obray Ramsay, Mel would switch to harmonica to let others play guitar and banjo, including Reggie and Jim Kweskin, and they mostly covered jug band tunes.[209] Mel kept urging Reggie to visit Leary's Center for Personality Research, just upstairs from Cravingston's office, and volunteer for one of their mind-expansion experiments with psilocybin, a substance derived from a certain type of mushroom revered by Mexican Indians.

So he worked up the nerve to visit Cravingston again, only to find his door locked. Upstairs, a group of graduate students were moving Dr. Leary's boxes of stuff to a new location, an address in Newton. The authorities were clamping down on student shenanigans. The winds had changed quickly, in a fast moment, focusing elsewhere, as if his attention had wandered after reading a book's last sentence, or hearing the final coda of the last song of an album. Something new blew in with this wind.

One day a young ragamuffin guitarist, a facsimile of the young Woody Guthrie, was strumming to nobody on the steps outside Tulla's. Reggie dropped a quarter in his hat, and the urchin introduced himself as Bobby Dylan, "D-Y-L-A-N". He glanced this way and that, as if looking for someone. Then he stared straight at Reggie's eyes, frowning, and asked about places to play in Cambridge.

Reggie decided to help him. "You know Ric Von Schmidt?"

"I know that name," Bobby sneered. "It's like a password up here."

They got to talking about folk music and about the coded instructions in songs. Reggie bragged about following the drinking gourd, the slave route to freedom, and Bobby broke into a smile when he heard the name Peg Leg Joe, a familiar name from his misty Minnesota past. "Heard about ol' Peg Leg, from a Negro disc jockey in Duluth, calls himself Jim Dandy." He told Reggie that he had to look up Dave Van Ronk if he ever got to New York. "Van Ronk knows all about these stories."

"I know that name," Reggie smirked, remembering Cornell's suggestion to look him up. "It's like a password up *here*. Van Ronk and Von Schmidt. We ought to get them together."

"There'd be some *world shakin'* goin' on."

When they arrived at Ric's, the elder folkie with smudged wireframe glasses was raving about having received his peyote buds mail-order from the Three Monkeys Orchid Farm in Texas, and was cooking them up in a large kettle and inviting everyone over to drink the soup, all the time winking at Reggie. Eventually Ric spilled the beans. "Given your father's background, I thought you might like this."

"What?" How did he know about my father?

"Peyote, and its other forms, like mescaline. Psychoactive substances."

"Waitaminute, how do you know…"

"Ol' 'Herb' Mention? He's one of those folklorists, y'know, part of the Alan Lomax bunch in New York. He brought a song back from Africa to give to Pete Seeger, the one they call 'Wimoweh'. You know, *A-wimoweh, a-wimoweh, a-wimoweh*.'" Ric kept singing it over and over until Bobby, impatient to learn something on the guitar, interrupted with a crudely rolled cigarette.

"Where'd ya learn how to roll like that?" Ric rolled his eyes, laughing, pointing at the bag of grass on the mantle. "That's some of Geno's mezz, knock you right on your ass, son."

Now Reggie interrupted. "What about my father?"

Ric squinted at him. "He's connected with Harvard, isn't that why you're here? Professor Leary and the others? I thought he was part of that government agency that helped them get started. Thought that maybe you knew how to get some of those Mexican mushrooms," Ric winked at Bobby and smiled wickedly at Reggie. Then Bobby took up one guitar, Ric the other, and Ric showed him how to play "Baby Let Me Lay it On You",[210] a Rev. Gary Davis blues…

Well I'd do anything in this god-almighty world
If you just let me lay it on you

Bobby didn't know how to make the country-blues phrases on his acoustic guitar. He wasn't particularly familiar with the Southeast country blues of Georgia and the Carolinas, and watched Ric closely. "It sounds like white folk music done by black people," Bobby snorted, laughing, "not like black music done by white folk people."

While Bobby practiced, Reggie showed Ric his father's Book. Uranium conspiracies, ancient adepts, lost civilizations, the secrets of Freemasons. "You need to talk to Fariña," Ric stated with an exaggerated rolling over the "ñ".

As if on cue, Dick Fariña bounded in with his wife, Carolyn Hester, bringing all other plans to a halt. Carolyn was staggeringly beautiful, a voluptuous Austin girl with sculpted features and windblown golden-brown hair. Bobby was instantly fascinated.

"Are we at the right place?" Dick joked, then buttonholed his wife. "Go get the Poem and park it out front." As she turned and left, Dick offhandedly explained. "We sold a poem for $50 and bought a used '50 Dodge, gray as a battleship. So we call it the Poem."

"What's the poem about?" Bobby wanted to know.

"It's called 'Celebration For a Grey Day'," Dick announced, and launched into verse. When he reached the line "There are so many things that must be told," Bobby snickered. "There are indeed, but ya gotta be careful about it."

"Y'know, the old Irish songs were very dangerous, they got people hanged," Dick retorted. "*Shan Bhan Bhocht*, the Poor Old Woman, that is what the shanachies called her in their songs. But that's so the English would think they were mourning a dead woman and not their own half-dead nation. 'Cathleen Houlihan', the woman shapely as a swan, or sometimes just 'the fair colleen', that was all code to deceive the English and other foreigners."

Fariña, as it turned out, was a dropout from Cornell University, a braggart born to wear a cape, who once said he'd been a gun-runner in Cuba and had bombed a British submarine for the IRA. "The songwriters were dangerous men. Every hamlet in Ireland has a history of brave lads hanging from trees, maddened by these songs that tore their hearts out of them. With these songs in your ears, Ireland is a woman you love that has been cruelly raped and beaten, and you must rush to her defense if you consider yourself to be a man. And that was how you ended up on a rope, covered in tar, swinging in the smoky dawnlight."

"Amen to that," Ric intoned solemnly.

Later, at Club 47, Reggie, Ric, and Bobby watched Dick and Carolyn perform. "She has beauty, talent, and charm; has it all, so to speak," said Ric. "She's been playing for a while now, in New York mostly. Has two solo albums already." Carolyn performed her usual set of traditional American and English ballads with a limber, casual voice that belied a powerful set of pipes, which she drew on occasionally to be more expressive, then backpedaled to a friendliness that charmed the audience. But it was Dick's old Irish and English ballads that had been brought to Appalachia, like "Riddle Song"[211] and his "Cuckoo Bird" interpretation, "Wobble Bird",[212] that captivated the audience. The energy popped way above Carolyn's professionalism to a sky-high intensity. Bobby, awed by Dick's lusty performance, leaned against a back wall like a frightened puppy. Ric and Reggie joined him to keep him company.

"He's got this European, Irish-English thing, with Appalachian overtones," said Ric.

"Yeah, this is really something," Bobby murmured, watching intently. There was something mysterious and unearthly in Dick's nasal delivery, especially the high notes, even out of tune. It didn't seem to matter. The audience could tell Dick was taking a risk, and they appreciated him all the more for it. Reggie could tell that Fariña also knew about some larger force, higher than governments, behind the events that unfolded in his life.

Next day, the five headed off to Revere Beach in Ric's old Buick, ham sandwiches and a large jug of "punch" made from orange juice, peyote broth, and plenty of rum. Sitting semicircle on a bed sheet in the sand in street clothes, they all looked too white, and Bobby in particular looked emaciated. No guitars, the salt air would have ruined them. This gave Dick Fariña the edge. He was a talker. He came on all explosive about his adventures in Cuba, sipping cocktails with Hemingway in Havana. He said he was writing a novel.

"Sure, uh-huh, everybody I meet is writing a novel," Ric laughed. "Next topic."

"No, listen, let me read it to you." Dick started quoting from the first page of his novel. "'I am the keeper of the flame, voyaged back from the asphalt seas of the great wasted land...'" On and on he went, through "glacier-gnawed gorges" and the "golden girls of Westchester and Shaker Heights," mind awash with schemes.

Carolyn yawned and turned back to her crossword puzzle.

Bobby saw this, stole at glance at Carolyn and accosted Dick. "I've been all those places, finger lakes and gorges, Faker Heights and Valley Forges, but I gotta ask you, man, have you ever heard Ric sing?" Bobby pointed to Ric. "I mean this here's a man who can sing the bird off the wire and the rubber off the tire. He can separate the men from the boys and the note from the noise." Everybody's giggling now. "The bridle from the saddle and the cow from the cattle..." Even Bobby can't stop laughing. "He can play the tune of the moon. The why of the sky and the commotion from the ocean."

"I'm an illustrator," countered Ric, "at least that's how I make a living."

Dick thundered, "That's it, illustrations! That's what the novel needs."

"Not decorative."

"No, not decorative, I mean illustrations that stand on their own."

"Advancing the story, so to speak. I can dig that."

"It's an entirely new genre! We're reinventing literature!" Dick was nearly exasperated with his own enthusiasm and how to direct it. Ric soaked it up and responded in his usual practical manner, let's exchange ideas, you send me some chapters, and so on.

Dick didn't want to get into details. He turned on Bobby. "We can reinvent music too! Poetry set to music. But not chamber music, or beatnik jazz, that's all been done before. I'm talking about setting poetry to a beat. Poetry you can dance too! Man, *boogie* poetry!"

Bobby couldn't resist. "On a fuckin' dulcimer? Like, how you gonna do that?"

"It's been done," Reggie pointed out. "A lot of the old country hillbilly songs could be poems. Even some blues can be poems. This one song I know, Robert Johnson..."

"You got a Robert Johnson record?" Bobby pounced on him. "Lemme borrow it."

Reggie nodded but continued. "Once you get into that old music, there's an incredible richness. You gotta know how to listen to those old ballads."

"Yeah, well," mused Bobby, "a lot of people don't want to hear you play 'em unless you play 'em exactly the way Aunt Molly Jackson played 'em."

"I think if you go back to the roots," Ric joined in, listing a bit and breathing rum, "you find that the songs we learned are just versions done in their own style, not in the original style. We don't even know the original style..."

It went on like that for a while, rum, sea, and sky, bathing beauties and a cornball tune sung by Dick *a capella*, "Cocaine, runnin' round my brain..."[213]

"Where'd you learn that?" Bobby wanted to know.

"Dave Van Ronk. Met him at Izzy's."

"Oh, everybody knows Van Ronk."

"Izzy's, the Folklore Center in New York," explained Ric to Reggie. "Your father knew Izzy."

Again with his father. Reggie couldn't believe that so many people knew so much more about his father than he did.

"Anyway, Van Ronk learned his version from the Reverend Gary Davis, but I learned my version from Cornell."

Reggie quipped, "You mean *at* Cornell."

"No man, I mean I learned it from an old Negro bluesman, calls himself Cornell. A friend of some people I know in New York."

"Cornell... Woodrow?"

"You know him?" Dick seemed frightened, as if caught in a lie.

"Hell, I know ol' Cornell," Ric drawled. "Showed me how to make my soup, how to bring out the best of the peyote buds, said he learned it from the old witch Mama Roux herself."

Reggie's insides twisted. Wasn't that the name of the maid at Johnny B's house back in Margate? Maybe a common name, for old witches?

"That man showed me the Monkey Demons," shuddered Dick, "and I don't ever want to see that again."

Bobby Dylan kept quiet. Couldn't be the same Cornell Woodrow he'd met back in Hibbing. Naw, 'twasn't him, just a common Negro name. The man I knew said he knew Robert Johnson personally...

Dick Fariña, haunted by the Monkey Demons, quoted again from his draft novel. "'I am invisible. And exempt. Immunity has been granted to me, for I do not lose my cool. Polarity is selected at will, for I am not ionized and I possess not valence.'"

A pause, a moment for the silent roar of the ocean. Reggie, higher than he'd ever been on grass, turned back to see his friends turn into wax statues, their features taut, faces to the wind. Their emotional valence measured neither positive joy, nor negative fear. Reggie could easily manipulate them and the environment around them, control matter and energy to produce that *field of force* Cravingston had been talking about. This field that puts him in what he called a "privileged position" with respect to them and everything else.

From this position, Reggie could see into their futures as if they were finished manuscripts in line to be published. Ric, settled on his blanket, weaving its wool through his fingers secure in his world, would forever be a folk artist, eccentric on the outside, rock solid on the inside. Carolyn, her lusterless eyes fixed on the freezing ocean, her frame as rigid as a dime-store Indian, would skip over the surface of this deep, growing folk movement. Dick, engrossed in the myth of his novel, mouth agape and eyes aflame, would strive for heavy valence, try to grab the brass ring, only to slip right over the edge.

Only Bobby, picking on an imaginary guitar an irrational note, a hard-fingered chord, searching the horizon for a sign... only Bob Dylan would make it out into the world unscathed and victorious.

The day stretched out to infinity, a day that would never end... but Fariña had a way of snapping it back to normal time, and gathered everyone around him. "All this running around, all this research, all this talk and debate, all these important works and important authors writing about it, but none of them and none of us can tell us *who*. And so I wonder, who."

"Who?"

"Who wrote the Book of Love!"[214]

Reggie nodded, smiling. "The Monotones."

* * *

Amnesty. Cravingston had sent out the message through his network.

Herbert Mention wore his usual three-piece suit and tie, creased trousers he could never really relax in, and a gray fedora perched jauntily on thinning brown hair. He was escorted through the main entrance to the E Street complex at Foggy Bottom formerly occupied by General William "Wild Bill" Donovan's Office of Strategic Services (OSS), now renamed the Central Intelligence Agency (CIA). By all appearances, it could have been a reunion luncheon of some sort. In an inner courtyard he was whisked into a limousine, and a few minutes later he was across the Potomac and entering the gated tunnel into the Virginia hillside which ran beneath the colossal new CIA building, finished just a few months after Kennedy took office.

Herbert thought back on his time working on Donovan's OSS task force from 1942-44 in London, supervising the testing of speech-inducing compounds on unwitting soldiers who'd volunteered for interrogation resistance training. The boys thought they were learning how to be strong so as not to crack if they were captured, but they were instead used as guinea pigs for potential truth serums. Donovan had insisted at the time that the need for such a weapon was so acute as to warrant any and every attempt to find it. "We should not be afraid to try things that have never been done before."

Herbert had gone AWOL after one of his subjects succumbed to hysteria and threw himself out of a sixth-story window at "The White Visitation" due to an incompetent mix of chemicals. "My God, there doing the same things at Dachau," Herbert had muttered during the subsequent investigation, and Donovan had given him a sharp look that sent Herbert over the edge and into the cold.

Although Army Intelligence hadn't been able to find "Herbert Mesh" and didn't have the budget to pursue low-level AWOL officers, the Corporation had no such limitations. According to the dossier in hand, they had subcontracted the project to the CIA, which had found him easily enough, in the guise of Herbert Mention, in Margate, New Jersey, living quietly with his new family. Herbert was important enough to them to let him have some peace and quiet. But Herbert must have got wind of the surveillance and somehow disappeared, and was gone for years as his children grew up.

When the Corporation discovered his reappearance as Herbert Mention, sometime in 1954, they had bigger problems on their hands. The Muslim Brotherhood had threatened stability in Egypt by trying to assassinate Nasser. The French had been thrown out of Vietnam and had been fighting to keep Algeria. And the Corporation's own bag men, the Mafia, had been tearing up the music scene, going way beyond their instructions. One of them, Frank Balzano from South Jersey, had engineered Johnny Ace's demise, sending a henchman backstage to one of his shows in Texas to "play" Russian Roulette. In fact, the only bright spot that year had been Mumblingore's cloud-seeding experiments that caused massive hurricane Hazel, which was termed a partial success because it leveled Haiti and helped to unseat the political power of the Vodou, but was also discontinued because the hurricane could not be stopped before wreaking considerable havoc across the Eastern Seaboard.

So, in the midst of these issues, the faceless members of the Corporation couldn't care less about his AWOL status or his name change. He could go on being Herbert Mention; in fact, with no history, the name was preferable. What they wanted at that time was his cooperation in silence. Now, as the decade of the Sixties dawned, they wanted more.

Through Freddie the DJ, Herbert had kept tabs on his old pals. He knew the Corporation was subcontracting investigations on ESP, subliminal perception, and other phenomenon associated with certain "mind altering" drugs. They were in contact with hypnotists, telepathists, and the organizers of séances and occult gatherings. They even suspected that it might be possible to communicate, through mediums, with dead agents.

Herbert's background with Donovan's task force, and his own interests in the power of music, would be very useful, and he would be paid handsomely for his trouble. They sat him down in a bleak conference room, with only a glass of water for comfort.

"You were one of Donovan's 'Dreamers'. We want to talk about your experiences with TD."

Herbert shot the CIA analyst a look. "TD? You mean cannabis. Marijuana."

"TD is our code name for it. 'Truth Drug'. It appears to relax all inhibitions and deaden the areas of the brain that govern a person's discretion and caution. The person's sense of humor is accentuated, to the point where any statement or situation can turn out to be extremely funny."

"Yes indeed," Herbert hissed. "A riot." Thinking back to riotous times in his youth, with his cousin Mezz Mezzrow. He took a drink from the glass.

"We've found that a subject, under strict interrogation, might be driven to babble on about psychologically charged topics. That whatever the subject is trying to withhold is actually forced to the top of his subconscious mind. But there are also subjects that get so paranoid that they don't say a word."

Herbert didn't say a word.

"What about mescaline?" Asked one of the other three operatives at the table. "You worked briefly with Dr. Savage in Bethesda, the Naval Medical Research Institute."

"Yes. Savage." Herbert snarled at them. "He started with notes from the Nazi doctors at Dachau, which the Navy picked up while scouring Europe for military secrets. They called them 'aviation medicine' experiments." He paused for recognition, but none was forthcoming.

"The interrogation techniques didn't work," Herbert continued. "But maybe you want to try some of the *other* experiments they did at Dachau. Injecting inmates with gasoline, infecting them with malaria. Crushing them to death in high-altitude pressure chambers. Shooting them in order to test blood coagulants on their wounds. Immersing them in tubs of ice water to see how long it would take before they froze to death."

The operatives just blinked at him.

"Well," drawled the lead analyst, "we can't coerce you, Mister, ah, Mention."

"That's right," Herbert snarled, and got up to leave.

"You will talk to us again," snapped the analyst, closing his notebook. It seemed that the meeting was over.

* * *

Herbert flinched when he ran into Will Cravingston in the hall.

"Like I said, full amnesty," Will said disarmingly. "But you were talking to the competition."

"What do you mean?"

"That group is MK-ULTRA. They're from the Technical Services Staff. They got their supply from the Office of Security."

"Supply?"

"The new psychoactive substance, d-Lysergic Acid Diethylamide Tartrate-25."

"Hoffman's lysergic acid, yes?"

"Exactly. The semi-synthetic compound."

"Why is this so important?"

"It's extremely potent, effective at doses of as little as ten-millionths of a gram."

"That's, what... five thousand times more potent than mescaline? Do you know what you're doing with these, ah, experiments?"

"ARTICHOKE is about to be phased out," replied Cravingston glibly. "Gottlieb and his people have other ideas about how to use it. They don't care about its therapeutic possibilities. They see it solely in terms of its ability to create toxic psychosis. To them, what we call 'tripping' is really just psychosis. We know the substance might be useful for interrogations, or for confusing the enemy, and in such tiny quantities we could deliver it to the bloodstream any number of subtle ways. But Gottlieb wants to take it a step further and use it for covert operations."

Cravingston paused, to see Herbert's reaction. Herbert shrugged.

"His group," continued Cravingston, "they want to secretly dose politicians, make them act strangely or speak foolishly in public. They're testing these theories by dosing agents on an impromptu basis."

The glass of water at the meeting!

As Cravingston was talking, Herbert started to feel the edges of his personality crumble. The coded messages he'd found in music were starting to appear in the gray metal office furniture, the cream-colored cubicle walls, the linoleum floors. Every little thing in the universe seemed to carry the message. Here he was, in the most powerful building in the Western Hemisphere, populated by human beings all scampering about like ordinary squirrels. The bureaucrats and operatives of the greatest spy network of all time ruminated over plans and provisions while farting and scratching their stinking, human bodies at their desks, in the cafeterias, and in the toilets of the lavatories, oblivious to the supernatural messages surrounding them.

Coded instructions led him out the front steps of the CIA building, and he looked back at the front entrance to see the inscription in stone, "And Ye Shall Know The Truth And The Truth Shall Make You Free". Herbert reflected on the verse it came from, John 8:31-32, in which Jesus had tried to explain to thick-headed apostles that seeking political freedom from Rome was not the issue; Jesus had meant a very different kind of freedom.

Caught in the full throes of a psychedelically-induced psychosis, Herbert shrank to the size of a molecule. And down here at the molecular level, down in the small time, without any kind of moral compass to guide you, all you can do is gaze upward at the colossal building, at the inscription in stone, at the gigantic planetary pyramid scheme of the wealthy and its smoothly delivered myths of the limitless.

He would disappear again, that much was certain. But before he departed, he glared back at Will Cravingston, and every argument they'd ever had was right out there in the open, decades of debate teetering toward a final judgement. All through the Eisenhower years, with everybody acting so quaint and cute, pure terror had inhabited some deeper level of Herbert's mind. In 1949 Truman had approved the development of the H-bomb. He thought he was going nuts, to be in such disagreement with his peers; then he realized it was *his peers* that were going nuts! Think tanks filled with geniuses carrying attaché cases and wearing horn-rimmed glasses, with every appearance of scholarly sanity, going to work every day to imagine all the ways the world could end. They would develop a bomb for every letter of the alphabet until they got to the Z-bomb.

And they would develop a secret network, transmitting and receiving data beneath the veneer of American life, to assure government command and control after a nuclear attack. And this network would grow with the Cold War and evolve toward civilian life, where it would creep through the smallest details of our lives, absorbing our energy, boosting their profits, and eating up our precious time.

And he finally found the words to say to Cravingston what he had meant all those years, what was truly wrong with the Corporation. "They carry within their hearts a bitter-cold death wish for the planet."

* * *

The Cambridge music scene had grown sharper with competition for gigs and, incredibly, recording contracts for folk singers like Joan Baez. It was getting harder and harder for blues purists like Eric Von Schmidt or straight-out country folk practitioners like the Charles River Valley Boys to get gigs. Reggie's roommate Tom Rush, an English Lit student who'd taught him a few Lowland Scots and Appalachian folk songs, featured them on his radio program, but the compass needle had turned south, toward the Newport Folk Festival and its New York contingent.

Bobby Dylan, Dick Fariña, and their rapidly growing entourage that now included Bobby Neuwirth and Geno, decided to take off for the gleaming metropolis. "Y'know, I'm proud of where I'm from," Bobby told Reggie, referring to the midwest, "but I would not be doing what I'm doing today if I hadn't come to New York first. I get my direction from New York. I get fed in

New York. Get beaten down, get picked up. New York keeps me going. Ya gotta come down, come to Van Ronk's place. If I'm not there, look for me at Izzy's."

Cornell had suggested Van Ronk, and had even predicted that Reggie would meet this kid Bobby who knew Jim Dandy. The memory of the crossroads haunted him. He wanted to skip out of Harvard and go his own way, but he had to reckon with the Selective Training and Service Act of 1940, signed into law, ironically, by Roosevelt, the hero of his own new liberalism. To keep from being drafted, one had to either be pursuing a college education full-time, or find some other means of exemption. One method was to fake homosexuality; another was to load up on speed and booze for three or four days, then smoke a lot of grass before walking into the induction center. Reggie was not prepared to do either, so he registered for only a short leave of absence from Harvard, and was off on the next train.

* * *

Izzy Young bustled about the Folklore Center at 110 MacDougal Street in New York's Greenwich Village, shouting at bill collectors on the phone, tacking up concert flyers, and handing out mail to itinerant musicians, as Reggie walked in. He was old school, horn-rimmed glasses hanging off his nose, and his tie aslant on his white shirt that slopped over the thin belt on his wool slacks. He wore work boots and his voice rolled like a bulldozer, always a little too loud for the room.

Reggie didn't have to ask Izzy for help. Dylan (who now preferred Bob to Bobby) was already there because he got his mail from Izzy. Bob referred to the Folklore Center, never to Izzy's face, as the citadel of New York folk music, "an ancient chapel, a shoebox sized *institute*."

They adjourned to the tiny back room and sat down on a bench, surrounded by shiny, intimidating banjos. Bob had been invited to Carolyn's recording session to play harmonica.[215] The session had been run at Columbia, by a man named John Hammond. "I told Hammond about your Robert Johnson record," Bob said. "He said he knew all about Robert Johnson. Said that Johnson could 'whip anybody.' But he wanted to know who *you* were, and how you'd heard about Johnson. When I told him, he said he knew your father. Y'now, there may be a thousand kings in the world. Hammond is one of them."

Before Bob left that day, Hammond had given him a couple of acetates of records not yet available to the public. Columbia had bought the vaults of '30s and '40s secondary labels such as Brunswick, Okeh, Vocalion, and ARC, and would soon be releasing some of the material on albums. One such album in the making was *King of the Delta Blues* by Robert Johnson.

Bob had the record with him, hidden between a Paul Clayton album of Scottish sea shanties and a Big Bill Broonzy record, because he didn't want anyone to ask him about it or ask to borrow it. The artwork for the Robert

Johnson album cover was an unusual painting. The painter's eye stares down from the ceiling at this fiercely intense singer and guitar player of medium height but with shoulders like an acrobat. "Look at that," said Bob, trusting Reggie enough to show it to him. "It's electrifying."

They were supposed to meet Fariña at Allan Block's Sandal Shop, which was jammed with musicians creating a suitable cacophony around the shop table amidst the odors of leather, tanning solvents, and glue. Dave Van Ronk, the unofficial mayor of MacDougal Street, was trying out a banjo, though he'd never played a banjo before. "God help you if you want to buy sandals," Van Ronk roared above the noise to Bob and Reggie.

Fariña arrived and poked Van Ronk. "You know, you can't play banjo," he shouted. "But you're the best banjo player I've ever heard." Laughter all around. Fariña was on a roll. "The problem with folk," he announced to everyone, "is that it needs a *beat*."

"Well we don't want to get *too* popular," Van Ronk said as he pointed to a notice on the bulletin board. "Look at what the public *wants*. Folk singers for parties. For a nominal fee, they'll hire some clown to come to one of their parties in East Hampton or wherever, and this clown will show up complete with beard, bongos, and beret, and wander around the party saying 'Wow' and 'Far out' and occasionally take a feckless thwack at his bongo."

Van Ronk was particularly angry at the flood of tourists on the weekends scouring the cellar clubs for the next Kingston Trio. And he had a few more words to say about a former club owner turned manager by the name of Albert Grossman, the "devil incarnate" as Van Ronk called him, who was looking for folk singers who could write, and trying to put together a trio with Peter Yarrow and Mary Travers. "He wanted me to change my name to Paul," Van Ronk sneered, "so that they would be 'Peter, Paul, and Mary'. What a joke." But Bob was intrigued.

Back in Van Ronk's apartment, Bob played the entire Robert Johnson acetate he'd received from Hammond. "Man, from the first note, the vibrations make my hair stand up. Those stabbing sounds from the guitar can almost break a window. And when he starts singing, he seems like a guy who could have sprung from the head of Zeus in full armor."[216]

Van Ronk kept pointing out that this song came from another song, and that one was derivative, another a note-for-note replica. Van Ronk put on some sides by LeRoy Carr, Skip James, and Henry Thomas. "See what I mean?" Bob did see what he meant, but as Reggie pointed out, Woody had taken some old Carter Family songs and put his own spin on them too.

"I've been playing this record over and over for an entire day, just staring at the record player," Bob confided to Reggie. "It felt like a ghost had come into the room, a fearsome apparition. The songs are layered with a startling economy of lines. But it's like he's already got all the styles and mannerisms of more than twenty men. His words make my nerves quiver like piano wires. They are so elemental in meaning and feeling. It's like I'm getting the inside picture."

Reggie was impressed. Bob had copied Johnson's words down on scraps of paper so that he could more closely examine the lyrics and patterns, the construction of the old-style lines, and the free association that Johnson used. "The sparkling allegories!" Bob exclaimed. "Those big-ass truths, wrapped in a hard shell of nonsensical abstraction. Themes that fly through the air with the greatest of ease."

Reggie thought that Johnson must have known about Walt Whitman. "Maybe he did," Bob replied, "but it doesn't clear up anything. He seems to know about *everything*, he throws in Confucious-like sayings whenever it suits him. And he could play everything, whatever the audience wanted, because he was a performer. But these recordings are *his songs*, like he's playing for an audience only he could see, one off in the future. And he's as serious as scorched earth."

* * *

John Hammond could sense Robert Johnson in Bob's studio performance, but Bob was more like Charlie Chaplin on the stage. After reading Robert Shelton's review in the New York Times, Hammond had gone down to the Gaslight club to see Dylan perform.

Bob was a very kinetic performer, with a lot of nervous mannerisms and gestures. He never stood still. He was obviously quaking in his boots a lot of the time, but he made that part of the show. There would be a one-liner, a mutter, a mumble, another one-liner, a slam at the guitar. Bob had that herky-jerky phrasing when he sang like Woody Guthrie, and especially when he took the talking blues into a new realm with songs like "Talkin' John Birch Paranoid Blues".[217] No one else seemed to be able to reinterpret and incorporate the old melodies into songs he could claim as his own. He moved swiftly through the folk canon and his own attempts at serious songwriting, changing his repertoire all the time. He'd find something he loved and sing it to death for a short while, and then drop it and go on to something else. Also like Robert Johnson, thought Hammond.

Above all, his sense of timing was uncanny: he would get all these pseudo-clumsy bits of business going, fiddling with his harmonica rack and guitar tuning pegs, and he could put an audience in stitches without saying a word. For one song he played a harmonica chorus that consisted of one note. He kept strumming the guitar, and every now and again he would blow this one note, and after a few measures the audience was completely caught up in trying to figure out when the next note was coming. By the end of two choruses, he had the entire audience laughing.

Hammond was frustrated with Columbia and, to be honest, with the world. Especially the mob's encroachment on the music business. Frankie Avalon, for chrissakes! Sing along with Mitch, on TV no less. The executives barely tolerated his Robert Johnson album and would probably be openly hostile about this kid. And Freddie, poor Freddie, doomed ever since he took that recording from the Spirituals to Swing concert. Did it really hold some kind of power?

But Hammond's advisor Cornell Woodrow had been right so many times before. Count Basie, for example. Integrating the Benny Goodman band. Billie Holiday. More recently, Cornell had brought Lead Belly to Café Society so that Hammond could hear his version of an old hillbilly song about a black girl in a whorehouse, "In New Orleans (House Of The Rising Sun)".[218] Not a raunchy number at all, but a story about a poor girl ruined by the House, and she tells her sister not to go there, but now can't pay the rent and must herself go back, as the House is her fate, and that's all there is to it. The hillbilly version had been more like a blues, but Lead Belly sang in a major key, not a minor. Cornell pointed out to Hammond that this was a reversal, for a white version to be more of a blues, more of a dirge, than the black version.

Hammond encouraged Lead Belly to make a recording, and Herbert Mention, who thought he heard something in it, produced a transcription disc that circulated among the new folk music revival crowd. The song was covered on several folk albums, including a pop-leaning, jazzy blues treatment by the Weavers.[219] What impressed Hammond was the writing, the lyrics. It seemed to be a more sophisticated take on the blues of Robert Johnson.

And here was Mention's son Reggie, showing up at just the right moment with Dylan, just as he's finishing up the Robert Johnson album. Hammond was taking a new approach in this experiment. He wanted an original songwriter, not another performer of Tin Pan Alley and folk songs. He had to move quickly but carefully. He had Bob audition a few songs for him in his office at Columbia, but secretly, without recording them. He didn't want any record of this kid's raw voice falling into the wrong hands. He could already hear them around the offices, referring to his latest project as "Hammond's Folly".

Bob was full of nervous energy in Hammond's office, his knees bouncing against the table, jiggling, herky-jerky, sitting on the edge of his chair. He had a lot of stories about who he was and where he came from, but he never seemed to be able to keep them straight. Hammond let it all pass in order to get the kid to sign a contract. Bob's first album would be a hybrid of authentic folk music and his own songs. But even the authentic songs sounded like his. It's the spirit of Robert Johnson, is how Cornell would put it.

* * *

Reggie couldn't tell at what point this circle of friends that included Bob had turned into a posse with Bob as the leader. Over time, Bob grew to be intimidating, hard to talk to. He'd toss off one-line criticisms at the jagged edges of wit. Reggie had seen grown men with steely eyes buckle under Bob's stare. He'd seen Dave Van Ronk, who could argue with God Himself and who still called him Bobby, cave in to Bob's subtle pressure and passive aggressive taunts.

Bob and his entourage, which now included Reggie, dropped into the Kettle of Fish after Bob's recording sessions with Hammond. Bob was being very mysterious about the whole thing, and no one else had been to the sessions. Van Ronk pumped him for information, but he was vague. Everything was going fine. Then Bob said to Van Ronk with a smirk, "Hey, would it be okay for me to record your arrangement of 'House of the Rising Sun'?"

It was Van Ronk's signature performance tune. Van Ronk had altered the chords in his arrangement and used a bass line that descended in half steps, which was a common enough progression in jazz, but unusual among folksingers. "Jeez, Bobby, I'm going into the studio to do that myself in a few weeks. Can't it wait until your next album?"

Bob turned to his posse and smiled. "Uh-oh."

Van Ronk didn't like the sound of that. "What do you mean?"

"Well," Bob said matter-of-factly, "I've already recorded it."[220]

Van Ronk sighed. How far could one arrangement go, anyway? But the gigs rolled in for Bob, and even though his first record hadn't sold well, Bob was already thinking that his career was taking off. He no longer had time for anybody, and his ambition seemed as wide as the Mesabi Range of his birth.

* * *

Mumblingore, just back from organizing Cuban exiles in New Orleans, still in his beret and fatigues, motioned for Cravingston to join him in the back room. "The results are inconclusive," he told Cravingston. "We can induce psychosis, but we can't control it."

"What about the rabbit…"

"Oswald, the one the Agency sent to Moscow? He's back, and we've tested him, and we know now that we can't control him. He's become, shall we say, *unreliable*. And how was your time with Herbert?"

"Fruitful in one way," mused Cravingston. "We know he can't be trusted, but there's nothing he can do to hurt us."

"And his son, the one at Harvard?"

"Coming along. Give him time."

"That's not what they want to hear." Mumblingore raised an eyebrow in contempt.

"Well, shouldn't we shift our focus away from the Agency's agenda? All this rabbit stuff. Put a rifle in one of their hands, it all comes unglued. What if the press gets hold of some report that some assassin under contract to those idiots had been part of *our* experiments? We need to do our own projects. Don't we have a lot of the stuff left over from Midnight Climax?"

Mumblingore smiled contentedly, as if this is where he had wanted the conversation to go all along. "Not only do we have the supply from 'Captain' Al Hubbard, we also have the operation's manager on board, George Hunter White. Not to mention Babbs, his very attractive assistant, the Grande Madam of the houses."

Cravingston shook his head in amusement. "Hubbard gets around, he's like a Johnny Appleseed, so it's amazing that the information hasn't leaked out. Testing drugs on unwitting subjects in brothels! Amazing that no one ever sued."

"Not yet. Of course I disapprove of our esteemed Dr. Gottlieb's premise and his methods. Yes, of course you can induce some kind of psychosis with these substances and maybe, just maybe, extract secrets from enemy agents, or send agents on impossible missions, but you're right. These subjects are having *revelations*, for heaven's sake. We can't trust what we hear out of their babbling mouths. We can't trust what they'll do under any circumstances."

"And this is with the new substance, d-Lysergic Acid whatever…"

"LSD-25, yes. Much stronger, more revelatory, so to speak, than the mushroom extract."

"This is precisely what I've been talking about. We need to use this substance on a higher level, with a much higher class of people, of intellect. It could be much more effective on a political scale."

Now it was Mumblingore's turn to be amused. "You're beginning to sound like Hubbard," he laughed. "Imagine, adding a drop to Khrushchev's tea at Kennedy's upcoming test ban meeting. He might just give up Cuba." But then he sighed. Hubbard had been a mistake, a loose cannon. His wanton Johnny Appleseed approach threatened the stability of the project, and must have contributed to his addled state. And once again he was late with his reports, his detailed observations of members of high society strung out on this new substance.

"We should make it available to Professor Leary, here at Harvard," said Cravingston, as if he were reading Mumblingore's mind that Hubbard should be ruled out. "I already handle someone in London with Sandoz connections, who can get it to him without his knowing that it has any connection to us. Leary's work for the Agency with the mushroom extract has progressed faster than the Agency will allow, and he's looking for positive results from these revelations, not negative states from varying degrees of psychosis."

"You *really* want to test it on our own politicians?" Mumblingore gave him that knowing look that said yes, I know of government secrets in your domain of expertise.

Cravingston paused. If knowledge has filtered down to Mumblingore in his lab, he must assume that the information he'd provided about his association with the Kennedy brothers had been useful. "One way or another, we must be in control."

Mumblingore frowned. "Meyer knows about you and his wife. He won't do anything yet, not with her tongue firmly planted in Kennedy's ear. You're lucky that he has bigger fish to fry in that department." Indeed, he thought, we are both lucky. The rogues in the intelligence community were threatening to take control of the experiment.

* * *

Back at Harvard to fulfill the minimum requirements for avoiding the draft, Reggie took time out from mediating Students for a Democratic Society disputes between the Kennedy liberals (of which he was the most radical member) and the progressives and old-line socialists, to go get coffee at Tulla's with Ric Von Schmidt and use Tulla's phonograph to play the acetate of Dylan's new album, which featured a tribute to Ric called "Baby, Let Me Follow You Down".[221]

Listening in were a group of excessive coffee drinkers that called themselves the Subtracters. They didn't consider themselves to be contributors to society; rather, with so many people in the world, there was no more room to add value. Like the old saying, "I have nothing to give," so their works of art *subtract*, rather than add value. Intrigued, Reggie took off with them to an art-desecration session at a house on Homer Street in Newton Center.

It turned out that they were wrong. The session today would be ego-death. A plaque on the front of the house showed the three monkeys in relief. And descending the stairs, clothed in vivid green velvet, was the love of Reggie's life.

Quite taken aback, Reggie fumbled his way out of the car and ended up half kneeling on the curb. Lucy, for it was indeed his unconsummated high-school sweetheart, last seen strapped to a gurney in an ambulance in Margate, approached quietly, and he could feel her warmth. Her soft face, fuzzy hair, sparkling eyes, and tongue-in-cheek smile made her look just a bit shy. Her feathery fingers rested on his arm in an earnest attempt at friendship, but also with a hint of lust. Baby, let me follow you down!

She helped him to a standing position, and at that moment a torrent of silk-wrapped freaks swarmed out over the porch and down the steps, singing various songs out of key, and waving colorful banners and streamers. Through the front door strode an older man with gray-streaked hair and a look of a gentleman about him, rakishly thin and serious, all in white, and as he held his hands together in prayer, the riotous group paused in silence. When the older man looked up from his moment of contemplation, he grinned a maniacal grin so wide and Irish that it crinkled every part of his face. This was Dr. Timothy Leary. And at his signal, the group erupted in frolic abandon to "Rip It Up".[222]

"Weird, huh? You'll get used to it." Lucy led Reggie up the stairs, through the twirling dancers, across the old porch with charred floorboards where Leary's roommates and visitors had lighted ill-advised bonfires, through a foyer with leaded-glass windows and walls covered with painted slogans, into a bare living room with a fleur-de-lis tiled fireplace filled with broken furniture, and over to a mayonnaise jar on the shelf. A miniature English flag on a toothpick stood sentry over the wavy, creamy, yellowish substance, which turned out to be vanilla cake icing with a special ingredient. "From London, the newest thing. Michael Hollingshead brought it," gesturing to a   balding, red-faced, paunchy troubadour strumming a ukulele on the porch with the dancers. "Lysergic acid."

Smiling sweetly, she dipped a dixie spoon, and held it to his lips. He licked it from the spoon, expecting an acidic taste, but the sweetness hid something else, almost but not quite metallic, that made his neck muscles twitch and his stomach tighten. Almost immediately he felt feathery wisps of incense assaulting his nose; he followed it to its source, an intricately detailed aluminum incense burner with a tiny buddha at its center, in whose lap the incense smoldered. The smoke floated up through a ragged hole in the ceiling to the second floor. She followed his gaze. "It's like an air freshener," she grinned madly. "We're a dysfunctional family. Tim's got his kids living with us, and all sorts of people crash here. The rule is that the men do the shopping and wash the dishes, and the women do the cooking, but we all have to take care of our own laundry, and, well… you know how that goes."

A side door opened, and Leary, still holding his hands together in prayer, shuffled across to them like an Indian swami but flashing the grin of a whiskey-soaked Irish barrister, and then shuffled past them without a word. An unspoken welcome. Reggie could sense that in this house no orders needed to be issued; simplicity had reached such a serene level that all things operated together without question in this soft womb. Only when unusual accidents took place was there need for speech; and little, even then.

Lucy held his hand and led him out to the porch to watch the dancers, now side-stepping to Fats Domino's "Rockin' Chair".[223] Reggie studied her, backing into a baffled smile that would soon occupy his face for the rest of the day and painfully through a weary dusk, from a rocking chair he could not get up from, feeling safe only as long as he kept rocking. And in an instant of eternity, in a single rock of the chair, he saw it all. How meaningless life was. How every mindful approach to the truth, across a range of approaches from the intensely spiritual to the most atheistic and dialectic, ended in a cul-de-sac of solipsism. Every life was a separate movie, and as long as he starred in his own movie, he'd never know its true meaning. It would take more than a leap of faith to get beyond the role that seemed to be laid out for him, of a Harvard-forged politician-in-waiting, or the role he wanted for himself, of a songwriter and an explorer of his father's mysteries. It would take a liberation of this psychic energy, to invent for himself a new role in this greater, larger-than-life movie, the center stage of humanity.

He tried to focus, to get another glimpse of his future, and it seemed at first that his gift had failed him… only to realize that it was not just a glimpse. He was immersed in an entire world of the future, three dimensional, completely alive, all around him like a never-ending panorama. All of his future journeys, loves, hates, trials and tribulations led up to a dramatic instant… beyond which there was nothing. It had all unfolded like one of those new tape-recording machines that sputtered out sound in fast-forward mode. And he knew, right then and there, caught in the throes of a mental hurricane, that all of this would be recorded in his brain in some inner recess he could never reach, at least while awake. He would not remember this when it was over. And in the next second, the next rock of his chair, he wouldn't remember any of it at all.

Lucy, sitting cross-legged before him on the porch floor cradling an open book in her lap, interrupted Reggie's reverie. "I know you like Woody Guthrie. But listen to this. He wrote an article called 'The Secret'. It's about people always asking him what the secret of life is, and whether he believes in God. And he writes, 'All is love, love is all, and love conquers all. I love the very sound of the naked word. The best and juiciest of our humanly truths are our naked truths. I work with naked hands and speak my naked words.'"

"And this is supposed to mean…" Reggie not quite sure he should be asking.

"It means he's been in love. Real, sexual, intimate love. Here, let me read this, his letter to a woman named Marjorie. 'So, I ask you and tell you, spread your legs apart now and let me put this several inches of new life and lights into your plowed grounds, inside your hole and your nest, inside where you can bathe and warm it in all of your slick oils and salves. Let me come slowly enough so as not to do you misery. Let me come in as slow as you want me.'"

"Woody wrote *that*?"

"My hole and my nest, Reggie," she closed the book, and let her hand guide the slit of her green velvet dress to show herself. No panties. Tiny black hairs curled like woodsmoke at the very top of her soft inner thighs.

Reggie lunged forward and buried his face in her, gripping her buttocks with both hands to bring her closer, and she hunched her hips to receive his tongue, and for the longest time all he wanted, ever, in all his life, was to just be there, in her quim without a care, lapping away at her sweetness.

At some point he thought he heard clapping, actually applause, and he realized that it was the dancers. They were congratulating him for leaving the rocking chair. Indeed, he had finally gone "off his rocker". Red-faced, to Sam Cooke's "Wonderful World",[224] he let Lucy take him by the hand and lead him upstairs to what he knew, through his recovered power of seeing the future, would be nirvana.

* * *

Reggie's expanded consciousness had somehow allowed an animal rapture to grow within him, an infatuation for Lucy's body that he'd never felt before. He could still taste her; his first-ever exploration of a vagina had suspended his worried mind and left him speechless in a complacency not unlike the reverie of an exhausted body turned toward sleep. He wallowed and snuggled in the linens holding her odor. A casual stroke of her buttock brought him up hard, achingly erect, and she guided him into her like the angel of the harbor piloting the Titanic to port. He had kept an image of her serene face with the impishly upturned nose and trembling chin like a photograph folded securely in the wallet of his everyday memory, as a charm against the raving indifference and petty vindictiveness of the competitive collegiate world. Her innocent face had gotten him through many weeks of lonely terror, outclassed in classrooms by day, ostracized from social circles at night. But now, as they were fucking, truly fucking, her face, veiled with sweat, grew in passion fiercely exquisite, and revealed to him the face of some other woman, a woman he didn't know, possessed as if by demons that were under no obligation to reveal themselves to him.

And another thing, and this was not a hallucination. This mind expansion that Mel Lyman had been pontificating about had sharpened his field of vision with regard to the future. He could still focus as before, but the revelation was much clearer. And as they untangled themselves, he knew he'd be asking this question and that she would answer it, reluctantly, even a bit defiantly, and would not kick him out of bed for it.

"What actually happened that night, under the Boardwalk?"

She didn't redden, she didn't even flinch. "I was raped. But I don't feel any animosity about it." Then, reluctantly, she tried to explain what had possessed her, where she had gone, and how she had met Dr. Leary, whom she now loved but not sexually. It's just that Dr. Leary had saved her life.

* * *

A butterfly net floated above Lucy in the pastoral sunshine. She instinctively knew what it was, and its purpose, to ensnare the animal soul of the planet. At the moment of conception, this animal soul would move into the embryo and become a living being, in a form resembling a man, possessing not only human qualities but superhuman powers. Her glorious moonchild, a transcendental consciousness capable, in time, of raising the consciousness of the human race. She remembered her Aleister Crowley: "We are but spirits trapped in bodies on this Earth, awaiting our chrysalis moment when we turn into star beings. For every man and every woman is a star."

She gasped as the butterfly net transformed itself into a shroud that enveloped her in darkness.

And then: white walls, a white ceiling. A warm, crinkly face with a maniacal grin blocked her view. He told some kind of drinking joke, as if they were regulars in a pub. Then he backed up and gestured around at what now appeared to be a hospital room. His name was Dr. Timothy Leary, and his lively eyes spoke to her and soothed her. Lucy had fallen in love with him even before she regained her full senses.

By the end of her seventh session with massive doses of LSD, she was no longer capable of recognizing the difference between reality, or what others told her was real, and her own fantasy. The government-sponsored therapy at Bordentown Reformatory in New Jersey had been focused on destabilizing and breaking down people under interrogation. They had experimented with her brain, disconnecting parts so that neuron connections were no longer made. She couldn't recognize melodies in one experiment, couldn't recognize rhythm in another. Over several months of rest with no treatment, these facilities came back to her, but now with far greater clarity and freshness, as if she had been deaf and could now hear for the first time. The researchers were puzzled.

She knew she had lost her baby, Johnny B's baby. They had taken it away during a surgical procedure that she could somehow watch from the ceiling, without feeling.

The dark curly-haired teenager in the next bed who introduced himself with a heavy Long Island accent as Lou Reed, explained that it had actually been her body on the surgical table, *her* baby that had been removed. Reed had received electroconvulsive therapy, "to cure my bisexuality" as he put it. "They put the thing down your throat so you don't swallow your tongue, and they put electrodes on your head. The effect is that you lose your memory and become a vegetable. You can't read a book because you get to page seventeen and have to go right back to page one again."

Over time, her memories came back, along with all her literary references. Lucy was once again recommending books to strangers, hoping to enlighten them, as if by enlightening *them* she would eventually recruit enough friends to watch her back, to warn her of danger, to squirrel away her medicine when she didn't want to take it. One of her recommendations would change Lou Reed's life: the poetry of Delmore Schwartz, and his book of stories titled *In Dreams Begin Responsibilities*. It seemed to her like a good fit for this confused, vulnerable, dark-haired boy. She could feel, as a low buzz in the pit of her stomach, the vibrations of the ridicule he'd been exposed to.

Dr. Leary hovered in the background and eventually got her transferred to a white-bricked psychiatric clinic hidden in a leafy forest near Lexington, Massachusetts. A Dr. Mumblingore, head of psychotomimetic studies at the clinic, had endorsed Leary's initial experiments with psilocybin, so Leary thought she'd be in good hands. Until he found out she had been dosed on LSD for six weeks. They wanted to see how the drug destabilized her. When she clawed a doctor's face with her nails and kicked a technician in the balls, they locked her up in solitary.

Leary sought out Professor Cravingston at Harvard, who knew Dr. Mumblingore, and got her transferred to Concord State Prison with Mumblingore's blessing, to continue with Leary's psilocybin experiments. And when the sparkle returned to her eyes, she joined Leary in Newton Center, where she spent most of her time hostessing the celebrities and making calls to friends of Allen Ginsberg to get them to come to Leary's for the next voyage into inner space.

* * *

Losing Lucy did not trouble Dr. Mumblingore, who had located another test subject, this time in McNeil Island Penitentiary in Washington State. Alvin "Old Creepy" Karpis, a member of the Ma Barker Gang, had passed along the info about one of his cell mates, Charlie Manson, a young impressionable sort who'd spent most of his life in institutions. The kid had picked up some ideas from books about the Masons and Rosicrucians, and he was a sucker for Scientology.

Mumblingore had quickly dispatched Lanier Raymer, a Doctor-level in the cult who could pass for a felon. Before long Raymer had Manson using the terms "to mock up," "cease to exist," and "to come to Now," and the concept of "putting up pictures." Manson was a quick study. Before long he was dabbling in post-hypnotic suggestion, planting messages in the headphones of sleeping prisoners over the prison radio, urging them to get out and root for the underdog prison basketball team, and then cleaning up when he placed bets with the over-zealous new fans against the team. He also planted suggestions to applaud his first performance as a singer, and he won the prison contest with a standing ovation.

Karpis, at Mumblingore's urging, taught Manson how to play guitar and gave him copies of Eric Berne's *Transactional Analysis* and *Games People Play*, which helped him develop his perverse doctrine of the Child Mind. "Now give him Heinlein's *Stranger in a Strange Land*, see what he makes of that," Mumblingore mused. "I think he'll be perfect in a few years. Ready to accomplish great tasks." Another one for the assassination squad.

* * *

Despite a ban on marijuana and a focus on the more benign psilocybin to preserve the purity of the chemical experiments, guests were now encouraged by Hollingshead and Lucy to strike out into the unknown with the mayonnaise jar. Soon they had all abandoned their clipboards and charts, and joints littered the porch ashtrays.

The mood was solemn. Olatunji's African drumming[225] floated in the background, conjuring the spirit of Shango in the interplay of mother drum and baby drum. The semicircle of subjects sat in lotus positions awaiting their doses. Leary, the control for this session, scratched out the starting time in a spiral notebook adorned with colorful crayon swirls. Mel Lyman tried unsuccessfully to control his fidgeting. The mayonnaise jar was passed around. Reggie took twice the normal dose and held Lucy's hand.

After a predetermined interval of contemplation, Leary raised his hand in signal, and spoke.

"Number one," Leary intoned in a sonorous voice more suitable for Gregorian chants than for a wild and crazy trip. "There is a dawning suspicion, based on considerable evidence, that the politics of the nervous system are such that man uses only a fragment, perhaps less than one percent, of his available brain capacity.

"Number two," Leary continued. "Certain psychophysiological processes, and we can talk about censoring, altering, discriminating, selecting, and evaluating… these are responsible for the restricted use of the brain capacity.

"And three. Indole substances, and here we refer to LSD, mescaline, and psilocybin, seem to *inhibit* or *alter* these restricting mental processes, so that a *dramatic* expansion of consciousness is triggered off."

Leary's words echoed in reverb, slowly receding as a Doppler effect, as Reggie began his whirl into the inner cosmos, now feeling like he's in one of those cup-and-saucer rides, the Tilt 'A Whirl on the Boardwalk. He's holding hands with Lucy and others in one of the cups. They're spinning mercilessly without any handholds. Round and round he goes through waves of nausea, circling ever wider, only to find he's really somewhere in the middle, and everything is expanding. The unfeeling machinery beneath them, he knows, is the force of nature. The beloved connectedness of all living things is the gravity that keeps him and his friends pinned in the seats of their whirling cups. But there is no love in these connections, only the nausea of being jerked around uncontrollably, indifferently, like superfluous cells of a writhing body. They all could be spun off and out into oblivion without a moment's thought or care.

The vision dissolves into a baseball game. Congressmen man the bases and the President hurls the pitch. But it is the umpire, the technocrat, the least obtrusive on the field, the one we pay no attention to, who stands above the contest and interprets and enforces the rules. Rules that They dreamed up to give each side equal weight, to keep the contest going, to sell tickets… rather than to resolve anything. And the game keeps going, never reaches a ninth inning, no matter if Democrats or Republicans or Marcuse or even Cravingston are at bat. Because it is a grand cultural imperative beyond question, beyond discussion. And so right off the bat, we have to question whether They have any legitimacy whatsoever, and then we're questioning Their institutions, and finally we're questioning Their meaning of life.

Our generation, my generation, Reggie thought, bred in modest comfort, now looked uncomfortably to a new, unstable world.

Lucy's hand in his own grew warmer, stickier. It occurred to Reggie that the ideal crucible for an alchemical transmutation is the human body. There is no other ideal crucible, no crucible so perfectly sealed and protected that it can be considered a truly closed system, a unit absolutely isolated from the rest of the universe. And if we are actually agreeing to create, from moment to moment, everything we perceive as real, then it stands to reason that we're also responsible for keeping it going in some harmonious manner. We may be the last generation in the experiment with living.

Lucy's eyes met his, and she gripped his hand harder as if to wring out any doubt about what was happening. She appeared to him as the Moon itself, and in her best periods she is Artemis, unassailable, a being fine and reflectively radiant. And yet she has a dark side; she is Hecate, the crone, the woman past all hope of motherhood, her soul black with envy and hatred of happier mortals. In between these extremes, to which she could spring back and forth at a moment's notice, is her animal soul; flush in the fullness of life, she is the sublime Persephone, for whose sake Demeter cursed the fields that they would bring forth no more corn until Hades consented to restore her to Earth, for at least half a year.

How sensitive is the formula for woman, he thought, that it can touch such extremes according to the nature of the influences upon her. Crowley had written that woman is the Moon, not illuminating, but reflective. Woman has no soul, he wrote, only sex; no morals, only moods; her mind is mob-rule. When attached to a solar soul, she reflected him, clung to him, Isis to his Osiris, sister as well as spouse; every thought of her mind being but the harmonic of his. She was not of a "scientific" mind; her aspirations to the Unknown had been fully satisfied by mere love. She could be happy in a commonplace cottage, tending her garden of love.

That didn't sound like Lucy at all. Lucy's thoughts were her own; her experiences the equal of any man. A true hipster, full of illumination. Reggie had been drawn to her like a butterfly to light. But now, to his distress, he could not see a flash vision of her future. And yet he still had the power. He could see one of his own future, a few years from now, leading a ragtag mob charge at the Pentagon.

* * *

A far more shattering experience than psilocybin, the LSD brought Leary to his knees, crouching in existential agony. Allen Ginsberg wandered into the living room wearing only his glasses and, raising his finger with a mad holy gleam in his eye, proclaimed himself the Messiah. "We're going to go out to the city streets to tell the people about peace and love. And then we'll get lots of important leaders on a big telephone to settle all this about the Bomb once and for all. Let's start with Khrushchev." Maynard Ferguson and his wife were spread out on the living room couch, Mel Lyman cat-scratching Dock Boggs tunes on the porch. Lucy tended to everyone, pouring carrot juice and vodka, arranging the tarot cards, cleaning up the puke.

This experiment, whatever it was, could not succeed or fail, thought Reggie. There would always be an infinite number of parameters, and unknown results. If the laws of physics and chemistry remain always approximate, so too are the laws of humanity. Laws created by humans no smarter than himself.

At some point in infinite time and space the Tilt 'A Whirl slowed down enough for Reggie to become aware of Mel Lyman, who was talking to no one in particular. "I am at the mercy of the blind ones, in the unyielding, unfruitful hands of the fanatics. They won't cop to objective beauty or acknowledge a God who never questions His own existence. They fear death because it is infinite and, thus, negative. They will do their ugly spider dance in the ugly web they have created. They will never have the courage to peer inward, dissolve the inner walls of lies, and discover that they too are in prison, doing time."

Lyman paused. The pause made everyone pay attention. "Love doesn't even exist on this planet except in rare fleeting moments. I have never met a truly loving person in my life. Love isn't something you find, something you do, something you study. Love is something you *become* after there is no more *you*. It's a complete sacrifice of the personality."

When no one replied, Mel intoned in a soft voice, for shock effect, "I am going to burn down the world. I am going to tear down everything that cannot stand alone, I am going to shove hope *up your ass*, I am going to turn ideals to *shit*. I am going to reduce everything that stands to rubble, and then I'm going to burn the rubble and scatter the ashes." He then looked up, and looked around at the others in childlike wonder. "Then maybe someone will be able to see something as it really is."

Reggie felt premonitions of creepy crawlers and murderous minions. Could this inner voyage wreak such havoc in one's mind? Was LSD that dangerous? Did other people think thoughts that I would never, ever, not in a million years... think? Was their reality *that much* different? And what about Mel Lyman, a musical partner in the jug band. How could a *banjo player* think such thoughts?

* * *

Signs were everywhere that science would soon take a back seat in the puppet show that passed for reality at the Leary house. Leary and Alpert still pretended to measure responses and doses, and still acted as controls in sessions. But one day Lucy introduced Leary to a cowboy she'd heard about, through Ginsberg, the wild one who Kerouac had written about.

Neal Cassady barged through the front door like a tornado. "Look here, I done the Magic Mushroom in Oaxaca, y'unnerstand, and felt the rainbow peacock tail brush my eyeballs, y'unnerstand. Done peyote with the Navajo in

Arizona, in a *hogan*, y'unnerstand, with the fire carefully guarded through the long, wolf-howling desert night and the chanting and the drums and the feathered scepter... Y'unnerstand? Psilocybin, though, that's new to me. Can you lay some on me?"

Leary stood rigid, thoughtful. "We don't work that way. We spend considerable time before the drug session training our subjects, alerting them to what they can expect. We've found that with adequate preparation, subjects have little trouble and can master the fears involved."

Cassady shook his head dubiously. "Why do you make it sound so dangerous? So how much is a dose?"

"Ah, ummm..." Leary looked down at his clipboard. "Two is what most experimenters use. Six is what I have found to be a good dose."

"Gimme twelve. Listen, you gotta stop this pedantic nonsense. You're defiling and corrupting something that is beautiful and free and wild and spontaneous. Why, you're running a *defloration* clinic, where people can lose their virginity in a sanitized mental health situation. Listen, there are no books written by scientists about ecstasy and cosmic orgasms. It's oral history and poetry, y'unnerstand? The history books are about meaningless events like wars and elections and revolutions. The only important things happen in the bodies and brains of individuals, y'unnerstand? That's the great secret of human life that scientists never talk about."

And with that, Neal gobbled up the twelve capsules. Lucy, giggling, led him to a back room and shut the door in Reggie's face. Reggie went right back to that rocking chair on the porch, and was still there when a sheepish Lucy emerged from the back room. Neal had gone off with a Radcliffe girl, and they were last seen double-clutching his Chevy toward Cambridge.

Reggie asked if she had ever fallen in love with anyone.

"Why do you doubt? Love is easy. I love you! And I have loved other men, even women."

"Maybe it isn't 'love'..."

"So what? We can do whatever we imagine. Are we not the world to come? Rules of proper conduct are for the aging, the dying, not for us."

* * *

The world had all but abandoned them to their hedonistic pursuits, it seemed, until Reggie was startled one day to see Cravingston himself on Leary's porch, accompanied by an attractive, thirty-something blonde with an angular nose, flamboyant eyebrows, piercing green-blue eyes, and sharp cheeks, tilting her hip provocatively in a red dress, perfumed for high society. She was introduced as Mary Pinchot. "So I see you've found Dr. Leary," Cravingston sniffed at Reggie. "Enjoy yourself, while it lasts." With an ominous look in his eye and an embarrassed Mary on his arm, he slithered off to a side room with Leary to discuss business.

Reggie could hear a murmur of argument, and then Cravingston's shout. "Poets!? Musicians!? That's not why I brought Mary in."

"But it works," Leary could be heard to protest. "Ginsberg is ready to call his friends in Washington."

The voices retreated to murmur again. Lucy arrived at his side. "I met her once before," she whispered in his ear. "Her last name is really Meyer. Her husband is Cord Meyer, works for the CIA. She could be useful."

Useful? In what way? "If she's CIA," Reggie replied, "what is she doing here?"

"Listen, the CIA is involved with lysergic acid." Lucy held his face in her two immaculate hands and met eye-to-eye. "You know, my stepdad was in the CIA, probably still is. And I'm pretty sure that guy is, too, 'cause I've seen him with my stepdad," indicating with her eyes the man behind the door. Professor Cravingston.

Reggie was about to *flip out* right about now, but he tamped down on his paranoia. "So what was your stepdad doing for the CIA?"

"Keeping an eye on Johnny's father, probably. You know he's the Mafia boss for south Jersey. I always wondered why we moved to Margate, it's twice the distance to my stepdad's office from where we were."

Well, that made sense, thought Reggie. But the connection with Cravingston, and my own father... "I think your stepdad was watching *my* house. Waiting for *my* father to show up."

Before she could ask what for, the door opened. Leary, beaming a thousand smiles at once, ushered out the wry-faced Mary Pinchot, who shot quick glances around the room as if looking for something hidden in the shadows.

Cravingston followed, and paused in front of Reggie, giving him a look. "I'll see you in a week, Mr. Mention?"

But the question was more like a statement, and Reggie didn't have to reply. A flash of a future vision showed him playing music with friends in a New York loft, with Lucy at his side, when suddenly a catastrophe begins to unfold over the radio and TV...

That night, after swirls of nauseatingly psychedelic panoramas retreated from his brain, Reggie dreamed he was attending Robert Johnson's meager wake somewhere in the Southern Delta, in a pasture behind a church marked with the sign of the three monkeys. He was wrangling for a view of the unevenly splintered closed box with black folks who wouldn't or couldn't believe that the actual man's body was in there. His father and Frank Balzano, Johnny B's father, arrived with bodyguards, and old bluesmen cat-walked across the lawn with flowers. Someone broke out coffee and doughnuts.

"Someone could get killed over music?" asked Frank Balzano.

"Money, maybe," said the record label executive, hovering over the grave. "Must be money involved."

"It's about a woman," said Muddy Waters at his side. "It's *always* about a woman."

* * *

Mary Pinchot Meyer brought some capsules and instructions back to her closet boyfriend in the Oval Office. They decided to try it in the Lincoln Bedroom since Jackie was away. Coltrane's new album "My Favorite Things"[226] purred on the phonograph. Kennedy had just left a meeting of his cabinet in a huff, rejecting all plans to invade Cuba, ordering the armed camps in Florida and Louisiana to stand down, shouting at one point to a secretary that the Bay of Pigs was not his fault. He smiled at the Secret Service in the hallway, thinking it would be an orgy, very relaxing, but then his brother Robert explained the situation. It would be more like a seance. He took his dose with relish, expecting colorful hallucinations.

But only hellish visions would appear in this setting. They hunkered down in an ornate room at the heart of the nation's heart, dominated by a portrait of saddened Abraham Lincoln and populated with bloody scenes from the Civil War. Every president since had worn that sad expression at one time or another, thought Kennedy as he gazed at the portrait. The nation was now connected to an artificial pump, a wartime machine belching forth dark clouds of nuclear annihilation.

Over the next few hours Kennedy would reject these visions and find his God, his very own Catholic Christ, among the chocolates and lime daquiris on the bedside table in the Lincoln Bedroom. In the days that followed, he would stand up to the raging maniacs in the Agency who wanted Cuba back. He would put his life on the line, stand on the Berlin Wall, force the issue with Khrushchev about missiles in Cuba, even take it to the brink like a Humphrey Bogart movie, and *get his deal,* get our own missiles out of Turkey, and seal a promise not to invade the starved island only miles from the Florida coast. The drama would galvanize public support for peace, and help him reverse the wartime machine's thrust into Indochina.

But before all that, he trembled uncontrollably at the end of his session in the Lincoln Bedroom, and he let Mary lead him back to the presidential bedroom. His morning appointments were put on hold.

Something in the Air

Something in the air, like a damp smell before a thunderstorm, suggested a force was reaching climax. Herbert Mention could always sense it: the suggestion that he was bearing witness to a magnificent turning point in history. The Bay of Pigs had highlighted the country's impotency in its own backyard, and the Missile Crisis had shown how a nuclear holocaust could be right around the corner. The long, slow pro-cess of destabilization suddenly accelerated and reached its apogee with the shooting of President Kennedy in Dallas on Friday, November 22, 1963.

Amid the chaos and confusion of the assassination, a hole quietly opened up in American history, a vacuum into which all accountability and Kennedy-related political assets vanished. Rumors circulated that it was the CIA or "some rogue operation" connected to the CIA, but for the Washington insiders a new enemy had risen above all of them, an enemy unnamable and not locatable on any organization chart or budget line. And, it seems, even some of Herbert's connections in the CIA were afraid.

He'd wrangled access to see the Zapruder film. Here was the lifelong turning point: a series of still frames, one by one, and then a jump cut to 24 frames per second, the sequence of the limousine taking off with agents jumping on board to rescue the First Lady. It was the pinnacle after a slow ramp up a roller coaster, when suddenly all hell breaks loose, and the world accelerates in free-fall to an unfathomable depth.

Herbert broke silence and called Beatrice for the first time in almost a decade. Gilbert didn't know what was happening, only that his mother talked quietly on the phone for over an hour, breaking into tears every five minutes, as if each revelation voiced over the phone took her to lower and lower levels of despair. The Kennedy assassination, and the subsequent killing of Oswald at the police station, would forever exist in Gilbert's mind as the point when he could no longer trust the world.

Johnny B watched it on the BBC with the Beatles on tour in Wales, and when Ruby shot Oswald, he made the connection. Ruby was a friend to the wise guys in Chicago, and even his father knew him. He wondered whether his father was out celebrating the event at Tony Mart's.

Reggie, Lucy, and Leary confidante Peggy Hitchcock were enjoying the party at the 112 Chambers Street loft that hosted Japanese artist Yoko Ono's latest conceptual piece, "Painting to Be Stepped On", which was a scrap of canvas on the floor that became a completed artwork upon the accrual of footprints. La Monte Young helped organize the loft events with Ono, and Marcel Duchamp had come by and dutifully left footprints. They gathered around the TV to hear the devastating news. Tears came freely. It was the end of all rational, political thought. The hopelessness of it all formed a lump in Reggie's throat. Back in his apartment the phone calls never stopped. It was a touchpoint of extreme heartache for almost everyone.

Barbault was an exception; his wife had to interrupt his experiments to tell him, and he waved her away. He was staring, quite astonished, at his beaker filled with liquid gold of the first degree, which might also function as a vitality serum, and he was eager to tell his backers in the Corporation.

Another exception was Harry Smith, who never stopped editing his latest film, *Heaven and Earth Magic Feature,* which he presented in New York City a week later. It was attended by hundreds who had heard that alchemical secrets would be unveiled in the course of the evening. A simple series of alchemical transformations were portrayed on the screen; they went on for hours, and hours, the result of years of pain-staking animation. But the audience was dropping like flies. They fled the theater until, at the transmutation, the theater was almost empty.

* * *

"Progress report?" The hierophant, now termed CEO, smiled at Mumblingore and Cravingston.

"We've taken over the coverup, as it was getting out of hand," reported Mumblingore.

The CEO was blunt. "The main thing is Kennedy, dead. The next thing is Oswald, dead."

"Yes," Mumblingore responded quickly. "Once Oswald's leftist sympathies are exposed, the authorities will conclude, will *want* to conclude, that Castro agents recruited him, used him, and... well, killed him."

"Hoover?"

"J. Edgar's on board," Mumblingore nodded. "Did you know he compiles lists? Subversives, leftist professors, poets, writers, musicians, known homosexuals. He's quite useful."

"Indeed," spoke the CEO. "And Dulles?"

"He's happy," spoke up Cravingston with a slight hesitation. "He didn't want the job anymore, anyway. It's funny, really. Kennedy gives them a new building, and they put that inscription on it, 'the truth shall make you free,' and at the same time Kennedy's about to dismantle the organization."

The CEO frowned. "These people are fucking serious. I don't think you get it."

"I get it, sir," Cravingston replied with deference. "And the resolution will pass. The war in Vietnam will give us all the capital investment we could ever want."

The CEO pivoted in his office chair in the nondescript office. "You know, I like the Hula Hoop. What a great idea! Take all that libidinous energy of the dance and reroute it into profit. The suburban white kids out there are all shaking their hips, doing the Twist, with these things, and their parents approve." He smiled at Mumblingore, who cleared his throat in agreement.

* * *

Bob Dylan was at a loss for words. He'd started several poems about the assassination, writing in one, "it is useless t' recall the day once more."

Reggie saw it as a turning point when Bob grumbled at him about promoting his poems to the magazines, *Sing Out* and Pete Seeger's new *Broadside*. With considerable audacity, Bob had penned poems in the "finger-pointing" vein such as "The Ballad of Emmett Till" based on a story Reggie had heard from Cornell. It was about the murder of a poor black kid from Money, Mississippi that had occurred a decade earlier. Other protest songs and poems followed quickly.

Bob's fame grew, though it hadn't yet put cash in his pocket. It was growing among people who hadn't heard him sing. It was becoming annoying. The pressure to satisfy the magazines and be a poet conflicted with making music. Bob kept picking a slave song he'd picked up from Cornell, "No More Auction Block",[227] over and over, as if to say, "Get the message?"

"That's what you ought to do," Reggie fired back. "Go back to the older music, the country music."

"That's exactly what I'm doin'," Bob acknowledged as he wove the melody of "Auction Bock" into "Blowin' in the Wind".[228] Van Ronk called the song "incredibly dumb" but it had been picked up by Albert Grossman for his new trio, Peter Paul and Mary, who used it to cross over into the pop charts.

For several months before the assassination the Poet had rambled onstage as Joan Baez's vagabond troubadour at her concerts, filled to capacity with middle-aged folkies and student activists.

Bob's fame grew, though it hadn't yet put cash in his pocket. It was growing among people who hadn't heard him sing. It was becoming annoying.

Three months before the assassination Bob sung with Baez in the March on Washington in front of more than 200,000 people. He'd already been back to Minneapolis to show his old friends how he'd been to the crossroads and had come back a real performer, just like Robert Johnson. But fame was beginning to eat at him. His past in Hibbing and his real name, Zimmerman, had been outed in the mainstream press. They'd come a very long way from the Cambridge coffee houses to the National Monument.

Reggie was partly responsible for their appearance by coordinating the stage appearances with CORE and SNCC. But even Reggie was becoming disillusioned with all of it. The leaders had decided against direct action and civil disobedience, so that they could get a friendly nod from President Kennedy. Malcolm X, spokesperson for the Nation of Islam, had derided it as the "farce on Washington."

Reggie spied Cornell accompanying Malcolm to the side of the stage, and saw him whisper in Bob's ear. After Martin Luther King spoke about having a dream of a future cleansed of the seething hatred of racism, Bob sang "When the Ship Comes In",[229] a joyously vengeful lyric in the vein of Pirate Jenny's song in *The Threepenny Opera* by Kurt Weill and Bertolt Brecht. It described the coming apocalypse, and was written in a fit of pique when Bob was refused entry into a fancy hotel because of his appearance. He secured the applause of the freedom fighters as he sang "the whole wide world is watching."

The audience had assumed the coming ship would be the freedom and dignity of civil rights, but all that was dashed with his next song, "Only a Pawn in Their Game",[230] which unfolded like a black hole from the stage, engulfing everyone in the confusing logic of the song. Medgar Evers, a leader and hero of the National Association for the Advancement of Colored People (NAACP), had recently been murdered, and the song portrayed the murderer as just a pawn, just another poor white dumb bigot caught up in Their game.

Among the stony faces on stage who could hear Bob's lyrics, only Cornell had been smiling, looking right at Reggie, as if to say, "Good work, you got some influence on him."

Had Cornell suggested to Bob that he play it? Bob had acted ornery in the face of fame before, such as stalking out of the Ed Sullivan Show because they wouldn't let him do his John Birch Society blues.

Reggie knew he was witnessing an important change in music, and it was something *he* had helped to bring about. All along he'd been arguing with Bob about the lack of energy in the protest movement, and especially in the songs. All the way down to Washington Reggie had shared with Bob his experience down South and his uncomfortable role as a *white* man working in the Civil Rights Movement.

Bob had sidestepped the issue in front of the Washington Monument with "Only a Pawn". He was moving on, expanding his intellectual frontiers with help from Reggie, Van Ronk, and Suze, who graced the cover of his second album, *Freewheelin'*. He had immersed himself in the French symbolists Rimbaud, Baudelaire, and Verlaine, as well as in the Old and New Testaments, fusing his apocalyptic vision with Jesus' words about the Last Judgement from the Gospel of Mark, "but many that are first will be last, and the last first," into his most enduring finger-pointing song, "The Times They Are A-Changin'".[231]

And now, all Bob could think to say of the assassination was, "They're trying to tell you, 'don't even hope to change things.'" The day after the assassination, at a concert in upstate New York, he opened with a dispirited version of "The Times They Are A-Changin'", explaining later to Reggie that the song was too much for that day, and that he couldn't understand, really, why he had even written it. "Something has just gone haywire in the country and they're applauding the song! And I can't understand it." The song had not yet been commercially released, and it had already been superseded by the event.

Three weeks later Bob spoke at the ceremony for receiving the Tom Paine Award for his contribution to the civil rights struggle, given by the Emergency Civil Liberties Committee, directed by Geno's father, Clark Foreman. Surrounded by well-heeled liberals donating to the cause, he grew uptight and drank heavily, vomiting in the men's room. Reggie helped him get to the podium.

Thanking the organization for the award, Bob started taunting the middle-aged audience about how proud he was to be young, compared to the people in the audience. "And I only wish that all you people who are sitting out here today or tonight weren't here... Because you people should be at the beach." After some nervous laughter from the audience, he plunged on, echoing lines from "The Times They Are A-Changin'". "It is not an old peoples' world. It has nothing to do with old people." In the quiet that followed, he rambled on about weird presents he'd received now that he was famous. George Lincoln Rockwell's tie clip, General Walker's car trunk keys, fallout shelter signs from Philadelphia. Then: "There's no black and white, left and right to me anymore; there's only up and down and down is very close to the ground." Traveling to Cuba occupied his mind for a while, and then he veered dangerously into Lee Oswald territory with this pawn-in-their-game theme. "I saw some of myself in him... I saw things that he felt, in *me*." Boos and hisses prevented him from continuing.

Reggie didn't know it, but his father, Herbert Mention, was in the audience, having shadowed his son for a few days in New York to see what he was up to. Herbert couldn't help thinking that this Bob Dylan character that Reggie traveled around with had either known or guessed the truth about Oswald. A pawn in their game, indeed. Anyone, anywhere, could have been gathered up and reprogrammed by the Corporation to do just about anything.

* * *

The assassination was covered extensively on the BBC, along with reports of segregationist rage and and fire-bombings in the Deep South. Crowds of Negro marchers bending to the charge of the riot police were toppled in clusters, smashed in their faces, and hit with rocks. A black man fell and the white boys moved in, kicking. Cops gripped billy clubs, one hand at each end, twisting hard. Firemen jumped off their trucks and turned on hoses that sent everybody spinning.

"America's falling apart," Gilbert said out loud, to the television. "And Reggie's in the middle of it." He kept Reggie's letter in his footlocker along with his father's *Special from Spirituals to Swing* acetate, the worn harmonica he no longer played (now that he had a full set with all the keys), the polished stone, and the pouch that contained dried roots, herbs, pill boxes, and a phial of some evil-looking liquid. In this climate of fear and uncertainty, and distrust for authority, it didn't take long for Gilbert to decide that he should try some of these herbs and find out what "getting high" was all about.

Johnny B was not enthusiastic. "Are you sure you want to do this?"

"C'mon, Johnny, you've been doing it for years."

"Don't let your mother find out."

Gilbert took the pouch to Brian Jones, always a willing participant. The Stones new manager, Andrew Loog Oldham, stood stiffly in the Edith Grove flat in his sunglasses, his arms folded in disapproval at something. At everything, really. Rubbish was strewn all about the front room Brian had been sharing with Keith. Mick's back room was smothered with dirty clothes. Food-caked dishes were piled high in the kitchen sink. Various mold cultures were brewing among the forty old milk bottles and the smell in there was hideous. The ceiling was covered with drawings done in smoke from lighted candles. The winter was the worse Britain had seen in a hundred years, and the water pipes had frozen solid, so the toilets wouldn't flush and they couldn't bathe. Every shilling they could scruff up went into the electric meter for the heater and the phonograph, which now belched out Brian's slide-guitar paean to Muddy Waters, "I Can't Be Satisfied".[232]

Brian yelled up from his fetal position on the stained couch. "'Would you let your daughter marry a Rolling Stone?' Hey mate, what the fuck is this?" He rolled into a crouch and approached Andrew menacingly, clutching a newspaper page.

Gilbert picked up the rest of the paper and read aloud, "If the Beatles are Christ, the Rolling Stones are the antichrist.'"

Andrew dismissed them with a delicate wave of his hand. "Don't give me that codswallop! You're getting press! They're comparing you to the Beatles. You're the nasty opposite. The Beatles are playing for the queen and all the adults, but you're playing for the young, the rebellious. You're the antidote, you snot."

Brian was still uncomfortable with it, but Andrew said that Mick and Keith agreed with the plan. And by the way, they were moving out, to live in a new apartment with him. Brian would have to find an apartment for himself.

"So your abandoning me, is that it? Are you even going to help me find a new flat? What's going on? The three of you left me on the way to the show last week. I came out of the apothecary's and you were all gone!"

"Well, Brian, we're all kind of sick of you holding everybody up. All these excuses. Look, it was a prank, that's all. Get over it." Andrew turned away, sniffed at Gilbert as if the condition of the flat was his fault, and excused himself.

"They're trying to undermine my leadership, because I'm the one on stage getting all the attention and they're jealous," Brian complained to Gilbert.

"Andrew's got Mick and Keith locked up in his apartment, trying to get them to write songs. They're missing the point! We've only scratched the surface of this music, we're only just now *getting* it, using its power. And we've got *plenty* of songs. We're *interpreters* of this music, that's more important than making pop songs. The blues is more authentic than anything they can come up with. What they're doing is taking the same blues progressions and adding trite lyrics. It's embarrassing."

Gilbert unrolled the savory substance and filled a pipe. With maniacal grins they took turns on the pipe, filling the flat with a thick, acrid smoke. The cannabis babble effect hit Gilbert first, and he stammered about the Kennedy assassination. "It's a vast conspiracy. You can't name names, 'cause it's like naming particles in the air, molecules or whatnot."

Brian was amused but not following this.

"This is something we can't see or name," Gilbert continued in a bit of a raving bewilderedness. "We can't measure it, or take a photograph of it. It's the mystery we can't get hold of, the plot we can't uncover."

"Sounds like you're paranoid, mate. This stuff does this to you."

"No no, just because I'm paranoid, doesn't mean they're not out to get me! It doesn't mean there are no plotters communicating by secret signs."

"I think it's something different," Brian said with a bit of a philosophical lisp. "It's like when one musician says to another, 'I covered this song.' The other musician knows the song. In an instant, they both have shared the entire song, all of its nuances, all of the emotions it conjures up. All without hearing it. How can they do that? It's the same way with the people in power. They act independently, yet they're all on the same plan."

Johnny B arrived half-exhausted from a Beatles package tour across England, and poked around inside the pouch. He pocketed the liquid phial, guessing that it was the new stuff he'd heard about, and realizing how devastating it might be on them if they weren't ready for it. One step at a time, Cornell had warned him.

Johnny showed them the half-open pouch. "I think the pills are a derivative of a mushroom. It's called psilocybin. Let me try one."

"Let's *all* try one," Brian grinned madly.

For poppers of pep pills used to the swift kick of speed, the effects of this substance came on too slow to notice, and Gilbert soon forgot he had taken it until he suddenly popped into a new realm, the madness of the moment. The flat had become the control room of a space ship, he was Captain McCloud, and Johnny B and Brian were his sidekicks, the Space Angels.

Brian, after a sudden asthmatic fit he had to subdue with his ever-present inhaler, screamed back at Gilbert that they were *not* in space. "Look at it!" Brian pointed at the scummy, ice-encrusted front window. "It's right in front of us!"

"What?"

"The center of it, of civilization, all of it! Right here in front of us. And Cornell gave us the seed! We're gonna plant it right in the host. We're gonna plant it like a virus!"

Gilbert, bewildered, poked Brian in the chest. "What are you talking about?"

With a maniacal cackle, Brian chased after Gilbert with two unconnected speaker wires as if to electrocute him. The general mayhem lasted until Johnny announced that Pat was outside in the snow, with Brian's child. "Don't let her in! Don't tell her I'm here!" They retreated, giggling, into the back room and huddled in the freezing cold, waiting for her to stop knocking.

This is Brian at his worst, mused Gilbert in his first clear thought in hours. He'd seen this routine before. Brian could talk his way out of anything, without repercussions. Brian would praise Pat for handling the situation, being the unwed mother of his son, but soon enough resort to intimidating, goading, berating, belittling, and even humiliating her to get what he wanted, which most of the time was the money she'd earned. He was insensitive to the severe damage he caused. It occurred to Gilbert that yes, indeed, the Stones *were* nasty opposites of the cheeky Beatles, and no, indeed, you would not want your daughter to marry one.

The knock had stopped for awhile, and they cautiously left the lavatory when a different one, a stronger knock, vibrated through the building. Johnny B confidently opened the door as if he knew who it would be, and sure enough, Cornell Woodrow made his entrance. The entire bit: big meaty smile, three-piece suit, somber homburg, black shiny oxfords, and a black cane with a gold fish head at the top. Gilbert blinked, checking to see if he was hallucinating.

"You always seem to arrive at the most opportune moment," said Johnny.

"I knows it," laughed Cornell. "You boys are having a good time with the magic mushroom, you got yourselves a good dose! But this boy's in trouble," pointing at Brian, now curled into a corner of the room in an introspective stupor. "He lacks the confidence he needs right now. Brian!" Cornell shouted at him. Brian nodded with a hazy smile. "Don't you know you're the brains of this outfit? The heart and soul too? You were playing this music before the others could tie their shoes. You're the one who got Keith up to playing this way, interleaving the guitar lines. You're the one with the power to shape the sound of this band."

"They're fucking with me," Brian retorted. "Mick and Keith, they resent me. They left me behind at the end of the last show, just left me to get mobbed by the fans, and the police had to fend them off." It sounded a bit like whining, but Gilbert had seen some of it, the gestures they made behind Brian's back, the disparaging talk. "And it's not fair, I got all the gigs, I made it happen, but they turn to Andrew for help, and when he tells them to sack Stu because Stu doesn't have the right image, they all turn to me to do the dirty work."

"You're the one with the gift," Cornell spoke soothingly. "You can play any instrument you want! Use the harmonica for awhile, see how far that gets you. Shake that tambourine! You got the power, you got the stone!"

Brian straightened up and pulled his thunder-stone out of his pocket where he always kept it.

"Let's break it down for you, get down to the specifics of it. Let me play something simple, a rhythm thing," Cornell said. Gilbert and Johnny B exchanged knowing glances as Cornell slipped a record onto the phonograph. "It's called a hambone.[233] One of the oldest rhythms on the planet, heard all around the world. You can play it by slapping your hands on your knees, you don't even need an instrument. Children all over the world learn it. You know it as 'shave and a haircut, two bits.' But now see how that rhythm can take you into a new world." As it finished, Cornell slipped another one on the turntable. "Now see how Bo Diddley stretches it out, and the sound he makes with it."[234]

Brian shook his hair and his tambourine to the rhythm as he felt it take over his body.

"The rolling stone was the key, to feeling the spirits of our ancestors," intoned Cornell, his voice softly seeping through the underbelly of the music. "It gave us harmony and rhythm, so that we could tap into all this noise and hear our ancestors. They want us to liberate all the people, to help them evolve into the ultimate beings that are ancestors have already become. So they sent the stones from the sky.

"The ancestors live with the ultimate beings, as *vibrations*. In order to gather us into the bosom of the ultimate being, they need us to radiate with vibrations. They need *all* of us to connect to each other through vibrations.

"Now music was, and continues to be, the method, you see," Cornell continued. "Music is how we connect, because music is what we hear from vibrations. As long as musicians tap into the sound they feel is coming from their ancestors, they can create vibrations that unite their people in a common cause. And as more people die and join the ultimate beings, they're like *recruits*, y'unnerstan, and their job is to send out *more* vibrations.

"And now we got the blues music, bringing people together through recording technology. The record can *hold* these vibrations in a static form, so that we can deliver them wherever we need to.

"But we also have resistance. The Corporation doesn't want to bring the people together. They don't want us to evolve. They don't believe in their *own* ancestors. In fact, they think they can conjure this magic without the ancestors, and just for the few of them, not for the rest of the world. They are out to determine their own destiny. They never realize their folly until right before they die."

Gilbert had started playing harmonica to the song and was now feverishly blowing a fantastic solo. Cornell pointed and smiled at him as the song ended. "Did you ever think, did music start out back in ancient times as coded messages in some universal language, before writing? What is the connection between alchemy, architecture, primitive cultures, voodoo, and ancient civilizations? And how is it that a good musician can suddenly 'get into it' like our boy Bert here with his harmonica, and a sound comes out that's magic?"

Brian got out his electric guitar, fiddled with his amplifier for a moment, and came out with the sound of Bo Diddley, right there on the floor. In just a few moments he had mastered the rhythm and the sound of the man's guitar with a cover of his "Mona".[235]

Cornell was amazed at Brian's performance. "Man! As Muddy once sang, it's the stuff you gotta watch."[236] And winking at everybody, he reared back to give a toast, in a fake Irish brogue,

Spirituality's imminent,
It's the price you pay to be into it.
Everything's so clear
You lose all your fear
With this massive dose of the infinite...

And at a snap of his fingers, he was gone.

Johnny B left shortly thereafter with the phial of mystery liquid. Cornell had connected him with someone who could have it tested and compared to the LSD-25 that some maniac called "the Captain" was handing out like candy to intellectuals and artists on both sides of the Atlantic. Cornell had slapped his hands and almost giggled when he explained to Johnny that the Corporation must have goofed when they let this stuff out. "It's like a synthetic peyote. Anything that can turn around the minds of these white kids must be good."

* * *

Herbert Mention, in disguise, shadowed the Captain in the rain through Soho. Cornell Woodrow had suggested tailing his former associate in the uranium business, to see what he was up to now, and who he was meeting. Al Hubbard, though not a captain of rank in any armed force, was a captain of his own fantastic mission: to introduce the most intelligent and powerful people of the world to the visions sparked by psychoactive substances.

Short and stocky with a large round head, a florid rum-drinker's face, and a razor crewcut, Hubbard looked like Hollywood's idea of a Southern sheriff as played by Rod Steiger, including a crazed smile suggesting nothing is real. Under the fake uniform of a captain in Special Forces, he carried a blue-steel Colt chambered for a .357 magnum cartridge, which was just enough gun for the type of situations a man of his standing could expect to run into at any time.

Herbert's goal was to see who was meeting "Captain" Hubbard, and who else might be following him. Wired directly into U.S. intelligence, the Captain had made his fortune in uranium, which Herbert, in his former identity as Herbert Mesh, had located for him in various parts of the world while studying ancient documents about energy. Herbert hadn't been involved in other Hubbard activities, such as running booze from Canada, but was still questioned about his relationship when the FBI finally caught up with Hubbard. The Captain did eighteen months in prison. But in the way such things happened in those days, he was released and then commissioned by Wild Bill Donovan of the OSS, before America's formal entrance into World War II. Donovan wanted to use his communication system to help sail ships under cover of darkness to Vancouver, where they were refitted as destroyers bound for Britain. Herbert, also working at that time for the OSS thanks to Will Cravingston's persuasive arguments, supplied the coding and encoding devices.

Herbert had no idea when the Captain had stumbled onto LSD-25. He knew the Captain had been an OSS source for mescaline, the psychoactive chemical isolated from the peyote cactus that the novelist Aldous Huxley had raved about, which Donovan wanted to use for interrogation tests on soldiers. Since the war, the Captain had been very busy. Traversing the art and music communities, he crossed paths with Cornell, who worked with him to set up several clinics in England bearing the sign of the three monkeys. With Cornell's blessing, the Captain had used the clinics to expose hundreds of prominent artists, musicians, and others to the far more powerful LSD-25. The experiments involved some of the best Beverly Hills psychiatrists, who, in turn, introduced the substance to actors, novelists, and filmmakers. Cary Grant, James Coburn, Anais Nin, and Stanley Kubrick were said to be devotees.

But Herbert was skeptical. Even with Cornell's involvement, it could all just be a cover for any number of Corporation-sponsored activities that Cornell didn't know about. At the 2i's Coffee Bar in Old Compton Street, the Captain met with a high official in the British government. Herbert strolled a little further down the road and saw, lurking in The Cat's Whisker, his old adversary Will Cravingston, awaiting the Captain's report. This confirmed Herbert's suspicion that the Corporation was also using the Captain, that sly old double-crosser. But for what project?

At the Colony Room in Dean Street, Herbert nursed a hot Earl Grey at a table close enough to hear the Captain's conversation as he greeted his next client. He nearly dropped the cup in his lap when he saw Frank Balzano's kid Johnny, all the way from Margate New Jersey, arrive looking every bit like a British ted. Herbert glanced around to see if any of his sons might be with him.

The Captain looked worried. "Where is Alexis Korner?"

"He sent me," said Johnny B. "He's busy right now."

"Busy how?" bellowed the Captain angrily. "We had a deal!"

"And I'm here to make that deal. It's okay, everything's cool."

"So where is he?" The Captain wouldn't let it go.

"Alexis has a gig this afternoon, Blues Incorporated, the matinee at the Marquee. He can't get into this right now. He needs his wits about him."

Herbert, hearing the conversation, smiled into his teacup. Earlier this morning he'd seen Cornell and his *brujo* Mustapha take Korner into a back room of a Kensington mosque that administered to the tiny African community in London, where they conducted some ritual involving the acrid stench of burnt ginger. Young Johnny Balzano must be covering for Korner at Cornell's request, or… branching out on his own?

The Captain grunted and slurped coffee, eyeing Johnny suspiciously.

"Look, *I'm* the one you want to talk to," Johnny thumped his chest. "Alexis is *my* client."

"And how do I know you will get this into the right hands? I don't want it to go to waste, and I don't want a scandal."

"You have ten thousand doses from Sandoz in a safe-deposit box in the Zurich airport," said Johnny. "You can spare a hundred or two."

When the Captain was alarmed, his eyebrows nearly popped off his bald pate.

"I have my own intelligence," said Johnny soothingly. "And I guarantee you will get the results you want."

Herbert put two and two together, came up with five. Johnny must have found the phial in the trunk. That means his sons also knew about the Book, the records, the herbs, everything. And their friend Johnny had graduated from being his father's mob courier to a fully operational agent of the opposition, thanks to Cornell's influence. He worried now that his sons had been drawn into it, and felt a deep pang of sorrow for their plight. He'd allowed Gilbert to remain with Beatrice and let Cravingston set up Reggie at Harvard, but even so, there had been no way to protect them.

As he stepped off the platform at the Ealing station, he saw a lanky man in a gray flannel suit walking ahead of him through the turnstiles, and Herbert paused. From the back he looked exactly like Cravingston. Fortunately Herbert hadn't been seen, and he was able to sneak into the club for a short while, and shed a tear, as he watched Gilbert sit in on harmonica with the Stones, bending chords with Brian Jones on the Gordy Berry classic, "Money".[237]

* * *

A few months after the assassination, Brian Epstein's experiment that put the lovable mop tops into uniforms of collarless suits had paid off handsomely in gold. America shook off its miserable mourning for its murdered king and embraced the Fab Four with gusto.

The Beatles arrived in New York to screaming hordes of fans, thanks to the advance work behind the scenes that goosed "I Want to Hold Your Hand"[238] up to number one in America and reserved them a slot on the Ed Sullivan Show. Merchandise deals alone would bring in millions for the Corporation and its cadre of manufacturers. Epstein, guided by Cravingston, had blithely made deals that left the Beatles with only about ten percent of the profits, when they could have had at least eighty percent. Oblivious to these backroom financial arrangements, Epstein glowed with pride for his boys. Beatle wigs never envisioned by Astrid and her friends started to appear on the balding heads of disc jockeys and impresarios. As they traveled, hotel owners would lose their door knobs to fans who thought the Beatles may have touched them. Some even began selling the sheets from their hotel beds for one dollar per square inch. Reporters were taken aback with their clever cheekiness.

Interviewer: What do you think of President Johnson?

Paul McCartney: Does he buy our records?

Interviewer: Do any of you have any formal musical training?

John Lennon: You're joking.

Interviewer: Will you sing a song for us?

John Lennon: No. Sorry, we need money first.

Interviewer: Do you plan to record any antiwar songs?

John Lennon: All our songs are antiwar.

Interviewer: Why do millions of Beatles fans buy millions of Beatles records?

John Lennon: If we knew, we'd form another group and become their managers.

Interviewer: Do you enjoy press conferences?

John Lennon: Yes, depending on the intelligence of the questions.

* * *

Reggie was driving across the Colorado flatlands with Bob Dylan and the folksinger Paul Clayton at the tail end of a grass, speed, and Beaujolais binge when they first heard "I Want to Hold Your Hand" on the radio.

"What the fuck is that, are they singing 'I get high'?" Bob wanted to know.

"Sure sounds like it," replied Reggie, lighting a fresh joint while steering with his knees. "The Beatles. My friend Johnny B over in England knows them."

"Well they're doing something here that nobody else is doing," Bob pointed out. "Those chords are outrageous, just outrageous! And the harmonies, man, that's what makes it all valid. You can only do that in a group."

"They're on Ed Sullivan next week."

"We gotta catch that. And I wanna talk to them. This is, like, pointing in the direction where *my* music has to go."

They wouldn't let Bob, an atrociously bad driver, to take a turn at the wheel, so he spent most of the trip in the back seat with his typewriter and guitar. Reggie heard the beginnings of a new song, adapted from a six-line coda Bob had attached to a half-finished poem inspired by the assassination. "The colors of friday were dull / as cathedral bells were gently burnin / strikin for the gentle / strikin for the kind / strikin for the crippled ones / an strikin for the blind."

In New Orleans, at the onset of an "acid" trip, as Bob called LSD, Reggie heard the first full rendition of "Chimes of Freedom"[239] with its chain of flashing images. At the triple-x marked tomb of voodoo queen Marie Laveau Bob speed-talked in elliptical, flashing images. Reggie kissed a statue and cried for freedom as Bob babbled on, "no one's free, even the birds are chained to the sky."

They debated the importance of this new experience as they hit the bars in the French Quarter until dawn. "I saw this before," Bob explained. "It's that switch inside yourself, you can turn it on. I did that. I did that way back when," he whispered, almost to himself, "when I went off to see the gypsy disc jockey out on the Iron Range." Jim Dandy, Robert Johnson, Woody Guthrie, Cornell Woodrow, and the voodoo backdrop were all of a piece. Bob tried to articulate how he'd gotten to this point. "If I hadn't heard the Robert Johnson record when I did, there probably would have been hundreds of lines of mine that would have been shut down, that I wouldn't have felt free enough or upraised enough to write. Johnson's code of language was like nothing I heard before or since."

It occurred to Reggie that Bob could have a lot more in common with the Beatles than he even knew. Remembering that he had sent a copy of *Freewheelin'* to Johnny B, he got in touch to see if the record had caused a stir. Across that lonesome ocean, Johnny B had given George Harrison the record, and the Beatles had worn it out on a portable turntable during their three-week stand at the Olympia in Paris. If he could get the Beatles together with Bob Dylan and his entourage, what kind of powerful music would be wrought? Reggie hatched a plan for a summit meeting.

* * *

It was Brian Jones, mischievous as always, who had the idea to bring his young doppelgänger. Gilbert snuck on the plane at Heathrow with the Rolling Stones as a stage hand for their first American tour, leaving in his wake an all-ports warning for a 15-year-old boy with long blond hair, and a distraught Beatrice to be consoled by Cravingston, who promised to look after him. The fake passport had been procured by Johnny B, who also procured a fake one for himself as "John T. Bassplayer" in order to tour with the Beatles. Johnny had no intention of alerting authorities that he was back on American soil.

The ongoing party, about to span the ocean, had started for Gilbert with a recording session in London. Johnny B had somehow found and invited Phil Spector, on tour in England with the Ronettes. Spector brought Graham Nash and Allan Clark of the Hollies, and singer Gene Pitney showed up from the airport with duty-free cognac. They proceeded to bash their way through "Little By Little"[240] with Brian providing the stinging lead guitar and Spector clinking a coin against the empty cognac bottle.

Brian had been practicing the hambone Bo Diddley beat, and he showed Keith how to work their guitars around it, with Keith taking up the driving rhythm and Brian playing a lead. At some point Keith had the bright idea to use the Buddy Holly lyrics to "Not Fade Away"[241] to anchor the chords, and Brian picked up the harmonica riff Gilbert had taught him. It was an instant hit in Britain.

The Stones had not yet cracked the New World. They followed the Beatles to America prematurely, without a hit single in American charts. They were unknown in the hinterlands, with each concert worse than the previous one. Farm country teenagers looking for lovable British mop tops were not ready for pimply-faced London punks singing Negro music. The police accosted them backstage and poured their scotch and Cokes down the green room toilet.

The bright spot was a visit to the Chess studio at 2120 South Michigan Avenue in Chicago. With help from Cornell, the band had managed to get in the door even though they were not signed to the Chess label. Brian considered it to be a pilgrimage to hallowed grounds, where Muddy Waters, Howlin' Wolf, Bo Diddley, and Chuck Berry had all cut their records. They arrived at the narrow two-story building to find Muddy himself at the door, ready to help with their equipment. "They're my boys," Muddy smiled to the other skeptical bluesmen in residence. "I like their version of 'I Just Want to Make Love to You'.[242] They fade it out just like we did. Only ten times faster!"

Cornell had sent Bobby Womack from the Valentinos over to the studio with his best song. After a few swigs from a bottle of Jack Daniels, they started the first take. In Brian and Keith's hands, the song "It's All Over Now"[243] took on a new life. The two guitarists meshed their notes on the introductory measures, as if to herald something new and different, like Gabriel's horn announcing a charge. Even the fourth note of Keith's lead, heavily laden with reverb, sounded just like a horn on a wrong note. In the initial half-measure they stepped down from major to minor, a descent from heaven to hell. The interval from the bottom to the tonic that completed the measure rose again to a street level that was no longer heaven. Drenched in reverb, the sound seemed to explode from the other end of a rain-drenched London alley. You can hear trash can lids smashing and traffic noise doppler-ing off the riffs into outer space.

But the intro ends after four measures, and the singer is going somewhere else, somewhere down to earth. The bass line comes up the major scale, one, two, three, four... and a sax should sound here, if it were a Fats Domino record. It's the natural dance, something everyone can do, the old high-step on outta here. At that point Jagger wrings out a blustering alcohol-infused vocal that recalls the menace in the air, of this city that harbors crooks and thieves and murderers and rapists hiding in dark alleyways and behind church doors, disappearing into shadows in the Jack-the-Ripper mists. "Because I used to (sneer) love you, but it's all over now."

"What's this song about?" asked Gilbert innocently in the control room with the other bluesmen.

"It's about a woman," chuckled Muddy Waters. "It's *always* about a woman."

* * *

Reggie almost didn't recognize his own brother. Gilbert had grown his blond hair long over the collar of his checked jacket and had lost much of his baby fat, appearing as handsome as the English actor David McCallum in the new *Man From U.N.C.L.E.* series. Standing with Brian Jones, the two looked like twins.

Johnny B had also grown out of his duckbill and brushed his hair forward, with bangs, looking more like a European artist than a biker from South Jersey. They embraced as an antsy Bob Dylan and Bobby Neuwirth looked around at the hundreds of teenagers that had crowded around the lobby entrance.

"How's mom doing?"

Gilbert gave Reggie a look that said, you don't even know the half of it. "Fine," he said, through gritting teeth.

Johnny led the party into the Delmonico Hotel, pushing their way through the crowds, the police, and the horde of fans in the lobby, and eventually made it up the elevator to the Beatles' floor. Even there, they found more police, journalists, Peter Paul and Mary holding guitars, the Kingston Trio holding guitars and even a *banjo*. Reggie's effervescent fervor for a pop summit went flat. What did all these folkies think, that they were going to jam on old folk medleys with the Beatles?

They found the door to the inner sanctum and knocked. The lads had just finished their room service meal. They were all startled to see Bob Dylan lounging in the doorway, shorter than they thought he would be; just a diminutive hobo in rumpled clothes. Brian Epstein welcomed Dylan and asked him if he'd like a drink.

"How 'bout some cheap wine?" Bob snarled as the rest of them crowded into the room. Epstein clumsily made introductions all around.

Reggie thought they all seemed shell-shocked. They were coming awake from a trance, from the never-ending pressure to present themselves as the Beatles to the press, to the hangers-on in the corridor, to the fans downstairs, and to outside world. And here he was, on Mount Olympus, having arranged a meeting of the gods of rock and roll and the god of folk, and dispatching aides to fetch wine.

Johnny B asked Bob if he wanted some speed pills, which were still the drug of choice for the Beatles.

"Naw, let's smoke some reefer instead," Bob said, surprising everyone. Johnny knew that the Beatles had never tried it. He looked at Epstein, who looked over at John Lennon for guidance. Lennon shrugged, so Epstein sheepishly admitted that they had never smoked pot before.

Dylan looked disbelievingly from face to face. "But what about your song? The one about getting high? You know…" and he sang, "and when I touch you I feel happy inside, it's such a feeling that I love, I get high, I get high, I get high…?"

"No, no man," John Lennon laughed in embarrassment. "Those aren't the words. The words are, 'I can't hide', '*hide*' with a 'd', it goes 'such a feeling that *my love*, I can't hide." He looked around nervously. "But let's try it, why not? Woody used to smoke it back in Liddypool" he said to Paul, referring to Lord Woodbine. Then he turned to Johnny B. "Remember that time in Hamburg? You brought it around and we tried it, but we didn't feel anything."

Paul nodded, but was uncharacteristically tongue-tied around Dylan. Reggie pulled out his bag of weed and some papers, and Gilbert, taking the cue, bolted the door and pushed a bathroom towel under the door crack. Bob took the bag from Reggie and deftly rolled a joint. Johnny B, who'd only just met the great Bob Dylan, was impressed with his rolling skills; the man had a habit. After Bob expertly licked the joint, he handed it to John Lennon.

Lennon, a bit apprehensive, handed it to Ringo with a brief laugh. "Ringo's my royal taster."

Ringo nonchalantly lit the joint and proceeded to smoke it down like an experienced viper. "Hey man, you're Bogartin' it," Bob laughed gleefully, breaking the ice, and proceeded to roll the next one.

"You should hear this," Johnny B spoke up, spinning the new Animals single on the turntable. The reverb-laden guitar and swelling organ of "The House of the Rising Sun"[244] filled the room, reverberating in their ears, lending the proceedings an eerie, ghostly effect. The Animals had effectively reinvented a song that Bob, Van Ronk, the Weavers, and others had covered, rerouting the melody into a dark derivative of a sixteenth-century English ballad, an entirely new form of music. "It's not folk, it's not blues, and it's *not* rock 'n' roll," Johnny B shouted.

"No! It doesn't roll," Brian Jones answered. "It's just the *rock* part. Maybe it should be called *rock* music. It's more serious than rock'n'roll. More like the blues."

All of a sudden Bob came to life and glimmered like a flashing light bulb. "This *is* something, like what I've been looking for. The only true, valid death you can feel today, put across as a pop song."

"You should record with a band," Brian Jones told him. "Have you heard the Paul Butterfield Blues Band, in Chicago? You should check them out, especially their guitar player, Mike Bloomfield."

"I heard him once, he played on Johnny Hammond's record. I don't know if I want a blues band," Bob replied, "but I've worked with a lead guitarist. Maybe I should try him."

The cross-pollination continued at a rapid pace as the smoke and wine loosened them up. Paul McCartney took it for granted that Brian Jones was still the leader of the Stones, and Brian pretended to have that power, as they discussed how to stagger their Beatles and Rolling Stones releases so as not to step on each other's toes. Lennon, famous for saying that no rock 'n' roll had ever topped Jerry Lee Lewis, found a kindred spirit in Dylan, who had emulated Lewis, Little Richard, and Buddy Holly in his youth. Both were fed up with albums that contained one or two hits and then eight tracks of rubbish. In the future they would spend whatever studio time was necessary to make each song as if it were a single.

It occurred to Reggie, listening to all this, how isolated they were. Alone, even when surrounded by people, none of whom understood what it was like to live in the fame bubble. The gods could share their experiences with no one else but themselves. But the world expected them to play their parts in this comedic drama. The Beatles had to be Beatles, and Dylan had to be Dylan. They could never drop their pretenses to play together, without causing some kind of huge sensation and expectations that they could never live up to. Only Brian Jones could flit like some phantom chameleon between the two.

After what seemed like years, Johnny B gathered the stoned Reggie and Gilbert in a corner. "We need to figure this out, compare notes," he said in a soft, conspiratorial tone. "Cornell encouraged this meeting to happen. It's part of his grand experiment, and as far as I can tell, your father was part of it."

Red eyes blazing, Reggie recounted some of his tale of the crossroads vision with Cornell. "*We're* playing a part in this. Remember that code, see no evil? Hear no evil?"

"Speak no evil," Gilbert murmured sheepishly.

"I get visions, every once in a while," explained Reggie. "Like a window into the future. It comes and goes really quickly, but I can remember some of things I learn. Like right now! I can see Bob strapping on an electric guitar. I can see the Beatles getting serious about their studio recordings. These different roots are going to converge. The result will inspire young people to organize."

"And I can hear the perfect sound they need to play," Johnny B. "I can fine-tune their vibrations, especially the bass guitar. I've been showing Paul some ideas about playing bass, stuff I heard from — get this — the bass player of the Beach Boys! Their songwriter, Brian Wilson. Not the surf sound, not the rumble, but his bass melodies."

They turned to Gilbert, who looked at them questioningly. "All I know is something I feel about rock 'n' roll getting more sophisticated, getting more interesting lyrics than 'I love you, you love me, ooka dooka, ooka dee.' We got to start our own band. I listen to some of this Dylan stuff, and I can't get over how good he is at emphasizing certain words, certain phrases. That's it, it's his *phrasing*. I want to bring all these things together, give this new music a voice." But Gilbert wasn't quite satisfied. He concentrated for a moment on the power of speech, and grunted. With a pop, the television set turned on.

Brian Epstein saw it happen and burst out laughing. Then he couldn't stop laughing, and the laugh virus started affecting everyone. Epstein's laughing grew hysterical, and started repeating, "I'm so high I'm on the ceiling! I'm up on the ceiling!"

The *Rocky and Bullwinkle Show* was on, and everyone turned to see the bumper sequence. Two frantic figures scamper along the cliff to a dramatic piano backdrop as violent lightning bolts seek them out. They reach to comfort each other, dodging lightning bolts, but the sky explodes and engulfs them. It is Shiva, come to destroy the world with a nuclear blast. The ground itself rises as the piano music shifts to a lighthearted tempo, as if to say, this is life, the way it is, you scamper about until engulfed. The figures are now dead, swallowed up, their outlines faintly glimmering underneath the ground. They have become the stuff of life, the fossilized life force, the basic fecund material of reality. From dust ye have come and unto dust shall ye return. Just then a smiling sun broke out above the barren field, and an army of fast-growing sunflowers pop up from the earth in the distance, marching toward the foreground, and ending with our two heroes popping up with them, sprouting from the ground like newborn babies.

"Wow!" Gilbert exulted in the time-honored phrase of the ultra-stoned. "The meaning of life, it's all right there!"

Everyone roared with laughter. How could it be, the meaning of life, hiding in plain sight on American television? Rocky, Bullwinkle, and the House in New Orleans.

"The meaning of life," Paul mumbled. All the others smiled back at him. "The meaning of life... Mal!"

Mal Evans, the Beatles chief aide, took several years, in Paul's stoned mind, to amble over to the couch.

"Mal! Have you got a pencil? It's seven levels."

"It's wot?" George Harrison on the couch next to him stirred from his near stupor.

"Seven levels," Paul answered him. "That's wot. Seven levels," Paul kept repeating.

"No, it's twelve. Twelve levels," George smiled as he pretended to argue.

Paul kept repeating, "It's seven levels."

"Ah, you're nuts, the pair of you," George dismissed him with a laugh.

"Mal, get a pencil, some paper."

Mal scurried about to comply. Befuddled, he couldn't find anything but the notepad and pencil by the hotel phone. Paul started scratching out "There are seven levels" and then stopped, staring into space. All forgotten.

* * *

Lucy and Reggie had their first real argument in the dusty one-room flat they shared in the Village. Neither had any real interest in domesticity, and when Reggie returned again from one of his jaunts as part of Bob Dylan's retinue and expected to find her there, he was perplexed.

He found her out at Yoko's loft, scissors in hand, giving Yoko opinions on how to present *Cut Piece* at Carnegie Recital Hall. The piece consisted of Ono, dressed in her best suit, kneeling on a stage with a pair of scissors in front of her, inviting audience members to cut pieces of her clothing off.

It was one more in a series of performances by a close-knit group of artists that were attempting to synchronize Dada and Surrealism with a neo-Dada that served as a critique of capitalism in the twentieth century. Underlying these performances was the Situationist concept of the *spectacle* of mass media, a development and application of Karl Marx's concept of fetishism of commodities, reification and alienation.

Johnny B had told Reggie about the Situationists in Paris. Experience and perception become commodities. In the society of the spectacle, the commodities rule the workers and the consumers instead of being ruled by them. Things that were once directly lived are now lived by proxy. The only way out is to construct *situations*, moments of life that deliberately reawakened authentic desires, experiencing the feeling of life and adventure, and the liberation of everyday life.

Ironically, Reggie believed in this art project, while Lucy had a different take. Yes, life could be lived this way "in the moment" but those who live this way rely on others to take care of them. She had seen first-hand, in Head Start projects put forward by the nascent Students for a Democratic Society (SDS), that the men, whose talents were put to use "in the moment" making speeches and writing mani-festos, were completely eclipsed by the women who ran the mimeograph machines, made coffee, and organized — one by one — each working class neighborhood family they wanted to radicalize. The men of SDS sought out these women and recruited them for their intelligence, and then demoted them to girlfriends, wives, note-takers, and coffee makers. Lucy pointed out to Reggie that he was being a shit-head, always jumping off to follow his pied piper.

So, "being in the moment" didn't apply to him? This was Reggie's first experience of the twisting turns of a woman's logic, for what she really didn't like was Reggie's selfish, manipulative, and emotionally immature friend.

Dylan had originally impressed her with his dedication to Woody Guthrie, to the point of riding all the way out to Guthrie's hospital bed in New Jersey to serenade him in his terminal illness. She had promoted Dylan to her artist friends, and to the folklorist Alan Lomax, who on the strength of her relationship with Herbert's son, had given her an archivist job. To help him extend his range beyond Guthrie, Lucy had given Dylan access to Lomax's extensive record collection and blues archive, and had even introduced him to Suze.

Bob and Suze were an ideal couple, for a while, appearing together on the cover of *Freewheelin'*. "She's the one who introduced him to CORE, and got him to do benefits for civil rights," Lucy reminded Reggie. "She's the one who introduced him to Brecht. And he's out there screwing every chick he can find on the road, expecting her to be waiting for him at home when he gets back. And now she wants to go off to study art in Italy, and he's upset at her. He's an asshole for treating her this way. So are you, if you think you're going to tell me what I can and can't do."

But a close reading of the album cover told the tale. As the self-absorbed country beatnik poet trudges down the winter street with a half-smile of wonder at the road ahead, Suze has her arm in his, and is barely in step with him, more like hanging on to him and slightly behind him at his side. She looks more like a fan than an object of his desire. Reggie remembered Bob's angst when Suze took off for Italy, and how he talked about her, how she had held him back. And it was so much nonsense! Her departure opened a floodgate of successful songs, at first maudlin and sorrowful, but in the end cynical and scornful, the best one about how he gave her is love but she wanted his soul. But don't think twice, it's alright.[245] In Bob's view, you can't be a wise hipster and in love at the same time.

Bob was hardly lonely going down that road. Joan Baez had begun to see her creepy little vagabond as the dream poet for her voice and activism, and invited him up to share her considerably larger stage. After a year of pretending to be the king and queen of folk, culminating in their performance together on the March on Washington, Bob turned his back on her. It turned out that ambition, expected in a man, looked suspiciously like ball-busting from the male perspective; an aggressive woman was "bitchy". Fooled into thinking she had been invited to join him in England for a pop-artist reception, Joan was treated like just another member of his entourage and was never called to the stage, and she departed in tears, sniffing to Reggie that Bobby had torpedoed her career.

Bob's spinning around on methedrine snarling at interviewers and putting down everyone and everything in his path had stranded him in a state of unresolved anger. He was contemplating leaving the music business altogether. Forcing the issue was the runaway success of the Animals' version of "The

House of the Rising Son", which prompted Dylan's producer to overdub an electric backing track on Dylan's version without telling him. Dylan, pushed to the limits of exasperation at the end of the tour, was not interested in a Fats Domino-style early rock 'n' roll thing.

The sound Bob heard in his mind was more akin to John Hammond Jr.'s new album, *So Many Roads*, that Reggie had given him. The son of the great producer, who had been perfecting an acoustic blues act in the Village inspired by his father's Robert Johnson records, had hired the electric guitarist Mike Bloomfield along with a Canadian bar band called the Hawks to back him. Dylan got closer to this sound with "Subterranean Homesick Blues" but it appeared like a surrealistic novelty in an album of acoustic music. The Beatles had surprised him with their harmonies, but after his tour of England, Bob felt new encroachment into his territory, again coming from England.

Gilbert had rejoined the Rolling Stones tour playing "Subterranean Homesick Blues"[246] over and over in their hotel rooms, cracking up whenever he heard the line about Johnny in the basement mixing up the medicine while he's on the pavement thinking about the government. Dylan's nonstop monotone "rap" was the perfect complement to the crunching, speeded-up blues rhythm.

The run-on verse style gave Mick an idea for Keith's riff, the folk song Keith had been working on loosely based on Martha and the Vandella's "Dancing in the Street"[247] but with a feverish guitar riff that kept him up all night.

An angry outburst against the life of endless motel rooms, highways, and commodities, "Satisfaction"[248] screamed about useless information and the emptiness of driving around the world, "doin' this and doin' that" and not really doing anything of importance. No matter how much we can consume, we can never get any real satisfaction from it. The song was an ironic and contemptuous comment on the prefabricated spectacle of modern life, even if the mainstream press and culture bearers thought it had something to do with masturbation. Overnight it became an anthem for disaffected youth, and no one knew it better than Bob Dylan.

In a sort of pseudo-competition with Richard Fariña, Bob had been threatening to write a novel, and out of hundreds of pages of notes and long continuous verses he'd come up with this "long piece of vomit," about twenty pages, about how it felt to be a rolling stone. Bordering on misogyny, the vengeful lyrics describe someone, perhaps Joan Baez, who has not really known hardship, but on whom hard times are about to descend as new situations unfold. He told Reggie it was "all about my steady hatred, directed at some point that was honest."

Reggie told Bob that this was his crossroads, his moment of decision. Reggie knew it was an important moment when Cornell showed up at the session with Al Kooper from the Blues Project in tow and a dour limerick to bestow on all the hangers-on,

Whoa, you're all dressed so fine,
I bet you can throw the bums a dime.
But soon you'll be stuck
On the back of bad luck
And lose your place in time.

Bob considered the arrival of Cornell to be good luck. Mike Bloomfield had arrived with a Telecaster on his back, no guitar case, and Al Kooper decided quickly to volunteer on organ rather than get in Bloomfield's way.

Bob had told Bloomfield, "I don't want you to play any of that B.B. King shit, none of that fucking blues, I want you to play something else."

Bloomfield had shrugged, whatever, okay man. Mike could see that Bob felt at home in the studio, where his method could be acted out in the moment. He'd try a song once or maybe a few times, and if anything about it didn't work, if something went wrong or somebody stopped a take, Bob would just give up on it. In two days he'd forgotten or thrown away far more verses than he wrote, abandoning them in moments of frustration. Somehow the magic was captured on tape. Anything, any change in the lineup of backing musicians, in their moods or feelings, in microphone placement, anything... even a change in the weather would have wrecked it.

In only two days of recording sessions, in fits of bad starts and sudden stops, only one take emerged, and that one was recorded early on day two. Reggie got together with the musicians to tell them, "Whatever you do, don't quit playing. If you quit playing, you're gone. You quit playing, you're never gonna hear that song again."

Bloomfield was to the point: "Man, it's a matter of pure chance. We're chuckle-fucking! We're stepping on each other's dicks until it comes out right."

So how did it feel to be without a home? The right take of "Like a Rolling Stone"[249] came together like an accident on the highway, and they couldn't improve on it no matter how many takes they tried after.

Bob sat cross-legged on the floor in the center of the control room, surrounded by dimly lit consoles with blinking lights, radioactive oscilloscopes, pulsating level meters. He felt safest in this artificial electronic womb in semi-darkness. It was at times a spaceship, a munitions factory, a Chapel Perilous, a bubble of artificial reality hidden in time and space. The control room of the universe. Everyone piled in around him to listen to the take. The organ part, faked by Al Kooper as he felt his way through the unknown song's changes like fumbling in the dark for a light switch, turned out to be brilliant, and Reggie recommended that it be higher in the mix.

They left the studio exhausted, knowing full well that this song, released as a single, would put the world on its ear. This was art made for radio, for the jukebox. Dylan pushed the envelope, as the new test pilots spoke of supersonic boundaries. Straining against censorship, his lyrics had consequences in real life.

With "Satisfaction" the Stones had pumped a charge into the youth culture of unspecified anger and revolt; but at what, no one could yet articulate. With "Like a Rolling Stone" hot on its heels up the pop chart, a new vengeful desire for justice lit this charge, and the condemnation of all that had gone before exploded the music scene. The loud snap of the snare drum that starts the song heralded the explosion. It was as if Dylan were telling everyone, the folkies, the politicians, and all the hung up people in the whole wide universe, get your act together. Nobody ever taught you how to live on the street, and now you're gonna have to get used to it.

When Frank Zappa heard "Like a Rolling Stone" he was almost ready to quit the music business. "If this wins and it does what it's supposed to do, I don't need to do anything else." It seemed suddenly quite possible that pop music could change people's lives, and even stop a war.

* * *

An attractive cosmopolitan woman hurried along the Old Chesapeake and Ohio Central towpath in Georgetown at 12:45 in the afternoon of October 12, 1964, harried and fearful, looking back and around her as if expecting to be jumped. And jumped she was. All in an instant an assailant emerged from tree-lined shadows, wrapped his arms around her, and shoved her behind the azalea bushes, forcing her to kneel. Then, without delay, the man shot her twice in the left temple and once in the chest.

Benjamin C. Bradlee, Washington bureau chief for *Newsweek*, was called upon to identify the body of his sister-in-law, Mary Pinchot Meyer. It was a path she had frequently walked with her best friend, Jacqueline Kennedy, before John F. Kennedy was assassinated. Almost a year after that tragedy she'd taken that walk alone, half-expecting that something would happen, half-expecting her own ex-husband, Cord Meyer, Chief of the International Organizations Division of the CIA, was planning it.

The tight-knit group of political housewives had unravelled. Some would disappear quietly into their households, and others would suffer Mary's fate. Leary, kicked out of Harvard, was preparing to leave for Mexico. Lucy, the emissary from Leary who had brought the light of the world down to Washington, had disappeared into the warrens of New York's Lower East Side. At division headquarters in Washington, Cord Meyer paced his office for hours until hearing the word.

"It is done," an aide spoke after hanging up the telephone.

"Maybe," remarked Cord Meyer, stopping his pacing. "But it is never finished."

* * *

Herbert Mention and Timothy Leary met at a coffee shop. Mary Pinchot's murder had made Leary jumpy and he was making plans to hibernate in Mexico for in spell. Leary didn't know for sure whether Mary had given LSD to the President, but the assassination closed that avenue permanently. The politicians would have no skin in the game of enlightenment.

Leary gave Herbert a progress report. "What we're experiencing is a quantum jump in intelligence. For the first time in history a large and influential sector of the population is learning to disrespect institutions of authority, not because they belong to some political group, but because they are free-thinking individuals. It's an individual's response to this, this... post-industrial world. It's so dehumanizing! As individuals, we can't be controlled by political groups. We demand something more from life, and none of the political parties or labor unions or dissident groups or alternative religions can provide it."

"So you are aiming for the intelligent youth," Herbert chuckled. "And McLuhan said you should use advertising?"

"That's what we're doing," replied Leary. "We're advertising a product: the new, improved, accelerated brain. McLuhan had some good advice, but we need help with this."

Herbert smiled. "You want *my* help?"

"There's a mystic you know, in Mexico. We want to settle there for a while."

"John Starr Cooke. He's connected, you know. High-level CIA."

Leary laughed in surprise. "And you're not?"

"Not any more," Herbert sighed. "You can use Cooke, but you shouldn't trust him."

"He's known as a healer," Leary protested. "There's a Sufi sect in Northern Africa that claims he can activate *shakti.*"

"Ah yes," Herbert nodded. "Kundalini energy. He could induce a blissful spinal seizure by touching you on the forehead. He's got quite a following, I hear. He's got Aleister Crowley's Tarot deck."

"He's already tried LSD. Don't know where he got it."

Herbert smiled. "Like I said, he's connected. You need to be careful with him. I'll get a message to him. Anything else?"

"Actually, what I want is your son's help, and his friend in England," said Leary. "They have the connections we're looking for. McLuhan suggested we contact the new pop musicians, turn them on, and get them to write jingles about the brain. Like this: 'Lysergic acid hits the spot. Forty billion neurons, and that's a lot.'"

"To help dispel the fear of this drug."

"Exactly. Slogans, man. Think of how powerful they can be. 'Give Me Liberty or Give Me Death.' 'A Nation Cannot Exist Half Slave and Half Free.' 'We

Have Nothing to Fear but Fear Itself.' 'Lucky Strike Means Fine Tobacco.' I spent a few days thinking about it, and I did LSD to think some more about it. I came up with 'Turn On, Tune In, and Drop Out.'"

"Turn on..."

"Right," answered Leary. "Turn on your neural circuits, explore the various levels of consciousness, learn about what triggers them."

"Tune in..."

"Tune into the world around you and to your own genetic circuits. Pick up on the vibrations of others, just like tuning into a radio station."

"And?" Herbert looked puzzled.

"Drop out. Detach yourself from involuntary or unconscious commitments. Learn to be self-reliant, mobile, and ready for change."

Herbert chuckled. "A slogan for increasing intelligence."

Timothy sighed. "Unfortunately, this has often been misinterpreted as 'get stoned and abandon all constructive activity.'"

"Because..."

"Because they're idiots. The press, the authorities."

"The Corporation."

Leary nodded and said nothing.

"You realize that they've taken on assassination coverups," said Herbert sternly. "What do you think they'll make of this? LSD, their own mind drug, on the loose? Their experiment gone haywire? They must be up to something, some backup plan. You trusted Cravingston, didn't you. Don't make the same mistake with Cooke." Herbert paused, then smiled. "But look on the bright side. It's quite a slogan."

Leary smiled. "I hear it like a soda jingle. 'Turn on to flavor, tune into sparkle, and drop out of the cola rut.'"

* * *

The lithe, serene Maureen Cleave of the London Evening Standard picked her way through the cluttered living room, stepping around a full-size crucifix to encounter a gorilla costume and a medieval suit of armor. The Beatles' newest single, "Day Tripper",[250] roared out of a garish jukebox with a stinging guitar riff suggesting a racing car, and lyrics echoing the misogynist fury unleashed in recent Stones songs. A smiling Cynthia Lennon led her across the hall of Lennon's home in Kenwood, Weybridge to a well-organized library where John sat in front of hardbound works by Alfred Tennyson, Jonathan Swift, Oscar Wilde, George Orwell, Aldous Huxley, and *The Passover Plot* by Hugh J. Schonfield. Cleave was writing a series of articles entitled "How Does a Beatle Live?"

At one point Cleave noticed the book by Schonfield and asked John if he was reading extensively about religion.

With an easy smirk, John nodded and responded. "Christianity will go. It will vanish and shrink. I needn't argue about that; I'm right and I'll be proved right. We're more popular than Jesus now; I don't know which will go first — rock 'n' roll or Christianity. Jesus was all right but his disciples were thick and ordinary. It's them twisting it that ruins it for me."

Cleave noted it, but moved on to more pressing details. "On your first tour of America, did you say that the one film star you wanted to see was Jayne Mansfield?"

"Oh sure," answered John bashfully. "She played the blonde bimbo in 'The Girl Can't Help It'."

Cynthia bowed her head and decided that now was the right time to fetch the tea.

"We *did* meet her, in Hollywood," John continued. "At the Whiskey A Go Go on Sunset Strip. I was annoyed because Jayne brought her husband along." John glanced around to see if Cynthia was close by, and then told Cleave, "I just wanted to be alone with Jayne. I've dreamed about it."

John didn't tell the rest of the story to Cleave. The club had been so crowded that it took the band twenty minutes to get from the door to the table, and instantly the whole of Hollywood paparazzi descended on them. Jayne Mansfield squeezed her way into the middle of the group and goaded the cameramen to take photographs of her and John. She curled up on her chair between John and George, riding her hand up John's leg and then George's. She tugged John's hair and squealed, "Is this real?" to which John replied, dropping his eyes to her most famous features, "Well, are those real?" She responded, "Well, there's one way to find out." At that point an angry George threw his drink at a photographer, and an ice cube hit another actress, Mamie van Doren, in the face.

That evening, at the Hollywood suburb of Bel Air where the Beatles were staying, Jayne arrived in a mauve cat suit ready to show John how real they really were. Later, a male friend of Jayne's arrived to take her home, and Jayne asked him to read the Tarot cards for herself and John. The man began to read them, and then dropped the cards in horror, exclaiming, "My god, this is terrible. I see an awful ending to all this." John was furious and threw the two of them out.

* * *

"Is he here yet? Has he arrived?"

Anticipation was running high at the Newport Folk and Blues Festival in the summer of 1965. The festival was sinking from the weight of its popularity, and the board members that ran it — a mix of old folklorists like Alan Lomax and folk stars like Peter Yarrow and Pete Seeger — were concerned, and more than a bit nervous. They had strangled the performers with rules.

"There are 26 performing groups on this Saturday night," complained one musician. "That means eight minutes for each performer. How can anyone be expected to do anything real, in that amount of time?"

"The sad fact is, every year it gets worse," said another. "We are always building on the ruins of the previous year. We don't change anything, we just add to the mess."

With so many performers on the bill, the atmosphere had become thick with restrictions on the performers' time, living quarters, and movement, stifling artistic expression. The large number of performers also meant long, enervating microphone rehearsals which increased the tension and irritability of the performers and the staff. And on Saturday night, the time pressure meant that Son House, Skip James, and Bukka White appeared together with about four minutes apiece in a performance that was a near disaster.

A stalwart of the festival, Cornell Woodrow was responsible for discovering and bringing to the stage many of the old bluesmen. He was uncharacteristically livid and lashed out at Alan Lomax and Theo Bikel for making it so difficult for an electric band to set up and play. "This festival is dying of complications. The attitude here seems to be, fall in, do your gig, and split. The workshops are so crowded they've become separate stages. And each member of the board has his favorites and wants to see them on the stage. This is not *Shindig*! For this experiment to work, you got to make objective decisions about who should perform, who is going to move the music forward and give the festival a meaning."

"Certainly *not* Dylan," groused Lomax, addressing the main concern for nervousness. "He's on his way here in tights and sequins. He wants to *trash* the festival." Albert Grossman, Dylan's manager, stood up abruptly and was ready to punch Lomax, but Cornell eased him back to his seat. Lomax was also incensed about the inclusion of the Paul Butterfield Blues Band, another act Grossman managed. "White boys trying to do the blues," he wailed.

And when it came time to introduce the Butterfield band at a Saturday afternoon workshop, Lomax had reached his limit and stood up to tell the audience, "Today you've been hearing music by the great blues players, guys who go out and find themselves an old cigar box, put a stick in it, attach some strings, sit under a tree, and play great blues for themselves. Now you're going to hear a group of young boys from Chicago with *electric* instruments. Let's see if they can play this hardware at all."

By the time the group took the stage, Lomax and Grossman, both oversized men, were at each others' throats, throwing punches and rolling around in the dirt. They had to be pulled apart. Lomax stormed off and gathered an emergency meeting of the board to ban Grossman from the festival. George Wein, the founding father of the festival, scotched this effort by telling the board that if they voted to kick out Grossman, they had better be prepared for a massive walkout of not only Dylan but also Peter Paul and Mary, Odetta, and Buffy St. Marie.

Dylan, the king of the '64 festival in blue jeans and work-shirt, now arrived with his entourage wearing puff-sleeved polka-dot dueling shirts, Beatle boots, and sunglasses. Reggie had found Al Kooper wandering around, and persuaded Bob to try the Paul Butterfield band as a rhythm section along with Bloomfield.

In his unwavering belief in the power of serendipity, Dylan had only thought of playing several of his songs on his own with an acoustic guitar. But the electric atmosphere of anticipation convinced him that his act would be boring, at least to himself. The time was right to fix it.

Reggie could see the immediate future. "Bob, they're going to boo."

Familiar with Reggie's grasp of the future, Dylan gathered the musicians for an all-night rehearsal before the show. He fingered his thunder-stone in his pocket. "Now there's gonna be some kinda circus out there," he drawled. "If they don't like it, too bad. They'll have to learn to like it. Just ignore whatever happens and play the show. Play it *fucking loud*." And he instructed Reggie to keep a firm grasp of things out at the sound console to make sure the show would be loud.

The crowd had been treated all afternoon to long bland ballads, good-humored homages to children, and schmaltzy sing-alongs. The Butterfield set drove many of them into the lines for the barbecue and the port-a-potties. As they settled back in their seats, they stared at the vacant stage, mysteriously populated with the previous band's equipment. A hush fell over the crowd as Dylan materialized on stage, all in black, like a motorcycle thief, followed by members of Butterfield's band.

The first measure of "Maggie's Farm"[251] hit like a tornado, louder than anything anyone had ever heard before, mixed with the ballsy camaraderie of kids cavorting in a candy store. Joe Boyd, the stage engineer, came running up to the sound board in a sweat. "They're freaking out! It's too loud, they want you to turn it down. They're very, very upset! Pete Seeger has an axe, and he wants to cut the power cable!"

Reggie, Cornell, Neuwirth, Grossman, Peter Yarrow, and the sound engineer were all grinning at the sound console. "Tell Alan Lomax," shouted Yarrow in glee, and he extended his middle finger.

"C'mon, Peter, gimme a break!" Boyd huffed.

"Well, just tell Alan that the board is adequately represented on the sound console," and he pointed to himself, Grossman, and Cornell. "We have things fully under control."

A booing sound rose from the front part of the crowd in the seats, where mostly folk purists and the older generation had gathered in order to sit through the show. Someone near the sound console yelled "Sell out!" He moved closer to the console and yelled, "Joan Baez would never sell out like this!"

"Joan Baez?" Neuwirth laughed. "What's she got to sell out?"

Oblivious to the boos and catcalls, the band powered on, even though the drummer had turned the beat around and was playing on the up-beats rather than the down-beats, throwing everyone off. Dylan led them through a brief "Like a Rolling Stone" but the rhythm section was floundering. Dylan switched gears, announced a simpler blues called "Phantom Engineer",[252] and the rhythm section found solid ground and took off, rip-roaring through the song with a jet-fueled frenzy.

As it crashed to an end in a field of boos, a tearful Dylan said "That's it," and walked off. The crazed audience screamed for blood, for salvation, for more songs... boos and hisses cut through the screams. Electric crap, someone yelled. Too loud! Everyone seemed to agree with that. No one was satisfied.

Pete Seeger walked out of the show dejected and solemn, his theme for the evening of "songs babies would like to grow up with" disappearing into the same dust bowl of irrelevance as the union songs he used to sing.

Backstage, Dylan was in tears, unable to speak. Johnny Cash came up and handed him a jumbo Gibson acoustic guitar, much too big for Bob, and told him to get on back out there. Bob stumbled back out and strummed a languorous "Mr. Tambourine Man",[253] to explain that he was ready to go anywhere, even to fade into his own parade. And, escaping on the run, he sang about striking another match and starting anew. "It's All Over Now, Baby Blue"[254] was a song originally directed at folk singer Paul Clayton, who had devolved from Bob's mentor to sycophant as a result of prodigious abuse of amphetamine. Many interpreted it as a message to the folk purists in the audience.

As the concert ended in chaos, confusion and rage, a pious Mel Lyman of the Jim Kweskin Jug Band, feeling Christ-like in ragged jeans, made an attempt to heal the wound by playing a mournful harmonica solo.

Lucy and Reggie caught up with Dylan, sitting in a dark corner table by himself at the festival after-party, for which the Chambers Brothers had been hired to provide night music of rhythm and blues. Lucy asked Bob to dance, but Bob declined. "I would, but my hands are on fire."

Cornell was there to offer condolences. "Musicians lose people as they go along," he told Reggie. "You see, people want the musician to keep playing the music that made them feel something once. They have some feeling they hope the old music might rekindle, or some dream they might recapture. But if a musician is at all alive, as an artist, the music he wants to play is well beyond that old feeling, that old dream. They say, 'Oh, you've betrayed us, why don't you play the music we expect, why don't you go back to your roots?' There are songs that people still want to hear today that are just inappropriate for these times."

* * *

Within a few days Dylan was back in the studio, sweating about how to follow up "Like a Rolling Stone" with something equally poignant. And then, with chilling accuracy, he penned a lyric that effectively put down all the folkies that had, in his view, ridden his coattails to rise above traditional folk songs and base their careers on their own songwriting. In "Positively Fourth Street"[255] he castigated the crowd he used to be with for pretending to be his friend, because when he was down, they just stood there grinning. He wanted folkie supremo Phil Ochs to know how it felt to stand inside his shoes. He wanted him to know what a drag it is to see him.

No song had ever shown so much nerve to be hurtful. So much of this music swirled over the airwaves, and the young people, especially the young white suburban kids, started to listen more closely, just as Cornell Woodrow had predicted. Reggie could see it shimmering on the horizon of his dreams. The kids were stomping at their dances to "no satisfaction" with a newfound anger at the people who try to hide "what they don't know to begin with" and the vengeful honesty of "how does it feel to be on your own?" It was a recipe for a youth rebellion.

"The electricity itself, not the volume," Bob had buttonholed Reggie at the bar of a Village nightclub, "not the amplification of voices and acoustic instruments, but the electricity *itself* that moves people like they've never been moved before." In search of that "wild mercury sound" he'd heard a hint of in his first electric excursions, Dylan wanted to find a band that could back him up without fawning all over him. Reggie told him about the Hawks, which were back in residence at Tony Mart's in South Jersey. "Ronnie Hawkins is no longer with 'em," Reggie explained. "But I think they have that sound you're looking for."

Before Reggie could finish explaining, Bob disappeared. Dylan had developed a camouflaged way of appearing at clubs in New York, slamming his friends with put-downs, and then disappearing, like a wise chameleon, ducking out of the joint the way Robert Johnson used to disappear from the juke joints into the hostile night.

* * *

An itch on Detective Delatore's backside would not let him relax. He'd driven out to the pine barrens for this meeting with Frank Balzano, which for some sick reason had been scheduled at night by the bottomless Blue Hole near the Egg Harbor River.

Balzano had phoned him to tell him that he had information about Freddie's murder. This was a surprise; mobsters typically didn't call the cops to talk about murders. Delatore pressed him for details, but all Balzano would say is that he had been there at the time, at the radio station, but Freddie was already dead when he arrived. All he did was shoot the body, to send a message to other DJs.

Someone else, an associate, had dumped the body under Lucy the Elephant. He had been acting under orders from a man in New York called Tony Just. "I'm just trying to keep the peace between families," Balzano had said on the phone. "I didn't kill him, all's I did was cover it up. And I'm talking about making a deal here, to get my son Johnny off the hook as well as myself. I'm gonna sell my record label and get out of the distribution business. I'm gonna live a quiet, peaceful life here in Margate. That's all I want."

Balzano told him to meet him out by the Blue Hole to receive some papers on this guy Tony Just. Delatore had been around the block; he knew Balzano's gratuitous gesture to get out of the music business was motivated by economics more than anything else. Payola was out. Money laundering was no longer viable. With the coming of the Beatles and others of their ilk, the music business was consolidating, with larger labels gobbling up smaller ones. No, Balzano wasn't doing this out of the goodness of his heart. The man was getting into something else, something that required a low profile.

Delatore got to the rendezvous point early, and got out of his car to check that none of Balzano's thugs were lurking about. He wandered over to the Blue Hole, filled with black water. Was it the crater of a meteorite or the work of the Jersey Devil? And where had the Jackal disappeared to? As he leaned over the edge to peer down into the inky blackness, someone came up from behind and gave him a push. Down he went into the water. As he bobbed up for air, a wrench split his skull open. His body sank into the immeasurable black depths.

* * *

Margate had not changed one bit. Across the bay in Somers Point, Reggie could see the Margate water towers that looked like giant golf balls on tees. Bay Avenue seethed with giddy teens and college-age kids poking their heads into the crowded Steel's Ship Bar, the Under 21 Club and the Anchorage.

Tony Mart's was full, standing room only, so Reggie bribed the doorman to get in through the backstage door. The Hawks launched into a menacing original tune, "Yazoo Street Scandal"[256] with Levon Helm chopping up the beat and Robbie Robertson pinching sharp, piercing notes from his Telecaster. The band now included three other Canadians, a young bass player, a lead singer, and a bearded organist that looked like a preacher. They seemed to have all the elements Dylan needed, including an icepick guitar and a cerebral organ. Reggie stretched the phone's earpiece outside the backstage phone booth so that Bob could hear the music. Bob told Reggie to bring the guitar player up to New York.

Frank Balzano appeared at the backstage door, nattily dressed in a three-piece suede suit. His hair had grown a bit longer, touching the tops of his ears. Reggie was startled, but quickly recovered and smiled. Ballzo smiled back, leaning backwards on his heels and hooking his thumbs into his vest. "Didn't think I'd know you're here? I know everything that goes on here. You were going to stop by the table on your way out, to say hello, right?"

"Sure thing, Mister B." Reggie held out his hand, and Ballzo shook it hard.

"You're in the music business now. That's what I hear."

Ballzo's stern voice made Reggie flinch, but he nodded, hoping for nothing more than a diatribe about this new rock 'n' roll.

"Well, be careful," Ballzo warmed up. "You don't know what can happen. You hear about that kid Bobby Fuller?"

"He had a hit with 'I Fought the Law'."257

"'And the law won.' Yeah, that's funny. Hear what happened to him? The record label's silent partner had a life insurance policy on him. They snuffed him for the policy."

Reggie was stunned.

"That's right kid. This stuff happens all the time. Managers sign an artist, record him, take out a million-dollar life insurance policy on him, record him again, put him out on the road and work him until he's bleeding, then smoke him and collect the insurance. Hell, they don't even have to kill him. Charlie Parker was jones-ing in the studio, and they'd have him signing away his composing, publishing, and artist's royalties before they'd let the dealer in so that he could shoot up."

Reggie could think of nothing to say.

"There's even a Dean Martin joke about it," Ballzo laughed. "If you see somebody being held by the heels outside a thirty-story window, that would be Jackie Wilson renegotiating his contract."

"Are you trying to tell me…"

"I'm trying to tell you to be careful. But what I want you to do is to tell Johnny. I know you're in touch with him. I know he was in town with the Beatles at the A.C. Racetrack. But he won't talk to me. Tell him that business with Freddie is over. I took care of it. That detective won't be bothering him. And you tell Johnny to be careful, in this new business of his."

"New business?" Reggie was genuinely surprised.

Ballzo looked him over. "Just tell him. He'll know what I'm talking about. He's already on their radar. He's working with the wrong dame. You tell him that."

* * *

Dylan would take the Hawks on the road in a brutal tour, with boos every night rising to a crescendo of hate and shouts of "Judas!" The audience synchronized its hand clapping as a rebuke, and Dylan would mumble through the hand-claps until they quieted down and strained to hear the nonsense he was mumbling. He would taunt them with his harmonica, as if he were about to do one of his folk hits[258] in the traditional folk style, and then tell them that the song "used to go like that, and now it goes like this." Then Bob would turn to the band and tell them to "play it fucking loud."

Drummer Levon, a veteran of chicken-scratch roadhouse knife fights, eventually threw down his sticks and declared Dylan to be crazy. But Bob persevered and punched through the boos with the loudest music ever to be heard on the planet until, spiraling out of a maelstrom of paranoia, he stuck out his middle finger at the music industry and disappeared into the woods of the Adirondacks.

* * *

She would never say where she came from, no matter how many times Johnny B would ask. She comes and goes as she pleases, trailing ambiguous desires in her frothy, perfumed wake. And even standing still, her ruby locks and spit curls, the color of pink grapefruit, flutter in the breeze of her movement in the direction of her next adventure. Her bleached white skin and solid frame suggests a country girl from Northern England, not quite Scotland, but her walk is Italian, each cheek of her perfectly round ass winking at you from down the street, and her laugh is pure American, with a hint of New Jersey. The gossamer folds of her blouse barely conceal dark unruly nipples punctuating her voluptuous, heaving bosom. It is a bosom you can't look away from, even when blushing, discussing other girls, or ordering another round of scotch and coke.

At the end of a Rolling Stones concert in Munich, Brian, loving the limelight, remained on stage as usual, laughing at the riot as screaming fans surrounded him. As Johnny B tried to reach him, two nearly identically dressed women blocked his path. Johnny looked up to see Babbs, the fantasy of his teenage years, and a woman that looked like a younger Austrian version of her. Johnny nearly fainted. They were both stunning creatures. It was hard to maintain one's gaze. They managed to corral Brian to the backstage area.

"I'm Anita," said the younger one, pouting into Brian's face.

"I'm Brian," he replied.

"Everybody knows who you are," Anita smiled and confidently snaked her arm into his. Brian was immediately smitten.

Babbs stood before Johnny B with a faint impish smile, pursed lips, darting blue eyes, and an entirely new ruby hair color. There were no traces of any bruises. Her smile curled into a knowing look, and her eyes hardened with lust. Johnny nearly swooned.

She held out her hand palm up, slightly open, cradling a phial of colorless liquid, the same type of phial that he had snatched from Gilbert's stash. For over a minute they gazed at each other in silence, without moving, as the chaos of the stage washed around them. Then he reached out to close her hand over the phial and gather her up to him. They kissed deeply for what seemed an eternity before they were jostled to the edge of the stage by the crowd.

Turned out that Babbs was working for a consortium that was producing the new "psychedelic" as she called it. "It's pure, of course," she told him with a broad smile. "Produced at Sandoz, in Switzerland."

"The Captain?"

"Forget him," she murmured, snuggling up to him. "I have the supply, and you have the market."

"Well," he patted her ass. "I think this is the beginning of a beautiful friendship."

* * *

All it took was a long-distance phone call to Manila. "Tell her it's Will Cravingston from MI6." A flustered Imelda Marcos, interrupted from her morning ablutions, picked up the extension and lowered the volume on "You've Got to Hide Your Love Away",[259] the Beatles newest single that featured Lennon sounding like Dylan.

"I got through to them, your highness. They probably won't be showing up at eleven. They don't like going to such affairs. I'm afraid I must tell you, the boys are not happy with Ramon Ramos. They're not happy with their hotel rooms, or about being in the Philippines at all. They are indeed an ungrateful lot. Their manager, Brian Epstein, just can't control them. I wouldn't be surprised if they sleep through it until their show at four."

Marcos was furious. She had already announced to the press that the Beatles would pay a courtesy call on her and her husband at Malacañang Palace. Ramon had promised to deliver them. Both afternoon and evening shows at the Rizal Memorial Football Stadium were sold out, with a combined attendance of 80,000. The Beatles would generate over a hundred thousand dollars in one day! Ramon's promoter take would be nearly a third, and his kickback to her quite considerable. She got back on the phone to the press, in time to make the ten o'clock deadline.

Cravingston had seen to it that the Marcos invitation would not reach Brian Epstein until it was too late. When the lads first arrived they were whisked off to the marina, and then to a yacht owned by his associate anchored two miles out from the port. Epstein couldn't reach them with the invitation himself, so he sent a local messenger, intercepted by Ramon Ramos, another Cravingston associate. Ramon saw an opportunity to cause trouble and skip away without paying the Beatles anything.

Imelda had set the lunch for 11 a.m. with 300 children. At 10 a.m., a delegation came to the Manila Hotel to collect the Beatles, but Epstein declined the invitation on the grounds that no earlier arrangement had been made and the Beatles were still in bed.

While the concerts proceeded normally, Ramon made a point of not being available afterwards for settling up. The next morning, with the newspapers screaming the headline "Beatles Snub President," the Beatles found no hotel services or transportation available, and their local bodyguards were gone. Bomb threats were phoned into the British Embassy and the hotel suite. A distressed Epstein hastily arranged a press conference at the hotel to apologize for the misunderstanding, but an unforeseen static blip cut out his interview from all the TV screens in the country.

Running a gauntlet of screaming Filipinos grabbing at their hair outside the hotel, the boys fled in separate cabs to the airport, where instead of the usual security they found themselves under arrest for failure to pay taxes. Epstein hurriedly forked over a bond for $18,000 from his own funds to get them to the gate. All security had vanished and escalators were turned off, so the Beatles hustled down several flights of stairs with their luggage, only to face an angry mob of several hundred Filipinos. Ringo, floored by an uppercut and kicked on the ground, had to be helped to the customs area. A booing crowd jeered and mocked them as they boarded the plane, and they sat on the tarmac for another hour as government officials stalled to await word.

Cravingston made another long-distance call, and they were released.

* * *

"Think they got the message?" Mumblingore wanted to know.

"That the world is no longer safe for them? I think they already knew that," answered Cravingston.

"The point is, we failed," Mumblingore grunted. "A pop group, for chrissakes! That queer Jew you have running things, what's his name, Epstein? The man wrote a book about them, for chrissakes!"

"I know. *A Cellarful of Noise* he called it. Know what John Lennon called it? 'A Cellarful of Boys'," Cravingston laughed. Mumblingore frowned at him, but he continued. "Keep in mind, the merchandise revenue is still pouring in."

"Yes I know, I know," replied Mumblingore with impatience. "But there were supposed to be *hundreds* of these teenage bands. Their banal music would have crowded the airwaves. Each year, a new crop of them. The old ones were supposed to dry up, but they keep going! They're adults now. We're losing control of them, completely. Especially the... the... really bad ones, what're they called? The Rollers?"

"The Rolling Stones. Anyway, we haven't lost control, not completely. We have a few more tricks up our sleeve. The first of many, uh, *psychological* operations."

"Good. Psy-ops, the oldest weapon in man's arsenal."

* * *

When the Beatles landed in America that August, the news showed the Ku Klux Klan setting fire to a wooden cross with a Beatles record nailed to it, and record bonfires and demonstrations across the Deep South. The remark John Lennon had casually tossed to Maureen Cleave had conveniently surfaced on the cover of a teen magazine in the U.S. just as the Beatles were to play Memphis. "More popular than Jesus!?," screamed the headlines.

The word was put out by unseen propagandists. Radio stations across the South immediately banned the Beatles. After a call from someone in New York, the Memphis city council chairman called a press conference to tell the Beatles that they were not welcome in Memphis, a city the group used to sing about. Even so, the afternoon concert in Memphis was well attended, but the Beatles had no stomach to visit the local recording studios and Beale Street after a firecracker exploded on the side of the stage.

As the controversy spread to Mexico, South Africa, and Spain, Epstein arranged a press conference, and Johnny B told Lennon to "just apologize, man, get it over with, don't think twice."

John Lennon stood before the merciless spider's nest of microphones, visibly pale and fidgeting, his cocky stance gone. "I suppose if I had said television was more popular than Jesus, I might have got away with it," he tried to joke, but no one laughed.

A reporter reminded him of what he had been quoted as saying. "Well, originally I pointed out that fact in reference to England," Lennon said in earnest. "That we meant more to kids than Jesus did, or religion at that time. I wasn't knocking it or putting it down. I was just saying it as a *fact*, and it's true more for England than here. I'm not saying that we're better or greater, or comparing us with Jesus Christ as a person or God as a thing or whatever it is. I just said what I said, and it was wrong." Lennon bowed his head in contrition, his voice cracking, nearly in tears. But he couldn't leave it at that. "Or it was taken wrong. And now it's all this," he gestured to the reporters.

A reporter pressed him. "But are you prepared to apologize?"

"I wasn't saying whatever they're saying I was saying," Lennon shrugged, his confidence returning. "I'm sorry I said it really. I never meant it to be a lousy anti-religious thing," he snarled at the reporter. "I apologize if that will make you happy. I still don't know quite what I've done."

By the time they returned to their limousine, all four Beatles had finally agreed to stop touring. They had taken a strong whiff of something sour in the air, of decay, corruption, and uncontrollable rage. They would produce albums from now on, in a studio they would one day make famous, and live in comfort in their new homes and gardens. As Cornell explained it to Johnny B, this particular experiment was entering a new phase.

A Movement is Accomplished

A movement is accomplished in six stages, and the seventh brings return.

"Ah," remarked Johnny B to Cornell Woodrow in the control booth, as Syd Barrett of the Pink Floyd sang his new composition "Chapter 24"[260] in EMI's Abbey Road Studios while the February storms of 1967 brewed outside. "The I-Ching. Wilhelm and Baynes translation of 1950."

"The Legge translation of 1899," Cornell Woodrow corrected him.

Johnny B inched up the volume on the bass, just in time to catch Roger Waters with his bass climbing from the depths of despair to a hopeful, optimistic note. The way Johnny mixed it, on the fly, gave the song the sound of church music. It was about persuasion, the power of the vibrations of the notes. The Pink Floyd took bass beyond its range, couldn't even be recorded properly without distortion. The blend of sounds of machines, gears, jet engines, explosions, all with computer-like precision, were at the heart of this new music.

Syd had found the melody by accident. Four notes, the first three part of the scale, the fourth out in left field somewhere. It suggested madness, and sadness.

As Johnny and the engineers managed the mix, Syd lay on a cot in the next room, his eyes like black holes in the sky. The band members could feel his presence, even hear his slight breathing. His daily LSD intake had put him on the dark side of the moon, and Waters, for one, was miffed. "He lays there, with unlimited choices he can make in his head, to paint, to write lyrics, to work on melodies, to listen to new music, to practice, to make love, to do more drugs. But in every choice is a limiting factor, a trap. If he makes a choice, he has to stick with it for a while. And so he lies there, unable to make a choice."

In "Bike",[261] Syd shows a girl a borrowed bike (not even his own!), a cloak, a homeless, aging mouse that he calls Gerald, and a clan of gingerbread men, all because she fits in with his world. He offers to take her into a room of musical tunes, which becomes a noisy collage of oscillators, clocks, gongs, bells, a violin, and other sounds, fading out with a tape loop of a joke laugh box reversed and played at double speed.

Pop music had come a long way from "she loves you, yeah yeah yeah."

Dada in music had reached its solipsistic nadir in composer John Cage's "4' 33",[262] which is notated as three movements, each marked "Tacet" (which means "do not play"). As "performed" by a musician seated at a piano, nothing happens. Background noises — the humming of the lights, the shuffling of the audience, the sound of traffic outside — are the actual music. La Monte Young took this line of thought to an extreme by suggesting that even sound itself was not necessary for a piece of music to exist. In "1960 #5", one of a series of similar pieces, he instructed the performer to turn a butterfly (or any number of butterflies) loose in the performance area. The piece being considered complete when the butterflies have flown away.

* * *

It's an awesome responsibility to be a musician.

Johnny B, consumed by this thought, gazed out across the river Thames at dawn, knocked out on a sample of his latest batch; and he realized within minutes, as his eyelids popped and his stomach churned, that the measurements had been wrong; the sample was too powerful. Take a note of that, he giggled to himself.

Wrapped in a soft mist, London revealed herself as a fairy tale of delicacy and wistfulness, of ancient stone monuments and mystic beauty. And yet, all was façade. He could break apart the scene into subatomic particles. He could hear the vibrations underlying these particles. All matter dissolved into vibrations; it was just a matter of zeroing in on a frequency to resonate with, and you could move mountains… And this is what is so important about music. Not just our history, not just our language, but our very *souls* are recorded in our music. It's an awesome responsibility, to be a musician.

And yet, it was not music he was out here to capture on his portable reel-to-reel recorder. Gilbert was advocating noise, to use noise as a role in music. McCartney had this rocking, rollicking number about a Sergeant Pepper and his lonely hearts club band, and a few other songs that reminisced of the bygone age of ballroom dancing, but with maddening sparks of brilliant over-amped electric guitar. Gilbert had suggested to Johnny that he record street noise, particularly the carnival-type sounds around Carnaby Street. Shielding his microphone, Johnny wandered through the morning crowd, spotting other refugees from modern culture, those who at one time or another had been stoned. He could spot them easily because they typically wore the latest in pop-inspired fashions. He wandered all morning in Kings Road and Carnaby Street, a never-ending festival of the young, all dressed up in anachronistic threads, lithe maidens in granny dresses just back from a druid castle, arm-in-arm with tall, laconic, long-haired and buckskin-jacketed Robin Hoods, celebrating awareness of ley lines and Stonehenge, meditation and astrology, inner space and radical politics, love and sex, and the cosmology of the universe. His recordings were used to permeate through the opening track[263] and second track[264] of the *Sgt. Pepper* album that would come to define the Love Generation.

* * *

Johnny B had found his calling in the studios, with Gilbert as his protégé, and McCartney and Lennon would take their advice. It was a year earlier that Gilbert introduced Lennon to controlled feedback. Lennon had pointed his guitar in the wrong direction, and his amp yelped into a piercing shriek. Gilbert was on hand and grabbed the neck of the guitar, and concentrating, he produced a lower pitch noise with an ominous tone.

Lennon had been intrigued. "You can't do that again, can you?"

Gilbert reproduced the sound again, exactly as before. After five takes of "I Feel Fine"[265] Lennon got it right. It sounded like a door opening, if you dared, to a yawning, gaping eternity, a mind-blown black hole at the start of the song. Lennon takes the wheel of the ship with a muscular guitar riff, and it falls back to straight-ahead rock. It may have been the first pop single to use feedback, and it signaled for many fans that the lads were on to something new.

Johnny and Gilbert were showing up regularly at the studios with reefer, LSD, and new gadgets to use with their amplifiers. The pair had been working with the Detours, now called the Who, to use feedback and put the bass front and center in the music, driving not only the rhythm but also defining the melody.

One day Johnny's hashish connection furnished him with a sitar, which he promptly gave to Brian Jones to see how quickly, how instinctively, he could learn it. After a single day Brian was ready to add the tasteful sitar licks to "Paint it Black",[266] turning a bleak folk song into a whirling dervish with a sinister aspect.

In search of otherworldly sounds to accompany their interstellar travels, George Harrison and John Lennon were intrigued with the sitar sound that embroidered the song like a Persian rug. It conjured up visions of Richard Burton the explorer, fording rivers in the valley of Death on an expedition to find the source of music. Johnny introduced George to the music of Ravi Shankar, and George applied this sound to a Dylanesque folk tune Lennon had written about a love affair with a journalist, using a bit of wordplay around the phrase "Isn't it good knowing she would?"[267]

Johnny and Gilbert were on a roll. McCartney took Johnny's advice to play melodic runs on bass like James Jamerson at Motown, and stay in unusual keys like Brian Wilson's bass in Beach Boys songs. "You don't have to play just the root notes," Johnny told him. "You're going from C to F to G. But you could be pulling on the G, or stay on the C when it goes to F." And so forth. Paul's bass modulation to introduce "The Night Before"[268] and his Indian raga-sounding bass on "Rain"[269] had impressed all of the other beat bands in England, who soon began to recognize Johnny The Bass Player as a Svengali.

Johnny had even heard from Brian Wilson, who was recovering from anxiety attacks from touring with the Beach Boys. Paranoid about competition from the Beatles and the other British groups, he wanted Johnny B to come out to Hollywood to play bass along with the superb jazz bassist Carol Kaye on his next album, *Pet Sounds*.

"The electric bass is more important than you think," Johnny T. Bassplayer was quoted in *Melody Maker*. "You can hear how the music changed, from rockabilly and the slap-bass, through R&B to Motown, where the bass defines the melody. Spector heard that too."

Even Brian Epstein, the Beatles manager, understood it. "He could affect some kind of alchemy in the lower registers. The vibrations down there are subtle but effect the body and the mind."

Johnny B encouraged McCartney to continue experimenting, playing an independent bass line against the arrangement and recording it separately, as he would never have tried to sing and play those lines at the same time. As they continued with sonic experiments, the new songs could never be performed the way they were recorded. It was just as well. Years of touring had been like years in a movable prison, with hotel rooms for jail cells. No one wanted to tour anymore, except through the mind. All of this new music subscribed to the ethic of the mind-blown state. The Beatles, dressed in flowery Carnaby Street fashions, made music for the inner mind. John, George, and Ringo had not only tried LSD but were tripping out at the *Sgt. Pepper* photo sessions.

There were minor setbacks. Mae West balked at being a part of the celebrity collage on the cover because she would never have joined a "lonely hearts club" and had to be cajoled into it by a cheerful Lennon. EMI's chairman pulled McCartney aside to say, "All well and good, my boy, but you can't use Gandhi!" The orchestra really didn't know how to follow the instruction, for the instrumental break in "A Day in the Life",[270] to start playing at one note and, no matter what your fellow musician is doing, play at your own speed up the scale to the final note. After a few takes producer George Martin threw up his hands; the musicians mostly followed each other up the scale because they couldn't think independently. Despite the production errors left out and a few left in, such as the egg timer to mark the beginning of the middle part, John Lennon had managed to accurately capture the wailing despair of a frightened man on the edge of a seething, technological wilderness.

At one point Lennon wandered out of the session in a haze and up to the naked edge of the rooftop of the Abbey Road studio. With no railing separating him from a killing fall, John was staring out into space wondering what was wrong. A familiar churn squeezed his stomach, and he recognized the metallic taste that precluded an attack of paranoia.

McCartney went looking for Lennon, and found him up on the roof dangerously close to the edge. John explained that he'd taken some of Johnny B's pills he thought were speed but, he now realized, were LSD. Not that he didn't like it, he told Paul, but he couldn't keep himself together enough to play. Paul pulled him away from the edge, whispering in his ear, "let's go over to my place," his place on Cavendish, just a block away. "Maybe it's time I tried it, too."

* * *

Johnny B's instinct had been to assemble some sort of infrastructure to accommodate these seekers of wisdom and truth, and Babbs' instinct had been to set up a business model to profit from them, just as Levi Strauss and the San Franciscans of the 19th century Gold Rush profited from selling shovels and jeans to the prospectors. The profits would finance all sorts of artistic and spiritual quests from art galleries and musical adventures to peace movements. Romancing the Stones, currying favor with the Beatles, wearing the latest in pop fashions, and distributing acid-laced sugar cubes were all of a piece, a performance on the grand stage of London's Carnaby Street and Kings Road with stores like Granny Takes a Trip. What better way to market the new freedom? Who could better put two and two together — the psychedelic experience and the youth market —than the upcoming rock music heroes?

Dawn had fled into morning on the London streets, and Johnny B, still caught up in his vision of the vibrations underneath subatomic particles, saw shoppers taking off their clothes, heard clerks saying gibberish instead of thank you very much, and felt the world shimmer in its molecules as if to shrug off reality altogether.

Buzzing, he entered the flat he shared with Babbs and poured himself into her bed, snuggling deep within her warmth. She awakened and turned herself to him. They enveloped each other in arms and legs and explored each other's tangy mouths in the morning light. As usual, he would energetically fuck her awake, and she would languidly fuck him to sleep. Then she'd get up, don a puffy blouse and miniskirt from Carnaby Street, and head on out to their clandestine LSD factory in Kensington.

Babbs had staffed the factory with members of a black-clad ex-Scientology group calling themselves The Method. The members wore black robes, silver crosses, and a triangular red magical sign known as a Mendez Goat, the symbol of Satan, sewn onto their cult capes. Their magazine eulogized Hitler, slaughter, and carnage, adorning itself with pictures of battlefield death; in one issue, Mick Jagger's girlfriend, singer Marianne Faithfull, was lying down holding a rose as if she's dead.

Babbs' actress friend Anita Pallenberg had led her to the Method's stately Mayfair mansion and all night coffee bar for one of their art shows. Anita had gotten a cape for herself and for Brian Jones, and had even dyed her hair blond to match Brian's.

Johnny B didn't mind the crazies Babbs had picked to manufacture acid in large quantities in the dead of night. Who else would do this kind of work? But Johnny B was wary of Anita. There was something devilish about her, besides the idiotic Satanic trappings that were pranks to call attention to herself. She could sense a person's weakness with incredible intuition and, if the mood took her, she'd exploit it. Recognizing Brian's weakness with his band members and his craving for the limelight, she had talked him into appearing on the cover of a German magazine in a Nazi uniform, causing a controversy that put him at odds with his bandmates. When Brian was cornered by a reporter in the Scotch of St. James and admitted to using acid and other drugs, it was Anita who whispered the name "Mick Jagger" to the reporter so that the *News of the World* would get it wrong. Mick was understandably enraged and filed a lawsuit with the tabloid, and this would in turn lead to all sorts of legal problems for the Stones.

Brian was plagued with insecurities, mostly fed by Anita, who spoke often of the others' jealousies. Then she would build him up by telling him how much she adored his sense of style. Collecting exotic clothes was still Brian's escape from the everyday paranoia, a kind of therapy. He shopped more frequently in times of stress and spent a small fortune at boutiques. At Chelsea Antique Market on a typical spree he would buy a mandarin coat, a pink fringed coat and velvet cape, a flannel-and-lace jacket, more embroidered and velvet jackets, velvet scarves, kimonos, strings of bells, and a pink beaded belt. He indulged himself in expeditions to ladies' jewelry departments. Johnny B joked about it with Lennon, that Brian was probably the first heterosexual male to start wearing costume jewelry from Saks and Bergdorf Goodman.

But photographs began to tell the tale. As Babbs told Johnny about another incident of Brian beating up on Anita, she spread out the Rolling Stones album covers, with the intention of showing Johnny how Brian had deteriorated.

On the cover of the first album, Brian stands with arms folded, no jacket, defiant, while the other Stones are jacketed. Brian and Mick stand as bookends with the others in-between. It almost seems like Brian and Mick are dueling partners, or even estranged lovers.

On the Stones second album cover, Brian is the focal point, his jaw set against the world as the obvious leader.

On the third, Brian sits at the bottom of the stairs, and all the other Stones are gathered above him. It looks as if they're all getting ready to leave the party, leaving him behind to explain the mess.

And then, *Aftermath.* The Stones are arrayed across the cover, looking straight at the album holder. Brian, on the end, is glancing over at the others with a look of suspicion, as if wondering, which one's going after me next?

Brian had evolved to be able to play almost any new instrument, coaxing music out of it within a few moments of touching it. It seemed to Johnny that his mastery of an ever-widening range of instruments, from marimbas to the Mellotron, had secured him the mantel of the most innovative of the Stones. So Johnny defended Brian, not only because he didn't trust Anita but also because he considered Brian to be a genius of some sort. Brian had created a masterpiece entirely with his own musicianship: the haunting, otherworldly "Ruby Tuesday"[271] that vied for best single in a year that featured heavy-handed productions from the Beatles and the Beach Boys that required orchestras and studio musicians. The composition came to Brian out of nowhere, and seemed to be about Anita, though Keith wrote most of the lyrics thinking of Linda Keith. Brian set up the song on piano along with Jack Nitzsche from Phil Spector's crew, and overdubbed the flute. Bill Wyman, who'd been quietly gaining inventiveness with each song, provided the double-bass, with fingers on fingerboard while Keith bowed the strings. From start to finish the song was perfect.

But paranoia had crept in with the increasing doses of acid. The Jagger-Richards songwriting team left no room for Brian. He had worked out the riff and some of the lyrics for "Ruby Tuesday" and provided "Under My Thumb"[272] with its signature riff on marimbas, but received no credit for either effort. Brian had always borne the weight of the paradox; he acted like a pop star, but was not at all inspired to play pop music, though he could add that extra touch to take a song to a higher level.

Uneasy about where the new pop music was going, Brian listened with Johnny to the run-through of "2,000 Light Years From Home"[273] that would anchor the Stones' next album, *Satanic Majesty's Request*, wincing at some of his own Mellotron runs. Only the flutes and recorders were original, the rest seemed to've been pilfered from the Pink Floyd.

They had all been there that night, at Club UFO, when Gilbert's favorite new band, the Pink Floyd, named after the Delta bluesmen Pink Anderson and Floyd Council, had launched "Interstellar Overdrive"[274] and Syd Barrett had piloted it to the moon. Syd had taken enough of Johnny's LSD to see through the very fabric of reality. As his onstage antics mushroomed into Dada-like insanity, his heavy-lidded unfocused eyes told a different story, one of supreme loneliness and distraction, of paranoid schizophrenia, of a desire to withdraw from everything.

Johnny could see the same look in Brian's eyes. In the mix, they were taking a wash of Mellotron and applying it to rather tepid lyrics. "Is this really the next flash?" Brian asked Johnny. "Haven't we missed it completely?"

* * *

A rush was in progress to try all manner of psychoactive substances. The torn poster on a coffee house bulletin board on Sunset Strip invited anyone to a new kind of party with the slogan "Can you pass the acid test?" It seemed absurd to Johnny B, in Los Angeles recording with Brian Wilson, to bring pop stars to such a public affair. But Gilbert, also in Los Angeles with the Stones to record follow-ups to "Satisfaction", saw it as an opportunity to connect Brian Jones and Keith Richards to the West Coast weirdos he'd heard about.

It turned out to be a hastily-assembled shambles of an event with a bad sound system, movies and mandalas flashing on the walls, and a makeshift band who'd just changed their name from the Warlocks to the Grateful Dead as if band names really didn't matter. They were pimply dead-end kids from Palo Alto that had crashed so many of the arty, wine-laden Stanford LSD parties thrown by the novelist Ken Kesey that, rather than throw them out, he installed them as the house band. At that very moment Cornell Woodrow was there, offstage in his usual getup, talking in earnest to the frizzy-haired lead guitarist named Garcia. The band then launched into "Cream Puff War"[275] with a frenzy of guitar stabs and organ flourishes that seemed to Gilbert like the American counterpart to the Pink Floyd.

What seemed like several hundred people were milling about, dancing strenuously, or puddled into corners, against the walls, and on the floor, all clad in colorful and exotic clothing, garish blouses, purple pants, native American outfits, and orange Day-Glo jackets. Several projection screens were showing vastly different sequences of images, film clips, or full-color quasi-protoplasmic blobs moving in time to what passed for music, which was a bed of ambient sound created from Mobius loops of wires and speakers, and enhanced by loud, incomprehensible, jagged, and not exactly lyrical shrieks, moans, expostulations, cries, murmurs, and laughter, as if there were hidden microphones everywhere.

A great strobe light flashed repeatedly, faster than a heartbeat, accidentally tuned to sync with brain wave patterns, and Brian Jones, who unknown to the others suffered from epilepsy, was nearly overcome with a seizure. Keith, annoyed as usual at Brian's flakiness, sat him down and Gilbert brought him something to drink, which turned out to be the acid-laced Kool-Aid.

"Never trust a Prankster." Reggie had warned Gilbert about the craziness he might find out here. Leary and his academic-minded pioneers of the new psychedelics, who'd already sacrificed their academic careers over it, were not happy with Kesey and his band of Merry Pranksters. It was hard enough to keep the straight press and government officials from going hysterical over LSD. They were devotees of the theory that you needed a proper *mindset* and a proper *setting* for going on a trip. They could not believe that the Pranksters were holding manic screaming orgies in public places. Any moment they were expecting the acid tests to explode in a debacle of mass freakout. LSD was still not illegal, and the police were growing frustrated with what journalist Hunter S. Thompson saw as a goddamn outrage: no laws broken, just every law of God and man.

The first "freaks" of the Sunset Strip — Vito, his wife Zsou, Captain Fuck, Beatle Bob, and Vito's group of about thirty-five dancers — cavorted about in superhero capes and tights. The fifty-year-old son of a Lithuanian sausage-maker, Vito ran a clay-making studio for Beverly Hills matrons, and Zsou started the first "hippie" clothing boutique. By most accounts, it was not the Mayan-tomb decor of the studio that many of the matrons found so exciting, but rather Vito's reportedly insatiable sexual appetite. Over in the corner, Gilbert spied two tender young girls, naked and entwined, tonguing each other's vaginas, while Vito and the others observed, as if the scene were part of some necessary training exercise.

"Hi! I'm Stark Naked!" announced a stark naked black-haired girl with a beautiful figure, weaving and twirling in from of him.

"Cosmo!" A young man in a buckskin suit and cowboy hat materialized next to Stark Naked and put his arm around her. "Once you find out about Cosmo, you know he's running the show."

Before Gilbert could react, an older woman, fully clad in black, approached him. "You know, you're not going to stop the war by playing their games, holding protest marches and rallies. That's *their* game. There's only one thing to do. One thing that's gonna do any good at all. And that's everybody just look at it, look at the war, and turn your backs and say, *fuck it.*"

More curious creatures came and went, some spouting nonsense, some showing too much sense to be there. Several members of the Hell's Angels motorcycle gang, in full regalia, sat in a circle crosslegged like blissed out Buddhas, exchanging glittering Angel esoteria, jewelry, chains, iron crosses, knives, greasy wrenches, filthy spark plugs. One by one they would get up, unzip their jeans, and follow the last one into a back room, where moans and groans were emanating in time to the music. "Oh it's great to be a Hell's Angel," said a stoned grinning fool, "and be dirty all the time!"

"You can't put it into words," a timid Leary follower said to Gilbert, clutching the *Tibetan Book of the Dead.* "This book talks about searching for the light, going to the light, immersing and then losing yourself in the light." The follower sought out the florescent bulb above the door to the men's room and stared intently at it until he could see nothing else.

Brian Jones was explaining it all to Keith Richards. "These are tools. Tools to enhance awareness, to expand our horizons, to access other levels of mind, to manifest the numinous and sacred. These are tools that have been in use for thousands of years by shamans, by oracles, and in the ancient mystery schools, by those who want to penetrate beyond the veil of illusion. It is not an 'escape' from reality. It is an exploration into super-reality, an inner voyage. You come back from it with a larger sense of what is real."

Keith wasn't buying any of it. The Kool-Aid had knocked him solid, and he was reeling from the experience. Brian, as usual he thought, didn't know what he was talking about, didn't know what kind of fierce tiger he had by the tail.

Gilbert wandered over to the control center, where Kesey himself was reaching over a galaxy of dials to tweak a control knob and flip a toggle switch. As Gilbert concentrated, he could feel the vibrations of sound coming off the stage through the sprawling mess of hundreds of wires and cables, presumably connecting every electronic entity in known space. The energy generated by Gilbert's synced mind started playing havoc with the conventional electronic gear; the amps started fuzzing and distorting, and when Gilbert made a gruesome face, twitching his lips and nose, the amps emitted piercing shrieks. Feedback roared to each amp's maximum volume as he opened his mouth wide, and stopped abruptly when he clamped his mouth shut. Crossing his eyes and spreading his lips caused howls, while staring bug-eyed at the equipment caused squeals.

Kesey was watching, and came over to shake his hand and take the measure of his stare.

They both turned to the stage just in time to see a plug leap out of its socket and scurry across the stage like an arachnoid rubber band. And then another! And another! It's a conspiracy, the electrons were freaking out in the presence of higher energy. Gilbert focused again on the vibrations, and more shrieks blared from the amplifiers. Then, as suddenly as the peak of a nightmare, over the speakers came a crazed scream of a woman. "Who cares?" She screamed, again and again. Someone seemed to be holding a microphone to a woman who was wrestling with visions of God. She kept screaming "Who cares?" over and over, then "Sex! Who cares?"

Gilbert looked at Kesey in panic, but Kesey just smiled and pointed to a tape machine. "A recording," he yelled above the din.

The speaker then blared an announcement by Hugh Romney, who wanted everyone to call him Wavy Gravy. "Ladies and gentlemen, there's a cop who's come apart in the next room. Will somebody go in there and put that cop back together again?"

And then, over the speakers, a litany of voices. "Don't fight it." "Go with it." "Neither accept or deny." "Go with the flow." "You're in the hands of experts."

"Control is the key," Kesey told Gilbert. "The point of this is to learn how to function on acid."

Function on *acid*? The world shimmered and disintegrated around him. And yet, what Kesey said was intriguing. If acid was a sacrament... and it was, wasn't it? Seeing God and all that? Not really *seeing* this thing called God, but a part of it nonetheless; an agent of God's great Experiment. So... to be a high priest of acid is a life's calling. A religion, complete with scriptures and commandments and a liturgy, and it promised not heaven but a new kind of liberating madness. The meaning of life, the universe, and everything, all in a cup of electric Kool-Aid.

A thin, desirable, barefoot, freckly-faced girl, just about Gilbert's age, appeared before him in what looked like a complete outfit of scarves that stretched sheer around her breasts, around her waist, and around and between her thighs. She smiled warmly at him, and said, "Today is the first day of the rest of your life."

Wow, how could she possibly know? Then he noticed that pinned to her scarf was a large button with the same slogan. She said her name was Shamhat, and she called herself a Digger. He told her his name, Gilbert Mention, but it came off his thick tongue like Mesh, his father's old name. She put her hand on top of his head and christened him Gilgamesh, her crown prince and lover, and then pulled him to her.

* * *

Johnny B gathered his thoughts. They were like wisps of cotton candy. He'd been here before, many times, at the brink of "ego death" as it was called by the psychedelic pioneers. Just sit there and let it flow over you. He was amazed at the Pranksters' expertise and mixed-media machinery, and their resolve to create a mind-blown state such as the world had never seen, totally lit up and amplified into a frenzy. Everyone would be in the "movie" because the show was not separated between audience and performer. He went looking for and eventually found the Prankster's mad chemist, and swapped information about his batch from Sandoz. The chemist was all business, probably not stoned, and promised to send some for further analysis.

He frowned as he saw Gilbert leaving with the freckle-faced girl, and Brian Jones leaving with two of the girls from Vito's pack. Keith had joined the circle of Hell's Angels. Johnny shook his head clear; he had to get back to the recording studio with Brian Wilson, where he would supervise the bank of bass violins on a song that would capture the meaning of what music was all about, "Good Vibrations".[276] He would then channel all of this acute molecular awareness of the acid experience into sublime bass lines for Carol Kaye to play on the instrumental "Let's Go Away For a While".[277]

As he stepped outside onto Sunset Strip, a riot of young people was in progress. Police were beating longhairs with night sticks. A radio blared a singer doing a bit like Dylan about something happening here and what it is ain't exactly clear. It was the newest hit by the Buffalo Springfield, "For What It's Worth".[278] Well, Cornell had been clear about one thing, Johnny B thought. The Corporation had lost control of its mind experiment. We could turn this thing around, to our benefit.

* * *

A pow wow. A gathering of the tribes.

"Man, that's what we need!" Michael Bowen, expressionist painter, pounded the table in his crowded apartment in the Haight-Ashbury district of San Francisco. Hashish crumbs scribbled to the floor and the water pipe wavered on its pedestal. He'd just gotten off a long-distance call with his mentor in Mexico, the mystic John Starr Cooke, and a gathering of the tribes was Cooke's suggestion. Bowen grinned. The party was in full swing. "We bring together Berkeley and the Haight."

"The antiwar and free speech people," responded Allen Cohen, editor of the *Oracle* underground newspaper, but Bowen beat him to it.

"That's right, the politicos. Jerry Rubin, Max Sheer, and even the New Yorkers, Abbie Hoffman, Reggie Mention, that lot."

"And we bring them into our celebration," Cohen interjected.

"And we bring them in to mix with us, to dance with us, to get spaced out. We turn them on! We tune them in on our wavelength, so that they stop thinking of us as a bunch of wastoids that are unwilling to fight on the barricades."

"Yeah, well, I don't know that *I'm* willing —"

"*I* am."

Gilbert unfolded from a cross-legged position on the floor. No one had noticed him before. The group must have been entangled in smoke and conversation when he had entered. Blond, blue-eyed, a Brian Jones lookalike, he had somehow failed to attract attention until he wanted the attention. The effect of the discovery and his reply was hypnotic. From being nothing in the room, Gilbert suddenly became everything.

"Who are you?"

"Emmett Grogan," Gilbert replied.

"No you're not. I know Emmett."

Gilbert smiled. "We are all Emmett Grogan."

"You're Reggie Mention's brother, right? What, you're a Digger now?"

"Yes. Reggie's with a group in New York, on the Lower East Side. They call themselves the Motherfuckers, but it's practically the same thing. I'm here representing the Diggers, which you all know already."

Gilbert, or Gilgamesh (his new Prankster nickname), had followed his penis, which much of the time was buried within Shamhat all the way up to the Haight-Ashbury in the back of a Volkswagen van. Her friends in the Diggers had grown out of the San Francisco Mime Troupe, which had been performing street theater. The Diggers were on board for this "Human Be-In" as the heads of the Haight were calling it. But unlike the peace groups, the Diggers didn't demand anything. To demand something from the "authorities" was to legitimize them as authorities. Don't demand food for the poor, go out and get the food, somehow, and give it away. Break through the "games people play" by force of sheer audacity.

They were living the life of the Situationists in Paris, creating spectacles that challenged the audience. Like the Dadaists of the early twentieth century, they wanted to inject art like some wild drug into the veins of society. As anarchists of the deed, they mocked the law banning public nuisance, stole sides of beef for the free stew they dished out every day in the park, gave away bags of pot and clothing, housed runaways, and put on the media. "We're like the executive branch of the hippie movement," said one of them, calling himself Emmett Grogan. When they went out on the street, they all called themselves "Emmett Grogan" especially for the reporters. The real Emmett Grogan was one of the more active members, an Irish outlaw from New York often seen on his motorcycle coiled like a snake and ready for menace and disruption.

Like the Situationists, they wanted action that would create the condition — the *situation* — it describes. They were life-actors because life itself was their act. They took the name Diggers from the seventeenth-century English revolutionaries who declared their faith in Love and endeavored to "shut out of the Creation the cursed thing, called Particular Propriety, which is the cause of all war, bloodshed, theft, and enslaving laws that hold the people under misery." They wanted everyone to treat the earth as a common treasury, and they proceeded, without asking permission, to treat it that way. They took over common land and started to dig it.

Well, can you dig it? By 1967, adolescents had drifted to the Haight-Ashbury section of San Francisco from all over the country. Over twenty thousand people, already dubbed the "hippies" by San Francisco columnist Herb Caen, came to the Polo Fields in Golden Gate Park for the Human Be-In. They treated the park as common treasury, feeding everyone, dancing on and off the stage, gobbling acid, smoking reefer, getting naked if they wanted to. The Diggers worked as the liaison with the Human Be-In security force of Hell's Angels, and set up the stage in the park for the Grateful Dead. Dr. Timothy Leary, out on bail from his bust at the Mexican border, was on hand to tell everyone to "Turn on, tune in, and drop out! Drop out of high school, drop out of college, drop out of graduate school. Turn on, tune in, drop out!" The new San Francisco bands played and Allen Ginsberg and other poets danced and sang with them. A parachutist dropped like an angel from the sky, and the whole world watched on the evening news.

* * *

Brilliantly splattered in costume jewelry and wearing a gold lame coat with beads and scarves, Brian Jones mingled with the hippies at the front of the crowd at Monterey Pop, the music festival put on by what was now called the "Love Crowd". He kept up the charm despite a massive dose of LSD, joking about seeing God and repeating over and over George Carlin's joke, "If God took acid, would he see people?"

There had been nothing like this festival before. A "board of governors" for the festival that included Jagger, McCartney, Paul Simon, Brian Wilson, and John Phillips of the Mamas and the Papas had decreed it to be a non-profit festival, and all the acts would play for free. Cornell Woodrow, unofficial advisor, secured a top slot for his new version of Robert Johnson, a black man named Jimi Hendrix who could play electric guitar like no one else on Earth. Mick had no plans to actually go, so Brian Jones took the opportunity to represent the Stones and to introduce the Jimi Hendrix Experience, an integrated affair of two English mods on bass and drums with Jimi in the lead role. Johnny B and Babbs accompanied Brian, mostly to make sure that the film crew sent by the Beatles management would be able to return from the festival to England carrying airtight camera lenses filled with enough liquid LSD from Owsley, the Prankster's chemist, to produce over a million doses.

Backstage, Johnny B played the release acetate of the Beatles' *Sgt. Pepper* while pointing out the sound effects he'd contributed, and Gilbert dispensed

Owsley purple tabs to any musician who wanted them, and before long the entire backstage area was buzzing like a spaceship, with impromptu jams forming among unlikely collaborators, such as Bob Weir and Paul Simon with Jimi Hendrix and Brian Jones. David Crosby of the Byrds got his first taste of singing harmony with Steven Stills of Buffalo Springfield. Otis Redding fell in love with the crowd and got them all to shake as if they were in a southern black church. Mama Cass Eliot in the front row gasped with astonishment over Janis Joplin's explosive performance. Mickey Dolenz of the Monkees led the cheer for Ravi Shankar, the Indian guru of the sitar, after Mike Bloomfield knelt in rapt attention at his feet.

Reggie had arrived with the Paul Butterfield Blues Band, which had backed Dylan at Newport. It was a reunion of sorts, with Johnny B laying out the details of his new venture. They had all agreed to form a band. Johnny would find the financing. When Reggie questioned him about it, Johnny just smiled back at him.

Johnny didn't want to tell him about the acid business. Certainly not Gilbert's participation in it. The Space Angels, a Gilbert inspiration based on Cooke and Bowen's Psychedelic Rangers, took flight at Monterey Pop. Whereas the shadowy group associated with Leary, called the Brotherhood, had specifically chosen the Hollywood scene and kept its recipes and customer lists absolutely secret, the Space Angels sailed from the Haight-Ashbury out into every home and castle in the western hemisphere, dropping acid on every corner of the nation. Babbs managed the processing with her shadowy friends in the Method.

Gilbert, now Gilgamesh, saw in Johnny B the spirit of Enkidu running naked with the wild animals. They had not fought, as the original story goes... but they had bonded as partners over this new, mind-blowing experience. And they both new what they were up against: a monster larger than governments as Cornell had put it, capable of snuffing people without retribution. And if Enkidu could grab this monster by the tail, Gilgamesh would find a way to slay it with his sword.

The band became a metaphor for this challenge. Johnny came up with the name, the Archetypes, loosely derived from a previous band called the Ancestors, in an extraordinarily lucid moment. "Reggie, you're the protestor, the civil rights marcher, the radical revolutionary. Bert, or Gilgamesh," Johnny smirked, "you're the hippie, the lifestyle artist. And I'm the arbiter of art and musical taste." And so they were, indeed, the Archetypes for the new generation.

The Archetypes began their musical odyssey in fits and starts backstage at Monterey Pop. With so much psychic energy from the purple tabs, they were bouncing off each other in crash jams. Johnny B would push the song with his influence, Reggie would see where the song's going but couldn't come in at the right time, and Gilbert would fool around with feedback from his harmonica mike. It took the intervention of Brian Jones to focus their energies to make real music, and a borrowed drummer, Mickey Hart from the Dead, to give it structure.

The Dead, in fact, were experimenting with a blend of studio and live recordings, which would eventually be released as *Anthem of the Sun*. No longer cute psychedelics, incense and peppermints. In "That's It For The Other One",[279] abrupt cuts from live to studio recordings made you think you'd been through a time warp and had forgotten everything in-between. The nascent Archetypes took root in this jamming style and recorded tracks for its debut album at the Wally Heider studio on Hyde Street in San Francisco, with members of the Dead and Jefferson Airplane.

The music was now ready to plug the listener into the actual experience of acid, or at least the sounds you might manufacture in your head while on acid. It was ready to throttle the listener in a miasma of sound effects, cajole the listener into believing the anecdotal evidence of acid enlightenment, and entertain the listener with embarrassing moments on acid, women trouble on acid, friends with hurt feelings on acid, and situations with law enforcement on acid. Even negotiating traffic on acid. Everything was in it.

* * *

In his mind, Brian Jones never returned from Monterey Pop, though his body traversed the continent in an oversized Afghan coat. Nervous, chain-smoking, Brian hung out in New York for a few weeks to see how much fun he could have with other musicians. The clubs in New York were open 24 hours a day, and Brian had been in one club for four days with an insane Welsh harpist called Hari Hari waiting for it to close. When Reggie, Dylan, Robbie Robertson, and the rest of the band caught up with him in the darkened club during the blackout, they dragged him up to his suite to jam all night. Reggie humored Brian with childhood stories about Gilbert, and Brian confided that he wished he could leave the Stones, join Dylan's band and move to America. He poured out his paranoia about Mick and Keith, identifying with the "Mr. Jones" Dylan sang about in "Ballad of a Thin Man"[280] as himself, the one who didn't know what was happening in his own band.

Reggie had heard all about Brian's falling out with his band mates from his brother Gilbert. Musicians were growing more uptight as the scene attracted money. Even the lingo had changed among the musicians, especially the British ones. Some kind of California influence, speaking half-English, half-hip code. "Far-out, man" was some kind of code for greatness. "Heavy" was something too real, something that needed to be dealt with immediately. "What a trip" was a commentary on life itself.

In earnest conversations, the celebrities combined the hip lingo with a code that omitted last names, key words, phrases, even entire paragraphs. They could express wholehearted concern, and anyone nearby who didn't know the code would lean forward and strain their ears in anticipation, or miss the next piece of the puzzle.

* * *

"You've heard Brian, you've heard his newest wild theories," drawled Lennon in thick Liverpudlian to Dylan, about Brian Jones and his trouble with the Stones. "You can't take any of them seriously you know."

They were in the back of Lennon's garishly-painted limousine with its portable record player somewhere outside London. Dylan was anxious; he'd been all over England playing his new electric music and getting booed by the minority of folk purists who always seemed louder than everyone else. The acid was coming on strong.

"He says there's a secret, shared down through the years," Dylan replied about Brian. "He says it has this effect on people, turns 'em into real entertainers. They know it when they hear it, that's all. Some minor chord, he couldn't make it for me, but then he always was a slide man."

Lennon shot him a look. "He has a knack for all stringed instru-ments. And I've heard all that before, from Cornell and Johnny B. We're all in search of the lost chord."

Dylan nodded, but his anxiousness had turned to nausea. The cameras had been rolling all this time in Lennon's limo, and the turntable in the back was spinning a new song by Procol Harum called "Whiter Shade of Pale",[281] which Lennon kept playing over and over, fascinated by the organ sound.

Dylan was never so tired as he was now, his nonstop amphetamine-fueled tour crashing to an end at the Royal Albert Hall. He had never truly grasped the inescapable fact that the heroin in his speedballs during intermission, which he used to temper his amphetamine rushes without becoming a raving lunatic at the end his performance, was growing into an addiction.

That evening Geno Foreman, the prodigal son and drug dealer who'd left Dylan's entourage two years earlier to seek another muse, showed up at the backstage door, and Dylan angrily had told him to get lost, in part because he was disappointed in Geno, and in part because Geno would have tempted him to do more heroin. Within a week, Geno was dead, purportedly of an overdose. As Dylan heard about this, he also heard that his former compatriot, Richard Fariña, had been thrown from a motorcycle in Carmel after the party for his first book. Previously Paul Clayton, who would never make the leap to electric, had committed suicide by electrocution.

He'd written songs about them. Could it be that he'd killed them by writing these songs about them? Without these songs, they would never have been pinned down by the spotlight, would never had been in the crosshairs... of what Cornell called the Corporation.

Dylan threw away the manuscript for his own book, which had quickly become irrelevant. He fled back to New York, scampered back up to a retreat in Woodstock, nearly killed himself in a motorcycle accident as if tempting Fariña's fate, and removed himself from his music industry obligations. The film of the limo ride with Lennon, *Eat the Document*, wouldn't be seen for another twenty years.

* * *

After three days of exhausting negotiations and phone calls without any sleep, and a 24-hour semi-coma as a result of too many bar-biturates, Brian Epstein, the Beatles manager, finally transitioned to a dream state.

He was 25 again, driving his shiny cream and maroon Hillman to his old parking spot near the circular public loo in the Liverpool suburb of West Derby. A handsome but slight young man with a patrician air, wavy brown hair always perfectly trimmed and in place, dressed in a hand-tailored suit, Turbull and Asser shirt, and a silk foulard about his neck, Epstein gave off the impression that everything worked, it was good to be English, it was great to be aristocratic. Only his nose betrayed him as the eldest son of one of the few devout Jewish families in this predominantly Irish-Welsh city. He was extremely fond of the truth, as he wrote in his book, but certainly not married to it or even engaged, as he kept his most feverish betrayals and sexual escapades secret. The only eyes that could see him were his mother Queenie's, and her eyes, shining with a keen intelligence and an indomitable spirit, transparently filled the night sky of Brian Epstein's dream.

The soundtrack to his dream was a new recording from Lennon, "I Am the Walrus".[282] Brian cut the engine, and this was the cue for the burly, older longshoreman to walk by, turning his head at Brian, giving him a wink. Brian met him at the dank urinal; the man's thick cock was out and Brian couldn't resist his own true nature, his longing. So what's the next big thing, the longshoreman, cock out, taunted him. Brian couldn't stop his reply. A good tune, a good tune is always the next big thing. The intense beating left him sprawled on the stained concrete floor of the loo, his watch and wallet gone.

Quite immediately he was standing before the tall, attractive Queenie in the parlor of their imposing home at 9 Queens Drive, Childwall. Her silence and knowing look devastated him as she learned of the blackmail; the longshoreman knew all about the Epstein family. All business, she rang up the family solicitor who was not in the least surprised; on the phone he joked with Brian, so what's the next big thing? Brian couldn't think of any other answer but a good tune, a good tune is always the next big thing. He could hear all of Lennon's friends, including Johnny B and Gilbert, taunting him with "Umpah umpah, stick it up your umpah!" and "Everybody's fucked up, everybody smokes pot!" And what did they mean by "stick it up your umpah"?

As the dream ended, all of Liverpool learned Brian Epstein's secret, and the smirking detectives waited in the shadows of a Whitechapel district shop entrance, ready to nab the blackmailer as Brian timidly handed over the money. And of course they whispered, over and over, so what's the next big thing?

The dream was painfully autoerotic as well as autobiographical, about an experience he kept in the background of his waking state, as a disclosure he couldn't quite bring himself to make to any friend or confidant, as a secret lurking underneath every business negotiation and threatening to expose itself through telltale effeminate mannerisms and slips of the tongue.

Peter Brown, as always the reliable businessman, had come to Chapel Street the day before to wake him, complaining about press calls. Paul McCartney had gone out on a limb with Fleet Street after the *Queen* magazine article appeared. It had detailed Paul's first indulgences with LSD. On television no less, Paul had complained about the press spreading it to all the homes in Britain. There was no room to maneuver in this situation, Brown was telling Brian, no way to issue a denial or say it was a misunderstanding, no possibility of a press conference like the Lennon apology they had held in New York. Brian Epstein was now more popular than Jesus on this late afternoon with the press calling every minute. More than likely to be crucified.

Yawning through grogginess, Brian felt stirring in his breast the impulse to surround his boys with his arms, gather them together, and then turn to face the danger. He should be standing between Paul and the horde. He should once again put Paul in debt to him, to ease Paul's fears. Paul had been snooping around at the office too much, learning bits and pieces about the merchandising fiasco, questioning Brian's competency and why Brian could never be reached before mid-afternoon.

But most importantly, Brian knew that he should be accompanying the Beatles to Bangor to meet the Maharishi Mahesh Yogi, in order to protect them. That master magician would find a way to con them into doing something like a free performance, or worse.

Brian sighed, fell back into the pillow. He reached out to his pills and counted out the usual dosage, not knowing that his pills had been replaced by ones that were ten times the dosage. He was gone by the next morning.

At Bangor, the Beatles gathered around the television cameras and microphones to pour out their sadness at Brian Epstein's death. How could they even go on without their manager, their Svengali? Afterward the conference, John Lennon muttered to the others, "We've had it."

* * *

"Do we have everything in place?"

It was not a good sign that the CEO had taken such an active interest in these projects. Every once in a while the CEO came out of hiding to tickle the creatures and make them do his bidding. He probably enjoyed controlling the fate of so many human beings. Cravingston, however, was not happy about his way of getting involved in the details. There were too many chances for slip-ups when the higher-ups started to meddle.

"Yes. The Beatles are likely to go into decline now."

"And are the drug arrests proceeding?"

"Well, Leary was busted at the Mexican border for grass, and Kesey is on the lam, but the FBI says they'll eventually get him."

"'Busted?' 'Grass?' You're beginning to sound like them."

"Yes, it's a habit you get when you're undercover, sometimes you can't shake the lingo."

"So," the CEO continued impatiently, "what are we doing now about this outbreak? A mind control experiment gone wrong. This could tarnish our reputation and hold us back for years."

"Not to worry, we have an ingenious plan. My friend Eugene thought this one up," he gestured at Mumblingore, who sat smugly to one side. "We're going to let them continue to spread LSD for a while longer, at least until it is declared illegal. When we've reached a certain, ah, level of penetration, we'll unleash a new form of the substance, a mix with a more amphetamine rush that will make them more receptive to opiates, such as heroin. Is that right?" He motioned to Mumblingore, who nodded.

"And that will go out through the same distribution routes?"

"Indeed it will. We have our best people on it."

"The Method Church."

"Yes," Mumblingore cleared his throat. "We rescued the best mind control experimenters from Scientology, and they're now organized as the Method. They're already involved in Babbs' operation, and they're moving their clan to Los Angeles. And Cooke is setting up training for the, eh, proselytizers."

"And what about the pop stars?"

"We're infiltrating the new rock groups," said Cravingston. "We have an operative ready to set up the Rolling Stones. We will bust them for hard drugs, and show their fans how decadent they really are."

"Don't you think that could backfire? They made their reputation on decadence."

Cravingston smiled at the CEO's grasp of previous objectives. The Corporation had indeed steered the Stones' manager to that particular press tactic. "No. Their leader, Brian Jones, is on the brink of insanity already. One push and he's done. The band has already moved toward Satanism and the occult, which are topics we control that can take this thing out of the political realm."

425

"Well." The CEO looked a bit more satisfied. "Speaking of the political realm, we have more work to do. The FBI call their latest project COINTELPRO. Infiltrating and discrediting so-called 'New Left' groups."

"We have been working on that, sir," Cravingston answered quickly. "As you know, we've been cultivating undercover and intelligence operatives." He was about to say more, but then stopped.

Cravingston was holding back on his big challenge. He needed to identify which infiltrators were from the FBI, and which were from local police forces. They were beginning to step on each other's dicks.

* * *

"Les, they're coming in the windows!" Brian Jones shouted into the telephone receiver to the Stones publicist. They were indeed coming through the windows and barging through the door. Like cockroaches, the police crawled all over Brian's London flat and searched everywhere. Brian was uncharacteristically clean. All they could find was a ball of wool with some hashish buried in it, and Brian knew immediately that the police had planted it.

That was just the beginning.

News of the World had enlisted the Corporation's help to prevent Mick Jagger's lawsuit from gaining steam. If they could show that Jagger was on drugs, the lawsuit would have no merit. Cravingston lent them his operative, known as the "Acid King" around Carnaby Street, who made sure that the right drugs would be found when the police stormed Keith Richards home in Redlands.

It was Mick's first acid trip, and they were all cosily playing checkers in the living room after a fine day at the beach, Dylan on the turntable, and Marianne Faithfull wrapped only in a fur rug after her bath. Bemused more than anything, Keith stepped aside as they searched. The police ignored the Acid King's briefcase on the table, which was loaded with all sorts of pharmaceuticals, but eventually found some Italian pep pills in Jagger's jacket pocket and traces of hashish in the ashtrays, which was just enough to parade them before the British public in handcuffs.

To escape the media frenzy, the defendants out on bail traveled to Morocco. Brian fancied himself a pioneer going off to some exotic land to learn exotic music, which he would integrate into the Stones music in order to surpass all the other groups. The plan was to have their driver, Tom Keylock, drive Brian, Anita, and Keith in Keith's Bentley Continental through France and Spain, crossing over to Morocco at Gibraltar. Mick was still angry at Brian for spouting the drug nonsense that had caused the *News of the World* fiasco, still unaware that Anita had planted that information, and had decided to fly with his entourage.

Brian succumbed to exhaustion on the drive and had to be hospitalized in Toulouse. Anita and Keith traveled on to Spain, where Anita inveigled Keith with some of the same coaxing she had used on Brian, seducing him in a Barcelona hotel. Keith had been aware of Brian's propensity to punch Anita during their many fights, and felt that taking Anita from him might sober the fucker up and provide some kind of retribution, as well as save Anita from more bruisings.

But when Brian called and asked for her to accompany him from Toulouse to Marrakesh, she dropped Keith like a hot bullet and went back to Brian. During a stop-over at the Rock of Gibraltar, they dropped acid and went to see the famous monkeys. The monkeys came out and clustered around them. "Look," Anita pointed out, "the three monkeys that Johnny B is always talking about."

Sure enough, three of the monkeys had arranged themselves in front of Brian. One held its hands to its ears, another to its eyes, and the third over its mouth. Brian decided to play them his music. He turned on the tape recorder and after a few bars the monkeys, with a collective shriek, ran pell-mell away, tearing off into the distance.

Brian took it as a terrible rejection. He screamed at the monkeys, trying to get them to come back. The acid didn't help; he began to weep, and then madly shouting "The monkeys don't like my music! First Mick and Keith, and now *you*! Fuck the monkeys! Fuck the monkeys!" The tourists around them backed away, appalled.

When they got to Marrakesh, Brian felt that he needed to prove his masculinity to Anita, and invited two Berber whores up to the room to have an orgy. When Anita balked at this obvious, vulgar attempt to gain power over her, she taunted him until he pounded his fist into the wall.

* * *

"I can explain everything better through music," Jimi Hendrix told the press, pointing to his own brain, at the reception for the Jimi Hendrix Experience album. His peon to Johnny B's acid, "Purple Haze",[283] was climbing the charts. "You hypnotize people to where they go right back to their natural state, which is pure positive, like childhood when you got those natural highs." Jimi laughed in a carefree style, and journalists noted that he was not at all hulking and menacing like his black friends in the Panthers.

Jimi had grown up in Seattle, as far north and west from the Deep South as a black man could get and still be in America. As a teen he'd seen Elvis in concert and met Cornell Woodrow, who gave him a record by the Jackal and told him to listen closely. Jimi paid attention and developed the electric guitar skills to surf the wave of rhythm-and-blues, playing with the Isley Brothers and with Little Richard, eventually getting fired for upstaging the Queen of Rock 'n' Roll with his fiery breaks. He then tried to form a group using white Village ex-folkies.

His mistress Fayne complained, they're just white kids, all about protesting the war and all that.

"I can't sit here in Harlem waiting for something to happen," Jimi snapped at her. He was holding a copy of Bob Dylan's *Bringing it All Back Home*. "These people are receptive, for whatever reason, to what I'm doing."

But Fayne remained unconvinced. "The Village ain't no place for a black man."

Cornell found him in the Village, at the Café Wha, playing loud, his fans spilling out into the street. Jimi hugged the man like his long lost uncle. Cornell was pleased. Here was the penultimate embodiment of the Robert Johnson spirit, with similar long fingers and a crackling bright attitude about what he was doing, and Cornell knew he had what he'd been waiting for all these years. The black musician who would cross over and take over.

Cornell had arranged the London session after his buddy Chas Chandler of the Animals had brought Jimi over from New York. True to the original Hammond paradigm, Cornell wanted to integrate Jimi's band. At first he had in mind a white supergroup backing for the black superstar, with Brian Jones on interleaving guitar and other instruments, Johnny B on bass, and Ginger Baker or Keith Moon on drums.

Brian, ecstatic about the idea after meeting Jimi and seeing him play, mentioned that it might be possible to woo John Lennon from the Beatles, now that John had second thoughts about the direction Paul was taking them. A super-secret jam session was hastily arranged with Lennon on rhythm guitar and organ.

Chandler, however, had other plans. He was indebted to the Animals' manager, Mike Jeffery, who had popped out of clandestine military service, some said MI-6, to run the Club-a-Go-Go in Newcastle. Jeffery and Chandler didn't want a supergroup to distract the audience from Jimi himself, but they took Cornell's idea of the integrated band and established the Jimi Hendrix Experience, with two of Brian's friends, Noel Redding and Mitch Mitchell.

Noel, a lead guitar player, had never played bass in this kind of combo before, so Johnny B took the opportunity to show him some things on bass guitar, but mostly how to tune up and go low, real low on the bass runs. The separation between Hendrix's wild guitar and Noel's deep down bass put space in the music between the highs and lows, accented with strategically placed quiet rhythm licks. "Hey Joe"[284] started this way, and Jimi shook Johnny B's hand and made Johnny his forever friend. "You're a messenger," Jimi told him. "A musician, if he's a messenger, is like a child who hasn't been handled too many times by man, hasn't had too many fingerprints across his brain."

* * *

Cornell had told Brian Jones to go into the hills near Marrakesh and look for a certain griot, a storyteller of great power, who could introduce him to the mysteries of hoodoo at its roots. But Brian, just another English clod on holiday, had been continually taking acid. He thought the experience in the Moroccan hills would not be strange enough by itself.

On the desert road between Fez and Marrakech, an old man's wicker cart full of oranges had been sideswiped by a gray-paneled truck. The old man lay dying on the road, his donkey dying next to him. Their chauffeured limousine pulled up behind a group of long-robed bystanders, and Anita jumped out in a candy-pink miniskirt. She elbowed her way to the dying man and wiped blood from his brow with her perfumed handkerchief. When she returned to the limo, she told Brian she would use that handkerchief in a ceremony to put a curse on a man who had spurned her advances, and the man would die. Kenneth Anger, the filmmaker who wanted Mick Jagger to play a role in his *Lucifer Rising*, had taught Anita about the power of blood taken from a man killed by violence.

Brian, filled with a paranoia so strong that he could no longer articulate it, fell into silence.

The next day, Brian went up into the hills with the painter and sound poet Brion Gysin with the hope of hearing local musicians and finding the griot. Gysin had told Brian about the exotic, thousand-year old music of the Master Musicians of Joujouka, but the timing was wrong to visit them. Brian didn't find the griot, and when he returned to the hotel in Marrakesh, he discovered that the entire Stones entourage had left him high and dry, without a note or any money for transportation. Anita was now firmly with Keith.

After frantic calls and telegrams, Brian made his way back to London in time for another tour. He no longer commanded the stage, giving way to Mick and Keith in his sorrowful, self-pitying state, and couldn't even look at Keith let alone weave his guitar patterns with him. In his drug-infused inertia, he spent hours in rooms littered with cigarette butts, album covers, and liquor bottles, with only the warm glow of a lamp draped with Batik scarves. He was in tenacious pursuit of doing absolutely nothing. He continued to feel disturbing influences, in tune with the new mood of student militancy, that he should be doing something more with his vast reputation than just playing slide guitar on the next album. His most pernicious fear was that the Stones would abandon him suddenly, just like the way they'd stolen his precious Anita. They just might hire Eric Clapton, whose supergroup Cream had started to go rancid.

The day after the tour, the police came after Brian again, at his Courtfield Road flat. Gilbert was visiting and both were asleep when the squad pounded on the door. In the next minute they'd flipped Brian's mattress and with a triumphant smile produced a purple leather wallet. Inside was some ridiculously green "grass" that looked more like oregano. What stupid chick left this? Gilbert told them there were always girls in and out, every day. The police eventually found roaches, crumbs of hashish in a tin canister, and several pipes with hashish resin.

But it was a phial with traces of cocaine that sent Brian into a panic. "Yes, the hashish, we do smoke it. But not that! I'm not a junkie. That's not mine at all!"

Brian and Gilbert were led away to Kensington police station, where TV news cameras were already in position. Gilbert didn't know it, but his mother had carried to the judge a letter from Will Cravingston, and he was inexplicably let off.

Brian, haunted by the fear of going to jail, and no longer trusting Gilbert, was easily convinced by his solicitor to plead guilty to a lesser charge. Gilbert told him to forget the plea bargain, plead not guilty, because you're *not* guilty! But it was impossible to talk Brian out of it. "Look, they're too strong for us," Brian cried.

Preparations for Mick and Keith's Redlands bust had been well organized, and their trial date had been speeded up. Not so with Brian; it would be six months of agony and alienation before his fate would be decided by the courts.

Released on bail, Brian celebrated with an orgy of drink and pills and went out to a club to play double-bass with the resident band. As he slapped at the bass, he also began kicking it, softly at first, but with greater and greater ferocity until he'd splintered it into matchwood. Even with the bass gone, as the audience looked on in consternation, Brian continued to play it with his fingers shaping notes and pinching the air, his face downcast and earnestly listening to notes only he could hear.

* * *

The audience of 12,000 at the stadium grew inexplicably out of control. Mick Jagger was knocked on the floor by a youth who'd broke through a cordon of 300 police. He grabbed Mick by his lapels, flung him to the floor, and began jumping on him. Keith's chauffeur Tom Keylock waded quickly into the melee to land a stiff uppercut to the kid's jaw.

Marianne was waiting for Mick back at the hotel, in bed in her see-through negligee. Mick strode in like a different person, not a word to acknowledge her, his eyes seething with fury. He had absorbed the intense violence from the audience and looked for somewhere, some thing, someone to unleash it upon. Without a word, he began circling her and slapping her in the face. She escaped to the bathroom, but Mick followed her in and continued to pummel her until the anger subsided. Then he collapsed in tears on the bathroom floor.

They never talked about it. Marianne, typically, had thought it was about sex, that Mick had somehow found out about her sweet night with Keith. But it was some other monster entirely, the bubbling kettle of bad karma, busts and trials, and the drama onstage and off between Brian and Keith over Anita.

In the studio, Keith began doubling and tripling up on guitar tracks so as not to need Brian. They brought in other players on piano, various symphony players for strings, and a horn section, all impinging on Brian's territory of touches and flourishes that were key parts of the songs. Keith's slashing, unadorned guitar took the forefront, percolating such an evil sound that Brian could only strum along, barely keeping up.

Johnny pointed out to Brian that Keith's slide work was nowhere near as good as his. "Keith's slide is just clunky, and he plays too much. You have that melodic touch."

"Ah," Brian whispered. "But no one seems to notice."

Brian played a barely audible harmonica on some tracks, but finally came alive on "No Expectations"[285] on acoustic slide guitar. It had been recorded at Olympic Studios with the band gathered in a circle like a family, singing and playing into open microphones without overdubs. Mick sang balefully, as if he knew what would happen to Brian, about their love, which is like their music. It's here, and then it's gone.

It was the last time Brian would play such an important role in a Stones song. *Beggar's Banquet* would provide the last image of Brian for the public, sprawled like a prince in his chair drunk and oblivious to everyone around the messy banquet, with a rabid dog jumping into his lap as he beckons with food.

* * *

Despondent after hearing that Jimi Hendrix would play with a new band, Brian Jones put off his big meeting with the Stones in which he had planned to quit. He would not quit, not now, not with the deadly uncertainty of a prison sentence hanging over him. Over the next few weeks, attended to by a Gilbert-lookalike from the Stones office serving as a personal valet who fed him Mandrax tablets, Brian grew less and less capable of playing in the studio. Normally he would know if a note is a quarter-tone off. Now, at Andrew Loog Oldham's direction, the engineers were secretly turning his guitar off in the mix, and Brian's habit of delving back into his corner without hearing the takes meant that he never knew it.

Johnny B saw this happening one day and freaked. After a few late-night telephone calls, Johnny convinced Brian to go back to Morocco and record the Gnawa drummers of West Africa and the Joujouka pipers in the foothills of the Rif Mountains, something Brian had wanted to do after hearing them play in a Morocco market.

Mustapha Abdeslam, a griot from West Africa recommended by Brion Gysin, took them to Joujouka. The musicians were playing a special song to a wooden sculpture of three monkeys. Where had he seen these three monkeys before?

"What are they playing?" Johnny whispered to Brian.

Brian played the same notes on his guitar, and wrote them down. "C to F sharp, also known as G flat. That's a tritone. Actually they do that, and then they do the diminished seventh, C to E flat to F sharp to A. Very common in the blues."

Brian's idea was to show the link between African and American black music by overdubbing layers of jazz and soul. He felt that if he could just illuminate the legions of youth on the origins of their music, they would *not* be turning from flower power, beads, and caftans to revolutionary badges, slogans, and military fatigues. Brian would never be, could never be a street-fighting man. "The movement has already been accomplished," he told Johnny. We don't need fighting. We need pure examples of the love we feel for each other. This is the message of the rolling stone. The spirit of love, of the universe, is buried within all of us. We just need to unlock this spirit.

Some of the musicians put down their instruments to prepare food for their white visitors. They walked past Brian and Johnny B carrying a snow-white goat. As Brian looked at the goat, with its bewildered, pale-fringed eyes, a strangled whimper caught in this throat. He whispered to Johnny, "That's me. I'm the one, the martyr."

Johnny smiled, recognizing the resemblance, but Brian was serious as they carried the bleating goat into a lean-to, and one of them drew out a long-bladed knife.

An Orgy of Meaningless Discontent

An orgy of meaningless discontent engulfed Reggie, caught in a nightmare of negotiating airport corridors, bus rides, subway turnstiles, which way to downtown or is it uptown? Suits and ties marched by on the sidewalk, their faces awed in childlike wonder, to the bolero of "White Rabbit".[286] The denizens of Madison Avenue, off to explore the realms of pills and mushrooms. Men on the chessboard, getting up and telling him where to go.

Cravingston's reedy voice kept repeating in Reggie's ears, a white knight talking backwards. You know the future. Is this what you want? This orgy of discontent, without meaning?

Feed your head. Reggie had been feeding Cravingston information, as promised. Reggie's deal kept both him and Gilbert out of the draft. Reggie had thought it would be easy to supply meaningless information, but he was compelled to educate Cravingston, and maybe to convince him. Playing both sides, he would help these groups organize, and be true to the cause. And he'd continue to report the truth to Cravingston, and let the chips fall where they may. Besides, Reggie couldn't make stuff up quickly enough. The truth was stranger than any fiction he could conjure up.

In the nightmare he stumbled out of the Yippie melee for peace and love in Grand Central Station, his head cracked and bleeding from a cop's billy club. He searched for a townhouse on the East Side, a safe haven, and then, there it is… and it explodes right in front of him, shrapnel spinning all around him…

Morning brought some kind of relief. He studied his face in the mirror. He looked old, maybe a decade older than he had last year. His face had a brutish aspect, with dark-circled eyes and puffy cheeks. He felt a cold, abiding despair in his bones.

He was in the Village, in the apartment he still shared with Lucy, although it seemed more like her apartment than his with all the stuff she accumulated. He was trying to start some kind of life after the Dylan tour whimpered to a halt. What were his choices, now that the movement was exploding?

Many of his peers were getting record contracts. Even Tom Rush, his former roommate at Harvard, already had a few records out. Sitting in with Rush and others at pass-the-hat basements like Café Wha, Reggie still lacked the confidence to get solo gigs. His only hope in music was to make the Archetypes a success. After Monterey Pop, Reggie, Gilbert, and Johnny B resolved to search for a drummer and get back together in time for the massive March on the Pentagon in a few months.

Reggie had already helped to secure the Students for a Democratic Society (SDS) endorsement for the March, and had recently introduced Berkeley activist Jerry Rubin to Abbie Hoffman, the leader of a very small New York "chapter" of the Diggers. Their charter of free-food-shelter and street theater had been eclipsed by a larger splinter group of Situationists calling itself the Black Mask. Its chief goal was the inte-gration of art into the political program of anarchist revolution. Reggie was expecting someone from Black Mask to arrive at his meeting.

Lucy, arriving with groceries, surprised him by announcing that *she* had joined Black Mask, and that they had sent her to negotiate on their behalf.

They argued about tactics over dinner until Michael Bowen and a handful of Psychedelic Rangers showed up. As the smoke curled, the debate spun out from the idea of the exorcism of the Pentagon as a media sound-bite and spectacle, to the idea that exorcism and even *levitation* of the Pentagon was a real physical possibility. A peyote shaman would direct magical and conscious energy towards the Pentagon in order to overcome its impregnability as both the symbol and seat of evil. They would form a ring of hippies with joined hands around the Pentagon, raise the entire building fifteen feet in the air, and turn it orange.

Lucy, on behalf of Black Mask, was giggly enthusiastic. Reggie stared at her in disbelief.

It was meetings like this that gave Reggie headaches, and no amount of pot or anything else could dispel the notion that he was dealing with lunatics, or worse, government plants. What Reggie really wanted to do was shake these shallow students out of their comfort zones, and hammer into their minds the practicalities of revolution. An infiltrator could easily make his way into the inner circles of these groups. Smoking pot and dropping LSD were certainly *not* credentials for trust in the New Left.

Reggie began to believe that a revolution would never happen without a progressive denial of all commercial pleasantries, that revolutionaries should not only give up pot and acid, tobacco, alcohol, and even chocolates, but also their privacy, their access to money, their masturbatory fantasies. There would be nothing left to tempt the revolutionary, who was then prepared for life in jail.

Now it was Lucy's turn to stare at him in disbelief. "Are you willing to sacrifice everything? Is this some new form of narcissism?"

Lucy was trying to learn how to relate to self-absorbed men. She found them everywhere, in the new rock music business, in the New Left, in her own partner. You were supposed to continually praise their accomplishments, but not so much as to sound fake, and certainly not so much as to boost their narcissism. You were supposed to continue to hammer away, softly, at the issues you wanted the man to address. But if he never addressed them… and if he grew worse as he grew older, which is what happens to everyone… If he takes himself too seriously, his life will end in disaster. Why doesn't Reggie see this? Isn't he supposed to have glimpses of the future?

Lucy had her own glimpses. The Black Mask pointed to a future that would turn protest into resistance, and resistance into revolution. They were opposed to and resisted on principle any attempt to take things seriously.

She had already been in verbal brawls with Maoist groups and other dogmatists, mostly men, who'd attacked her personally rather than address her ideas. Men joked about "putting chicks up front" at the barricades to soften the onslaught of police brutality. And even the sober, idealistic, sexist-aware SDS warriors were inclined to cheat on their movement women when tempted in the back rooms of debate halls and occupied school buildings.

Reggie and Lucy's first movement-related fight was also his last. It involved Lucy's cartoon, drawn for an underground paper, showing a woman holding a screaming infant, washing a sink full of dishes, and saying into a telephone, "He's not here, he's out helping the struggle of oppressed people."

"You don't understand, it's not good to be so divisive," argued Reggie. "What you want and what I want are the same things. Why are you alienating the very people we need in this fight?"

"Because you don't treat our intelligence with dignity. You may be proud of our work in the movement, but you want us for cooking, typing, and fucking. Did you hear what that SDS asshole said? 'The movement hangs together on the head of a penis.' No wonder we feel incapable of making important contributions, and we're so tongue-tied at these events. Resentful, is what we are."

Reggie had no comeback. He hung his head and ignored her.

She looked hard at him. It seemed, suddenly, that he was a stranger to her. He had never been anything more than a frame of reference, on which she had hung the shining garments of her ideas. She had let him diffidently make love to her, not because she cared, but because she no longer cared. The relationship no longer mattered.

And with that thought, she walked out on him.

Like any man obsessed with his own righteousness, Reggie thought that her departure would be temporary. It's true, he sighed, men wanted only pussy, but that should be a blessing to women who don't want to be tied down, either. Could men really trust the women who wanted so much to change them, to tie them down to their agendas? Geno used to say, be wary of a woman who only shows up when you are winning.

* * *

Emmett Grogan, Peter Berg, Billy Fritsch, and Gilbert as Gilgamesh seized an opportunity to take the Digger show on the road with a trip to an SDS "old guard" conference in Michigan. They wanted to freak out the stodgy New Left, and call the white radicals' bluff. Gilbert knew Reggie would be there, and he wanted to impress upon him that the New Left was square and hypocritical. They're just middle class kids comforting themselves with plans for the future while supporting themselves with checks from Mommy and Daddy. He thought that maybe Lucy was there with him, and he wanted so much to see her even if Reggie was with her. Maybe they would have it out and he could finally put Reggie in his place.

There was no time like the present. They got in a car with plenty of whiskey, wine, and speed pills, and drove at breakneck speed from San Francisco to the camp in the middle of Michigan.

The meeting was in full swing. Reggie had just introduced Tom Hayden for a keynote in the wood-beamed camp dining hall. "My own radical journey began with MAD Magazine," Hayden told the crowd. Reggie quickly flashed on the thought that maybe Hayden had also been looking in issues of MAD for codes to a conspiracy.

But Hayden left that topic quickly, and spoke with renewed urgency about the burning war in Vietnam and the burning ghettos at home. A faction styling themselves as potential urban guerrillas were talking, with nervous humor, about rifle practice as the next step. Many others were still arguing the need to bore into the system through President Johnson's War on Poverty programs.

The door suddenly burst open, and out of the pouring rain came three men, one in a leather vest and another in a fur hat, shouting "Is there a fucking lawyer here? We need a lawyer."

The Digger show had started, grinding Hayden to a halt, sowing confusion and astonishment. They claimed to represent all the kids fleeing to the Haight-Ashbury in San Francisco. They had driven all the way from San Francisco, and had been nabbed by the highway patrol for swimming naked in the Platte River. They were nabbed again for speeding, narrowly missed getting arrested for shoplifting, and escaped from a barroom brawl they had started. Finally they had skidded into a canal down the road, and one of them was in a local jail.

Gilbert, his blond locks tucked into a fur hat, began beating his tambourine.

Who are you guys, the audience members started asking. What are you doing here? Are you provocateurs?

"You don't know what is happening," Berg began lecturing as he moved around the hall with a microphone. "You're abstract, ineffectual, hopelessly middle class, irrelevant, derivative — why, without Vietnam, without Cuba, you wouldn't even exist! You are all a bunch of rich dentists, out protesting the war for the weekend."

Murmurs of resentment, but Berg continued, full of stagecraft and menace. "You have to make up your own civilization! Property is the enemy. Burn it, destroy it, give it away. Don't let them make a machine out of you. Get out of the system, do your thing."

Grogan jumped up on a table to take over where Berg left off. To a mother, he said "You'll never understand us. But your children *will* understand us. And we're going to *take your children!*" Spying a black man, probably the only black man in the entire room, Grogan screamed at him. "You! Spade! You're a nigger, what are you doing here? Your people need you. There's a war on. They got fucking concentration camps ready."

"If the CIA wanted to disrupt this meeting," one of the self-assured old guard yelled back, "they couldn't have done it any better than by sending you."

"Please give us back our meeting," another one pleaded.

Grogan would not show respect to a hall full of wimps who couldn't even lock arms and kick out three intruders. Some of the audience members were turned on by the Diggers' theater of cruelty. Others were merely transfixed and confused. The older ones were appalled at the anti-politic frenetic madness; it was a disaster for the youth movement, pure and simple. The hippie throng had already been co-opted by a business culture. Wasn't there already a cheap burger joint in the Haight selling "love burgers" and a Bay Area radio station advertising its own "flower power"?

Reggie was incensed at Gilbert. How could you allow these capricious, irresponsible idiots to come here and fuck up our conference?

"You sold out, brother," Gilbert stood before him, clenching his fists, ready for anything. "You made a deal with that guy, Cravingston. You're out to save your own ass."

"I did it for you too," Reggie frowned. "You're also safe from the draft."

"Don't do me any favors," Gilbert sneered back. "That asshole is sleeping with Mom, in Dad's bed. It's been happening the entire time I was in England."

Reggie was stunned.

Gilbert studied him, searching for recognition in his eyes. "You didn't know."

Reggie came back to life. "It doesn't change anything. All he wants is information. All we gotta do is feed him information. Bad information, if you want. Foreign influences. Communists. Whatever. He won't know the difference. We gotta string him out, for our own sake. And for Johnny's sake too, because they're looking for him." He paused, then extended his hand. "C'mon, brother. Peace. We got to stick together."

Gilbert shook his brother's hand, but his eyes wandered. He resisted the urge to penetrate with his gaze any of the women around him. Lucy was watching him. He could feel her watching him, enjoyed the feeling of her watching him, sizing him up, now that he was a good-looking activist musician. He spread his cape, nodded to Reggie, and left the hall.

Reggie looked over to where Lucy was, but Lucy had disappeared.

Back in New York, the Diggers were invited onto a television show. "Watching people on the box puts yourself in a box," Berg cautioned on the show. "This is how you get out of the box. You stand up, and you at home can join me in this. Stand up, and start walking to get out of the box. Now, here I go, now, just keep the camera on me, and I'll keep walking." He walked to the exit door, opened it, looked right into the camera, said, "Now turn off your television sets and go to bed," and walked out.

* * *

The promise of an evil undoing of the Love Generation could be felt as a shiver in the wind on Haight Street. John Kent Carter, a.k.a. Jacob King, a.k.a. Shob Carter, a.k.a. any number of different identities that pointed to the same man at the same address just four blocks from the Psychedelic Shop, sat in his armchair in the living room chilling out before leaving to meet his connection in L.A. Handcuffed to Carter's right wrist was a briefcase that could be opened only by removing the cuffs. The chafing of the cuffs on his right wrist kept him alert, despite the odd mixture of vodka, seasickness pills, and Afghan hash pulsing through his head and nauseating his stomach. The impromptu tribal gathering outside had been going for about an hour, its primitive-sounding cries and percussion mixing like a Johnny Weismuller Tarzan movie into the background of the electronic crescendos of Pink Floyd's "Take Up Thy Stethoscope And Walk".[287]

They came at him from all angles, and before he knew what was happening an arm appeared from someone behind him and plunged a scarab-encrusted, pearl-handled knife into his chest. The first stab was the killer, straight through the heart; the others inflicted eleven more stab wounds. As Carter felt his life slip away, the leader of the hunting party wielded a primitive-looking machete and neatly sliced off the entire wrist. The handcuffs clattered on the floor.

Shub Carter, acid dealer, had become the first murder victim of the Summer of Love in the Haight-Ashbury.

A local motorcycle racer was picked up in Sonoma County driving Carter's car; the police found $2,600 in cash, Shub's pistol, a severed right arm wrapped in a black and red suede cloth bag, and an acetate marked "Archetypes" autographed by someone named "Johnny B". The next day the motorcyclist claimed he shot Shob Carter in self-defense. His lawyer entered a plea of not guilty, on the grounds that the killer had lost his mind on LSD.

Two days after Carter's murder, a bearded black man was found dead about forty feet down a cliff near the Pt. Reyes Lighthouse in West Marin County. He was another acid dealer, known around town as Superspade. He had been shot in the head execution-style, stabbed ceremoniously in the chest, wrapped up in a sleeping bag, and tossed off the cliff.

Rumor on the streets had it that Carter and Superspade were in on the same deal and had ties to a shadowy LSD distribution network based in the Haight called the Space Angels. Superspade was more well known, and would often complain about the "state of mind called Mafia" to his friends. The murders would inspire Donovan to write "Season of the Witch".[288]

* * *

A day after Superspade's murder, Johnny B and Gilbert got out of a limo at the corner of Haight and Masonic with George Harrison, his wife Patti, and Derek Taylor, the former Beatles publicist and Monterey Pop organizer. George wore flowered bell-bottoms, a denim jacket, heart-shaped sunglasses, and a button that said "I'm the Head of My Community". They strolled up Haight toward the park, just another group of colorful mods touring the scene, and it took quite a while before anyone recognized George, who looked pretty much exactly like the pictures of him on the *Sgt. Pepper* album cover. Someone handed George an acoustic guitar, and soon they were part of a parade down Haight Street with George as the pied piper. Someone asked George what he thought of the Haight. "If it's all like this, it's too much," a theme he would repeat in the song "It's All Too Much".[289]

About two hundred people were gathered on Hippie Hill in Golden Gate Park to witness a debate between members of the Council for a Summer of Love, now calling themselves The Flame and proposing a self-sufficient community that lived off retail sales, versus the Diggers and the Free City Collective, who wanted everything to be free. To many of the gathering the debate seemed moot in the wake of the news of both murders. They argued about everything under the sun, and uncharacteristically in San Francisco that late summer of 1967, there was a great deal of sun.

By the time George and his parade reached the park, word had reached Hippie Hill. Hundreds gathered around George, who was obliged to play a few Beatles songs. Johnny B thumped a set of bongo drums and Gilbert, as Gilgamesh the Digger, wrangled a few mournful notes from his harmonica. Amateur musicians came running with their instruments to join in. George, sensing danger, decided to leave early for his flight, so his entourage left Johnny B and Gilbert in the midst of a throng of eager musicians.

Johnny kept looking over his shoulder. The murdered acid dealers had been part of his and Gilbert's network. He had a nagging suspicion that his father knew who'd done it. The murders had wise guys written all over them. The organization must have awoken to the lucrative acid trade and decided to move in. That would explain Shob Carter's sideline deals with cocaine.

Cocaine. The mobsters' touch. Johnny was no prude, but cocaine was poison for musicians. It screwed up their timing and dulled their pitch. Singers couldn't even tell when they were flat. And after doing too much, they needed heroin to come down. That's what Babbs had said when she scored cocaine from somewhere to feed the Method members so that they'd work all night. She considered it a substitute for relatively harmless Prellys, but the experiment backfired when the Method members spun around in circles babbling in tongues. She had to get some heroin jacks to calm them down.

Johnny hadn't approved, and they had argued. Babbs had said that she had scored the cocaine through one of Cornell's connections, and Anita had gone with her to get some for Brian Jones. Now that Johnny thought about it, that simply didn't make sense. Cornell was not into that scene, was he? And Brian didn't do cocaine. The cops had planted it when they busted him. Or *someone* had planted it... Would Anita have gone that far?

With the coming of other drugs, especially drugs from the previous jazz age, Johnny could sense a new unsettling vibe among the dopers, as well as a lack of trust. Instead of the ritual handshake or smile, everyone was giving him the same greeting, "Where you *at*, man", suggesting a high level of discomfort.

At parties Johnny began to notice men in the shadows, older, rigid, unsmiling, there and not there, holding out in a defiant posture, unwilling to fade. He recognized them vaguely. He had seen enough of them in his father's business. They went out to collect cash debts, they broke rib cages, they got people fired, they kept an unforgiving eye on anything they interpreted as a possible threat. If this dream of a revolution was doomed, and the faithless money-driven world was ready to reassert control, it would be agents like these, dutiful and silent, out doing the shit work to make it happen.

Was it possible that at every gathering, every love-in and peace rally, those dark crews have been busy all along, reclaiming the music and the resistance to power, the sexual freedom, all they could sweep up, for the ancient forces of greed and fear?

* * *

Gilbert stood in the doorway naked, the same pose he'd taken way back as a kid in that Margate bay window. Lucy had often pictured it, the vulnerable boy standing before the world, reaching for a climax. Now his blond locks and lithe body looked terrific. He had told her about his penetrating gaze, how it could stimulate a woman without her knowing it just by staring at her, even from behind, and cause her to twitch, to scratch, to squirm in sudden awareness of her very private parts on display for... someone...

He had even tried it on her, staring at her stomach, and she felt a warmth spread across her groin and down her thighs. She was delighted.

But now, as he stood there, she could tell that his penetrating stare wouldn't work on her. Nor did his fake bravado about harmonica players, good with their tongues and all that. What he wanted, what he needed, was adoration. Someone to adore his body, his penis. To swallow his come. Ick. Wants to fill me with his meaningful stuff. Wants a "groupie," that's what they call the sluts who hang around backstage. It might be fun to oblige him, for a while, but...

Their blissful union lasted about two days before she grew tired of the vacuous conversations. Gilbert was not as philosophical as his brother, and unable to see beyond himself to have real empathy for someone else. That last thing he could ever handle would be a relationship, she thought as she watched him plow his way through a throng of eager groupies to reach the stage.

When Reggie finally called her, he sounded resigned and quite reasonable. Abbie Hoffman had contacted him about a Digger-Black Mask collaboration. He wanted to set up a press conference before the March on the Pentagon. Abbie had seen Peter Berg's act on television and was convinced that the movement could grow to a mass scale through televised events.

The Washington police had already announced that they were ready to use a new chemical called Mace that stung the eyes and temporarily blinded people. Abbie was ready to announce Lace, which he claimed was LSD mixed with DMSO, a skin-penetrating agent. "When squirted on the skin or clothes," he solemnly announced to the press, "it penetrates quickly to the bloodstream, causing the subject to disrobe and get sexually aroused."

On the stage behind Abbie, Gilbert and Lucy sprayed each other with water pistols full of a fluid that was actually Schwartz Disappear-O, a strange product imported from Taiwan, which made purple stains that would then disappear. The couple then proceeded to tear off their clothes and perform the act of love in the middle of the conference. Reggie, who had set up the conference, didn't stay to watch, claiming that he had other work to do.

Afterwards, Lucy and Gilbert went their separate ways without saying goodbye.

* * *

"You haven't been in contact," said the reedy voice on the phone belonging to Cravingston.

Furious, Reggie nearly slammed the telephone receiver on the table, but caught himself. Thinking quickly, he decided not to let Cravingston know that he knew about the affair with his mother. He sighed, then took up the receiver. "Nothing to report," he answered slyly. "The march is supposed to be peaceful. There may be a handful of activists who are looking for a fight, but the vast majority just want to stand up and be counted. What are you afraid of?"

"I'm a staunch liberal, remember? Adlai Stevenson? Jack Kennedy?" Cravingston was back to cajoling.

"You're afraid you'll be outflanked by the New Left."

"Indeed, just when we need to rally behind our President. You want Vietnam to end, don't you? Johnson wants peace as much as you do. Back in '65, he offered Ho Chi Minh a billion-dollar Mekong Delta development program, just like the Texas dam project that put him in power in the Senate. Johnson wanted Ho to get behind this dam, but Ho turned it down! Johnson is frustrated with that tinhorn dictator, that posturing fool! Ho Chi Minh is one big fool. He never got the hint from Johnson that he could have had South Vietnam in due time, without a war."

"It's not just the war," Reggie retorted. "We're drawing on the anarchist tradition. The spirit of Prince Kropotkin."

"Yes, yes, I've heard it all before. So it's 'we' now? You've joined these idiots? You pick up a guitar, wear a beret, grow a mustache, learn how to play music like the poor country blacks. Is that it? Some kind of holy mission?"

Reggie took the bait. "Well, that's why we're considered dangerous. Governments fear spiritual uprisings more than economic ones."

"You have more to fear than the government," chuckled Cravingston, but something about his voice suggested exasperation. "Your affinity groups and hippie groups are going to push you over the edge. You remember your friend Mel Lyman, the banjo player who volunteered in Leary's experiments at Harvard? He's got a harem now, and soldiers, and they just took over the *Avatar*, an underground paper in Boston. He's a raging psychedelic Nazi, or something. *That's* the kind of lunacy you and your hippie friends have to look forward to."

* * *

The audience had been entertained by "some electric folk rock group" for an hour, according to Time magazine, so the young were more or less happy, grooving with the music of the Archetypes, while the middle-aged liberals were feeling dim, out of place. The cavern of the theater resonated with electronics on the march: the public address system hissed and rang in a chorus of electronic noise, of cerebral mastication by some horrible machine from outer space, and a hum like the squeaky hinges of the Gates of Hell. Reggie strummed his Martin at the edge of the stage with an ultra purple spotlight shining on him from the balcony. Here out in the penumbra of society, the psychedelic netherworlds seethed with the shocked brains cells of adolescents on acid. Gilbert included.

Reggie wouldn't look at his brother, and tried to avoid the gaze of people in the front row looking to him for guidance. They sat there, stricken, inert, in terror of what the Saturday march would entail, and were unable to rise to any word from any speaker, not even the blunt literary shit-kicking Norman Mailer, who tried to instill vigor in this new haphazard army by shouting "FU-CK YOU!" to a heckler and pronouncing "shee-it" in his best Southern accent imitation of Lyndon Johnson.

For an encore, the Archetypes covered the Beatles newest single, "All You Need Is Love",[290] which had appeared via satellite on televisions in 25 countries that summer. Many had not seen the lovable mop tops since the heyday of Beatlemania and were surprised to see them as grown men with mustaches and wire-rimmed glasses and decked out in the latest Carnaby Street fashions. Singing for the entire world, they had honed their message to the simplest idea possible in the modern age, an idea that couldn't be misinterpreted: love is all you need. Never mind the fancy clothes, the limos, the eternal cocktail parties…

"There's nothing you can do that can't be done." Switching instruments, Lennon had played the harpsichord and banjo, McCartney had doubled down on double bass, and Harrison had picked up a violin for the first time. They had recorded the vocal and orchestra overdubs with a host of friends in the studio under the watchful eyes of video cameras. Johnny B had painstakingly rehearsed the changes with the other Archetypes the night before — the two 7/4 measures for the verse, a single bar of 8/4, followed by a one bar return of 7/4 before repeating the pattern. The chorus, however, maintained a steady 4/4 beat with the exception, another Lennon touch, of the last bar of 6/4. The effect was to shorten and punch the line "love is all you need," as if Lennon were patting the listener on the head and murmuring "that's a good boy." No one could escape the conclusion that they had become hopelessly naive about the world and how it really works.

And yet, Reggie could repeat the line over and over, love is all you need, to stop arguments and defuse any crisis. It was a simple mantra in a perilous time. Before the show Reggie had accompanied Carl Davidson of SDS to the press conference. A spectrum of left and liberal diversity had invested the podium, gathered together by David Dellinger and Jerry Rubin of the Mobilization, ranging from a Catholic Monsignor to a now-pacifist former Green Beret, from Dr. Spock to Women Strike for Peace, from comedian Dick Gregory to SNCC leader H. Rap Brown. Reggie tried to make sense of these proceedings and quotes from Rubin ("We're now in the business of wholesale disruption and widespread resistance and dislocation of American society"), Abbie Hoffman ("We're gonna raise the Pentagon three hundred feet in the air"), and H. Rap Brown ("I would be unwise to say I'm going there with a gun because you-all took my gun last time. I may bring a bomb, sucker!").

All you need is love, indeed. Despite Reggie's best efforts, Davidson had been noncommittal about SDS involvement. The organization had sworn never again to take part in large but largely ineffectual demonstrations. It did its work in the field, organizing students to do social work in ghettos, and radicalizing them in the process. But the back-and-forth between the Mobilization and the authorities over permits had caught his attention. Some kind of violent confrontation was inevitable, and SDS had to be there, leading the vanguard of the new student shock troops.

On stage entertaining the radical leadership, Reggie could visualize the opposition — happy and healthy suburbanites, ex-Marines, state troopers, professional athletes, movie stars, rednecks, mill workers, city officials, cops, and more cops —all with the light in their eyes for a life they enjoy, all for the war in Vietnam for no other reason than the government says it's right. And here we are, Reggie thought, standing up to them. An intelligentsia, with the Freud-imbued embers of Marxism rising from our stomachs like bile, harnessing the resentments of the younger, more ambitious liberal inheritors of the middle class, in a resistance that was a hopeless melange. They're on a freakout from the suburbs to a love-in in the Pentagon parking lot, lobotomized against sin, nihilistically embezzling all of the moral funds of their middle-class parents, lusting for an apocalypse.

And here they were, the very next day, fearing that very apocalypse under a late morning sun that baked Reggie's hangover into a vague headache. Gilbert had wanted to bring a small stash. He couldn't greet the day without his customary toke. Reggie split the hotel room, disgusted with him.

Johnny B didn't answer his room phone. Of course, his comings and goings were never predictable. He'd left the late night rally early, after arguing with Reggie about the future of the band. "We're going in different directions," he had told him. "This left-wing revolution thing is getting more unhip every day."

"The revolution has to be more than just hip," Reggie had scolded him, and in an instant regretted saying it.

"You're wrong," Johnny had told him with a look that ended further conversation. "Hip is more important. If there's one thing we learned from Cornell, it's more effective to be a trickster than a martyr. The point of being hip is to be one step ahead of all this shit. And yes, to be hip, all you need is love."

* * *

The air was violent, yet full of amusement. Washington D.C. was vividly awake, alert to all the possibilities of this day. Echoes of voices a block away promised violence. The whores were out, and motorcycles gunned up and down the streets. Gilbert followed at a distance, but Reggie lost him as they merged into the crowd. At a street corner massed with people, a group of troubadours were singing Dino Valenti's song of doomed hope that the Archetypes had covered the night before, "Let's Get Together".[291] Love one another right now! Everyone cried and hugged, and Gilbert lost count of how many women he'd kissed.

A bit later a trumpet sounded. The masses streamed along the sides of the reflecting pool, all got up in costumes from the *Sgt. Pepper* album that had been released only months before, but also garbed as Arab sheiks, dime-store Indians, Davy Crockett in a possum hat, or Wyatt Earp in vest and greatcoat with Paladin's mustache, and a man imitating Claude Rains in *The Invisible Man*, his face wrapped in a turban of bandages topped with a black satin top hat. There goes Charlie Chaplin, the Friendly Martian, and a knight in full authentic armor. They had picked up the costumes wherever they could, flowing capes and colorful Hindu junk in Digger Free Stores and the new blow-your-mind head shops that had popped up in major cities, inspired by the ones on Haight Street, Bleecker Street, and Carnaby Street. Some were on safari in tropical bush jackets and tattered Foreign Legion uniforms, some were in Confederate drag to remind us of all the parallels this event had with the Civil War more than

100 years earlier. A Roman Senator in toga, lost on his way to the Forum, scrambled to keep up with Superman, Batman, and the Green Lantern.

And many looked like scarred working class people hovering and pleading for food outside the rich man's ball, innocent bystanders and victims of a national plague. Middle-class runaways were eagerly heading into battle, and here and there stood out a stoic defense lawyer, a whispering priest, an ebullient rabbi, a guilt-ridden poet, a celebrity novelist, and a blinking child psychologist, conspicuous in their conventional clothes amidst the sea of madness.

Flanked by the all-seeing eye of the giant penis of the Washington Monument, the march began on a road that separated the upper and lower steps of the Lincoln Memorial, watched over by a sad, brooding Lincoln who would never have sanctioned a structure as obscene in the sweet Virginia countryside across the river as the Pentagon. Bored numb for hours by speeches, and now suddenly elated as if woken from a trance, this mass of circus performers swarmed into ranks that billowed and sheared under the pulses of inertia and momentum from behind, and flowed onto the bridge with police on both sides, gunning their motorcycles. Helicopters roared overhead, and TV crews with hysterical technicians in open convertibles filmed out in front of the front line. Just as they left the road on the Virginia side of the Potomac and topped a rise, the formidable target of the Pentagon appeared in the distance, rising like a Sphinx from the soft placid field of Virginia grass, its pale yellow walls reminiscent of a electric plug, a gigantic connection to some invisible underground machine that remained insulated from any nature surrounding it.

The North Parking Lot was physically separated from the building by a four-lane highway, and the early arrivals scampered out in the vast and empty lot as if they were the early arrivals for a sports event. No enemy was visible. At the far end, a crane rose up in absurd defiance with a speaker's platform on the end of its arm. The Fugs, led by Ed Sanders and Tuli Kupferberg dressed in orange and yellow capes with rose-colored trousers, had gathered underneath on the rear bed of a truck to play music that sounded medieval, and in fact was the overture to a Shakespearian farce. Participants cavorted about like musketeers disguised in Hindu guru rags and Confederate cavalry gear.

Reggie recognized the formation as the beginning of the exorcism of the Pentagon. Abbie Hoffman had indeed asked for a permit, a *permit* no less, to encircle the Pentagon with twelve hundred people in a ring of exorcism that would raise the building three hundred feet into the air. And the General Services Administrator who ruled on the permit, had, with a twinkle in his eye, consented to allowing the building to rise ten feet (ten feet!), but had ruled against complete encirclement. That was alright with Hoffman, but not with Michael Bowen and the rest of the Haight contingent, who had not batted an eye before exclaiming with all seriousness that without encirclement the levitation of the Pentagon would never work.

And so, in a solemn voice from a caped crusader on the platform, "In the name of God, Ra, Jehovah, Anubis, Osiris, Quetzalcoatl, Thoth, Allah, Krishna,

Shango, Jesus Christ, Buddha, and Rama, do exorcise and cast out the evil which has walled and captured the pentacle of power and perverted its use to the need of the total machine and its child the hydrogen bomb..."

And while the Indian triangle rang, the cymbal slashed, and the trumpet let out a mournful subterranean wail, while finger bells tinkled and drums beat, "In the name of the amulets of touching, seeing, groping, hearing, and loving, we call upon the powers of the cosmos to protect our ceremonies in the name of Zeus, in the name of Anubis, god of the dead, in the name of all those killed because they do not comprehend... In the name of Dionysus, in the name of Dion and the Belmonts, in the name of Jesus, Yahweh, Hermes, in the name of the Beak of Sok, in the name of the Tyrone Power Pound Cake Society in the Sky, in the name of Ra, Osiris, Horus, Nepta, Isis, in the name of the flowing living universe, we call upon the spirit to raise the Pentagon from its destiny."

And then, the troupe shouted "Out demon — OUT!" Voices in back cried "OUT!" over and over, a doppler effect of "OUT!" across the parking lot, mournful as wind in a cave. Reggie tapped his foot to the rhythm, whispering "out demons, out" as if by some remote possibility this might work. And how would the military inside the Pentagon take this? Do they have experts in levitation, experts on vibration? Are they peering out of this steel and glass structure in fear of their lives?

On the fringes of the crowd, another crane rumbled forward, protected by a phalanx of Virginia State Police, with another makeshift stage on its arm, manned by a horrified Catholic priest who held a large silver cross sideways, as if to block Satan himself. The fuse of blasphemy had exploded in this reverend's mind. He began barking the centuries-old incantations of the Roman church in an effort to stop this madness, this tornado of religious hatred that had spun out of a respectful demonstration against the war.

Red-bearded Ed Sanders intoned, "Seminal culmination in the spirit of peace and brotherhood, a real grope for peace! These are the magic eyes of victory. Victory for peace. Money *made* the Pentagon. Melt it! *Money* made the Pentagon, melt it for love!" And the voices out on the fringes, that doppler effect again, "*Burn* the money. Burn it, burn it, burn it..."

Reggie could understand Sanders, even *dig it*, as the expression goes, but he also could see the point of view of the reverend. After several years of bland reports from acid explorers of enlightenment and awakenings, vague Tibetan lama goody-good auras of religiosity, rumors of natural mysteries and sunken Atlantis continents, now suddenly we have witches, warlocks, hippies being murdered over acid deals... Have we said goodbye to our visions of heaven? Have we fallen from the high of Tibet to the mundane Christ, and down further to the Middle Ages of revolutionary alchemists and anarchists?

On cue, an anarchist push from the rear staggered Reggie and the others surrounding the troupe. A battle cry unheard, only felt, surged through the crowd, and a rush of motorcycle-helmeted rebels, some wearing football shoulder pads, wedged their way through in an intense hush of silence. At the

446

point in front, two members carried standards, the blue and gold of the National Liberation Front, the NLF, for they were the presumed American wing of the Vietcong. On they pushed to the Pentagon, sweeping others with them in their wake, for who did not want to witness the attack? They all moved forward in a forward posture as if keening at the wind, rolling on a collective wave of purpose, and their leaders scrambled forward with their flags, flinging their legs this way and that, with Groucho Marx torsos too large and humped over for their limbs. And Reggie knew where he had seen this posture before — a painting of Union soldiers attacking across a field of battle during the Civil War.

Now the leaders of the wedge were jammed up, something was wrong, and even as the crowd pushed forward, others came running back, screaming, tear gas in their eyes. Reggie saw the look of terror in their faces. And yet, from behind, came the yells, "Why don't we move? Just move ahead! Let's go!" A burly man in his twenties, in overalls and a cotton plaid shirt, pushed forward. "I came here to get into the Pentagon," he growled. "Let's get going! I want to get to those soldiers in the Pentagon! What are you all, yellow!?" But the man's voice had no ring of truth to it. His dialogue was all wrong.

Reggie knew it would make sense for the Corporation to play a hand in this, to send out provocateurs, to start violence in order to discredit the movement. And he had assumed Cravingston would be here, lurking in the shadows, switching sides whenever it was convenient.

Orders had come down to arrest at random, to avoid martyrs. The person arrested, having done nothing in particular to warrant the arrest, would feel more like a fool or victim than a hero. He may be treated as a hero by his peers at first, but eventually he would disappoint them. The technique would also disrupt the demonstrators' careful planning for press coverage of notables being arrested, and generate exaggerated rumors of brutality that would scare the more peaceful demonstrators into leaving for the buses in the parking lot.

In fact the random arrests were brutal. Verbal provocations from the protestors were ignored, but if one of those filthy degenerates accidentally touched a soldier, a U.S. Marshall would reach from behind, between the soldier's legs, and drag the perpetrator, preferably by his or her long hair, back behind the ranks of soldiers for a quick beating with skull-cracking billy clubs and a kick into the waiting wagon. One soldier spilled water from his canteen on a sitting female demonstrator, and when she tried to shift her body away from the stream, her shoulder touched his rifle, and that was enough to haul her off and beat her nearly blind, using a billy-club not only to crack her head but also as a blunt sword thrust between her protecting hands and into her face. Two more troops dragged her away, her face covered in blood. A startling disproportion of women were beaten and arrested, and this served to humiliate the protestors, who could not protect nor even make a charge against the forces that took their women. It broke their resistance, taking it down several notches to that woeful passive disobedience of the juvenile, hapless sit-in, where you sang along with bad renditions of old worker folk songs and waited your turn to be clubbed, Maced, and cuffed.

Reggie was arm-twisted by a Marshall into handcuffs and tossed into, of all things, a Volkswagen van, very much like the type of vehicle that gypsy hippies always refurbished with psychedelic Day Glo paint, but this one had been drafted into the armed services and painted drab white with gray interior. He thought he would be arraigned, fined, and released before nightfall, but the gloomy interior of the van suggested otherwise. There were enough of these vehicles in the parking lot to hold hundreds of protestors. Hopeful rumors about getting out were quickly followed by cruel rumors of weekend court delays, and followed again by hopeful rumors of judges working overtime. And so Reggie felt like a yo-yo, back and forth, hopeful and crushed. He was helpless to do anything; self-absorption and apathy would be the poles of his emotions.

He was deposited in a seat next to a solemn leather-clad man in his early twenties, cradling a white motorcycle helmet in his lap, and a Lenin button in the lapel of his leather jacket spouting the slogan "Turn the imperialistic war into civil war!" Reggie learned his name, Terry League, and remembered seeing him in the vanguard of the first rush on the Pentagon carrying those NLF flags, though he didn't know him or his organization, if indeed he had an organization.

League seemed to have one because he acted so professionally. He set his helmet against the window of the van and used it as a pillow, and fell immediately to sleep, as if he already knew what would happen — and in fact knew that nothing would happen for several hours — and he needed sleep in order to be effective later. Reggie recognized the pose: the revolution needed people who would work, sleep, think, and eat revolution twenty-four hours a day. They would organize, proselytize, explain, instruct, and inspire. Above all, they would work.

And so it was no surprise to Reggie later that evening, inside the makeshift jail at the Alexandria Post Office, that League, who had slept to conserve his energies, came wide awake and took advantage of the situation by conducting a free school about revolution. A crowd of prisoners surrounded his bunk to get involved with the only active theater in the prison. He talked about the collective experience of the revolutionary activity, and how one could analyze it and extract the appropriate revolutionary content from the non-revolutionary mixed bag of intentions, compromised programs, sellouts, and cop-outs. He argued that the entire assembly, rally, and march on the Pentagon had been wrong from beginning to end — too ambiguous in its promises, and too timid in its execution. And way too compromised in its collaboration with the government over the march route, the use of the South Parking Lot, and so on.

Reggie listened with interest, and partially agreed with some of it, but League's indictments of the leadership of the Mobilization to End the War, of Dave Dellinger and Jerry Rubin and the others, were too easy. Reggie had heard too many communists and Trotskyists expounding on similar themes with just this same misconstrued militancy and precise but ultimately useless analysis.

Overnight and into the morning, League was the happiest man in the prison, the most active and awake, resplendent in his element. He had convinced many of the prisoners of the total inadequacy and incompetency of the Mobilization, and had drafted a series of points in a letter he proposed to send out to the media. And so, the free school had revealed its purpose.

Counter-arguments were mounted from the fringes with shouts of "This is just divisive!" Reggie stepped into the fray to neutralize League's momentum, for he suddenly realized that League just might be an agent provocateur. "Wait a minute, there may be as many as ten million Americans out there right now who think we're heroes. Heroes! Can't we let them think that? Can't we let them be happy with that thought, at least for a few months, before they find out we're not?"

The prisoner vote against the letter spoiled League's efforts, but as a consummate professional revolutionary or actor, he never showed rancor. He decided to redraft the letter and present it to the Mobe internally.

Later, Reggie walked with League down the corridor to the courtroom, still suspicious of his motives. "What would you have done," Reggie asked him, "if you had managed to get into the Pentagon and hold a corridor for a while?"

"Oh, I don't know," said League, grinning. "We could have painted the walls or something, y'know, just create some disruption."

Later, the courtroom drama over, Reggie caught a glimpse of the news on TV. He saw a sequence captured on video of Gilbert at the front lines, along a line of soldiers holding their rifles with fixed bayonets. Gilbert had captured the "flower power" zeitgeist perfectly when he placed a carnation in one of the rifles. The sequence, and the key shot of Gilbert placing the flower in the barrel of gun, would be repeated in newscasts and documentaries for years to come.

* * *

"Just then Tom Paine himself"[292] came running, sang Dylan on his new album, which had come out of nowhere, recorded as far away from the hippie scene, the revolutionaries, the Village, and the psychedelic madness as he could get — in Nashville with country music people from the Grand Ole Opry who'd never heard of the Haight-Ashbury. The album was full of allegory and Biblical imagery; its cover showed Dylan smiling with some Indian gypsies and outlaws out in the bleak American sticks. "Shouting at this lovely girl," thought to be America itself, or the spirit of liberty, as the song continued, "and commanding her to yield."

The album blew a cold wind of imminent war through the Lower East Side flat that Lucy still shared with Reggie, in a state of truce, with the stated effort to "repair their relationship." She endured hour after hour of Reggie's incessant playing and talking about the album. "The song creates its drama with a D minor chord and an insistent, almost menacing rhythm," Reggie tried to explain to her, like it was so important. "It's about the dark side of seduction, not just from women, but from anything that promises far more than it can ever deliver, and ends up leaving you worse off than when you started. And Thomas Paine's common sense is no balm for the wounds you'll receive. All he can say is that he's sorry, sorry about what America has done."

But Lucy had other thoughts. The repression that followed the March on the Pentagon grew swiftly and forcefully. Demonstrations at army recruiting centers and hundreds of college campuses were put down with Mace and billy clubs. Flowers, peace, beads, and caftans gave way to badges, slogans, and military fatigues. Peaceful happenings gave way to sporadic street fighting. At Christmas gatherings the talk between liberals and radicals, and between men and women, grew more divisive as the new Beatles songs in *Magical Mystery Tour* poured out of stereo speakers referring to fools on a hill, friends who've lost their way,[293] pretty little policemen in a row, you say yes and I say no, how does it feel to be one of the beautiful people? And, almost an afterthought, all you need is love.

Reggie continued to repeat this, all you need is love, whenever confronted by the reality of their lives. But Lucy knew he was pretending. He was still jealous of her quick affair with his brother. He acted so professionally when they started rehearsing as a band, but he wouldn't cut Gilbert any slack, complaining about his sound, even going around Gilbert's back to lower the volume on his amp. And they would never talk about their mother.

Lucy was done with musicians. Reggie had been sweet but was coming unglued with this revolutionary craziness. And Gilbert is so immature and self-centered now, completely unable to manage a relationship. And Johnny B, well… Johnny had simply ignored her, as if he'd learned all he could from her. They are such assholes! So full of themselves! Reggie used to complain about not being invited to sit in with some of his famous friends. Now, with his own band, he and his brother were acting like prima donnas. Bickering over who should play a solo break, when the audience couldn't give a shit.

"You had that keyboard player sitting backstage the entire set, waiting for a cue to come on stage to sit in," she yelled at Reggie one day, "and you didn't care that he was back there, anxiously waiting, playing the song in his head. You don't want to be upstaged, not even for five minutes! And if he gets applause, you'll hate him."

Reggie shrugged. She just didn't understand how important it was for the band to develop its "sound" on its own, without interference. How it must build on the egos of its members to create something more than the sum of its parts.

"Bullshit," she replied. "The audience loves to see others sit in. They like the serendipity, the possibility for something magical. Instead they get a bunch of uptight assholes with rigid playlists."

Reggie shook his head, but she continued, mocking him in a sing-song voice. "And who's on the guest list? And who else is on the guest list? It's such a bribe you hand out, for friendship. Because you're up on stage the whole time and you have no time for real friendship."

Lucy didn't tell Reggie this, but she'd also grown disillusioned with the Black Mask, which had changed its name to Up Against the Wall Motherfuckers, based on a phrase in a LeRoi Jones poem, "The magic words are: Up against the wall, mother fucker, this is a stick up!" She had been taken by the Situationist's romance of deliberately constructing events for the purpose of reawakening and pursuing authentic desires, experiencing the feeling of life and adventure, and the liberation of everyday life. Now it seemed that the male impulse to violence had taken hold. "This movement is like a masculine midlife crisis," she'd criticized them. "You're all living in a bubble, talking to yourselves, comparing cocks. Narcissists, admiring yourselves in the TV screen."

She had wanted to conduct women's studies at Columbia, but that university was embroiled in a student action that made headlines around the world, stupidly over a gymnasium the university wanted to build in a ghetto that was plagued with a housing shortage. As she wrote in the *Rat*, "All this madcap brainstorming, all these proposals for courses on anti-culture, anti-families, anti-poetry, anti-theater, students taking over classes, all this superheated radicalism of rejection, this white-hot discontent, always runs the risk of evaporating into a wild, amorphous steam. It degenerates into a semi-articulate, indiscriminate celebration of everything in sight that is new, strange, and noisy. You're fondling ideas like an infant playing with bright, unfamiliar objects."

She was blithely ignored by the males. To add insult to injury, several of them surrounded her at the magazine's party, pumping their fists in glory at the newest misogynist exploits of the Stones. "Jumping Jack Flash",[294] destined to become their most often played song in concerts to come, started with Bill Wyman and Brian Jones sharing a piano to come up with some riffs, which were then picked up by Mick and Keith, who seemed driven by divine guidance to replace the soft psychedelia of their previous album with muscular, two-fisted rock. Jagger had picked up Johnny B's line about being born in a cross-fire hurricane. Each verse was a concise nightmare that drove like a train to a hedonistic and sardonic refrain about everything being alright, "fact it's a gas!" By the time it was recorded, in a whirlwind of rejuvenation after Mick and Keith's drug trials, Brian was still fighting his legal battles and had only time to add a tambourine.

* * *

By 1968, ordinary citizens could not avoid the televised images of carnage in Vietnam and unrest at home. One by one, the events shattered any hope of complacency. Martin Luther King, Jr. was killed by a gunman and riots erupted in all the major ghettos as nonviolence went to the grave with him. Robert F. Kennedy, looking to save the Democratic Party from its own divisiveness about the war, was gunned down just as he was about to win the California primary for the presidency. Leftists in America were inspired by student riots in Germany and France, where Rudi Dutschke and Daniel Cohn-Bendit were bigger than the Beatles. The French and German students read translations of *One-Dimensional Man* and elevated Herbert Marcuse to the status of a hero of the Paris revolution. Yves Dormant and his group tacked a message onto the main entrance of the Sorbonne, reading in part, "The revolution which is beginning will call in question not only capitalist society but industrial society. The consumer's society must perish of a violent death. The society of alienation must disappear from history. We are inventing a new and original world. Imagination is seizing power."

Reggie, along with Tom Hayden and others of the "old" New Left, wept at Robert Kennedy's casket. Not because Kennedy would have been a savior. None of them were happy with Kennedy's centrist politics. But in the back of their minds, they had wanted the system to work, and now hated that system for failing them. The opportunities for peaceful change had gone with the wind. It was time to redouble their efforts. A rising call went out to all the organizers of youth movements around the country to go to Chicago that summer to disrupt the Democratic National Convention.

Seizing an opportunity to warn his son without revealing himself, Herbert Mention planted a story that would be published in *Ramparts* about the liberal National Student Association serving as a recruitment arm for the CIA. It mentioned Cravingston by name.

By the time Reggie saw it, he considered it old news, something he had figured out long ago. And he thought it no longer mattered. Lucy was not so sanguine. "Your left-wing credentials are at risk. You'd better not contact that man again."

* * *

Rehearsing and recording with different drummers in New York, Reggie and Gilbert set aside their differences and fell in with the Lower East Side Diggers and Abbie Hoffman. Johnny B, apolitical as always and nihilist to a fault, thought the new revolutionaries were fools, rogues, and followers, but he recognized Abbie as an actor that could stir up an audience. As the Archetypes, they agreed to provide the soundtrack for the Yippies, as they now called themselves, and play the Festival of Life in Chicago. It would be a gas, gas, gas.

As Abbie explained it, "The coming of radio and records influenced the people who are now over fifty; they have to *hear* it to believe it. The coming of TV influenced the thirty-to-fifty set, who have to *see* it to believe it. But those of us under thirty grew up with TV and we're hip to the ways it can manufacture images. We have to *feel* it to believe it. We don't respond to articles, speeches, or even rallies where we all feel like bystanders. What we need is to *participate*. And if reality as everyone knows it is determined by the mass media, if reality is only just the perception of reality as the mass media shows it, then we must engage the mass media. Not just provide information, but provide the context for that information, the myth that we are large in numbers and resolute in spirit, that we really can change things, and we can do it right now in the face of the political war machine."

Jerry Rubin and Paul Krassner arrived from Berkeley, fed up with the movement as it now stood. "We can't be sending out boring letters or making tedious phone calls. We can't march with picket signs. It makes for bad TV. We need mass media attention, to reach the audience we would never reach any other way, the audience that would never have considered radical politics. We want the people who see us on TV to think again about the way things are, and after seeing us acting absurd, with no spelled-out meanings or messages, no 'end the war' or 'fight poverty' but some kind of street theater, the people will have to figure things out for themselves. The way to do this is to create a 'blank space' in the national media. Let them fill in this space with whatever they want, let them be critical, let them repeat the endless myths about our counterculture. Let them do *anything* except ignore us."

The Yippies knew that the turned-on generation they were playing to desperately needed their acid visions and their dope dreams, the energy of their rock 'n' roll hearts, and even the jaded sophistication of their TV sound bites. They hoped the young people would accept their posturing, their contradictory content, and their wild hyperbole as just a lot of noise aimed at putting on the straights, making the six o'clock news, and giving them all something to laugh along with.

To prove their point, Abbie, Reggie, Gilbert, and Jerry went down to the New York Stock Exchange, joined a tour of the exchange, and when they reached the balcony overlooking the floor of massed stockbrokers, Reggie took out $300 in small bills and handed the wad to Abbie, who threw them over the balcony. As if on cue, as if a puppet master had taken over their bodies, the stockbrokers stopped everything and charged after the dollar bills, grabbing them out of the air and rooting them off the floor. It was pandemonium for five minutes, and it made headlines across the nation.

The myth of Yippie! was born, that blank space of Dada, the actively absurd spectacle that irrationally promised magic and freedom.

"Join us in Chicago in August for an international festival of youth music and theater. Rise up and abandon the creeping meatball! Come all you rebels, youth spirits, rock minstrels, truth seekers, peacock freaks, poets, barricade jumpers, dancers, lovers and artists. It is summer. It is the last week in August and the National Death Party meets to bless Johnson. We are there!"

Gilbert wrote the last line of the manifesto. "Demand respect from the stodgy porcupines that control the blob culture."

In all seriousness, Graham Nash, now singing with David Crosby and Steve Stills, wrote a song.[295] "Won't you please come to Chicago? Or else join the other side."

Another anthem emerged from the Stones camp, a piece of supernatural Delta blues by way of Swinging London. Originally a song about paying dues, "Street Fighting Man"[296] starts off with Keith attacking his electrified acoustic guitar, Charlie Watts smacks out a marching rhythm, and Brian Jones underlies everything with a sinister sitar. Inspired by the street fighting in Paris, Mick injects a bit of reality by asking, what can a poor boy do, but to sing in a rock 'n' roll band?

The anthems provided just the right elixir of anarchy and battle music, a soundtrack for the tear-gassed streets.

* * *

Reggie jogged, in clothes caked with sweat, down Chicago streets glazed with tear gas. Gangs of youths were playing cat-and-mouse games with shotgun-toting cops, calling them "pigs" and throwing rocks and beer cans at them. He'd been running in the streets for two days, and had lost track of Gilbert and Johnny B after their abortive concert in Grant Park in which the stage crumbled in the wake of police riots. The Chicago cops had been indiscriminate, clubbing reporters along with demonstrators and even some delegates to the convention who happened to be in the wrong place at the wrong time.

Many had said that the Chicago action would be a trap. Many had stayed away, leaving the Archetypes as the only band besides the MC5 to make it. Even the Hog Farmers had canceled along with their prize pig Pegasus, slated for the Yippie Presidential Nomination ceremony. The Yippies had to scrounge in the Indiana countryside for a suitably large hog as a replacement.

"Watch the man who casts the first stone," Reggie had told Gilbert. "He may be a cop." Reggie had been keeping track of suspicious characters that might be provocateurs, especially the ones who were encouraging others into acts of stupid violence against property. His estimate of about one provocateur for every six demonstrators turned about to be close, as he found out when he ran into Cravingston after ducking into the Haymarket Lounge of the Hilton across from Grant Park.

"And that's only the local Red Squad, Mayor Daley's boys," Cravingston smiled over a scotch and soda. "Who knows how many infiltrators there are in all these peace groups?" Cravingston was wearing a Clean for Gene button on his suit jacket lapel, even though Gene McCarthy and his peace plank had already gone down in defeat over beyond the barbed-wire in the tear-gas shrouded convention center.

Reggie wiped tears from his eyes from the gas, took a drink, and said nothing.

"Oh, the silent treatment, eh? Look how satisfied you are with your scotch, now that you need it so much. Look at how the 'establishment' as you call it," Cravingston gestured around the lounge and lobby of the Hilton, "has the capacity to provide satisfaction in a way which generates submission, and weakens whatever rationality you may have for protest."

Reggie rose to the bait, flushed with anger. "Cultural revolution is more important than political revolution. Bugs Bunny should be adopted by anarchists everywhere. The nomination of the boar hog Pigasus for President by the Yippies is the most translucently lucid political act of the twentieth century. What we need are mass orgies, acid in the water supply, and fucking in the streets, these are the acts that help us take the next step toward liberating the world from tyranny. As the Airplane sings, we are all outlaws in the eyes of America.[297] In order to survive we steal, cheat, lie, forge, fuck, hide, and deal."

Cravingston looked smugly at him from the other side of the table. "This Chicago action is all a trap, you know. They want to catch the movement leaders in the act, and they'll prosecute them, you can be sure."

Just then Reggie had a flash of the immediate future. Surrounded by plate glass windows in the lounge, he could see the tear gas billowing thicker outside and the people streaming past like fish in an aquarium. He stood and pointed to the plate glass, because he knew in the next 30 seconds that it would smash. "The key to liberation is magic."

Cravingston frowned, but before he could think of something to say, the plate glass window smashed, spilling tear gas and stumbling demonstrators into the lounge. The cops had broken into a riot, clubbing and macing demonstrators in front of the TV cameras at the Hilton, and the whole world was watching... again. In the confusion Reggie slipped away. It didn't matter to him anymore how many provocateurs there were. He couldn't trust anyone.

* * *

"We as women are oppressed," Lucy addressed the Mobilization crowd weeks after the Chicago riot. "Women must take control of our own bodies. We must define our own issues."

"Take it off!" a man yelled from the back.

"Take her off the stage and fuck her!" another one in back yelled.

"Take her down a dark alley!" another man, laughing, shouted from the side.

Lucy, shaken at first — this is not fucking burlesque! — put her hands on her hips and pointed at the laughing man, shouting angrily, "Okay motherfucker, let's start talking about where *you* live." Boos all around, but Lucy roared on. "'Cause we want to know if capitalism and all those other '*isms*' don't just begin at *home*. Because we women often have to wonder if you *mean* what you *say* about revolution, or whether you just want more power for *yourselves*. White men! *You* are the most responsible for the destruction of human life and the environment on this planet! Now who is controlling the revolution to change all *that?*"

Pandemonium broke loose, fist fights were started, and Dave Dellinger had to stop the session. While the revolutionary men were agonizing over their defeat at the hands of the armed State and didn't want to hear this, the revolutionary women were just getting started, and their actions were exhilarating. With amazing speed the women's groups had spawned health collectives, clinics, legal centers, newspapers, therapeutic groups, communes, abortion counseling services, and battered women's shelters. The white women's alliance with black women was the only real connection between the white revolutionaries and the Black Panthers.

Lucy had found her calling, and it no longer mattered to her what her former lovers were doing.

* * *

Back in London, Johnny B arrived at the Abbey Road sessions to find the Beatles in a state of disarray. No one was talking about it, but they were acting like four individuals now, recording songs by themselves or with friends sitting in, each feeling something inside that was always denied. A cold wind blew through the double album, released in an all-white cover, that frightened some early Beatles fans. The singsong-coated profundity of *Pepper* and the frivolous whimsy of *Magical Mystery Tour* had given way to a much heavier end-of-a-decade vibe with stinging guitar and a satirical look at themselves through a glass onion.

Responding to a comment Johnny B made about the goofs in Chicago wearing pictures of Chairman Mao, Lennon wrote a song about revolution that at first was ambivalent about violence and destruction, singing "you can count me out" or "you can count me in" depending on his mood at the rehearsals, and eventually singing "count me out, in" for the single version.[298]

Lennon screamed the finale of the slower album version,[299] stretching out "all right" to nihilistic visions of a utopia gone wrong. With his new lover Yoko Ono, Lennon mixed all sorts of noise and Johnny B's field recordings into a pastiche of the avant-garde, "Revolution 9",[300] a roaring mushroom cloud of the thoughts in his head, the thoughts he would try to drive *out* of his head with meditation.

Lennon had learned all he could about meditation on the Beatles' trip to Rishikesh, where the Ganges flowed out of the Himalayas. "You just sorta sit there," Lennon told Johnny B, "and you let your mind go, wherever it's going, doesn't matter what you're thinking about, just let it go. And you just introduce the mantra, or the... the *vibration*, just to take over for the thought. You don't will it, or use your willpower."

Johnny B nodded sagely; it's just what he feels when he concentrates on hearing the vibrations in music. It's what Reggie feels when he can suddenly see the future, and what Gilbert feels when he projects his voice through his harmonica to articulate the spirit of the moment.

Lennon had expected something more from this trip. When the Maharishi invited one of them to join him in a helicopter ride, John jumped ahead of Paul to get in. Afterwards, Paul had asked him why he was so eager for the ride. Lennon had winked and whispered ruefully, "I thought he might slip me the answer."

But the only answer had been to write new songs and grow beards, as if growing a beard somehow conveyed peace and tranquility. They left their Indian holiday camp disillusioned with the Maharishi, and not just because the holy man had cast a lustful eye on the young actress Mia Farrow and her sister, who were part of the entourage. Lennon could not let the irony pass without a song, "Sexy Sadie",[301] barely disguising the Maharishi's name at the last minute to avoid a libel suit. One can almost hear the end of the Sixties as Lennon describes the guru as the latest and the greatest con man of them all.

Before releasing the "white album" they launched Apple as an independent company. "A beautiful place where you can buy beautiful things," McCartney told the assembled press, "a controlled weirdness... a kind of Western communism."

Lennon explained that they needed a company involving records, films, and electronics, and — as a sideline — manufacturing or whatever. "We want to set up a system where people who just want to make a film about anything, don't have to go on their knees in somebody's office... probably yours," he said fiercely, looking directly into the cameras.

* * *

Folks in the bleak area of North London were accustomed to the odd limousine now and then, what with the TV studio in their midst. And this particular December weekend in 1968 was too cold and rainy to go outside to see what all the fuss was about. But there were no less than *ten* limousines pulling up to the studio, including John Lennon's fabulous all-white Rolls with the ultra-modern TV antenna. The folks couldn't resist dawning shawls, slickers, boots, anything to fend off the wet and cold weather, to go have a look.

Besides the usual giggling teenage girls, a new set of older fellows decked out in all sorts of costumes stood by, taking it all in, leaning against the high wire fence surrounding the studio. Many of them had longer hair than anyone had ever seen before on a man; some had patched jeans and ragged shirts and looked forlorn, not at all hip or trendy. A greasy Hell's Angel, with "Their Satanic Majesties" stenciled below the Angel death's head, stood near the gate as if either on guard duty or selling contraband, or both, his bike leaning against the fence. Elsie Smith, Mick Jagger's schoolteacher from his boyhood days, handed out photographs and entertained the girls with stories of how quiet and polite Mick had been as a child. The entire staff of the Rizla cigarette paper factory across the street came out to watch from the rooftop just in time to catch Mick arrive with Marianne Faithfull in a finely embroidered Tunisian coat, followed by nameless fair-skinned nymphs in simple dresses made from old newspapers, giggling as they were chased by an old geezer in a dirty raincoat carrying a bucket of water.

"Brian wants to do 'I Wanna Be Your Man' the little snot." Andrew Loog Oldham glanced up from the poster he had just signed with a felt tip pen in Elizabethan script larger than any other autograph, larger even than Mick's. He crinkled his upper nose and brow a bit, something akin to a smirk, his best facial feature. "He's been spotted lurking about with that crazy top hat with the horns on it."

"Fuckin' moron," was all Mick Jagger could manage in reply, sprawled on the couch, decked out in his circus ringmaster outfit complete with a black top hat, a bright red waistcoat trimmed in white, white riding breeches and knee-high black riding boots. The whip lay on the floor. Later he would take to wearing a crucifix around his neck, as if to protect himself from his own lyrics in "Sympathy for the Devil",[302] the band's hit off *Beggar's Banquet*. He was now a man of wealth and taste, and he could afford — or the band could afford — to put on this culmination of British rock, the Rock and Roll Circus, featuring the Who, Jethro Tull, the Archetypes, Beatle John Lennon, and of course the Stones.

Mick thought about Brian Jones and the day that Lennon and McCartney had shown up, at Andrew's urging, to provide the Stones with a pop song. Brian had been adamant about not doing pop songs. Brian had been their leader, the one who named them, the expert arbiter of taste. Brian had to be convinced by Andrew to go along with this new direction. Brian only agreed to do it if he could somehow subvert the traditional pop song and inject real blues into it, and he did that, he really did that. He really was, as Andrew put it, "the anti-christ" to the Beatles in pop. And that's how you do it, that's how you become successful. You make a deal with the devil.

Mick slowly came to life at this thought, widened his eyes and protruded his ruby lips before giving Andrew that trademark smile, tongue between his teeth, cheeks puffed out like a cheshire cat. "It's because Lennon's here, at's it?"

Just as he spoke the man appeared, dressed in a comical juggler's outfit with silver sequins and black lace ruffles, Yoko on his arm all in black with a pointed witch's hat, quite seriously in the spirit of things, having received an invitation to be part of a circus. John Lennon chewed gum furiously, his fierce eyes darting about and finally settling on Mick, focused and implacable. "Chaotic, right?" Lennon stopped chewing, blinked at Yoko, then back to chewing like his life depended on it.

The moment grew long and involved, as if extending far back in time to when they were entirely different people, Mick a serious accounting student, John a bohemian drinker with a fabulous record collection… back to when there was little hope, if any, that there lives would be any better. And yet the moment also extended to their shared future as revered clarion callers of the new millennium, and as the stakes grew higher, the danger of what they might lose grew more terribly clear.

Andrew watched from his corner of the dressing room. Capturing Lennon for this gig had brought the project into clarity and focus, from murky napkin drawings to actual blueprints. Capturing Lennon meant getting his attention first, before managers could step in; only Brian Jones could pull that off. Brian had made the phone call for him, but that's all Andrew would allow him to do.

Lennon broke the ice with a smile straight from the Liverpool docks, just back from lunch, ready for work. "So we're here to do our thing, man, where do we go? I'm taking your lead men, you know. Brian and Keith said they would play with us. We got Eric Clapton too, and Mitch Mitchell."

"I don't think Brian is up to it, but you're welcome to have Keith," replied Mick as if bored with the entire thing. "What do you want to play?"

"The voice of reason," replied Lennon. "So where's Brian?"

* * *

The scene in Brian's dressing room was problematic at best. Tom Keylock knew trouble when he saw it: Mustapha, the little wog Brian had brought back from the Joujouka tribe, stinking up the limo with his incense and body odor, was now holding a six-foot wooden staff engraved with twisting, curling snakes and a gold swastika planted on top, reciting from an old dusty leather-bound book in some foreign language. Brian lay spread-eagled on the bed swooning in a warm fog of self-pleasure, stark naked and attended to by two Anita lookalikes stroking his penis. Three asthma inhalers were balanced on the rim of an ashtray, and hashish and cigarette smoke billowed in the upper regions of the windowless room. Champagne bottles and fresh flowers littered the floor.

Keylock, a massive V-shaped man in a gray pin-stripe three-piece, stood in the doorway watching, weighing the possibilities from a safe distance. His job as Keith's chauffeur had eagerly pleased his handler in MI6, and now he'd become Brian's personal manager. An excellent position from which to gather intelligence. *News of the World* reporters were just outside the steel-plated studio door not 20 feet away with two-way radios tuned to the police band. Keith was in the next room with Anita, keeping to themselves with a bottle of Jack Daniels; just a knock on the door and a word with Keith would lead to a row that would probably put Brian in the hospital, if not out of the group for good. Brian, you little shit, thought Keylock, you don't realize how fortunate you are to have me here to keep the dragons at bay, even if I am selling your soul to the devil.

Down the corridor Keylock could hear the Lennons consulting with the stage manager. He quickly shut the door and stepped between the mumbling griot and the bed. Mustapha stopped his mumbo jumbo and faded into the background as Keylock slapped Brian to get his attention, disturbing the nymphs in the process. One of the nymphs, a beautiful nordic blonde called Monique, with shiny teeth and pert breasts, wrapped her legs around Keylock's trousered leg. The girl had an arrangement with Keylock that took care of her monthly rent and expenses in exchange for details of Brian's contacts and whereabouts at any given moment. All she had to do was participate in a sort of group masturbation — so sweet, really, not as destructive as Brian's relationships had been. Nothing to go to the police about, was it? Keylock played fair, respected her feelings, and didn't force her to do blow jobs, but there was the occasional invitation.

Keylock took off his glasses, bent all the way over and shoved his face into her wide-open crotch, smacking his lips loudly and nuzzling her most sensitive organ, purring a vibration that oscillated up her spine. Her moans caught Brian by surprise and he quickly yanked the other girl's hand from his cock and stood up. Keylock stopped, disentangled his leg from hers and stood before Brian. The two looked like they were about to wrestle each other.

"You have about 15 minutes, Brian." Keylock smiled and wiped his face with a monogrammed handkerchief, TK. "And John Lennon is here to see you."

By the time John and Yoko arrived, Brian's dressing room was presentable and Brian had put on his trademark wide-striped trousers. Lennon's eyes swept the scene, and as usual he got right to the point. "Brian, what is all this?"

"John," Brian yawned. "So nice of you to come. Sorry I'm a bit groggy."

From out of nowhere Keylock produced an acoustic guitar, and then another, handing the first to John and the second to Brian.

"Thanks Mal," John mustered in a mock low voice, like a carnival barker on the sly to his crony. Yoko smirked because she knew John was mocking Brian's handler by referring to him as if he were the Beatles' Mal Evans. They were all the same to John, servicemen to the stars, procurers of aspirins and Cokes, backstage passes and guitar strings, pot and prostitutes. But as Lennon practiced guitar riffs, Brian was again distracted by one of the nymphs, and Yoko frowned with impatience. This wasn't going to work. Brian was simply in no shape to play.

Fifteen minutes later Brian emerged from his room with a velvet sack, tied in a knot at the top. "I expect all of this to make it to Paris," he said to Keylock, eyes fierce from lack of sleep. "Most particularly the hashish from Mustapha."

"Trust, Brian," said Keylock, frowning. "You need to have trust. It will all be at the hotel when you get there."

* * *

The camera caught them joshing each other backstage. "Winston," greeted Mick in a daze, "Welcome to the show." Mick proceeded to admire his work and apologize about not having seen John in so long, and Lennon, in character, retorted "It's not been my fault, Michael."

Mick countered, "Didja remember that old place off-Broadway, we …"

"Oh, those were the days, I want to hold your man. Remember that."

"John, I want to talk to you about your new group, the Dirty Mac, which you got together for tonight's show, comprised of yourself and…"

"Myself, Winston Legthigh. And we got Mitch Mitchell from the Jimi Hendrix Experience."

"Are you really?"

"Oh yes —"

"Experienced?"

"Oh very, very... You've read my file," Lennon sneered. "And we've got Eric Clapton from the Cream, the late great Cream."

"Cream... fantastic."

"And we've got Keith Richard, your own soul brother."

"Dirty."

"I'd like just to give you this mate," Lennon handed Mick his paper dinner plate, "on behalf of the British public."

"Thanks John," Mick took the plate and looked on admiringly. "Yer Blues, John. Yer Blues." He kept repeating it, watching Lennon walk away, admiringly to the point of maudlin, "Yer Blues, John…"

* * *

The scene clapboard snaps.

John Lennon stands at the microphone on the stage like a captain of a pirate ship, staring fixedly at the camera, eyes brimming with implacable rage and contempt at something, no one knows what, not even the sound and video crew assembled at his feet. The camera light turns red, and John suddenly lightens up, manages almost a smile, and counts off in businesslike precision, 1… 2… 3… 4…

Yes I'm lonely, wanna die…[303]

Lennon had called this a simple blues, but simple it is not. A master of timing and raw energy, with a dash of showmanship, Lennon conjures the spirit of Robert Johnson in posture, attitude, and ambition, sneering the lyrics like they meant his life. He sings an intense, over-wrought and stylized blues conjured from the British style, popularized at first by the Animals, of emphasizing attitude over expertise; it's a gesture more than a real song, exploited as a ready-made cliché to mock the very roots of the Rolling Stones. Reversing traditions, Lennon places his mother in the sky and his father of the earth, and you can feel the earth's resonance occupying blood vessels and bones with each bass note Keith plucks, bringing everything down to the basement of blues magic, while Mitch pummels his snares and punctuates each phrase with a thump of the bass drum. Building around the same slow pounded-out twelve-bar frame, Lennon manages to unnerve the listener with the subtle contrast of alternate A and B verse sections, hiccuping one intentionally spastic extra beat in all but the last verse, midway through the song, where he feels so suicidal, he even hates his rock'n'roll.

Lennon omits the extra beat and modulates the backbeat into four-square with eighth-note triplets that are twice the speed; suddenly the song is a parody of rock'n'roll, complete with a sick-of-it-all guitar solo.

On the "White Album", the song ends with a rough and rude splice to the beginning A-verse structure that fades as an outro — a clumsy four-track studio trick that becomes a special effect in the hands of the Beatles and the minds of their fans. Lennon reproduces the sound of the splice live by stopping everything, then resuming the A-verse structure as an outro.

Eric Clapton had rehearsed this song only twice, the first time in the studio a few months back when he added a lead guitar part. At the time he thought the track fairly reeked of self-congratulatory narcissism, a slap in the face of the British blues purists like Eric, a parody of Eric's original Yardbirds, the Animals, the Stones, any British band that copied the American blacks and their music. As if to say, I'm John Lennon and I can do this music as a parody better than you blokes can do it for real. And the fucker *can* do it, the song just rolls off him effortlessly, and that's what cuts. So Eric had it in mind to add a stinging authentic blues riff to the solo, and to devil up the rhythm with riffs so that it would call to mind the Hubert Sumlin heaviness that reinforced Howlin' Wolf's howl... But in the end they didn't use that take on the album.

Eric is caught up in this thinking again when it comes time for Lennon's solo, and he watches with wry interest as Lennon attacks his guitar with a dark force yet unknown in the rock world; an attack that is also a parody of that dark force. When it comes time to do his bit, Eric jumps into character and plays a stinging parody of a blues riff, indeed a parody of his own riffs from Cream, a statement of Eric Clapton as God and here it is, a very short riff from God. Eric's parody of himself completes the picture.

The decade seems to have come to an end prematurely, with the authentic blues giving way to hard rock parodies, and the revolutionary spirit of the young giving way to hip capitalism.

* * *

When the Stones showed up at Brian Jones' door to fire him, he was playing over and over the takes for "No Expectations", the last song to which Brian had contributed some brilliance. Brian had stopped using drugs and had sobered up as he prepared for the trial that might put him in jail for several years. He'd moved to Cotchford Farm in East Sussex, which had once been owned by A.A. Milne — the very same one-hundred-acre wood where Milne had dreamed up Winnie-the-Pooh and Christopher Robin.

The Stones left after promising Brian a share of the band's royalties that he would never receive. When Gilbert arrived with some tapes from the sessions they'd done together, Brian told him how depressed he was, not only by the Stones, but also by a frightening Tarot reading done for him recently. The Star (number XVII) signifies hope but can also portend loss, and deals with the immortality of the soul. "You will die at the hands of someone or some spirit of lesser abilities, his heart infused with jealousy. You will die for no good reason, maybe even accidentally, as the lesser spirit may be incompetent as a killer. But you will die at an early age. And everyone will think you died before your time. It is the curse of awareness."

Gilbert stared at the figure of a young naked woman on the card, down on one knee and pouring water from two vases. He laughed at Brian. "C'mon, man, let's listen to the tapes."

The supergroup had come together without a name, though Lennon came up with "Balls" for the tape labels. The Archetypes trio of Johnny B on bass, Reggie on rhythm guitar, and "Gilgamesh" Gilbert on harmonica and vocals, were augmented by Brian Jones on slide guitar, sitar, and other exotic instruments; John Lennon on vocals, guitar and keyboards; Mitch Mitchell on drums; and Jimi Hendrix on lead guitar.

Their sessions in the basement of Apple's headquarters on Saville Row had been held in strict secrecy. After a brief warmup of rock 'n' roll standards and instrumentals, they'd attempted several takes of the Archetypes' signature jam, "The Experiment", and a very hyped up "Crossroads" featuring a caustic Lennon lead vocal. They broke down, unfortunately, with only two takes of "Stagger Lee" with Gilbert on lead vocals.

Bob Dylan, traveling incognito, had arrived with an acetate of *Nashville Skyline*, his parody of pure country, and with him they recorded a lazy version of "I Threw it All Away", a frenetic "Drifter's Escape", and a positively hypnotic version of "Went to See the Gypsy" with Brian Jones on lead guitar.[304] Bob stayed three days and then split for home. Lennon had already decided that the music would be produced under the new Apple label.

Brian listened to the entire tape before asking, "Will Johnny B mix this?"

"Yeah," Gilbert said, "Just as soon as we all get back from the States. We've got a slot in the upcoming Woodstock festival, and then we'll be back at Apple to do the mixing."

"Woodstock, I wish I could go, but I can't get a visa. Will Bob be there?"

"Dylan *lives* there," Gilbert replied, "but he can't stand the idea of it. He's leaving town before it starts. Listen, we'll get you over to the States soon. The Dead want you to play slide guitar with them, and Paul Kantner and Grace Slick want you to play with Johnny B on their new album, something about hijacking a future starship, filling it up with hippies, and taking off into outer space."

"Great idea. I'd love to be a part of that!"

"Yeah, but Brian, listen. This tape is the only copy. Lennon didn't want any copies sitting around at Apple for someone to steal. He doesn't want anyone to know yet that he plans on leaving the Beatles. So you have to hold onto this until we get back."

* * *

Brian Jones knocked at the door of the Scotch of St. James in Masons Yard. The bouncer behind the peephole took less than a second to open it, as Brian was well known at the club. He stepped down the twisting staircase past the cloakroom and found his guest at a table. He was holding drafts of some promotional material to use for an album of recordings he'd done with Johnny B of the Joujouka pipers of the Rif Mountains. He had not yet overdubbed Jimi Hendrix and the band's contributions.

Mustapha Abdeslam, the griot from West Africa, abruptly informed him that he could not use the recordings. The commercial use of this spiritual music would incur the wrath of his ancestors. The pairing of this music with Western music would be sacrilegious, tantamount to insulting the entire culture. The griot's followers were particularly incensed that a British musician would be doing this, as they have long memories of the British slave trade.

"Am I not your friend?" pleaded Brian. "So I've wandered out past the edges of what's acceptable in your world, but haven't others as well?"

Mustapha sat across the table, his eyes downcast, saying nothing.

"Have I not thrown off the yoke of the British Empire and all that it represents?" Brian continued pleading. "Have I not been patronized and placated and even betrayed by my best friends? They think I'm mad, and perhaps I am, but I am the root and they are just branches, leaves."

Mustapha eyed him curiously.

"They don't connect to your world," Brian continued. "Nor to the history we all share. But I do. I understand this music. Whom would you share this music with, if not me?"

Mustapha considered the situation. "If I allow you, and you use the secret vibrations in your recordings, in your album, then your life will be in danger. Those who fill the world with evil sights and sounds will block your progress."

He paused. "You may be safe here, in England, but if you travel anywhere else, such as France..."

Tom Keylock was waiting by the car, his contempt for Brian barely concealed. He would be driving the pathetic sod around only for a few more weeks, at best. Dropped from the Stones, careening about complaining about Mick and Keith, tying up profit-making talent like Hendrix and Lennon for his silly projects... Brian was less than useless. Keylock's handler had given him the green light. Frank, his steely-eyed fixer, had firmly established himself in Brian's country estate as the construction foreman, patiently dealing with Brian's absurd modifications. With any luck Brian would take some sleeping pills, and the deed would never be detected.

* * *

The conjunction of Uranus and Pluto was in opposition to Saturn. Barbault's 20-year experiment to create a form of liquid, potable gold reached its second inconclusive result. Sinister influences from natural psychedelic experiences and from West African voodoo — Cornell Woodrow's lifelong involvement with a four-hundred-year experiment to raise the spirit of Legba — had corrupted the mix. Both experiments had become contaminated. The quest for gold corrupted the experiment in spiritual fulfillment, while the spiritual experiments devalued the quest for gold.

The Corporation suspended contracts with its occult consultants, fired its resident mystics, and returned to the drawing board. The best and most creative musicians perished or dropped out, while the most practical cashed in their tickets to ride and tailored their music for commercial success. Those that lasted were the ones more capable of business and numbness than of heroism.

It was early July, 1969. Gilbert stood weeping with Johnny B at the funeral for Brian Jones, who'd drowned in his pool while horsing around with Frank, the estate's foreman. The coroner recorded a verdict of death by misadventure, taking into account the amount of alcohol in his system. A placard lay on a wreath at the entrance to the Priory Road Cemetery in Cheltenham, only yards away from the Anglican church where Brian had once sung in a sweet high choirboy voice the lyrics of common prayers.

A grand, spacious English town, Cheltenham in Gloucestershire squats at the feet of the Cotswolds. It's a museum brought to life, brimming with warm beer, cricket matches, and old ladies cycling to church in the Sunday morning mists. Brian had been on the run from this place for years. Only in death could its pathological spell draw him back.

Tearful fans and curious onlookers flooded the flower-choked cemetery, surrounding a spectacular eight-foot arrangement from the Stones with hundreds of red and yellow roses, and the words "The Gates of Heaven" written out in flowers. Brian's parents did not attend, but sent instructions to create a floral grave marker in the shape of a guitar. But there were many members of the hip aristocracy of Swinging London in attendance including Charlie Watts, too shaken to sort out the details, and Bill Wyman, annoyed that Mick and Keith hadn't shown up. Neither had Brian's former lover Anita Pallenberg, now shacking up with Keith. Press photographers swarmed like wasps, buzzing Brian's grave. As the gold casket paid for by Bob Dylan was lowered into the ground, teenagers shoved and jostled to toss their flowers into the hole.

Canon Hopkins, conducting the service, admonished the youth of the world. "And why is it that this younger generation is so drawn to such extravagant behavior that could destroy their lives?" He asked the assembled to pray for Marianne Faithfull, another musician caught up in extravagant behavior, who'd eaten a mess of pills in a suicide attempt after flying with Mick Jagger to Australia. He then read aloud to the crowd Brian's own epitaph, "Please don't judge me too harshly."

There was talk of murder. Theories revolved mostly around the many people who visited Brian's home that night, and whose police statements all clashed with and contradicted each other. Johnny B knew something. Gilbert could tell by his demeanor, how he kept staring at Brian's chauffeur.

* * *

The day before, in London, Gilbert heard Pete Townshend's eulogy at the Speakeasy. "Brian was such a pretty sheepdog. On stage, he could thrust his head and strut like a cockerel. The girls always screamed more at Brian than Mick. But Brian was a pleasant and quite well-educated fellow. Really.

"The Stones have always been a group I really dug. Dug all the dodgy aspects of them as well, and Brian Jones has always been what I've regarded as one of the dodgy aspects. The way he fitted in and the way he didn't was one of the strong dynamics of the group.

"When we played the Rock And Roll Circus I was very upset about Brian's condition. I was upset at Keith Richards' green complexion, too, but he seemed in good spirits. Brian was defeated. I took Mick and Keith aside and they were quite frank about it all; they said Brian had ceased to function, they were afraid he would slip away. They certainly were not hard nosed about him. But they were determined not to let him drag them down, that was clear. Brian certainly slipped away that evening.

"Brian should have been put in a straitjacket and treated," Townshend finished. "A little bit of love might have sorted him out."

* * *

Now Gilbert regretted wearing his Carnaby Street jacket, black jeans, and wicklepicker shoes to this funeral. It was too much of a reminder of the lifestyle that had killed Brian. The heat wave that British summer had settled on him like an indictment. Swinging London had swung back with prejudicial cops and rabid fans, and it was time to get out of the way.

Johnny kept staring at that chauffeur. Tom Keylock had first driven for Keith. But when Keith suspected Keylock of setting up their headline-splashing drug bust the year before, he had lent Keylock to Brian, ostensibly to take care of Brian and keep him sober, but mostly to get Keylock out of the day-to-day Stones business. Johnny wondered who the driver *really* worked for.

With no notice and out of nowhere, Cornell Woodrow appeared next to Johnny. Despite the heat, his black skin was dry within his dark three-piece suit and somber homburg. He carried his usual black cane topped with a gold fish head, and used it to gently push forward a stocky brown-skinned man wearing an orange cloth turban decorated with blue and purple sea shells.

Cornell spoke to Gilbert in a deep baritone. "Brian was the archetype. He could play any instrument. He had an incredible feel for music and an even more incredible desire to play it."

Johnny B turned his gaze on Cornell's companion.

"My friend, Mustapha Abdeslam," said Cornell. "He doesn't speak much, he doesn't know English very well." Cornell smiled, a single gold tooth glinting in the sun. "He's from the village of Jajouka, near Ksar-el-Kebir, in the Ahl Srif mountains. Northern Morocco. Brian had made quite a strong impression on him. We want to collect his spirit now. It's the spirit of a pale houngan, and we need to grab it before the left-handed ones get ahold of it."

"The left-handed ones?"

"The ones that practice the Petro rites with the Left Hand."

"A bit late, mate," spoke up Johnny B in false Cockney, a touch of anger in his mocking voice. "Brian's pushing up daisies, gov, he's broken on through to the other side."

"Murdered," whispered Gilbert. "Strangled in his pool, left to drown."

"Never too late," Cornell smiled, his mouth a slice of lemon floating in a dark brew. "The Long Ju Ju of Arno was killed many times but lived thousands of years. He lives even today."

"Don't know about the Long Ju Ju, mate, but Long Brian Jones is no longer," Johnny snapped at Cornell in Cockney, and then dropped the accent to show how serious and angry he was about this. "The Stones, they used him up and spit him out. All his power, all his musicianship gone to waste with these motherfucking egomaniacs. Is that it?" Johnny blazed in Cornell's face. "Is that all there is? To be useful for this experiment of yours? Useful up to a point, and then done?"

"We are *all* useful up to a point, and then done." Cornell replied quietly, his eyes twinkling.

"And that's what happened to the Jackal, too?"

"His spirit lives," Cornell answered him serenely. "Like Brian, his body is no longer needed. It would be fertilizer if your culture didn't enclose it in such an ornate box."

"This just doesn't seem like an appropriate conversation to have now," Gilbert scolded both of them.

But Johnny wasn't finished. "I thought we were supposed to be the good guys," he demanded of Cornell. "Babbs told me she used *your* connection to get cocaine and heroin. And she's somehow responsible for Freddie, isn't she? Is she working for you? Is that driver over there working for you too? I thought it was the Corporation, they're supposed to be the bad guys. Are you working for them too? Are you good or evil?"

Cornell smiled back at him. "It's not about good and evil, who's good and who's evil," he spoke soothingly. "We all have different good and evil aspects. I can't say who Babbs works for. The driver, my guess is that he's connected to the Corporation, just like Loog and many of the other band managers. But I work for myself. And I don't approve of cocaine or heroin, or managers either," his eyes twinkled, "even though many of the best musicians have used them."

Johnny looked away, fuming.

"Look, these are *distractions* that are derailing you, all of you," Cornell spoke solemnly. "The managers foist these distractions on you. Loog for the Stones, Epstein for the Beatles, Colonel Parker for Elvis, Grossman for Dylan *and* Janis, and now Jeffery for Hendrix. The managers bring stress and fame into the musician's life, and with both come the temptations, the wrong drugs, the pressure to produce. All of that stifles the creativity and the experimentation. Well, maybe Brian Epstein is the exception. He loved his boys, and he stayed out of their way in the studio for a very long time. But they got to him, you see. The Corporation needed results.

"What you got to do is avoid these distractions. The most influential musicians and bands are influential *before* they get tied up with managers, bad drugs, and the lot. When they're influential — *that's* the most important time in their careers. And maybe they get influential again *after* they dump their managers and bad drugs. The problem is that the spirit of Legba has the potential for what you call good *and* evil. It's up to you to channel it."

Cornell pointed at Johnny. "Now, you hear no evil, but you're *distracted* by acid. You think you can make white people better, *hipper* to the situations that are going down. And Gilbert, you speak no evil, but you're so distracted by lust and the freewheeling lifestyle that you haven't yet demonstrated your power, which is to *communicate*. And your brother Reggie, who sees no evil, is so distracted by all this talk of a political revolution that he can't see the *cultural* revolution, the force of Legba, happening all around him.

"What you also got to do is show some *empathy*," Cornell continued. "Even for the people who want to bring you down. Remember, recognition of 'no evil' is the source of your power. You got to remember that they don't know what they're doing, either. They are fighting the rising spirit of Legba, but they don't know *why* they're fighting it. They think the music is poisoning young minds. But from my perspective, from my viewpoint, it's liberating those young minds. But good and evil, these are just perspectives. We're all the same, all human."

"Funny," Gilbert interjected. "That's what Reggie said about that guy Cravingston. There is no good or evil. Or actually, one can't exist without the other."

Cornell turned to sternly confront Gilbert. "Have you been in touch with Cravingston?"

Gilbert was flustered. He'd never seen Cornell acting sternly. "No, all I know is what Reggie told me."

Cornell pounced on him. "Did you get the tape? The one you were all working on last week over in Saville Row?"

Gilbert was not surprised that Cornell knew about the secret Balls sessions in the Apple basement. Cornell seemed to always know everything.

"Everything of value is gone," Gilbert told him. "The place was ransacked. Someone lit a bonfire out on the front lawn with some of his furniture. Guitars, a sitar, marimbas, all sorts of instruments are gone. Recording equipment too."

For the first time ever that Gilbert could remember, Cornell was cross, his brow furrowed. He stood in thought for a long embarrassing moment. Then he broke his frown, smiling freely at Johnny B.

"Perhaps the time has come to tell you," Cornell said solemnly to Johnny. "It is unfortunate the recordings are missing. They would have meant so much, representing, as it did, the most influential set of musicians ever to be imbued with Robert Johnson's spirit. Indeed, the spirit of Legba, in his musical phase. The Jackal, Brian Jones, John Lennon, Jimi Hendrix, even Reggie and Gilbert, all vibrant receptors of the Robert Johnson spirit."

Cornell paused, and his smile grew even wider. "And you, my friend. Johnny B! The very flesh and blood of Robert Johnson himself."

"Wha…"

"You are, you know," Cornell put his hand on Johnny's shoulder. "*You* are the cross-over, from black audiences to white, that Robert dreamed about. You remember that pretty woman minding the store at Mad Records? She's the daughter of Robert's first marriage, to Virginia. Raised by Mama Roux. You know, the old woman who cleaned your father's house? Her daughter, Marie Laveau Johnson. She's your real mother."

Johnny gulped. All the anger drained out of him. He began gurgling, then coughing, then choking.

Gilbert grabbed him. "It's okay, man, take it easy…"

Cornell continued as if nothing was wrong. "No problem. The recordings? We'll try again. We'll get you all back into the studio with Eric Clapton. He has the spirit."

Johnny straightened up. He gave Cornell a look. He cocked his head. "Why did you wait…"

"Until now?" Cornell completed the thought. "Did you really want to know that your father would do that, would impregnate the sixteen-year-old daughter of his maid? Listen, my boy, the world is wide," Cornell gestured with his arms held wide. "It's wide and wooly and full of mystery and surprises, and human beings are capable of just about *any*-thing."

Cornell's eyebrows popped like Groucho Marx.

"Wait," Johnny interrupted, smiling ruefully. "You… you're not about to hit us with one of your nasty limericks?"

"Of course!" Cornell then sung in a false Scottish accent,

There was a young man from Leeds
Who swallowed a packet of seeds.
Within an hour
His cock was in flower,
And his balls were all covered with weeds.

And with a sweet wave goodbye, Cornell and his mute Moroccan companion Mustapha slithered effortlessly like pythons through the crowd to the edge of the gravesite. Standing tall, eyes up to the heavens, Cornell poured mumbo jumbo from his lips while Mustapha raised his eyes and arms to Allah.

A heavy air floated down to quiet the crowd. Johnny B balanced to one side, as if his entire world had gone tilt. Gilbert still held Johnny's arm. He squinted into a paisley sun beam to catch a glimpse of God, swearing later that what he heard at that moment were the opening licks before the drum beats of "Paint it Black". Instead of the drum beats, the casket lid slammed shut.

The tension dissipated in the slam's echo. Gilbert looked to where Cornell and his companion had stood. They were gone.

"I'm going back to Margate, to see her," Johnny sniffed, on the verge of crying, into the wind.

"I'll go with you," Gilbert said. He felt proud of this role reversal. Johnny had always helped him, had been even more like a big brother than Reggie had been. But with a twinge of guilt, he thought about his brother. "Reggie too. We'll both go, in case your father gives you trouble. We'll be there with you. Right after Woodstock, we'll go."

Something Brian Jones had said stuck with Gilbert, had filled the flimsy sails of his ambition. "Music carries messages past the censors." Brian had been talking not about lyrics, but about melodies and rhythm. Slaves transmitted survival messages through song. Their ancestors communicated by drum and sung their histories. As long as humans have been on this Earth, music has been a measure of the order of the universe, of the proportions of the planets and stars, and of the proportions of the human body. To many cultures, music is an expression of God's greatness.

Brian Jones knew all this, and wanted to bring powerful world-music rhythms to rock. Now Gilbert began to feel like he could see the future the way Reggie could. The three of them would make music to carry this message past Brian's grave.

"Gimme an F!"

"Gimme an F!" Country Joe McDonald and the Fish screamed from the Woodstock stage to the half-million throng.

The audience wavered, a few shouting back "F!"

Stage manager John Morris looked at Gilbert and blinked. Gilbert looked back to the stage. Did he mean, give me the key of F? Gilbert had just grabbed a capo and had literally thrown it across the stage to a stagehand standing next to Country Joe, who had said he wouldn't go on without it.

* * *

An hour before, Richie Havens had agreed to open the festival by himself because the opening band was stuck out on the New York Quickway with their equipment truck. After an hour, Richie was too exhausted to keep time with his two-man percussion section. He retreated from the microphone, his eyes closed as if he were locked in a voodoo trance. Morris wrapped an arm around Richie's sweat-soaked robe and pleaded into his ear, "You gotta go back!"

Havens didn't pay attention. He completed a four-bar progression, lolled his head forward, opened his eyes for a second, and gasped, "Can't go back!"

Morris had no choice but to shove him back on stage. Richie had already played every song he knew. He started vamping on "Freedom" and "Motherless Child" until he couldn't move his fingers anymore.

Gilbert spent a half-hour crazily shaking down every acoustic guitar player for a capo, while Morris convinced Country Joe that now was the time, the perfect time, to step out and launch that solo career he'd been talking about.

Country Joe balked at playing someone else's guitar. "It doesn't have a strap," he said, "and I can't play without one."

Morris threw up his hands. Belmont, sensing a moment of glory, ripped a piece of rope off the side of the stage and fashioned it into a strap.

"Very neat, Belmont, but I left my picks back at the hotel. I guess that puts a lid on my going on next —"

"Bullshit, Joe, I've seen you play with a matchbook cover. C'mon, man, no more excuses."

"Just give me a capo and everything's cool."

Ah yes... Gilbert scrambled. "I'll find one. Stall Havens for a few minutes."

* * *

Will Cravingston pondered the situation from a perch at stage left. The operation was too sluggish. The Food for Love gambit to knock out the concession stands was taking too long. But he was making progress. His contact at Coca Cola had come through and sent only half-filled cans to the concessionaires, guaranteeing complaints. Six refrigerated trailers of hot dogs and hamburgers had been stalled in traffic and were spoiled.

But this wasn't like the festivals in Miami, or Atlantic City, where the cops were available to do obvious harassment. He had only state troopers. They were duly bribed; they'd done a good job, looking dumb, blocking the wrong intersections, pulling kids out of cars to search for dope, and putting a stranglehold on all the traffic. The point was to delay everything, the bands from arriving, the utility trucks from removing the waste, the food trucks loaded with spoiling meat out on the highway. The point was to make the crowd a bit more restless.

His first bit of sabotage had already been successful. Reggie had told him about the group known as Up Against the Wall Motherfuckers, but he had had little use for them at that time. More recently, he had realized their worth, had gathered them up, and had fed them the rhetoric. The festival would be hip capitalism at its worst, a stupid bonfire of all the great ideas the youth movement has had up till now. Power to the promoters? Motherfuckers to the rescue; they would be sure to tear down fences and blow over ticket-takers wherever they stood in the people's way.

The ordinary crowd beat them to it. Before the festival even started, most of the fences had been torn down and over a hundred thousand people were already in the audience bowl. John Morris had announced the inevitable, that this was now a free festival. "The show's on us," he had cheerfully shouted, but had also blurted out that the promoters were going to take a big bath on this one.

Cravingston shook his head. Big mojo was preventing him from spoiling the opening act. Cornell must be here. It must have been his idea to put Richie Havens on, an old has-been folkie. Havens had hit a nerve with his freedom cry; the audience loved him. And now here was Country Joe and the Fish, dumb-ass volunteers for lost causes.

"Gimme a U!"

Cravingston still had some tricks left. The Up Against the Wall Motherfuckers were ready to burn the concession stands. With the traffic hopelessly snarled, the helicopters they'd deployed to get around it would cost them a fortune. And a storm was due. Mumblingore's little rain-making experiment might just work.

Nevertheless, big mojo had launched a counteroffensive. Cornell Woodrow was here. He had to be.

"Gimme a C!"

By now the crowd had a pretty good idea where this was going, and enthusiastically shouted back "C!"

* * *

Cornell Woodrow had caught the winds of change. He felt the wild spirit rising again. Live music was now the thing. It goes beyond the high-fidelity record. It was now possible to put across the music from a large stage, with amplification that could knock the beat into the feet of every member of the audience and send throbbing bass notes straight into their hearts, while keeping the subtle notes floating in the air.

He began to bet heavily on festivals. They offered stages where black and white musicians could jam together and bands could learn from each other. He was not so pleased about the young blacks turning their backs on black rockers and the blues, favoring that smooth shit out of Detroit. Festivals were the keys to opening it up to black as well as white audiences. Stages that put on Jimi Hendrix, Sly and the Family Stone, even Santana, a colored band with a white drummer! What a trip!

Cravingston saw Cornell's moves as the beginning of a battle for the supremacy of black voodoo over white alchemy. Cravingston already had the communes and fringe groups in his pocket, and had infiltrated and ruined the radicals. He followed Cornell into the festival business for the purpose of disruption. At the same time, Mumblingore had prepared batches of psycho-changing drugs to foist on these human guinea pigs. By the time Woodstock got underway they were heavily invested in many aspects of the festival, including a fair portion of the off-duty New York City cops in their red shirts emblazoned with the Woodstock logo over their potbellies.

* * *

"Gimme a K!"[305]

The crowd wildly shouted "K!"

"What's that spell?"

"FUCK!" The audience roared.

"What's that spell?"

"FU-U-CK!" The audience roared again.

"WHAT'S THAT SPELL?" Country Joe and the Fish screamed as loud as they could.

"FU-U-U-U-U-CK!"

Country Joe just leaned his head back, laughed, and launched into song. "Come on all of you big strong men, Uncle Sam needs your help again..." And

475

something magical transformed the stage and the crowd at that moment as the sun set. The Woodstock Music and Art Fair had just turned into a festival.

* * *

The white Peterbilt tractor sat idle in the backstage area, serving now as a "green room" for the Archetypes. It had groaned the entire trip, from the sands of Death Valley to the green pastures of upstate New York, and was now shimmering the air around it with its heat. Its trailer held the Archetypes' sound system and a half-million hits of pure unadulterated LSD.

Herbert Mention's notes of the early 1950s had told of the stash that "Captain" Al Hubbard had buried in a secret location in the Valley, in what he called a sacred parcel. The Captain had been slowly receding into the paranoia of apocalypse, and wanted to preserve this cache against what he saw as the massive spiritual deterioration sweeping the planet, to keep it out of the hands of the death-dealing messiahs.

Johnny B had found the stash and had driven the white Peterbilt in a sweat-soaked frenzy, as if his life depended on getting to Woodstock on time. A blonde waif had ridden shotgun wearing only a long t-shirt. Johnny told the story of how he had saved her, had found the stash, and had dodged the killers waiting for him.

* * *

Two weeks before, as Johnny B got ready to leave London, the mailman dropped off a manila envelope with no return address. Assuming it was fan mail, Johnny left it for Babbs to open. It turned out to be a year-old issue of MAD Magazine.

Babbs handed it over, and Johnny thrashed through its pages until he found the marginalia with a drawing of the three monkeys. It adorned a parody of a senator named Hubbard who'd been dosed on acid and was declaiming all sorts of new legislation, from psychedelic posters and light shows in the Capital to the legalization of marijuana and dopey behavior.

Johnny put it together, with some help from Babbs. The musical notation above the three monkeys could have meant anything, but he took it to mean latitude and longitude, which put the stash in the Panamint Valley next to Death Valley. Johnny placed a long-distance call to Reggie to verify the notation in his father's Book.

He had promised to avoid distractions like this, but a stash of half a million hits of acid was something else entirely. He had always been wary of the manufacturing operation in England run by the Method. "With a stash like this, we wouldn't need them," he told Babbs. "We'd have all we need here. We're losing our distribution in the States anyway. The Space Angels are disintegrating. The murders in the Haight freaked them out. They want to turn everything over to the Brotherhood in L.A."

"You want to get out because you're afraid of your father," she argued. She knew just what to say to cut him down to size.

"Of his friends," replied Johnny acidly. "You don't know where they're gonna pop up next." A wall of ice rose between them as she put on her stone face. Johnny retreated to the bedroom to pack for his trip, and Babbs took off on business.

While packing, he searched her drawers and came across a familiar object. A gold pendant with a pinkish stone set at the center. Where had he seen that before? When it hit him, his legs gave way. He stumbled to the floor. A wave of nausea swept over him.

Freddie had always worn the pendant around his neck. "A gift from God," as Freddie had put it. He would hold it in his fingers, to "pick hits like a water-dowser picks wells."

There could be only one reason that Babbs would have it. He knew how much she liked souvenirs. Had Freddie been an assignment? From his father?

His father had always said a woman like Babbs would break his heart, and broken hearts are for assholes. Stick to cheerleaders, he had told Johnny.

His heart pounding in his chest, Johnny returned the pendant to its hiding place, and split before Babbs could return.

* * *

The next day Johnny B was in San Francisco loading the Archetypes road equipment into the Peterbilt for the trip to Woodstock. He left early to make the detour into the Panamint Valley in the blazing sunset. Dark shadows loomed under the cliffs and up the steep gulches of the Panamint Range. He reached the crossroads near the coordinates and found the marker stone from the Herbert Mention book, chalked with ancient petroglyphs.

As he moved toward the spot in the twilight, dark figures approached from a nearby abandoned ranch. He could just make out the nude bodies of women, smeared with mud, with red faces grimacing in horror. They were holding knives.

"Now wait a minute..." he barely had time to say.

The leader of the gang moved forward swiftly and swung her knife. He grabbed her forearm as she swung it, and she toppled backward, off-balance. In less than a second he had her pinned on the ground on her back, his knees straddling her and squeezing, holding the arm with the knife. "What the fuck are you trying to do!?" he shouted at her.

"Charlie says he has a contract," she shouted back defiantly, her nipples bouncing as she struggled under his grasp. The other girls circled them, uncertain about how to proceed. "You have to die!" she screamed. "You're just like the other filthy piggies, living piggie lives. Just like the song!"[306]

A blonde beauty, with blonde curled hair peeping out from under her armpits and perfect, mud-smeared breasts, stepped up with a long knife held to his chest. "Charlie says the black people will rise up and slaughter all you white rock 'n' roll groups that are stealing the blues."

"Charlie?"

"We're getting ready for the race war," the blonde sneered at him. Where had he seen her before? "The Beatles are hip to it, they know what's coming, that's why they sang that song 'Helter Skelter'. We're gonna use that message to get all the kids in the Haight-Ashbury to join us. When the blacks see all the hippie chicks leaving, they're gonna get angry and rise up in a murderous rampage, and that will trigger the race war. And we are out here to wait for the war to end."

Could music really do this to people? "Helter Skelter"[307] was the loudest, rawest, dirtiest song the Beatles ever recorded, with Paul screaming his head off.

"Um…" Johnny began, "A helter-skelter is what the British call an amusement park slide. You go for a ride, top to bottom, that's all it is."

The blonde shook her head, grimacing.

And that's when he realized who she was. "Maxine?"

"That's right, Johnny."

"What happened to you?"

"I left Margate," she laughed harshly. "And I aborted our baby in the Bahamas, like you said to do. Big Dom helped me out. *You* didn't help at all." She looked down at the ground, dejected.

Poor doomed Maxine. She had come out west and lost control. Fell for the first man who could give her an orgasm. Johnny took advantage of her moment of reflection and jumped off the first girl. He grabbed Maxine, and shook her arm hard until the knife fell. He then grabbed her by the throat and leered at the other girls. "Any closer and I choke her," he shouted at them. Then at her: "Who's this Charlie?"

"Charlie Manson. God. Christ the Lord."

The way she said it, Johnny knew. They were sex slaves. He could see the acid tinge in Maxine's eyes and in the eyes of the others. They were all on fantastic voyages into gore and sex magick, willing to do anything for Charlie. It was a fantastic, incredible story that no one would believe. This sex-crazed Charlie must have put together all this looney crap and combined it with Crowley's Law. He was dosing these girls, quoting absurd philosophies to them, laying his cock on them, and arming them for murder.

Cornell is wrong about evil, Johnny thought. This was pure evil, pouring out of their eyes.

Maxine squirmed to get away from him, so Johnny sucker-punched her. He grabbed her knife, and moved to crouch, ready to strike if any of the other girls wanted to continue with this attack.

But the girls sighed and lowered their weapons. Some even smiled at him with the unmistakable come-hither look, twisting their nude bodies to show their rears. They could switch on the sex at will. They were like sirens, and Johnny's mission would be dashed to pieces.

He grabbed Maxine and pulled her up. He tenderly dubbed her bleeding nose with his t-shirt. "You're coming with me. I'll get you some clothes on the way."

So this Charlie character had a contract on him, Johnny mused as he made his way east through the mountain passes and Maxine slept. But who had told Charlie that Johnny would be near Death Valley? Who knew these coordinates? Reggie knew, and…

Babbs. Of course. She had set him up. For all he knew, she might have even planted the code in the magazine. Anything is possible with the Corporation.

* * *

Cornell had just told them backstage at Woodstock that the "white lightning" showing up in large batches was a new kind of mind poison mixed with nalaxone, courtesy of the Corporation. Trippers were freaking out because the music suddenly didn't make sense or didn't provide any pleasure. Johnny had no doubt that Babbs had something to do with it. Her Method buddies were probably distributing it.

Hog Farmers were talking the trippers down, taking them to a quiet space, reintroducing the sound from outside, and showing them how the melodies and harmonies were constructed. Wavy Gravy reassured and calmed down the first wave of freak-outs, enough to suggest to them that they should serve as nurses for the second wave. Later, Wavy took the stage to tell the audience that *acid* isn't bad, it's just that there's a *batch of bad acid*, or acid that was prepared poorly. So avoid it, or if you must, try taking only half a tab! It turned out that half a tab was enough for some of the hallucinogenic properties to emerge but not enough to suppress the pleasure of music.

Fortunately the backstage area had been purged of the bad acid; it would have been disastrous for musicians to forget their own melodies. Johnny B made his rounds with the pure acid from the Captain's stash. The demand was extreme. All of the musicians were beyond nervous, with something like half a million people out there waiting to hear them play live, with their instruments, through this rickety sound system under tarps heavy with rainwater. It came to be accepted as wisdom that a tab of acid could make this unreal reality seem more like a dream, and therefore easier to cope with. The exception was a frail Janis Joplin, who drank herself to a near stupor for eight hours before going onstage.

Dosed to the gills, except for Reggie who wanted to see it all for what it really was, the Archetypes took the stage after Joe Cocker and the Grease Band. The enormity of it all took Gilbert by surprise. It was too much information to process at once. He started having a complexity catastrophe, otherwise known as a bad trip, when you're forced to process more information that you can. Frequently, victims of this syndrome exhibit signs of fibrillation, otherwise known as "quivering and flailing about" before experiencing a total system collapse. As he teased music out of his harmonica, Gilbert's flailing began to resemble Joe Cocker's epileptic contortions, spasmodically slapping at an imaginary guitar and twisting his lithe body in pretzel-like contortions. From the audience it may have looked like the band members were being electrocuted.

In the middle of "The Experiment" a sharp crack announced the sudden arrival of a thunderstorm. Water poured down in sheets. "Hit the power!" someone screamed from behind a bank of amplifiers. "Hey, no fucking around man, cut the power! Shut it off and get the hell out of here!"

"No! Leave it on!" John Morris faced the crowd, paralyzed, bathed in sweat. His white knuckles were wrapped around a live microphone just two inches from his lips. Winds buffeted him, and garbage swirled through the air. The latticework towers holding the massive sound speakers began to sway out over the crowd. "Would you please get away from those towers! Keep your eyes on those towers!" He looked up to see thousands of pounds of speakers shifting with each movement. It was only a matter of time before they either toppled off or the towers snapped, and hundreds would be hurt, maybe even killed. "Get off those towers!" And then, lightheaded, giddy with the prospects of total catastrophe, he shouted, "If you think really hard enough, maybe we can stop this rain!"

The chant went up in the audience. "No rain, no rain, no rain, no rain…"

Cornell smiled from a distant hilltop. They were doing it, they were countering the rain with their thoughts, their sheer willpower.

The rain drizzled while Reggie, Gilbert, and Johnny B came out without their drummer and finished their set acoustically, dodging electric sparks from the microphones. Battle-scarred and tense with their instruments, the band would never again play "The Experiment", having established this rendition as the final version.

* * *

Gilbert, energized after the set and all night afterwards, bounced around at the side of the stage as the Who started up. Pete Townshend introduced him as

"Gilgamesh, the original pinball wizard" and beckoned to him to join them on harmonica.

A completely stoned Abbie Hoffman, sensing his moment, charged up on stage and grabbed the microphone stand in front of Townshend. Hoffman yelled into the microphone, "I think this is a pile of shit! While John Sinclair rots in prison!"[308]

Townshend, wheeling off one of his trademark windmill guitar sweeps, shouted back at Hoffman. "Fuck off! Fuck off my fucking stage!" He then gave Hoffman a well-placed kick that catapulted Hoffman into the audience.

As the Who climaxed with a transcendental version of the anthem "See Me Feel Me"[309] Gilbert realized that Reggie had predicted this rift. Gilbert could join the band, but Abbie could not. The radical political movement could not survive the flood of hip capitalism. Lifestyle trumps revolution.

They had been half a million strong, as Joni Mitchell later put it in song,[310] but they were "caught in the devil's bargain." The counterculture had won only a Pyrrhic victory by dancing in the streets of revolution. Because, as Townshend would sing the following year, they would have to "meet the new boss, same as the old boss."

* * *

"Ho Ho Ho Chi Minh, dare to struggle, dare to win!"

Two months before Woodstock, the chant overwhelmed the SDS convention. Reggie's former lover Bernadette, the raven-haired, square-jawed Irish beauty who had left him in the middle of the Freedom Summer riot, took the stage in military fatigues and a Ché beret and bellowed, "You don't need a weatherman to know which way the wind blows!"

That line from Dylan's "Subterranean Homesick Blues" coalesced the idea of the hip outlaw impatient for action. It was a cue for the new Weatherman faction to take control of the convention. Bernadette and her cohorts had forged shaky alliances with other frustrated splinter groups against the white-shirted, short-haired, anti-drug Progressive Labor faction, which had tried to redirect the movement into Marxist allegiances with the working class. The Weatherman had already concluded that the working class had been bought off by consumerism. They identified with Ho Chi Minh and the North Vietnamese, and wanted to be part of the worldwide struggle against U.S. imperialism.

The clash had broken up the convention. Bernadette basked in the glow of many a radical male's erotic fantasy of an Amazonian leader. She met up with Reggie and was contemptuous of his pleas for sanity. But her fiery green eyes still mesmerized him. "You are part of the wimpy old guard that's holding us back," she shouted at him. "If you don't do it our way, you're up against the wall."

"Why are you so hostile?" Reggie couldn't believe they could take themselves so seriously. The acid test had given way to the gut check of the armed revolution: Were you willing to be more violent, to prove your commitment? Bernadette explained how members proved themselves with long LSD sessions and orgies. They wanted to smash monogamy. No longer would couples be tolerated. Any of the men and women could sleep with each other. Sex was the ultimate intimacy, and they were going to build a political collective bonded with this intimacy among all members.

At another time in his life, Reggie would have agreed with this lifestyle as a strategy. He'd pretty much lived that way with Lucy, as equals — or so he thought — and as partners who were open to having sex with others. But, as enticing as orgies on LSD sounded, the shrill rhetoric and muscular posing of these revolutionaries was just a downer, it marked the end of a noble intellectual struggle.

The only alternative had been the humorous antics of the Yippies, but Reggie had felt guilty when he had helped Abbie Hoffman strong-arm the Woodstock promoters for ten grand "for the cause, or else." The "or else" had happened anyway, with the festival in free-fall. Abbie and the Yippies were pure of heart, but these younger hippie refugees from the suburbs would never form a revolutionary class. He resented their deceitful charade, their sleepy-eyed grin and puerile demeanor, always with their heart open and their hand out. The young hippies had hoodwinked him into believing all the gibberish about brotherhood and peace. But all they were interested in was the same type of self-gratification that his brother Gilbert was addicted to.

Reggie wanted to know how much of this collapse of the New Left was due to the influence of undercover informers and provocateurs. He understood cause and effect when he could see its physical aspects. Police undercover agents had been in the front lines at the Chicago protest, inciting the police riot. Some, such as the one posing as Tom Hayden's bodyguard, had testified at the Chicago 8 trial. Rumor had it that one of the most active Weathermen who had been instructing SDS members on the proper method of creating Molotov cocktails was an FBI provocateur.

Reggie hadn't seen Cravingston since the summer before, in Chicago. He hoped that his new career in the Archetypes would excuse him from any further involvement. When Cravingston got word to him to meet up in South Jersey after Woodstock, Reggie shivered. The man had been keeping tabs on them, and knew about Johnny B's planned detour to Margate to see his real mother. Maybe this was a trap, to find out where they'd been hiding the Book and records and other things from his father's trunk.

But Reggie reluctantly agreed. One more clandestine meeting with Cravingston would, Reggie hoped, put his and Gilbert's draft statuses on indeterminate hold.

They met outside Fralinger's Salt Water Taffy on the Boardwalk. "So your family is in town? Johnny Balzano too, I see. Saw you at Woodstock. Too bad about the rain."

Reggie froze.

"You look concerned," Cravingston spoke easily. "Don't worry. The Selective Service will not be calling, not for quite a while. All I want to know is, who in the Black Panthers is most sympathetic to SDS."

That information would be easy for him to come by, so Reggie told him. "Fred Hampton, chairman of the Illinois chapter."

"Ah yes," Cravingston nodded. "I hear he's a great speaker."

"He's not violent," Reggie spoke forcefully. "He's not going along with the split either. He thinks the Weathermen are like a children's crusade gone mad, just like I do. He compares them to Custer's Last Stand."

Cravingston guffawed. "How right he is! Sock it to 'em!"

The *Laugh-In* reference made Reggie angry. "*You* caused this. Your informers and your provocateurs. *You* drove them crazy."

"Nonsense. They invited their own suppression. The counterculture is and will always be parasitic, hung up on affluence and indulgence. It will always be blocked when it moves into opposition with the institutions and the economic system, which, by the way, all of you depend on for existence. The wilder and more uncontrollable it gets, the more useful it becomes as a myth of irresponsibility, and we can use this myth to regain control. You sow the seeds of your own destruction."

Reggie frowned. "We tried to establish our own institutions. The underground press, the rock culture, street theater."

"And we took them out," Cravingston responded with a bit too much glee. "Legal challenges, IRS raids, evidence-planting, even kidnapping. Come on, Reggie, you are a part of this whether you like it or not. What is it they said in Paris, during the struggle last year? A revolution is not a spectacle. There are no spectators. Everyone participates whether they know it or not."

Reggie frowned again, but kept his cool. It would not do to tip his hand just yet. "Okay, I'll give you a report on the Weathermen. But you have to tell me who is *also* involved in this. What other infiltrators you have on the inside. We don't want to be stepping on each other's dicks."

Cravingston nodded and smiled. "They're from the FBI. Squad 47. You already met one of them at the Pentagon action. Terry League."

* * *

The muscular guitar riff from Robert Johnson's "Come On in My Kitchen" replayed in Johnny's head, and he began whistling the riff, to the chagrin of

Reggie and Gilbert, who were silently suspended in trepidation as they crossed the first bridge. Margate City appeared across the bay in suspended animation, still exactly the same, its paved streets and brick homes locked in a time warp and vacant as Summer subsided into Fall. Lucy the Elephant, shabbier than before, brooded over an empty beach and a troubled ocean.

Johnny B still had the key, somewhere in his belongings, for the maintenance closet in Lucy the Elephant's hindquarters. The hiding place for his very first stash. Reggie's idea was to create a diversion for anyone following them by parking right in front of the old Mention house down the street from the Balzano house. Johnny would go on alone, taking the beach route.

As dusk approached, Johnny stealthily made his way inside Lucy, and then down into the underground passage. They'd hidden the Book and everything else in the passage underneath Lucy. It all looked undisturbed as he probed with his flashlight.

He scampered up the ancient wooden ladder that led to the closet in the storage shed behind Mad Records, ecstatic about the possibility of meeting his mother. He remembered the time he'd last seen her, when he didn't know who she was. Just a middle-aged black woman in scarves, smiling at him. But the trapdoor to the closet would not budge. There was no sound coming from above. He knocked, but no one answered.

Then he heard it. Without a doubt, it was the same sound he'd heard long ago, when he had stolen his father's truck and driven through the pine barrens. The menacing howl, the shrill whistle. The shadows of the tunnel formed the shape of a horse's head and long neck, a tapered body with flapping wings. And then, a whiff of animal frenzy, and all at once, the smell of fish. The Jersey Devil! Caught in its lair, Johnny tried to flee, jumping off the ladder and stumbling onto the tunnel floor. His flashlight went spinning down the tunnel and pointed away.

Think yourself not there. He covered his eyes, his ears, and his mouth with his hands. *See no evil, hear no evil, speak no evil.*

Something was on top of him in the blackness. A hand reached under his armpit and dragged him up to a standing position. Johnny could just make out the man's sweating face. A black man with eyes blazing white. The man turned to retrieve the flashlight, and shined it on himself. He was an old, wrinkled version of the Jackal. Shirtless, in moth-eaten wool pants and dirty sneakers. He looked like he'd aged 50 years.

"Johnny B, am I right?" He rasped in a whispered, gravelly voice somewhere between Howlin' Wolf and Miles Davis. "You okay?"

Johnny nodded. "What happened to you? After that concert on the Boardwalk?"

"They were after me. I took off, back to the woods. I wanted to live, to play another day."

"Cornell didn't help you?"

"Nothing he *could* do. Cornell's always moving forward, always finding new musicians to take on the spirit."

"Take on the spirit?"

"You know what I mean. You got it in your soul-ness," he laughed that Cornell belly-laugh. "You still got things to do with it. I'm recuperating from it all now. Guess I just got lost in the transition, from blues to electric rhythm and blues, to rock 'n' roll. I'm waiting for my time to come again. I'm gonna make a comeback, someday, when the people get nostalgic, you know, for the old stuff."

Johnny was distressed. "I wanted to meet my real mother."

"She's just fine, just fine," the Jackal chuckled. "Treats me very well! Leaves food for me all the time. Wonderful woman, she is."

"Where is she?"

"She's gone now, into hiding. The heat's on. You got them Corporation folks after you, they've been all over this town looking for you."

"What should I do?"

"What I suggest is," the Jackal put his arm around Johnny's shoulder, "you go on back the way you came, and don't forget to grab that book and the other stuff. Take the whole trunk, and get the fuck outta here. Otherwise they'll find it."

Dejected, Johnny returned to underneath Lucy to find a new envelope on top of the Book. It was his birth certificate, listing Marie Laveau Johnson as his mother. Her birth certificate was also included, listing Virginia Travis as Marie's mother and Robert Johnson as her father. Among the documents were adoption papers that gave custody of Marie to Marie Laveau "Mama" Roux.

Also included were stock certificates, made out to John Balzano, in the Uranium Corporation of Vancouver. Clipped to them was a handwritten note. "Cash these as soon as you can. HM."

* * *

Gilbert and Reggie saw Johnny emerge from the dark beach into the glare of the streetlight at the beach stairs, clumsily carrying the trunk. Reggie jumped out of the car first.

"Are you crazy? They may be right around the corner."

"Gotta move it, all of it," Johnny choked as he maneuvered the trunk toward Reggie. By now Gilbert had joined them, and they carried it to the car.

"My dad wanted this stuff to be safe," said Reggie resolutely. "He wanted us to put it to good use. If it falls into the wrong hands…"

"Too late for that!" Gilbert pointed up the street.

A Lincoln Continental was pulling up in front of the Balzano house.

Ballzo himself was standing in the doorway with his arms folded, looking right at them. Johnny B swept away Reggie's grip and strolled right up the sidewalk to his father.

"You're a draft dodger, son," Ballzo boomed proudly as a greeting, pointing his thumb back inside the house. The entire neighborhood could hear him. "You should see the pile of Selective Service letters. This is your only known address."

"You lied to me," Johnny leveled his gaze at him. "About my mother. And about Freddie. *You* know who killed Freddie, don't you. They worked for *you*, right?"

"Not me." He paused, looking over at the Lincoln. "I'll bet she can tell you all about it."

The Lincoln's door opened. Out stepped a tall thin white-haired man in his seventies, dressed dapper in a pin-stripe three-piece suit and two-tone shoes, holding a Colt .45 revolver. Behind him stepped out Babbs wearing a slinky glitzy cocktail dress that barely covered her breasts. Johnny noticed that her breasts had begun to sag, and the stress lines in her face had aged her ten years in the space of a year. But he stared at her anyway, and didn't even notice that the man's revolver was aimed at him.

"Now wait a minute..." Ballzo shouted as he quickly stepped in front of his son. Tony Just fired. The bullet ripped into Ballzo, and as he began to fall backward, he pivoted to cover Johnny with his body.

Another quick shot zinged by Johnny's ear as he slumped underneath his father on the sidewalk. Then another shot, muffled, came from somewhere else, and Tony Just crumpled and fell onto the street. Babbs, behind Tony Just, was holding a smoking .38 Smith and Wesson Special.

Johnny scrambled out from under his father, who sighed once more.

"I don't know how it happened with Freddie," Babbs started talking, and Johnny turned to look at her, with menace in his eyes. "It seem like a bolt of lightning hit him," she continued. "We were there, your father and I, but not to kill him. Freddie was all set to turn over his Jackal recordings. He didn't want to be involved anymore, he just wanted some money for it. But we never got the recordings, and then this bolt of lightning, I don't know, maybe the transmitter... He just got electrocuted, right there at the controls. Frank... your father... decided to take care of the body. We didn't want to be implicated in this, but he wanted to send a message to the other DJs who might be talking to the Feds about payola. Frank could arrange to have someone shoot him in the head without leaving a bullet behind. We decided to take advantage of the situation, that's all. Johnny," she sobbed, "I'm not a killer!"

Johnny looked at her quizzically, then his eyes scanned down at her body to the gun in her hand. She called my father Frank. Of course. They must have been an item.

Babbs could see that Johnny had put it all together. She raised the gun again, but suddenly a shotgun blast knocked her back onto the hood of the car. The shotgun cocked again, but there was no need to fire again.

Lucy emerged from the shadows at the side of the Balzano house, holding the shotgun. She sidestepped over to the doorway of the house. "Never could stand that bitch," she muttered. She looked over at Reggie by the car.

Reggie felt his legs go weak. He grabbed Gilbert to steady himself, and found Gilbert ready to collapse. They both leaned against the car.

Lucy wandered over, the shotgun loose in her arms. She laughed. "Thought you'd do this by yourselves, huh? It's a good thing Cornell sent for me. Good timing on his part, for sure."

"Who is that guy?" Reggie staggered to regain his balance.

She looked over at Tony Just's dead body. "That bastard never even knew who he worked for. Neither did Johnny's dad. They worked for something called the Corporation. Cornell told me that *your* father, Herbert, was determined to put a stop to this, but Cornell didn't want him to risk it. So I volunteered."

"My father..." Gilbert whispered.

Lucy looked directly at Gilbert. "He loves you both, but his work is not done and he's not about to get caught, so he's not going to contact you. That's why Cornell's looking out for you."

* * *

Johnny, dazed, knelt by his father. All the things his father had said to him, all the backhanded advice, swirled through his mind. He loved him, hated him, loved him. Hated what he stood for. Loved him for saving his life.

"Your father was a good man." Mama Roux appeared out of nowhere, and placed her hand on Johnny's head. "He didn't deserve this, on account of *your* business. He kept you safe from *them*. And he kept us together. He was a good man. You keep him alive in your memory. He was always good to my daughter. To your mother."

Johnny looked up at her. "Where is she?"

"She's safe. She's expecting to see you at some point, but not right now."

"What am I supposed to do?" What could he possibly do? The only people he ever loved, Babbs and his father, were gone.

Mama Roux just smiled. "Keep on doin' what you're doin'," she laughed. "Keep on doin' it until they stop you. If they can. My my, all grown up now! And you look just like the picture I have of your granddaddy, Robert Johnson."

She helped Johnny up. He saw Big Dom behind her, now holding the shotgun Lucy had used. Big Dom just nodded at him.

"Now you just git on outta here," Mama Roux told Johnny. "Get your friends and go." Then she added, triumphantly, smiling at Big Dom, "We'll clean this up."

* * *

Babbs was no longer around to give orders, but someone else was, as the Method members were still distributing the bad acid. Maybe they were out of control. "That Charlie Manson character you were so enamored with," Cravingston spoke acidly to Mumblingore. "He used it to brainwash his girls. They're off murdering people."

"I know, I know," Mumblingore assured him, "but at least they were able to catch him. He was a mistake, as bad as Oswald really. Not like Sirhan. But you have to admit, he was useful. California was turning into a serious problem. Your girl didn't have it under control. They were supposed to be out there recruiting, not holding human sacrifices, for chrissakes. Now they have their boogie-man. But what about the music business?"

Cravingston paced around the room. "It's like a period, menstrual or something. Every few years the business hits a peak and suddenly loses its ear, starts signing talent that simply resembles previous talent and should have been left to wander the streets. So right now the current trend is to hire the young, still with soap in their ears, but the feeling is that the young understand their own market. These entry-level kids who, only yesterday, had been content to trip out on weekends with their dates from the local high school, are now elevated to executive status and given stupendous budgets. They sign just about anybody who can walk in the door, carry a tune, and slice up lines of coke on the desk without sneezing. This business is running on dreams, or perhaps you'd call them hallucinations."

"But are we still in control?"

"We give them advances, we give them cars," laughed Cravingston. "This is how we control them. Advances against record contracts, and then we charge production and studio time against their meager royalties. The point is, we keep them in debt. By advancing credit we put them in fear of us. It gives us power to control their output. Once they're in debt, they're like a flesh and blood form of money, a walking investment."

"And once they are too big to fail, like the Beatles?"

"Well, you see what has happened. They squabble in the studio like prima donnas, but their records and merchandise still make a fortune. And isn't it funny that at this stage of their careers, they would turn into cartoon characters? They have a hit with this animated movie of theirs, *Yellow Submarine*."[311]

"I've seen it. The little bastards put us in it!"

"What do you mean?"

"They've caricatured us! Look at them, they look exactly like us. The Blue Meanies!"

* * *

Jimi Hendrix had been just talking and smoking in a stranger's flat in Piccadilly after meeting the man at the Speakeasy, when the man suddenly stood up, glared at Jimi, ran out to the balcony and hurled himself over the bannister, landing on the floor below and breaking both his legs.

Jimi could not believe it. Did that man just jump like that? Because of me? Weird things were happening to him ever since he took on the Jackal's repertoire, the Jackal's rhythm style. Jimi could sense the power he emanated, the power that Cornell had told him would come from his immersion in the Jackal's music. It had grown within him and elevated him to this new level, but now he could feel it spinning and cartwheeling out of his control.

He'd been moving randomly, connecting and disconnecting with friends, lovers, and other people, never explaining and never telling where he was going next. He was dodging his management and the process server from Chalpin, due in a London court any day now, and yet he could not leave Billy Cox in the state he was in, a vegetable, hiding from the press in a secret apartment across town from his decoy room at the Cumberland Hotel. Billy hadn't spoken a word since the dosing, the freakout, and the Thorazine. Management had cancelled the rest of the tour due to "Jimi's exhaustion" because they couldn't find Jimi.

Shy, quiet and unassuming, Billy had never taken acid before. Drugs were not his style. He concentrated on his bass playing and that's it. Not even much alcohol. In Copenhagen on tour, someone triple-dosed Billy with powerful Owsley acid in a glass of punch. Jimi wondered whether the hot dose had been meant for him, not Billy. He'd noticed shadows following him for the last year or so, but never paid too much attention to them. Some kind of facet of this show business thing. He could even believe that Mike Jeffery, his manager, had put these men on his tail, just to keep track of his movements.

Jimi collected his thoughts. Jeffery ran a tight office. Every time Jimi asked to see the agreement he'd signed years earlier with Jeffery, he was stalled, redirected somewhere else, or rebuffed. Management got thirty percent of everything he earned, off the top and before expenses. Any royalties he had were funneled into accounts in the Bahamas over which he had no control.

Jimi knew that Jeffery was dismayed at his new direction and disliked Billy. The manager had hated Jimi's Band of Gypsies and hadn't wanted to field an all-black band. Jeffery wanted Noel Redding back in the band, and he wanted Jimi to go out with the original Experience, doing the original songs. A lot of money was involved. This whole enterprise had gotten out of hand. Jeffery could have arranged this thing with Billy. Anything was possible now.

Jimi was dosed with bad acid backstage before his last Band of Gypsies show in Madison Square Garden. He could play only "Who Knows" and "Earth Blues"[312] before telling the audience, "That's what happens when earth fucks with space — never forget that." He stumbled over to the drum riser, and then left the stage.

Buddy Miles was convinced that Jeffery had been the one to dose Hendrix, in an effort to sabotage the current band and bring about the return of the Experience. When Johnny B heard about what Jimi had said on stage, he interpreted earth as Cornell's experiment, and space as the Corporation.

* * *

Woodstock had been held in fertile farm country not far from an artist colony, a garden as green and muddy as the abundance of nature. Cravingston's exploits had been overkill and essentially ineffective. The Corporation had sent in more than 400 people and had failed to create the catastrophe they were looking for. The promoters lost their shirts but gained a movie deal, and the festival was deemed a success.

Altamont, later that year, was held in a harsh dustbowl of a speedway on the redneck side of the East Bay Hills, littered with the wreckage of its demolition derbies. The naive managers of the rock groups had thought it just fine to have the Hell's Angels on hand to keep order. The Corporation needed only to send in one man with a gun.

* * *

Charlie Watts regarded Mick Jagger's knee-high burgundy suede boots, yellow crushed-velvet pants, red silk shirt, brown suede vest with red piping, and a leather cape with a collar of chicken feathers. "Never top Brian Jones at Monterey."

"I'd never try to top that," answered Mick, tossing his hair. "So overdressed."

"Brian at the London Palladium, then," Charlie said.

"That was the purity of that style," Mick responded. "After that he lost all sense of simplicity."

The helicopter descended at a crazy angle to a spot near the backstage area surrounded by crowds, landing with a bump. Mick got out first, and a boy ran up to him and hit him in the face, screaming "I hate you!"

Everyone moved quickly except Charlie Watts. Johnny B coaxed him through the sea of bodies, sleeping bags, wine bottles, and dogs. The most polite rock star in the world hesitated like a stuck mule as he gingerly placed each foot. "Come on Charlie," Johnny prompted him. "Just step right on them, they don't mind, they can't feel a thing."

Hell's Angels were everywhere backstage and on the stage. Whoever had suggested using them as a security force had known only the boisterous, layabout, and ultimately timid British version of the Angels; these were the real burly, bearded, beer-matted, and brutish monsters, wearing fascist insignia and wielding pool cues like lances to protect their Harleys. Marty Balin of Jefferson Airplane had jumped down from the stage to stop an Angel from beating up a black man, and got himself beat unconscious as the band members pleaded for peace from the stage.

Keith had been at the site mingling with the audience all night and all the next day on Johnny B's acid, smoking opium to keep the edge off. He didn't want to know about the escape route planned for the band after the set ended. Apparently they had lined up four Highway Patrol cars, the only vehicles available to take them to the airport. Mick shook his head. "Not with the cops," he told the road manager. "I ain't going out with the cops." At that statement Gilbert proudly put his arm around Mick.

The Maysles brothers, filming the concert on behalf of the Stones, announced their presence at sunset with bright quartz lights, circling the outside of the crowd so that the light was always shining directly into someone's face.

"Turn off the lights," Mick said. "No lights." But they had ignored him, so Mick turned to the road manager. "Tell him no lights."

"Mick says no lights," the manager shouted into Albert Maysles' ear.

"Far out," Albert replied with his Boston accent. The California term had become a slogan of the tour, "far out" in that Boston accent, as it fit so many situations as the ultimate answer. As in combat, language had become code, and they could practically read each others' minds because they were feeling the same terrors. In this case "far out" meant "we can worry about it later."

Reggie told the Dead's Jerry Garcia about Marty Balin getting punched out. Garcia knew all about the Angels and their propensity for unrestrained violence, even though he had partied with the Angels at Kesey's. The band had even used the Angels to guard the power lines at their much smaller Golden Gate Park events, usually for just a few cases of beer. But Reggie's fearful attitude convinced Garcia and the rest of the Dead to leave. One of the results was a hole in the schedule after the Archetypes' set and before the Stones were scheduled to play.

A busload of Angels were throwing a fusillade of full beer cans to their friends on the stage as Johnny B tuned up. Sam Cutler, the emcee, offered the head Angel $500 for the entire beer supply so that the beer could be brought on stage without Angels turning them into missiles.

The Archetypes started up, and all around the fringes of the stage Angels were beating up kids who were getting too close. Crazies in the audience found there way up front to offer themselves like human sacrifices. A blond kid had stripped off his clothes and was crawling to the stage as if it were an altar, only to disappear beneath a hail of fists and pool cues. A fat freak with a Mexican mustache stripped naked to reveal his pendulous breasts and, clutching his penis, endured a pool cue beating for over a minute before toppling. A photographer trying to record the incident was hit over the head with a pool cue, kicked to the ground, and then stomped as he lay bleeding. The Angel who'd hit him then smashed his camera.

A pall of wariness and fear shown on the faces of the earnest members of the audience there to hear the music. The drums were not properly miked and Reggie's guitar seemed to separate and disappear in places. Johnny's bass vibrations were absorbed immediately into the ground just a few feet from the stage. Their harmonies were barely audible over the deteriorating speakers. Gilbert, dressed up in scarves as Gilgamesh, could not summon emotions. He reached into his pocket to find his thunder-stone missing. Numbly he looked out at half a million people in the climbing dusk. One surge forward and people would be crushed. Without rules on how to conduct themselves, the sheer physical weight of so many people would create terrible destruction. As darkness fell and the cold intensified, fires were lit from garbage and the remnants of the speedway fence, and a pall of smoke, rancid with singed wax paper and burning cellophane, drifted across the stage. They lamely started running through their last number, which had been "The Experiment" for the past two months of touring.

Johnny B looked tortured. Every bass note was a repudiation of his past, a reminder of his conflict with his father, a lesson to be learned about love from Babbs, an acknowledgment of his own misguided role in the spread of bad drugs. At some point he couldn't take any more, and he signaled the ending walkup only halfway through, skipping the entire jamming break in the middle. And at the very end, Johnny B played a coda on bass alone, the riff to Robert Johnson's "Come On in My Kitchen". Then he parked his bass guitar against his amplifier, and without a word, disappeared.

* * *

The Stones waited until total darkness to take the stage. Doctors in a nearby medical tent, overwhelmed with casualties from the bad acid, asked for extra light. They were told that the light would spoil the impact of Jagger's entry in his stage costume. When the Stones finally materialized on stage, a demon red spotlight picked out Jagger surrounded by a phalanx of Hell's Angels, looking every bit the part of Lucifer in an orange and black satin cloak.

The sound was no better than it had been before, scratchy and pockmarked with dropouts. Cravingston's initiative took place even though he wasn't there. A young black man, Meredith Hunter, had been lit up by the bad acid, and dressed in his Beale Street iridescent blue-green pimp suit, had flashed his nickel-plated revolver at one of the Angels near the front of the stage. Several Angels fell on him with pool cues, and one stabbed him in the back with a long knife. Hunter was killed in front of them, but the Stones continued playing without realizing what had happened. They also had not realized until much later that their "Gimme Shelter"[313] had become the soundtrack of the new realism. The song frightened everyone, including the Stones as they watched the Altamont murder unfold on the Maysles brothers' editing screen. They could not summon any sort of optimism after it, because it was as true as any situation could be. Rape, murder, and war were just a shot away.

They all threw themselves into the helicopter that had been chartered for the Stones' escape to shelter. Gilbert walked the Haight-Ashbury that night, which had turned unfamiliar and sinister. Many of his Digger friends had migrated to communes in the countryside. The hypocrisy of the street counterculture was all too clear. Love burgers and head shops. Speed and heroin. Rape in the back alleys of Haight Street.

The Band and Dylan's "Tears of Rage"[314] drifted out from a back alley. What kind of love is this, that goes from bad to worse? Gilbert talked himself into thinking that he'd never really believed any of it. Not the magic, not the spiritual forces in the music. None of it. It had all turned fake.

* * *

Word had reached the Beatles that their "white album" had been the soundtrack for human sacrifices committed in the Los Angeles mountains and beaches. They heard about nomadic hippies, cult followers, drinkers of dog blood, producers of sado-masochistic orgies and snuff films, bad actors who hung rotting goat heads up in their kitchens, rich people who rented corpses for Bel Air parties, and predators and victims of every persuasion. A band of nude, long haired thieves in stolen dune buggies had lit out from a movie ranch near Burbank to a remote area in Death Valley after splashing "Piggies" and "Helter Skelter" in blood on their slashing victims' walls. They practiced free love and murder in the desert hills with a group of a few men, more than twenty women, and eight children.

The Beatles took this news in shock, and triple-bolted their doors. Lennon nervously joked about all the Beatle fans who'd read mysticism into their songs. He was working on a song called "Come Together"[315] that started off with "shoot me" whispered three times.

Fog dripped from mysterious trees in the British dawn on Lennon's estate. Lawns spread out to small forests obscuring the borders, giving the place a sense of limitless territory, an ancient druid Britain. And in the center, a small man-made lake shimmered with an island in *its* center, the island a microcosm of the outer property, as if someone had first created the island, then the lake surrounding it, then the property surrounding the lake, as a set of concentric circles. At the target center sat an unhappy, disheveled, long-haired man in a tattered buckskin jacket, rumpled army trousers, and imitation cowboy boots. He was a young American hippie, and he was cradling the "white album".

The manservant, with a scowl that framed his handlebar mustache, thought it might be one of these crazies from the Los Angeles hills. He brought the young Yank to Lennon's front door and knocked, hoping to get Derek Taylor to tell him what to do with him.

The manservant had successfully avoided Yoko Ono for at least two months after the altercation about the second limousine, but here she was, wearing, god help us, a billowy see-through nightgown barely covered by a white housecoat. Before he could even think to look away he'd taken in her body curves, voluptuous breasts, steamy wisps of black pubic hair, the warm dank odor of her sweat, and felt the inexorable pull of her animal spirit.

But he did look away. "Sorry, ma'm," he said to the half-smiling Buddha statue to the right of the front door. He explained how he'd found the Yank out on the estate, but before he could ask what he should do with him, an unsmiling John Lennon in pajamas appeared next to Yoko, his face unshaven and his hair clumped about in odd angles. The American stood in silence, not looking at either Lennon or Ono but staring dejectedly down at the nicely trimmed lawn that surrounded the front patio in a semicircle.

Just then a bustle of activity inside the house caught their attention. Yoko withdrew to the inner sanctum and could be heard giving instructions to someone. As she came back to the front doorway a film crew appeared from the side of the mansion, advancing slowly, filming everything; an extremely thin blonde woman, girl really, walked ahead of the cameraman holding a light meter.

John Lennon spoke to the American, asking him what he wanted.

Even in the unedited footage, the American is unintelligible in his first comments. Lennon shifts to lean against the side of the door frame and folds his arms in an attempt to make the American feel more comfortable. The American sighs and finally looks up at John with starry eyes. The talk is about a song John had written, and how it had so strongly affected the young American, as if it had been written just for him, and that he had to seek out John and find out if John would have anything more to say to him.

Lennon points out that he wrote the song for himself, about his own life with Yoko, and that if others found meaning in it for their lives, well that's fine. But he didn't write it for others, he wrote it for himself. He didn't write songs for other people, and he is thinking about Manson, about every possible creep out there that might turn his lyrics upside down to rationalize whatever violent fantasy they harbor in their heads.

"I'm just like everybody else," Lennon finally says in his comically thick Liverpool accent, the "else" seemingly to take off from his speech and go elsewhere. "I eat, I sleep, I take a shit like everyone else…"

The talk resumes in quiet tones until Lennon sighs and asks the American if he'd had anything to eat. The manservant and film crew follow them all into the kitchen, and the film shows them eating a wonderful breakfast that brings color back to the American's cheeks. At some point the American even smiles, a doe-like smile with his head bent down, looking up through sleepy red eyes.

The Beatles had already recorded *Let It Be*, an album that showed, but only through a keyhole in a locked door, how they could get back to their roots and play honest, live music. Soon they would break up for good.

* * *

A six-foot cardboard machine gun was suspended from the stage of the dilapidated, bullet-ridden dance hall in the ghetto of Flint, Michigan. Across the back of the stage and the side of the hall were psychedelic posters of Ché Guevara, Fidel Castro, Ho Chi Minh, Lenin, Mao, Malcolm X, and Eldritch Cleaver of the Black Panthers, with an entire wall devoted to alternating red and black posters of the murdered Panther leader Fred Hampton.

Reggie looked out across the hall, only partially filled with the new insurgents in army fatigues, work shirts, and Ché berets. Only a smattering of former SDS members had shown up, and Reggie figured that some of them had to be police agents.

Nixon had convinced the public that he was actually trying to end the Vietnam war, even as he secretly authorized an escalation and the bombing of Cambodia. Reggie felt double-crossed. He had told Cravingston about Fred Hampton assuming that Hampton already knew the Man was after him. The FBI had pumped hundreds of rounds into the apartment, killing Fred Hampton in his sleep. The murder of Brian Jones, completely unrelated and across the ocean, also unsettled him.

Where was Cornell and his tiresome limericks? What good had he done with his experiment? What good did it do *me* to participate in it? Cornell had never endorsed the student movement with its Marxist rhetoric, nor had he endorsed the Black Panthers and their black pride rhetoric, even though he had befriended Malcolm X and Eldritch Cleaver. Now they were all dead or underground. The movement's contradictions within itself had polarized SDS. It was no longer flowers and doves and spontaneity, but another vicious system, the seed of a heartless bureaucracy vying for power.

The remnants of SDS leadership in Flint were determined to avenge Hampton's death. Some were talking about how wonderful it would be to "kill a pig". Bernadette had seized on the unfolding coverage of the Sharon Tate murder and praised Charles Manson. "Dig it!" She exclaimed from the podium. "First they killed those pigs, then they ate dinner in the same room with them. They even shoved a fork into the victim's stomach. Wild!" The Weather Underground adopted as a salute the gesture of four fingers held up in the air to represent the fork.

After Flint the organization broke into smaller regional collectives and tribes that would act independently. Many of the Weatherpeople didn't think they were going to live through this serious confrontation, with a government that was willing to murder their leaders. Others wanted to escalate that confrontation, and not all of them were police provocateurs.

Reggie's close confidants in the New York City collective were determined to go through with a plan to bomb an officer's dance at Fort Dix. A tough greaser who had been recruited from the Cincinnati streets had helped them build crude antipersonnel bombs using dynamite and sixteen-penny nails for shrapnel. The justification for the action was to make the officers and their wives pay with their blood for the American bombings in Vietnam. There were no innocents in this war of aggression. The army used sophisticated fifteen-thousand-pound "daisy cutter" antipersonnel bombs on the Vietnamese, with curlicued plastic shrapnel that were undetectable by X-rays.

The idea of the Fort Dix action was the ugliest possible expression of the zeitgeist. Reggie had been suspicious of the Cincinnati greaser, who was a bit more aggressive and hyper-militaristic than the others. His thoughts focused on the future, and he thought he could see the blast, or something like a blast — a great wind, and then pieces of a building pummeling his body. When he heard that Terry League, the informer Cravingston had mentioned, was involved in the planning, he immediately drove to New York to warn them. Reggie could see himself going up the steps of a townhouse with one of his Weather friends. That part of the visualization was clear. But he couldn't see what happened afterwards. He had no premonition of going inside and warning them. There was nothing afterwards, just a blank space.

* * *

On March 6, 1970, in a basement of a townhouse on West Eleventh Street in the Village a half a block from Fifth Avenue, two wires crossed to complete an electrical circuit to a detonator cap, which set off the three bombs the collective were working on. The blast rumbled up from the basement, and the four-story building collapsed in a roar of thunder. Several of the Weather collective were killed instantly. Two women who were upstairs when the blast hit, one of them naked, struggled out of the wreckage and disappeared into the night.

News reports listed the dead. Each story opened with a photo of Reggie Mention playing at Altamont. His body, and the bodies of two others, were never found, and were presumed to have been incinerated in the blast. Reggie was identified by the remnants of a pendant he had worn everywhere and at the concert, in which was embedded his thunder-stone.

* * *

A memorial concert was held for Reggie, but Gilbert, who'd been crying for days, was in no shape to play with any of the tributes made by various bands and artists. The Stones were on tour in Australia, and Dylan would not leave his Woodstock retreat. John and Yoko held a vigil during one of their bed-ins for peace, but the other ex-Beatles were unavailable.

Cornell brought with him another experiment that Reggie and Johnny B had worked on, originally with Hendrix, Lennon, and Jones in Balls, but recorded again with Jeff Beck and Jimmy Page. "Beck's Bolero"[316] had been performed live in the studio, in a single take, inspired by Johnny's Purple Haze acid. A fitting epitaph, this muscular instrumental marched through all the distractions and ambitions of the Sixties, encapsulating all of that wild energy in a sharp, dissonant, excruciating bolero. If you would dance to it, you would have to be in the costume of a matador. Johnny gave the song its bass foundation, and Reggie's its rhythm, while the others snatched riffs soon to be classics from the deepest reaches of outer space. The effect on Gilbert was to remind him of how proud he had felt to be a part Cornell's experiment.

Jimi Hendrix was scheduled to play but had been found dead a week earlier, having choked on his own vomit after a fitful, fearful night of sleeping pills and red wine. After the Isle of Wight concert, Jimi had hidden out in London trying to avoid his manager Jeffery, and was in the process of signing a new management deal with Alan Douglas. Douglas phoned Hendrix's New York lawyers, informing them that he would be relieving Jeffery of his management duties.

Jeffery was losing his cash cow. His nemesis Douglas, in taking over the books, would discover Jeffery's embezzlement and mismanagement over the years. This would be the end of Jeffery's career, if not imprisonment. Jimi's death, by coincidence, enabled Jeffery to cash in on an insurance policy and continue managing the Hendrix estate. Jeffery's luck ran out a year later when a plane he was flying in crashed with no survivors.

* * *

With Reggie gone, Gilbert lost his voice. He could no longer write songs. For a year he searched for Johnny B, looking in all of his old haunts. One late afternoon he reached Margate, and he jimmied his way inside Lucy the Elephant's maintenance closet. There was nothing but graffiti to remind him of Johnny.

There was a big hole in Gilbert, a hole he couldn't ever fill to satisfaction. The experiment was supposed to fill that hole, but the experiment had turned in on itself. Those who controlled the gold were pumping out evil. Hollywood movies were getting more twisted and sinister. Television stations were broadcasting more and more disturbing and graphic programming. Music continued to grow more violent it its lyrics and album covers. Bombarded by evil, one could no longer see no evil or hear no evil. Gilbert could no longer concentrate on seeing it, hearing it, and turning it around.

Rumor had it that Johnny B had stepped in anonymously, in disguise, to play bass in a number of different bands, on a number of different albums. No one would confirm anything. But it certainly seemed to Gilbert that he could hear Johnny's bass propelling songs by new bands on the West Coast.

The rumor was confirmed when Gilbert heard the *Blows Against the Empire* album by the newly formed Jefferson Starship. Johnny B's unmistakeable bass lines drive the last track "Starship"[317] through the floor. The climax is a futuristic fantasy of wanderer hippies hijacking a starship to take their tribes and families away from the dreadful Earth. "America hates her crazies," they sing, so you got to let go.

And at the very end, a voice challenges youth everywhere to make this fantasy a reality. Gilbert heard Johnny B's halting voice whisper, "Well?"

* * *

You lose friends, you lose family. The experiment takes you like a moth to flame, and burns you up.

Gilbert, as Gilgamesh, limped on with a phantom version of the Archetypes, hiring Ashley to sing and fill out the sound with pedal steel guitar. Eventually Gilbert's fame deteriorated like body armor rusting away and he no longer recognized the music.

And when the band you're in starts playing different tunes...[318]

To fill the time, he brought his old friend Syd Barrett, whose mind had left him helpless and a recluse in a British suburb, back to Abbey Road Studios. Syd, now fat and bald, watched and giggled from a sofa in the control room as Gilbert lent his feedback-generating services to Pink Floyd during the recording of their most influential album, a piece for assorted lunatics called *Dark Side of the Moon*.[319]

Every single day Gilbert walked into Abbey Road, and he would wave at the aged doorman, who would give him the high sign. Gilbert had no way of knowing it, but the doorman was none other than his father, Herbert Mention, now retired from his mission, and keeping an eye on his son, but too ashamed of his years of absence to reveal his identity. You can hear Herbert Mention speaking in a false Cockney accent in the run-off groove at the end of the album. "There's no dark side of the moon really, matter of fact it's all dark..."

Epilogue: The Roar of the Audience

The roar of the audience woke the Professor in the Fillmore balcony; a premature roar, offered in earnest but only to a guitar tech who'd walked out on stage to fix something and simply resembled a band member.

It was a recurring dream he awoke from. He is driving on a twisting, curving road along a cliff that could be the Jenner Grade on the Sonoma coast or Devil's Slide south of Pacifica; he'd driven both, back and forth, from excruciating jobs that never let up, to anxious wives that were never satisfied. But now the world is fogging up, the simplest details and signs of the road are disappearing. Nature itself is receding, leaving only the crumbling edge of the asphalt and the potential, unseen cliff. Sometimes he's alone, and sometimes he's with someone who is doing all the talking. Either way he can't account for his inability to steer.

The fear comes on suddenly, like having your arm stuck in the sleeve of a coat and you're suddenly, inexplicably unable to pull it out, and for a moment you tug and tug at it, getting nowhere, feeling even more stuck. It's a claustrophobic fear that can happen even in the great outdoors, out in the endless fog. He can't steer, but he's still driving, going forward, seeking escape from the fog. He knows he must eventually steer, that the cliff is somewhere on his right side, or his left side.

The fog suddenly clears, and gravity is suspended in a timeless weightlessness. The car has only two wheels on the road on one side and two wheels in air on the other, with nothing but the yawning depth of the thousand-foot drop into the ocean, nothing but certain death under silently spinning wheels.

He pulls the steering wheel with all his might, but the car only sluggishly responds, only part of it turns, and it is not enough. The car floats as it leaves the roadway.

This is when he woke up, and realized that the dream was a metaphor for the failed experiment of the Sixties.

The song about the boxer[320] echoes in his head. We hear what we want to hear and disregard the rest. He carries the reminders of every betrayal of his generation. He had cried out many times that he was leaving it all behind, but he remains, stuck in his Sixties. So many of his musician friends had not escaped. They were unable to steer away from the cliff.

* * *

The Fillmore Auditorium, highlighted in neon and attended to by limos, stood in formidable ownership of the corner of Fillmore and Geary in San Francisco. In the Sixties the building had been a squatting dark brown hulk with a dusty marquee hiding secret enclaves in its shadows, and attended to by a few psychedelically-painted Volks-wagens. Now, half a century later, bearing the heaviness and displaying the evidence of every rock band of consequence, the Fillmore had transcended anachronism. Limos now pulled up at its entrance. Its terra-cotta ceilings and archways, its dull white crystal chandeliers, and its heavy dark red curtains gave it the look of a musty cathedral in disrepair, or the set of Rocky Horror Picture Show before the props were put in.

On the altar of a stage, tonight's ritual sacrifice called for a reenact-ment of "The Experiment" from decades ago, a sop to aging Archetypes fans. From the back of the hall the Professor could see the stage laid out like a grand electronics experiment gone wrong, a roped-off crime scene, a murder among the massive speakers, amplifiers, pedals, foot switches, and miles of cable. Guitars in their stands were clustered behind each microphone; the more prima donna the band member, the larger the cluster.

One microphone stood out from the others with no cluster behind it, and he thought, just for a moment, that the band had set up a vacant position as if to honor someone. But they would need two positions for his fallen brothers, one for his best friend Johnny B, and one for his real brother Reggie.

Not a chance. A technician was adjusting it for a smaller person, someone who would sing lead, a limelight position. The names of Johnny B and Reggie, missing for three decades, would only be whispered in corridors backstage where soul vampires stalked the dressing-room doors with posters to sign.

Techies wired up an elaborate foot-pedal platform for one of the guitarists. Musicians quietly materialized at their instruments and stood there adjusting knobs, tweaking strings, flipping drumsticks, and waiting interminably for the techies to finish. The concert had originally been billed "An Evening with The New Archetypes" which would have meant no opening act, but ticket sales had been overwhelming, so the promoter had acquiesced to including an opening act that would settle the audience latecomers before the New Archetypes took the stage. Which meant they had only a few minutes for a sound check in order to accommodate the other act.

They worked up a serviceable "Experiment" for the sound check, but without the vocals, as Gordon MacAdam and his wife had not yet materialized. According to Ashley, disintegration had been the theme of the new band's mid-set jams for weeks; each buildup to a crescendo frozen mid-arch and then dissected from the inside out, first with precision and then with a staccato carelessness that left the musicians in chaos, the pieces of the jam falling where they may. Perhaps they were getting, in sonic terms, closer to describing the original band's slow disintegration.

By '69 the original band had reached the brink, the Hilary Steps of the Mt. Everest of rock fame, the stairway to greatness, at Woodstock. When a band reaches this point, climbing becomes an act of faith, the essential ingredient of religions and Faustian pacts. Blind faith, to quote Clapton. As a band, to a man, you make your choice and you stick with it, hell or high water. You push your concept, imbue it with whatever history you can muster or fake, set a background, declare your influences, and create a series of albums each better than the previous one. You think that if you could just make it to the top, you would shine brilliantly.

For a short while.

Then comes the moment when you are aware of writing songs *as you write them*; that moment when all influences fail to make each new note relevant. The notes are stripped of meaning; they exist only to have one song follow another, right off a cliff...

Three decades ago, the heart and soul of the Archetypes, Johnny B and Reggie, left this world. Legba fell asleep, bored with human shallowness and greed. Stagger Lee took a long vacation elsewhere. The Crowley mystics slithered off into hiding. Christian charlatans paraded around the square dropping leaflets of doom. The energies of millions of teenagers were divided and ultimately dissipated with the cyber-onslaught of millions of bands and billions of songs. Everyone was indoctrinated into a false theory of "innovation" that ensured a rapidly churning economy favoring the rich and powerful.

Gilbert survived by reliving the past. He taught history and music to a generation of thick-headed self-absorbed brats.

* * *

The sound check ended in a whimper. The Professor quickly vacated the upstairs balcony and was prepared to leave without a trace, when Ashley came out to the lobby with a backstage pass. "Do you want me to introduce you to Gordon? He'll be here shortly."

The Professor shrugged, and took the pass. "Going out for a smoke. Don't know if I'm coming back."

Outside, he lounged hipster-style against a lamppost, brandishing his Winston like a sword, a contrarian in the world of nonsmokers. The line stretched around the block, and those at the end knew they would never get in. The venue had reached its limit, but they would party on anyway, out on the pavement rolling joints, taking up a collection for beer. After finishing his smoke he took out a harmonica and began to serenade them. They cheerfully clapped along, happy for any kind of show.

Two of his students, Dish and Dash, surrounded and engulfed him like circling wagons, their chaotic outfits bristling with blinking electronics. Dash, vaguely black, leather-skinned, with tightly-wound curls of brown hair, had a twinkling pirate earring in his right ear. Dish, vaguely Oriental, melon-skinned, with wispy-thin black hair and no jewelry, did most of the talking. They were amazed to find him here. They were here for the opening band, having never even heard of the Archetypes.

"They got to get some mojo," was Dish's summation of the sound check.

The Professor smiled. Dish and Dash, forever in each other's company, wrapped in a culture of instant messages, hip hop fashions, and diet rock, had trivialized the performer's voodoo. How does one "get" mojo? You must be born with it, it must be part of your DNA. The Professor thought that he had once come close to acquiring the state of mojo, out there on a stage shaking his blond mop of hair, as Gilbert, stage name Gilgamesh, gyrating with each harmonica lick. But it was Johnny B who had mojo. Built right into his thin torso. Gilbert had merely followed him to clubs and scenes, on stage, and in the studio, larking about like a tourist. When it came to exploring the secrets in music, Johnny B was the only one who hadn't acted like a fucking tourist.

Parting a curtain, they entered a busy green room and right into the middle of a whispered argument between Jorge the drummer, a casual-suit recruit from the Seventies version of the expanded Ashley-led band, and Ashley in a sunny hippie outfit of jeans, tie-dye t-shirt, and headband, who was trying to quiet him. "You've forgotten how green *you* were back then," Ashley whispered.

"But where are these amateurs coming from?" Jorge spoke with a Spanish accent. "The music! It goes everywhere, it's not stable."

Ashley ignored him, and with a gotta-get-high smirk, grabbed the Professor's arm. "Hey I need your opinion on something." He led the Professor over to a makeup table with a laptop showing a vividly psychedelic fan page for The 27 Club: the stars of rock, each of whose meteoric rise to success was cut short by a drug-related, accidental, or intentional death at age twenty-seven. The Big Five of the 27 Club were Brian Jones, Jimi Hendrix, Janis Joplin, Jim Morrison, and Kurt Cobain. The founding father was bluesman Robert Johnson.

And there was a photo of Johnny B, in a glorious moment at a festival in 1969, looking like he was about to paddle a canoe with that Fender bass. His brother Reggie, and a young fuzz-cheeked Gilbert were like ghosts behind the dominating figure of Johnny B, the navigator of a doomed crew posing for the cameras just before hitting the rapids.

"He's listed as disappeared."

"Wishful thinking," the Professor put it softly.

"Wow," blurted Dish, never one to pick up on social cues. "Another one's just joined the 27 Club."

Dash crowded him at the display. Navigating more rapidly than anyone from an older generation could, Dash brought up the latest deaths.

"Disco D." Dish began reading from the screen. "Also known as David Shayman, purveyor of underground booty tracks. He was twenty-six.' Wow, man."

Dash, who seldom spoke at all and never against Dish, decided on this point to argue. "That's not twenty-seven."

"'He was bi-polar, a prodigy, and a genius in high school, with vision and talent and the ability to live at the intersection of art and commerce,'" Dish intoned, reading off the display. "'He was chemically unbalanced, and estranged from his Brazilian model-actress fiancee. He took his own life before reaching twenty-seven.'"

"That don't make him twenty-seven."

"Maybe they should call it the Twenty-Six to Twenty-Eight Club," spat out Dish in frustration. "That way they could let in Shannon Hoon, and Jason Thirsk."

"Not to mention Gram Parsons, Nick Drake, and Tim Buckley," interjected the Professor, amused at his students' antics, shooing his eyebrows up on each syllable. "Maybe if you know your time is up at twenty-six, you short out your amp. Or at twenty-eight, you've outlived all your medications except one. You die in a flash and leave behind a handsome corpse, or none at all."

"'Fesser, you think it's a conspiracy?" Dish was earnest.

The Professor smiled ruefully. Ashley looked slyly at him, expecting wisdom. "A conspiracy indeed. To kill what you were talking about, mojo. They all had mojo, in spades, that's why they're remembered. And if they're remembered, they're immortal."

A family drifted into the green room looking for Gordon and Brigit, looking for snacks. There was no cognac for the cognoscenti, no coke but Diet Coke. The green room had become an oasis for families wearing ear plugs, sons and daughters, grandsons and granddaughters, with cupolas of candies and ice chests filled with fruit juices and natural sodas. The band members were off in another room, an inner sanctum.

"What about a Sixty-Four Club?" Ashley wouldn't let it go as they navigated the room. "Twice the number of years, quadruple the drugs, and what have you got?"

"You got Paul McCartney singing 'will you still need me, will you still feed me,'" the Professor laughed. "And you'll need to be fed intravenously, Ashley, 'cause already you can't count. Twice the years would be the Fifty-Four Club, and as Dylan said, we're way past it."

Maybe his headband was on too tight. Ashley had confided in the Professor that during these last months on tour, Jorge and Gordon hadn't trusted him to remember a particularly intricate part of "The Experiment". "It's supposed to happen suddenly, Ashley, not when you get 'round to it!" Gordon had had to signal Ashley by swirling around, mike in hand, crouching, and then rising with the theme, and finally holding up three, then two, then a single finger, usually his middle finger.

Ashley, poor deranged Ashley, the folklorist, the history nut... here was a guy who could make a pedal steel sound like the Mormon Tabernacle Choir on a

Bartok binge, could play the Hendrix break in "All Along the Watchtower" note for note on a modified Fender Stratocaster with a vintage Fifties wah-wah pedal, had even spent a week on Sir Paul's farm in Scotland auditioning for Jimmy McCulloch's spot in Wings. McCulloch was another casualty and junior member that didn't quite make it into the Club, dead of an overdose at age twenty-six. Ashley always thought he could have been in Wings, but, according to Ashley, Paul had been spooked about theories, some kind of counterforce, that wreaked havoc on bands. Paul had told Ashley back then not to leave the Archetypes, that Johnny B would return, and he didn't want to see another band break up the way the Beatles had.

Johnny B's disappearance, his sudden departure from everyone and everything he'd been a part of, had tainted them all, like a failed sit-com that forever brands its actors to play similar parts in B-movies.

* * *

"An entrepreneur in Palo Alto walked in front of a train yesterday." Dr. Will Cravingston frowned and sighed as he sat down on a stool beside his colleague in the chilled, serene Stanford lab. With his thin eyebrows, angular nose, and thin face, he looked to be always scrutinizing.

Dr. Eugene Mumblingore raised a thick eyebrow, shifted his wide girth, and suppressed a growing blush across his florid face.

"First to go is the ability to distinguish versions of the same song," continued Cravingston. "Eventually you lose the ability to identify melodies. They arrive in your head like buzzing bees, without discernible pitches. Without soundtracks, movies and videos are just a jumble of blurring images. All you can recognize is talk, noise, and silence. You drive without the benefit of rhythm, barely able to pass a truck gracefully, because you have no melody to boost your courage. You walk with a jaunty, disconnected gait like a puppet dangling from loose strings. In less than a day of experiencing the effects, you may just walk out on your job and your life."

Now he stood up for emphasis. "These are not side effects. This is what it does. It puts the subject's mind in jeopardy."

"Nonsense," grumbled Mumblingore, looking up at him. "A variety of social factors, unemployment, financial ruin."

"So then what's the point? The substance exacerbates all the contradictions in their lives. Things they will never be able to resolve."

Mumblingore, now growling, "The point, the point. We use it on psychopaths. Think, man. Every killer has a soundtrack. Charles Williams with his Tupak CDs. Manson with the Beatles white album."

"Yes, yes, don't give me the cover story," Cravingston interrupted. "We're using it on musicians, on artists. We keep repeating the same mistake. The

Corporation has a history of failure to suppress, going all the way back to the beginning of recorded music, the ban on ragtime. Just look at how quickly Spector degenerated on the stand!"

"Well, so what? Charles Manson was a musician. And he's a model prisoner now. Couldn't recognize his own songs, and now..."

"Now he's comparing notes with Spector in the next cell."

"Ah, Cravingston, you miss the point! We've taken it this far, and we've covered the depression symptoms with new drugs, which, by the way, guarantees continued funding from the pharmaceuticals. The experiment is self-funded, and self-perpetuating. We're suppressing the old neural circuits to make way for the new, throwing away those useless circuits that once preoccupied our minds."

"We're throwing away music."

"Music is a pleasure-seeking behavior," countered Mumblingore at his most unctuous. "It pushes the pleasure buttons for language ability, emotional signals, motor control, flexing our muscles to the rhythm for walking and dancing. But it's *useless*. By design it does not help us attain human goals such as a long life, grandchildren, or an accurate perception of the world. It could disappear and our lives would be virtually unchanged. It has no role in the survival of our species."

"Disappear?" Cravingston rejoined. "No role in our survival? Nonsense. Music is something we respond to. It's based on the lives we led fifty thousand years ago. It takes *that long* for an adaptation, the endless reproduction of genetic mutations, to show up in the human genome. And today, we all have an ear for music. And we've come so far in our efforts to control music. The music business, for example!"

But Mumblingore was already miles away in his fantasies. "If we could only devise a way to design an internet of dreams... Indeed, we could then insert commercial messages into the dreams! Just imagine," he gushed like a teenage prom queen, "the sources of funding that would open up for us!"

Cravingston betrayed his unsettled attitude by not making a comment.

Mumblingore returned to reality, grunting. "Look, it obviously works, we just need more test subjects. We could use one from *your* old pipeline."

Cravingston frowned deeper. "You mean the Professor."

"We have an opportunity to test our theories about musicianship with this drug."

"Gilbert Mention. Don't you think the subject is played out, with everything that has been done to him already?"

"Having a professor of music on board is a good thing." Indeed, it would help convince their backers that the drug posed no threat to art and culture. "If it's just a question of one agency taking responsibility for him over another, why not us? He'd be a perfect subject. He tried everything, was subjected to everything, and went through all the changes that his generation went through. If he's somewhat of a burnout, well, so are many others his age. But he has that capacity for melody that we want to test, and our younger subjects just don't have that."

Cravingston's resolve was beginning to wilt. "You *do* realize that it may not have any effect at all? With a musician, the specific pitches of a melody retain their identity. The musician still recognizes the melody if you change the first pitch and then change all the others in relation to it."

"Yes, yes," Mumblingore replied impatiently. "You can play a melody in the key of C on different instruments and still people would recognize it. Play it at half-speed or double-speed, doesn't matter. Start playing it in D, or E, and still people would recognize it. Even impose all these transformations at the same time, starting in E, on a different instrument, at a different speed, and *still* people recognize it. That's why we all know how to sing Happy Birthday."

"So you think Mention is the ultimate subject."

"Results with other, what you might say 'normal' people, have been unpredictable. Subjects walking out of their jobs and their lives. Their social graces fail, and they turn rude and arrogant. Well, musicians are *already* rude and arrogant! Let's see what we can see, hear what we can hear."

Cravingston began to pace the room, a sign that he was about to acquiesce. "And you don't care what happens to him? Look at the results so far. Hip hop is taking off, no melodies at all, just rhythm and words. It sounds like an apocalypse in the making. They are deluding the next generation, casting a spell with pounding, thumping subwoofers spewing unintelligible lyrics, repeating exact intervals of prerecorded bass notes like a strobe light, a strobe thump really, hypnotizing the young head-shaven white kids into believing that they could be gangsters, with Glocks in their armpits... at least on weekends."

Mumblingore blinked at him, asking wordlessly if he could kindly come off his soapbox.

"Okay, we'll get Professor Mention," Cravingston acquiesced. "But you can't contain this music thing, it's just one more game of whack-a-mole."

Mumblingore let out one of his rare heartfelt sighs. "What's happened to us, Will? We used to be such splendid fellows."

"It's the passage of time I guess," Cravingston shaking his head.

"But I still can't contain the fury, in my heart. I want to kill every damned one of them, beatniks, musicians, communists, sexual degenerates. Every one, no hint of remorse, none of the mercy I'd show even to a deadly microbe." Mumblingore gazed out the window at a civilization once fair but now infested with deviants. "Their aim has always been the same, all the way back to the free spirits of the middle ages. To take away our hard-won gains, to subdivide our lands among their hordes, to pull us down, you see? Pull down our lives, all that we love, all for some ideal of 'equality'."

"You? In love?"

Mumblingore ignored him. "I am so tired. Centuries of struggle. I have sailed too long in thankless waters. The future belongs to the Asiatic masses, the pan-Slavic brutes, even, God help us, the seething black hordes from Africa. We cannot hold. Before these tides, we will go under."

Cravingston left him to his depressing thoughts to stir the cauldron for the solution to give the next test subject. Tonight, the Fillmore Auditorium would host an entirely new kind of experiment.

* * *

The opening band, Gut Fury, would make any band that followed anti-climactic. Drumming burst forth like rapid machine-gun fire; screaming guitars scaling Wagnerian progressions meshed into an enormous wall of sound, each bass note punching the chest. This was some new genre called Scandinavian Thrash Death Metal. What was once known as "heavy metal" was now a meta-genre. It seems there were infinite ways to slice and dice extreme anarchy and screaming negation.

Gut Fury had been screaming negation in relative obscurity for twenty years, and eventually built a reasonable following. The mosh pit seethed with them, hairy, bare-chested, muscular men raising angry fists and two-finger accusations, bouncing off each other viciously, jumping over the heads of the crowd only to fall back, floating over hands until they're dumped to the floorboards in a gaggle of guffaws.

The lead singer preened and shook his shaggy head, but from the left balcony the Professor could see the rangy bald spot he was trying to hide. He would bow forward as far as possible to flip his shaggy mane over his face, then flip his head back so it would fluff up at the top of his head. But it made no difference; within a minute or two the sweat would flatten it out, and from above he looked more like an aging troll than a rock singer. The repeated gestures — the bass player kept wagging his tongue in an annoying impersonation of Gene Simmons, the two lead guitarists flicked their fingers across fretboards as if playing the nipples of strippers — made them seem like puppets. There was nothing original about any of it.

The Professor held his footing against the noise like a captain in a storm, but only for a few minutes before retreating backstage again, where other members of his generation might be lurking about. Amidst the unquiet milieu of band members rustling through their knapsacks and instrument cases and grandsons munching potato chips, the Professor glanced at Ashley's set list, attached by duct tape to the pedal steel's foot pedal, to see that the first song would be his own "Johnny B" in the key of C.

It's time to remember the great ones
The leaders and the seekers of truth

You were always a fast gun
Your energy a fountain of youth
And they never could understand you
No they never could pin you down
You were always pushing the limits
You were always changing the sound
Johnny B., Johnny B., where did you go?
Johnny B., Johnny B., where are you now?

A perfect target, thought the Professor, giggling over the prank he would set in motion. His song would be the perfect moment for them to experience firsthand the humbling, voiding effect of feedback gone berserk.

* * *

Look not at what is contrary to propriety; listen not to what is contrary to propriety; speak not what is contrary to propriety; make no movement which is contrary to propriety."
—Confucius, c. 500 BC

The stage lights tripped, a pulse of light blinded nearly everyone, and then pixie dust from the light settled on the shoulders of the stagehands. The Professor stood at stage left and watched, transfixed, as time slowed down and everything turned historic. In the back of the hall, shining with some inner light, a tall, gaunt black man of indeterminate age, country-bent yet city-slicked in a dire three-piece pin-stripe and classic porkpie, bumped and ground his way through the slow-motion audience like Jiminy Cricket at a mint julep barbecue. A good look at his face confirmed it: he was the "Un-Cola Nut" man in all those 7-Up commercials from the 1960s, now slithering rapidly around the guard at the backstage curtain who couldn't even see him, snake-charming his way up to the stage, to stand beside the Professor.

"Cornell Woodrow."

"My man Gilbert! You look beat up!" Cornell gave him that gold-tooth smile that preached everything's gonna be alright. "How's your woman?"

"The first one, I tried to make her happy for, I dunno, 26 years..." The Professor sighed. Conversations with Cornell were always like this, squirming in a quiet bubble. Time lurched forward, slowly, the stagehands moving like puppets. "The second one, she was unhappy most of the time."

"Yeah, well, a woman gets like that when her man doesn't meet her expectations." Spoken like a man who knew his way around. And then Cornell put on the fake Irish accent, always strange for his husky voice,

The lass I brought home was a prize,
With alluringly bright blue eyes.
Her bottom and breasts had passed the tests,
But her penis was quite a surprise!

The Professor smiled ruefully, all too familiar with Cornell's penchant for dirty limericks, but didn't drop his seriousness.

"C'mon, Gilbert!" Cornell slapped him on the shoulder. "Gilgamesh! Don't you remember the story of your namesake?" He adopted a stance for reading poetry, with his hand out as if holding a book. "He saw the great Mystery, he knew the Hidden. He recovered the knowledge of all the times before the Flood. He journeyed beyond the distant, he journeyed beyond exhaustion, and then he carved his story on a rolling stone."

The Professor winced. These were the lyrics to one of his songs. "Do you still believe all that hoodoo shit? Legba, or whatever it is, the spirit, runs through us? That it started all the way back in the 1700s? That a slave, a single man, cast a spell? The experiment, the music going through all those changes to become rock, that all of it can be traced to this one event?"

"Why not?" laughed Cornell. "You white folks believe in a single event, a single man who got crucified 2000 years ago. What happened in West Africa back then is also such an event. One man, a powerful man, my ancestor, cast a spell to keep his kin and all his people from committing suicide to escape slavery. He appealed to the very forces of nature to deliver his people to freedom some day in the future, and to keep them aspiring for freedom until that day would arrive. And he also cast a spell on the white enslaver, to wander the earth uneasily, without spiritual guidance and without good music, and with a burning desire to feel what the black man feels in music."

Cornell jabbed Gilbert in the chest. "You know what happened to you? You fell apart. Reggie and Johnny B were gone and you went to sleep. You were supposed to stay awake, like Gilgamesh, to learn the secret of immortality. But you fell asleep, and the snake came and stole your magic plant. You've been asleep all these years."

"Immortality?" Gilbert was genuinely frightened.

"Immortality," Cornell answered. "It's a state we achieve by joining the vibrations in our brain with the vibrations out in the universe, out *there*, outside our eyes and ears. Vibrations that travel through space itself, and connect us with other versions of ourselves."

Had he blown it? He had stopped believing. What could he do now? "What's going to happen to me?"

"What's the worst thing that could happen?" Cornell's eye twinkled.

"I'll die soon."

"OK. Then what?"

"No one remembers me?"

Cornell belly-laughed, put his arm around Gilbert like a coach reassuring his prize fighter. "What do you think happens? You go *back*, that's what. You go back and *do it again*, just like the song. This is the rehearsal, next comes the performance. You just don't remember that you did it before."

"You go back..."

Cornell flashed his gold teeth. "Jack. Do it again. Only this time, do it better."

"Back to the past?"

Cornell grinned, neatly disappearing behind the grin. "Past, future, all illusion," said his voice. "But you got the gift. You can hear what's in the music. And when you *sing* and *play that harp* boy, you will remember. Middle-age whitey rap! That shit is the dope!"

"Cornell..." But the silent bubble dissipated in a maelstrom of feedback from the stage, and Cornell's tall, gaunt figure floated back into the audience. A familiar chord was struck on the electric guitar and rang high above and around him, suggesting what Cornell had told him once, that a powerful memory would follow.

There were moments at concerts that transcended all notions of entertainment, getting high, getting laid, putting on the hair, the clothes. Moments signaled by a familiar chord progression the way an epileptic seizure is forewarned by an odor, a color, an intolerable clarity of a piercing tone; moments that carry a truth so intensely bright and joyful and also painful that your memory can't hold it, you can't remember what it was, as if returning from a nitrous oxide rush. And like an epileptic who can remember the signal but nothing else that may have been revealed in the experience, so Gilbert remembered chord progressions that had set him off on trips to the wondrous wilderness of the unknown, from which he had always returned empty-handed, spent, delusional. Memory was both crutch and banana peel, propping him up on his journey, slipping away when he needed it most.

Not this time.

The familiar chord progression resolved into a truth so intensely bright and joyful that it materialized as a real person, standing before him. A gray-haired man in the seaman's cap and a tie-dye cape, carrying a guitar. There was something familiar about him.

The man said "Gilbert."

It took Gilbert a second. Then he was shocked. "Reggie?"

"Been a long time. Sorry, brother, but it couldn't be helped."

"Wha — you're supposed to be dead!"

"I thought I was dead. But it was just New Jersey." Reggie laughed, then leaned in to whisper to him. "I'm Gordon now. Gordon MacAdam. That's my name now. Reggie is dead, as a name, as a personality."

It was true. Reggie no longer looked like Reggie. His nose was crooked, and his jaw set in a different way.

"Look, this was Dad's idea. I'm just sorry I couldn't tell you. I think Dad told Mom, but swore her to secrecy."

"Dad?" Gilbert was incredulous.

Reggie explained. "Dad was there, in front of the townhouse, after it exploded. I was on the steps, got smashed by the front of the building. Broke my nose and my jaw. He pulled me out and got me out of there, got me all bandaged up and everything. He told me to *use* it. Use the fake death. I didn't realize it, but he had pulled the pendant off from around my neck and threw it into the smoking ruins, so that the police would find it."

"And you've been…"

"Underground. Then I became Gordon. And I learned how to use my power."

"You're a billionaire."

"Yes."

A waiter appeared with a single beer bottle, meant for Gilbert. "This is courtesy of the backstage manager," said the waiter.

Gilbert took the bottle and was about to sip it, but Gordon swiped it out of his hand. Glass shattered against the backdrop behind the stage. "Don't ever drink from an open bottle! Remember what happened to Robert Johnson?"

Gilbert nodded and looked around. The waiter was retreating with an impatient look, and starting to run backstage as if to report back to someone.

"One of Dad's old enemies, I believe, is trying to dose you with something."

Gilbert looked at his transformed brother. "Where's our father now?"

"Retired," Reggie/Gordon smiled, and put his arm around Gilbert. "I've been doing all the leaking for him, over the last decade or so. All that stuff about the CIA's acid experiments? You know what I mean, you can Google most of it."

"What about Johnny?"

Reggie/Gordon frowned. "It took a long, long time for me to find him. And it took a long, long time to convince him to come out from the cold. But you see, the experiment, it's not over! We're still working on it. He was doing the work in his own way. And we kept in touch with Cornell, and that's how I learned about the Robert Johnson estate, the lawsuit. Johnny's the true heir, you know. Millions. Together we can fund the experiment for another century."

Reggie/Gordon took Gilbert's arm. "Look yonder."

She was standing on the other side of the stage. Abigail Hucke from Dewey, Cheatem & Howe. Next to her stood an older woman, a mulatto, dressed in stage scarves and an Egyptian headdress.

Lucy.

"She's Brigit now," said Reggie/Gordon to Gilbert. "We've been married for about 20 years. Two kids, both sons."

From behind Lucy/Brigit stepped a lanky dude in a pocket vest and jeans and a Charlie Chaplin hat, carrying a bass guitar.

Johnny B. Looking exactly the same as he ever looked, as if in a dream. He winked at Gilbert.

Reggie/Gordon poked Gilbert. "You need to do this with me. We need to take the stage."

All of the pain in Gilbert's life had come to this. He had to be recognized. He had to be loved, and the only place he could get that kind of love was on the stage.

They stepped out together into the spotlights.

The crowd went wild. Johnny B stomped over to his usual position on bass guitar like a god from Olympus. Lucy swirled on the stage behind him to take up a position at a microphone. Reggie/Gordon raised his guitar in the air, and then sliced it down, Pete Townshend style, for the opening chord.

The roar of the audience greeted Gilbert as he stepped up to the microphone.

About the Author

Tony Bove has written more than two dozen books on computing, desktop publishing, and digital music. Tracing the digital revolution back to the 1960s counterculture, Tony produced a CD-ROM interactive documentary in 1996 titled *Haight-Ashbury in the Sixties*. As a founding member of the Flying Other Brothers, which toured professionally and released three commercial CDs, Tony performed with Hall of Fame rock musicians.

Web site: www.tonybove.com

To play the music in this novel, visit: www.rockument.com/experiment

Non-fiction works:

iPod and iTunes For Dummies (Wiley, 2012)

Just Say No to Microsoft (No Starch Press, 2005)

Haight-Ashbury in the Sixties (Rockument CD-ROM, 1996)

The Art of Desktop Publishing (Bantam/Random House, 1986)

Playlist

To play the music in this playlist, visit:
www.rockument.com/experiment.

[1] "Hurrian Hymn No. 6" (c.1400BCE) Ancient Mesopotamian Musical Fragment – Michael Levy, *An Ancient Lyre*. This hymn to Nikkal is oldest written song ever discovered.

[2] Alla I'aa Ke – Alhaji Bai Konte, *Kora Melodies from The Republic of the Gambia*

[3] Jato – Alhaji Bai Konte, *Kora Melodies from The Republic of the Gambia*

[4] Cewe Lenkele Wecho – Alhaji Bai Konte, *Kora Melodies from The Republic of the Gambia*

[5] Gaudete – Steeleye Span, *Below the Salt*. One of the first Christmas carols.

[6] John Barleycorn Is Dead (Live) – The John Renbourn Group, *Live in America*. An ancient folksong from Britain.

[7] Tartini's Sonata In G Minor for Violin and Basso Continuo, "Devil's Trill Sonata" – (Giuseppe Tartini) Joshua Bell and John Constable, *Vivaldi: The Four Seasons*

[8] Akiwowo (Ah-Key-Woh-Woh) – Babatunde Olatunji, *Drums of Passion*

[9] Fayunkunko – Alhaji Bai Konte, *Kora Melodies from The Republic of the Gambia*

[10] Stones In My Passway – Robert Johnson, *The Complete Recordings*

[11] Wind and Rain – Kilby Snow, *Country Songs and Tunes with Autoharp*.

[12] Dalua – Alhaji Bai Konte, *Kora Melodies from The Republic of the Gambia.*

[13] Sail Away – Randy Newman, *Sail Away*

[14] A Salty Dog – Procol Harum, *A Salty Dog*

[15] Wreck of the Hesperus – Procol Harum, *A Salty Dog*

[16] Old Jabo – Brownie McGhee & Sonny Terry, *Classic Blues*

[17] Black John the Conqueror – Dr. John, *The Sun, Moon and Herbs*

[18] Stack O'Lee – Mississippi John Hurt, *Avalon Blues*

[19] Chimes Blues – King Oliver, *Ken Burns' Jazz*

[20] Heebie Jeebies – Louis Armstrong & His Hot Five, *The Best of the Hot 5 & Hot 7 Recordings*

[21] Be My Baby – Ronettes, *The Ronettes*

[22] We Shall Not Be Moved – Mavis Staples, *We'll Never Turn Back*

[23] Sympathy for the Devil – Rolling Stones, *The Rock and Roll Circus*

[24] 55 (Hamsa oua Hamsine) and War Song/Standing & One Half (Kaim Oua Nos) – The Master Musicians of Jajouka, *Brian Jones Presents the Master Musicians of Jajouka*

[25] Love in Vain – Robert Johnson, *The Complete Recordings*

[26] Love in Vain – Rolling Stones, *Let it Bleed*

[27] Down The Dirt Road Blues – Charley Patton, Founder of the Delta Blues

[28] Nobody Knows You When You're Down and Out – Bessie Smith, The Best of Bessie Smith

[29] Memphis Blues – Lieut. Jim Europe's 369th Infantry Band, *Ken Burns' Jazz*

[30] Oh Didn't He Ramble – Preservation Hall Jazz Band, *50th Anniversary Collection*

[31] Livery Stable Blues – Original Dixieland Jazz Band, *The 75th Anniversary*

[32] The Pearls – Jelly Roll Morton, *The Complete Library of Congress Recordings*

[33] Hellhound on My Trail – Robert Johnson, *The Complete Recordings*

[34] Walking Blues – Robert Johnson, *The Complete Recordings*

[35] How Long, How Long Blues – Leroy Carr, *Leroy Carr Vol. 1 (1928-1929)*

[36] Drunken Hearted Man – Robert Johnson, *The Complete Recordings*

[37] Phonograph Blues (Alternate Take) – Robert Johnson, *The Complete Recordings*

[38] County Farm Blues – Son House, *Classic Blues from Smithsonian Folkways*

[39] They're Red Hot — Robert Johnson, *The Complete Recordings*

[40] Come On In My Kitchen – Robert Johnson, *The Complete Recordings*

[41] Stop Breaking Down Blues — Robert Johnson, *The Complete Recordings*

[42] Preaching Blues (Up Jumped The Devil) – Robert Johnson

[43] Cross Road Blues – Robert Johnson, *The Complete Recordings*

[44] Traveling Riverside Blues – Robert Johnson, *The Complete Recordings*

[45] From Four Till Late – Robert Johnson, *The Complete Recordings*

[46] Walkin' Blues – Muddy Waters, *His Best*

[47] Teenager in Love – Dion and the Belmonts, The Very Best of Dion and the Belmonts

[48] Personality – Lloyd Price, *Greatest Hits*

[49] What'd I Say (Parts 1 and 2) – Ray Charles

[50] Rollin' Stone – Muddy Waters, *His Best*

[51] (I'm Your) Hooch Coochie Man – Muddy Waters, *His Best*

[52] It's Late – Ricky Nelson, *Greatest Hits*

[53] Just a Gigolo – Louis Prima, *Le meilleur des années 50, Vol. 3*

[54] Bo Diddley – Bo Diddley, *20th Century Masters - The Millennium Collection: The Best of Bo Diddley*

[55] Rock Around the Clock – Bill Haley and His Comets, *20th Century Masters - The Millennium Collection: The Best of Bill Haley & His Comets*

[56] You Can't Catch Me – Chuck Berry, *Chuck Berry (box set)*

[57] Stagger Lee – Lloyd Price, *Greatest Hits*

[58] The Creation, Hob. XXI:2: The Heavens Are Telling – (Haydn) Academy of St. Martin in the Fields, Heather Harper, King's College Choir, *50 Best Classical Hits - The Greatest Classical Music Ever!*

[59] Mountain Blues – Sonny Terry, *From Spirituals to Swing*

[60] Charleston – James P. Johnson, *Ken Burns' Jazz*

[61] One O'Clock Jump (1937 Version) – Count Basie & His Orchestra, *Count Basie's Finest Hour*

[62] Swingin' the Blues — Count Basie & His Orchestra, *Count Basie's Finest Hour*

[63] Phonograph Blues – Robert Johnson, *The Complete Recordings*

[64] Last Fair Deal Gone Down – Robert Johnson, *The Complete Recordings*

[65] Hey! Ba-Ba-Re-Bop – Lionel Hampton and His Orchestra, *Swing Essentials: Swing Like Kings*

[66] Cavalcade of Boogie – Meade Lux Lewis, Albert Ammons, Pete Johnson, Walter Page, Jo Jones, *Spirituals to Swing*

[67] Strange Fruit (1939 Single Version) – Billie Holiday, *20th Century Masters - The Millennium Collection: The Best of Billie Holiday*

[68] Really the Blues – Mezz Mezzrow and Tommy Ladnier, *Mezzrow Ladnier and Newton Play the Blues*

[69] Good Rockin' Tonight – Wynonie Harris, *More Greatest Hits - Good Rockin' Tonight*

[70] Me And The Devil Blues – Robert Johnson, *The Complete Recordings*

[71] That's All Right (Alternate Take) – Elvis Presley, *Platinum: A Life in Music*

[72] That's All Right – Arthur "Big Boy" Crudup, *That's All Right Mama*

[73] Blue Moon of Kentucky – Bill Monroe & His Bluegrass Boys, *The Very Best of Bill Monroe*

[74] Cool Drink of Water Blues – Tommy Johnson, *Essential Blues Masters*

[75] That's All Right – Elvis Presley, *Elvis At Sun (Remastered)*

[76] Just Walkin' in the Rain – The Prisonaires, *Sun Records: The Definitive Hits, Vol. 1*

[77] I'm on My Way – Golden Gate Quartet, *Spirituals to Swing*

[78] Tomorrow Night – Lonnie Johnson, *The Very Best of Lonnie Johnson*

[79] Blue Moon of Kentucky – Elvis Presley, *Elvis At Sun (Remastered)*

[80] Good Rockin' Tonight – Elvis Presley, *Elvis At Sun (Remastered)*

[81] Tutti Frutti – Little Richard, *Here's Little Richard (Remastered)*

[82] That'll Be The Day – The Crickets (Buddy Holly), *The Buddy Holly Collection*

[83] Heartbreak Hotel – Elvis Presley, *The Essential Elvis Presley*

[84] Cold, Cold Heart — Hank Williams, *20 of Hank Williams' Greatest Hits*

[85] Go 'Way from My Window – John Jacob Niles, *The Best of (Remastered)*

[86] Ramblin' Man – Hank Williams, *20 of Hank Williams' Greatest Hits*

[87] Way Down The Old Plank Road – Uncle Dave Macon, *Go Long Mule*

88 Going Down The Road Feeling Bad – Woody Guthrie with Sonny Terry, *This Land Is Your Land: The Asch Recordings, Vol. 1*

89 Not Fade Away – The Crickets (Buddy Holly), *The Buddy Holly Collection*

90 Suzy Baby – Bobby Vee, *Jukebox Playlist Vol. 2*

91 This Train Is Bound For Glory – Arlo Guthrie, *Tribute to Woody Guthrie*

92 Sh-Boom – The Chords, *Atlantic Top 60: Doo Wop, Rock, and Bobby Socks*

93 Tour De Floyd – Harmonica Frank Floyd, *The Great Medical Menagerist*

94 Poor Little Fool – Ricky Nelson, *Legacy*

95 I'm Walkin' – Ricky Nelson, *Legacy*

96 Hey! Baby – Bruce Channel and Delbert McClinton, *Delbert McClinton: The Definitive Collection*

97 A Worried Man – Kingston Trio, *Their Greatest Hits*

98 Tom Dooley – Kingston Trio, *Their Greatest Hits*

99 Cannonball – Duane Eddy, *$1,000,000 Worth of Twang*

100 Gee – The Crows, *Doo Wop Classics, Vol. 1*

101 I Only Have Eyes For You – The Flamingos, *Doo Wop Classics, Vol. 1*

102 Maybellene – Chuck Berry, *20th Century Masters - The Millennium Collection: The Best of Chuck Berry*

103 Hound Dog – Elvis Presley, *The Essential Elvis Presley (Remastered)*

104 Hound Dog – Big Mama Thornton, *Hound Dog: The Peacock Recordings*

105 I Put a Spell on You – Screamin' Jay Hawkins, *Cow Fingers and Mosquito Pie*

106 Sick And Tired – Fats Domino, *They Call Me the Fat Man (The Legendary Imperial Recordings)*

107 John the Revelator – Blind Willie Johnson, *The Essential Blind Willie Johnson*

108 Conjur Man – Memphis Minnie, *Chess Blues (Box Set)*

109 Who Do You Love – Ronnie Hawkins & The Hawks, *Kansas City*

110 Got My Mojo Working – Muddy Waters, *The Anthology 1947-1972*

111 Tipitina – Professor Longhair, *New Orleans Piano*

112 Travelin' Man – Ricky Nelson, *Greatest Hits*

113 You Always Hurt the One You Love – The Mills Brothers, *20th Century Masters – The Millennium Collection*

114 Mystery Train – Little Junior Parker, *Sun Records - 60 Years, 60 Singles, Pt. 1*

115 Mystery Train – Elvis Presley, *Elvis At Sun (Remastered)*

116 Down the Line – Buddy Holly, *The Buddy Holly Collection*

117 The Wah Watusi – The Orlons, *Cameo Parkway: The Best of the Orlons*

118 The Bristol Stomp – The Dovells, *Cameo Parkway: The Best of the Dovells*

[119] Mack the Knife – Bobby Darin, *The Ultimate Bobby Darin*

[120] Follow the Drinking Gourd – Richie Havens, *Songs of the Civil War*

[121] Stackolee – Woody Guthrie, *My Dusty Road*

[122] Stag-O-Lee – Professor Longhair, *Rock 'n' Roll Gumbo (Maison de Blues Series)*

[123] That Old Black Magic – Tiny Grimes, *Atlantic Rhythm & Blues 1947-1974*

[124] Terraplane Blues – Robert Johnson, *The Complete Recordings*

[125] America – New York Philharmonic with Leonard Bernstein and cast, *West Side Story*

[126] Hello Mary Lou (Goodbye Heart) – Ricky Nelson, *Ricky Nelson Greatest Hits*

[127] Teenage Idol – Ricky Nelson, *Ricky Nelson Greatest Hits*

[128] Walkin' The Boogie (Alternate) – John Lee Hooker, *Chess Blues (Box Set)*

[129] Hawaiian Boogie – Elmore James, *The Best of the Modern Years (Remastered)*

[130] Pledging My Love – Johnny Ace, *Greatest Hits and More*

[131] Come On In My Kitchen (Alternate Take) – Robert Johnson

[132] Shine – Django Reinhardt, *Ken Burns' Jazz*

[133] Scrapple From The Apple — Charlie Parker, *Ken Burns' Jazz*

[134] No Expectations (live) — The Rolling Stones, *The Rolling Stones Rock and Roll Circus*

[135] Manteca – Dizzy Gillespie and His Orchestra, *Ken Burns' Jazz*

[136] Moaning At Midnight — Howlin' Wolf, *The Chess 50th Anniversary Collection: His Best*

[137] Little Red Rooster – Howlin' Wolf, *Howlin' Wolf*

[138] Standing At The Crossroads – Elmore James, *Shake Your Money Maker: The Best of the Fire Sessions*

[139] The Hallelujah Chorus – The Roches, *Keep on Doing*

[140] Rock Island Line – Lonnie Donegan, *Rock Island Line - The Singles Anthology*

[141] Whole Lotta Shakin' Going On – Jerry Lee Lewis, *Sun Records: The Definitive Hits, Vol. 1*

[142] Power and the Glory – Phil Ochs, *All the News That's Fit to Sing*

[143] Rain and Snow – Obray Ramsey, *The Music Never Stopped: Roots of the Grateful Dead*

[144] Butcher's Boy – Buell Kazee, *Buell Kazee Sings and Plays*

[145] Ommie Wise – G.B. Grayson and Henry Whitter, *The Recordings of Grayson & Whitter*

[146] Peg And Awl – The Carolina Tar Heels, *The Very Best Country & Western Vocal Duets*

[147] Stackalee – Frank Hutchinson, *American Folk Legends*

[148] Gonna Die With My Hammer In My Hand – Williamson Brothers and Curry, *Old-Time Music of West Virginia, Vol. 1*

[149] Grizzly Bear – Eric von Schmidt and Rolf Cahn, *Rolf Cahn and Eric Von Schmidt*

[150] He Was a Friend of Mine – Eric von Schmidt and Rolf Cahn, *Rolf Cahn and Eric Von Schmidt*

[151] When That Great Ship Went Down – William and Versey Smith, *Never Let the Same Bee Sting You Twice - Blues, Ballads, Rags & Gospel In the Songster Tradition*

[152] Fast Acne – Eric von Schmidt, *Living on the Trail*

[153] The Magic Flute, K. 620: Overture – (Mozart) London Philharmonic Orchestra & David Parry, *The 50 Greatest Pieces of Classical Music*

[154] So What — Miles Davis, *Kind of Blue*

[155] Stewball – Eric von Schmidt, *Living on the Trail*

[156] Silver Dagger — Joan Baez, *Joan Baez*

[157] Wimoweh – The Weavers, *The Weavers At Carnegie Hall*

[158] Fatal Flower Garden – Nelstone's Hawaiians, *American Folk Music, Vol. 2*

[159] This Land Is Your Land (Alternate) – Woody Guthrie, *Woody At 100: The Woody Guthrie Centennial Collection*

[160] Follow the Drinking Gourd – The Weavers, *The Weavers At Carnegie Hall*

[161] Tom Joad Pt. 1, Tom Joad Pt. 2 – Woody Guthrie, *Dust Bowl Ballads*

[162] Go Down, Moses – Paul Robeson, *The Power and the Glory*

[163] The Coo Coo Bird – Clarence Ashley, *American Folk Music, Vol. 1*

[164] Be-Bop-A-Lula – Gene Vincent, *Blue Jean Bop!*

[165] Ramrod – Duane Eddy, *Have 'Twangy' Guitar, Will Travel*

[166] Money (That's What I Want) (Live) – The Beatles, *Anthology 1*

[167] Twenty Flight Rock – Eddie Cochran, *The Best of Eddie Cochran*

[168] Jeanie, Jeanie, Jeanie – Eddie Cochran, *The Best of Eddie Cochran*

[169] One After 909 (outtake) – The Beatles, *Anthology 1*

[170] Some Other Guy – The Beatles, *Live at the BBC*

[171] My Bonnie — The Beatles with Tony Sheridan, *Anthology 1*

[172] Roundhouse Stomp – Alexis Korner, *Kornerstoned - The Alexis Korner Anthology 1954-1983*

[173] Eyesight To The Blind – Sonny Boy Williamson, *King Biscuit Time*

[174] I Believe I'll Dust My Broom – Robert Johnson, *Complete Recordings*

[175] Santa Fe Blues – Lightning Hopkins, *The Best of Texas Blues*

[176] Up-Town — Alexis Korner's Blues Incorporated, *Kornerstoned - The Alexis Korner Anthology 1954-1983*

[177] Jack O'Diamonds – Lonnie Donegan and His Skiffle Group, *Rock Island Line - The Singles Anthology*

[178] Rave On — Buddy Holly, *The Buddy Holly Collection*

[179] My Babe — Little Walter, *The Chess 50th Anniversary Collection: His Best*

[180] Only The Lonely (Know How I Feel) – Roy Orbison, *The Essential Roy Orbison*

[181] Ain't That Loving You Baby — Jimmy Reed, *The Very Best of Jimmy Reed*

[182] I Can't Be Satisfied – Muddy Waters, *The Anthology*

[183] Little Queenie — Chuck Berry, *The Chess Box*

[184] Around and Around – Chuck Berry, *The Chess Box*

[185] Dust My Broom – Elmore James, *Delta Blues Vol. 2*

[186] I'm A King Bee – The Rolling Stones, *The Rolling Stones*

[187] Please Please Me – The Beatles, *Please Please Me*

[188] I'm the Face – The High Numbers (The Who), *The Who: Thirty Years of Maximum R&B (Box Set)*

[189] Come On – The Rolling Stones, *Singles Collection: The London Years*

[190] I Want to be Loved – The Rolling Stones, *Singles Collection: The London Years*

[191] Everybody Needs Somebody To Love – The Rolling Stones, *The Rolling Stones, Now!*

[192] You Can't Catch Me – The Rolling Stones, *The Rolling Stones, Now!*

[193] I Wanna Be Your Man — The Beatles, *With the Beatles*

[194] I Wanna Be Your Man — The Rolling Stones, *Singles Collection: The London Years*

[195] Little Red Rooster — The Rolling Stones, *Singles Collection: The London Years*

[196] Shout – The Beatles, Anthology

[197] Wade in the Water – Judy Henske, *Judy Henske*

[198] Joe Hill – Joan Baez, *Rare, Live & Classic*

[199] We Shall Overcome (Live) – Joan Baez, *Rare, Live & Classic*

[200] I'll Be All Right Some Day – Reverend Gary Davis, *Have a Little Faith (Remastered)*

[201] No More Auction Block For Me – Paul Robeson, *Paul Robeson Sings Negro Spirituals*

[202] Catfish Blues – David "Honeyboy" Edwards, *Honeyboy Edwards: Missisippi Delta Bluesman*

[203] Dry Bone Shuffle (Take 2) – Blind Blake, *Too Late, Too Late, Vol. 11 (1924-1939)*

[204] Rock Me – Sister Rosetta Tharpe, *The One and Only Queen of Hot Gospel*

[205] Follow the Drinking Gourd – Roger McGuinn, *22 Timeless Tracks from the Folk Den Project*

[206] Follow the Drinking Gourd – Taj Mahal, *In Progress & In Motion*

[207] Train That Carried the Girl From Town – Frank Hutchison, *White Country Blues, 1926-1938*

[208] Sowing On The Mountain – Woody Guthrie, *Muleskinner Blues: The Asch Recordings, Vol. 2*

[209] Jug Band Music – Jim Kweskin & The Jug Band, *Jug Band Music*

[210] Baby, Let Me Lay It On You – Reverend Gary Davis, *Blues and Ragtime*

[211] Riddle Song – Dick Fariña and Eric von Schmidt, *Dick Fariña & Eric Von Schmidt*

[212] Wobble Bird – Dick Fariña and Eric von Schmidt, *Dick Fariña & Eric Von Schmidt*

213 Cocaine Blues – Dave Van Ronk, *Folksinger*

214 The Book of Love – The Monotones, *Doo Wop Classics, Vol. 1*

215 I'll Fly Away – Carolyn Hester (with Bob Dylan), *Carolyn Hester*

216 Ramblin' On My Mind – Robert Johnson, *The Complete Recordings*

217 Talkin' John Birch Paranoid Blues – Bob Dylan, *The Bootleg Series, Vols. 1-3 (Rare & Unreleased) 1961-1991*

218 In New Orleans (House Of The Rising Sun) – Lead Belly, *Absolutely the Best*

219 House of the Rising Sun – The Weavers, *Vanguard Visionaries: The Weavers*

220 House of the Risin' Sun – Bob Dylan, *Bob Dylan*

221 Baby, Let Me Follow You Down – Bob Dylan, *Bob Dylan*

222 Rip It Up – Little Richard, *Here's Little Richard (Remastered)*

223 Rockin' Chair – Fats Domino, *Blues Kingpins: Fats Domino*

224 Wonderful World – Sam Cooke, *The Man Who Invented Soul*

225 Jin-Go-Lo-Ba (Jin-Go-Low-Bah) – Babatunde Olatunji, *Drums of Passion*

226 My Favorite Things – John Coltrane, *My Favorite Things*

227 No More Auction Block – Bob Dylan, *The Bootleg Series, Vols. 1-3 (Rare & Unreleased) 1961-1991*

228 Blowin' in the Wind – Bob Dylan, *The Freewheelin' Bob Dylan*

229 When the Ship Comes In – Bob Dylan, *The Times They Are A-Changin'*

230 Only a Pawn in Their Game – Bob Dylan, *The Times They Are A-Changin'*

231 The Times They Are A-Changin' – Bob Dylan, *The Times They Are A-Changin'*

232 I Can't Be Satisfied – The Rolling Stones, *More Hot Rocks (Big Hits & Fazed Cookies)*

233 Hambone – Ella Jenkins, *Adventures In Rhythm*

234 Hey Bo Diddley – Bo Diddley, *The Chess 50th Anniversary Collection: His Best*

235 Mona (I Need You Baby) – The Rolling Stones, *The Rolling Stones*

236 Stuff You Gotta Watch – Muddy Waters, *The Anthology 1947-1972*

237 Money – The Rolling Stones, *More Hot Rocks (Big Hits & Fazed Cookies)*

238 I Want to Hold Your Hand — The Beatles, *Past Masters, Vols. 1 & 2*

239 Chimes Of Freedom, Bob Dylan, *Another Side of Bob Dylan*

240 Little By Little – The Rolling Stones, *Singles Collection: The London Years*

241 Not Fade Away – The Rolling Stones, *Big Hits (High Tide and Green Grass)*

242 I Just Want to Make Love to You – The Rolling Stones, *The Rolling Stones*

243 It's All Over Now – The Rolling Stones, *12 x 5*

244 The House of the Rising Sun – The Animals, *The Best of the Animals*

245 Don't Think Twice, It's Alright – Bob Dylan, *The Freewheelin' Bob Dylan*

[246] Subterranean Homesick Blues – Bob Dylan, *Bringing It All Back Home*

[247] Dancing in the Street – Martha Reeves & The Vandellas, *The Ultimate Collection: Martha Reeves & The Vandellas*

[248] Satisfaction – The Rolling Stones, *Singles Collection: The London Years*

[249] Like a Rolling Stone – Bob Dylan, *Highway 61 Revisited*

[250] Day Tripper – The Beatles, *Past Masters, Vols. 1 & 2*

[251] Maggie's Farm (Live) – Bob Dylan, *The Bootleg Series, Vol. 7: No Direction Home: The Soundtrack (A Martin Scorsese Picture)*

[252] Phantom Engineer (It Takes A Lot To Laugh, It Takes A Train To Cry) – Bob Dylan, *The Bootleg Series, Vols. 1-3 (Rare & Unreleased) 1961-1991*

[253] Mr. Tambourine Man (Live) – Bob Dylan, *The Bootleg Series, Vol. 6: Live 1964 - Concert At Philharmonic Hall*

[254] It's All Over Now, Baby Blue (Live) – Bob Dylan, *The Bootleg Series, Vol. 4: Live 1966 - The "Royal Albert Hall" Concert* (lyrics)

[255] Positively Fourth Street – Bob Dylan, *The Essential Bob Dylan*

[256] Yazoo Street Scandal – The Hawks (The Band), *Music From Big Pink (Expanded Edition)*

[257] I Fought the Law – The Bobby Fuller Four, *Never To Be Forgotten*

[258] Baby Let Me Follow You Down (Live) – Bob Dylan, *The Bootleg Series, Vol. 4: Live 1966 - The "Royal Albert Hall" Concert*

[259] You've Got to Hide Your Love Away — The Beatles, *Help!*

[260] Chapter 24 – Pink Floyd, *The Piper At the Gates of Dawn*

[261] Bike – Pink Floyd, *The Piper At the Gates of Dawn*

[262] 4' 33" – John Cage, *4'33"*

[263] Sgt. Pepper's Lonely Hearts Club Band – The Beatles, Sgt. Pepper's Lonely Hearts Club Band

[264] With a Little Help From My Friends – The Beatles, Sgt. Pepper's Lonely Hearts Club Band

[265] I Feel Fine – The Beatles, *Past Masters, Vols. 1 & 2*

[266] Paint it Black – The Rolling Stones, *Aftermath*

[267] Norwegian Wood (This Bird Has Flown) – *Rubber Soul*

[268] The Night Before – The Beatles, *Help!*

[269] Rain – The Beatles, *Past Masters, Vols. 1 & 2*

[270] A Day in the Life – The Beatles, *Sgt. Pepper's Lonely Hearts Club Band*

[271] Ruby Tuesday – The Rolling Stones, *Between the Buttons*

[272] Under My Thumb – The Rolling Stones, *Aftermath*

[273] 2000 Light Years From Home – The Rolling Stones, *Their Satanic Majesties Request*

[274] Interstellar Overdrive – Pink Floyd, *The Piper At the Gates of Dawn*

[275] Cream Puff War (Live) – Grateful Dead, *So Many Roads (1965-1995)*

276 Good Vibrations – The Beach Boys, *Smiley Smile*

277 Let's Go Away For a While – The Beach Boys, Pet Sounds

278 For What It's Worth – Buffalo Springfield, *Buffalo Springfield*

279 That's It for the Other One – Grateful Dead, *Anthem of the Sun*

280 Ballad of a Thin Man – Bob Dylan, *Highway 61 Revisited*

281 Whiter Shade of Pale – Procol Harum, *Greatest Hits*

282 I Am the Walrus – The Beatles, *Magical Mystery Tour*

283 Purple Haze – The Jimi Hendrix Experience, *Are You Experienced*

284 Hey Joe – The Jimi Hendrix Experience, *Are You Experienced*

285 No Expectations – The Rolling Stones, *Beggars Banquet*

286 White Rabbit – Jefferson Airplane, *Surrealistic Pillow*

287 Take Up Thy Stethoscope And Walk – Pink Floyd, *The Piper At the Gates of Dawn*

288 Season of the Witch – Donovan, *Sunshine Superman*

289 It's All Too Much – The Beatles, *Yellow Submarine*

290 All You Need Is Love – The Beatles, *Magical Mystery Tour*

291 Let's Get Together – Jefferson Airplane, *Jefferson Airplane Takes Off*

292 As I Went Out One Morning – Bob Dylan, *John Wesley Harding*

293 Blue Jay Way – The Beatles, *Magical Mystery Tour*

294 Jumping Jack Flash – The Rolling Stones, *Singles Collection: The London Years*

295 Chicago (Live) – Crosby, Stills, Nash & Young, *4 Way Street (Live)*

296 Street Fighting Man – The Rolling Stones, *Beggars Banquet*

297 We Can Be Together – Jefferson Airplane, *Volunteers*

298 Revolution (Single) – The Beatles, *Past Masters*

299 Revolution 1 – The Beatles, *The Beatles (White Album)*

300 Revolution 9 – The Beatles, *The Beatles (White Album)*

301 Sexy Sadie – The Beatles, *The Beatles (White Album)*

302 Sympathy for the Devil – The Rolling Stones, *Beggar's Banquet*

303 Yer Blues (Live) – The Dirty Mac (John Lennon and Friends), *The Rolling Stones Rock and Roll Circus* (lyrics)

304 Went To See The Gypsy — Bob Dylan, *New Morning*

305 The "Fish" Cheer / I-Feel-Like-I'm-Fixin'-To-Die-Rag – Country Joe and the Fish, *The Life and Time of Country Joe and the Fish - From Haight-Ashbury to Woodstock*

306 Piggies — The Beatles, *The Beatles (White Album)*

307 Helter Skelter – The Beatles, *The Beatles (White Album)*

308 Abbie Hoffman Incident — The Who, *Thirty Years of Maximum R&B (Box Set)*

[309] See Me Feel Me (Live at Woodstock 1969) – The Who, *The Kids Are Alright (Soundtrack from the Motion Picture)*

[310] Woodstock – Joni Mitchell, *Ladies of the Canyon*

[311] Yellow Submarine – The Beatles, *Yellow Submarine*

[312] Earth Blues – Jimi Hendrix, *Rainbow Bridge (Original Motion Picture Sound Track)*

[313] Gimme Shelter – The Rolling Stones, *Let It Bleed*

[314] Tears of Rage – The Band, *Music From Big Pink (Remastered)*

[315] Come Together – The Beatles, *Abbey Road*

[316] Beck's Bolero – Jeff Beck, *Truth*

[317] Starship – Paul Kantner and Jefferson Starship, *Blows Against the Empire*

[318] Brain Damage – Pink Floyd, *Dark Side of the Moon*

[319] Eclipse – Pink Floyd, *Dark Side of the Moon*

[320] The Boxer – Simon and Garfunkel, *Bridge Over Troubled Water*

www.ingramcontent.com/pod-product-compliance
Lightning Source LLC
Chambersburg PA
CBHW061505020726
47502CB00006B/1946